WHITE PENITENT

࿐*࿐

Book 3 of the

Kestrel Harper Saga

࿐*࿐

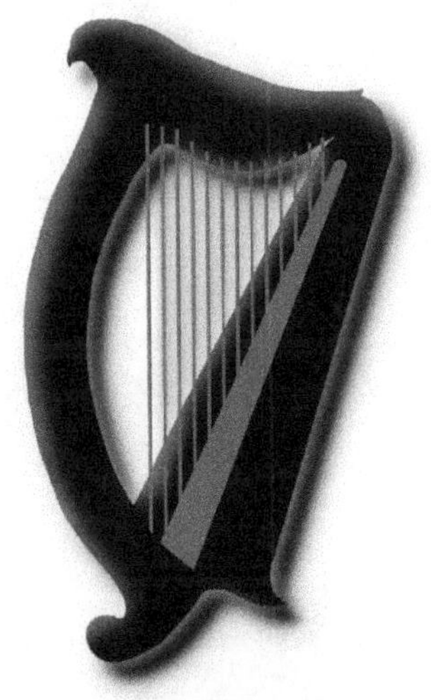

Tamara Brigham

Cover Design by: Tamara Brigham and Amanda Kazanowski

Published by:
Tamara Brigham
PO Box 151
Clearlake, CA 95422

Printed and bound in the United States of America

First Edition

ISBN #978-1-7320024-6-3

❧ * ❧

For Drew...
whose musical inspiration fueled so much

❧ * ❧

❧Prologue❧

"I thought she would be over this by now." The prince, nearly the spitting image of his grandfather except for his blonde hair, laughed warmly as he twirled the braided gold band upon the middle finger of his right hand. Though he spoke to the ivory-skinned man next to him, his eyes followed the movements of a young woman across the courtyard of her family home, laughing with two other young women he was only marginally familiar with. When he became aware that the man beside him was watching his absent fiddling, he laughed again, though this time there was a note of embarrassment to the sound. "It is going to take some time to get used to wearing this," he murmured, looking at the ring again.

"It will come, Muir." The soft intensity of the pale man's lyrical voice caused the prince to inch unconsciously towards him. The man's voice had always had that effect on him, as far back as his memory reached. "Change takes time to assimilate, even when it is welcome."

As the young woman left her friends and glided across the courtyard with her mother, he shifted away from the prince, making room for the woman who now belonged at Muir's side. The younger of the two women draped her arms possessively around Muir, aware of the stares she drew and delighting in the attention. Crushing her airy white gown of Elyri lace and Káliel silk against him, she kissed the

❧❧

prince upon the mouth. He returned her ardor eagerly enough, though with noticeably more self-consciousness. Upon her middle finger on her right hand, a gold braid that matched the one he wore.

Turning her face to the prince's companion, she smiled. "You will not object if I steal my new husband to dance, Lord Cliáth?" She rested her hand playfully on his arm until her mother's disapproving expression caused her to withdraw it. It was there long enough, however, to make the bard uncomfortable. Her smile did not falter.

"Would it matter if I did?" he countered as Muir stepped away.

"No," both husband and wife laughed simultaneously.

Muir looked back. "We are not finished speaking about this, Lord Harper. And you must play for us privately before you leave."

"Yes," his bride agreed, whirling the prince into the crowd, "you must."

The second woman, the mother of the bride, settled on a nearby bench, watching the bard's face as his gaze followed the movement of the dancers. Lost in the music, she knew. It was his sole earthly love, the only passion he allowed himself. Despite the fact that she was younger than him, he looked as if he could be her son, so regal, so beautiful. Those thoughts, and the old emotions brought with them, caused her to swallow uneasily and look away.

There had been enough changes in her life since they first met, and enough time had passed, that she no longer felt as she once had for this elusive man. Yet there were times such as this, when the light caught the silver in his thick waves of white hair, reflected in the emerald of his eyes, or played upon the calm serenity of his features, that she longed to touch him. Longed to make him smile or laugh. Candlelight such as what surrounded them here was particularly seductive. However, unlike those early days, she no longer tried. Even now, as he joined her on the bench, her hands remained in her lap. Experience had taught her what this man desired from her, and physical affection and intimacy were not part of it.

"Not finished talking about what?" When he did not reply, she smiled and asked, "Or is it none of my concern? Man-talk perhaps?"

The bard looked at her with an expression of confusion until the twinkle in her eyes told him what she meant. His skin flushed. "Nothing like that, Gabrielle. You know me too well. Muir was asking about the state of affairs in Rhidam, his sister in particular."

"Oh."

She was disappointed, having hoped for some cherished tidbit of his life. But what he said was the truth, though not all of it. What he had not said, she did not need to know. To change the subject, he asked, "Where is Owain? I have not seen him since the ceremony."

Gabrielle smiled. "Piran demanded to see the boats, so Owain obliged him. He's not old enough to be interested in weddings and adult gatherings and there are few children here today. The boats are his favorite diversion. Owain says he has several wooden ones, a whole fleet, which he sails in the horse troughs and fountains in Fiara."

Hearing her melancholy, Kavan asked, "It is hard to let him go?"

She sniffed, though the smile on her face did not fade. "Of course, Kavan. He's my son. But," she shrugged, "Owain missed Muir's youth, and it is good that Piran spends more time with him. Also, on the practical side, there are skills I cannot teach him."

"Such as how to wield a sword."

"Yes." Her tone was resigned. "A man cannot survive long without one. Well…you can, and Ártur does; most Elyri do. But Piran does not carry the power, or if he does, it is too weak to be of use. He wants to be a swordsman, to be a man worthy of being both a Lachlan prince and a Dilyn diplomat. There are many in the Káliel Guard who could train him, but it is more fitting for his father to do so. Even if Piran did not desire those things, I cannot teach him how to be a man. He needs his father."

Kavan looked back to the dancers, his thoughts drifting to his childhood. "He will find his way, Gabrielle. Everyone does."

❧ ❀ ❧

"Perhaps. This is the best we can offer. I cannot live in Fiara, and Owain cannot live here. Our duties will not allow it. At least I get to see them both, and perhaps Piran will return here to live one day."

The subjects of their conversation came out of the house into the rear courtyard. Piran's deep strawberry blonde hair was windswept, the edges of his white sleeves and hands still dripping with water. While his eyes were green like his mother's, his face and build, even at such a young age, were clearly his father's. Owain Lachlan did not share his son's disheveled appearance, but with the small hand held in his, his face exhibited the same joy as the child's. That brought a rare smile to Kavan's face. It pleased him to see Owain happy.

The spectacle of the wedding festival was overlaid in his vision with the image of a considerably older Piran surrounded by Káliel council members. When his vision cleared, Kavan said in a low voice. "He will come back to you, Gabrielle. You can be sure of it."

Having seen that look come over his face, one she had seen before, her mouth opened to speak but there was no sound. The Sight had shown Kavan her son. It was enough to let her relax and rise to greet her family with an expression of relief and joy.

"Dance with me, mother," Piran squealed, extracting his hand from Owain's and pulling her into the midst of the dancers. She paid little heed to the sorry state of his sleeves or his dripping hands. Owain took Gabrielle's place on the bench at Kavan's side, stretching his legs out before him as he leaned against the stone wall behind.

Neither man spoke. Like Wortham Delamo, Owain could remain silent in the bard's presence without feeling the need to speak. He was content to watch his sons and his wife and relish the Elyri's quiet, soothing company. It was a comfortable relationship, except in those moments when Owain felt overcome with guilt at how he had once treated this gentle man. But Kavan never spoke of that time, rarely spoke of times past, and when those memories came, Owain pushed the guilt down to be examined at some other time.

Prince Muir and Clianthe left the company of dancers with few realizing it. Gone into the house, Owain presumed. The sun had nearly set, the courtyard lit only by the glow of dozens of tall, yellow candles. If this were Enesfel, a great feast would ensue, the festivities lasting far into the night. However, this was Káliel. Owain had shared these customs before. Shortly, the new couple would reappear, bestow their tokens of thanks upon their guests, and the public festivities would end. The majority of the guests would depart and the families of the new couple would proceed indoors for a shared meal, to which Kavan was invited, as much family to Prince Muir as anyone else he knew.

Once Gabrielle and Piran completed their dance, they went into the house as well. The troupe of musicians played a few more numbers, jigs and reels that encouraged one final flurry of dancing, until the Prime Magistrate returned with her son, now in dryer apparel. She spoke to the performers and beckoned to Owain. The man nodded to Kavan before joining her, leaving the bard alone.

The next song was of native origin, with a hint of both Elyri and Hatuish influence that spoke of the long history the Islands shared. As the song began, Muir and Clianthe emerged from the villa, both once more wearing the fine metal mesh black veils and pale blue wedding robes of Káliel's custom they had briefly abandoned after the morning ceremony. In Muir's hands was a black enamel chest. From it, as they stopped before each guest, Clianthe withdrew an item and placed it in the hands of that person, uttering ritual phrases of blessing and thanks for friendship, support, and acknowledgment of their union as husband and wife. As had been arranged beforehand, the couple made a point of speaking to the other guests first, saving Kavan until the end. The place of distinction.

"Blessed brother," began Muir as he handed the chest to his bride. "Of the guests here, you are he who has had the greatest influence on my life. If not for your wisdom and guidance, I would not be standing in this hallowed place of commitment. When I mourned, you

❧❦

comforted; when I erred, you judged wisely and brought me back. There is no truer friend. May the forces that grant happiness, and k'Ádhá's love and peace, grant you all you have ever given me. Accept this and wear it close to your heart, the guardian and protector of the memories we share."

From the enamel box, the prince withdrew a smoky gray crystal hung upon a silver chain. He intended to draw it over Kavan's head but the bard did not move, unexpectedly overwhelmed by the emotion in Prince Muir's voice. In many ways, this was a parting, a farewell to what they had shared before. With the King's indifference to his bastard stepson, Kavan had been the man most responsible for raising Muir. If he accepted this gift, he was severing his former ties with Muir and allowing Clianthe to take the place of supreme importance in Muir's life…where Kavan had once been. To refuse to take it was an indication that he did not approve of this union and was a curse upon the marriage. Having been through this ritual one other time, he knew the ramifications of his actions. This occasion was no less difficult for him than that one had been, for the last time he had given in to Gabrielle's union with Owain. For a few brief seconds he could not move, but then he resolutely bowed his head and accepted the cold, heavy crystal.

There was a static spark and pop as the crystal touched the half-moon medallion he always wore. He wondered why. Power in the stone, perhaps, the thought making him curious to study it later. Muir kissed the top of his bowed head and whispered, "Thank you, Lord Cliáth." Turning to the other guests, he said, "I know it is customary to sing the Cra Nique hymn. However, with the approval of our parents, Clianthe and I have opted to forgo that custom."

Surprised murmuring interrupted his speech. Clianthe lifted her hand and the gathering fell silent. "Instead, we have chosen to take advantage of the talent of one of our guests. It is not often that our islands are graced with the presence of the White Bard of Bhryell."

From beside the bench, Kavan retrieved his ever-constant companion, the black kestrel harp, his most treasured possession. People around him were applauding already and he had not even begun playing. Ah well. He had agreed to perform for this blessed event and expected such a reaction wherever he traveled. Play he would. The notes from the brass strings soared into the evening sky, mingling with the breeze and the cries of evening seabirds before blowing out across the ocean. He had rarely been able to turn down the opportunity to make music.

❧Chapter 1❧

Coiling and uncoiling her ebony tresses, Princess Diona Lachlan tried in vain to find a style that pleased her. For some reason, none of them did. At least none of them adequately complimented the gown she wore, the gown that would mark her twenty-third birthday. She allowed her hair to tumble down her back and smiled. Most of the men she knew preferred her hair down. Fortunately for them, regardless of popular fashion, she did too.

She should have attended Muir's wedding, but there was too much to do before tomorrow night. At least, that was what Owain had said when he convinced her that Muir would forgive her for not attending. She loved the man dearly, as she did her half-brother, but she suspected he had convinced her to stay in Rhidam to get Kavan away from her. True, Owain rarely saw Kavan, and she knew how much he desired to be alone with the bard, if only for a few minutes. She could not blame him for that. And she knew there was no way Kavan would miss Muir's wedding.

And there were many details to see to in preparation for tomorrow, giving the correct guest count to the cooks, having her dress fitted, deciding upon a hairstyle and accessories, and most importantly, greeting the guests who arrived continuously from outside of Rhidam and seeing to their comforts. Why her father did not do that, she was not sure, except that he said it would be proper for her to greet those she had invited…as well as those she had not but were attending anyhow. She had requested this banquet, as she did every year, but this year her father had placed obligation for it in her hands, to teach her some degree of responsibility she was sure. But Arlan was King; she would not question his decision if she wanted this banquet to proceed.

Nevertheless, she had wanted to go to Káliel, both to be with Kavan and to see Muir again. In the last fourteen years, she had not seen much of her half-brother; he spent his time between Fiara and Káliel, stopping in Rhidam when he could to visit her and the bard. After Bertram's death and Muir's departure from Rhidam, Diona had felt isolated in an unexpected way. Hagan and Bianca had been initially too young to make good companions, and she and her cousin Wilred had little in common. Muir was her closest friend, and now she had missed his wedding. And he was going to miss her birthday.

As might Kavan, she realized with an irrational flash of anger. Perhaps that was the real reason behind the timing of Muir's marriage, to provide the bard an excuse not to attend her ball. Not that he needed a reason; he was a nobleman, with business that often took him away from Rhidam. If Kavan wished not to attend, he would not. However, he had promised to be there if he could, and she could think of no time when he had broken an arrangement with her. It was not in his nature to go back on his word. She smoothed the azure velvet of her dress as she studied her reflection in the mirror. It was for his benefit, this gown; he had said this color complimented her eyes and complexion, and that he approved was what mattered. Princess Diona had a mission for tomorrow night.

The sound of children screaming in the courtyard below drew her attention to the window. Of the five children scampering over the stone benches and around the trees in the near darkness, two were boys. Diona quickly identified four-year-old Llucás Phaedr MacLyr. As usual, though he was the youngest and the shortest, he was the leader, coaxing the other children to jump from the bench. Although not a far drop, Diona had often heard Lady MacLyr tell her son not to do it. Like any child, however, Llucás was determined to continue, particularly since his mother was away and his father was otherwise occupied. Besides, he had other children to impress.

Shades of Bertram, she sighed, motioning for her lady in waiting, Belda, to unbutton the back of her gown. Bertram had used more physical means of persuasion however; Llucás used words. A budding master spokesman at four years old, learning the intricacies of language and argument from Princess Diona. He might not be a healer like his parents, but he had other talents the Lachlan Crown could utilize if he chose to remain in Enesfel.

There was a knock on the door behind her; she waved Belda to answer it as she pulled free of her gown. Belda returned shortly, alone.

"Who was it?"

"Lord Flannery, milady."

"And you did not show him in?"

"Milady!" The servant looked and sounded appalled. "You are not properly dressed to receive male visitors."

Diona chuckled and cut the woman off. "Why should it matter? Men receive guests in their underclothing; why can't I? Besides, if a woman receives a caller as handsome as Lord McGrannis, I think she should welcome him immediately, regardless of her state of dress…or undress." Belda was unsure how to interpret the flippant remark, though she had heard many such comments from the princess during her years of service, thus she said nothing as she helped the woman dress. "What did Lord Flannery want?"

"He wished to inform you that Prince Harcourt has arrived and is waiting in the library to see you at your leisure."

The glibness fell away. "I cannot receive the prince dressed like this!" Diona cried, struggling to get out of the plain yellow gown she had started to don. The serving woman sighed, wondering why the yellow gown would not suffice to greet the Prince of Hatu if her underclothing was suitable attire to greet Lord Flannery.

Thirty minutes and four dresses later, Diona paused outside the library, smoothed the gently gathered pleats of pale blue linen, and then entered the room. Prince Espen Harcourt stood at the window, his back to her, his deep purple turban in his sun-browned hands. She liked this image of him, dark in his cream-colored tunic, his curly sable hair cut above his collar. He looked exotic, more than Kavan or any Elyri ever appeared to her. It made her pulse quicken and her hands tremble to see him thus, particularly when he was not aware she was watching. He might be foreign, but he was still Teren, that detail she had learned well over the last fourteen years.

"Welcome back to Rhidam, Prince Espen."

He turned, surprised by her voice, warmed by the nervous tremor it held, his face turning vaguely crimson beneath its darker tone. "I did not hear your arrival, milady. I apologize."

"Oh, none of that, Espen," she smiled, the formality dropping away now that they had both spoken. "I think we can be casual with one another, can we not? Celebrating the fact that I am another year older is not cause to act like we have just met."

Prince Espen, the younger brother of the King of Hatu, agreed in theory. But the women in his land were more reserved around men, less forward and visible, and it took time to adjust to Diona's candor and strength after being away from her for any significant length of time. He appraised her appearance without seeming to. "You look remarkably well…and as beautiful as ever."

"Thank you." Her words were spoken casually, but her eyes and the flush on her cheeks indicated she was flattered at his notice of her appearance. "I am pleased you have come. I was not sure you would."

"You know you have only to ask, and I will abandon everything to come to your side." He took a step closer. "I have waited too long to abandon you."

Like a skittish horse afraid of its rider, Diona took a step away. "Espen…" she started in a whisper.

He did not pursue her. "Aye," he said through clenched jaws, "you do not wish to speak of this when I have just arrived. I will leave the matter for now, if you will think on this. Neither of us is getting any younger. Other women your age have long since married…as have men of mine. Noreis has no heirs, and with three wives is apparently incapable of producing any. Hence, it falls to me to see to Hatu's future and survival. There is any number of women at home I could choose, should I find it necessary, but you are the only woman I have ever…"

She turned and cut him off. "Would you care for a game of dice, Espen? I am weary of being alone, occupied by nothing except preparations for the ball. I could use the diversion and it is too late to ride. Will you join me? You can tell me all about things in Hatu, about your journey here."

He rolled his eyes, annoyance behind the smile he kept on his face. Once she had been willing to listen to his rationale for their union for hours, for as long as he wished to confess his feelings. Recently her inclination to hear such platitudes had decreased. He wondered if her resistance was weakening, meaning she would soon accept his proposal, or if she was weary of him and was nearing the day when she would deny him irrevocably. He did not think that true, as she still desired his company; if she did not, she would not continue to summon him to Rhidam. And she would not have asked him to dally over dice. She wanted him near, and that was where he wanted to be.

"Of course I shall play. What game do you wish?"

❧*❧

"Tusánt, tomorrow you will go to Alberni to take stock of how the chellé's construction is progressing. Lord Cliáth wants to open for the

❧ 13 ❧

Feast of Kóráhm, thirteen days from now. Notice from gdhededhá Khwílen indicates they are ready, but I want you to be certain."

"Of course, Your Grace," Tusánt replied, meticulously jotting down the instructions upon the parchment stretched before him. The k'gdhededhá did not understand why the Elyri gdhededhá did that; the other man's memory was like a trap. He never forgot anything.

"If they are ready, you are to perform the dedication and conduct the Feast's Gathering. Lord Cliáth requested it. Please do not disappoint him. Once you return, there will be altar attendants to train; consider this your chance for respite. I expect a full report on the chellé; please take your time in assessing it."

The Elyri gdhededhá nodded, his eyes twinkling at the honor of being chosen to open the new chellé hábhai, or Seeking House.

k'gdhededhá Jermyn turned his attention to the brown haired gdhededhá beside him, his hair tonsured in the latest ecclesiastical fashion. "Rankin, prepare the Feast here; I am sure the Lachlans will attend, so everything must be impressive. You are also to begin preparations for the Dhágdhuán and Udhár High Gatherings, as they will be here before we know it. Try to convince Lord Cliáth to play for at least one of them."

Rankin frowned. "He has rejected requests in the past, Your Grace. What makes you think he will accept this year?"

The older gdhededhá chuckled. "I don't believe he will, but it cannot hurt to ask. I think he expects it; I do not want to offend him by not asking. Perhaps this time he will change his mind. I also want you to see about repairing that hole in the roof of the residence hall before gdhededhá Hazen asks for my head. If it starts to rain before it is repaired, I am going to send her to see you, is that understood?"

The younger man nodded gravely, his expression showing he held great respect for the wrath of the ancient gdhededhá Hazen.

"One more thing. When you tally the donations between now and Udhár, set aside any funds not directly needed for our upkeep. The orphanage sees an increase around that time; we should donate something to them again. Do not give them the money or we will never know what becomes of it. Buy clothing, food, or any other goods they need. We will take it to them before the Festival."

Again, Rankin nodded, making notes as Tusánt had done.

"Claide?"

The balding Teren gdhededhá sat apart from the others, his feet propped on the k'gdhededhá's desk, his heavy eyelids nearly closed. He looked at Jermyn when spoken to, however, and removed his feet from the desk when he noted Jermyn's annoyance. "Yes?"

"I have some tasks specifically for…"

Tone dripping with sarcasm, Claide asked, "There are some you have not already delegated?"

Jermyn frowned. "You know I must distribute the burden as evenly as I can, according to a man's talents. St. Poul's in Levonne claims need of major repairs upon their facilities and has requested funds. I don't know how that can be true; everything seemed in good condition when I was there last spring, though I admit I did not climb upon their roof or crawl in their basement. Please pay them a visit and see what they need. Do not hesitate to turn down their requests if the need is not there. While in Levonne, they have a young man ready to take vows. You are sanctioned to perform the Initiation, and I want you to bring him to Rhidam afterward so I may interview him."

Though his head nodded, his slightly offended expression did not change. "Is that all, Your Grace?"

"No. One of our parishioners has asked that you bless and dedicate his new house near the southern edge of town. I told him I would inquire if you were available; if you would agree to do this, I will arrange for you two to work out the details. Is that acceptable?"

"Of course."

Thankful that there was no fight over the assigned duties, as had increasingly become the case over the past ten years, Jermyn smiled with relief. "Good. You can see to that on your return from Levonne. I should go to St. Poul's and the chellé myself, but k'gdhededhá Dórímyr has sent word he plans to arrive within two…"

"k'gdhededhá Dórímyr is coming here?" Tusánt sounded skeptical and thought Claide looked ill at the suggestion.

Jermyn shrugged. "Well, he says he is. With his schedule, one never knows. But I cannot risk being away or not being ready should he come this time. Besides, I have to review náós appointments, find a home for our newest gdhededhá, and see if there are others who need to be reassigned. If there are problems, please let me know, and if Rankin needs assistance with preparations, I expect each of us to do our share to help him. It is late and I have an appointment with the King in the morning. Goodnight, brothers."

He waited until the other three gdhededhá had departed, noting that, as usual, Claide was the last to exit. Claide was the last to do anything, the last to arrive, the last to speak. There was a great reluctance to the man that had not been there when he had first taken vows. Over the past ten years, Claide had grown quieter, more withdrawn, until he barely spoke to k'gdhededhá Jermyn except in the line of official business. Jermyn wondered if it was his fault; he had never felt entirely comfortable with Claide and preferred Tusánt's easy-going temperament to the Teren gdhededhá's pricklier one. Once Rankin arrived, the youngest gdhededhá's company was his favorite as they shared enjoyment in many of the same things. The bonding of Rankin and Jermyn seemed not to trouble Tusánt; the Elyri gdhededhá went about his business as he always had. But Claide had, it appeared, not appreciated becoming more the outsider.

Jermyn tried to include Claide in as many functions as possible, tried to make him feel welcome in every way he could. He had thought it was working until Claide stopped accepting invitations, and eventually, Jermyn stopped trying, except on the rare occasions when guilt made him feel that the effort was necessary.

Scratching his ear, the heavy man settled behind his desk. He was looking forward to the arrival of k'gdhededhá Dórímyr with a mixture of anxiety and excitement. The Elyri pontiff had not stepped foot outside of Elyriá in his entire career, except when he had journeyed to Rhidam to appoint Jermyn as k'gdhededhá of Enesfel and had then gone to Aralt to appoint Tymothy Borlad as the k'gdhededhá of Cordash. That had been over twenty-five years ago. If he could be certain of the man's arrival, Jermyn would have invited every gdhededhá in the Teren kingdoms.

But the ancient pontiff had announced his coming many times over the years and each time had canceled his trip. There were valid explanations and reasons for each cancellation, but to Jermyn and the clergy around him, they amounted to the same thing. Excuses to avoid Enesfel. Though Jermyn knew that the same was likely to occur this time, he still allowed himself to hope the pontiff would come. It felt imperative that he do so.

❧*❧

"I apologize for our tardiness," Bhríd chuckled, watching Tayte being pulled out the door by his younger cousin Llucás. "Gaelán is recovering from an illness and Madalyn was reluctant to leave him. But he finally convinced her he would survive for a few days without her hovering. He has to be the strongest-minded child I have ever seen. I hope the princess has not been hounding you for our whereabouts."

King Arlan shrugged and motioned his chamberlain to a chair. The castle library was brightly lit at this hour and empty for the first time that morning. It was the King's first choice for greeting guests, or for welcoming his friends and advisors back from their travels. "I doubt she realizes you are late. She spent nearly all day yesterday preparing her wardrobe. Once Prince Espen arrived last evening, she has had no time for anyone else."

"Do you think she will ever marry him?"

The question made the King groan. "I have given up trying to understand her mind. She thinks like no one else I know. She should be wed; her peers are. Yet she refuses. Given her focus of attention, I do believe if she ever marries it will be him or your cousin."

"Kavan?" the dark-haired Elyri asked with a snort of amazement. "Come, sir. You know that will not happen. Kavan will not allow it."

"I know. But," he rubbed his temples, "it is not a union I would object to…no matter how awkward it might be to have my best friend, older by seven years, marry my daughter."

The chamberlain chuckled, trying to imagine the quiet Elyri bard married to the outspoken Lachlan princess. "Enesfel would object."

Arlan nodded as he stood to pour a glass of wine. "You are likely correct in that, Bhríd. I think she turns her attention to Kavan because he is safe; she knows he will not dishonor her. I cannot believe her affections are serious. Once she decides to marry, her attention will settle where it should. Are you certain Gaelán will be well?"

"Quite. A fever and sneezing, nothing a few days in bed did not cure. He is rarely sick for long, whereas Tayte can spend weeks in bed. I think Gaelán was not feeling up to a long journey yet, but I'm sure he is on his way to being healthy again. He will be running about by the time Madalyn returns home, I suspect."

"Good. I have considered asking you to bring him soon, making him one of my pages. The experience should prove beneficial."

Again the chamberlain laughed. "Beneficial for whom? You would likely find him trying. Once he gets an idea in his head, nothing can turn him from it, regardless of the consequences. He is not necessarily the most cooperative child, not good at taking orders."

The wine glass was drained and set on the mantle. "Like Phaedr."

Remembering his brother fondly, Bhríd nodded. "Yes, I suppose he is. I had not thought about it, but that is exactly who he is like. I will discuss your wishes with Madalyn. I doubt there will be any objections. Has there been any other news during my absence?"

"k'gdhededhá Dórímyr might pay a visit."

"We have heard that before."

"Precisely," snorted the King. "I put no stock in the notice, but I want you to see that the grounds and staff are in top condition in case he does decide to make an appearance."

"Of course. May I change first and rest before the ball?"

"By all means. None of that is pressing for today, and I will not have my daughter accuse me of keeping you away with duty. Before you settle in, however, you should announce your return to Ternce and Minos, if you have not done so already. They have been anxiously awaiting you."

Bhríd stood with a grin and bowed. "No doubt, My Liege."

The men to whom King Arlan referred were, at that moment, arguing about the availability of funds required to increase patrols in Rhidam's streets. It was less a fight than a spirited debate, concluded Ártur MacLyr who was in the dayroom painting when the two entered. The sound of their bickering was commonplace since Guthrie McHador's death; it was one thing everyone in the keep expected to hear at least once during their daily routine. Kavan more than once commented that the men were actually good friends, but no one quite believed it. Ártur only believed it because his cousin said it was true.

Minos Cornell was sensitive to the need for more men to patrol the streets; he had once been the Lord High Justice himself. He knew what it took to maintain a presence and the latest series of brawls and petty thefts had not gone unnoticed. But recent expenses had left the kingdom's coffers short; there were no funds available to hire even a single man until taxes were gathered at year's end. That was several weeks away. He had nothing to give the general or the justice.

The leader of Enesfel's army had no doubts that the chancellor spoke the truth. It did not, however, keep him from requesting resources. He knew what was needed too, as Lord High Justice Darius Corbin did. While Darius was not about to pressure the chancellor for additional resources, the general was not so squeamish. It was better, he felt, to be vocal about his needs than to remain silent and risk being overlooked when the resources became available.

That they did not notice the Elyri healer's presence as they entered, debated over details found in a book they drew from the shelves, and continued out of the room made the healer chuckle. He appreciated that some things never changed.

❧*❧

Behind him, Caol Dugan could hear Asta laughing politely at some comment Prince Hagan made. He could not define the relationship between his daughter and her cousin, the heir to Enesfel's throne. Prince Hagan was a quiet young man, shy and gentle. Asta, on the other hand, was boisterous, fun-loving, and would have been a perfect candidate for the Association if Caol were still part of that life. At her request, and perhaps against his best judgment, Caol was teaching her the skills he had learned as a boy, picking locks, climbing, eavesdropping, anything that had ever been useful to him, and some things that had not. His son Wilred had shown no interest in those things, likely because his brush with that part of Caol's life had led to the kidnapping and the death of his cousin Prince Bertram. If her mother were alive, or if King Arlan learned of Asta's schooling, it would be halted at once. Asta's interest sprung from the tales of her brother's rescue and she was secretly proving to be a capable and willing pupil.

Prince Hagan knew nothing of her inclinations; secrecy was part of the agreement if she wanted her father to school her. And, as Caol had taught her, secrecy was one of the most important tools of that trade. As far as the inquisitor knew, the only person aware of Asta's side schooling was Lord Cliáth, and that was because he had caught her attempting to climb into his room through the window late one night. The bard kept silent about the incident, but it taught Asta two important lessons. Do not underestimate the target, and take extra precautions if that target was Elyri.

Today, at Prince Hagan's insistence, they scoured the city for a gift for his sister. They started early that morning and it had taken until mid-afternoon to find the right items. At last, they were returning to the keep. Asta demanded it since she claimed it would take her the rest of the day to prepare for the ball.

Caol had no doubt about that. At thirteen, Asta was still boyish in figure and took great pains to emphasize her feminine features as compensation. Her blonde hair was nearly straight, her eyes a deep azure. Traces of Deidre, though the woman's hair had not been straight, but in Caol's eyes, his daughter did not look like her mother. Deidre had been beautiful, loved by everyone, but being a realistic and practical man, Caol had few doubts that Asta would surpass her mother's beauty. Quite soon, he suspected he would be fending off a number of suitors for his daughter's hand.

Unless she decided to marry her cousin the heir or one of the Cáner boys as he suspected she would. She was quite fond of each of the three young men and had no difficulty sharing her affection with them. But only Prince Hagan was old enough to consider his future and no doubt his father was thinking about that future as well. Asta was in no hurry to form romantic ties. She was too intent upon what her father had to teach her. She wanted what no woman in Enesfel, or elsewhere, had ever held, the position of High Inquisitor.

❧*❧

❧2❧

Diona fingered the parchment, admiring how the light glinted off the sapphires set into the pair of Cordashian combs in her other hand. She had to admit her cousin Wilred had perfect aesthetic taste; the combs were exquisite. But she had hoped he, Bianca, and Lady MacLyr would attend her ball. Wilred and Bianca had not been in Rhidam since their wedding a year ago. She wanted to blame their absence on Bianca but she could not. Bianca could be erratic and fickle, but she was not spiteful or cruel and she was fond of Diona.

Besides, as the letter stated, Wilred's first child, Coriana Deidre Dugan, had been born the day the letter was written. Bianca was in no condition to make the journey from Durham to Rhidam, and Wilred would never leave her alone. He was more devoted to his wife than any man Diona knew, and Bianca would go nowhere without him, as inseparable now as they had been as children.

The princess wondered absently if she would ever inspire that kind of devotion.

The combs that matched her dress had arrived in time for the ball, and Wilred sent his love. That mattered as much as whether he could attend or not. Tonight would be a happy occasion despite his absence. She wished her twin Bertram were here to share it. It should have been his birthday too.

❧*❧

Kavan rolled over, waking to sunlight in his eyes. It brought him to a sitting position at once, wondering how long he had slept. The wedding celebration had lasted far into the evening and he had played more in a single night than he had in many years. His fingers still tingled from the effort but they did not hurt. He could not recall a time when they had.

Blanket falling away, he allowed the autumn island air to chill him as he stared at his hands. There had been freedom in his three days on

Káliel, away from demands, expectations, and courtly pressure. The only duty expected here was music, something he gladly gave.

The great clock in Gabrielle's entrance hall clanged three. Mid-afternoon. Already. There was little time; he must bid those here farewell and return to Rhidam. The princess would be growing anxious and he did not wish to face her wrath should he fail to attend her ball, in spite of the growing cold gnawing within every time he thought about tonight's event. There was no rational explanation for the feeling except that something in the princess's voice and eyes of late made him increasingly uncomfortable.

After dressing in the white robe and gray suede boots he usually wore, he rubbed his fingers over the black wood of his harp, closed the case, and went downstairs with it, pausing at the bottom to study the záryph on the rail as he fought with himself over returning to Rhidam.

"Kavan, you're awake. I didn't realize we'd tired you. I apologize for that."

The prince, currently alone, looked blissful and content. Kavan eyed him curiously, wondering not for the first time what it was about marriage that caused such changes to come over some soon afterward. He doubted he would ever understand. "Perhaps sleeping late was an unconscious attempt to avoid the inevitable. Where is Clianthe?"

Muir clasped Kavan's arm reassuringly. "With her mother in the back garden. I did not think it prudent to linger and hear what the women were planning to discuss." He grinned, though his face still showed concern for the bard. "Father and Piran are in the dining room, I believe. You look ready to return to Rhidam."

"Ready? I do not think…resigned is more appropriate."

Seeing pain flicker in Kavan's eyes, Muir said, "Perhaps I should go with you, talk to Diona. I am one of the few she will listen to."

Kavan shook his head. "In this, I do not think she will be swayed. I have no idea what can be said to convince her I do not want marriage."

The hand on Kavan's arm tightened a little and Muir stepped back to allow Kavan to come down the final step. "But you do, Lord Cliáth. That's it. I saw it on your face yesterday. You want that sense of belonging so badly it is unmistakable sometimes. I think Diona sees it as I do, which is why she persists. She believes she can be the one to ease your loneliness."

Kavan glanced at his hand, wondering what it would be like to see a ring on his slender white fingers. The thought made him shiver. "It will not happen, Muir. I am resigned to it. Regardless of what I might wish. I have no desire to marry Diona, yet I cannot make her see that."

"She will. Soon. She wishes for children and will realize that if she does not accept Prince Espen's proposal…or someone's…she will spend her life alone. I think she knows it already, which is why she tries fervently to change your mind."

"Her desperation is intolerable."

The prince sympathized with Kavan's predicament but was also at a loss of how to approach his sister. "I tell you what. After the celebration tonight, you are welcome to come here for as long as you feel necessary, until Diona gets the message. I know Gabrielle would welcome you, as would Clianthe, and I do not think Arlan will object."

Kavan shook his head. "I will not intrude on life with your bride."

"You are never an intrusion. I wish you would realize that." Muir leaned forward and kissed the bard's cheek. "If you will not come here, then go to Fiara with Father; you know he would appreciate your company. He does not like to be far away from you…like the rest of us." He had to smile at Kavan's embarrassed expression. "Or if solitude is what you desire, go to Alberni. You said the chellé will open soon, devote your attention there. That is one place you can go where none can accuse you of shirking duty. Alberni is your responsibility."

Though he agreed with Muir's logic, he felt no less obligated to attend the ball. "When did you become wise, My Prince?" he asked.

"It has been a gradual process that I owe to my wise tutor. I'll retrieve our gifts for Diona and send the others to bid you farewell. Please give her my apologies again."

"I shall."

It was nearly an hour later before Kavan, Owain, and Piran arrived in the upper oratory of Rhidam's keep. Over time, Owain had grown to accept the Gates, but he thus far allowed no one other than Kavan, and occasionally the healer, to take him through. Piran, still young enough to find the new and unusual exciting, looked forward to each trip, though it had taken his solemn promise to keep the secret before Kavan agreed to take him. Knowledge of the Gates was too widespread for the bard's liking, inevitable with the large number of Elyri employed in Rhidam's castle, and he had ceased taking anyone through unless it was an emergency. Today had been an exception, as the timing of Muir's wedding and Diona's ball allowed no other means of travel if they were to arrive on time.

Owain led his son to the room they shared when they were in Rhidam, leaving Kavan in the oratory. The Elyri spent several minutes in prayer, longing for music yet knowing that to play would alert others to his return. He was not yet willing to speak with anyone, particularly the princess.

In his room, he found new clothing laid out on his bed. Crisp blue linen trousers and a royal blue silk tunic. Not his clothes, and from the color, he knew who had left them. There was a note; half curious, half dismayed, he read it, then let the message fall from his fingers.

Sinking upon his bed, Kavan hung his head. Gift from the princess or not, he did not intend to wear anything other than his usual robe.

He placed the clothes in a drawer and undressed to bathe. There was water in the washbasin, cold but acceptable, and after changing into a fresh robe, he settled to read while he waited for the evening's torment. The princess would not be pleased with his decision, but it could not be helped. He would not let guilt manipulate him into something he found even more uncomfortable than attending this ball would be.

&cChapter 2&s

"Thank you, milord!"

Diona bubbled with excitement as she kissed Owain coyly, and then maneuvered to let him clasp the string of pink pearls around her neck. She grabbed his hands in a manner that made them linger longer than appropriate upon her neck, and then released them with a laugh and a quick flash of her eyes towards Kavan. Her attention turned to the other gathered guests, waiting for the next gift to be bestowed.

To one side of her, on the dais, lay her current horde of treasure: the small cedar, gold, and abalone jewelry chest given by Tayte, Gaelán and Llucás and a book of poetry from Asta and Caol. The princess speculated it was Asta's choice by the few verses she had peeked at upon opening it. There were six bottles of the finest Dubuais wine, two bolts of Káliel silk and two of Káliel linen…all deep blue…delivered from Muir and Clianthe since they could not attend, and from Hagan, two porcelain dolls, the kind with rosebud lips and delicately painted features she loved. k'gdhededhá Jermyn offered an expensive bound prayer book, a rare commodity outside of Elyriá or outside of the náós walls. She was not particularly pious, but she appreciated the value and the artisanship, and she did value the tenants of the Faith. Beside them, the painting Diona had requested from

Ártur, one of her and her twin Bertram when they were much younger, before Bertram's premature death. In her heart, it meant more than the other gifts, both in its size and significance.

It was not customary for such gifts to be given publically, but Diona had demanded it from the time she was old enough to be considered an adult. Despite a host of admonitions from her father and others, that such a custom would result in the awkwardness of guests being envious of the gifts of others, feeling overshadowed or ill-favored if another's gift outweighed their own in expense, sentimentality, or extravagance, Princess Diona would not be swayed. This was her day and she would celebrate it as she chose. And judging by the host of other gifts already revealed from other Lords, Ladies, and families of wealth throughout Enesfel and beyond, the King doubted his daughter would relinquish this custom anytime soon. She liked pretty gifts and public adoration.

They helped her, on this day, think less about the twin she had lost.

"Milady," Prince Espen spoke, bowing as he presented her with an ebony scroll case. She looked at him quizzically, wondering what significance such an item could have in Hatu as a gift between a man and a woman he expressed interest in marrying. "Please…if you will."

Her mouth formed a perfect O. She had to break the seal on the enclosed scroll before reading it, aware of Kavan's piercing gaze from across the room. He had not worn the clothes she gave him, which angered her initially. Nor had he made any mention of her gown. But her anger passed as the festivities commenced. At least he was present. She wondered about his expression, what he was thinking as she opened Espen's gift. She hoped he was jealous, both of Espen and of the others she flirted with.

"A deed?"

Espen bowed. "It is a region of fertile, forested land not far south of Natrona. There are several farms upon it and a modest fortification.

I have Noreis' permission to bestow it upon you, in order that you and your family will have somewhere to stay when you are in Hatu. The income from those farms will be directed into the upkeep when you are not there. A goodwill offering, if you please."

"A castle?" she whispered, her blue eyes wide. "I have my own…" She looked as if she would throw her arms around him but for once restrained herself. "Thank you, milord. No one has ever been this generous."

King Arlan smiled. He had watched his daughter flirt with Flannery, Owain, Kavan, and Prince Espen for years. Tonight was no exception. Owain was married and Kavan had no interest in his daughter's affections. Flannery was often flustered and unsure of how to behave around her, but Prince Espen was not. The prince of Hatu had made an impression on her with this gift, and upon her father. Such a gesture between the nobility of other lands was a good sign. Perhaps Arlan would live to see his daughter wed after all.

"My gift is not as grand as Prince Espen's," he said, presenting his daughter with a small box while she nursed the scroll case and its contents on her lap, "but it is special."

Within the box, a cameo, the woman's face upon it etched in pink coral. Diona looked at her father, who smiled. "That is your grandmother. She gave it to her daughter, and I am giving it to you."

"This belonged to…mother…?" She stopped, not trusting her voice. Arlan thought she might cry, which had not been his intent. Others looked as if they too believed she might weep. Instead, in a gesture that reminded Arlan of himself, her expression grew calm and neutral. She pinned the brooch to her royal blue almost too revealing velvet gown with its white lace bodice panel. When she looked up, she smiled, any thoughts of her mother's absence locked away inside.

"Lord Cliáth, do not think we have overlooked you. Do you have anything to add?"

Kavan did not like the seductive tone of her voice; neither, he noticed, did King Arlan or Prince Espen. The implications seemed lost or ignored by most of the gathering, however, though both Owain and Ártur looked at her, and then at Kavan, with concern. Though tempted to drop his gaze, Kavan did not. Doing so would suggest that her words affected him, and he had learned that nothing quelled her advances faster than denying their effect.

"I have but a single gift to bestow, My Princess, the only gift I have to share."

She clapped her hands and grinned like a little girl. "You have written a song for me?" When Kavan nodded, she said, "Play it, milord, if you please."

In this, he could oblige her. Notes swelled and soared to the highest corners of the Grand Hall, filling the room in a way that nothing else did. The melody was complex, intense, full of joy and excitement, the way the princess lived. Beneath it, the countermelody carried a touch of hollow sadness so typical of many of the bard's works. Most failed to hear that part of his music, as was evidenced by the reproductions he heard played by other minstrels. It was assumed that the White Bard wrote only of the joy, love, peace, and passion he brought to the lives of others, that these songs came from a life of wonder. The White Bard could never write or know despair, except upon the death of those he loved, and thus when those darker elements were present, they were most often ignored. No one in the room appeared to notice it, not even Ártur or Owain. Kavan bit the inside of his lip to keep it from quivering.

There was silence upon completion of the song, a pleased hush he treasured even if he knew the music was misunderstood. He did not need words, expressions, or applause to know his audience approved. He could feel it. But the princess broke the stillness of his enjoyment by throwing her arms around his neck; he turned his head so that her lips found his cheek rather than his mouth as she intended.

"That was the most beautiful song I have ever heard, Lord Cliáth," she declared, and then whispered against his ear, "and the most seductive." He could not keep the flush from his face as he looked away from her. Pleased that she had gotten a reaction, she added in a louder voice, "I think I shall ask you to play that every year."

"As you wish," he murmured, grateful she had risen from his lap.

"Shall we dance?" Knowing better than to push him at that moment, the princess was already pulling Flannery onto the open floor. The quintet hired for the night began a spirited number, calling other dancers to join the princess. Asta Dugan, with her blood-red gown swirling around her feet, was quickly claimed for this dance by Tayte Cáner while Prince Hagan slouched sullenly, watching. He was spared the need of moping when Ordelia Cornell, the granddaughter of the chancellor, approached him, struck up a conversation, and then agreed to dance.

After seven more songs and watching Diona work her way through the same number of partners, Kavan discreetly made his retreat. He had no desire to linger long enough for her to ask him to dance because he knew of no graceful, diplomatic way to turn down the request, particularly on her birthday. Better not wait to be asked. No one observed his retreat, though eventually, someone would notice he was gone. It was something he had done at nearly every formal function held by the King and his family; no one would find it unusual.

He went first to the oratory but did not stay long; that would be the first place anyone would look for him. The back garden, amongst the grave markers of Lachlans long departed, would be the second place. He should take Muir's advice and leave the grounds, go to Alberni. But he wanted to see Wortham, let the man know where he was going to be. Even more than his cousin Ártur, Wortham Delamo was the one person in Rhidam that usually knew the bard's whereabouts.

But it was late and Wortham would likely be asleep. He wondered why the Captain had not attended Diona's ball. Either ill then or the man had watch duty tonight. Regardless, the bard would leave him to it and find him in the morning. Kavan felt weary to his bones, though he knew it to be an emotional weariness and not a physical one. It would be safe to sleep in his room. That would be one of the last places anyone would expect him to be if he desired to be alone.

He awoke some time later to a tendril of alarm, a dream perhaps that he should not have been having. He rarely dreamed; if it was one, he could not recall it. The Sight tapping into his consciousness, he wondered, but memory showed him nothing, left only that snaking feeling of discontent, thus he tried to relax, hoping sleep would reclaim him. But there came the distinctive brush of skin and breath against his bare shoulder at the same moment he became aware of a body lying beside him, and his eyes flew open and he jerked into a sitting position in alarm.

"You are shocked, milord? Do not tell me you wish me to leave."

Confronted with the sickening, embarrassed horror in his stomach, Kavan backed away and tumbled off the bed, the sheet coming with him as he fell. He had not sensed her arrival, unless that, or her lying down beside him, was what had roused him. He knew he had not invited her, and knew her presence here meant only one thing.

The princess pursued him, crawling across the bed, over the edge, and then across the floor like a cat stalking prey until he was against the windowsill. Only then did she stop, her body inches from his. Her eyes sparkled with a hunger he recognized but had never seen directed at him, and he could feel the rapid beat of her heart radiating with each quickened breath she took. He tried to breathe but his throat closed around the attempt, causing him to struggle to remain conscious. There were no words he could utter as apprehension filled his eyes.

Misunderstanding his expression, she continued, "Do not look surprised. You have wished me here as often as I have wished it."

Had he, he wondered in the part of his brain that could still form thoughts. Had he somehow led her to believe that was true? The answer that clawed out of his soul was a resounding no.

"My…this is not proper for a…"

"For a lady? Or a princess?" Diona laughed as she ran one finger down his bare white chest. He shivered, a response he knew she read as positive though for him it was a reaction of fear. She wore fine cotton, her sleeping gown he knew, having seen it before though never at this proximity. The scent of flowers surrounded her, caught in the waves of dark hair that tumbled over her shoulders. "I would not be the first woman to take a man before she wed him."

"I have no intention of marrying…" he murmured, trying to escape but realizing he was trapped by a dresser on one side and the corner of the room on the other.

She bit her lip, a gesture that made her appear uncertain for a moment, and then she shrugged in a way that suggested she had anticipated his argument. "Even so, I would not be the first to know one man and marry another. You want this, milord…as much as I."

Did he, he asked himself again. Her hand on his face rooted him in place. She traced his narrow jaw, his high cheekbone, and then touched her fingertips to his mouth. This had to be a dream. He could not imagine how this could be real. But the press of her young body against him when she closed the distance between them, the way he became acutely aware of every curve and round softness of her form, was too real to be a dream, too real to ignore, and might have been pleasant if he wanted this attention.

"No!" He jerked free, ramming into the corner of the dresser hard enough to topple items from it and leave a bruise on his fair skin, the sheet trapped beneath her knees falling away from his nude body as he stood. Panic-stricken, he fumbled for the fabric in the near darkness while Diona watched. "I do not want this ever. It is not something…I will not. And you should be ashamed…" he sputtered.

"Ashamed that I love you?" Two steps closer, until her face was caught in the moonlight shining through the window. Tears glistened at the corner of her eyes and she spoke in the tone of a child begging from her parents. How much of it was genuine, and how much of it was a play for sympathy, Kavan did not, at the moment, care to know.

"You do not love me." He was certain of it. Long ago, he had concluded that no woman would love him, and what he sensed from her now did not feel like love. He found a short tunic on the dresser and clumsily pulled it on while trying to maintain the covering around his hips. "You do not yet know love, Diona. To love is not to force, not to act thus. You desire me in a physical capacity of which I…"

"Of which you are not capable? Is that it, Lord Cliáth?" She drew near again, backing him against the bedpost, attempting the only other tactic she could think of to convince him to have her. Her hands found the bare skin of his stomach and she pressed her mouth to his. He shook from the intimacy of it and from the emotions he felt within her; there was fear and anger behind her play for passion, and not simply anger at him for not being what she wanted him to be. There was more beneath that anger than he cared to investigate. Yet how could he be anything other than what he was? He felt nothing except a growing fear of her increasing wrath but he could not even respond to that.

When he did not kiss her back, would not touch her, she withdrew abruptly and struck his face. "You are a pathetic waste of a man."

Her expression hardened, a darkness descending over her features that Kavan had never seen on any woman. Was that hatred? Did the girl he had raised, taught, befriended, now hate him? "Any man would beg for what I offer, but you…you do not know how to…I do not think you could please a woman if you tried."

He shrank from the force of her unexpected words, their barbs striking deep and rooting there. "Milady," he started, but she was beyond listening.

"I often wonder why you…such a handsome face…you do not know desire; you are as cold as the Kármár. You write of passion, your music is filled with it, but you know nothing of it. You have the physical attributes of a man…" she ripped the sheet from his hands, leaving him mostly uncovered before her cold gaze, "but that is all. The outward appearance…and more of a child in appearance at that. You do not look like a man. Even your voice betrays you. You are a fraud, not a man at all. Coward! I will make certain every woman in the Sovereignties knows you are nothing. A statue, heart of marble, beautiful to behold but dead in every other way. No woman will seek your bed, milord. You drive me from it; now no one will have you. It is not that I am who I am…it is that you are incapable of giving a woman the one thing she wants."

Her words stung in a way he had not imagined possible. Was it true? Was he incapable of knowing that bond? No, he had felt it once, with Gabrielle. But he fled anything more intimate than a kiss and had not felt those soul-consuming stirrings with another. And he knew that feeling passion was not the same as completing the union. Perhaps he had known he would fail and that was why he had run from Gabrielle. White. Marble. Beautiful. Searing thoughts swam in his mind; he could not sort them out, could not think clearly. There was a great ripping pain in his chest, in his soul. Not a man. He heard those words over and over. It was the one slur he had never wanted to hear, the one truth he had feared from his earliest realizations that he was different, the affirmation of his separation from what he longed most to be. Not a man. But if not a man, what? Fake. An imitation. Cold. Unfeeling. Dispassionate. Dead.

Not a man.

Mind and heart crying in horror and frustration, he yanked the tunic over his head and fled to the oratory, away from the princess' knife-like words, past Captain Delamo without seeing him. Not a man. Dead. Coward. He ducked into the k'dhín bhólibh, the Chamber of Purification that housed the Gate, where he pulled on all of the energy he could command and reached for the first point of contact he recognized.

Wortham stopped in the hall as Kavan fled by, stricken by the expression on the man's face and stunned by the fact that Kavan had nearly crashed into him without noticing. Such terror and pain were not like the bard. The Captain pushed the oratory door open to follow but then heard the sound of the chamber's curtain pulled harshly open. No point in entering; Wortham could not pursue through the Gate. As he let the door close with a heavy sigh, the princess exited Kavan's room, her nightdress slightly askew, her face dark, angry and tear-streaked though Wortham failed to notice the latter. Biting back the first words that came to mind out of the habit of diplomacy, he was certain he knew what had happened.

"I hope you know what you have done," he snarled.

Diona tossed her head. "Do not speak to me thus, Captain, or I shall have you flogged."

"Aye, and I would accept that flogging…but that he wishes otherwise for me is what restrains my tongue from what I might say. But I tell you this; you have made a grave error in judgment this night."

She snorted. "I did nothing, Captain, except show him the truth."

As she strode to her room, Wortham crossed his arms with a grunt. The truth? Perhaps, but whose truth? And at what cost? He growled low in his chest and entered the oratory to await Kavan's return.

The bard emerged from the náós into city streets he did not immediately recognize. His eyes saw little except the sheet falling away from his nakedness and Diona's look of scorn at what she had seen when he was exposed before her. Not a man. Dead. Coward. Her words had become his mantra, the only thing he could focus on.

He stumbled down several mostly empty streets, not knowing what he was looking for, why he was here, or what he wished to do. Coward. Not a man. It was too dark, the streets too poorly lit, his sight too blurred by the turmoil in his mind, to accurately judge where he was heading. He bumped into corners, into crates and carts and people, until he stopped beneath a garishly painted signboard with a dancing pig wearing a bonnet. The Merry Sow. He shook his head to clear it of the distorted, swaying image and pushed through the doors to stagger inside and settle on a barstool. His head fell onto his arms, crossed on the sticky wooden surface of the bar, in despair.

Not a man. Dead. Coward.

"What do you want?"

Not a man. Kavan looked at the bartender, a thick fellow with wide lips, unruly gray hair, and bulging dark eyes. Were the man's features naturally distorted, he wondered, or was this part of the nightmare he was caught in?

Not a man.

"Order something or get out."

The words came from far away, and his reply seemed to come from even further. "I do not have money…"

Were they his words, his voice?

Dead.

"Then out. Paying customers are welcome, beggars are not."

Not a man.

Kavan began to rise, to obey the forceful order, but staggered and sank down on another stool; no doubt, the man thought he was drunk already. There were raucous words in a distant corner of the room. The bartender shot a look in that direction and started around the bar to help Kavan out of the building.

"Out with you, now. I don't need trouble, and you're asking for it. No money, no service. Out." He pulled Kavan up by one arm and the bard slumped against him. Noting his partial state of undress, the fellow stared and asked, "By the saints…where are your clothes…?"

"Don't fret, Horace, honey. He's with me."

Coward.

The woman who took Kavan's weight, gently settling him onto the stool and then plopping down beside him on another, was large, buxom, dark, and smelled of cheap wine and even cheaper perfume. Her face was as full and round as her body, made more so by heavy usage of cheek and lip rouge. Part of his mind screamed in protest as she draped one fleshy arm around his slender shoulders and put one hand on his exposed knee. He was shivering but he could only stare with a numb expression and wonder where she had come from.

Dead.

The bartender snorted and resumed his duties, keeping his eye on the corner group quietly hunched over the table with their heads huddled together. "You look as if you've lost everything, love," the woman commented, her painted mouth inches from Kavan's ear. "Including most of your clothes. Why don't you come upstairs and tell Cora what happened?"

Coward.

"Cora?" he whispered roughly, realizing that she was correct. Other than the short, sleeveless tunic, which barely made a decent covering, he wore nothing, not even shoes. His feet were dusty and bleeding, his legs bruised and dirty. No wonder he was drawing stares.

"Me, of course. You're Elyri, right?"

Not a man.

"Yes." As if I could hide it, he thought.

"Well then, I know you won't drink, but order a bottle and bring it up. Cora has what it takes to cure what ails you."

Dead.

She was a harlot, he realized, though it failed to cause a reaction. A woman had to make a living too, and he knew some were not given favorable choices in life. "Burgundy," he muttered to the bartender, who produced a bottle and handed it to the woman; Cora wriggled to her feet from the stool and beckoned. Snickers and a few whistles followed them.

Not a man.

What harm could there be in going upstairs, in talking to this woman? Kavan had learned long ago that those on this darker side of life had knowledge and wisdom not often found in his world of courtiers and kings. Perhaps she could help. They slowly staggered up the stairs and passed several poorly closed doors. He stopped outside of the door she passed through, looking beyond her with glassy eyes, listening to the sounds emanating from the other rooms. It occurred to him that the other rooms contained similarly paired occupants.

There were no furnishings, only a lumpy stained mattress that was likely infested with lice, fleas, and worse. When he realized he would have to be on a bed beside her, else upon the floor, the panic and terror resurfaced. He would have fled if his legs would have allowed it, but Cora took hold of his arm and pulled him gently into the room, with nothing carnal in her touch or actions.

Coward.

"Sit," she said in a matronly tone that was devoid of anything resembling sexuality. She produced a pair of dented mugs and a pitcher of water from a wall shelf beside two candles and then settled her bulk upon the mattress as gracefully as she could.

He was still trembling and his mouth had gone dry, but he managed to speak. "I should not…I cannot…if anyone…"

"Honey," the woman smiled, patting the mattress, "I don't talk to nobody about what goes on here. No one will know. You don't have to do anything you don't want to. Stay and talk. Or not. Pull yourself together in a safe place. You don't look like you should be alone."

She poured water from a dark stained pitcher into a mug and held it to him. He looked at it, took it from her hands, and hesitated before drinking its contents quickly. When she offered to refill it, he motioned for the bottle of burgundy.

"Are you sure, honey? Trying to kill yourself? I don't need a man dying here."

Man? Dying? Not a man. Dead already.

He swallowed hard and gestured. "I'm sure. I promise to die somewhere far from here."

Coward.

"I don't see why you should want to die. With a face like yours…" Beautiful. Cold. Dead. Not a man. "It can't be that bad…bad enough to want to die over, whatever it is."

He reached out, motioning for the bottle again. She hesitated but reluctantly put it in his hand. Resisting the urge to drink the entire bottle, he took two large swallows and gave the bottle back as the red liquid burned its way into every fiber of his body. It weakened his muscles, causing him to collapse onto the mattress.

Coward.

He was still conscious and vaguely aware of his surroundings, though the sick warm haze of alcohol replaced the numbness he had previously felt. He wondered how long it would be before the alcohol either caused him to pass out or killed him. Cora was talking but he could not respond. He could not even make out what she was saying, other than knowing it was an attempt at small talk to which he was oblivious. His tongue was thick, his mouth swollen from the liquor. He wanted to lie here alone, in this insect-infested closet of a room, and die in peace.

Dead.

Not quite dead. He was aware when she kissed him, touched him, running her plump hands over his body in a way he knew should produce results, would produce results in other men. Nothing happened, not the smallest response, positive or negative. His head started to pound. Not a man. He groaned.

"Easy honey. No use fretting. Alcohol gets the best of them, and you're Elyri. Can't expect it to be easy. Let it work out of your system. We've got time."

They stayed in the silence lying side by side beneath the light of the two candles, listening to laughter below and the nighttime sounds of the city streets. She ceased attempts to arouse him and instead propped up on one round elbow and ran her other hand up and down his arm. There was unusual peace in lying there, in doing nothing, drifting in the haze the alcohol produced in his mind, free for the time being of the screaming that filled it not long before.

It occurred to him in that haze that perhaps his participation was required to produce a response from his body.

Desire. Cold. Coward.

He touched the heavy thigh that rested on his leg and shivered, fighting the alcohol-fueled nausea burning in the back of his throat. Coward. With an extreme effort of will, he rolled on top of her. Cora smiled, wrapped her arms around him, and pulled him down until his mouth met hers. He let her do what she would, sick, afraid, waiting for the response that would disprove Diona's accusations, yet dreading that moment with everything he was.

It did not come. It would not come. Something within him snapped, and he pulled free, pushing weakly to his feet. What in k'Ádhá's name was he doing? Retching, his mind screaming again, he fled through the door, down the stairs, and into the dark streets, not heeding the calls of the woman behind him or his disheveled state.

Not a man. Coward.

Dead had dropped from the sequence. No one could be dead and feel as much pain, disgust, and horror as he felt.

He wondered if she knew who he was, was aware of the identity of the man she had tried to bed. What would she have said if she had been successful? What would she say in the face of his failure?

Not a man. He lurched, the alcohol in his system blinding both his psychic senses and his physical ones. Unable to see clearly, unable to think coherently, he blundered along, seeking shelter. Coward.

Ah yes, he was that. Everything Diona said was true. And before k'Ádhá's eyes, he had tried to bed a whore. The one thing she had wanted, the only thing, and he was unable to give it. Repulsed, he leaned upon a stack of crates and his stomach rejected its contents.

"What have we here?"

The garbled, drunken voice echoed the length of the passage; in his state, Kavan could not tell where it came from. Looking ahead revealed he had entered a dead-end alley. He turned to face the way he had come.

Not a man.

There were six, at least six he could count. He vaguely recognized one from the tavern; perhaps the others had been there too. He could not recall. They blocked his avenue of escape. As they approached, he noted that only one was armed. The others carried no weapons, at least none he could see.

"Looks like we've cornered a prize. One less of your cursed race to litter our streets and bed our women. Should've taken Horace's advice and left while you could, instead of opting for a little tumble with Cora. She's not too bright and your face is pretty enough to tempt the saintliest to vice. We'll see to her later. She'll not make this mistake again…and neither will you. Haven't you heard prostitution is a sin? Our Duchess may've wed one of you, but that doesn't mean we want you living here."

He was in Levonne?

They circled him as the leader spoke, taunting him with swings not meant to connect. He spun away from one then another, drunk and dizzy, until he could barely remain upright. With one final effort, he charged, hoping to break through the ring to freedom. Two of the men caught him and flung him back into their midst, knocking him to the ground.

The blows fell, hands and fists and boots, striking with a drunken fury he could not endure. Nor could he fight back; he did not have the strength or clarity of mind to accomplish anything except attempt to avoid each blow. When he fell, he fought to get up but a leaden kick shattered bone in his lower left leg, toppling him. Another kick by the same assailant broke the other leg, shattering his kneecap. There was pain, but not enough to penetrate the haze of alcohol and self-deprecation that enveloped Kavan.

As someone pinned his arms to the ground and the armed member of the group drove his dagger into Kavan's side, the Elyri felt the ball of energy bubble up within, more swift and powerful than he had ever experienced. His body might not have the strength or capability to fight back, but his spirit apparently did.

He attempted to restrain the deadly ball, half-hoping they would kill him, half-hoping someone would put a stop to this insanity before they did. When a heavy heel ground into one hand, crushing bones, shattering fingers, he yowled and the energy released. Someone mangled his other hand in the same manner as Kavan watched one man's head explode and another man collapse when his chest erupted into a spray of blood and bone and flesh. He heard a woman's plea, and then a thunderous growl echoing the length of the alley. The last image Kavan saw as something struck his head, was a large cat ripping its fangs through its first ill-fated victim.

❧Chapter 3❧

Artur entered Captain Delamo's stark room, hoping to find the man with the other the healer sought. Instead, he found both King Arlan and Prince Owain there, wearing similar expressions of perturbment. From the looks on their faces, the healer suspected there was bad news.

"You have come in search of Kavan as well?" asked Arlan.

The healer frowned. "I have not seen him since the ball. I meant to compliment his composition, but he was asleep when I stopped by his room last night and have yet to find him this morning. I have looked everywhere else I can think of…"

"As did I," the King agreed. "Owain suggested he might have returned to Káliel…"

It was a testimony to how time could change people that King Arlan and former King Owain could remain in the same room without visible animosity. The King no longer blamed the man for the death of his wife, and Owain had long ago gotten past any anger he felt after being forced to give up the Lachlan throne to King' Innis' youngest heir. Life felt the way it should. Almost.

"I said Muir invited him back," Owain corrected. "He could be any number of places."

Wortham did not look up as he finished pulling his boots on. "You assume I know where he is."

"To be fair," said the King, "you usually do."

The captain grunted. "I am sorry, milords…I have no idea where he is. I only know…" He stood and went to where his cloak hung.

"What? What do you know?" snapped the King impatiently. Though not normally an impatient man, King Arlan was known to have a temper, and when it came to Kavan, the monarch was not often logical or practical. Few of them were.

Squaring his shoulders, refusing to be intimidated, Wortham replied, "I do not gossip and I cannot tell you more than I know. I encountered Lord Cliáth last night; he ran past into the oratory, his expression…unsettled. He took the Gate."

Ártur ran his hand through his pale red hair. "Then something bad has happened. The Sight must have shown him something."

Wortham grunted. "I pray that is all it is."

The King grunted too. "Let me know as soon as he returns. I have much to speak to him about. And I want to know what has happened."

He left the bunkhouse, satisfied with the answer or too busy to press the issue, but Owain and Ártur remained, looking at Wortham expectantly. The captain wrapped his cloak around his shoulders, pretending he did not know they were seeking more than he had given them, until Ártur asked, "There is something else?"

"Why do you suspect it to be so?" He knew why. Ártur was Elyri. They knew things. And the healer knew him well after so many years serving the King together.

Ártur leaned against the wall. "I know my cousin. It's unusual he chose to go to his room when he normally retreats as far from everyone as possible when he desires solitude. That he stayed in Rhidam is odd enough. If something happened, something distressing as you suggest, I want to know. You look to know more than you're telling."

"Lord Healer," Wortham sighed, "the rest I do not know, only surmised from what I witnessed. I do not think the King should hear my speculations when I may be in error."

"Why?" Owain asked with a grave expression, feeling the air grow suddenly heavy.

The bear-like captain crossed to the window with his hands clenching and unclenching at his sides. Ártur exchanged looks with Owain but did not speak. It was obvious that Wortham was angry and as worried as they were. As Kavan's most constant companion, if the captain felt something was wrong, it probably was. If they should know, he would tell them. The man stroked his beard and turned to meet the healer's gaze, his muddy brown eyes rimmed with tears.

"He was more than unsettled, Lord Healer. He was terrified. He did not see me; he nearly knocked me down in his haste to flee. He wore little, a short under-tunic, nothing more. I cannot imagine where he would go dressed thus. I followed to the oratory, but when I realized he had taken the Gate and I could not follow, I turned and saw…the princess was coming out of his room in her nightdress…"

Ártur sank against the wall. "záryph á málneagthé," he whispered.

"She was exceedingly angry…threatened to have me flogged…" That, each man knew, was quite unlike the princess. "She said she had shown him the truth about himself. I do not know what she meant, but judging from what I saw, I do not think it was…whatever she said or did hurt him deeply."

Owain growled. "I did not…what could she do that would…?"

The men were silent, each thinking their own thoughts. This revelation explained Ártur's restless and anxious night, but it did not tell him where his cousin had gone. He remembered what had occurred when Gabrielle kissed Kavan many years ago. Knowing the princess as he did, the healer suspected she would not stop at something so innocent to get what she wanted; she had already tried and had not gotten the response she desired. While Kavan was older, more mature and experienced, and in some ways wiser, the healer doubted his cousin could easily deflect, or come to terms with, any flagrant displays of physical ardor directed at him. He clutched his head between his hands, his temples beginning to throb.

The captain squatted before him and put his large hand on the Elyri's knee. "Lord Healer?"

"I was recalling the last time…" He paused to look at the men with him. Kavan's closest friends, the two men who, other than Ártur and Prince Muir, probably knew the bard best. He saw no harm in speaking to them if it would help find his cousin. "You must mention this to no one," he cautioned in case he was wrong. Both nodded. "Wortham, do you remember what Kavan was like when you first met him?"

The captain furrowed his brow. "I recall he was morose, troubled. Haunted. I had never seen that demeanor on any other man in my life."

"Has he ever told you the cause?"

"No. I did not think it prudent to ask. Might it have a bearing now? What happened, milord?"

The healer stood. "Gabrielle kissed him. He believed it a moral affront, believed he had committed an unforgivable sin by feeling attracted to her."

Wortham's face expressed his comprehension. Owain's revealed his surprise to learn that Kavan had loved, to any degree, the woman he had married. It almost made the blonde man feel guilty as he realized it; it explained a lot about both Kavan's and Gabrielle's behavior when the two were in each other's company. "But surely…"

Ártur shook his head. "He had not experienced anything like that before to my knowledge…not a kiss, not desire…he was convinced from an early age that no woman who truly knows him will love him. His face draws people…but few have the ability to see beyond his face, his music, his faith. I don't know how he came to the conclusion that desire was wrong, that a kiss would damn him…but he did."

"k'Ádhá knows how he would feel if a woman did more."

"Exactly," the healer nodded. "It took a long time, but I thought he had finally worked through that. While he has come to understand that there are things that cannot be helped, that there are bodily functions he cannot control, that the heart loves who it loves and such responses between men and women are normal, it does not mean he accepts it."

Owain rubbed his face. "We have seen how he reacts to her flirtation. He is always uncomfortable. I never believed she might…if she was to pursue him further…where would he go? A náós?"

"Perhaps. The chellé in Alberni. Or home to Bhryell." Ártur shrugged wearily. "Maybe he has gone to Káliel. I do not know…and until Syl returns, I cannot afford to look." No matter how much he wanted to, the Lachlan House needed a healer on hand, and his wife was not due for many more days.

The captain rose as well. "It is equally probable he has gone to none of those since he knows we would look there. And he has not taken his harp."

"Then perhaps he is nearby," Owain said, knowing that Kavan rarely went anywhere without his harp. "Let us search Rhidam. Maybe he went to the k'gdhededhá for absolution if he felt he needed it."

The healer tried to cling to that thought as the three men left the room. "I hope your optimism is well founded," he said quietly. If not, he feared for his cousin's life…and his soul.

❧*❧

"I will be leaving in the morning," Prince Espen announced as he entered the solar where Princess Diona was speaking with her serving woman. Belda bowed to the prince and left, taking the other servants from the room with her. Proper or not, they knew the princess would demand to be alone with the Hatu prince. She always did. When the others were gone, Espen returned his attention to Diona and noted at once her odd expression. Angry, repentant, confused, ashamed…any of those descriptions would be appropriate but none of them were easily explained.

He wanted to stay, to ask what troubled her, to ease her burden, but he would not. There had been a change in the air since the Elyri bard left the ball last night, a change the prince did not like. It felt more pronounced this morning. If it concerned their relationship, he did not wish to know. His discomfort made him more determined to leave Rhidam before he learned the truth.

"So soon?" Her question was tired and distracted, not disappointed as he hoped.

"I have duties. I cannot dally at your whim. I came to the ball as requested. I am accommodating of your wishes because our customs are different and I do not desire offense. However…" He cleared his throat. "I am no longer at your disposal, Princess. Should you have honest need of me, or should you wish my presence here as something other than a distraction from boredom, I will come. But I shall not speak of marrying you again."

She closed her eyes, thinking about what he said in the silence that grew between them. "I have been…improper…haven't I?" she asked in almost a little girl voice.

Espen found it hard not to respond apologetically to that lost and sad tone, but he held his ground. "You have been inconsiderate of my position and my feelings. I have waited many years; the wait grows tiresome and an end does not appear to be in sight. If you do not wish to marry me, pray tell me that I may seek a bride elsewhere."

Watching him toy with his turban, she knew she had hurt him. She did not want him to look elsewhere; she could not bear the thought of him married to another. She slipped her hand into his, squeezing tightly to keep him from pulling away. He tried once and then relaxed into the gesture that meant so much to him. "I am sorry, milord. I do not mean to hurt or offend you. It is not that I do not want to marry you…I…do not know if I am ready to marry anyone. When I think I have an answer, something happens that makes me rethink my feelings. I need more time…"

He growled softly. "Ten years is not enough time?"

She managed a sad smile. "I was a child when you first posed the question. I liked the idea of marriage well enough then, but I was in no way equipped to answer you. I didn't understand what marriage entailed…and with our differing customs, sometimes I still do not know how we could make such a union work. I do not feel any better equipped to answer you, but your offer is still under consideration."

This time his hand did pull free of hers. "While you pursue other potential husbands."

"Other…?" She looked and sounded more confused than she felt. "Do you mean Lord McGrannis? I like him, it's true, but I do not consider him a potential husband. He would resent a woman more outspoken than himself. I don't want a man to live in my shadow…or to shadow me. I want one who can stand as equals in all things. Besides, I am told he's considering betrothal to one of Duke Niall's daughters."

"I was speaking of Lord Cliáth."

She almost grimaced and stepped back. She had not realized he suspected that, that many in Rhidam did, despite how obvious her flirtations had been. "He is older than my father."

"But he looks little older than you…younger some might say. Even so, many women wed older men…I am older than you…and I do not believe you would let a man's age interfere with your plans. Is he the man you wish to marry, Diona?"

His bluntness pushed her into an honest answer, perhaps the most honest one she had ever given where Kavan was concerned. "I do not think I would be opposed to it," she admitted, "and I have pursued him…but he has no interest in marriage or love…or in me." That hurt more to admit than expected, especially because she knew it would hurt Espen. "For him, age is one of many problems that exist. To consider him a potential husband is…foolish." She sighed, feeling the truth of those words for the first time.

"But you hope to change his mind." She might have said it was in the past, but he did not think it was behind her. Or behind them. "I cannot say I am happy about this, but I wish you well in your pursuit."

"Espen…"

Thinking she had made her choice, he shook his head and stepped away from her distracting proximity. "Enough. There is no more to say. Should you change your mind, you know where I can be reached. But I stress to you, do not wait much longer. I love you, but I cannot tolerate this game you are playing with my affections. It is painful to watch you pursue others while I await an answer. It makes me look the fool, both before your people and my own. Either you want me or you do not. When you have an answer, I would like to know what it is. Until then…I must pack."

"Espen." She was unsure if she should return his gift since it felt as if he wanted to be free of her, or whether he would be more offended by such a gesture and take it as a final severance of their friendship. "Thank you…for coming…and for the gift. I will come to Hatu to see it as soon as I can."

Regretting that he had made a public show of that presentation, that he had given it to her at all, he nodded and left her alone.

❧*❦

málneag Kóráhm's chellé hábhai, also called Saint Kóráhm's Abbey in the various Teren tongues, had once been a sprawling single story, gray stone manor carved from the mountainside on the southern edge of the city of Alberni. It fell under the jurisdiction of the Duke of Alberni, and once Kavan assumed that title and position, he began to renovate the abandoned building and add to it. The groundwork and some of the existing structure were Elyri in origin, but much of it had been rebuilt and expanded many times over the centuries, resulting in a mixture of at least five architectural styles. Kavan spent much time, energy, and expense in returning the entire building to its original Elyri form and spent an equal amount of effort to outfit the interior in a fashion he felt most conducive to pursuits of faith.

While it was more aristocratic in structure than similar facilities meant for the gdhededhá and the Faithful, Kavan intended málneag Kóráhm's to be a place of learning, of knowledge, of enlightenment. A place worthy of bearing the name of the saint who was his patron. There were rooms full of books and scrolls and several more with shelves waiting to be filled. There was more money invested in those documents than in the abbey itself, showing where Kavan's interest was. There was a large, airy room furnished for the scribes he hoped to attract, men and women who could translate and copy those works and make them available in every language of the Sovereignties for anyone who desired to read them.

gdhededhá Tusánt gazed in wonder at the domed ceiling of the grotto-like sanctuary adorned with painted záryph, clouds, and stars. He was not privy to the details of its construction, but Tusánt wished he knew who the painter was. Such a master could be commissioned to do similar work in Rhidam. The carvings in the wooden benches and prie-dieu, the marble statue of Saint Kóráhm that loomed beside the entrance, the towering white pyre that seemed to float behind the altar in the midst of a dark chasm, were awe-inspiring to behold. It was impossible not to note that the figure of Dhágdhuán was absent. The pyre was barren except for what looked like charred areas at the base where the flames of his death would have eaten at the wood.

"Welcome to málneag Kóráhm's, gdhededhá Tusánt."

The Elyri gdhededhá turned, startled, so engrossed in the splendor that he had not heard anyone approach. He recognized the man from previous meetings and smiled. "k'gdhededhá Khwílen. Excuse me for not hearing you. I was…enthralled by what Lord Cliáth has inspired here."

Khwílen was an ideal choice to head a place such as this. He was a brilliant author, master painter, and skilled speaker. His shoulder length, un-tonsured, butter-blonde hair and child-like face made him blend in with the painted záryph in a way that some found unnerving. It was easy to understand why Kavan had chosen him.

"That is the function, to lift us from the ordinary into the sublime. While Lord Cliáth did not do the actual construction or artwork, it is his concept, his vision. I merely painted what he saw. Though he has yet to see its completed form, I am confident it is exactly as he envisioned it." He gestured at prayer cubicles filled with foliage and bubbling springs as if they were in hidden grottos in paradise. "You approve?"

"How could I not? It is the most beautiful place I have ever had the privilege of seeing. I thought to hire the artist," he grinned, "but I am not sure commissioning the new k'gdhededhá would be appropriate…or that Lord Cliáth would give you up even for a short while. The pyre?"

Khwílen smiled. "Lord Cliáth wishes this to be a place of joy and peace. Rather than dwell upon suffering, he wants those here to dwell on the result…the fact that Dhágdhuán conquered mortal death to be taken into the divine. The fact that divinity is in each of us if we strive for it. Some will undoubtedly find his vision unorthodox but I agree with it, as I do with Saint Kóráhm's."

Tusánt studied the image from a perspective he had not considered before. The yawning darkness behind the pyre did seem like an empty grave, its gloom dispelled by the pinpoint of light from above that showered warmth upon the pyre in a way that offered hope. "I know little of Kóráhm's teachings," he admitted, "nor have I thought about this in this way. I think there is virtue in such belief. Is the rest of the facility complete? Is it anything like this?"

"Except for the final half of the living quarters, the work is complete. Those rooms are scheduled to be done by next autumn; I doubt they will be needed before then. We have many empty rooms and if we need more for residents before the rest are finished, there are guest rooms we can utilize. We are prepared for opening."

"Good. I am granted leave to remain until the Feast, to open the naós on the most fitting day. May I view the rest?" Tusánt was eager to see how the other areas measured up to this one.

"Follow me," Khwílen said with a smile, gesturing to the open door through which they had both entered.

❧*☙

Swabbing his patient's forehead, Gaelán Cáner sat on the edge of the bed, a worried frown on his young face. He had been wandering town last night, taking the opportunity of his parents' absence to visit a young woman who had recently caught his eye. It was late when he started for home and he had been fearful of traveling the streets in the dark, even though he was the Duke's son, or perhaps because of it. Title meant little to those who hated and feared Elyri. When he heard the sounds of brutal fighting in an alley ahead, his first instinct was to flee. He was only a boy. But a woman's voice, calling his name, begged for help, encouraging him to enter the alley against logic and wisdom. He followed the voice to find the most beautiful woman he had ever seen kneeling over the broken, beaten body of his cousin, the bard. There were dead men lying around them, horribly mutilated. There was no time to stare in revulsion, surprise, or awe. Rather than fetch a healer or the city guards, Gaelán did as the auburn-haired woman instructed, discovering in the process that he carried the same healing abilities as his aunt and uncle, something he had only recently begun to suspect and had refused to believe possible.

The woman helped transport Kavan to the Dubuais-Cáner house and stayed long enough to be sure the bard would be comfortable and likely live. It took Gaelán several agonizing hours to heal first the puncture wound, and then the cranial damage, his inexperience hindering his progress. Eventually, his perseverance meant success, and when he turned to thank the woman, she was gone. That had been early this morning. He had not gotten her name, learned how she had found Kavan, or how she and the bard had come to be in the midst of what had sounded like a drunken street brawl or wilderness ambush. He had not learned why his cousin had been so badly beaten and wore so little. He was afraid to know.

Not long after her departure, Kavan's eyes flickered open while Gaelán was trying to heal his legs. Being untrained, the boy had no idea how to gather more energy for the task, and it took nearly an hour of healing, pausing, and healing again to mend the left leg. Kavan's knee would have to wait, as would his hands, as by this time Gaelán was more exhausted than he could ever remember being. The bard had shown little indication of knowing where he was and was silent until Gaelán mentioned that he should send for Ártur to heal the other injuries before permanent harm set in.

"No. You cannot. Ártur must not…this cannot be undone. Please, leave me."

He drifted back into unconsciousness, muttering the same words over and over. Coward. Dead. Not a man. Gaelán had no idea what those words meant and no idea what he should do. He was fond of his cousin, awed by the power he wielded, and had wanted to be like him for as long as he could remember. Gaelán had no musical talent and had not thought he could carry any ability to manipulate Elyri power. His brother certainly did not. That he suddenly discovered he could heal was a stunning revelation. He wanted to respect the man's wishes, yet how could he not send for Ártur? If Kavan did not receive medical attention from a trained healer, the use of his hands would be lost. He would never make music again. Gaelán did not want to be responsible for that, not even partially responsible.

He decided to wait until Kavan awoke, to press upon him the necessity of sending for a healer. The older man would have to listen to reason.

But evening came and then faded into night and Kavan still slept. Gaelán slept as well, his head upon the man's chest, his dreams full of ugly images he could not, did not want, to recall upon waking. Now he stared out the window in the direction of Rhidam, wondering how long it would be before one of the servants discovered what had occurred, wondering what his family would think when they learned of his newly discovered talent.

A noise behind interrupted his thoughts. Kavan was awake, staring at him with a haunted expression that chilled Gaelán as if the window was open mid-winter. He looked at the window to see if it was closed, and when he saw it was, he approached the bedside slowly.

"How do you feel, k'aendhá?" he asked.

Kavan's eyes closed and Gaelán feared he was going back to sleep. He reached to touch the man, but the bard spoke. "I…ache. But much of the damage seems to be…repaired. I told you not to summon Ártur."

"I have not, k'aendhá," he shook his head. "That which has been healed was done by my hands."

The bard stared as if looking for something, and then he relaxed into his pillow. "It is so. I remember, k'tydhá. This is good."

Gaelán frowned. "No, it is not good. I do not know what I am doing. There may be damage that will kill you if not tended…"

"Then so be it."

The resignation in the bard's androgynous voice made the boy stare, slack-jawed. "You cannot mean that! There are people that need you, love you…it is stupid to allow yourself to die when it can be prevented!"

Kavan sighed. "I do not think I am going to die, kyá, however much I might wish it. I do not need Ártur to keep me from dying."

"Then let me send for him for your hands."

The response was vehement and cold. "No."

Begging, Gaelán said, "If I do not, if the damage sets, you may not play again." He might not have been a trained doctor, but he had seen what untreated injuries did to soldiers.

Kavan stopped him with a withering look. "This is punishment, k'tydhá. There is nothing Ártur can do. Only k'Ádhá can do it when he feels I have atoned for my transgressions."

"What could you have done that could warrant such punishment?" Kavan's expression told Gaelán he was not going to answer, and it brought tears to the boy's eyes. "At least allow Ártur to try…"

Kavan's gaze grew colder. "I want you to swear you will not summon him. I do not want him here. Swear it, or I shall not speak to you again."

A threat of that nature coming from Kavan was unusual and not to be taken lightly. Gaelán began to tremble as his tears spilled free. He was thirteen years old, not prepared to cope with such threats from the man he worshiped. "I swear, k'aendhá. I will not ask Ártur to come. But is there anything more I can do? I have slept; perhaps I can tend your other leg?"

Stirred by the boy's tears, but not enough to change his mind about summoning Ártur, Kavan nodded, allowing Gaelán to heal his other leg if he could. He focused on the touch and energy flowing from Gaelán's hands. Yes, he was a healer, raw and untrained but the potential was there. Odd that no one had seen it earlier, when potential healers were usually recognized at birth. Perhaps his Teren blood had masked the power. It took the boy nearly an hour, but at last, he declared that he had done as much as he could, that as far as he could tell, Kavan's knee was whole. That Kavan found mobility restored confirmed it, though there was still residual pain, the ache of bruised muscles that would take days to dissipate.

"May I…is it possible to get food? And water?"

Gaelán stepped away from the bed and wiped his face. "I'm sorry I did not think of it sooner. Of course, you are hungry. I shall fetch something." As it was the servants would be worrying about him; putting in an appearance would save him from questions later.

When he was alone. Kavan chose to do what he had been dreading since opening his eyes. He looked at his hands. They were crushed, twisted, swollen, and dark with purple, red and black bruises that looked more hideous because of the natural whiteness of his skin. If he had known the words to use, he would have cursed himself for his foolishness. Instead, he let his head fall back into the pillow and wept.

To never play again. This was punishment of the worst kind, to be bereft of the one love in the world he cherished. No more music. The end of the career of the White Bard of Bhryell. All because he turned in his weakness to the arms of a whore whom, in the end, he had not been able to bed. Coward. And not a man. Diona was correct. He would not be able to face her, never return to Rhidam. Even fleeing to Alberni or Bhryell was out of the question. He could face no one he knew with what he had become. Fate had brought Gaelán to save his life, but no one else must know of this.

When Gaelán returned with a tray of food, Kavan pretended to be asleep, not wishing the boy to see his misery. The tray was left on the nightstand, the candle extinguished, and then Gaelán left the room for the second time in his long vigil. Kavan curled into a tight ball and stared into the darkness.

❧*❧

It would be good to leave Levonne and gdhededhá Picus in the morning. Claide had once tolerated the differences between himself and many other gdhededhá in Enesfel, but over the years that tolerance had faded into barely concealed loathing. Self-righteous gdhededhá who preached open-mindedness and universal acceptance were the worst, and while he was not suspicious of Picus' loyalties, the gdhededhá's sermon that morning had annoyed him more than ever and convinced Claide that he did not like gdhededhá Picus. Picus had no right, in his eyes, to demand that people accept everyone they meet, that they tolerate differences and embrace each other in the spirit of unity and goodwill. There was no brotherhood between Teren and Elyri. Such sermons made Claide ill.

It would be good to take young Valgis, the gdhededhá he had initiated, away from Picus' putrefying influence. Claide saw something in the young gdhededhá, something he could use if it was molded properly. As much as it went against his nature to be friendly, Claide planned to make every effort to befriend Valgis, win him over before they returned to Rhidam. If he was not successful, he would lose Valgis to the k'gdhededhá's fatherly force. That, Claide decided, could not be allowed to happen.

❧*❧

Over the next five days, Kavan drifted in and out of sleep, and though he requested food that first day, and Gaelán brought him more each consecutive day, he did not eat. The cook was suspicious of the requests for extra food, forcing Gaelán to try his best to charm and assure her that he was a growing boy recovering from illness and thus needed more to eat. That excuse worked at first, but he was unable to eat as much as he was taking, no matter how hard he tried, it was obvious the woman was beginning to doubt his truthfulness.

What worried Gaelán more was knowing that his mother and brother would be home soon. He would not be able to hide Kavan's presence from them as he did from the servants. They would be angry that he had failed to send for a healer, even if they did believe he had the healing gift.

As he watched Kavan's flushed face twitch in slumber, feeling the lingering fever begin to spike, Gaelán feared his kinsman would die. He had promised he would not summon Ártur, but he had not promised that he would not tell the healer where Kavan was. It seemed a fair and reasonable compromise. Providing the healer with information was not the same as summoning him. As he penned a letter and gave it to one of his mother's retainers for delivery to Rhidam, he hoped Kavan would see it the same way. If it came to a choice of Kavan not speaking to him, and Kavan dying, the first choice was the better alternative.

❧*❧

Ártur was giving up hope of finding his cousin. When the King could spare him, he searched Rhidam, searched Alberni, and had searched Owain's home in Fiara. Kavan was in none of those places. No one had seen him. Káliel would be a last resort, as he saw no point in worrying Prince Muir this soon after the young man's wedding.

Today, five days after Kavan's disappearance, the healer decided in desperation to visit Bhryell. He went first to bhydáni Tíbhyan's home, but the sage was not there. At least, he had not come to his door or bid the healer enter. It left one other place. Using Kavan's key, Ártur opened the door to the brick structure Kavan once called home.

The house had been empty for too long; the layers of dust proved it. Objects had been undisturbed, it appeared, since the healer and his wife had last been here. He wondered if Syl wanted to return when their second child was due. She had not said it, as that event was still four months away, but Ártur knew how much it meant to her that her children be born in her hometown. As if their place of birth made them more, or less, what they were. They had been pleasantly surprised to conceive so soon after Llucás' birth. That the pregnancy had progressed this far was a good omen. As rare as Elyri children were in their long life spans, such a quick conception after their son's birth was incredible. The Sight had not revealed whether this child would be a boy or a girl, but Kavan had told him that this child would be a healer. That announcement, knowing that the child was likely to live and heal, had given Ártur as much joy as knowing he had fathered a second child.

Coming down the stairs after having searched Kavan's room and private náós, Ártur heard the front door creak. He raced the rest of the way down and into the front hall, calling, "sínréc? Is that you?"

"No, ílMairós MacLyr, it is me," a wizened voice replied. "I saw the door open and wondered who was here, if perhaps Kavan had come. I take it," the visitor chuckled, "you have lost your cousin?"

Seeing the ancient sage instead of Kavan, Ártur wilted against the wall. "bhydáni. I hope Kavan is not lost in any real sense. He left Rhidam in a state of distress and no one has seen him in five days. I am worried."

Those words made the old man frown. "I have never known him to show distress, not even when your father expelled him, or when he brought Mílne home. Composure is his strength. What has happened?"

"I do not know. What little I do know would lead to speculation and I don't want to do that. You have not seen him?"

"I have not seen him since your son was born," Tíbhyan admitted, sounding sad. "I have hoped…I do not have much time left, I fear, and I want to speak with him, to share as we once did." He brushed away the man's hand, not wanting his privacy invaded by a healer's probing touch. "I have new tidbits for him, and I am sure he has much to teach me. He always does when he comes. I would like to be able to depart this life knowing I was the wisest, most learned man in Elyriá, and have passed that mantle on to young Cliáth."

Ártur's hand dropped. His senses did not register any ailment in the sage, but there were some things about Elyri that no one understood. The ancient ones were known to walk away from their homes, never to be seen again, and no one, not even other Elyri, knew whether they died or met some other end. As ancient as the sage was, it was entirely possible that time was drawing near for Tíbhyan.

"I will tell him you asked for him. Please…if you see him…tell him I am worried…we all are. Tell him to come home. And please, do not tell my family I was here. They will feel slighted if I do not call, but I do not currently have the time for a visit." Nor did he want to be pushed into a position of explaining Kavan's situation, or rather what he did not know of it, to their less than sympathetic family.

"As you wish," the old man agreed.

Ártur helped the sage down the steps, realizing how frail the man had become though he respected the bhydáni's wish not to be read. He was frail, but his life force was strong, suggesting he would not be leaving life as soon as he feared. He would wait for Kavan's return, if he could. Tíbhyan shrugged away further assistance and they parted in the street, the bhydáni tottering towards his home and Ártur returning to the village náós and its Gate rather than using the one in Kavan's room. Kavan had gone to that náós often as a troubled younger man. Ártur had not sensed him earlier, but perhaps he was there now.

He saw Elys from a distance, her familiar blonde hair worn high upon her head, the shape of her neck so intimately familiar that the sight stole his breath. There was a small girl tagging along behind her, straining against the matronly hand that kept her from straying. It stopped him in his tracks. He had intended to marry Elys once; now she had a child and he had his. He shivered as he mused on the path their lives had taken, paths Kavan had foreseen, and returned to Rhidam with a befuddled, heavy heart.

❧*☙

k'gdhededhá Jermyn hesitated to leave the three Elyri manuscripts he had found in the hands of anyone other than Lord Cliáth, but learning that the bard was not there, he reluctantly gave the books into the care of Wortham Delamo. Not that he lacked faith in the captain. If that had been the case, he would not have left them. No, Wortham was the next best choice. Jermyn's reluctance was due only to the value her perceived in his find. Priceless, he had said.

And Wortham believed him.

The books lay upon the bed, wrapped in wax canvas to protect them from dust and moisture. Rubbing his hand across them, Wortham wondered what kind of books they were. Ancient books, according to Jermyn. He wanted to open them, to look, to know what secrets had been uncovered in the bowels of the náós. Religious manuscripts most likely, or historical texts, possibly even confiscated items the k'gdhededhá of Clarys had not wanted the Faithful to read. Wortham doubted he could read them; he could not master High Elyri despite Kavan's attempts to teach him. There was no use in unwrapping them, exposing them to possible damage. He locked the books in his chest of personal items and left the bunkhouse to learn if Owain or Ártur had found any trace of the missing bard.

❧*❦

Madalyn detected the peculiar aura in her home the moment she arrived, though there was no Elyri in her blood. It was likely, she mused, a product of her close relationship with Bhríd and her familiarity with the home she had been born in. It was prevalent in the silence of the servants, who welcomed her and Tayte but did not otherwise speak. It crept out of the darkness of the unlit halls. There was no sign of her youngest son, who should have been lighting the lamps at this hour if the servants had not. Fearing his illness had worsened, she sent Tayte about his business and hurried to Gaelán's room. She stopped and stared in distress at what she found.

Inside the door at the foot of the bed lay a pile of bloody, soiled sheets. Nearby, a wash basin full of water with a damp cloth hanging over the edge. On the nightstand, a tray of uneaten food. She started to rouse Gaelán from sleep but froze when she realized it was not her son in the bed. It was Kavan.

"Welcome home, mother," said the quiet voice behind her as she pressed deeper into the room.

"Gaelán, what is this?" She kept her composure as she turned to look at her son, relieved to see he was well but worried about what she saw around her. "What has happened?"

Gaelán shifted his weight from foot to foot, wondering how much he should reveal. "I was in town," he finally began, leaving out mention of what hour he had been out and the fact that he had been out alone. "A woman found him in an alley, after a brawl. We brought him here to care for him. Except for his hands, I do not find any other damage…"

"Ártur…the whole Lachlan house has been looking for him for several days." She knew her son well enough to know he was leaving out details. "How long has he been here?"

The boy shrugged. "I don't know. I lost track. A few days…"

"And you did not think to send word to Ártur?"

Insulted that his mother would think him irresponsible, even though he knew he had hesitated at Kavan's demand, he replied, "I have, mother. I hoped he would come with you."

"His search has kept him out of the keep for much of the last several days. Perhaps he has not gotten your message. I hope you stressed urgency." Madalyn reached for the blanket covering Kavan, intending to pull it back and examine his condition.

Not wanting her to see what Kavan was clearly trying to hide, Gaelán moved fast, knocking the meal tray from the nightstand with a loud crash. As Madalyn jumped, her efforts to pull the sheet back thwarted, he murmured, "I am sorry, mother. And yes…I did."

She looked at the spilled food, the need to inspect Kavan temporarily subverted. "Has he eaten?"

"No. He asked for food once, but he has not touched it…only water. He sleeps most of the time. His fever has risen though I cannot determine why."

"That," she sighed, "is what a healer or physician is for. Come, help me clean this up, take the sheets to be laundered, and then we shall see what more we can do for Kavan."

From his mother's demeanor and tone of voice, Gaelán thought it best not to mention that he was, in fact, a healer.

❧Chapter 4❧

Hes á Redh Náós felt barren with both Tusánt and Claide out of the city. Tusánt would not return until after Kóráhm's Feast, which left Jermyn more shorthanded than usual. Thankfully, Claide's stay in Levonne should be a short one and he would bring back the new gdhededhá with him. That would fill the gap until Tusánt returned. Perhaps, Jermyn mused, I will assign this youngster right here. He could certainly use some young strength.

Particularly since the task of cleaning the chambers below the náós was proving too much for his aging back and failing eyes. The old sepulcher had been the first area to be cleared, as the k'gdhededhá disliked the idea of rot and decay existing below the floors of a hallowed place. The bodies had been there for centuries, perhaps longer; the task of removing them had been put off long enough. For Jermyn, bodies buried in the yard around the náós was acceptable, beneath the floorboards was not. He, Rankin, and six townsmen had spent the last month clearing it. The crypt was now empty and clean, and yesterday their efforts revealed a small wooden chest at the rear of a now-vacant burial shelf. It was but one of the small treasures found in that room, jewelry and pottery and ornamental weapons all representative of people of wealth now forgotten and nameless. Most of the time, the items were easily reached, but the chest had been beyond Jermyn's grasp. Fortunately, Rankin, with his longer arms, had been able to hook the metal handle and pull it from the back of the burial shelf.

As with every body, every item they found, Jermyn wondered who the buried individual had been and why such items had been important to them.

There was great excitement at this discovery, as with the others, for no one knew how old that chest might be. None of them could read the High Elyri script engraved on the chest's exterior, nor on the books found inside, but Jermyn did recognize the numeral on the defaced cover of one of the books. It was a three. And he recognized the first letter. His pulse quickened at the thought that here, in his hands, he might hold the banned third volume of Saint Kóráhm's writings. As a member of the institution that had banned such books, Jermyn should, perhaps, destroy what he had found and the other books found with it. Even those members of the Order of Saint Kóráhm were not allowed to read the Saint's words. To hold such a book in his hands might be an offense in the eyes of some, as would be giving the books to Kavan.

But Jermyn sent them to the bard anyhow. If the Saint saw fit to manifest to and through Kavan, then it was right and good that the Elyri should have any words the Saint may have written. All of them. If Jermyn was wrong, if this book was not what he thought it to be, then he could think of no one else who might be interested in their contents and could tell him what they were.

"k'gdhededhá?"

Jermyn shook his head to clear his thoughts. "Yes, Rankin?"

"Can you look over the list of motets and readings for the Saint Kóráhm Gathering? I do not want to neglect or forget anything."

"Of course. Sit. Let me see what you have."

❧*❦

❧68❦

Princess Diona paced the back garden, conducting a silent dialogue with her mother and twin entombed nearby. She had expected that, as usual, harsh words would roll off Kavan easily and that he would have returned home by now. Life should have gone back to normal. That he had been missing for a week left her much time to think about what she had said and done and to experience the early stages of profound guilt and remorse.

She wanted him to love her. That was all she had ever wanted. Since the first stirrings of womanhood, she had been unable to think of him in any other way. He was gentle in everything he did and said. He would never hurt her. She believed that loving him would pave the way for her acceptance of other men, if he would but love her back.

And he had the face, the physique, of a záryph. Not a boy, not a man, but something ultimately superior. She could admit that to the dead; she could admit it now that Kavan was not here to hear it. But she knew he did not want to be a záryph or a saint. He wanted to be himself. He wanted to be a man…and her angry words of emasculation had devastated him. She knew it but did not want to believe it. He had always seemed strong; she did not want to believe that perhaps he was more fragile than he appeared, or that she had done irreversible damage to how he must see her, to how he must see himself, to his dear, loving heart. She wondered if she would have the courage to face him, to seek forgiveness, when he returned.

Yet he did not come, and Diona feared he never would. She had driven him away from his home, his friends, his family, in the cruelest way possible. There was no one to talk to about this, no one to confess her burden to.

Confession. Yes, she needed to seek out k'gdhededhá Jermyn. Then, perhaps, she would go to Káliel. If anyone could set her thoughts straight, it would be Muir.

❧*❧

"A message for you, Lord MacLyr, from Master Gaelán Cáner."

"Thank you, Darius," Ártur said with a nod as he took the scroll. He gave Wortham a quizzical look and shrugged. It was peculiar that his nephew would contact him instead of his father, but as he read the message, he understood why. His throat constricted and he had to read the message a second time to be sure he had read it correctly.

"Milord?" asked Wortham, watching the color drain from Ártur's face.

"Kavan has been injured...he may be dying...in Levonne." He stood hastily. "I must go at once."

Wortham rose as well. "By Gate?"

Ártur shook his head. "I cannot concentrate enough for that."

Understanding, the captain said, "I will get horses and travel with you. You may need protection."

The captain let his words stand. Ártur knew Wortham would follow if not invited, and to be honest, he did not trust himself to be alone.

Kavan. Dying. Those words in one sentence caused unimaginable pain. Not thinking to tell anyone where he was going or why, Ártur fled to his room, gathered his supplies, and met Wortham in the courtyard where the man had two horses and a pack waiting. That it was not long before sunset did not matter. Kavan needed him. Ártur would ride all night if he must.

❧*❦

Kavan felt consciousness approaching, realizing as he woke that Madalyn must be home. It must be her presence he sensed, as he had grown familiar with Gaelán's company over the last several days and he knew it was not Gaelán with him. He felt hot, stiff, and his hands throbbed painfully. Without opening his eyes, he sighed. "You do not need to linger. There is nothing you can do for me."

"You are sure of that, átaelás mai?"

"Kóráhm!" He jerked up; the pain of the effort made him dizzy and nauseous. Scarred hands steadied him, taking away some of that dizziness and nausea, though it did not lessen the pain elsewhere in his body. Their eyes met briefly until Kavan looked away, humiliated.

"Were you expecting someone else?"

"Anyone. It has been so long since you…and after what I have…"

"What have you done?"

He shuddered and closed his eyes. "You know."

"Perhaps I do not." The quite real form of Saint Kóráhm the Heretic settled into the chair at his bedside, pushing his hood from his head. "Unless you are reading my thoughts, you do not know what I know or do not know. But if you will not speak freely with me, I shall not pursue it. It is up to you to trust me or not. I do have a question to put to you, however, that you must answer before we proceed with any discussion. Why have you refused Gaelán's offer to heal your hands?"

"He cannot do it. He is not a trained healer."

The auburn head of hair bobbed once. "He is not…but he has healed the rest of your injuries…though not completely I admit. I see no reason he could not tend your hands to offer mobility. Even so, he could have summoned Ártur to aid you."

"This," Kavan held his twisted hands before Kóráhm, choking at the sight, "is punishment. No healer can undo what k'Ádhá has done."

"k'Ádhá? Did you see k'Ádhá amongst the men who beat you? Did you see him crush your hands?"

Kavan grunted. "He allowed it."

Kóráhm narrowed his gaze. "k'Ádhá gave us freedom of choice to do what we will, and then stepped away from creation to allow it to function alone, to find the path back to him. Some events may be predestined…experience tells us this, and he knows what the outcome will be of a man's choices, but he does not dictate every moment of our existence. He allows many things, most of which he has no hand in. He might have allowed those men to attack you, but he did not make them do it; it was their choice, not his."

"It is punishment," Kavan said, conviction intact. "I want to be healed, to play my harp, but it will only come after I atone for my…"

The saint rose, shaking his head with regret. "You think you are privy to the mind of k'Ádhá, phyl haeles. That is a dangerous path, and one many do not come back from. If you wish absolution, you must first know what your sins are before they can be forgiven. Only then, since you have chosen misery and self-destruction, will your hands be restored."

Not understanding what the saint meant by self-destruction, not believing he had chosen any of this, Kavan cried, "But I have confessed, milord! You know I have! I became needlessly drunk. I tried to bed a whore. I have admitted this…and that I was wrong…"

"Then there must be something more damning to which you have not confessed."

"More damn…" Tears sprung to his eyes. "I am not a man. Is that a sin?"

"Not a…Kavan…kyag…" Kóráhm knelt by the bedside and touched the bard's face lovingly. "You are as much a man as I was at your age. You have considerably more willpower and self-control than I did; perhaps you are more of a man. If it had been me," his hand dropped and he stood, "I would have bedded the whore. And likely the princess too."

"You…?" Kavan was visibly shocked.

Kóráhm's expression grew mournful at the betrayal in Kavan's eyes. "You have much to learn about life, kyag, but you are, in many ways, a better man than I ever was. In this, there is nothing more I can do. I leave you with one final instruction." He laid his hand over Kavan's eyes, closing them as he spoke. "When it is time," he whispered, "go where she leads; do as she instructs. Trust her as you once trusted me. If you do, you may find what you seek."

There was a quick discharge of static in that touch, and though the sensation of the hand over his eyes lingered, Kavan knew Kóráhm was gone. The man's words tore at Kavan's soul. Kóráhm was a saint, after all. How could he have been anything less than an ideal role model and be taken into the Faith's Hall of Saints? However, Kóráhm had been mortal once, and it was possible, with information about his life lacking, that he had been the same as any other man. Now Kavan's sense of betrayal had caused Kóráhm to depart. Even the Saint had abandoned him. He was certain of it. His transgressions had taken his hands, his music, and driven Kóráhm away. Kavan wept again, hoping to convince himself that Kóráhm would return, that surely Kóráhm had been a much greater man in every way than Kavan would ever be.

❧*❧

"Diona has done what?" Arlan snapped at his son, dropping the wine glass he held. It shattered, splattering its contents over the stone floor.

Hagan attempted to rephrase his thoughts. He feared his father and had only brought him this news because Diona begged him to. "She asked me to tell you she has gone into seclusion under k'gdhededhá Tythilius' direction. She said it is her fault Lord Cliáth left, and that, to atone for her actions, he instructed her to spend time alone to meditate on what she has done."

In a low, gravelly voice, the King asked, "What did she do?"

"I…"

"Damn it, Hagan! Lord Cliáth is lying in Levonne gravely injured, possibly dying from what Bhríd tells me, and Diona claims responsibility. I want to know what she has done!"

Hagan stepped away, hoping he would be out of range of the man's hand should he strike. "I do not know. She did not say. She said she offended him greatly. She wouldn't tell me anything more."

The King came close to kicking something, a chair, the wall, or Hagan if he had been closer. Instead, he knocked the decanter and remaining glasses from the countertop and listened to them splinter against the floor and wall. The violence of the sound made him feel a little better. "I want to see her the instant she returns. I want you to see that she gets that message. Is that understood?"

Deciding that the best way to do that was to give the message to k'gdhededhá Jermyn, Hagan squeaked, "Perfectly, father."

❧*❧

It was late afternoon when Ártur and Wortham rode through the iron gates of the Dubuais-Cáner estate at their mounts' top speeds. Gaelán, seated upon one of the many courtyard benches, looked as though he was awaiting their arrival. Without speaking, other than initial words of welcome, he led them through the halls and up the stairs, taking them first into the empty adjoining sitting room.

"Where is Kavan?" the healer ground out, not in the mood for delays. If Kavan was dying, he must go to him immediately.

Gaelán dropped into the nearest chair and fretfully clenched his hands in his lap. "I will take you to him, but there are things you need to know." He explained how he had found Kavan, the extensive damage the bard had sustained, and his condition over the days since. "He ordered me not to send for you, which is why it took me too long to write, and why I did not ask you to come, but rather told you he was here. He said if I asked you…he would never speak to me again."

Knowing how the boy idolized Kavan, Ártur understood why Gaelán had hesitated before such an unusual threat. "I will take responsibility for being here. Now…I must see him." He had waited long enough, too long, and he could not bear to wait another second.

Gaelán reluctantly took them into the adjoining room where Kavan slept. With Kavan's hands clutched to his chest beneath the blanket, none of the damage Gaelán reported was visible. The healer pulled the blanket free, and though there was little visible damage on the rest of his body except the array of mottled bruises spread across the white skin like a map, he swallowed hard at the sight of his cousin's hands. He heard Wortham choke behind him.

"sínréc?" he moaned, but there was no response.

Placing his hands upon the smooth white skin, Ártur's healing sense shifted into full power, seeking the source of Kavan's fever. There was residual damage in his knee and ribs, and some in his side where a dagger had penetrated, but the majority of the injuries were properly healed. Ártur tended to the minor damage, fought down the fever, and then withdrew his senses, though not his hands, as he looked at Gaelán. "You have already had a healer here? Why did they not complete what they started? The fever would not have developed if…"

"I am the healer," was his embarrassed, hesitant reply. Rather than accuse the boy of lying, Ártur reached for Gaelán's hand with a befuddled, disbelieving expression. It took no more than a shared touch between them for the elder healer to know the truth.

He cleared his throat. "You are indeed. I did not think…how long have you known?"

The boy shrugged. "I thought something was different when I got sick. I would probably still be abed, except I told myself I was getting better…and I did. There was a kitten with a broken paw…when I touched it, trying to see how bad it was, it was not broken anymore. I did not realize what I had done until the woman who found k'aendhá told me…"

"Then you have saved his life. Thank you." He turned back to Kavan, touching his hands, hoping to heal them if it was not too late.

But the sensation of hands upon his, and the pain it caused, brought Kavan awake at once. "Do not touch me, Ártur."

The healer withdrew at the venomous tone. He was not surprised that Kavan recognized his touch. They had known each other for too long, been through too much together, for Kavan not to know his touch. "It is too late for that, sínréc. I have already ensured that you will live." He watched as Kavan gave a quick glance at his hands and then relaxed with a peculiar mixed expression of anguish and relief.

"My hands…"

"Yes…you have seen to it that there is nothing I can do for you. Do not blame Gaelán for my presence here. I also warn you not to blame this," he indicated the bard's hands, "on anyone else. You should have…"

"This is no one's fault but mine; it is my punishment. There's nothing you could do, even if you were here. Nothing anyone could do."

Kavan curled up, his eyes meeting Wortham's when he realized the man was there. There were tears on the captain's cheeks, a heartbroken expression Kavan could not bear. "Wortham, why are you…you should not be…you must go…"

Wortham shook his head. "I will not, milord. I have brought you a gift."

The look on the captain's face, the set of his jaw, was something Kavan had seen many times. He did not think there was anyone more stubborn than Wortham. "A gift?" he whispered. One of the last things he expected was gifts. He did not deserve gifts.

The captain approached with purpose in his movements but hesitancy in his eyes. Laying the satchel he carried upon the bed, he opened it to remove the books. "k'gdhededhá Jermyn found them in the sepulcher below the náós. They are written in High Elyri; you should have them. Perhaps they will bring you comfort."

Kavan wanted to touch Wortham's hand, to share the gratitude that filled his heart, but he could not find the courage to do so with his damaged fingers. Instead, he rolled away, burying his face in the pillow to stifle the rising grief. "Leave me. Please."

Wortham placed the books on the nightstand, and with great reluctance, the three returned to the sitting room. Wortham looked back one last time before closing the door, but his hand refused to release the latch.

"I do not want to leave him alone," the healer admitted, his face and voice drained of color and any emotion but sadness. "It could be the fever, but he is not thinking clearly."

"He was like this before the fever," Gaelán admitted.

"Did he say anything before? Anything about what happened?"

"No…other than warning me not to send for you. When he was asleep it was always the same few words. Dead, coward, not a man."

"She did this," Wortham spat, certain he knew what the princess had done.

"Wortham," the healer gripped the heavily muscled arm, feeling the man's anger in the tension there. "Anger will not help Kavan. Nor will confronting her. We must think of what is best for him. He may not want us with him, but one of us can sleep here to keep watch."

"I am across the hall…I've kept the door open," Gaelán added. "I am a light sleeper. If anyone opens the door, I will hear it."

Wortham grunted. "But that still leaves the window through which he could leave…and a Gate in the náós." He did not know if there was a Gate in this estate, if there were any others closer than the náós. He released the door handle at last and slung the satchel over his shoulder. "I will be in the courtyard, under his window. He will not get past me if I can help it. If he leaves, I will follow. No further harm will come to him if I can prevent it."

Their vigil was for naught, since the following morning, Kavan was as they had left him. Ártur tried to convince him to return to Rhidam, but each time, Kavan expelled him from the room with unmistakable fury. In desperation, Ártur finally sent Wortham to him.

Perhaps the bard would listen to his best friend if he would not listen to his cousin.

The captain entered the room to witness Kavan try, unsuccessfully, to open one of the volumes Jermyn had sent. "May I assist, milord?"

The light in Kavan's eyes shifted swiftly from angry to anguished. "I must learn to do…"

Ignoring the protest, Wortham came closer. "No reason you must do it today. The damage is still painful. When the pain is less, it will be easier."

Kavan looked at the man fondly as he beckoned him nearer. "Why are you willing to accept me, what is, without blame or question?"

Wortham perched on the edge of the bed. "Blame is a tricky beast. I try to avoid it." Except for now, as he unrepentantly blamed the princess for what he saw. "As for questions, what use is there in asking questions I know you will not answer?" He opened the book Kavan was holding. "But there is one you must answer for me, milord. Why do you not wish to return to Rhidam?"

Kavan's eyes grew shadowed. "Not you…"

Hand lightly upon Kavan's arm, Wortham said, "I have not come to convince you of any path. If something unpleasant occurred between you and the princess…"

Not trying to hide his horror, Kavan asked, "You know?"

"Nothing more than that you fled past me with a look of terror and she emerged from your room with claims that she had shown you the truth."

"She did…yes…"

The captain scowled and his hand on Kavan's arm tightened. "Whatever she said, she is wrong. I know it as surely as I know I am here with you. There was a light in your eyes once, and whatever she said or did has taken that away. It was wrong. However, she is the princess. If she has made it so you can no longer return to Rhidam, I will support you and your choice. Just tell me if she is the reason…please."

"Her…and this…" The bard stared at his hands but Wortham gave them no more than a glance.

"Where shall you go? Alberni? Bhryell?"

That was a question for which there was no answer. "I do not know. As it…I am an outcast. I shall be welcome nowhere my name is known. They will see me and…I do not want their pity, their ridicule. I do not…"

He started to sob again, this time against Wortham's broad shoulder, and the captain held him like a child. "There is no need to decide now. You will know what is best when the time comes. I am here to support you."

When Kavan lifted his face he said, "You are…"

Shaking his head, Wortham silenced him. "Do not speak, milord. Rest. Read for a time if you wish. It will distract your thoughts. I will tell Lord MacLyr that you will not return to Rhidam unless you wish for me to stay and assist? I should like to know what the books say."

"Go. Tell Ártur the truth, Wortham. That I cannot go back as I am a coward of the worst kind."

"Milord! You are not…"

But Kavan motioned him away and stared at the page without seeing it, a gesture the captain knew meant further words would be ignored. He leaned against the doorframe outside in the hall, his chest aching, wondering how much Ártur had heard. In the years he had known the bard, he had never seen Kavan so full of anguish. The captain met the healer's gaze, wishing the man had not insisted on waiting in the corridor.

"He is not returning to Rhidam."

Ártur looked stunned. "I thought you could convince him…"

"He is more than injured in body, milord. She wounded him in a way no one should ever endure. She cut into his soul and he believes her words to be truth. He does not understand that words spoken in anger may not be accurate or honest. He does not wish to face her, and after seeing what she has done, I do not blame him. I will stay until he is ready to travel. Then I will go wherever he wishes to go. I shall draft my letter of resignation for you to deliver to the King and pray he understands."

"That you are breaking your oath of fealty?" Not that the healer blamed him for it, but the simple fact that Kavan would not be coming back was a heavy burden to bear and made him irritable.

"That I am upholding a far more sacred oath," Wortham said evenly, "to protect a man, whom k'Ádhá has given great blessings, in his darkest hour. Someone needs to see to his well-being. I may be the only one he will allow to look after him, the only one who can give up their duties without detriment to others." Ártur had a family, as did Owain, and both had responsibilities that would not allow them to leave indefinitely. Wortham was a soldier, nothing more, with no family to tie him. He was the only choice, the best choice, and he was making it without the King's permission.

Ártur's stomach tightened into a hot, jealous knot. Though he hated to admit it, Wortham spoke the truth. Kavan would welcome no one else into his private hell, not even his cousin. Likely, if he accepted Wortham there, it would be because he knew that the captain was too stubborn to leave him. "I am not going until I am certain he is healthy. Madalyn has asked me to keep her informed. Will you stay here in case he needs anything?"

"I would be nowhere else."

Kavan was not up to reading after Wortham's dramatic display of loyalty. He did not deserve it, he who was not a man but a coward. He wanted to believe Wortham's words to be a lie, but no matter how he tried, he could not. Wortham carried no deception in his soul.

The town crier called four in the afternoon. Wanting to sleep, Kavan had barely closed the book when dizziness struck and his vision blurred. There was a woman, her long auburn hair lifted by the wind as she perched on the bow of a ship. A ship pulling out of Levonne's harbor, a ship with the markings of a Hatu merchant vessel. She looked at him, though across the distance separating them Kavan could not see her features. He felt as if he knew her, as if he had seen her before. She reached for him, and then her hand dropped as the vision faded.

Shaking, he awkwardly pushed the book onto the nightstand. Who was she and why did she call to him? Kóráhm had said to follow the woman, do as she bid. This woman? Was he to follow her bidding to Hatu?

"Very well, Kóráhm. I shall follow her. I only wish to know why."

❧Chapter 5❧

He had forgotten how cold it was this close to the sea this time of year. The overpowering stench of old fish and wet nets turned his stomach, but there was no other option if he was to be away from here. Wearing a pair of Gaelán's boots, a tunic and breeches Madalyn had left for his use when he was recovered enough to rise, and the cloak Wortham left on a chair in his room, Kavan wove unsteadily towards the docks. He questioned several captains until he found a boat bound for Natrona, the boat he was sure he had Seen. There was money in the cloak's inner pocket; while he hesitated using it, he had none of his own and passage had to be paid for. He needed to get as far away from Rhidam as possible and he was certain Wortham would forgive him the use of it.

He was less certain Wortham would forgive him for leaving without a word of farewell.

It did not occur to him that he was more likely to suffer seasickness in his current condition until he settled into the room that served as passengers' lodgings. The room swayed as the tide beat upon the wooden sides of the ship, and little by little, the rocking prodded his already unsettled stomach. It was not yet dawn and the ship would not set sail until the sun rose. The only thing Kavan could do was wait and fight against the gnawing discomfort in his belly.

"Who's here?"

He peered into the corner from where the voice had come, to find a portly, middle-aged man huddled there, his clothing marking him as a monk of the order of Saint Bhenádíctus. He had not seen or sensed him there when he had entered. "I am a traveler aboard this vessel as you are, gdhededhá. I mean you no harm."

"And Elyri, too," the man chuckled with a welcoming tilt of his head.

"How do you know?" Kavan had guessed, from the man's milky white eyes, that he was blind; it was surprising therefore that he might know Kavan was Elyri from his voice.

"A man without eyes learns to utilize other senses to their fullest. You carry an accent…though it is faint, suggesting you have spent many years abroad…probably in Enesfel. And who else would call me gdhededhá?"

Kavan was glad the monk could not see his embarrassment. Of course that word gave him away. Most Teren preferred the shortened term dedhá. "I am Urian Jayr, on a pilgrimage to St. Bhenádíctus' shrine on Káliel. Where are you bound?"

Until then, Kavan had not considered his destination; he was running to escape, not to arrive. But the mention of a saintly shrine sparked something, an idea he had not considered before. "I…Kílyn I believe." It seemed a logical choice.

"To Kóráhm's shrine. A good place for troubled souls. Perhaps I will travel there myself, after Káliel. What is your name?"

He hesitated giving it, as his name would reveal the status from which he had fallen. But he could not lie, particularly to a man of the Faith. He did not need another stain on his soul. "Kavan."

"Kavan. It appears I am blessed with a traveling companion for this journey. Sea travel is tedious; don't you agree?"

He did. If this monk knew who he was, he had the courtesy not to say. Kavan listened to the monk's chattering until he felt the shudder of the lifting anchor and the ship's creaking lurch into motion. Goodbye, Ártur, he sighed, his thoughts reaching out to touch the single individual he knew he could reach.

❧*❧

A tickle in his mind caused Ártur to wake, but it was gone as soon as he opened his eyes. He rose from the settee he had slept on and looked out the window, but Wortham was not in the courtyard. It was likely the man was already awake and with Kavan, though the healer had not heard the captain pass through the sitting room. Light was barely peeping over the horizon and the healer was in no hurry to rise if he was not needed. He would allow Wortham to tend to Kavan. It was what his cousin wanted.

❧*❧

It was not the sort of structure the leaders of the Faith were usually asked to bless and dedicate unless the owners were dedicating it to a religious purpose, feared it held a curse or some other form of evil, or were particularly superstitious. Since this was a new house, an average-looking, plain, wood and brick building, with wooden shuttered windows and a wooden door reinforced with iron bands, there was no cause to think it suffered from such indignities as deceased previous occupants. Yet the brothers who had built it, who would be living here, had specifically asked for gdhededhá Claide to give it his blessing. He knew these men and knew better than to question why those of station desired such an unassuming residence. When he arrived, they followed him as he strolled from room to room, listening as he gave each room the ritual cleansing and blessing prayer, and whispered among themselves as he talked until Claide could tolerate their insolence and rudeness no longer.

In response to his admonitions, the two offered him the chance to do something he had desired most to do with his life. They discussed the matter in detail over a noon meal, laying their ideas and plans before him, asking for his suggestions, and, in the end, pledging that if he backed them, they would, in turn, back him. They had the resources, and the connections, to make it happen. They wanted the same end; if they worked together, they could achieve it. Claide departed with a head full of ideas and schemes and his heart more hopeful than ever. At last, he believed, the Enesfel he dreamed of could come to pass. The Faith could be everything he believed it should be and he would be its leader.

❧*❧

Wortham had seen no point in going below deck when he bought passage and came on board. He had watched Kavan board this ship; he knew he was here. He waited until moments prior to her lifting anchor to board as well. With both of them stuck on this ship for the next few days, there was no reason to confront the bard now. Kavan was not going far. Night would come, at which time the captain would go below to sleep. That would be soon enough to meet.

When he heard footsteps behind him, he knew his effort to give the bard space was for naught; Kavan was on deck and had seen him.

"Wortham?"

The captain turned. "Aye, milord. I followed from the house to the dock and booked passage when it was clear you were staying aboard."

"Why?" The question was not angry, but was, instead, intense and pleading. "I am nothing…"

Wortham resisted embracing his fragile friend; Kavan would not want that. "You have my cloak," he started with a smile before growing more serious. "You are my best friend. I told you, wherever you go, I will go, that I will remain beside you regardless of what that entails. I do not know your plans, but I think you will need me. I know that I need you."

Kavan tried to grip the rails with useless hands and ended up leaning his arms on it instead. The effort sent throbbing pains shooting up his arm and it took several moments to speak because of it. Without looking at the man beside him, he asked, "You can call me friend knowing what you know?"

"I know you are in a place of great personal need. After what you have given me over the years, restoring my sight, protecting my life, this is my chance to repay you. You have been the truest friend a man could hope for. That is cause enough to cherish your friendship and stay with you."

How often had Kavan longed for someone to love him in that fashion? Unconditionally. He could not count them. Though he had known Wortham was loyal, and he treasured that, he did not think he had ever understood the strength of Wortham's love and loyalty before. "What of the King?"

Wortham shrugged. "I gave my letter of resignation to Lord MacLyr to deliver to the King. As of last night, I am no longer in the employ of the Lachlan House, but in your service, if you will have me. My first loyalty has always been to you, milord; you know that. Tell me I may follow you."

"I cannot prevent you from doing as you wish. I will never be your master." Finally, he lifted his head to look into the brown eyes that studied him calmly. "I think, if you truly desire it, I should appreciate your company," he admitted. "You may not, however, be able to tolerate mine."

Wortham smiled, a warm, almost giddy look on his broad face. "I can tolerate anything, milord, as long as you allow it." The ship tossed suddenly to one side, causing Kavan to stumble. Wortham caught his hand to steady him, regretting the pain the gesture caused but not regretting the action itself, and noticed the discoloration on Kavan's face beneath the light of rising dawn. "Milord, you should be below," he encouraged, knowing how easily the bard grew seasick. "I have brought more clothing if you wish it. You left with very little…"

Nodding, Kavan accepted both the offer and the support required to get below deck before he grew too sick to remain on his feet.

❧*❧

Ártur was not pleased to discover Kavan gone, or to learn that Wortham too was missing. His consoling thought was that if Kavan ran into trouble, the Káliel Captain was more than a match for most men. They had been correct to assume Kavan would flee at the first opportunity, but Ártur wished he knew where his cousin was heading. He did not look forward to returning to Rhidam and trying to explain this to the King.

He found solace in the knowledge that the tickle in his mind that morning was Kavan bidding him farewell. Wherever he was going, regardless of whether he returned to Rhidam, Kavan thought enough of his cousin to say goodbye, even in the midst of torment. As far as he knew, it was more than Kavan had done for anyone else. Ártur had not even been able to give Kavan Tíbhyan's message.

Madalyn found him in the garden, leaning wearily against a barren tree. "No luck?"

"None," the healer sighed. "He is not on the grounds. If Wortham has not returned by morning, we can assume that Kavan is gone and Wortham with him."

"Could he have taken a ship? To Káliel perhaps?"

"He hates sea travel, but I suppose anything is possible after what I have witnessed." He shifted to face her. "Which brings me to something I need to address. Did you know your son is a healer?"

Madalyn stared at him. "My s…Gaelán? A healer? But he is…"

"Half-Elyri. It is extraordinary, yes. I did not think it possible, as he showed no signs at birth as is the norm, but he is quite adept already it seems. If he had not healed Kavan, he would be dead in the alley where he was found."

"He said nothing about being in an alley, said that a woman found Kavan. And he said nothing of healing Kavan…" Madalyn frowned, wondering what else her youngest son was keeping from her.

"Perhaps I have spoken out of turn in telling you, but I want you to know I am eternally grateful to him. He has expressed interest in coming to Rhidam; if it is acceptable, I would be honored to assume responsibility for his instruction."

"Is this how it is when an Elyri child gains this…ability…?"

Ártur shook his head. "If a child is to be a healer, it is apparent at birth; it is a quality of their physical contact that another Elyri can sense. Other children do not experience an awakening of power until they are about eight or nine years old. At their ages, it was fair to judge that neither Tayte nor Gaelán would be gifted. Perhaps the Teren in his blood diluted his initial sensitivity, but it is as strong as in any other Elyri his age. He can be trained if you allow it."

She glanced towards the house, wondering where her son was. "I suppose it does not matter what I wish."

"On the contrary," the healer assured her. "It will not harm him to be untrained…as long as he does not display dangerous tendencies. If you and Bhríd do not wish…"

"But he may not forgive me for denying him this. Tayte is heir to my holdings. What is the future of a second son? In many ways, Gaelán has always been more…Elyri-like than Tayte. He has emulated Kavan for as long as he has known him. And a healer…I think I should allow him to pursue this if he wishes." She smiled and offered her hand. "Take him with you, Ártur, and present this to Bhríd. If he has no reservations, then my son will be the first half-Elyri healer in the Five Sovereignties, and the first healer in the Dubuais family."

Wortham did not return to the manor by evening, nor by the following morning. Heavyhearted, Ártur departed, accompanied by Gaelán and several of Madalyn's retainers. They camped for the night rather than ride in the darkness and then continued on with the sunrise. It was cold for the tenth month of the year, but there had been no snow or rain yet this autumn and their journey was uneventful. The healer prayed continuously that they would see Kavan riding towards them, or that he would wake from this nightmare to find Kavan safe in Rhidam, wake to a time before Diona's ball. Maybe then Ártur would have been able to spare his cousin much misery.

☙*☙

Watching gdhededhá Rankin methodically instruct gdhededhá Valgis in the procedures of Hes a Redh Náós made Jermyn grimace. While Valgis was devoted to his vocation and was eager to please, Jermyn noticed an occasional rebelliousness in the young gdhededhá, a trait to be expected in the young, perhaps, but one in Valgis that Jermyn found unsettling. It manifested in the way he did tasks a little differently from what he was instructed, or in an order other than what was described. This morning, Valgis' attitude had resulted in an unpleasant confrontation between the k'gdhededhá and the newcomer that wrung the older man's heart.

Knowingly or not, Valgis had misplaced the consecrated serbháló for the Gathering; it was later found in Tusánt's sleeping chamber and was nearly empty when gdhededhá Hazen found it. Tusánt was not in the city to blame, and Jermyn had never seen Hazen drink serbháló, or any other alcohol, except during the Gathering. It had been Valgis' duty to replace and fill the items after the Gathering, which meant he was the last to be seen with them. It suggested guilt but did not prove anything. After considerable protestation, Valgis admitted he had not put the serbháló away as required, but swore no knowledge of how it had come to be in Tusánt's room or why the flask was empty.

Even this, Jermyn might have overlooked. Men had their vices, and once Valgis discovered that Jermyn was not an ogre but tried to be understanding of such shortcomings, he hoped the young gdhededhá would be open with him rather than resorting to sneaking the Holy Gathering serbháló when he felt in need of a drink.

What bothered Jermyn most was that Claide had taken a special interest in Valgis and appeared to be sheltering the young man under his wing, defending him, siding with him whenever Valgis erred. Perhaps he was wrong to disapprove of that relationship; every man needed friendship and Claide had been alone on the fringes for too long. With Claide's declining attitude over the last several years, however, his standoffishness and resistance to any attempts at inclusion his fellow Faithful made, and the way Claide appeared to be drawing Valgis into those same questionable attitudes, the k'gdhededhá could think of nothing good that could come of this new friendship. Nothing good for Enesfel, for the Faith, and especially for Valgis. Unless Valgis could somehow turn Claide's head around.

Kavan appreciated the dark gray robe Wortham had procured for him, as well as the matching hooded cloak. He also appreciated that the man thought to bring the books Jermyn had given him, since Kavan, in his haste to leave Levonne, had not remembered them. He spent his hours of confinement reading, stopping occasionally to converse with Urian or to sleep. As expected, he became seasick and Wortham spent many hours wiping Kavan's forehead with a cool, damp cloth to soothe him. It was akin to being a child, he thought, though he had never been sick as a boy, save for that one peculiar incident when young Prince Arlan had been poisoned, and thus Kavan had not experienced this sort of compassionate attention. There were many times when he wanted nothing more than to curl up in Wortham's arms and weep, particularly when he grew frustrated that he could not use his hands as he wished or when the captain's tenderness overwhelmed him. Yet he did not.

How could he prove himself worthy of divine grace if he could not be strong?

Of the three books, Kavan began reading the smallest first. It was a journal, detailing a young woman's account of her life during the years of the Great Persecution. She had been Elyri, not much older than he was, Kavan suspected, and passionately in love with a man she feared was in great danger. He often spoke against the violence and prejudice of the time, trying vainly to convince Teren that peace was best for both peoples, that Teren and Elyri could harmoniously coexist if the Teren would allow it. She quoted phrases from several of her beloved's speeches but did not reveal his name. Perhaps, Kavan thought, it had been an effort to protect him, or herself, should the journal fall into the wrong hands.

The final third of the book was empty, incomplete. The last entry made mention that her lover, for that is what Kavan deduced they were, had suggested she join her family in their flight behind the Llaethlágárá, out of Enesfel forever. She refused, telling him that if he was staying amidst the Teren, she would also.

What had happened, Kavan wondered, that the journal stopped there?

The gentleman's perspective filled the second book, not much larger than the first and also written in High Elyri. Whereas her language had been that of common discourse, his was sophisticated, educated, and he wrote of his people's plight with an eloquence and passion that struck Kavan as both familiar and personal. This man witnessed the abuses, the torture, and the chaos first hand, and wrote about it with great sadness. And the woman, the woman he claimed to love more than his life, the woman he longed to wed, had been killed in that chaos mere days after she was warned to flee. Murdered. Sacrificed. He called the woman Yhsábhel.

Yhsábhel. It was a common name in Elyriá, particularly in Clarys, but Kavan was sure there was a greater significance to this woman's name than its commonality as if he had read about her somewhere before. As he pondered where he might have read it, why the name felt familiar, he studied the man's handwriting on the open pages. Small letters, eloquent, simple, a beautiful hand, similar to his own.

The journal tumbled from his lap as his hands began to shake. Not only could he not make music, it dawned on him he might no longer be able to write. Every day brought a new loss and the scope of his injuries became more apparent with each revelation. Each time it grew a little harder to accept Wortham's steadfast loyalty when he was convinced he did not deserve it. He had nothing to give any longer. Of what use could he be to anyone?

He fumbled with the book, trying to pick it up, thankful that he, Wortham, and the monk Urian were the sole passengers on this journey and that Wortham was above deck now, enjoying the sea air. It was something the big man missed more than he admitted, though Wortham never complained. And Urian's blindness meant he could not see Kavan's hands or his frustration.

But as he reached again for the fallen book, Urian found it first and held it out to Kavan. "Here, lad."

Kavan hesitated taking it. "How could you…?"

"The ears," the man replied with a smile. "They show me much my eyes do not."

"Were you blind from birth?" The question was both one of curiosity and an effort to direct attention away from himself as he took the book awkwardly back onto his lap.

"No. I fell ill when I was a young man; the sickness took my sight away slowly. I can see nothing, and have not been able to for…" he paused in thought and continued, "must be fifteen or twenty years. I know a new handicap can cause tremendous pain…both emotional and physical." Kavan choked back any response he might have made, having no desire to talk about his hands. "I know, you see," Urian added in a low voice. "Your hands trouble you. I hear frustration in your breathing, can feel it in the air. I have no need to know what happened or how bad it is, but I assure you, life will improve. You have other faculties; your life is not over."

Sliding from the bed, Kavan sank to the floor beside Urian. "It might as well be, gdhededhá," he admitted. "I was a harper; my hands were my life. Without them, I am nothing."

Urian patted his arm. "Nonsense. You are alive. Quite brilliant, I suspect. You have a loyal friend in Captain Delamo. That is more than many can claim. To him, you are everything. Live for that until you find a way to be useful and live for yourself. If you were a musician of merit, there are more ways to perform than with your hands."

Silent for many minutes, Kavan stared at his fingers, mulling over the holy man's words. Kóráhm had said much the same. But that did not make it true. Kavan had spent his entire life as a harper; people loved him for his music. Without his harp, without his hands, no one would accept him. No one but Wortham and Ártur would love him. The White Bard of Bhryell must have a harp. It was who he was.

"Is it possible, gdhededhá," he finally asked, "that if I make some act of penance k'Ádhá might restore the use of my hands?"

Urian leaned back into his corner. "Is that why you are going to Kílyn? To seek forgiveness and healing?"

"I do not know why I am going. Kóráhm told me I must first know what I seek clemency for; I admit I do not understand what he means."

There was a low whistle of breath as Urian's eyes widened. "Saint Kóráhm told you…you are the miracle worker! The Elyri bard who performs miracles and talks to Saint Kóráhm! I have heard many tales of you…should have recognized you sooner."

Kavan shook his head violently. "No. k'Ádhá once used my hands to perform miracles…but he has taken them from me. I am nothing." Not a man. Coward. The mantra started again, pulling him towards a depression he had no desire to fight.

"There is a purpose to all things. k'Ádhá does not take something away without giving something in return. Just because you cannot see the gift does not mean it isn't there. Perhaps you'll regain the use of your hands…perhaps you will not. Perhaps you are being tested to teach you another way…"

"If this is a test, I have already failed." Kavan returned to the bunk and lay with his arm across his eyes as if hiding "I have failed because I have admitted I cannot tolerate this. I would sooner be dead."

"Then take your own life," Urian said nonchalantly."

"That would be another sin to burden my soul…and I am too much of a coward to do it."

The monk chuckled. "Suicide is the coward's way, son. To live with what you find intolerable is the mark of a strong man. You persevere because you know it is the right thing to do."

But Kavan was no longer listening. He rolled over and buried his face in his bunk to muffle the anguish.

❧*❧

King Arlan's face was ashen as he collapsed against the back of his chair. Across from him, Owain's face wore a nearly identical expression of shock and loss, as did three of the others in the room, Caol Dugan, Bhríd Cáner, and Jermyn Tythilius. Ártur's face was a numb mask; he had lived with the news he bore for more days than he wished.

"His hands are his life," muttered the King. "His hands…"

The first time Arlan Lachlan had met Kavan, the Elyri was playing his harp. Arlan could not imagine Kavan without it. He understood the bard's pain at that loss. But he did not understand what his daughter could have done to cause Kavan to flee and leave himself vulnerable to attack.

Unable to think of anything better to say, he growled, "Knaves…"

"Are dead, according to Gaelán," Ártur assured him. "From what he described, two of the bodies looked as if they had exploded." He decided not to hint that he suspected Kavan was responsible for that. "The others appeared to have been ripped apart by wild beasts. Whoever stopped them from killing Kavan did us a favor."

Caol leaned his elbows on his knees. "Do you think it was a deliberate attack? They must have known who he was if they intentionally smashed his hands. I will look into it if you think this warrants investigation."

"Of course it warrants investigation," the King snapped, angry at the situation rather than at his inquisitor. "No one attacks my best friend and gets away with it. Learn everything you can about those responsible, and if any of them live, I want them brought to Rhidam."

"This is likely to stir great chaos," Bhríd murmured. "Kavan is a…he is practically a saint in the eyes of many…and nothing but a cursed Elyri to others. That he has suffered such injustice will indubitably raise a fuss."

"Let it. Perhaps when people learn of this, it will drive those who are sane and tolerant to manage those who are not," the King snorted.

"Or it will be the beginning of a string of violence we might not be able to contain…"

The King looked at Jermyn as if he had not considered that possibility. In truth, he had not. His concern was how he might help, or at least avenge, Kavan. "Do what you must, Caol," he said with a sigh as he stood. "I want the men who did this. If you can find them without stirring trouble, without hiding the facts, so be it. The responsibility for any negative reaction to this investigation will belong to the men who nearly killed Kavan. And to me."

The inquisitor left with the King, discussing how best to proceed with his investigation. The k'gdhededhá got to his feet, realizing the business he had come to discuss with the King would have to wait for another day. "I will pray for Kavan night and day. I owe him; prayers for his health and soul are the least I can give."

There was a long silence when the two Elyri were left alone in that room. No words could express how either felt, or make the other feel any better. This was the second time anti-Elyri violence had struck close to home and it was no easier than the first time.

"Do you think we should tell anyone at home?" asked Bhríd.

"So my father can gloat that it is a product of our insisting on living amongst Teren? Or that Kavan got what he deserved?"

"He did not…"

The healer shrugged. "I know, but it is what bhydhá believes. I should tell bhydáni Tíbhyan; he asked for Kavan and now it looks like he might not return to Bhryell…"

Bhríd leaned forward. "We must have faith he will come back, Ártur, else we shall fall into despair."

"We already have."

Changing the subject to ease the healer's heart, Bhríd asked, "You said there was something about Gaelán you wish to discuss."

The healer nodded and rubbed his eyes. "If not for Gaelán, Kavan might be dead. He is a healer, Bhríd; he saved Kavan's life."

The ebony-haired Elyri's face broke into a surprised but pleased smile. "I did not think…does Madalyn know?"

"I told her before we left and asked about assuming responsibility for his training. He wants it, or seems to, and it would be better than sending him to Elyriá where he knows no one."

"Not to mention how much of an outcast he would be there…half-blood. Here he can be with me, and you are the greatest healer in the lands. I can think of no one better qualified to train him. Where is he?"

Flushed at the praise, Ártur looked away. "He met Asta when we came in and the two of them headed towards the stable with the horses. Find her and you will probably find him."

"I must read him myself, commend him…but I will not forget my prayers for Kavan. You can count on them."

"I appreciate the prayers of anyone who will give them." So, he mused, would Kavan.

❧*❦

Once his depression subsided, Kavan turned his attention to the third manuscript. It was night, leaving him the smoky glare of the swaying lamp to read by. He had asked the others if he should extinguish it, but the light was of no consequence to Urian and Wortham claimed it would not disturb his rest. The captain was in a hammock, wrapped in his blanket, snoring softly, a sound oddly noticeable over the gentle roar and slap of the water outside, and comforting in its proximity.

There was a growl in Kavan's stomach tonight, but he knew that to eat would aggravate his seasickness. He had not eaten since Diona's ball and the alcohol he had consumed was no suitable substitute for food. There was water, but it did little for hunger. Doubtless, he looked more gaunt than usual after twelve days of fasting.

Succeeding in opening the third volume caused the first two pages to fall to the floor. The cover had been defaced by fire and some sharp instrument and was unreadable except for the High Elyri numeral three and the first two letters. Could it be? His hopes soared for the first time in days with the knowledge that he might have obtained the forbidden Third Volume of the Articles of Kóráhm. One of the two pages on the floor confirmed his hope, but they were dashed again by the overall condition of the book. Many pages were water damaged, others stained with rot, and the upper edges of most were scorched and charred. It looked as if someone had rescued it from an attempt to burn it. The book had been saved, but age and attempts to destroy it left it unreadable.

Kóráhm's third volume at last and it was useless. After all this time. He did not attempt to catch it as the book slid from his lap and landed on the floor with a thud.

"Milord?"

"It is nothing, Wortham. Go back to sleep."

But the big man, shirtless despite the cold, had already rolled out of the hammock, retrieved the fallen book, replaced the two pages, and put it back on Kavan's lap. "You are upset. What is this that it has dismayed you?"

"The Third Volume…" Kavan started in a whisper to hide his cracked voice.

"Saint Kóráhm's writings? k'gdhededhá Jermyn found it?"

The bard nodded. "Yes…but it is worthless, unreadable…"

"Unreadable, perhaps, but not worthless. You have proof it exists, and you can claim to own a copy even if you cannot read it. Perhaps there are words you will be able to see under a better light."

Kavan stared into Wortham's eyes for many moments as the captain brushed pale silver-white strands of hair from Kavan's face. Wortham did not retreat from the stare. He did not know what Kavan was hoping to find in those moments of contact, but whatever it was, the bard must have found it as his eyes closed and a contented sigh escaped him. "Do you find something positive in every situation?"

Wortham smiled. "I try to, milord. If I did not, I might spend too much of my life in a profound state of sadness."

"Like me."

The captain began to contradict him. Instead, he shrugged. "Like you," he conceded. "Perhaps you should seek to do likewise. It cannot hurt to try."

"Perhaps. Go back to sleep, Wortham."

The man returned to his hammock but did not immediately doze. "Are you going ashore at Káliel tomorrow? It would do you good to get off the boat for a few hours."

"And risk Prince Muir seeing this? Gabrielle…?"

"Without a white robe, and with the hood of your cloak up, I doubt anyone will recognize you. Brother Urian has asked us to go to the shrine with him. Perhaps k'Ádhá will find such a thing pleasing? At least it would give you a chance to pray there."

When Kavan did not answer, Wortham cast him a quick glance. The bard was staring into the glare of the lamp, tears on his cheeks though he was silent. This time Wortham resisted the impulse to dry them. Kavan wanted solitude. And perhaps, the captain thought, he needed to show Kavan that, while he was beside him always, he would not always be the one to dry the man's tears. Kavan had to relearn how to stand on his own.

❧Chapter 6❧

The Hatu merchant ship docked at Káliel mid-morning. Harbor patrol was not willing to allow visitors until they learned that one of those visitors was Captain Delamo, a native of Káliel and a man well remembered there by many. That the captain was willing to vouch for the two pilgrims gained them permission to go ashore, although Kavan secretly hoped they would be disallowed. The risk of being recognized terrified him. Still, once there, it was a relief to be on solid ground, even if it was on shaky legs.

With Wortham's aid, Kavan and Urian passed through city streets and up the rocky, shrub-covered hill south of the city's limits. Atop that hill, overlooking the ocean, the small limestone náós stood alone. There were no trees to shelter it, no vegetation or windbreaks, leaving the ancient structure exposed to the elements, and it showed in the wear the external walls bore. It looked desolate, abandoned, small, and vulnerable, as vulnerable as Kavan felt, buffeted by a world of storms. Gazing over the crash of the rough surf below, it occurred to him that, as alone and vulnerable as it appeared, the Shrine of St. Bhenádíctus had been there since being built over eight hundred and seventy years ago, and it was still visited and revered by many. Untold storms had pummeled those sturdy walls, rain and wind and sleet, and it had not fallen, the loving care of its visitors enough to prevent its collapse.

Thinking about those things, he squatted near the ledge, staring at the horizon, giving the monk privacy inside the building. Wortham had gone back into the city, but for what purpose Kavan did not ask. As long as the man did not reveal their presence here, Kavan did not care what he did. It gave him time to be alone. While he appreciated Wortham's steadfastness and everything the man did for him, and did not object to Urian's constant company aboard the ship, it was difficult for Kavan to maintain composure around them when he felt shattered into a thousand irreparable fragments.

His thoughts were not on himself today, however. He was not thinking at all. The rhythmic pulsing of the choppy surf was soothing from this distance, where he was neither surrounded by it nor rocked on constantly swaying water. He listened, watched, and occasionally closed his eyes. When he thought at all, it was of the building behind him and of Urian.

The monks of St. Bhenádíctus were an exception to the usual religious orders that had sprung up over the centuries. There were Orders in Elyriá that took vows of poverty, that sent proselytizers into the world, but the Teren gdhededhá of Saint Bhenádíctus were truly poor, true missionaries. They had less reason to fear the Teren they traveled amongst than Elyri missionaries did. There was a single, small náós in southern Cordash where those seeking union in the order went to take vows, a náós with no wealth to its name and a single gdhededhá and two apprentices to maintain it. Most in the order claimed no residences and few trade skills with which to earn a living. They existed by wandering from town to town, taking odd jobs, or by accepting the kindness of others. It took great conviction to enter their ranks, as it took great certainty to join the gdhededhá in Elyriá. Kavan knew he did not have that conviction, had never had it. He had too many questions that disallowed reconciliation between his private beliefs, the reality of what he was, and the teachings of the Faith. It was sobering to realize that Urian's conviction was greater than his.

Footsteps alerted him to Urian's emergence from the shrine; Kavan struggled to his feet to stop the monk before he tumbled over the cliff into the sea. Thus far, there was no sign of Wortham.

"You are finished, gdhededhá? Did you find what you sought?"

The monk chuckled. "I came to leave an offering, to speak prayers, and to ask guidance for my next destination. My lot is to wander, to help others. I did not come to seek, but to give. When you spoke of Kílyn, I knew that would be my next destination."

"How could…may I ask why?"

"I believe you are my messenger, as are many travelers I cross paths with. Where they are going, I often go. You are in a place of great need; though I cannot see, there may be other ways I can aid you…even if only for company until our paths diverge. My prayers are said, my offering left, and my next path is clear. Are you willing to accept company as far as Kílyn?"

Though his impulse was to refuse, as he did not want companions, Kavan kept that thought hidden. Who was he to turn the man from a path k'Ádhá might have set? "I will not obstruct your spiritual quest, gdhededhá. If you wish to go to Kílyn, we travel together." He made no mention of offered aid. There was nothing Urian could do for him.

The captain was trudging up the hill, a bundle slung over his shoulder. Food other than the ship's rations, Kavan suspected, and other supplies perhaps. He hoped there was something in that pack that might soothe his hungry aching stomach. Knowing the man's fondness for Káliel's port wine, Kavan suspected he had brought at least one bottle for the journey.

The thought of wine, however, made Kavan's stomach churn and filled his head with images and memories he was trying to forget. The mantra started again. Dead. Coward. Not a man. His hunger vanished.

Wortham scowled at the swift change of expression on Kavan's face and he wondered at the cause. "The ship is preparing for departure. We should return to it. Are you remaining here, dedhá, or traveling with us?"

In response, the blind monk grasped the captain's arm, a grin on his soft features. Kavan followed behind them.

❧*❧

Clianthe clutched the front gate of the Prime Magistrate's villa, her knuckles white, staring into the midst of the city, and then in the direction of the shrine with a puzzled expression. She had seen Captain Delamo but twice in her life. The first time she had been five years old, when Prince Bertram had died. The second time she had been fifteen and her mother had married Owain Lachlan. Both contacts were brief, yet she felt confident that the man she had seen this day was the same. Anyone of such stature and build, with wild dark curls and a thick bear-like beard, would be easy to remember. But if he was on Káliel, why had he not come to visit her mother? Why was he accompanying two monks to the shrine? She wanted to approach, to learn why, but by the time she got up the nerve, he was gone.

❧*❧

In the courtyard, several of the keep's youngest members were gathered in a circle, heads bent low as they shared some secret. Princess Diona could not see what they were doing as she passed through the front gate, but she noticed her brother amongst them as Piran and Hagan began to laugh raucously. Llucás looked confused, while Asta and Gaelán were grinning with self-satisfaction. The princess had hoped to arrive home unnoticed, which was why she had waited until nearly dark. Hagan saw her, however, as the men escorting her home left her just inside the gate, and he motioned for her to wait. She stopped reluctantly and chewed the inside of her lip.

The Lachlan heir left the gathering and joined his sister, pulling her nearer to keep others from hearing his words. "I'm glad I am the first to find you. Father asked to see you as soon as you were home…"

"I know," she murmured. k'gdhededhá Jermyn had told her the same. "Was he angry?"

"More than angry," the prince replied with a vexed expression. "Lord Cliáth has not returned…from what Gaelán, says, he was in Levonne but left when he was fit enough to travel…and no one knows where he has gone, not even Healer MacLyr."

Diona's face lost color. "He was ill?"

"No…attacked and beaten…nearly dead as I hear it. His hands were…" Hagan shuddered. "He will never play his harp again."

"Never…?" She closed her eyes to blink away tears, but it did not work. They spilled down her cheeks. She could not be directly blamed for an attack, but she was the one who had driven him away. Her memory of his expression when he fled was vivid enough to suggest he might not have been in any state of mind to fight attackers. Kavan was not a violent person by nature; perhaps he was not capable of fending off an attack, particularly in an emotionally vulnerable state.

"I suppose," she whispered, staring at the castle doors, "Father is waiting."

"He doesn't know when you are due. I think he is meeting in the stateroom with Lord Cáner and Lord Cornell this evening. You might be able to get in without seeing him…at least until morning."

She leaned into her brother and kissed his cheek. "Thank you, Hagan." With a nod, she hastened inside and up to her rooms. No one saw her. It gave her the chance to pack several things into a satchel, and then after scanning the corridor to be sure no one was about, she made her way to the healer's room. She did not know if he would be there and was grateful when her rapping brought Ártur to open it. His cold expression upon seeing her, however, caused her to drop her gaze.

"May I speak, Lord MacLyr.?" She did not expect him to agree, despite her noble status, and was surprised when he silently bid her to enter. Once inside with the door closed behind her, she murmured, "I beg you, take me to Káliel." She knew Elyri had a quick way of getting from place to place, though she had yet to experience it. Anything that might get her away from her father's wrath was welcome.

He folded his arms across his chest. "Why should I do that?"

"I wish to speak with Muir," she replied nervously.

"And avoid your father…and what you have done?" She turned her face away. "Do you know that Kavan…?"

Not wanting to hear how bad his condition was, and reasoning the healer would tell her if she did not stop him, she interrupted. "Hagan told me he was beaten, that his hands have been…"

The words were almost spat out in his hurt and anger. "His hands are useless. More importantly, he is a broken man, Milady. I saw him, spoke with him. He believes he is a coward. That he is not a man. That he does not deserve to live. Captain Delamo has left service to travel wherever he goes; I pray he can keep Kavan alive and offer solace after what you have done."

She paused before letting loose the insulting words that first came to mind. She deserved the healer's outrage, but that did not mean she liked to hear it. Twisting her hair around her hand as she often did when distressed, she swallowed hard, finding it difficult to look the man in the eyes. "I never intended to drive him away, to do any of this. I was angry and said things I should not have, words I did not mean. Vicious, vile words. I regret them sincerely, but I cannot take them back. I assumed…he has always been strong. I did not believe he would take them to heart. I thought he would be home so that I could…I did not mean for…" Tears again slid free but she did not try to hide them or brush them away.

The healer groaned. He knew she was telling the truth, that Diona was not the sort to wish hurt or pain on Kavan. But she had, and he could not forget that. "From what he said to me…and to Captain Delamo…it is doubtful he will ever return to Rhidam. That is how affected he has been."

Never return? Diona could not believe her selfishness could have had such an effect on anyone, that her thoughtlessness could drive away her father's best friend. No wonder he wanted words with her. It was the same, she realized, with Espen. Had she driven them both away, out of Rhidam, out of her life? How could she undo what she had done?

"I wish…I wish I could tell him I am sorry. I wish he would be angry with me rather than direct his anger and pain at himself. k'gdhededhá Jermyn gave me penance, part of which is begging forgiveness, and he suggested I speak to someone I trust as I would not speak frankly to him. I thought Muir might be willing to listen…if you would take me to him." She stared, taking the time to wipe her face with the back of her hand, and waited for his reply.

The prospect of helping her grated on the healer's nerves, but he could not deny her request. She was royalty, after all, a member of the family he had sworn to serve, and if there was even a marginal chance of Kavan's return, Diona learning the lessons this unfortunate series of events taught would be necessary to keep him here. "I have promised Owain to take Piran to his mother for a few days; I can take you if you will meet me in the oratory after dinner."

"I will. Thank you, Lord Healer." She curtsied, faltered, and turned to go.

"One more thing, Princess." She hesitantly looked back, expecting the harsh words he had not yet said. "Think on this while you ponder what you have done. I know my cousin better than most. He seeks acceptance but he is afraid of intimacy. To have it forced on him is one of the worst things anyone could do…rivaled closely by telling him he is not a man. You have done both. If he comes back, if you love him in any way, think of him before you act. He is not as secure in himself as he appears. Please remember that."

In her eyes, Ártur thought he saw a spark of understanding, the birth of empathy she had not had before. He wondered what he had said that resonated within her, but she nodded gravely and sighed. "I will endeavor to never hurt him again for as long as I live."

꙳*꙳

bhydáni Tíbhyan shuffled around the lower level of his home, hanging clothes to dry on ropes and cords strung for that purpose, or over the backs of furnishings as he found room for them. He stopped periodically to light the candles that continually sputtered out because of the draft blowing through his open door. He should close it, but he relished the sensation of the cold upon his skin. It was a reminder that he was alive, that he could still feel such things. Though he detested rain and snow, cold temperatures he did not mind.

Healer MacLyr's news troubled him. It had been a pleasant surprise to see the healer twice in such a short span of time, but the pleasure of it had been short-lived as the news about Kavan's serious injury had not been the sort the sage longed to hear. He thought back to when he had first come to know of young Cliáth. It was the faint tinkle of a harp echoing through the streets of Bhryell from the open windows of the MacLyr house at first, a breathtaking sound even then, one he heard many times over the years yet found new and refreshing each time. When that sound was connected to the boy the sage began to tutor, Tíbhyan had grown to understand both the boy and himself in a deeper way than he had ever imagined possible.

Music was a factor in nearly everything his pupil had ever done. Almost every major event in Kavan's life that Tíbhyan could think of involved music. Being stripped of that gift was worse in some ways than losing his life.

One aspect of the situation troubled the sage more than others. He knew first-hand that Kavan was insecure, but he was also innately wiser than anyone Tíbhyan knew. The sage wondered how the younger man could believe that the same deity who had given him that gift, and had made such use of it in the past, would capriciously take it away. Tíbhyan believed it was merely one of those random acts in life that held no purpose, not a form of divine retribution.

But Kavan believed everything served a purpose, believed everything occurred for a reason. If he could not deduce a rationale, it made sense to the sage that he would attribute the event to divine intervention. That must be the answer, the man thought as he strung up his last damp tunic. To think the cornerstone of his Faith would cruelly shatter his life would be more than the bard could tolerate. No wonder he had fled. He was not only fleeing the pity of others, he was hoping to flee the reaches of k'Ádhá.

Tíbhyan hoped he would live long enough to learn that Kavan had come home and he prayed that when that day came, Kavan would be whole. Physically, mentally, and spiritually. He would like to hear music from his student one last time, would like to see him smile. Tomorrow, he would go to the Feast Gathering of Saint Kóráhm for the first time in decades, an event likely to be sparsely attended because of the Saint's dual heretic status. There he would light a candle and pray for Kavan to know peace.

"How could you have said such spiteful things?" Muir cried, aghast, shocked, and hurt by the tale his sister shared. He had hoped her actions and intentions towards Kavan were a childish passion. There had been no reason to believe it to be more, that she could do these things to the man who raised and cherished them from infancy.

Blinking against the steady stream of tears, Diona did not shrink from her half-brother. She deserved these harsh words and more. If she could not hear them from Kavan, she would hear them from Muir…and probably later from her father. "I know my faults in this, Muir…I am a hateful creature for what I have done and there is no excuse for it. I do not expect anyone's forgiveness, especially Lord Cliáth's. I will ask him for it, as I am asking you…if I get the opportunity, but I will not blame him if he denies and rejects me."

Muir was tempted to strike her as he had sometimes done when they were argumentative children, but he did not believe in undue force or violence and knew it would solve nothing. "If he comes home, I expect you to treat him with the respect he deserves. Your affections, your actions, are inappropriate…"

"I have discussed that already with the k'gdhededhá. I know. What I don't know is why. I mean…" She shuffled to the window and stared at the fading flowers outside. "I knew he would turn me away; he always has… why did I think this time would be different? Why was I so hurt, angry, offended…by his rejection? I came hoping you might be able to…that you might help me understand why I fail to let him go. I don't want to do this again. I am asking for your help."

Muir stepped closer and wrapped his arms around her. "You are welcome here Diona…even if I want to strangle you for what you did. Clianthe will be glad to see you. For Lord Cliáth's sake, I will help if I can. This must not happen again. Come…I will see you settled in a room and then we will go to the garden and talk more."

❧ * ❧

There was unusual bustle in the pre-dawn hours of Hes á Redh Náos. Unusual for most days, though not for the feast day of Saint Kóráhm. No other náos in Enesfel celebrated the day with as much enthusiasm as Rhidam, though Jermyn prayed that the new chellé in

Alberni would grow to rival their celebration. He would not even object if it surpassed Rhidam's efforts. It was fitting that Saint Kóráhm's Abbey should mark the occasion, while Hes á Redh did so because the k'gdhededhá had been a monk in the Saint's order and because the King wished it. Wished it because he believed the Saint had a hand in his gaining the throne. Wished it because it was said the Saint had personally escorted his wife across the bridge between this world and the next. Wished it because he knew that his bard and best friend, the Elyri who bore the Saint's name, felt the occasion worth the attention.

If k'gdhededhá Dórímyr had planned to come to Rhidam, he would have done it before today. Kóráhm's Feast was a major week-long event in Clarys and the days between that Feast and Udhár were the busiest of the year for the Faithful. There would be no time for the patriarch to come until after the Feast of Dhágdhuán, probably not until late spring when the winter weather passed. Jermyn knew, as did his parishioners and fellow gdhededhá, that k'gdhededhá Dórímyr was not likely to return to Enesfel. Not this year. Not ever.

Rankin lit the last of the tall green candles as Valgis dusted the wooden benches. Claide could not be found. That was not unusual; the Teren gdhededhá frowned upon celebrating the sainthood of a man many in the Faith called a heretic. Fortunately, Valgis did not seem to share that view. Jermyn would rather Claide be somewhere else today than have him interrupting the Gathering and putting questionable ideas into Valgis' head.

❧*❧

The procession of gold robed gdhededhá, men and women, circled the nave with green candles, bowls of incense, and hymns of praise, led by gdhededhá Tusánt who quaked with every step at the honor of participating in this holy event in this place. Similar candles illuminated artwork and the dais with an ethereal glow; from the choir loft, a harper led the hymns accompanied by seven young boys and three girls whose pristine voices soared over the congregation's heads and were sent back into their midst by the painted záryph upon the ceiling. Dawn broke as Tusánt stopped at the altar, waited for his assistants to take their places, and began the Gathering.

Though the sanctuary was not full, it contained approximately eighty people, both gdhededhá and townsfolk who had come to the Faith through the work of the men and women their Duke had brought to this place. The náós was designed to seat perhaps three times that many for a Gathering, but this many in attendance was, in Tusánt's eyes, impressive for the first Gathering within the chellé's walls. It was many more than he expected to see.

If only Lord Cliáth were here for the opening, to see the numbers who flocked from the surrounding countryside and the twenty-seven men and women who had taken holy orders to support the Abbey. Tusánt knew nothing of what was going on in Rhidam that kept Kavan from being unable to be here, but he knew that if the bard could see the rapt face of k'gdhededhá Khwílen, hear the music of his handpicked musicians, see the beauty surrounding them, Kavan would know that what he had built here was a good and needed thing.

ॐ * ॐ

He could not kneel in prayer; his weak legs would not allow him that. But he could lean against his walking stick to light a prayer candle and give to k'Ádhá the most heartfelt prayer he could remember giving. There was little he could offer in exchange for his favorite student's well-being, but he offered everything he had, whatever k'Ádhá felt inclined to take. Even his life if it would help. He had lived long and full, four hundred and sixty-two years of it. He might as well die for this cause than for any other. If he had to die for any cause, he would prefer it to be Kavan's well-being.

"bhydáni."

He glanced to the side where Bhendhámyn MacLyr joined him. The young man smiled as he lit his candle and knelt to pray. His grandmother, Dháná MacLyr, stood to the other side with a timid glint in her eyes. Tíbhyan had little contact with the MacLyrs since Kavan left Bhryell, yet he liked what he saw in Bhendhámyn. The young man finished a quick prayer and clasped the old man's hand. "Good morning, bhydáni."

"Here for the Gathering or to pray?"

Dháná looked away uncomfortably but Bhendhámyn replied, "I never miss málneag Kóráhm's Feast. It is right I am here; one of us should be. Until someone offers me one good reason," his glance challenged his grandmother, "as to why Kóráhm is rón, I will venerate him according to the status the Faith gave him." He grinned when the old man smiled proudly. "aendhá is away, so aene came with me."

The sage nodded. "That explains it." He was not intending to discuss the private matter further, but Bhendhámyn, ever the talker and almost gossip, was not going to let the chance to talk before the ceremony started to go unused.

"You rarely come to Gathering, bhydáni; it is a long walk. Did someone accompany you?"

"I came on my own."

"Why? You would not come on a whim. What has happened?"

Tíbhyan met the young man's gaze, marveling at his discernment and curiosity. "Yes…you are his kin…you should know."

"Who, bhydáni?"

"Kavan."

"Of course he is kin," Bhendhámyn insisted as Dháná visibly retreated into herself.

That was good to hear. "He was attacked, beaten, nearly killed. From what I was told, his hands are damaged so badly that unless k'Ádhá sees fit to spare him, he will never play music again."

Tíbhyan suspected Bhendhámyn was weeping, this one who did not know his cousin except by name and reputation. The young man clutched the rail, his head hanging, blonde hair hiding his face while his shoulders shook. The older man covered one strong hand with his frail one. In that touch, he learned that this particular MacLyr had deep empathy indeed. His grandmother, on the other hand, looked as if she did not want to believe it.

"How do you know?" she asked in a brittle voice. "Is he in Bhryell? Have you seen him?" She might have grown distant from her nephew but she still cared for him.

"I wish I had. No one knows where he is."

"Then how…"

"Your son was looking for him. He told me."

The woman looked stunned. "Ártur came without bringing us the news?"

Her grandson spoke bitterly before Tíbhyan could. "What would aendhá have said if he had? Rather than be considerate of Ártur's feelings and Kavan's suffering, he would…" He stopped as she raised her hand. His point was made. Avoiding Tám's ridicule was the best reason for Ártur not to return to his childhood home with such news. Bhendhámyn looked at the sage. "You have come to light a candle for Kavan. That is generous and thoughtful."

"For him, it is no effort. For him, I would travel to the edge of the world. I come for him. But may I suggest something, young MacLyr?"

Bhendhámyn bent his head closer. "Please do, sir."

"If you can manage it, I think your uncle is in need of amity at this time, at least for a few days. Let him know, if you can, that he is not the sole member of his family to care whether Kavan lives or dies."

The blonde nodded as determination set in his eyes. "I will do that, bhydáni, as soon as I can. May I assist you home after the Gathering?"

"It would be gracious, but not necessary…"

"I would be honored to do it. Consider me at your service, bhydáni." Bhendhámyn did not acknowledge his grandmother's resigned sigh. Unless she wanted to walk with them, she would be returning home alone.

❧*❧

The bundle upon his lap was small and light, wrapped in several layers of Káliel's finest pale green linen kerchiefs. Kavan studied the bundle for many moments but did not touch it. Near him, Wortham waited with an impatient sparkle in his eyes. Finally, more to appease Wortham's patience than his curiosity, Kavan did his best to tug on the length of ribbon that held the linen in place. The cloth fell open to reveal a pair of loose-fitting gray leather gloves and a small silk pouch. Kavan glanced at Wortham curiously.

"What is this?"

The bearded man grinned. "It is your birthday, milord."

Kavan blinked. It was. The Feast day of Saint Kóráhm. "You remembered," he murmured, more surprised that he had not realized it then that Wortham had remembered.

"Of course. It is a simple day to remember since it is also Saint Kóráhm's Feast. I would remember it even if it were not, simply because it is your day. I thought you could use the gloves. They might not erase the disfigurement, but they will keep your hands warm and mask the severity of the damage." In Kavan's shifting, a metallic object slid from the pouch and started to slide to the floor; Wortham caught it before it fell. "I saw this in a shop window as we journeyed to the shrine. I thought you would like to have it."

It was a cloak clasp, wrought of silver, square and nearly the width of his palm. The T-shape of Kóráhm's Cross was in relief, at its center, etched and adorned with a small red stone at its heart. Its mechanism was simple, such that Kavan could open and close it despite his injuries.

"You are a thoughtful man, Wortham," Kavan murmured, "both to remember and present such appropriate items. But I fear wearing this might be blasphemous."

"How so, milord? You still wear the other?"

Kavan shook his head sadly. "I cannot undo the clasp. Kóráhm has abandoned me; to wear this…"

Not knowing why Kavan believed that, Wortham interrupted. "Might bring him back to you. I do not know why he would abandon you…but prove you do not blame him for what has happened, that your faith and love in him and in k'Ádhá have not diminished, and perhaps you will find favor."

"My faith in k'Ádhá remains strong. As for Kóráhm…do you know that he came to me…that he told me that if he had been in my place…he might have taken what the princess offered?"

Wortham's face was thoughtful, though if he comprehended the unspoken nuances of that statement he hid it. "All men have weaknesses. Perhaps beautiful women were his, the one temptation he found difficult to avoid or cast off. He was only a man after all."

Only a man. Not a man. Kavan choked on his words. "But I could not…how could he have become a saint if such is true?"

Why that should matter, Wortham did not understand. "The k'gdhededhá make saints, usually long after a person's death. The committee that anointed him would not have had many details about how he lived his life unless someone bothered to write it down. All they would have had was the stories and legends. He helped others; he lived his life according to the Faith as he believed it and succeeded more than he failed. In the grand scheme of things, would it have mattered? Men fight their weaknesses every day; sometimes we win, other times we lose. Some of us lose more than we win but are accepted back into the Faith if we desire to be. That you can avoid temptations most men cannot speaks highly of your spiritual constitution. As long as we continue to fight, I think in the end we will be forgiven our transgressions. Is that not what the Faith teaches?"

Kavan did not speak, deep in thought over the words Wortham had wisely spoken. The captain patted his arm reassuringly and went above deck where he had left Urian basking in the sun.

❧*❧

The oratory was undisturbed this day, which was fortunate for Ártur though disheartening. He rose early after a troubled night and came to the stone steps of the oratory altar to pray. The single thick white candle still burned there after a day of contemplation.

The one time he had been away from this spot was when he accompanied the Lachlan household to the Gathering of Saint Kóráhm in Hes á Redh. While he had not wanted to forsake his vigil, he felt compelled to attend in support of the King and as a testimony that anti-Elyri violence would not sway him from duty. Also, he felt he should be there in Kavan's stead, since for all he knew, Kavan was unaware of the day's significance.

Despite the beauty of the service, the elegance of the décor, and the poignant quality of the music, the Gathering felt wrong. In the past it had felt as if Kóráhm was present, celebrating life and sacrifice. But today that feeling was absent because Kavan was absent. That the Saint had not seemed to acknowledge Rhidam's Gathering darkened the healer's mood. He suspected the future would hold much more unpleasantness without Kóráhm, and Kavan, to stabilize it.

Ártur should not have knelt here alone. It was Kavan's birthday. The bard should be here with his friends, his family, people who loved him. He should not be wandering far away under the impression he was insignificant. No one else seemed to have remembered the day's importance; they had acknowledged Saint Kóráhm's Feast day and nothing more.

Ártur knew how much Kavan feared complete solitude. Not self-imposed solitude, but the solitude that came from rejection. He had Wortham with him, if the captain had been able to find him, but would that be enough? Would being unable to gain the acceptance of people as he once had destroy whatever part of Kavan's spirit the princess had not devastated?

Ártur had no way of knowing. Unlike other times when he and Kavan were separated by great distances, there was no attempted mental contact except for that brief farewell. Any time the healer was not otherwise occupied, he left his mind open for such contact, but it did not come. He felt certain that Kavan lived, but in some ways, it felt as if he had lost his cousin and sínréc forever.

"Do not fret, son of Llyr," came a voice from the air, a soothing sound that caressed him like silk over his skin. The healer looked up from his prayers and musings but there was no one to be seen. Yet the presence of someone in the room was unmistakable.

In reply, he scoffed aloud, grating against the calm voice like a petulant child. "Do not fret? If you know I fret, you know why."

"Your cousin is safe, at least for now."

"Safe does not mean happy."

"Happiness is relative, MacLyr. It may be a long time before he achieves that state. However, he is learning much about himself and what it means to live and be content. Perhaps if he is observant and open, he will make discoveries that will bring him peace."

The words, more than the voice, were suddenly recognizable. The Saint had never spoken to him before, but Ártur felt confident it was him. "Am I speaking with Kóráhm?"

The air in the room reverberated with an amused chuckle. "You are more perceptive than I thought."

Some might have found that insulting. Ártur did not. "You have not revealed yourself to me before."

"There was never a need. I must choose the times and places of return carefully. And your cousin has my full attention, whether he believes it or not. Why did you summon me, Healer MacLyr? What may I do for you?"

Summoned? While Ártur had prayed to the Saint for Kavan's sake, he had not sought a visitation. No man ever did…except perhaps Kavan. "I know I am not the man my cousin is, that I do not share the great strength of his faith. But may I ask a favor?"

He was embraced in warmth. "You wish me to convey your affections to Kavan." The intimacy with which he spoke the bard's name made Ártur shiver. "I would, but he has shut himself off from me. He has learned details that were not…to his liking." The healer heard the melancholy in the disembodied voice and closed his eyes. "I have lost status in his heart. But there may be another way to convey the message. I will do what I can."

Then the voice and its presence were gone. Ártur realized he was shaking. Saint Kóráhm had never come to him, only to Kavan, and once to Wortham and Prince Muir. It would have soothed his fears if not for the painful knowledge that Kavan had turned his back on Kóráhm. He did not like that, and from the Saint's tone of voice, neither did he.

❧*❧

The wine in his cup was bitter and stale. Arlan knew that from the smell; it had not been that way when he had poured it several hours ago, but after a single sip, he had not touched it again. He had paced his bedchamber irregularly since the Gathering, unwilling or unable to bring himself to leave the room. Every meeting, every engagement was canceled the moment he stepped into the náos that morning. It was not until that moment that the impact of the day hit him. It was not merely the Saint's day. It was also Kavan's. Or it should be.

The bard was not here and the King's daughter had driven him away; Arlan felt that loss deeply. Yet it was other secrets that he alone knew that troubled him, secrets that kept him in self-exile away from his advisors and his children.

Not for the first time in his life, did the King realize that he, like others within these walls, took the bard for granted, demanding time, attention, advice, support, and music without a thought about what the man might need. That Kavan gave selflessly and rarely complained or asked for special treatment, and indeed seemed to have a need to give to find self-worth, made it too easy to abuse his generosity. And Arlan, as the King, was perhaps guiltiest of that offense. Every time he realized it, he vowed to change, to make it up to Kavan, to repay him somehow, but he never had. And now the bard was gone, possibly forever.

Squeezing the cup in frustration, he felt its tin sides give to the pressure of his hand. The moon had risen; it was too late today for action. He had made the same promises throughout the day, promises meant to appease Kavan if the man would return. Promises he knew he would probably not be able to keep, even if his wish for Kavan's return was granted.

He was annoyed for forgetting Kavan's birthday. The bard rarely accepted gifts except from Captain Delamo, but Arlan gave him something every year, forcing it upon Kavan by finding something the bard needed. Horses. Ancient books. Harp strings. Furnishings and art for Alberni. Gifts to the Faith on his behalf.

This year, however, Arlan had forgotten. He had gotten nothing, done nothing, given nothing, nor thought about it until he stepped into the náos.

He would rectify that in the morning. He would scour Rhidam, Enesfel, all of the Sovereignties for a perfect gift and hold it until the bard returned. While the Elyri might never know the reason for an elaborate gift, might not know that the King had forgotten, Arlan would never forget the offense. This time, k'Ádhá willing, he would make up his errors to his friend.

At least one other person in the Lachlan stronghold remembered the significance of the day. In the back garden, Owain paced in the moonlight, stopping sometimes to gaze upon the burial markers of those he considered family. Waiting in the keep for his son to return from Káliel, knowing the King was tolerant of his being there even if he did not seek his company, Owain had ample time to wonder where Kavan was and why he had left. Something Diona had done, yes, but was there something more? Had those who loved him done something, or failed to do something, that contributed to his belief in inadequacy? The wondering had taken its toll today, making Owain irritable and unfit for the company of others. It did not help that he felt slighted; Kavan had bid farewell to Ártur, had taken Wortham with him it seemed, and had left Owain with nothing, to worry and miss him alone. There was no one here he could confide in, as they had their own troubles and cares to fret over. Perhaps he should go to Káliel with his family. At least his sons and Gabrielle could offer solace.

That Kavan had forgiven him for his transgressions and accepted him as one of his closest friends still left Owain with an occasional pang of guilt. He noticed the stiffness in the bard's shoulders once and made the unthinking mistake of questioning it. Kavan would not tell him, but the healer had. It was caused by residual pain from the beating Kavan received when Owain, then the King of Enesfel, imprisoned the bard many years ago. Owain could not imagine wanting to cause Kavan pain but he knew he had done it, and would have executed him if the bard had not escaped. Owain praised the fates every day that

Kavan had fled that death. Otherwise, Owain's life would have taken a much different course and likely have been considerably shorter.

Thus, he made a point of acknowledging the bard's birthday every year, almost as if it were a Feast Day unto itself. Regardless of how the rest of his life progressed, Owain would set aside the day to remember, to be thankful, to renew his personal vow to live up to the faith Kavan put in him, whether the bard remembered him or not.

❧*❧

She was alone, her auburn hair loose around her shoulders, but she was too far away to see her image clearly through the mist. She waited at the foot of Kóráhm's shrine, barefoot, her hands at her sides. He thought she was smiling, for there was warmth and welcome in her presence that he had not felt with her appearance before. There was also an aura of tremendous power about her that made Kavan weak. He tried to call to her, to summon her closer to learn more, but she either did not hear him or did not intend to oblige his request.

But he did hear her voice, a low, husky, melodic tone that made him tremble. Her mouth did not move but he heard her nonetheless. She revealed that Ártur, and others, held him in their hearts today, were thinking about him on this day more than any other, if that was possible since he remained close in the thoughts of those who loved him throughout every day of his absence. He wanted to ask how she knew this, but she was gone, as was the vision of the shrine.

Kavan awoke from sleep but could see no light coming through the small porthole that provided air and light. It was still night and Urian and Wortham both slept. Something about the experience suggested it was not a dream, yet nor had it been the Sight. She was real, as real as Kóráhm ever was, though Kavan could think of no saint that fit her description. If not a saint, what was she? Who was she? How did Kóráhm know her?

Though not eager for contact, Kavan relented to her unspoken suggestion, opened his thoughts and reached for his cousin.

On the steps of the oratory altar, Ártur awoke with a pleasant start. Kavan's mind in his! He could not contain the joy the contact elicited, and his elation momentarily drove Kavan back. The communication was stilted, restrained, but two things were clear; Kavan was as physically fit as he could be, and that this was the last time he would contact anyone until he found the answers he needed. Before he broke away, Kavan emitted a brief wave of both misery and love for his cousin, Arlan, Muir, and Owain. Then the link was broken and the night around Ártur felt immediately cold and empty.

Alone, Ártur wrapped his arms around himself and fixed his gaze on the Pyre above him as he wept tears of joy, remorse, and loneliness.

❧Chapter 7❧

Minos Cornell was a practical man and had grown more so in the years since accepting appointment as Enesfel's Chancellor. He was not prone to hysteria or quick action unless there was an immediate need for it. When he first read the letter left for him that morning he was disconcerted but nothing more. Threats themselves did not necessarily require action, only a little extra caution, thus he paid closer attention to his surroundings and the people he worked with as the day wore on. He reported the threat to High Justice Corbin and forgot about it.

Or he tried to forget about it. It was the reason behind the threat that left him off-balance and gave him cause to consider more definitive action as the hours passed. What if it was true? What if the threat was the beginning of some larger danger? If the accusation was accurate, was it then his duty to learn the truth and report it before the situation escalated?

Yet how could it be true? Would he not have known it before? He did not understand how such things worked, and thus he eventually concluded he needed to seek the facts. If it were true, it could explain many things and open up a chapter in his life and Enesfel's future that might be significant.

"Lord MacLyr?" He found the healer in the dayroom completing a portrait of the late Princess Deidre. The detail was exquisite, much more beautiful than the chancellor considered the late princess to have been. Yet over the years, Ártur's paintings had gradually taken on some other dimension that revealed the soul of the subject as well as their features. Her soul had been as beautiful as the woman the Elyri healer portrayed.

Owain was also in the room, reading near the window, but gave the chancellor no more than a casual glance. The man no longer viewed Owain as the previous King of Enesfel. He was merely Owain Lachlan.

"Is there something I can do for you, Lord Cornell?" the healer asked without looking at him.

"Aye, I wish to ask something of you."

Assuming the chancellor wanted privacy, the prince lay his book aside and began to rise. "I shall go…"

Minos stopped him with a wave of his hand. "There is no need, milord. I have nothing to hide, and your input on this matter might prove beneficial." Curious, Owain sat back down and Minos focused on Ártur. "I received a written threat this morning…"

Ártur put down the paintbrush and turned. "Why come to me?"

"I've already reported it to Justice Cornell. I am little concerned with that. What I require is of a more personal nature." He paused and took a deep breath. It had to be now. "Is it possible to prove if there is Elyri in my blood?"

Owain was as startled by the question as Ártur and more surprised than before that the chancellor had asked him to stay. "In your…?"

The chancellor nodded, clearly not happy but still determined to find answers. "It is far-fetched. I find it hard to imagine, which is why it has taken me so long to come to you. But there is a possibility it is true. Lord Cliáth asked once if there is Elyri in my family; I asked him why he thought this and he commented that he finds me easy to read, as if I project my thoughts."

"I often thought that of you," Owain remarked. "It is easier to know what you are thinking than most."

"I am aware of it," admitted Minos with flustered consternation. "There have been other moments in my life that I have not been able to explain, such as my irrational gut reaction to anti-Elyri violence and my low tolerance for alcohol. It may be nothing more than my sense of morality and a weak constitution, but since this threat indicates I will be the first of many to die, it seems prudent I know the truth."

Ártur wiped paint from his hands on a cloth hanging over the corner of the easel. "Are either of your parents Elyri?"

"No. But I did not know my grandparents, and relatives on my mother's side were never spoken of. I have no living elders to ask, and though I can send inquiries to my cousins, if any of them know the secret, they may be disinclined to share it. I was hoping you can resolve this without the need of dredging up awkward family history."

"I can read you if you wish."

"Will it help? If it will answer the riddle, then I am willing." He sat, nervous despite his conviction to learn the truth. The healer took one of the chancellor's hands in his, and laid his other upon Minos' chest. Minos felt nothing but the normal pressures of a man's hands. It was eerie sitting like that, with the healer's eyes closed and Owain watching in fascination, but fortunately, the experience and silence did not last long.

Ártur dropped his hands and leaned back. "I cannot be completely accurate, as such things rarely are when the bloodline is many generations diluted, but I am fairly certain there is Elyri in your heritage."

The chancellor let out a long slow breath and made every effort not to appear shaken. Ártur admired the man's fortitude. It could not be easy to discover at the age of seventy that his entire life was based upon inaccuracies. Minos' jaw twitched, but that was the only expression he allowed. Owain gave a low whistle.

"How…certain…are you?"

"There is an eighty percent likelihood of Elyri in your bloodline, probably a grandparent or great-grandparent…or before."

Minos nodded. That was good enough. "I should alert the King. The threat might be a hoax or…"

"It might not be. Someone has gone to great lengths to learn this about you and to make it known. You know the threat of violence against Elyri is high, especially for those most vulnerable or in positions of influence to the Crown."

"Owain's right…like Kavan…" Ártur murmured.

"Lord Cliáth? Has something happened to him?" Surprised the chancellor had not already heard the story, the healer repeated it, finding the retelling no easier than learning of it the first time had been. He watched the chancellor's expression grow increasingly grim. "What of his estate? Who is tending it? Has Lord Dugan learned anything? Were the bodies of the dead identified?"

The healer shrugged. "I do not know what Lord Dugan has learned. You know he will not report anything until he is sure of his facts. As for the Alberni estate, Kavan has made certain it is self-sufficient."

"But who makes the major decisions in his absence? Who governs the lands?"

"I do not know…he never told me. Ask Bhríd; if anyone knows, he likely does as he and Kavan and Muir set up the original transfer of deeds and title."

Worried about details like governing and taxation in the face of a potential crisis, Minos was back on his feet. "I shall do it at once. If this threat has anything to do with an attack on Lord Cliáth, if there is a conspiracy at hand, we must deal with it swiftly."

He did not escape the healer's grasp on his arm. "Will you be…?"

Minos cleared his throat. "Fear not, Lord Healer. This changes nothing. But thank you for asking. While unnerving, this does little to affect the way I live and would not have affected me years ago if I had known then. If someone wishes me harm because of something beyond my control, then it is better I learn of it after I have lived a full life and made a contribution to the kingdom."

Owain rose and offered the older man his hand. "Milord, I will be in Rhidam until my son returns from Káliel. I ask that you allow me to serve as your protector until the perpetrators are seized or I must leave for Fiara."

"You…protect me?" The chancellor paled. "That was my position once, to protect you; I did a poor job of it."

Shrugging, Owain ignored the awkwardness those words birthed. Those events had occurred long ago; he rarely considered the changes his abdication had wrought, except for those entangled with Kavan. "Events have unfolded as they should as Lord Cliáth would say."

"But you are a Lachlan prince."

The blonde man smiled, still harboring a secret few knew. "I have nothing else to do and the King would appreciate if I was busy, out of his way. It will make me feel useful. What do you say?"

Minos hesitantly agreed. "If you insist. Come, We will discuss this with the King. And I think, perhaps, I should alert my son."

❧*❧

Gaelán's dark gelding raced ahead of the others though Asta's pied mare was not far behind. Perhaps continually winning these races against Prince Hagan and Dayly Niall was not the wise thing to do, but the races were usually at Prince Hagan's insistence and Gaelán could not help that his gelding was the swiftest. He had gotten this horse when he turned nine and had won every race the prince proposed in the last four years. But today he realized Asta's new mare might pose a challenge to his continual winnings.

He said nothing as he reached the tree that was their designated goal. He saw no point in gloating, but Asta had her own plans. She pulled her mare alongside him and kissed his cheek.

"A trophy for the winner," she said with a smile.

Gaelán blushed, aware the Crown Prince was glaring at him. Unlike Hagan, who had recently begun to develop an interest in girls, despite being the oldest of the boys, or Tayte who had yet to show any interest, Gaelán, the youngest, had long been interested in the opposite sex, longer than his parents cared to admit. Normally, however, he did not blush when a girl paid him a compliment. Asta alone brought out that reaction. Also, he did not normally object to another boy's interest in whichever girl he might be chasing. Today, however, he did not like the way Hagan was looking at him, as if Asta were the prince's property and Gaelán should leave her alone.

"Shall we rest the horses before we start back?" he asked to divert attention from the race and the kiss.

The four soldiers with them, the remaining four Káliel guardsmen, dismounted as the younger riders did. Their ranks did not seem complete without Captain Delamo, but as much as the captain was missed, most were relieved he had stayed with Kavan. Rhidam could make do without Wortham; Kavan could not.

As she dismounted, Asta's foot slipped from the stirrup and she slid to the ground. Not a far drop, and she was experienced enough on a horse to minimize the impact of such a fall, but she still gave a startled yelp as she scraped her hand upon the stony earth.

Already thinking like a healer, Gaelán began to wash the wound with water from his flask. It was not deep, but her entire palm was scratched and bleeding. Hagan pushed closer to see if she was injured and in the hopes of possibly getting between her and the youngest Cáner. He was close enough to see Gaelán put his fingertips to the clean wound. Pulling upon the small, unfocused pool of energy within, Gaelán directed it into her hand and within moments, the broken skin was mended.

Prince Hagan gasped; Dayly swallowed loudly and shifted on his feet. But it was Asta's wide eyes Gaelán met, with no real thought as to what the reaction might be to what he had done. "Does it hurt still?"

Asta shook her head. "You are a healer? Like Lord MacLyr?"

He nodded, suddenly embarrassed. He had not considered how his friends might react the first time they discovered his secret. "I just found out. This is why I'm in Rhidam. k'aendhá is going to train me."

"You will stay in Rhidam?" Asta asked expectantly. Prince Hagan appeared to have been about to ask the same, though the emotion in his eyes indicated a different motive behind the question.

"More than I have in the past, yes," Gaelán said, nervous because he sensed the prince's jealousy.

Asta squeezed Gaelán's hand with her newly healed and cleaned one. "Thank you for tending my hand, Healer Cáner."

Healer Cáner. He liked that. He smiled, no longer caring what Prince Hagan thought.

❧*❧

The halls of Harcourt Castle were dark when Prince Espen arrived. It was not yet dawn; his ship had caught a swift current and made better time than foreseen. He had not expected to arrive until evening.

The guards allowed him to enter without a word. Espen stopped to look at the yellow-gray stone structure he called home. Sterile was the best word he could use to describe it, since it bore no mark of distinction and no banners on its square parapets. The castle's size and the high stone walls surrounding the main building were all that revealed that it was not the home of a peasant, merchant, or mere nobleman. It was the home of the Hatu kings, a home and title Espen was destined not to possess, a kingdom he would never rule.

Not that he had always thought of home in such a way. Though it was sparsely furnished and mostly unadorned, it had seemed a grand place while growing up. Compared to the homes and shops that comprised Natrona's port city, small, mostly single-story buildings of the same yellowish gray stone and clay shingled roofing, the palace was lavish to behold. Compared to the rest of Hatu, the small towns and villages periodically destroyed and rebuilt in wave after wave of internal unrest and instability, Natrona and its keep were a marvel.

But traveling into Enesfel for the first time had been an awakening for the prince. Even the peasants in Enesfel lived better than those in Hatu and the homes of the lowest lords appeared more opulent than the Harcourt palace. To Espen, it was no wonder the people of his homeland frequently revolted. Conditions in Hatu had begun to improve in the final years of King Geir's reign and Noreis was continuing their father's efforts to stabilize and strengthen Hatu, but there was still much progress to be made.

What most astonished Espen in that first visit was the intermingling of men and women. In Enesfel, women could move about freely, both at home and in the streets. They could own private lands although that was a rare thing to find. They could be educated, if they could afford it, and were not shunned for having, or speaking, opinions, though not all were eager to do so. Seeing it, speaking to some of those women, allowed the prince to discover that women could be as intelligent and outspoken as any man. Princess Diona certainly was both of those things and more. He had not considered that women could be as competent as men in some matters, better in others, as there were few women in his life in Hatu to allow him to make such a judgment. There had been his mother and his nurse, but both abruptly disappeared from his life when he turned six, as was the custom in lives of Hatuish nobility. He was told that he and Noreis had three sisters, none of whom Espen had ever met. Occasionally he was able to see and speak with his mother, but for the most part, the women in his family did not exist for him.

Going to Rhidam, being in the company of Lady MacLyr, Lady Cáner-Dubuais, and Princess Diona was a little like stepping back into his childhood. At first, he had almost resented the constant company of women, except for Diona, but eventually he had grown accustomed to it and had come to find conversation with them stimulating.

Which made returning to the nearly empty, male-dominated halls of Harcourt Castle feel ever more sterile. Noreis continued to teasingly mock him about his hesitancy to marry, but in this atmosphere, Espen could see little reason to take a wife. He had come to believe, after spending time with Diona, that marriage should be about companionship, not merely an arrangement made to reproduce and continue a bloodline. If one simply wanted to father children, there was no need to marry to do that. What was the point in marrying a bright, beautiful woman, a princess, if she was not welcome in the Hall, not allowed to speak before the men, not able to stand with those whom she was, by birth, on equal footing?

Princess Diona would not be welcome here. Her customs would annoy every official in Hatu's court. And she would be uncomfortable and unhappy, probably not even like this warmer, barren environment. A lesser, more docile woman might be content, but Espen would never be drawn to such a person. Being forced to keep silent, to keep apart, would anger the princess, and in time, Espen as well, if he was forced to hide her against their mutual wishes.

Perhaps it would be for the best if she decided against marriage. He adored her; his chest ached when he imagined life without her. He had no desire to condemn her to the sort of existence she would have here. In her little piece of Hatu, she could do as she wanted; Espen had included that stipulation as part of the agreement when he chose the site and secured the contract with his brother the king. She could rule it, entertain guests, and make the decisions for its upkeep, pursuant of course to the laws of the land. Yet of what use were those stipulations if every lord in Hatu shunned her because she was a woman?

Weary, Prince Espen trudged to his room and crawled into bed after shedding sea-worn clothes in a trail across the carpeted floor. He would think clearer after rest. Sleep would also help him avoid his brother and questions about Espen's marital status that much longer.

❧*❧

"No, I have not found anything useful about the attacks on Kavan," Caol groaned in annoyance as he removed his gloves and threw them on the table. "I examined the corpses; not pretty work, I'll tell you. Without an Elyri on hand, I could not identify them and thus far there is no one willing to come forward with information."

He took the glass of wine the page offered with a nod of gratitude. "The citizens of Levonne are scared to go out, either because they fear being attacked by their neighbors or by the beast that killed two of those men…and it definitely was a beast. And of course, the fact that the others appeared to have exploded has left many wondering if this is something all Elyri can do or if it was an act of k'Ádhá."

The King grimaced. "I hope you reinforced that Elyri cannot…"

"Of course. I made it quite clear that Lord Cliáth had no hand in those deaths, that no Elyri is capable of making a person explode."

Remembering what Kavan had once told him, King Arlan's serious expression did not change. "You told them a lie."

Caol shrugged and drained the wine glass. "Not exactly…if Lord Cliáth did that, it was not with his hands. I saw no other choice, unless we want to watch anti-Elyri violence escalate unchecked. I told them I had no idea what caused those deaths because it is true, but I am continuing to investigate. Honestly…I do not see how any man could have done something like that." Of course, he remembered watching

Kavan turn a boulder to dust before his eyes; there was no reason something similar could not be done to a person. Kavan, as many who knew him knew, was no mere man. "Father Picus pushed the divine intervention angle since Lord Cliáth was outnumbered by stronger opponents and is widely regarded as a…"

"Saint," the King sighed, knowing how it would pain his friend to hear that. "Keep looking, Caol. Someone had to see something or know who those men were. They must have families, friends. Someone will report them missing eventually."

"My thoughts too, Sire. I've got my people on it."

The King chuckled darkly. "I should like to meet your 'people'."

"I am sure you would," Caol replied with a twinkle in his eyes, "and many would like to meet you. But it is better for you, and them, if it never happens."

ᕫ*ᕬ

Minos glared at the general with his usual annoyance. "Can't you see I am busy, Lord General? Why do you pester me with requests you know I will turn down when I am in the middle of something?"

Ignoring the chancellor's grumpiness, Ternce Wyndham said, "Pardon the interruption," with a bow, directing his apology at Flannery rather than Minos. "I have not come to make a request but to inform you that the King has ordered Justice Corbin to increase palace security and patrols in Rhidam. The justice has already informed his men they will have to take a temporary pay decrease to fund more men. We are aware," he smirked at the chancellor, "that there are currently limited funds, but the King would like you to look into ways of increasing the treasury to support this necessity. Now…if you will excuse me."

Folding his arms across his chest, Minos did not attempt to hide his frustration after the general was gone. "Do you see what I have to contend with?"

Flannery, who had been preparing for the duties of Chancellor since he had come into the Lachlan employ years earlier, looked thoughtful. "There is land near Theron which the Crown confiscated a few years back, I believe. And some of the old Neth territory that Lord Lachlan set aside as property for the Crown."

"Are you suggesting we sell it?"

"Sell it, auction it, award it to someone who will make it profitable, whichever will bring the most income the quickest. As I recall, the land near Theron is not bringing much income, and no one lives in the old Neth acreage. Perhaps someone can make it profitable, so the Crown can benefit from additional taxes…or parceling it and creating new lords might serve us similarly."

The chancellor scratched his cheek. He had not considered using those lands and was surprised to have the younger man suggest it. "I can see why Lord Cáner selected you and insisted I continued your training. Keep on this path, stay abreast of matters, and the day may come when you are asked to fill this position. I'm not a young man; no one else is better qualified to fulfill this duty." And given the threat he had received, that day might come sooner than expected. "I will see what the King thinks of your suggestions."

❧*❧

Finding Tusánt quickly gulping down his morning meal in the nearly empty thóres kitchen, Jermyn smiled as he sat on the bench beside him. "Good morning, Tusánt. We have not had opportunity to talk since your return from Alberni."

The Elyri gdhededhá chuckled and swallowed. "When you said there would be new altar attendants to train, you did not specify there would be this many. And as you know, Rankin has placed the choir in my hands for the Dhágdhuán and Udhár Feast days.

"You knew he would. Yours is the best voice we have, making you the best person capable of conducting others." Tusánt bowed his head in humble thanks and pushed his empty plate back. "You've had a chance to meet Valgis? What do you think of him?"

"I have." Tusánt considered his words before asking, "Honestly?"

"Of course."

He kept his face neutral as he spoke. "I will reserve judgment a little longer. He strikes me as a zealot, and you know I dislike fanaticism. But he is young and new to his calling and gdhededhá his age often seem over-zealous to me. Perchance some of it will wear down with experience and time. I think you are right to keep him here, where we can observe him more closely in the meantime. A zealot in the wrong place, and under the wrong influence, would be trouble."

The k'gdhededhá agreed. "Good…I did not want to think I alone felt this way." Changing the subject, he continued, "I have not been able to look over your report but I am eager to know what the new chellé is like."

The memories of that place made Tusánt smile. "It is…too exquisite for words. I could not do it justice. Lord Cliáth told me it would be a place of great beauty, but this…the art, the architecture, the gardens…even the gdhededhá who serve there…They have this look about them, something that makes them seem as ethereal as the place in which they live."

"Are they Elyri?"

"Most are Teren…to be expected with anything connected to Saint Kóráhm. k'gdhededhá Khwílen is expecting another five Elyri scribes to arrive soon; after that, he is not anticipating many more, since few Elyri are willing to travel outside of Elyriá these days."

"Who can blame them when their patriarch will not travel here?"

"k'gdhededhá Dórímyr did not come?"

"Did we think he would?"

Tusánt shook his head. The náós outside Elyriá barely existed to the patriarch.

"Is the chellé complete?"

"Some of the living quarters are not yet finished, but Khwílen is not expecting to need those for some time. There are also a few security measures not in place, and the grounds have not been fully planted as it is too cold, but there was nothing to delay the opening."

Jermyn cocked his head. "Security? For a chellé?"

"It sounds unnecessary to me as well, but Khwílen explained that Lord Cliáth wants a place that will attract Elyri and Teren, a place where both, and the books housed there, will be safe. A haven. There are guards at the outer gates; those inside are free to leave but no one enters without permission. I do not know what Lord Cliáth plans that is not already done. Though concerned about the image of sentries at the gates, the k'gdhededhá is more concerned with the welfare of those who live there."

"And he should be," Jermyn thought with a sigh, thinking about the attack on Kavan. "You opened the chellé?"

"I did. You must see it, Your Grace. If you do nothing else in your life, you must see this place. It is like living in paradise."

"Like looking into Lord Cliáth's soul."

Tusánt wholeheartedly agreed.

❧*❧

Kavan was grateful that the ship would dock in Natrona tomorrow morning. Fourteen days at sea with short stops at more than one port along the way was more than he could endure. He was truly sick, both from the motion of the boat and lack of food. Wortham made every attempt to coax him to eat and had been successful a few times. But because of the sickness, just the thought of food made Kavan nauseous. The bard spent most of his time trying to sleep. Twice more he saw that woman, always in dreams, her face hidden. She did not speak, did not communicate with him again, and her appearance had little effect upon his well-being or disposition. She merely stood upon the shore and appeared to be waiting. For him, he wondered. Would she be there when the ship docked? Where would she lead him?

Today, however, perhaps because he knew relief was drawing nearer, he felt capable of sitting and resumed reading the man's journal, which he had not yet completed. Much of it was as he expected, the other side of the woman's tale. The author mentioned her frequently and made occasional references to someone named Dhyóti. While the man's story did not differ significantly from hers, there was one passage that disturbed Kavan, causing him to reread it several times in an attempt to grasp its meaning.

It has happened. My brother has found the ancient náos that I have made it my life's mission to preserve. Not only has he discovered it, he has defiled it. During my absence, he gained passage below the castle…I do not know how…and violated the altar with Teren sacrifices and other unspeakable abominations. It is my failing; I was lax in my diligence and k'Ádhá has seen to it I have paid for my errors. It has cost me Yhsábhel. Never has a man loved so much…lost so much…as I. Her body broken upon that stone, her blood spilled in the name of hatred and revenge. If I had the fortitude, I would tear the temple apart stone by stone with my hands, or collapse it upon myself as my final resting place. As things are, I will do what I bid Yhsábhel do, flee behind the Llaethlágárá, away from these people who know nothing of love, flee to Dhyóti. Perhaps I will return one day to make what reparations I can. As for the temple, it is for my descendants to rectify that wrong, for I cannot. I am cursed to never enter it again. The key to its purification has been left with Bhóité in Enda. I pray he will do what must be done when the time arises, though it will cost him much I fear. I would need to kill my brother to right the wrongs done, and for that, I do not have the courage.

The ancient náós below the castle? Though the manuscript did not specify which castle or náós it referred to, Kavan knew. He had not been there since the night Arlan took the throne from Owain, and he had not thought about it except on the day Prince Bertram suffered his fatal wound in a similar náós on Káliel. Similar in age and power, if not in features. Kavan recalled the negativity the room elicited despite its religious paintings and the four saintly statues keeping watch. The destructive energy in that altar was explained, it seemed, the energy like that which emanated from the final resting place of Dawid Coryllien on the island of Pháne, Káliel.

Staring towards where Urian whittled a block of wood into a tiny figure, Kavan pondered the connections and threads of his life. It was during the Persecution that Coryllien was said to have lived, and sacrifices, Teren and Elyri alike, filled the stories surrounding that mythical man. Coryllien was more than myth; Kavan had uncovered that truth already.

Had Coryllien been involved in the desecration of the náós? And who was the man who wrote this journal, the man who claimed to be the defiler's brother? How had they gained access to the náós, the Gate, or the keep? Coryllien was said to be Teren. If his brother, presumably Teren, was the author of this book, how had he learned High Elyri, and how had he fled to Elyriá with Yhsábhel's family at a time when Teren were not allowed beyond the Llaethlágárá unless they already lived there?

Kavan recalled the moment when he touched the mummified body of Coryllien; the word tágdhedokag, brother, had echoed within his skull as loud as any screaming voice. There had been no opportunity to ponder it at the time, and Kavan had not thought about that day since. The black hatred that consumed the corpse had filled Kavan in that touch, suggesting that Coryllien would have been fully capable of such acts of violence as Teren and Elyri sacrifices. But who was his brother? What had become of him? Or had it been an Elyri follower of Coryllien's instead, as illogical as that notion seemed? What was the importance of that ancient náós?

It gave Kavan a purpose. He could not return home, could not face those he had left. And his career as a musician was behind him. He could, however, devote his life to research, and perhaps find a way to restore the sacred aura of that náós. He prayed that, if he were successful in the endeavor, k'Ádhá would see fit to restore his hands and his music.

❧Chapter 8❧

Though unable to walk of his own volition when they debarked the ship, Kavan felt certain that no one was as grateful as he was to be on firm earth again. If he could prevent it, he did not intend to set foot on another boat for the rest of his life. They wove through Natrona's streets until they reached Heart of Humility Náós, the single operating náós in Hatu, where Urian's Faith affiliation was enough to gain them beds for the night. Although Kavan doubted any of Hatu's citizens realized it, Heart of Humility Náós was possibly the oldest example of Elyri architecture in the Sovereignties, though its Elyri name, Hes Onyhéc, had been converted into the Trade tongue when Elyri hatred was at its height. To be within its walls should have been uplifting and redemptive.

For Kavan, however, to be within the walls of a náós for the first time since leaving Rhidam, kneeling before the altar as had once been his custom, felt profane. How could he kneel in the seat of the highest divine light when there was darkness within? He yearned for the peace he once found in such places, but instead, he found silence and the empty chasm in his soul. Though tempted to leave the sanctuary, to abandon his penitent prayers, he planned to remain throughout the night with the hope that his diligence would be rewarded.

But he had been on the altar steps since their arrival that afternoon; now it was after midnight and nothing had changed. His hands were limp and useless in his lap, he felt spiritually dead, and he still suffered the effects of seasickness and lack of food. Defeated, he left the steps, deciding to return to the room he was to share with his companions in the adjacent building, hoping sleep and a morning meal would help.

He paused outside the náós door, looking towards the ocean through the early Veerhill fog. Though unable to see the water, he could hear the pulse of the surf as the sea was no more than four hundred paces to his left. The náós had once been shielded from the winter storms by a barrier of trees, but those had been cut away for building purposes long ago. Still, these structures, like the shrine on Káliel, appeared undamaged, a testimony to the makers and wardens, another example to Kavan of strength against the evils of adversity.

As he wrestled with the ever-present despair, he became aware of a voice through the mist. A woman's voice. Singing. A song without words that rivaled many of his works in its intricacy. The sound rose and fell over the rumble of the tide and he strained to see who was there. He saw no one. On shaky legs, he took a few steps towards the water, in the direction where the voice seemed to rise. The moon thrust a pale finger through the fog but it did little to light a path.

It did, however, reveal a figure gliding along the surf's edge. Her feet were bare beneath the white of her shift, her hair dark in the dim glow of the moon. Without the wind, it fell around her shoulders to the middle of her back in thick waves. The cold air seemed not to trouble her despite her sheer raiment. Though he could not see her face and she moved away from him, Kavan knew he had found her. The woman Kóráhm had sent.

When she sensed she was not alone, she halted but did not turn. The singing ceased. Kavan took a few steps towards her, which caused her to hasten away.

"Wait. Please. Do not go. I must speak to you. I must know who you are…what you want of me…"

Rather than stop, she disappeared into the mist as if she had never been there, as if she was a vision only. Kavan reached the place she had been to discover footprints in the sand that the waves had not yet erased. No vision then. She was real. Squatting, he touched them with his fingertips, looking in the direction she had gone. He could follow her, but he suspected that, whoever she was, she did not desire to be found. Besides, he knew he did not yet have the stamina for pursuit.

Kóráhm had said to follow where she led. If she knew enough about him to convey Ártur's wishes, then she must know he was in no condition to track her. Perhaps she had wanted him to see her, to know he was on the right path, or she had not been aware he was there. Which might mean that, while she had unusual abilities, she, like Kóráhm, was not omnipotent.

Kóráhm. If nothing else, the days of contemplation at sea had revealed to Kavan one truth. The individual known as málneag Kóráhm, or Kóráhm íth rón, had once been a man. He had possessed the physical capacities, needs, and desires of a mortal man. He had failings. He had not been perfect yet k'Ádhá accepted him. Shortcomings and all. The leaders of the Faith had sanctified him. While Kavan felt no better and still believed himself a coward and something less than a man, he was willing to concede that Kóráhm was what he was. The bard had reached a place where he could accept that realization and accept Kóráhm as he once had. Whatever the man had been, whatever he was now, Kóráhm existed. The Saint was the link to everything Kavan had been, everything he desired to be again. Kavan did not know, however, if his renewed faith would be enough to bring Kóráhm back.

❧*❧

"Would you be angry if I said Lord Cliáth might have been here?"

Muir looked at his bride curiously, aware Diona's breath caught and her face grew pale at the mention. "Here? At the house?"

Clianthe shook her head. "On Káliel. I cannot say for certain…but a few days before Diona came, I was near the docks. There were three men going to the shrine; two appeared to be gdhededhá in dark robes, neither able to climb the path without help. The third, the man helping them, looked much like Captain Delamo. I only saw them from the rear…did not see them return, but the Captain is quite recognizable."

"It could not have been Kavan," Diona said with downcast eyes. "He always wears…"

Her brother reached for her hand. "He could have worn something different to avoid recognition, particularly if he hopes to avoid pity. Bhenádíctus is not his patron, however…"

"Perhaps he is looking for healing?" Clianthe offered, glad no one was angry that she had not spoken sooner. Many made the climb to the shrine of Bhenádíctus for healing. For a desperate man, any shrine would do.

"Or absolution," the prince murmured, meeting his sister's gaze. It was too like Kavan to blame himself. Both suspected their assumptions were correct.

❧*❧

Wortham drafted the letter to King Arlan not certain he should send it. To his knowledge, no one in Rhidam knew where they were or whether they lived. While there would be little concern for his well-being, he knew that everyone of import in the Lachlan House would worry about the bard. He also knew Kavan had no desire for anyone to know the truth of his condition. He wanted to fade; he wanted no one to miss him as much as he feared he would not be missed.

It was that fear of no one caring if he was gone upon which Wortham based his decision. That, and the fact that the captain held much respect for his former employer, brought him to the gates of the Harcourt castle in the early morning hours, before he set to purchases for tomorrow's journey.

"Hold!" called one of the sentries at the gate. Wortham did as he was told. The guard approached, one hand resting upon his short sword, and circled the much larger man. "What business do you have here at this hour?"

"I am Captain Wortham Delamo of the Lachlan Guard. I come to deliver a message to Prince Espen Harcourt, if he is here."

The fellow laughed. "He returned a few days ago. Another message from the Enesfel Princess so soon?"

It sounded to Wortham like the prince's unproductive infatuation with the Lachlan princess had become a joke amongst the Harcourts' soldiers. Wortham felt bad for the prince. "No. I am on a pilgrimage to Kílyn. I have information for my king regarding one of his men who was injured during the journey. It is important this message is delivered to King Arlan as quickly as possible and I pray Prince Espen is willing to see it done." He held forth the scroll he carried, closed with his personal wax seal. "Please, tell him it is urgent."

The soldier took the scroll. "Would you rather speak to him yourself?"

"It is too early for social calls, and currently I do not have time. I have duties to complete before we depart." He bowed. "Thank you for this, sir."

"Aye, you are welcome." The sentry took the scroll inside. Relieved that the message was on its way, trusting that Prince Harcourt would see it delivered, Wortham went about his business.

❧*❧

It was gdhededhá Claide's assigned duty to visit the sick parishioners today, but after spending over an hour searching for him, Tusánt asked Rankin to do it instead. The Elyri gdhededhá would have gladly accepted the duty, but he had learned long ago that some Teren parishioners did not want him to administer the sacramental blessing to them, as if he were somehow less a gdhededhá because he was Elyri. He could feel slighted, but he knew that many Elyri felt similarly about having a Teren gdhededhá tend them. Since Rankin had no further pressing duties today, he was the most logical candidate for the task.

More and more of late, Claide could not be found. Most of his duties were performed as usual; today was the first time he had failed to carry out an assignment as far as Jermyn knew…but it was not the first time he had failed to appear. While Jermyn worried that perhaps Claide had acquired some vice to draw him from the Faith, Tusánt felt a much deeper concern. Though he could not identify it, and could not offer support to explain why he felt as he did, he could not shake the feeling that his life was in danger.

He had lived with the threat of death once; that had passed after his time away from Rhidam with the Enesfel troops and his mission to convert the people who had once been Nethites to the Faith. There had been peace since then. Lately, however, that chilly feeling of dread had resurfaced, with no actual threats and no perceived danger. Being Elyri, Tusánt listened to his inner voice even when he thought it was being irrational. There would be trouble but he did not know in what form it would come.

❧*❧

It was dawn the following morning when two sets of travelers left Natrona. One was a single rider on a fast horse, bound for Rhidam with instructions to travel as quickly as he could. The other group consisted of a blind monk on the back of a mule, an armored bulk of a man carrying a sword and large pack, and a shaky figure in a dark cloak who clutched the arm of the armored man every time his still weak legs threatened collapse.

Despite his condition, Kavan insisted on starting out today. After a day of resting and eating what little he could stomach, he saw no reason to remain in Natrona. He forced himself to take each step, to endure the hardship, which Wortham reluctantly admired, but when it became too much for Kavan, Urian gave up the mule and strolled beside the captain, both men forcing the bard to ride or else set camp.

Currently, Wortham and the gdhededhá were involved in discussion about how the holy writings pertained to the status of women in Hatu. Kavan half listened, half dozed, pulling as much energy as he could gather with the hopes of restoring his depleted strength, as he felt guilty about making the blind man walk. It helped little, but the noon meal and a brief nap did wonders. He had not wanted to sleep, but Wortham insisted upon taking the time to sharpen his sword, newly purchased in case they needed it, and Kavan was unable to stay awake. Afterward, the bard was grateful for the unexpected rest though he did not express his gratitude.

When they stopped for the night, long after dark, Kavan realized again how grateful he was that Wortham was with him. His hands prevented him from gathering firewood or cooking, though he was capable of awkwardly lighting the fire with a handlight. He could not even tend the mule as he wished. His hands still hurt too much. He was capable only of resting, of listening to the sound of Urian whittling in the darkness. He almost asked how the monk could do that in the dark but realized that the gdhededhá lived in darkness.

He slept almost at once after the meal was complete; he ate more than he had in many days and his body was exhausted. It was not long, however, before he awoke, recoiling in astonishment and horror from the dream and the condition of his robe.

She was there again, on the beach. The night was cold; the fog thick. She wore the same white shift and a partial veil that revealed nothing of her face except dark eyes, but she was near enough that he could smell the scents of fern, sea salt, and exotic fruits. His heart beat wildly as she reached for his face. Her fingertips touched his lips as if to prevent him from speaking and then she was gone, waking him with the abruptness of her departure.

Not as erotic a dream as he had once had about Gabrielle, but it produced the same effect, his body responding as any man's would to such a woman. Not a man? The dream stirred something in him long dormant, a very male response. He was not sure whether to laugh in delight that perhaps the princess's accusations were false, or cry in despair that he could not escape that primal response.

What do you want, the voice whispered in his head? Kóráhm's voice, though he could not be seen or felt. You mourn that you are not a man, yet cower when presented with the truth that you are. Decide, phyl haeles. Accept what you cannot change; be what you are.

Kavan wept with the truth of the Saint's accusation.

∾*∾

Reading the sheets of parchment that fell from the King's fingers, Ártur felt cold and vulnerable in a way he had not in many years. The letter and accompanying documents were from Felicity Colson-Menir, wife of General Catald Menir, Duke of Seres. A young Elyri woman had been raped and slaughtered in a public square in Seres by four young men. The Duchess found the woman shortly after the violence ended, and while the victim was alive then, she died in the Duchess's care soon after. Several witnesses identified the guilty parties and the four were quickly apprehended. They were sons of one of the wealthiest merchants in Seres; their father had not been in the city at the time of the incident.

A trial ensued with fourteen witnesses coming forth against the brutality. The four showed no remorse for their actions and proudly asserted they had given the woman what every Elyri sorceress wanted. They claimed she had enjoyed their affections, claimed they were not responsible for her death. After all, she had been alive when they left her, had she not? They also indicated that they would do it again if the opportunity presented itself. Appalled and outraged, Duchess Menir ordered them hung. Their father arrived during the pronouncement and seemed as surprised as his sons about the outcome of the trial. While bigotry was not a punishable crime, the Duchess was tempted to give the young men's father the same sentence, because he supported what his sons had done. She was also contemplating punishing the witnesses who had done nothing to intervene.

Despite the merchant's verbal bullying, the Duchess remained firm in her decision. The merchant threatened action against the Menirs if his sons were not released, and expected either the Menirs or the Crown to compensate him for his anguish. She agreed to stay the sentence long enough to present the issue to the King for judgment, a declaration the man eagerly agreed to in his belief that the Crown would support him. The records of the trial, as well as the sworn testimonies of the witnesses and the statements of the young men were included with her letter, signed by those involved as an indication that they had read the pages, or had them read to them, and found them to be accurate. The decision was placed in King Arlan's hands.

The King shared the documents aloud to his core advisors, Bhríd Cáner, Ternce Wyndham, Darius Corbin, Caol Dugan, Minos Cornell, and Ártur MacLyr. There was little discussion afterward, as everyone agreed that the Duchess had made an appropriate ruling given the nature of the crime. The King decided to send twenty-five soldiers to Seres, under the command of Minos Cornell, Owain Lachlan, and Duke Menir, to give his royal pronouncement and diffuse the situation.

He also did something he had not done in many years. The King prepared a kingdom-wide proclamation stating that any violence against Elyri would be met with the same punishment as would be meted out in violence against Teren. All foreigners, including Elyri, were welcome in Enesfel; such violence as what had occurred in Seres, and what had happened to Kavan in Levonne, would not be tolerated. Threats against Elyri would be investigated. Duchess Menir had made an acceptable and right ruling in accordance with the laws in effect throughout the land. The four men guilty of the rape and murder of the Elyri woman would hang as ordered. The Menir estate did not owe their father compensation, nor did the Crown.

Ártur remained in the chair against the window, his wan expression unchanged. The stateroom was empty since the King had stormed out and the others who gathered to hear the news had gone to carry out their orders. Anti-Elyri violence was not uncommon, but this latest string of events weighed heavy on the healer's shoulder, perhaps because it had begun with Kavan. When he realized his hands were shaking, he clasped them tightly in his lap.

"Ártur?" He looked at his wife who had returned that morning from her stay with Bianca and Wilred and their newborn child, and from her expression, he knew she had just heard the news. She nodded to confirm his thoughts. "Bhríd told me. Do you think it is safe here?"

Sagging further into the chair, he shrugged. "I cannot say. I do not have the Sight like Kavan. I do not think we are in immediate danger; we are protected here, but if this continues…"

She knelt beside him and put her hand on his knee. "I was thinking…I know Llucás is not old enough to take full apprenticeship, but perhaps your brother will make an exception."

He blinked. "You want to send Llucás to Elyriá?" He did not know why he asked. Seeing to his son's safety was the logical and right thing to do.

"It might be safe for him for many more months, or even years, but he is too young to be exposed to the likes of violence such as this. He will not understand it and it might frighten him into never wanting to come back. Besides, we will be there with him…"

There was the catch he had waited for. He shook his head. "I cannot leave Arlan."

Syl tried not to scowl. "You have done more than anyone expects; you have served the Lachlan house all of your adult life. It would be fair of them to allow you to leave before you are endangered."

But Ártur's resolve stayed firm. "I cannot, aeslag, not while Kavan is out there. I know you want our baby born in Bhryell; if you wish to take Llucás home, I will not prevent it. I want you safe."

She entwined her fingers with his. "I would rather you come too."

"I know," he murmured, leaning forward to place kisses into her hair. "But there are the Gates. I would be with you as often as I could be, and if the situation becomes too dangerous, I can stay in Bhryell then. Please…do not ask more of me than I can give."

Nuzzling against his face, she sighed. "I knew you would stay, but I had to ask. I will talk to Sámel. If he agrees to apprentice Llucás, I will take our son there then return to Rhidam to stay with you until the baby is due…then I will go to Bhryell. If he will not take Llucás yet, then I shall be forced to stay there with him. Do you think Kavan will let us use his home?"

"Of course he will," Ártur said automatically. Even if he was staying there, Kavan would open his doors to Ártur's family.

"Good." She stood, kissed the top of his head, and left the room.

Sámel, Ártur thought as he watched her go, take care of my son. If Syl left him here alone, he was sure he would go mad.

⮞*⮜

Seven days after leaving Natrona, Kavan caught sight of Saint Kóráhm's shrine as the sun set behind the white marble T-shaped Kílyn Cross atop the small hillock believed to be the location of his attempted, or successful, execution. Its success or failure was debated by those not afraid to discuss Kóráhm's mythos. The Saint was said to have pulled free of the nails that held him to that burning pyre, and then disappeared, leaving his unburned mantle draped over the arms of the cross. His followers had taken the mantle it was said, and it was never seen again, only rumored to have survived in secret corners where the Faith could never find it. When Kóráhm began to appear to believers many years later, the Kílyn shrine was erected and the patriarchs of the Faith declared the man a saint.

Kavan had never been to the shrine; the one time he had been in Hatu his goal had been to gain the Harcourts' assistance for Prince Arlan and there had been no opportunity for side excursions. He had not asked Arlan for permission to come here in the years since. Perhaps that was his failing, he mused; Kóráhm was his patron and he had never paid him proper tribute.

Directly behind the marble cross was a grove of trees, mostly cedars, sheltering the shrine from the wind and afternoon sun. There were pilgrims here, come for the Feast of Kóráhm many days ago and remaining for reasons only they knew. Their presence should have bothered Kavan, but for the first time since his injury, he refused to let others intimidate him. Let them see him. He was here and he would not turn away. He found a vacant spot near the foot of the cross, knelt, and began his vigil. Nearby, Urian found a comfortable place to kneel and did likewise, although his prayers were more vocal and formulated than Kavan's private ones.

Wortham, however, hesitated to approach the shrine of the man that, through Kavan, he had come to admire. He knew Kóráhm's stories by heart and felt as if he knew the saint personally. To be where zealots had murdered an innocent Elyri man made the captain uncomfortable. He did not feel worthy to stand on that ground and was thus content to set camp at the base of the hillock, about forty yards away, keeping the bard and monk in his sight.

That night passed uneventfully, as did the next day, the following night, and the day after. Urian came to the camp to eat and sleep, but Kavan did not. If the bard slept, it was at the foot of the shrine. If he ate, it was but morsels that Urian brought whenever he approached. The other pilgrims departed, alone or in groups of two and three, until Kavan alone remained. Supplies were running low but Wortham had no idea if they would stay longer, journeying somewhere else, or returning to Rhidam. He ventured from the shrine late in the afternoon to barter for food in the nearby town, hesitant to leave Kavan but not wishing to spend the night hungry.

He had no cause for concern, as Kavan was still at the shrine when he returned. The captain prepared a meal for himself and Urian, watched Kavan until it was too dark to see him, and then fell asleep, propped up against his pack.

Tonight, Kavan was restless. After hearing Kóráhm's voice during the journey here, he had hoped to see him again. This seemed the most likely place to make amends, the most likely place for the Saint to return to him. Yet there were no stirrings in his soul as he often experienced when in prayer, there was no gathering of energy and no spirits lingering about him. He was hungry, and though he had not spoken to Wortham, he knew the captain was growing impatient, wanting some indication of what the future held. The captain wanted to speak with him after his return from the market that day, and Kavan knew it. He decided reluctantly that if he did not receive a sign this night, some clue of what he must do next, he would talk to Wortham in the morning and bid the captain to part company. If he must, Kavan would spend his life at this shrine waiting for an answer, a life that might not be long, he knew, if he starved.

"You are tremendously stubborn."

"Milord Kóráhm!" His relief at seeing the auburn rimmed face of the man at his side was momentarily greater than the sum of his despair. He reached for the Saint's hand to kiss it but Kóráhm was beyond his reach. Kavan's crippled hand fell to his side as a whimper escaped. "I have waited for you, prayed…"

"I know," the saint said quietly. "Your diligence has not gone unnoticed, but I fear it may have been a wasted effort."

"Wasted?" Distressed, Kavan struggled to his feet. "Milord, I have done as you asked! I have searched my soul, poured my faults out before Dhágdhuán and k'Ádhá, have begged forgiveness…"

"And what have you learned?"

"That you are a…or at least were, a man. That all men have faults. That I am a man in the ways that matter most. I have not spent as much time in prayer and contemplation as I should, perhaps, and I have excess I should donate to the needy more than I do. Despite your steadfastness, I have not come here to thank you or honor you properly…"

Kóráhm shook his head with a heavy sigh. "It is not enough, Kavan. Those are good things to know about oneself, but unimportant in the end. You give more than most and you do it with a proper heart. And few spend more time devoted to their faith; more is not required. This you know, though you seem to believe you must spend your life in poverty and cloistered in a closet to be pure. If that was expected of you, you would have been called to a vocation in the Faith. Works you have, but works will not gain forgiveness. I am thankful your faith and love for me are restored. I have missed you. Coming here is not a requirement to keep my love; I seek only your love in return. But you must search deeper, Kavan. You have failed to discover that which will give you what you seek."

"Kóráhm! No! Please! I beg you…I will do anything." Kavan reached for him, panic and terror filling him.

The saint drew back and shook his head. "It is out of my hands. There is nothing I can do. As you recently admitted, I am not omnipotent; I can tell you what I know, nothing more. And what I know is that you are not yet ready to get past this."

Kóráhm walked into the grove and vanished from sight, his steps those of a man in great pain. Rending his clothes, Kavan fell to the ground, barely stifling the scream that tore at his throat. He had confessed to the faults he could think of, only to be told they were not spiritual faults but rather failings in his own eyes. He could think of nothing else. What more did k'Ádhá want of him? His life? What could he give that he had not already given?

Miserable, feeling abandoned and worthless, Kavan curled into a ball and cried himself to sleep before the Cross of Saint Kóráhm.

And dreamed. He dreamed that he held the woman in his arms, that she kissed him in a deep, sensual way he had not known possible. That her hands touched him and his touched her. Her face was hidden behind the veil, too close to study, and she did not speak, but there was no need for words. Soft moans escaped as she drew away; he wanted her against him, not distant. She drew near again, pressing her body against him as if to make him a part of herself, as if to fulfill his wish for her closeness. He was drowning in a pool of sensation, of one wave of new feeling after another, each one more incredible than anything he had known. It pulled him higher and higher until there was a blinding flash. That peak reached, he was left in his dream sweating, breathless, weak and alone.

Opening his eyes, Kavan discovered he was still before the cross, feeling as he had in that dream, weak, out of breath, and chilled with uncharacteristic sweat. The sky was dark and he was alone. Trembling with cold and exhaustion, he examined himself to discover that his dream, more intense than any before, had left no trace of its passing, though he was sure there should have been something. His dream had not soiled the shrine or himself. He was certain it had…or should have.

As realistic as the dream had been, he could smell her still, could feel her softness against him, leaving him aware of the throbbing she awakened. Shivering, he rolled to face the cross, marveling in the realness of that dream, wallowing in self-loathing, not expecting sleep to overtake him again.

ॐ*ॐ

"What is the meaning of this, Caol?" The King waved the six parchments under the man's nose.

The inquisitor squared his shoulders. "You cannot think I had anything to do with those."

"Why are they in your possession? Where did you get them?"

Caol snatched the parchments back and then looked at Arlan with a touch of contrition. "One of my people found them outside the Eagle's Nest and near the náós. She did not see who posted them but took them down and brought them to me. I asked her to be sure that no more of these vicious things are posted and to remove every one she finds. No more appeared this morning, and there don't appear to have been others. I think this may be all of them."

The King growled low in his chest. "Why?"

"Why did I ask her?" Caol asked.

"Why is someone posting anti-Elyri notices in my city? Right outside the palace? Do they think to get away with it?"

"Unfortunately, they did. All it would take would be for a few people to read them and start talking. Even if there are no others, these may have already had the effect their creator desired."

"This is getting…Caol, we must do something…"

The Inquisitor agreed. "My people are already looking into it."

"I hope they are efficient in this, as everything else…please tell them they have my faith."

Knowing what that would mean to many of his contacts, Caol bowed. "I shall."

❧*❧

"Milord?" Urian's voice woke Kavan from his restless sleep. Dawn was breaking as the bard opened his eyes to discover he had badly torn his robe in mourning during the night and was thus lying before Kóráhm's shrine unclothed. He began to rise with a worried glance around him; no one else was here and Wortham still slept. Urian held forth a robe for him, the extra brown one from Kavan's pack that Wortham had procured in Natrona. He was afraid to ask how the monk knew he needed clothes when the man could not see.

As if reading his thoughts, the monk chuckled. "A woman told me you looked to be in need of new garments. I found this amongst your things."

What woman, Kavan wondered, as he donned the robe in haste. Either he was projecting his thoughts or Urian's ability to detect his distress was greater than expected. While not the dark gray he had been wearing, this was better than a white robe he did not have and could not bring himself to don.

The gdhededhá continued. "Your friend learned something he is eager to share. He did not tell me what it was but mentioned something about Saint Kóráhm. Perhaps it is the sign you seek."

"Perhaps," Kavan said with a shrug, his voice weary and flat. He left the shrine for the first time in days and followed Urian to where Wortham was camped. The blind man poured three mugs of water before Wortham was aware of their company and awoke. He made a quick visual appraisal of Kavan but did not speak until he retrieved bread and cheese from his pack.

Noticing his silence, and deeply worried after last night that Wortham was turning his back on him, or that the captain had overheard some part of the dialogue with Kóráhm and was upset or offended by it, Kavan asked, "Are you not speaking to me, Wortham?"

"Milord." Wortham met his sad gaze. "I am unsure what to say…except that I am happy to have you with us."

Kavan nodded, accepting those words at face value though he felt the captain wanted to say more yet was afraid to. It would be unusual since Wortham had never been afraid to speak to him in the past. Hoping to encourage the man to be open and frank, Kavan asked, "gdhededhá Urian says you have learned something about Kóráhm?"

Relieved to be speaking, the captain swallowed a mouthful of bread and nodded. "I know the stories, the ones you have told me. Are there others you have not?"

"I have no reason to keep such tales from you."

Wortham nodded. "I am not suggesting you have…only thought perhaps there are more I do not know. If there are none, then what I learned yesterday should be of interest to you." He shifted on the hard earth to face Kavan fully. "I encountered an elderly woman telling a group of children about the saints. She spoke in such an inviting and exciting manner that I felt compelled to listen. She told a story about Kóráhm's martyrdom, that when he pulled free from the burning cross, he stumbled from the gathering on the arm of a young woman."

"I have told you that story," Kavan reminded him.

"Aye, but your version stops there. According to this woman, after his escape, his female escort bought a merchant's wagon and the two traveled south. The wagon was found abandoned many weeks later in the southern city of Enda. The owner of the wagon could not be located, she and Kóráhm were not found, as you know, and the story was discarded as a fable meant to draw travelers to Enda."

"Enda?" The journal entry regarding that subterranean náos mentioned Enda as well. Perhaps, as Urian stated, this was his sign. To travel to Enda, find the key to the purification of the náos, and perhaps learn something about Kóráhm he had not previously known, something that might clear the charge of heresy from Kóráhm's name. "Wortham?"

Hearing a long-missing note of excitement in the bard's voice, Wortham eyed him expectantly. "Aye, milord?"

"Would you be interested in accompanying me to Enda? I think that is where I am destined to go."

The captain, pleased that the bard had discovered a new purpose, even if it was taking them further away from Rhidam, could not refuse. Anything that encouraged Kavan to live, to persevere, was welcome. "I shall follow you to the ends of the world."

"The chance to learn something new for the Faith would be a great opportunity," said Urian. "May I travel with you?"

There was no hesitation in Kavan's reply. "If you wish, gdhededhá."

Standing, Wortham brushed off his pants. "I will prepare our supplies to be ready to leave tomorrow morning. No sooner, milord, because you have had little food or sleep in the last few days. dedhá, will you stay with him?"

Urian smiled, happy to be included. "Of course."

Gloved hands in his lap, Kavan watched Wortham hurry into the heart of town. Except for his useless hands and the nagging worry about what lesson he was unable to uncover on his own, Kavan's spirit felt lighter than it had in several weeks. He was on the right path. He knew it.

❧Chapter 9❧

"I do not have many men to spare; they're spread thin. How many more such incidents do you think there are going to be?"

Caol read his son's letter a second time. He was familiar with the Bull's Head Tavern; his father had frequented it when Caol was a child. It had changed ownership several times since those days, as the Association's business took its toll, but it still felt as if a friend had died to learn that the establishment had burned to the ground.

The circumstances surrounding its destruction were the reason for Wilred's letter. It had caught fire late in the evening and attempts to halt its destruction had failed. The owners were not in it at the time, the inn had been peculiarly empty of patrons. A man and his wife had been the sole guests, and according to a barmaid, the couple was Elyri, traveling home from trade on the fringes of the great desert.

Wilred, as Duke of Durham, detained the innkeeper and his family for questioning, and since they refused to talk, he sought permission to send them to Rhidam where his father might learn the truth.

"I'll get my people on it…"

The King, not in a good mood that day, snorted, "Your people? How many do you have? How much do you pay them?"

"Most aren't paid…we work on a favor system…" Caol began.

"Are you saying the Crown is supporting the Association by turning a blind eye to their activities?"

"Not at all. Murders, large thefts, major crimes…those things are pursued if they fall into my jurisdiction, and if Darius gets them, that is not my problem. I don't care much about the petty details. The favors I am doing them is not revealing everything I know about the organization and members, and I do not testify against known members. In exchange, I get information when I need it. Since what I want to know typically does not interfere with their activities, they are satisfied to assist. You could not get this kind of a network, this sort of information, without me."

King Arlan crossed his arms over his chest. "That is what I am afraid of. What will happen when you leave my service?"

"I'm not planning on going anywhere, Milord," Caol assured him.

"Not planning, yes, but…"

"I am training someone. You will not be left unstaffed…"

"Pardon me, My Liege." Darius entered the dayroom carrying a crumpled scroll. "This arrived from Prince Espen; the messenger said it was urgent I give it to you immediately.

The King took it, expecting some sort of bad news from his ally to the south. As he prepared to break the seal, he noticed that it was not the seal of the Harcourts, but rather that of Captain Delamo.

"Lord Corbin, please find Lord MacLyr and Lord Cáner and send them to me. They will want to see this."

"What is it?" Caol asked, narrowly avoiding the temptation to read over the King's shoulder.

"A message from Captain Delamo."

"About Lord Cliáth?"

The King shrugged but did not speak as he read. The two men arrived before he completed it; he handed the pages to Ártur.

"He and Kavan were well and in Natrona when this was sent. Bound for Kílyn," the King muttered with a strained sigh of relief. The letter did not say they were coming home, but at least Kavan was well.

"We should have guessed," Bhríd said. Kóráhm's shrine was a logical destination for the bard in a time of distress.

"Kavan is unhappy," Arlan continued, "his hands are useless, but there is hope that Saint Kóráhm's shrine may provide an answer."

"Don't see how." Caol shook his head and rubbed the back of his neck as the two Elyri read the pages side by side. A shrine was just a place, and though the Saint was said to speak to and through Kavan, Caol could not see how praying at the place a man died would help. "They would have made it to Kílyn by now. If his hands are restored, he should have come home already."

"He could be coming by land rather than by Gate," offered the chamberlain.

Without thinking, Ártur muttered, "After what Princess…" When he remembered the King was in the room he fell abruptly silent.

Arlan was not about to let the issue slide this time. "What did she do? Hagan told me she is responsible. k'gdhededhá knows something but he cannot tell me. What was bad enough to drive Kavan away?"

"I should not speak of it…it should be for her to explain," the healer said with his head bowed.

"Was it that bad?" He knew it was, but he was hoping his intuition was wrong. "I will hear it in private. Caol, tell Wilred to send those people here. Bhríd, Caol will update you on events in Durham, perhaps you will have suggestions. I would like all of you to spread this news about Kavan to those who should know." Once the two men were gone, the King looked expectantly at the nervous healer.

"Do you want me to intrude on your daughter's privacy, Milord?"

"You know about it, Wortham knows. Owain probably knows. The k'gdhededhá knows and Muir likely does too. It is not a private matter any longer. I am King, I am her father, I have a right to know…and Kavan means so much to me…"

Ártur conceded, swayed by the grief in Arlan's voice. It was not fair for the man who had befriended Kavan first to have no idea why he had left the kingdom. "She tried to…she used unfortunate methods to convince Kavan to marry her. When her inappropriate words and actions did not sway him, she said things that wounded him. She called him a coward…accused him of not being a man."

The King groaned. "More than anything he wants to be seen as a man like any other."

"Exactly," the healer agreed. "I do not know her exact words, but they cut him in a way I did not think anyone could. His eyes were so haunted…he was so…broken. On top of his injuries, he believes he can not face us if he is less than a man and a coward as she asserts."

"This makes you angry," Arlan said softly, feeling more hurt than angry at this moment himself. He wanted answers, wanted to know precisely what his daughter had said and done to so slight his best friend, but he was as impotent as Ártur.

"I try to hide it, but it is hard, My Liege. I have never been so angry with anyone except my father who treats Kavan in a similarly abysmal manner. Fortunately, I do not believe she meant what she said, unlike my father…but Kavan does not understand that."

Arlan offered his hand and Ártur took it. "I shall talk to her when she returns, convince her that marriage to Kavan would be a costly mistake, and demand she drop her efforts to convince him otherwise. Convince her to choose someone closer to her age, who can love her as she deserves. And I will demand she desist from speaking to him again in such a way. He does not deserve that, especially from her."

Squeezing the King's hand, the healer said, "I hope it works. If Kavan ever does return, he will not stay if her pursuit continues."

❧*❧

When Justice Cornell and Owain reached Seres, the tension could be felt as they rode through the city's stone gates. The presence of Duke Menir did much to dampen it, since the citizens trusted their Duke to resolve the situation more than they apparently trusted his wife. His first action was to call a private meeting between the King's envoys, his wife, himself, the four convicted men, and their father. The Justice read the entire proclamation, aware that the four convicts, though sorry that their actions would lead to their deaths, had no remorse for what they had done and did not comprehend why they should die when they believed they had done the kingdom a favor in killing the Elyri woman. That their father shared their opinion struck the chancellor as extraordinarily sad.

The merchant started to swear, wanting to do or say something to change his sons' fate, but there was nothing he could do. The King had spoken, had quoted written law. All of his sons would die.

The five were shaking as they were lead to the place where the gallows had been constructed. A crowd was already assembled as if they had known what to expect of their monarch; Minos found it reassuring to see that King Arlan's beliefs and mandates were known and respected…by most. This time, the Duke read the proclamation to his subjects. There was a mixed reaction, but overall it was a favorable one. Even those who did not like Elyri could concede that such violence in their town was not good, regardless of whom it targeted.

At noon the four brothers convicted of rape and murder were hung by the neck as the Duchess had sentenced. Their father was not in attendance to watch them die.

&*&

"Good morning, Bhen," Syl called in greeting as she climbed the steps of the MacLyr house. "Is your father here?"

"k'aene! Llucás! How wonderful to see you!" Bhendhámyn lifted Llucás and spun him around as they laughed. When they faced Syl, both were smiling. "bhydhá is in the shop. k'gdhededhá has placed an order for two new full scales and of course, he wants them yesterday."

"You are not helping?" she asked warmly.

"aendhá believes he and bhydhá are the best qualified to construct these particular harps. Granted, they are the most experienced harp makers in Elyriá, but it was one of my instruments selected last year as the finest in the land." He smiled mischievously, looking much like Ártur when he did. Setting the child down, he watched Llucás scamper into the house following the smell of baking bread.

"I have come to discuss Llucás' apprenticeship."

"He's young, k'aene…"

"I know. But the situation in Enesfel is unstable, and while I do not believe there is immediate danger, I do not want him exposed to such violence."

The blond man's expression grew grave. "Does this have anything to do with k'aendhá Kavan? bhydáni Tíbhyan told me what happened. Was it as bad as he described?"

Syl nodded. "From what Ártur showed me, yes." She took Bhen's hand and passed the images Ártur had shared before releasing it. His face lost color and his mouth formed a quivering pout. "Llucás has no knowledge of Kavan's condition or of the other events in Enesfel. Duke Cornell has been threatened, a woman killed, because they carry Elyri blood. I would rather Llucás not be exposed to such things…at least not until he is older and wiser."

Bhen nodded. "I understand. I cannot say if father will accept Llucás or not, but I do know aendhá will not want it. However, if you think he should remain in Bhryell, I will gladly accept guardianship and apprenticeship of him…unless you think my skills are inferior."

She smiled at his mirth; he was a charming young man whom she loved dearly. "That would be welcome, Bhen." If his harps had won awards, he had the skill to mentor her son. And it was obvious that he and the boy adored one another. Syl could think of no better choice.

"Then it is done. Talk to bhydhá, if you wish, but I do have one favor to ask in return. I have hoped to visit k'aendhá Ártur, to share my sympathy for k'aendhá Kavan. Since I am not needed here for a time, I would like to make the visit before I take Llucás in. It may be my sole chance to see Rhidam. Would that be acceptable?"

She frowned but nodded. "You must be careful if you go. Rhidam may be the safest place for Elyri now, given the Lachlan stance on anti-Elyri violence, but conditions could change at any time. If you promise to watch yourself and bring Llucás' clothing back with you, I'll stay while you visit. It will give me the chance to see my family."

"I will get some things together. aene is in the kitchen if you wish to see her. I wager that is where Llucás has gone."

Knowing Llucás' fondness for pastries, Syl chuckled. "You are likely correct."

☙*❧

"I have come as requested, milady. Are you ready to return?"

Diona dropped her gaze at the bitterness in Ártur's voice. Her mistakes had cost her the respect and friendship of Healer MacLyr, and probably more. It would take a long time to right the wrongs she had committed.

"Would you be terribly upset if I said no?"

"Would it matter if I were?"

The princess blanched at his words. "I have made progress in making sense of the mess I have created, but I think there is more to unravel. Muir is most helpful, and the time away from Rhidam…"

"…means you do not have to see the damage you have caused."

Refusing to turn away or succumb to the ache his words brought, she whispered, "Yes."

With a snort of what she thought sounded like disgust, the healer replied, "There is no need for you to return yet. Lord Lachlan is on an errand in Seres and will not return for a few more days; Piran is to remain here in the meantime. Your father has extended Owain and Piran an invitation to his birthday feast. You will return for it?"

"Of course." She knew that if she did not she would have even more outrage from her father to face.

"Please tell Muir…"

"Healer MacLyr." Gabrielle entered the study, surprised to see him there. "Has there been word about Kavan?"

"Very little…unfortunately. He was on his way to Kílyn, but that is all we know." He looked again at the princess, feeling no desire to speak of his languishing cousin in front of her. "Would you please extend your father's invitation to Prince Muir? He is adamant about his attendance; please convince him to come. I will return for you, Princess, when Lord Lachlan returns from Seres."

Being dismissed like one of the servants stung, but Diona felt she deserved such treatment. She curtseyed and murmured, "I shall…and I shall be ready," before backing out of the room with her head down.

Once the princess was gone, Ártur focused on the Prime Magistrate. "Owain asked me to tell you that he was called away from Rhidam for a few days; Piran may stay until he returns."

The woman smiled. "I'll let him know. Kavan is well then?"

"His hands are still…but he is in no danger of dying. As I understand Captain Delamo, he is on a spiritual quest. He will either learn to live with his loss or he will find the miracle he needs to bring him home whole."

"I pray it will be the latter."

Ártur nodded. "As do we all."

❧*❧

A fit of coughing caused the King to drop weakly into the nearest chair. He was alone in his study, a room he allowed no one to enter except Kavan and the servants who came once every few days to clean and polish the ancient wood surfaces. Since the bard was not in Rhidam, and he had chased the servants from the room earlier, Arlan knew he had little chance of being disturbed. He retreated here more and more over the past few months, whenever he felt the dizziness overcome him, the cold spells he could not ward off. It was a bad sign, the ever-increasing recurrence of these episodes, but the King fought to believe it was not a serious problem, that it was merely a symptom of his increasing age and of the time of year.

He could not die. There was too much to do. Hagan was the heir to the throne, but Arlan had little faith in his ability to rule; he was little more than a boy. Diona appeared to have taken leave of her senses, and the specter of the Elyri Persecution was once more rearing its head. He saw no way for his children to deal effectively with such a menace when he knew of no way to disarm it himself.

Caol had found and apprehended the woman responsible for the anti-Elyri flyers. She was wild-eyed, ranting that an Elyri had killed her son. From what the inquisitor was able to learn, her son had died fifteen years before at the age of twelve of a fever. Her ramblings were more paranoid delusions than malicious attacks, but Arlan could not risk releasing her to the streets to spread more damaging tales. Instead, she was sent to Saint Bhílycá's in Dorshur where she could be cared for and, he hoped, made well.

He wished he understood why and how this violence had been birthed a second time. His father had made Enesfel safe for Elyri and other than King Bowen's brief reign of terror, there had been little anti-Elyri violence in the land. Until now. The King had hoped that restoring the Faith, returning the kingdom to stability, would strengthen the peace King Innis had fought to attain. Instead, something had gone wrong. The attack on Kavan had uncorked a bottle of chaos Arlan was finding difficult to close.

No, he could not die. Not until Kavan returned to reassure him. Not until peace was restored. Not until he saw the Elyri's beautiful face one more time.

❧*❧

The newly constructed house at the southern edge of Rhidam had seen a great deal of traffic in its first few weeks of use. Caol knew this because several of his spies had told him so. It might not have seemed unusual, new houses usually attracted visits from friends and relatives, but his informants were the best and if they believed there was something suspicious about the comings and goings, it was likely true.

Caol scoped the place for several days himself, watching who called, and though he recognized none of the visitors, he did concur that something about their movements was odd. He knew the identity of the owners and was puzzled by their choice of home. He could not afford to let them know he was watching, however, thus he delegated the tasks back to others and returned his focus to Lord Cliáth's attack.

He had learned the identity of two of the four corpses when their families finally reported them missing. Fortunately for the families, the men they sought were those who appeared to have been attacked by a wild beast. Caol doubted they would ever identify the man whose head had exploded. There had been nothing to identify him, not even a bit of jewelry, a scar, or tattoo. With the identities of two of the four known, however, Caol was confident it would not be long before he had as much of the story as he could get.

Whether the attack tied into the rising anti-Elyri current or was the spark that set the blaze would be much more difficult to prove.

❧*❧

Bhen stopped, breathless, and exited the k'dhín bhólibh. He rarely used the Gates but was grateful he had learned to do so. This journey to Rhidam would have taken weeks without it. It was not the rush of immediate travel that excited him, however. Stories he had heard as a boy portrayed the Teren kingdoms as barbaric, certainly not capable of magnificent architectural works of this magnitude. The basic style of Hes á Redh Náós was Elyri; the renovations were not. Despite his belief in his wayward kinsmen, he had not anticipated that the stories might be wrong, that Teren might have redeeming qualities, that his uncle and cousin might have ample reason, other than rebellion, to live amongst them.

"May I assist you, sir?" said a voice behind him.

Bhen turned, smiled, and bowed to the man approaching from across the room. "You are k'gdhededhá Tythilius?"

The man chuckled. "You have me at a disadvantage, young man."

"Bhendhámyn MacLyr," he replied, offering his hand.

Jermyn was surprised. "I did not know Healer MacLyr had any young relatives. A brother?"

"He is my uncle. I have come to see him, provided I can find my way. I stopped to admire the náós. It is not what I expected." He continued looking around in awe.

"Better or worse?"

"Better," Bhen assured him. "Much better. But different. My grandfather would have us believe Teren are brutes, incapable of anything more sophisticated than huts and clubs. I am delighted to see that this is not the case. Can you point me in Ártur's direction?"

"I shall do better than that," the k'gdhededhá said with a gesture towards the door. "I was planning to visit the King later, but I can go now and take you there myself. It will give me company, and given the tensions lately, my presence should keep you safe. Come along."

Rather than talk, Bhen listened as the k'gdhededhá pointed out structures of interest while they strolled. Though the houses and shops were different from what he was used to, Bhen did not see that they were in inferior. And while the Lachlan keep was not built with the same graceful, artistic lines of many great Elyri structures, it suggested Elyri base construction and conveyed the strength and solidarity needed by its occupants to rule.

The k'gdhededhá led him into the library and bid him wait. Bhen agreed on the condition that Jermyn did not reveal who Ártur's visitor was. He set down his bag and fidgeted, adjusting the dark cord that gathered his straw-colored hair at the nape of his neck. He had seen Ártur twice in his life, when the healer and Syl had come to Bhryell for the birth of Llucás and when Ártur had gone home to express his grief over Mílne's death.

He turned when the door opened and met the man's surprised grin with his own smile. "Bhen?" The healer rushed in and embraced him roughly. "By k'Ádhá it is good to see you! What are you doing here? Has something happened at home? Are Syl and Llucás well?"

"They are fine, k'aendhá, as is everyone else. bhydáni Tíbhyan told me about k'aendhá Kavan; that is why I came. I felt one of us from home should show our support. I know aene supports him too, but she will not say it."

Ártur nodded, gesturing to a chair. He knew how his father intimidated his mother. "How much did Tíbhyan tell you?"

"As much as he knew, I suppose. Syl showed me the damage, though it did not look as bad as the bhydáni described. Is there more?"

Sitting as Bhen did, the healer sighed. "Four attackers were dead when he was found; one has yet to be identified and no one knows if there were more. Kavan was…devastated…when he left Levonne. He was traveling to Kílyn, but I have no idea where he is now."

"He has not tried to contact you?" He had been told Kavan and Ártur were close; no contact between them seemed significant.

"To say goodbye and to reassure me he was alive and would not be returning or contacting me until his quest is complete. Nothing more. The message received from his traveling companion, Captain Delamo, indicated they made it as far as Natrona and were bound for Kóráhm's shrine. I wish there were more to tell you. I think Kavan would be touched to know his predicament brought you to Enesfel."

Bhen laughed. "I am not relocating, k'aendhá. I came to visit and see Rhidam before I take on Llucás' apprenticeship."

"You?" the healer asked with surprise.

"bhydhá does not feel Llucás is old enough, and you know how aendhá is about such matters. But Llucás can live with me and there are duties a child can do around the shop, cleaning up and such, as he begins to learn the trade. Leave him to me. I will make Llucás the youngest harp maker in Elyriá; you shall see. Syl is visiting her parents until I return. She wants me to bring his things back when I go."

Ártur's face was momentarily sad. "You aren't leaving already?"

Embracing him again, Bhen said, "Not for several days, unless you tire of my company and wish to be rid of me."

"That is not likely to happen. Having you here is one of the best things that could happen to me. Besides, I know Bhríd and Gaelán will love to see you. Gaelán is the newest healer in our ranks," he added proudly.

Bhen rolled his eyes. "Another one?" he asked with a teasing grin. "As if you and Syl are not enough."

"The world can never have too many healers. If it wasn't for Gaelán, Kavan would be dead. I read him; I saw how bad Kavan was when he was found. I chose not to share that with Syl." He took his nephew's hand and watched the young man grow visibly weaker as the imagery filled his thoughts. "I am sorry…but if you are to be in Rhidam, I thought you should know the truth. Let me give you a room. Once you are settled, I will show you the grounds and introduce you to the King."

Wiping his eyes on his sleeve, Bhen forced a smile. "I look forward to meeting the man great enough to keep you out of Elyriá. k'aendhá?" The healer looked at him. "Thank you for showing me."

❦*❧

They discovered the brown-haired man in red breeches and black tunic camped alongside the road shortly after sundown, a man barely older than Prince Hagan but with a hint of more worldly experience about him, as if he had seen more of life than one his age should have. Kavan had no desire to make camp with a stranger, but Urian had been asking to stop and Wortham saw no reason not to accept the young man's offered hospitality at his fire. The bard also did not wish to lower his hood or reveal his identity, but the monk was making introductions before Kavan could stop him. Fortunately, the young man did not appear to recognize Kavan's name.

"I am Eridel," he said merrily. "Happy to meet you."

Wortham began unpacking the mule. "Why are you traveling these roads alone? You are not armed. I would think it a dangerous choice for one so young."

Laughing cockily, Eridel replied, "I am old enough. My sword was broken in the last squabble and I had to sell my horse to pay the tavern owner for the damages. But I played the village long enough; it was time to be on to the next village anyhow."

Those words caused the captain to cast Kavan a worried glance. "Played the village?" he asked in a small voice.

"I am a harper; this is my one possession and friend." He patted the leather case that lay beside him and Kavan groaned. "Milord?"

Rather than answering because he knew words would not come out of his suddenly closed throat, Kavan stalked away from the campfire, keeping his back to them until he was barely visible in the dusky light. Eridel pouted. "Did I misspeak?"

"No," Wortham sighed, preparing Kavan's bedding with the hopes of appeasing his guilty conscience. "It is my error. He is a harper as well, though an attack has left him unable to play. It was a recent event and he has not yet recovered. The loss still pains him."

Eridel nodded sympathetically. "As it should if he was a harper of any merit. Was he good?"

The captain began again, wanting to spare Kavan the indignity of sharing the tale with another musician, but Urian was faster with his reply. "Boy, have you not heard of the White Bard of Bhryell?"

The young man's hazel eyes grew wide as he stared into the darkness, trying to see where Kavan had gone. "He is the White Bard?" Neither man replied as Kavan's appearance alone made the answer obvious. "Why would anyone…to deprive the world of his music…it is a tragedy. I shall express my sympathies…" He began to get up, but Wortham caught his arm in the steel grip of his big fist.

"No. He does not want sympathy or pity. He wants to be left alone. If you wish to earn his respect, do not speak of his injury and do not remind him of what he has lost."

"Truly?" The young man sounded as if he did not believe those words, as if they seemed illogical, but he did relax, watching the darkness. "I shall do as you say. He is my…I first learned to play listening to his works. I wish to cause him no grief when he has given me so much joy." He gestured to the scattered goods around the fire. "Please, I do not have much food, but I have wine to share if you like."

"Splendid," Urian exclaimed, holding out his hand for the flask.

"Sell us out to the witches, will you?"

Owain heard the shout moments before a shower of rocks began to rain from the forest around them. He had known someone was following since leaving Seres, and though he expressed his concern about departing without the twenty-five soldiers they had come with, Minos was eager to return to Rhidam. The chancellor had correctly pointed out that Catald Menir could use the extra men to restore peace to his city, and it was possible that whoever was following on the fringes of their perceptions were merchants traveling on business or hunters in the forest curious about the pair on the road.

That was apparently not the case, since the eight individuals overtook them and prepared an ambush, somehow getting ahead of them in the trees to attack. The chancellor fell from his horse when the animal balked, but Owain's shield deflected most of the rocks aimed at him. He maneuvered his horse to shelter Minos, dismounted, and drew his sword.

"Come out, cowards," he snarled. "If you think you are in the right, come and face the King's Chancellor and the prince who was once your king!"

The projectiles stopped flying long enough for two of their attackers to come forth, rushing Owain with swords drawn. He easily dispatched them, but his divided focus left Minos, who was climbing to his feet, vulnerable. Though armed with shield and sword, the elderly chancellor was no match for the two who attacked him. Owain spun at the tumult behind him to see Minos fall beneath their blows.

"You were warned, Cornell. How foolish to think…"

The speaker did not finish; his head was separated from his shoulders in one blow. Minos' other attacker required considerably more effort to dispatch, since three others came from the cover of the forest to engage the prince, making the battle four against one. They underestimated their one-time king, and in the end, Owain killed each of those who crossed swords with him. He was not without injuries, however. His left bicep bled profusely, he was bruised and sore, and there was a pain in his lower back and accompanying wetness spreading across his tunic that he doubted was a good sign. That injury made it difficult to bend, but he did so.

Minos was alive but he was not conscious. Several open wounds were scattered across his chest and arms. Owain was not a healer and he doubted the chancellor would live long enough to get him to Rhidam. Still, he was determined to try. He did his best to bind the wounds and stop the bleeding, tied four of the seven bodies to his horse and three to the other, and then after lashing the animals together, tied the lead horse to his waist. Lifting the chancellor as gingerly as he could, he began the long journey to somewhere they could find help. The ride to Rhidam should have been two more days. At this pace, he would be lucky to make it in four…if he did not die first.

❧*☙

Having come from a long visit with his cousin Bhen, Bhríd found the King in the stateroom, looking over a scatter of documents on the long oak table. "You wished to see me, Sire?" he asked, not wanting to disturb the monarch if he was busy with some other matter.

The King did not hesitate but came straight to the point. It was the easiest thing to do. "Please. I want to update my final statement."

The chamberlain's face turned white. "Milord…?" He could not have heard that right.

Wanting to dispel the tension in the room, the King chuckled. "A formality, Bhríd. I plan to be here for many more years. These events of late have set me to thinking about the future of the kingdom, and I should be prepared. Hagan is of age to rule, but I have doubts about his readiness. I hope I can share some wisdom with him in writing, if nothing else. It seems a good time to put down my thoughts, put my affairs in order, before times grow more chaotic and I forget."

Those words should have been enough to reassure him, but like all Elyri, Bhríd's sense of empathy was higher than a Teren's. He worried that something might be wrong that he was not aware of. "Are you sure that is all there is, Milord? Should I summon Ártur?"

"No," the King said with a wave of his hand. "There is no need for that. I am fine. I should have done this long ago; it should be put off no longer." The last time he had considered the matter, had addressed the future in this way, had been after the death of Bertram so many years ago. It was time to review his words and update them as necessary. "No one needs to know; it is standard procedure and no cause for alarm. Oh…and I want to include something for Muir. He deserves better than I have given him."

The chamberlain came further into the room. "He has forgiven you, Milord. The circumstances were understandable…"

"Understandable does not make it right. Kavan reared him well, that is why he has forgiven me. I think that leaving him something when I go is the proper thing to do. He is Brenna's son. He is Guthrie's grandson. I owe it to both of them to see he is provided for, as much as I owe it to him."

"Very well," Bhríd said, "When do you wish to do this?"

The truth was Arlan did not want to do it. Admitting his mortality was not something he enjoyed. But he knew it had to be done and he was not one to avoid the unpleasant for long. "Now…if you have the time. Do you have what you need?"

"I need parchment, ink, and a quill." Those items were found in the side cabinet, and he joined the King at the table, pushing aside the nagging anxiety in order to better do his duty.

❧ * ❧

The journey deeper into Hatu was accompanied by an increasing warmth in the air. All of his life, winter had been cold, usually snowy, but here, Kavan had no reason to continue wearing his hooded cloak or his gloves. No reason except to hide his identity and the state of his hands. Eridel traveled with them, having nowhere else to be and wanting the attention he hoped Kavan would give. On more than one occasion, he asked why Kavan continued to wear such awkward clothing, but Kavan chose not to reveal that his Elyri abilities afforded him the luxury of comfort regardless of the outside temperature or what he was wearing. In the summer, he was cool, in the winter he was warm. As long as it was not raining or snowing, the weather had little effect on him.

The cloak and gloves were not the only things Eridel used to try to spark conversation. Kavan had to admit Eridel was a likable fellow, friendly and easygoing, and an above-average musician even if his works were not original. But the constant attention, along with the ever-present reminder of what he had lost, was a heavy yoke. It was bad enough that Urian had told Eridel who he was, but having to endure night after night of music on a quarter-scale, redwood, kestrel-shaped Cliáthan harp was like a knife twisting repeatedly in his heart. It was watching a younger, cheerier version of himself. Kavan spent every night staring at his hands without seeing them, his back to the others to hide tears he refused to shed, while Eridel played.

It was fortunate that Wortham took control of the situation, drawing Eridel's attention away from Kavan as often and for as long as he could. He felt guilty for having been the one to insist on sharing a fire with this stranger and made every effort to rectify his mistake. Gossip, tales of his exploits as a soldier, details about the Káliel islands where Eridel had never been, tips on swordsmanship, all were expedient tools for pulling Eridel from his fixation, though nothing proved useful for long.

Not having dreamed of the auburn-haired woman since leaving the shrine, and not sensing the saint near him, Kavan was beginning to feel lost and alone again. Nothing eased his spirit. Perhaps, reassured Wortham, Kóráhm did not come because Kavan was on the right path and he had no reason to show himself until there was something more to reveal. Kavan and his companions were three days from the city of Yd Haszafni, with many more to travel before they reached Enda according to Eridel. The increasing weight in Kavan's soul made him hope fervently that he would find what he sought when they arrived…and that Eridel would leave them long before that.

ॐ*ॐ

His arm tingled where Gaelán removed his hands, but at least the pain was gone. Nearby, the King and Bhríd talked over the body of Chancellor Cornell. Arlan's face was twisted with rage; his chamberlain was trying to calm him, a difficult feat considering that his balled fists indicated he was angry too. Owain was surprised the King agreed with his assessment of the attack, that it was connected with the threat Minos had received as well as retaliation for the execution of the four young men in Seres. Arlan also agreed that the events in Seres had been more than coincidence. It had been a trap.

The question was, what could be done about it? Owain had killed every one of the eight attackers, leaving no one to question. If there had been more in the trees, Owain had not seen them. The King had already asked Caol to investigate the matter and while the inquisitor's network was extensive, spread throughout the kingdom, Owain could not help but wonder how long it would be before there were no men left to employ. Could they hope to find anything more about this incident that they did not already know or suspect?

"Any other pain or injuries that I have missed, Lord Lachlan?"

Owain glanced at the boy, amazed that he possessed the same abilities as Ártur, who supervised Gaelán's work silently from one side. The other man next to the healer looked to be family, though Owain had not heard his name spoken. Shifting his back and then flexing his arm, he shook his head. "None that I can feel. I am still a bit numb…"

"Numb?" Thinking it might be a physical symptom of something seriously wrong, the older healer placed his hands on Owain, but then quickly withdrew them with a relieved sigh. "Emotional numbness is something we cannot heal, I'm afraid."

Owain sighed. "I did not think you could, but it was worth a try. I cannot…" The humor fell away. "I warned him not to leave the troops in Seres."

"No one is blaming you, milord. The King is fully aware of Lord Cornell's stubbornness. He might not say it, but I am sure he is grateful you lived to return the chancellor here and bring the bodies of the murderers with you. Their identities will be easier to ascertain. Arlan might not be comfortable around you, but he does not wish you dead."

"Like he used to," the prince admitted with another sigh. "I do not suppose there has been any news of Kavan while I was away?"

Sensing that hopefulness in the man's question, Ártur was pleased to be able to give him a morsel of good news. "Actually there is a letter; Wortham sent it from Natrona, where they stopped on their way to Kílyn."

"To Kóráhm's shrine?"

"Apparently. That is a logical place for Kavan to go; we should have thought of it. Wortham said that, considering the circumstances, Kavan is doing better, although his depression runs deep. He gave no indication when they might be returning to Rhidam, or if they even would. Would you like to read it?"

Craving that meager connection with the men he called friends, Owain nodded. "I would appreciate that, Ártur. Thank you."

❧*❦

A Memorial Gathering for Chancellor Cornell was held the next morning in Hes á Redh Náós. His body would be sent to his home in Theron, to his son Rostryn, with a letter expressing the King's grief and his sincere appreciation for Minos' years of service. The turnout was moderate, as Minos had not been the type of man to collect friends. Those who attended were those who had worked for him, his military and political equals, and the Lachlan household. The k'gdhededhá had known how it would be and was not disappointed with the turnout, although he was disappointed that Claide refused to attend. He had never been aware of animosity between Claide and the ex-chancellor, but there apparently had been. Why else, he mused, would Claide refuse to attend the man's funeral?

The new Chancellor of Enesfel, Flannery McGrannis, led the procession to the altar, at King Arlan's insistence. Jermyn had no problem with that. It would have been Claide's position, had he been there, and neither Tusánt nor Rankin felt slighted about being replaced by the new chancellor. Valgis, however, sulked at being denied such an honor, and seemed to be more upset after overhearing Jermyn express his concerns about Claide to Tusánt and Rankin. Jermyn tried to assure him that his exclusion from leading the procession was nothing personal, but Valgis would not accept that answer.

From his place at the head of the room, Jermyn caught the looks that passed between the King and those around him, and between some of the parishioners. He wondered, as he celebrated the Gathering, what secret Minos Cornell had taken to his grave, what secret everyone knew but him.

❧Chapter 10❦

B hen smiled, though a reluctant shadow crossed his face when his cousin came into the oratory, his arms full with sacks of Llucás' belongings.

"You are leaving?"

The younger Elyri held out his hand. "I have learned much while here, the most important thing being that Teren are not as different from us as many want us to believe. Not that I ever thought they were, but I have proof to present before those who claim we are better. They lack the power, but I think many of us lack the passion for living, the need to push forward that their shorter life spans gives them. I have had the honor of meeting King Arlan, an honor few Elyri can claim. But yes, I must go. I have harps waiting to be made, and your son to train. If you want k'aene to be here for the celebration tonight, I should leave this morning."

Ártur put down what he carried and took the offered hand. "Will you come back?"

"I intend to. I see no reason why I shouldn't. I don't know when it will be, but I want to see more. I may journey to Alberni to see Saint Kóráhm's. From what gdhededhá Tusánt tells me, it has to be a magnificent work. Have you seen it?"

"No. I want Kavan to show me, but since he might never…" His voice trailed into a choking cough. "Perhaps we can go together."

Bhen's smile grew wider. "I would like that. I want to know him better…and you. Would you please let me know when there is news? And if you can, let him know my prayers are with him?"

Ártur nodded. "He will be touched by your concern. It will mean even more that you wish to spend time with him."

They shared one tight embrace before Bhen stepped into the k'dhín bhólibh. Ártur waited for the familiar discharge of static that indicated Bhen was now in Bhryell, and then entered the chamber to bring Piran and Princess Diona home.

❧ * ❦

Rolling the cherry over his tongue, Arlan watched the dark clouds gather over Rhidam through the window of his room. He wondered if it would rain on his birthday, and then wondered if it mattered. Tomorrow he would be forty-five years old. And he looked it, unlike Ártur whom he had passed on his way downstairs. The healer was eighty and looked to be in his mid to late twenties. Remarkable, that one difference between Elyri and Teren. On his birthday, that anomaly bothered the King; the rest of the year, it rarely crossed his mind.

It troubled him more today than usual because he felt cold. There was a tingling numbness in his fingers and toes that was not there yesterday, almost enough to make him seek the healer this morning to ask for an examination. He had not. He knew what was coming, or believed he did, and that was enough. He did not want anyone else to know. Especially not tonight, when such knowledge would darken the celebration of yet another year of life, and he did not want that. No, there was no reason to worry anyone with what might be nothing.

But he wanted Kavan with him, at the end, whenever it came, to take him across as he had Brenna, Guthrie, and Bertram, even if

Arlan's passing could not have music. Kavan had been there at the beginning, on the day he was born, as had Ártur, and they would be here when he was gone. The thought of Kavan's continued existence made what lay ahead bearable.

On the table was a ring, a large garnet circled with gold. A gift from the Harcourts', from Prince Espen. A beautiful jewel, a flawless complement to the Lachlan regalia. Arlan had not had the courage to put it on his finger. Would it be a bad omen for a dying man to wear a new ring?

Kavan, his thoughts reached out, where are you? Why can't you be here? You've always been here when I needed you. I need you now.

❧*❧

Their arrival in Yd Haszafni was uneventful; it was late in the afternoon and Kavan chose to spend his time in the small clay brick náós while Wortham and Eridel procured supplies. He hoped Eridel would go his way now that they had reached civilization, but the younger bard showed every indication of traveling in Kavan's company for as long as he could. Kavan's intolerance of the situation grew daily, though he made every effort to remain cordial. It was difficult, however, when he did not feel cordial. Even the monk's idle whittling, which he did often, and his consistently cheerful banter made Kavan irritable.

When they departed Yd Haszafni this morning, it had been with a dark cloud smothering his soul, an ominous feeling that grew heavier as the day progressed. Kavan was cold, faint, and occasionally dizzy. Wortham worried that Kavan had taken ill, though he did not recognize the symptoms. Kavan did not recognize them either, but he did grow, little by little, to recognize the cloud within. Death. His own, he presumed, causing a flare of panic that he found difficult to combat. As black as his soul and thoughts had been of late, he did not feel ready to be judged before k'Ádhá. In an effort to cleanse his spirit, Kavan lingered behind the others, deep in prayer, and made it known he did not desire to be disturbed. They would reach the town of Palil by nightfall. Then he would bid farewell to Wortham and part company with him to die alone.

❧*❧

Gaelán watched his brother toss his head and saunter into the keep to find Asta. He could not understand how Tayte could be cruel, calling him evil simply because he had the power to heal. A power that Tayte did not possess. Pointing out that Ártur and Syl were both healers caused Tayte to remind him that he was part Teren and Teren could not heal. Gaelán would never be full Elyri, would never share their other powers or their lifespan; why was he pursuing training? Why was he turning his back on their family?

Gaelán did not think he was turning his back on his family, but Tayte had made one good point. He had a decision to make. Did he wish to pursue this unexpected Elyri gift as far as he could, be Elyri as much as was possible when he would inevitably fall short, when it would mark him as a monster in the eyes of many, set him apart from all things Teren? Or should he deny this gift, accept his life as Teren among Teren, and be unfulfilled but safe?

It did not feel like such a difficult choice to make. If he could heal others, help others, Gaelán felt he must. If it meant that he clung to things Elyri and offended his brother in the process, that is the way it would have to be. And while Tayte believed he could convince Asta to show Gaelán the error of his choices, Gaelán knew she admired this gift. It set him apart from the other young men she knew. Teren men.

What Tayte also did not know was that Asta was not in the keep today. Let him look, Gaelán thought bitterly. Let him look all day.

❧*❧

Prince Muir stepped from the chamber into the upper oratory, catching his breath at the swiftness with which he arrived in Rhidam. Being here at the King's request, no less, which was odd unto itself. Diona stood beside him, looking as nervous at being here as he felt. Soon Gabrielle and Piran came out of the chamber behind them, followed by the healer.

"Prince Muir?"

Having been staring at the pyre figure on the wall behind the altar, a figure he had once seen shed blood, Prince Muir was startled by the voice. "Did you say something, Lord Healer?"

Ártur gestured towards the door. "Are you coming? The King is waiting for you both in the solar. One of you needs to go first."

The princess nudged her brother. "If he asked you here it will certainly not be to berate, ridicule, or punish you. He wants to see me for an entirely different reason."

Muir knew that to be true. He swallowed his apprehension and nodded. "Very well…I shall see him now." He sounded calmer than he felt as they traversed the castle halls together.

At the solar door he paused, smoothed his crimson tunic, and after a glance at Diona that asked for her support, he knocked on the door.

The King bid him enter, looked, up, and smiled when he came into the room. Actually smiled at him, an expression Muir had longed for often as a boy but never received from his surrogate father.

"Welcome, Muir. It is good to see you. Please, sit. How is Clianthe?"

Wondering if he looked as nervous as he felt, Muir did as he was asked. "She is well and asked me to send her best wishes; she has remained on Káliel to oversee the Council while her mother is in Rhidam. Lady Gabrielle has come to see you."

"Wonderful," the King remarked. "It will be good to see her, though I would like to meet Clianthe too. Did Diona return with you?"

Thinking that his being asked here was due to his sister's recent misbehavior, Muir straightened his shoulders. "Yes. I wish to say on her behalf, that while I know what she has done is terrible and cruel, unthinkably foolish, I believe she has learned a great lesson from…"

"Easy, Muir," Arlan said, holding up his hand to beckon the prince to stop. "I am grateful for your loyalty to her. She will continue to need your calm strength I suspect, as she can be too hot-headed for her own good…rather like her father." He chuckled and leaned back in his chair. "I have words for her that are not your concern, but it is not my place to condemn her. I believe Lord Cliáth's absence and the knowledge of how she has hurt him may be punishment enough. I asked you here for two reasons, neither of which has to do with her. The first, of course, is because I want you to attend the celebration tonight. You are family. You should be here."

Muir bowed his head. "Thank you, sir."

"The second reason…" Arlan paused and stared across the room for many minutes. "I owe you an apology," he admitted. "I have rarely been fair to you, and was unnecessarily cruel without intending to be. Lord Cliáth often pointed it out to me, but I was too blinded by arrogance and pride to see it. I should have thanked you for killing Bertram's murderer, and for participating in the search for him. When I learned that Guthrie was Owain's father…your grandfather…I should have paid you more respect than I did. It was too late by then, of course, to be the father to you I should have been. You were a man; you left to pursue your own life. And over the years, I could not bring myself to say it. But I am saying it now. I am sorry. For every wrong I have ever caused you. Will you accept my apology?"

Muir studied him, noticing how thin the man's face had become since the last time they had seen one another, how dark the circles were under his eyes. Undoubtedly, he had not been sleeping well since Kavan's attack and departure. But there was sincerity in his voice. "I forgave you when I learned the truth from Lord McHador," he admitted, unable to call his grandfather by anything else. Guthrie had been Lord McHador all of Muir's life, and grandfather only at his death. "That knowledge put many details into perspective and showed me where I needed to be, where I belonged. I did not belong here. Lord Cliáth knew it all along. He knew so much…"

As his voice faded with a mournful note, the King reached across the space between them and squeezed Muir's hand. The prince met his gaze. It was an awkward gesture for both of them, a fatherly one that Arlan had not made before to the boy he had raised. "Your concern for him runs as deep as my own. Our love for him is the one thing we have always shared and agreed upon. Perhaps it will be enough to see him through this."

"If it was enough," Muir sighed, "he would not have left. I sincerely believe, regardless of how much we love him, it will not be enough. He needs something we cannot provide…but I pray that someday he finds what he needs. All that we can do is give our best and hope it is satisfactory." He withdrew his hand and they both relaxed, deep in thought, thinking about the same man, until finally, Muir cleared his throat. "I have something for you."

The King shook his head. "I told Ártur I want no gifts…"

"He said nothing to that effect. Please," he said as he held forth a tiny box. "Take this."

Arlan hesitated but took it to satisfy Muir and appease his curiosity. When he opened the box, he discovered Guthrie McHador's rank insignia. "I…cannot take this, Muir. He left it to you."

The prince smiled. "I have other tokens and I have my father. You have nothing of the man who raised you save memories. Take it, please."

"I cannot." The hinged box was snapped closed and pressed back into Muir's hand. "Do not be insulted. It is a meaningful gesture and I appreciate what you are trying to do. But I would not feel right having it. Guthrie gave it to you, not to me…I think he would understand."

"But I do not wish you to think…"

"I want no gifts, Muir," Arlan repeated. "I have everything a man could ask for, except the presence of my best friend. It is enough. Please, keep it."

Muir tucked the box back into his pocket, murmuring, "As you wish. Is there anything more you wish of me, or shall I send Diona to you?" There seemed no reason to stay. The air was cleared between them, forgiveness asked for and given, but that did not mean they shared any grounds upon which to converse as friends.

And the King knew it. "Send Diona in, please. And Muir, thank you…welcome back to Rhidam."

The prince bowed and covered any lingering tension with his retreat. Diona squeezed passed him, showing unusual anxiety when entering the room. She had never looked afraid of her father before, but until now, she had done nothing to warrant great anger. She was afraid to sit, afraid to look at him, afraid to get too close. Arlan knew from her expression and behavior that she was deeply sorry for what had occurred.

"You wish to speak to me?" she asked in a small voice.

Arlan grunted, expressing more anger than he felt any longer. This was not the time for anger. "I have a single question for you, and I want honesty. I know you tried again to convince Kavan to marry you. Ártur told me that much. I do not know what you said or did, nor am I sure I want to. But Kavan rarely succumbs to an assault of words and because of you, he is not here. What happened?"

The princess shook her head and answered without looking up. "I cannot tell you, Father. Suffice it to say, I have done penance, will continue to do so, and will never attempt such a thing again. My failings have cost us, but him most of all. I wish I could relive that day, take back those events and words, but I cannot. I can but ask that he forgive me…and you as well. Can you?"

Arlan had to admire his daughter's courage, even as it annoyed him that he still did not know what had happened. Hagan would have told him anything to avoid his wrath. Seeing that he would never get the story from his daughter, that it embarrassed her too much to speak of, he let the matter drop. "I am not the one who must forgive you, Diona. Though I miss him, I am not the party you have wronged. I hope you learned from this…and that you are home to stay."

Relieved, she nodded and dared to glance at him. "At least until I decide to see the gift Prince Espen gave me."

"Speaking of Prince Espen…we know Kavan will likely never marry, and for you to wed him may be perilous for Enesfel, especially now. However, there is at least one eligible man who would be delighted to be your husband. I want to see you marry before I die," he teased. "I want to know you are happy and well-cared for."

"Father…I am happy. No one takes better care of me than you. But," she smiled, her face looking enough like Brenna's that Arlan hugged her and did not want to let her go, "I will endeavor to do as you wish. I love you, Father."

As she hugged him back, he murmured into her hair, "I love you as well, my princess."

❧*❧

The náós in Palil was decaying around him as he knelt in prayer. Kavan could hear occasional pieces of the rafters or walls peel away and crash to the rotting floorboards. No one used this building any longer, had not used it in centuries he judged by the barely detectable power in the altar. The pews were tipped over, broken, or missing, and the entire room was covered with a layer of thick yellow dust. No one would find Kavan here; no one would recognize this as a náós or enter such a dangerous hovel in search of him.

Except, perhaps, Wortham. There was a crushing pain in Kavan's heart as he thought of his parting with the captain. He claimed to want time apart, that he was looking for a place to pray alone. He had hugged the man tightly before departing, and knew Wortham detected his desperation but did not interpret it as a final parting. All the better, for if he had, he would not have allowed Kavan out of his sight.

But how would the man feel in the morning? Would he forgive the Elyri if he found him dead in this place, or did not find him? Or would Wortham resent him forever for not allowing him to say a proper farewell, for denying him the right to be with him at the end?

In the barrenness of this decrepit place of worship, Kavan tried to pray but was distracted by the increasing nearness of death. It was there, beyond his sight and grasp, waiting patiently for its opportunity. What must he do, he wondered. Let his guard down? Sleep? Or was his passing to be more violent and he had to await the arrival of whoever was to take his life? Perhaps, he thought as another bit of rafter fell behind him, the collapsing building would kill him. Restless, he paced the width of the crumbling stone platform, clutching his gloved hands to his chest.

He could die. Violence, injury, and sickness killed Elyri as they did Teren. He had seen it often enough to know it was true. But he had never known Elyri to die of age. Those elderly he had known had not died to his knowledge; they simply left their homes and did not return. There were no graves for the elderly in Bhryell. Kavan was not ill, thus it seemed safe to assume that his death would be violent. As the night wore on, violence became more and more the outcome he could envision as his end.

Hours passed, or rather, it felt like hours. His internal clock had stopped the night Diona drove him out of Rhidam and he had yet to regain his sense of time passage. The darkness grew deeper, taking with it the vestiges of starlight and moonlight. The sound of movement outside the náós caused him to halt his pacing as his heart leaped into his throat. He held his breath, expecting whoever, or whatever was there, to come in and claim him.

Nothing happened. An animal then, or passerby. But death was closer than it had been, and he knew it would not be much longer.

Arlan.

The image flashed before his eyes for a moment but was burned into his mind. Not his death then, he knew, but Arlan's. His unnatural connection to the boy he had made a king caused him to feel the strong emotions or physical sensations Arlan experienced. And Arlan was dying. Panic seized Kavan and he felt outward with what energy he could gather, hoping to find a Gate within the ruins around him. Arlan needed him. He could not abandon his quest, nor could he face others in Rhidam. The hour was late, however, and surely, most of the palace staff and family would be asleep. If he could find a Gate, he could go directly to the King's chamber. He must. Arlan needed him.

But unlike many, this náós had no Gate, at least none that left a detectable trace of energy. In despair, Kavan was about to sink onto the altar steps, certain he would die alone when Arlan did, when the creak of the rotting floorboards in the doorway made his heart stop. The massive cat, sleek in its gold, black and white stripes, sat on its haunches staring at him expectantly. He had never seen another animal like it, save the night he was beaten, and he had been certain that memory was born of hallucination and despondency. Was it here to kill him now? Would Arlan's death come because it was Kavan due to die by what he guessed were large teeth and claws?

But the cat did not move, and nor did he. Soon it stood, circled as if preparing its bed as dogs often did, still watching Kavan with yellow eyes trying to communicate unspoken thoughts. Mesmerized, not perceiving the animal as a threat despite his conviction that it was here to kill him, Kavan took one step closer. The cat went outside and hesitated at the bottom of the steps when Kavan did not follow. It returned to the threshold, repeating its actions, until Kavan sighed and murmured, "Very well…I shall follow you."

Brushing his hair from his eyes, he chose to meet this challenge despite his fears. The creature might lead him to where he needed to be, or it would lead him to his death. Either way, pursuing this unexpected visitor seemed to be his path.

Through the night, he journeyed, through tangled vegetation and over rocky terrain, following the cat that remained several bounds ahead as it led westward into uninhabited scrubland. The perfect place for an attack, Kavan mused. But the animal shared his urgency, matched his speed, until it lay down at the center of a crumbling ruin of massive rocks, each taller than a man and wider around than any two men could reach. Many lay on their sides, toppled by ancient forces. Most had chunks chiseled from their weather-worn facades. Few were erect any longer, but they still formed a crude circle; he could determine that much by the moon's glow. There was energy here, potent and ancient, emanating from a point in the center where the cat rested.

It did not retreat as Kavan drew near, trying, despite his steps, to remain beyond what he thought the cat's jump radius would be. He had yet to reach the center, but the cat finally rose and moved back as he drew closer. Then his senses, so focused on the animal that he paid little attention to his surroundings, prompted him to stop. His heart hammered at the unexpected find.

A Gate.

One of those ancient Gates like the one in Owain's home in Fiara. One of two that showed destinations, behind his closed lids, that had no other access, destinations which were brighter than the rest but much further away. But those were not the destinations Kavan was looking for. There was no time to investigate them now. It was the familiar he wanted, particularly one that would take him to Rhidam.

Realizing that he was vulnerable to attack with his eyes closed, he opened them to see that the cat had gone. He had not heard it leave. A manifestation of the phae k'kairá, he wondered, or Saint Kóráhm? Or something else? There was no opportunity to ponder or investigate. He had somewhere he needed to be. He must go to the castle. Arlan needed him.

The King tossed beneath his wool blankets in a vain attempt to get comfortable. Despite the multiple coverings, he still felt cold and his extremities numb to the point that he could barely feel them. He was restless, unable to sleep, though when he left his celebration he had felt exhausted. Weary of the crowd, perhaps. After a few hours of sleep, he awoke refreshed, ready to tackle the problems plaguing his kingdom. If he had not felt so cold, he would have risen and found something to do, but he could not imagine leaving what little warmth his bed offered.

His guests seemed to have enjoyed themselves despite the painfully obvious absence of the harper who should have been with them. There had been more than enough food, ample wine, and a quartet of musicians who were quite good. While his guests danced, Arlan watched, studying them as if for the first time. He watched Asta float from Gaelán to Tayte to Hagan, and then repeat the process. Diona, contrite and well mannered, restricted her dances to Muir, Owain, and a few with Caol. The inquisitor was surrounded by women and danced much of the time. He had been unmarried since Deidre's death and it was good to see his friend's interest in women resurfacing.

It never had for the King. Unlike Caol, or indeed most people, he had not spent his adolescence exposed to girls; Brenna had been his sister's servant and confidante, his friend, his first love, and eventually his wife. When she died due to complications of childbirth, part of Arlan had died too. The idea of remarrying seemed unnatural to him but he did not begrudge Caol a second chance at happiness. In fact, he hoped his redheaded friend found it.

The two healers had eyes solely for one another, as did the Duke and Duchess of Levonne. The King noted the changes in his friends, how different they looked from the first time he had met them. The Elyri were the same, however, with only Ártur appearing to have aged.

Tonight, for the first time in years, the King decided to dance and gave his dances to his daughter and to Gabrielle Dilyn when she was not at Owain's side. He knew many eyes had watched him, as he had not danced since Brenna's death with the exception of a single dance with Bianca when she and Wilred married. Arlan could almost hear their thoughts, hear them wondering if he was ready to accept the late Queen's death.

None of them knew how far from the truth they were.

When he grew weary and cold, he excused himself from the celebration, bidding his guests to continue as long as they wished. Ártur accompanied him into the corridor, asking if all was well, and the King reassured him that it was. He was simply tired, he said, the stress of recent events, and Kavan's absence this night, taking their toll. He wanted to sleep. Fortunately, the healer had not touched him and had been eager to return to his wife's side. Arlan knew that if he had, the healer would have learned the truth and the night of celebration would have come to an abrupt end.

A sound within his dressing chamber roused the King from his remembrances of the evening. He rolled to face the door and then pushed into a sitting position, his hand finding the dagger kept beneath his mattress as he maneuvered to defend himself. He did not speak. In the dark, he was hoping that anyone hiding there, assassin or kidnapper, would not be able to see that he was awake.

A dark cloaked figure emerged and stopped. The King held his breath, awaiting the intruder's next action.

"Arlan?"

The monarch could not throw his blanket off fast enough in his haste to get out of bed. Entangled, he fell, but the other man caught him before he hit the floor and obliged him with a tender embrace.

"Kavan! It is you! I did not think…" He stopped. He pulled back to look at the bard's face with reluctant comprehension. "I am dying. Aren't I? I prayed I would not until I saw you…and you are here."

Rather than answer the question because he did not want to admit it, to either of them, Kavan lowered the hood of his cloak and said, "Death is near. I feel it, but I cannot say whether it is yours or mine."

Arlan touched the bard's cheek, catching a strand of thick, silver-white hair in his fingers. "It is my death that approaches. I know it, even if you will not acknowledge it. But I thank k'Ádhá you have come. Your hands?"

Hesitating, Kavan sighed before settling the king back upon the bed and awkwardly removing his gloves and holding forth his hands. There were tears in his eyes, and the pain of shame thumping in his chest, but he felt strongly that Arlan needed to know what had taken him away. There was no room for lies this night.

"By k'Ádhá," Arlan whispered, "It is worse than Ártur described. I am glad the four who did this are dead."

"Four…dead?" Kavan remembered the two he had killed. The fate of the others he had never known.

"Two…one's head exploded, the other's chest suffered a similar injury. Your doing, we supposed. The others looked to be torn apart by beasts…"

The memories came back, clearer now that distance from the event had stripped away some of the emotional trauma. "A cat…larger than any wolf. Striped, I think, but it was dark and I did not see it clearly. And there were at least six of them. They followed me, I believe, from the Merry Sow."

"The Merry…" The name of the place sounded like somewhere Kavan was unlikely to frequent. "Caol is working on it. He will find everything there is to find. What were you doing in Levonne? How did…?"

Kavan shook his head, his eyes closed in the hopes of blocking those particular memories. "I do not wish to talk about it. Please."

Sighing, respecting Kavan's wish to this one bit of privacy when he could have demanded an answer, Arlan said, "Of course. I am sorry, Kavan. As is Diona. She will be pleased to know…"

"She must not know I am here. I will leave…when my time is finished. I do not want to see anyone else."

There was pain, anger, confusion, and fear in the bard's voice, causing Arlan to fall silent and stare at him for many long, silent moments. Hoping to cover the looming awkwardness, Arlan leaned against Kavan's shoulder and said, "Before I die, there are things I need to know…things that will put my mind to rest. Things I hope you can answer."

Relieved to no longer talk about himself and his injuries, the bard nodded and replied, "I will try."

Arlan eased against the headboard, wanting to watch Kavan's face as they talked. The Elyri's expression often said more than his words. "Do you think Hagan will be a good king?"

Kavan lowered his gaze, wondering how much he should tell. "That is up to him," he said. "You have taught him well; he has the potential for greatness if he is given the chance to use it."

"Meaning?" Arlan asked around the lump in his throat.

It was something he had never mentioned to Arlan, but tonight he saw no reason not to speak of it. "When I first met you…you touched my hand and there was a tingling sensation…something I had not felt from any other infant. You became king. I did not receive that touch from Bertram…and he died. I did receive it from Hagan; I know he will be king, but I also know that Diona is destined to rule Enesfel."

"Diona…? What will happen to Hagan?"

Kavan shrugged. "I do not know. I know he will become unable to rule, while Diona is capable, but I know no more than that."

"My daughter…a queen. Will you ever forgive her for what she has done?" Arlan started shivering and Kavan pulled the blankets up around him. Hagan could die of disease, of age, or in combat. He could suffer some ailment or injury that left him alive but infirm and incapable of ruling. The thought of what the young man might endure hurt the King, but by focusing on his daughter, he hoped to push away worry and despair for events he would not be able to change.

"You are cold," he said instead of answering the question, but the King knew from his friend's expression that forgiveness from a man who easily forgave was still a long way off. He smiled a little as Kavan finished with the blankets. "Is there anything else I can tell you?"

"You do not…you must find these matters petty…"

"The concerns of the…your concerns are never petty, Milord. Your heart is with your kingdom, where it should be."

Arlan squeezed Kavan's wrist. "You are a wise, compassionate man."

The touch, more than the words, unsettled him, causing Kavan to rise and shuffle to the window, keeping his back to the King as he wiped away tears that gathered in the corners of his eyes. "Compassionate, perhaps, but I would not claim to be wise."

"I do not know what has happened to bring you this much pain, Kavan, to cause you to doubt yourself, but I assure you, you are the wisest man I have ever met. If fate had not brought us together, Enesfel would be a much different place. The kingdom owes its prosperity to you as much as it does to me. I would not be king…"

"You were meant to rule. Fate would have found a way…"

"It did," Arlan smiled. "It found you. It brought us together. I have no illusions about my successes, but I would not have chosen this path if not for you. But there is one more duty I wish I could perform for Enesfel before I die."

"What is that?" Feeling calmer, Kavan came back to the bedside.

"I want to rid Enesfel of its anti-Elyri sentiments. This violence…first, there was you. Then an Elyri woman was raped and murdered in Seres. Wilred told us of an Elyri couple killed in Durham in what appears to be a suspicious fire. Minos…did you know he was part Elyri? He was killed a few days ago after receiving threats. There have been flyers posted around Rhidam…" He scrubbed his face with both hands. "I wish I knew what has caused this, how to stop it…if it even can be stopped."

Kavan listened, filing each incident in his memory. "I do not know, Arlan. It is possible that it is connected to some historical details I have recently discovered. Do you remember the náos beneath the keep, that we used the night you claimed the throne?" Arlan nodded. "It may have been used by Dawid Coryllien to conduct Teren and Elyri sacrifices…

"Dawid Coryllien is a mythical…"

"No. He was real. I discovered his remains in the room where Bertram was…Wortham and I…that corpse was destroyed, but it was Coryllien. I am sure of it. He had a brother, someone who claims that the key to cleansing the evil from that place is to be found in the Hatu city of Enda…which is where I am going. The náos was connected to those years of violence and persecution and may be connected again. Once it is cleansed, the violence may cease."

The King looked skeptical. "You are not suggesting there are sacrifices going on there?"

"Not unless an Elyri is behind it. There is no direct way in and out of there other than the Gates, without you discovering that someone is entering the maze through the dungeon. I hope to learn more soon."

"Then Enesfel's fate rests once more in your hands." Taking note of the Elyri's crestfallen expression, he added, "I am sorry to have brought you into this, Kavan."

"You have not…"

"It was my request that brought you to Enesfel…when I asked you to help me gain the throne. If I had not…"

Kavan awkwardly fingered the half-crescent resting on Arlan's sunken chest. "This bound me to you before that request was made. My fate was sealed when you were born. I came because it was where I was meant to be."

This meant, he realized, that even this night was pre-ordained. Nothing could change it. Arlan realized it too, and after another awkward pause, he changed the subject. "Kavan, open the top drawer of the night table."

"Milord?"

"Do it, Kavan," the King chuckled. "There is a pouch there; do you see it? And the book beneath it. Take them. They are yours."

"Mine?" Kavan asked as he removed the pouch and the book, ancient though without a title or author engraved upon the leather cover, and closed the drawer.

"Did you think I would forget your birthday?" He paused uncomfortably, wondering if Kavan would see through those words to the truth, wonder if the bard would reject these gifts as he tried to do with others in the past. For the first time in the years Arlan had known him, however, Kavan opened the pouch without protest, signaling acceptance of these gifts without question. Arlan sighed and swallowed back tears. The end was truly near.

"A key?" Not merely a key. Taking it out of the velvet that embraced it, he could see that it was made from the same silver-like metal the crescent pendants were fashioned from. That in itself was significant, though he did not know what it meant. He had yet to learn where that sort of metal was fashioned or what it was fashioned from. And there was power in the key; power in a crafted object such as this was rare, making this an object of importance.

"I don't know much about it. I was looking for something appropriate, and this arrived with a message from Wace Elotti…"

Arlan noticed the spark of interest in his friend's eyes, something he had not expected to see this night on the bard's otherwise melancholy face. "He said you would appreciate it, that its significance would not be lost on you. It looks like any other key to me…except for the metal it is made from."

"It is possible there is Elyri in his blood," Kavan said, fingers still on the key. "Perhaps he felt in this what I feel…the power. When it is important to know its purpose, I suspect I will know." He replaced it into its bag and tucked it safely inside of his pocket. The book, whatever it was, would wait. He did not have the heart or will to lose himself in it tonight. "Thank you for your thoughts…for the gifts."

Arlan shrugged, unable to find words to express his thoughts and feeling as if he should have offered some other gift as well. He said nothing as Kavan set the book upon the bedside stand, a difficult task with his twisted hands. Observing that difficulty, knowing how Kavan was suffering, and thinking about what Kavan had said about the mission he was on, Arlan finally asked, "I thought your quest was for restoration of your hands?"

Kavan's jaw clenched and Arlan immediately regretted the question. Before he could retract it, however, the bard said, "Restoring the naós may be part of what is required of me. I do not know. I do not know," he admitted, "if they will be restored."

"They will be. They must be. Have faith that things will be as they were."

"I am trying to have faith…but things cannot be as they once were. Not after this," he looked at his hands and then into the King's eyes, "not after tonight…that is too much to ask."

"Kavan…" For the first time since he had been a young man, Arlan threw his arm around his Elyri friend and held him tightly, more to fend off his grief than to comfort Kavan in his. In the bard's voice, he had heard that he would be missed when he was gone, and the thought of adding more suffering upon Kavan's already burdened shoulders was too much.

In that embrace, Kavan was stiff, uncomfortable with such a display of affection, yet Arlan refused to release him. Finally, he forced himself to relax simply to ease Arlan's conscience and the King's hold upon him. It worked. Kavan pulled back, but Arlan refused to look at him.

"I have offended you," the Elyri said with a sad sigh.

"You? No…it is I who has offended you. I should have known…"

Kavan touched Arlan's hand self-consciously. "It is nothing, Arlan. You desired something I should have given…for once in my life. There is nothing I can say in my defense except that I am sorry. Please forgive me, Milord."

Arlan turned his hand to hold Kavan's gently. "Always, my friend. It is enough that you are here." He tried to hide a yawn and another shiver that raced through his body.

"You are tired, Arlan. You should sleep…"

"No!" Hastily, not wanting Kavan to misunderstand him, he continued, "I mean…I do not want you to go. I do not want to part company with you. You…my first and truest friend. The one man who has always told me the truth, even when I did not want to hear it and would not listen. We have made quite a team, you and I."

Kavan smiled. Almost. "Yes, we have. My life would be very different if we had not met. I promise I will stay as long as I am able. I have no music to soothe you, but I pray my company is enough."

"It is more than enough. With you here…I can go in peace. She's waiting…but I couldn't leave without…" Still holding Kavan's hand, he changed the subject, asking, "Will you stay in Enesfel, help Hagan and Diona as you have me…and their children too if they need you?"

Kavan did not need to think about that answer before giving it. "My destiny became intertwined with the Lachlan House long before you were born. An old woman, whom I suspect was k'kairá, foretold that I would find my destiny the first time I came to Enesfel. I found you. I shall do what I can for your House as long as I am able, or for as long as they will allow, whichever comes first."

"That means," Arlan smiled, catching Kavan at last, "that you will come back to Rhidam. Someday."

Kavan started to speak, to deny the possibility, but realized he could not. "Someday," he conceded. "Right now, I do not know when that will be."

"It is enough to know you will come back." His smile stayed in place as he settled into his pillows, closing his eyes wearily, keeping Kavan's crippled hand firmly in his.

"Arlan?"

The King opened his eyes. "Yes, Kavan?"

"I do not believe I have ever told you…I love you." It was, to Kavan's knowledge, the first time he had said those words to anyone.

Arlan's smile reached into his eyes. "You have not…but I know. I love you as well, my friend."

The King drifted into sleep, leaving the room silent and still. Closing his eyes, Kavan attuned his senses to his surroundings, watching over Arlan with everything he had. When the záryph came, Arlan Lachlan departed the world with a sigh of relief, his heart stopping within his breast, his hand holding Kavan's. The bard sensed a warm presence he had not felt in many years, that of Brenna Lachlan, and knew Arlan was where he longed to be. With the woman he loved. Somewhere nearby, the presence of Guthrie McHador was felt, as well as Prince Bertram and those Lachlan kings who had gone before. Arlan was home, at peace, with his family and forefathers.

Though the feeling of bliss faded and the hand around his grew limp, it was many long minutes before Kavan could open his eyes. Pulling his hand away from Arlan's was one of the most painful acts he had ever committed. Arlan had been his first friend in a world of people who did not understand him, who worshiped or rejected him, who could not give him the friendship he craved. This loss was like nothing else. At last, he understood how his cousin felt when King Donal had died. Lifting Arlan's body, he clutched it to his chest until long after the warmth had gone out of it and his tears stopped falling. He did not want to leave. Once he did, he would never see Arlan's face again, would not feel his touch or hear his voice. But dawn was not far off and there was one thing Kavan knew he must do before returning to Palil.

Removing the crescent pendant from around Arlan's neck, Kavan forced himself to step away from the bed. Not knowing what to expect, he touched the Lachlan half of the pendant to his own and felt a painful, rending snap. It knocked him to his knees, that final, total separation from Arlan. He could not breathe, could not see, and could not move. For several seconds he could only kneel, his chest aching as his lungs fought for air. Then, as if someone opened a window, air rushed into his lungs and the pain subsided. Trembling, he remained on his knees, clutching the two halves together, until he began to feel something unexpected…his strength seeming to ebb out of his body. Arlan had died, and it felt to Kavan as if he would follow.

Terror-stricken, Kavan lurched to his feet. Hagan's room. He had to get to Prince Hagan. No one was in the corridor as he stumbled blindly towards the prince's chambers and the young man did not wake when Kavan entered. He dropped to his knees at the bedside, studying the sleeping man as long as he dared, praying that k'Ádhá would give the prince the strength and courage to survive the days to come. The pendant was slipped carefully around Hagan's neck in order not to rouse him; when it touched the prince's skin Kavan felt the half he wore begin to tingle upon his chest. Gradually, the feeling of weakness, real or imagined, subsided. A connection was established with the new king, yet it was not the same as what he had shared with Arlan. Nothing would ever match that.

Kavan returned to the King's room and knelt beside the bed again, not yet ready to say goodbye. He gently brushed the man's hair from his face and straightened the blanket to suggest that the king had died in his sleep as naturally as any man might. Kavan knew, however, that Ártur would know he had been here. That could not be helped.

A rooster crowed in the distance. The servants would be arriving soon with the morning meal. Kavan kissed Arlan's forehead, allowing his tears to drop silently onto the King's peaceful features, and then, with the book clutched to his chest, trudged with agonizing slowness to the dressing chamber where the Gate was located. He looked one last time at the face he would lose forever once he departed. "Goodbye, Arlan. There will never be another man like you."

❧Chapter 11❧

The crash of a breakfast tray stopped Asta in her tracks. Already awake for several hours, she had practiced climbing from her window to the ground outside before the rest of the palace stirred and then roused Gaelán to show him the puppies born during the night. Gaelán remained with the puppies in the kennel while she went to tell her father of her latest exploit. Normally, noises within the King's chamber were none of her concern and she ignored them, but this time a servant threw open the door directly in front of her, making the occurrence hard to ignore.

"Bring Lord Healer at once!"

Asta was composed and quick-witted enough to obey without questioning the order. She knocked loudly on the healers' door, hoping they would not be angry with her for waking them.

"Milady?" Ártur asked, his eyes bleary with sleep.

Asta curtsied and said, "A servant in the King's room asked me to fetch you." There was nothing more to say. Ártur pushed past her, his strides long and purposeful and she had to hurry to catch up. He closed the door as he entered the chamber, however, leaving her in the hall. Curious, and assuming it was nothing more than a matter of broken glass or pottery, Asta was content to wait in the corridor to learn more.

The healer, on the other hand, did not know what he expected. An injured servant, perhaps, judging by the food scattered across the floor. But the woman who should be cleaning up the mess was staring at the King. Ártur followed her gaze and felt his heart drop to his knees.

There was no need to touch the man, no need to perform an examination. Arlan's pasty gray skin was the only explanation needed. Ártur had seen death often enough to recognize it. Still, perhaps to obtain tangible proof that his eyes were not deceiving him, he touched the King's hand. It was cold, indicating the man had been dead for several hours.

There was something else too, something more than the too neatly arranged bedding. There were gloves upon the bed, indicating that someone had been here. Murder? Surely not. There was no evidence of blood, and no evidence upon the king's features, or in the initial touch, to suggest poison. No, this death had been natural. It was not until Ártur picked up the gloves, however, that he knew what their presence meant. Kavan had come. Arlan had not died alone in his sleep but had shared his last moments with his best friend. Perhaps, the healer thought, clutching those gloves to his chest, they had been left to let Ártur know his cousin had been here. Or Kavan may have forgotten them in the stranglehold of grief. While Ártur regretted not having seen his cousin, he was thankful the bard had come for Arlan.

But the knowledge did little to ease or eliminate the icy pit in his stomach or quell the shaking that overtook him. Arlan was gone. The first Lachlan prince he had welcomed into the world, the prince he had rescued from danger, the young man he had helped make into a king. It had hurt when Kings Innis and Donal had died, but Innis had been a man in the middle of his life when they met, and Donal, a few years older than Ártur, had suffered a weak heart. This time, he had known Arlan his entire life. How many kings would pass before his eyes before he died, or before he decided he could bear to lose no more?

Fingering the man's hair, Ártur wept, trying unsuccessfully to will the emptiness away.

"Please, clean this up," he said politely to the shocked woman behind him as he spread his hands over the King's chest, pouring energy into the body to preserve it, to keep it from decay until burial. He straightened but did not otherwise move for many minutes, not wanting to face what he knew would come next. There was a gathering in the corridor; he could sense it beyond the door. The longer he took to emerge from the room, the more anxious they would be and the larger that gathering was likely to become. Swallowing hard, he pocketed the gloves and went among them. This was something he could not hide.

Syl, Bhríd, and Caol had joined Asta and looked at the healer's not quite blank face expectantly. Syl's presence did not surprise him as she had stirred at the knocking on their door, but he wondered what had brought the Chamberlain and Inquisitor so quickly. Did they notice the trace of tears on his face or the red that rimmed his eyes in the deceiving light of the lanterns in the hall? "The King is dead," he said matter-of-factly, trying to block the wave of emotion from the others as best he could.

Caol stuttered, trying to push past the healer to get into the room, "Dead? How can that be? He was…" The chamberlain caught his arm and held him back, his expression sick-hearted.

"He was ill and did not let us see it, did not let me tend him. He died in his sleep during the night." Arlan had been just as stubborn that way as Donal had been; his death came as no less of a shock

"Arlan…" Bhríd leaned against the wall, his face losing color, his hand sliding away from Caol's arm at last. He was not a man prone to displays of emotion, but he was fond of the King. That fondness had brought Bhríd out of Elyriá into Enesfel and kept him here when many of his countrymen would have left. Syl placed her hand in his and squeezed, though her eyes were on her husband's face. Ártur looked away, unable to maintain eye contact; it would lead to an emotional collapse he did not think he could afford.

"I should have known," the chamberlain continued. "He asked me to update his final statement… a formality he said…"

"And it could have been," Syl said to soothe her brother. "There was no way to know otherwise."

No longer trying to see what he would not be able to unsee if he opened that door, the inquisitor muttered, "He was trying to get his affairs in order. He insisted on having his birthday celebration early…had the k'dedhá here yester…" Caol's eyes widened. "The k'dedhá! I must send for him. The final rite!"

The healer nodded. "Do that. Though it is unnecessary to make a formal announcement yet, there is also no reason to hide this…"

"May I find Gaelán?" Asta asked her father, wanting the company of her peers to confide in while the adults dealt with the intricacies of the death of a friend and a king. Caol led her down the corridor, his arm around her shoulders, keeping her close as if afraid to lose her too.

Ártur waited until he was alone with Syl and Bhríd before speaking again. Producing the gloves from his pocket, he murmured, "At least Arlan was not alone."

"I thought…" Syl said, reaching for the gloves, fearing the King had been murdered and what that would mean to every Elyri in the kingdom. But with one touch upon the gloves, she gasped, "Kavan was here?"

"I detected him when I touched Arlan…he must have Seen what was coming…and came to see Arlan over, to say goodbye."

"I think it would have done much for our grief if he had stayed," Bhríd mused, though he understood why Kavan had not. Heavy of heart, musing that Kavan had foreseen what none of the rest of them had, he wiped his eyes.

"He did what mattered to them both…made sure Arlan was not alone. I think we share this news no further…except with Prince Muir and Owain. They should know he was with us last night, even if we did not see him."

Brother and sister nodded in agreement. "Shall we wake Prince…I mean King Hagan?"

Ártur shook his head. "We might as well let him sleep, Syl. He will learn of this soon enough."

❧*❧

Prince Hagan yawned and stretched, waking to light in his eyes. It was cold but at least the sun was shining this morning, making him smile. No clouds to darken the day King Arlan had been born, the way it should be. He began to dress before noticing the heaviness around his neck and upon his chest.

Touching it made him stumble to the mirror, wanting his eyes to confirm what his fingers were telling him. His father's pendant? How had it come to be around his neck? He knew, as did everyone else, that Arlan never took it off, not even to bathe or swim or sleep. They also knew Lord Cliáth possessed the mirror half. It held symbolism for the two men, but Hagan did not know what it meant. He could not imagine his father giving it to him. He certainly did not remember anyone coming to his room and he knew his father had gone to bed long before Hagan had. It made no sense unless his father had come to him in his sleep, but why could he not remember that?

Dressing hurriedly, he was interrupted by a knock on his door, a servant bringing breakfast. The woman's behavior seemed abnormal; she curtsied, averting her eyes, and then scurried out in a fashion she never had before. Hagan glanced at the meal but the tight knot of confusion in his belly would not allow him to consider food. He needed to know why he wore this pendant. Puzzling out the servant's behavior could wait.

In the corridor, he paused, not sure where he should begin. Seeing no one about, he started towards his father's room. Perhaps he had too much to drink before bed; it would explain his lapse in memory if indeed his father had come to him. He rounded a corner in the hall in time to see two of the Káliel guardsmen, Avner and Denyan, carrying the body of the King from his room with Healer MacLyr following. A strangled choking sound escaped Hagan's throat but he was unable to act or call after them. He had to be dreaming. The healer must have heard him, however, since he turned to meet his gaze. The soldiers continued away with their burden while Ártur came to Hagan.

He saw no way to speak of the matter gently, particularly since the prince had seen his father's body. Looking into the stunned hazel eyes, Ártur bowed. "Your father has died, Milord, in his sleep during the night. A servant found him this morning."

"Died? That means…he is…I am…" Terrified, Hagan shook his head. The last thing in the world he was ready for was to be king.

"King, Milord. Is there anything I can do?" Ártur was tempted to touch Hagan soothingly, but the look on the young man's face showed he was too much in shock to welcome contact or sympathy.

"I…no…see to my father…please…" he mumbled. The healer bowed and followed the soldiers reluctantly, looking back several times. Unable to lift his leaden feet, Hagan remained where he was until the healer disappeared into the stairwell. Jarred suddenly by being alone in a uniquely terrifying way, the new King fled to his sister's room. It was the only place he had to go. Pounding on the door, he called, "Diona! Diona? Wake up!"

There were muffled noises within the room, the sounds of someone getting out of bed and shuffling across the stone floor. His ever-beautiful sister let him in, looking annoyed as she closed the door behind him. "What is it at this hour, Hagan?"

"Father is dead!" he wailed.

"Dead?" For a moment, she thought her brother was pulling a prank, as they often did to one another, but Hagan's distress was too real for that. As the realization began to sink in, her face lost color and she stumbled backward into the armoire, shaking her head in disbelief. "He can't be…"

"I saw Avner and Denyan…and Lord MacLyr was with them. He told me…Diona…I'm not ready to be King! I don't know how!"

His sister did not respond. She crossed to the window and watched a line of soldiers gathering in the courtyard. General Agis was speaking to them but she could not hear him. Informing them of the King's passing, she wondered, if it was indeed true. Is that how it was done? It took great effort to refrain from crying when she realized that, because of her actions, her father had died without his friend at his side. He had been utterly alone. He had seemed young, too young to die. She had not even known he was ill.

"Diona!"

She looked over her shoulder at her little brother. He was taller than her, bearded as the men of Lachlan often were, but he did not look like a king to her. Still, perhaps to make herself believe it, she said, "You will do fine, Hagan. Lord Cliáth taught you everything you need to know. You need confidence, and that will come in time."

He shook his head, not believing her. "What I need is someone older and wiser to assist…"

"That is why you have advisors. Don't you think Lord Cáner and Lord Dugan…?"

"I was talking about you. You always know what to do." As children, she had been the one he turned to for advice. They both realized that perhaps it had not been a good thing for him to rely so heavily on her.

"If I was wise, I would not have driven Lord Cliáth out of Rhidam," she said in a weary voice of defeat.

He hugged her as if afraid he might lose her too. "You made a mistake. We all do. But you know how to talk to our elders, how to get what you want from people. You know how not to back down when you believe you're right. Will you show me how such things are done? Help me be a good king?"

The princess knew her brother was right. He had many good attributes but lacked backbone. "I will do my best," she agreed as she pulled from the embrace. She noticed her father's pendant hanging around her brother's neck and assumed Lord MacLyr had given it to him. With a pang of jealousy, she said, "Let me dress and go down with you. We will find out the truth."

And maybe, she hoped, they would learn that Hagan was wrong and their father was still alive.

❧*❧

The sun had been up for nearly an hour before Kavan rejoined his traveling companions. Wortham was the first to see him, and the worry in his eyes deepened when he noticed the profound ache etching the bard's face. This was a new, fresh pain, one that added to Kavan's already sagging shoulders. The captain greeted his friend with an outstretched hand that Kavan did not accept, also noticing then that Kavan was not wearing his gloves and his hood was down.

"I was concerned, milord," Wortham said in a low voice. "We are ready to be off but could not find you…"

Kavan met his gaze. "My…friend…you should know…during the night…King Arlan has died."

Wortham gripped Kavan's shoulders to remain standing when his knees began to buckle. "Died…? You were with him…?" Kavan nodded and the captain groaned. It explained Kavan's temperament over the last several days and his disappearance last night. Something, either the Sight or one of Kavan's other abilities, had warned him of what was to come. Beneath his hands, he could feel the bard trembling and sensed the conflict within him, the wish to be held and comforted and the wish to be alone in his grief. In compromise, Wortham clasped Kavan roughly to his broad chest for several moments and then pulled away. Kavan lowered his eyes, accepting that compromise for the gesture of friendship it was. "It is good you could be there with him. I am sure he appreciated it. Did any of the others…?"

"No one knew, but I suspect Ártur will soon and tell the rest."

The captain turned to watch Urian and Eridel involved in conversation far enough away that they could not overhear. He gestured to Kavan, and when he reached the others, he asked, "dedhá, can you perform a memorial Gathering? Here? Now?"

The monk nodded. "Of course. Has someone died?"

Taking the matter out of Kavan's hands, giving him no reason to talk about his pain, Wortham replied, "We have received word that King Arlan of Enesfel has died. Both milord and I served in his house; it would mean much if we could mark his passing and pray for his repose in the proper way."

Urian began to fumble in his bag. "I lack proper articles, but we can devise or arrange suitable substitutes while Lord Cliáth eats."

Eridel groaned. "So we are not going anywhere today?"

Not appreciating his disrespectful tone, Wortham grunted, "No."

"Then I shall unpack the mule."

Kavan remained by the dwindling fire staring into its flames, not hungry, hurting too deeply to be useful today.

❧*❧

"I come here once and the queen died. Now I come and Arlan dies. Perhaps I am not welcome in Enesfel." There was forced levity in Gabrielle's words but it did not mask her sorrow.

Owain held her in his arms. "Bad timing, my love, nothing more. Besides, you have been here other times when no one has died. No one knew Arlan was ailing."

She pulled back far enough to look into his eyes. "This must be difficult for you."

He agreed, although until that moment he had given it little thought. "Awkward. We were not close but…I think we had gained respect for each other. He was my junior by eight years, yet he is gone. I was king before him and now…" He shrugged. "If it had been me…"

"You might have been killed by your subjects, the way I understand it."

Owain nodded grimly. "Maybe. It might have been better if I had been. If Muir had been Arlan's eldest son rather than mine, he would be King…where he belongs. We are not Lachlans by blood, but our upbringing has made us part of them. My mother assured me I was meant to be the king my father should have been. I could not be…but Muir…I do not know. Things are jumbled. They make no sense."

Muir's presence in the doorway interrupted his ramblings. It was a welcome distraction, though he wondered how much the younger man had heard. Gabrielle stepped back and offered the prince her hand. He accepted it, and her embrace.

"I think," she said, "I will go to the princess and see if there is anything I can do. I know what it is for a daughter to lose her father. Owain…I will return soon."

The men watched her go, Muir rubbing his neck wearily before saying, "You have heard then?"

Owain nodded. "Lord Dugan told me. I cannot believe it is true."

Muir grunted. "I should have suspected it. I wanted to give him grandfather's rank insignia, but he would not take it. Lord McHador was the closest thing to a father he ever knew and he refused."

"My father was a father to him…his father was a father to me…" muttered Owain. "Perhaps he and I are more brothers than we realized." An air of anguish passed over his face. It would have been nice, he thought, if he had grown up with a brother close at hand.

"Lord MacLyr told me something he thought you and I should know…Kavan was here."

"Here…in Rhidam…last night?"

"At the end. Lord MacLyr found gloves on the bed next to Arlan. He thought it might lessen our grief to know that Kavan is thinking of us even if he cannot be with us now."

Owain's sad smile was proof that Ártur's assessment was correct.

❧*❧

General Agis, the sole Cíbhóló in the Enesfel military, mounted his charger, wanting a few hours of privacy to mourn the passing of his leader in the custom of his people. While he had not been a friend of the King, they had respected one another, and his belief in the near-divinity of his sovereign tore at him in a way he could not explain to those who were not of the desert.

But Lord High General Ternce Wyndham waved him into the barracks, preventing him from departing. Duty was the one thing that could make Agis dismount and a summons by Ternce was a duty.

"Yes, Lord General?"

"Where are you off to?"

The question sounded innocent, but Agis took nothing for granted. He might have served the King unfailingly for years, but he was still a foreigner and believed he would always be treated as such. "I was seeking a place of solitude in which to perform the rite of mourning my people conduct for those who have led us."

"Can't you do that here?"

Agis squared his shoulders. "No one would understand."

Snorting, Ternce shook his head. "Give us some credit. Grief is grief, no matter how it is expressed. I think if you asked to incorporate your rituals into the funeral, you might be surprised by the response."

"I shall consider it," he said, not having thought to try. "Is there more?"

"I want to know how you might feel about taking charge of Enesfel's military. Not that I have control over who King Hagan appoints, but it is time I retire my post."

That surprised the nomad. "You are stepping down?"

"I am an old man," Ternce muttered. "We are not in a state of war; there is no reason to think the troops will be needed soon. Even if we were, I am too old to lead them afield. McHador tried and got himself killed. I will not die like that. I have a home I would like to spend a little time in before I die. I have served the Crown my whole life."

Agis waited, expecting Ternce to say more. When he did not, the dark-skinned man cleared his throat. "To accept the responsibility is my duty if the King requests it. What must I do?"

"Duty, yes…but do you want the job?"

Agis nodded. "It would be an honor."

"Then wait for King Hagan to approach you. I will present my letter of resignation after King Arlan is buried and his final testament is read. I will make my recommendation to the king then. I did not want you to be surprised if he agrees with my choices."

"Very well." Understanding that he was dismissed, Agis turned to leave then asked, "Sir? Who should I speak to about this…final rite?"

"The King? k'dedhá Jermyn? Both? I'm not sure. You will do it?"

"I will consider it," the nomad admitted.

Ternce almost smiled. "Good. I would like to share it."

❧*❧

Around the room, the gathering of thirteen gdhededhá sat or stood in stunned silence. Jermyn called them together as soon as he returned from the keep in response to Caol's summons. No one wanted to believe this news; King Arlan had been a stabilizing factor for the kingdom for many years, had brought prosperity back to Enesfel and the Faith. His death, particularly its abruptness, was a shock. Claide's face was blank, but more and more of late that was normal. Jermyn repeated what he knew and waited for questions. There seemed to be none until Tusánt leaned forward, elbows on his knees.

"When will he be buried?"

"Tomorrow evening in the Lachlan crypt. He currently lies in state in the Hall, should any of you wish to pay respects. He will be brought to the náos before dawn for the Gathering, in which I expect each of you to participate, and then, afterward, a procession will transport him back to the grounds where General Agis will perform a..."

"What heathen rite is he...?"

The k'gdhededhá bristled. "Different is not heathen, Claide. The nomads view the passing of their leaders differently. He has discussed it with me and with King Hagan and we find nothing sacrilegious in it. He wishes to express his grief in a manner to which he is accustomed. He shall be allowed to do so; we think King Arlan would be honored to see it. Anyone wishing to speak during the service is welcomed to do so. He will be interred at dusk. Since this will be a full day affair, I need at least one volunteer to remain here with Hazen after the Gathering to clean up and comfort parishioners."

"I will." Jermyn thought Claide's acceptance of the task a little too abrupt.

"As will I," both Rankin and Valgis remarked at once.

Jermyn stopped them. For some reason, he could not help feeling that leaving Claide and Valgis together would be a disaster. And bringing Claide with him would be awkward. He was certain of that. "We don't need all of you here; I will need two of you to assist me.

Hazen and Claide will stay. Valgis, I would appreciate if you would join me. It is not every day that a gdhededhá must attend to the nobility in this manner; I want you to experience this early in your career so that you do not forget it. And Rankin…if you will assist me as well…"

Not seeing it as an attempt to keep him away from Claide, Valgis smiled. "I would be honored, Your Grace." It was not often that the k'gdhededhá asked him personally for help.

"Good. It is late. Tomorrow shall be a long, trying day; we should get some rest." He did not fail to notice the look Claide gave Valgis. He could not describe it, did not know what it meant, but he did not like it. Tusánt, silent and morose, noticed it too.

❧*❦

It was dark again, and Kavan had not died as he had feared. He had, instead, lost a man he considered one of his best and closest friends even though their rapport as sovereign and subject had wedged between them over the years. The closeness they once shared eroded gradually after Arlan's ascension to the throne but it had never ceased. Now it was gone. It felt like a stone weight in his core, and the pain, coupled with the loss of music that would have brought him comfort, felt to be an unbearable burden. Yet he could not end his life to escape that hurt. He had duties to see to. He had to live for those duties. Saving Enesfel might be in his hands since Arlan was not there to do it. He would tolerate personal pain and loss as best he could, as he had always done and he would sacrifice all in the service to Enesfel. Arlan would expect nothing less.

❧*❦

The procession wound from Hes á Redh Náós through the widest streets of Rhidam until it reached the Lachlan stronghold. The townsfolk that followed were stopped at the palace gate and not allowed to enter while k'gdhededhá Tythilius led everyone else to the back garden where a new tomb had been prepared in the familial crypt. King Hagan wanted to allow everyone to attend who wished to, but after his advisors pointed out the risks of allowing unlimited numbers of commoners on the grounds unescorted, he permitted only Lachlan staff, closest friends, and family to come to the gardens. The rest of Enesfel had to be content with the public Gathering.

Not that the Gathering had been anything less than an opulent and stirring pageant of grief. Each gdhededhá said words about the late King, there had been songs hastily composed for the occasion, and the k'gdhededhá lovingly decorated every detail of the náós with candles and ribbons of gold and crimson and winter flowers of pale blue and white. The biggest tribute had been that, while King Arlan had not ruled over the established Faith, there had been such a degree of cooperation and respect between them that there was rarely any conflict. Hagan intended to maintain that tradition.

The procession stopped before the tomb and the four pallbearers, the Káliel guardsmen and one other, set the body upon the stone slab that would be Arlan's resting place. General Agis came out of the throng, dressed not in his armor but in the thin gauze shirt, gray trousers, wide black cloth belt, and ceremonial dagger of the men of the Cíbhóló tribes. He was barefoot, his face adorned with intricate red markings, and he carried two clay pots. Speaking in the language of his people, which most of those present did not understand, he recited what sounded like a genealogy of the Lachlan house, surprising many with that knowledge. Meanwhile, he poured the contents of the first pot over the King's hands, some sort of fragrant oil that he also used to bathe the monarch's face. Princess Diona could smell its bitter tang from where she stood at the front of the gathering with Hagan beside her. She wondered if everyone else could smell it. The odor made her weak, but Ártur's hand under her elbow steadied her. She glanced at him sadly before turning her attention back to Agis.

The cleansing complete, Agis continued his monologue in praise of King Arlan's deeds as he sprinkled gray dust from the other pot over his own head, and the King's. Ashes, they had been told, meant to be the ashes of previous rulers. What, or who, those ashes belonged to, no one in attendance knew. King Hagan felt a giggle rise in his throat at the spectacle the general was making but it was cut abruptly short when Agis pulled his curved dagger from his belt. With a roar of anguish, he drew it across the palm of his hand and allowed his blood to drip into the remaining ashes in the pot. He stirred the mixture with the blade and then drew symbols similar to those on his face upon the King's. Hagan's mirth turned to shock.

No Lachlan king had ever been marked thus.

"This is the symbol of earth, from which we are made, to which we return. This is water, this is air, without which none can live, to which we owe our existence. And this," Agis drew the final symbol on Arlan's forehead, "is fire. It is the custom of my people, wanderers that we are, not to bury our dead in the shifting, transitory sand, but to allow the gods of fire to consume us at a place where waters flow, so that the air and water can carry our deeds to the corners of the earth. Those who lead give our ashes to those who come after in blessing. Great King, whom I left my home for and swore to serve, though your ashes will not pass to your kin, you will remain close to them. I shall remember you in death as you were in life. Leader. Fighter. A man like no other. I place myself at the disposal of your heirs, that I might continue to serve them faithfully until my death."

The remainder of the bloody ash was sprinkled over the body before Agis moved a half step. The two clay pots were smashed upon the ground near the slab; he gathered the shards and placed them on either side of the man's head. Two of the Káliel guardsmen approached when Agis moved and pushed the stone into the marble crypt. It dropped into place with an echoing thud. The brass grave marker was sealed into position and then some of those gathered departed, heads low, voices hushed with sadness, leaving the family and closest advisors in the near darkness, mourning. They awaited the reading of Arlan Lachlan's final testament, which the monarch had wanted to be done here, beneath the sky, for those closest to him rather than in the confines of the Great Hall before a host of lords and ladies.

It was short, succinct, to the point, the way Arlan had been much of his life. A separate missive had been written for Hagan, to be given to the new king for reading in private, and another had been written for Kavan, with no knowledge, at the time of writing, whether his best friend would ever read it. In the main document, Arlan bid his kingdom, his family, and his friends farewell, wishing them long and prosperous lives. He begged forgiveness from Owain for wrongs overlooked between them. Knowing Caol would accept neither money nor an estate, all Arlan could leave him was the guaranteed right to live in the keep so long as he chose to do so. To his daughter, he bequeathed the Lachlan family estate in Kamin, and to Muir, he left a large portion of the Crown's land surrounding Fiara, a gift which placed that land almost directly under Owain's power once more, and which surprised both Owain and Muir. Neither had expected to be mentioned in Arlan's final testament.

The reading complete, everyone waited. This was supposed to be the opportunity to reminisce, to talk about the deceased, yet no one seemed to know what to say. They looked at one another, expecting someone else to break the mournful silence, until finally the k'gdhededhá began speaking of the first time he met Arlan, how surprised he had been to learn that Kavan's tales of a savior prince were true. This started others talking about those days before Arlan was king, of the campaign that brought him to Rhidam and the throne. While it made Owain uncomfortable to hear his part in these tales from the opposing side of that turmoil, he learned a great deal about the history he had been a part of, as the younger generation around them learned more about the King's life and rise to power. In the end, he gained a deeper respect for Arlan and his vision.

Inevitably, throughout the conversation, the remembrances were as much about Kavan as they were about the King. It seemed to Owain that, without the Elyri bard, Arlan might not have won the throne. In the history books, if the chroniclers were honest, the story of King Arlan's rise and reign would also be the story of the Elyri bard, and others, beside him. Owain wondered if the historians would include those facts or delete the Elyri's involvement altogether.

The assembly began to disperse as the air grew colder, the gdhededhá returning to the náós and the soldiers to their barracks. Agis laid his hands on the stone that entombed the king, kissed it, and then ambled alone into the darkness. After a few quiet words to Owain, Ártur and Syl departed, taking the youngest members of the Lachlan household with them. Muir and Gabrielle sat upon one of the stone benches, leaving Owain alone before Arlan's grave, his head bowed, wrestling with the demons of his past. King Hagan watched him from a distance, wondering what the man was thinking. When his sister tugged on his sleeve, the new King, silent in his musings, chose to follow her and the chamberlain inside.

"Lord Cáner?" Hagan said as he began to walk

"Yes?"

"I…" He looked over his shoulder at Owain but kept moving. "I must admit I know little of recent events, other than Lord Cornell's being killed. May I call the staff together in the morning to learn what has transpired, what I need to know?"

Bhríd nodded. "You can do as you wish, Milord. Am I to be retained as chamberlain? Shall I see the others are informed to meet?"

"Yes," murmured Hagan. "To both. Tomorrow morning, eight, in the stateroom, I suppose."

"Milord?" Ternce approached from the shadows to his left, having waited for his chance to speak to Hagan when he would not be intruding on the young man's grief. He had overheard the dialogue between King and chamberlain, and assumed he would be included in that early morning briefing. This seemed to be his best opportunity to speak on his own behalf.

Resisting the urge to look to his sister for support, the King coughed and said, "Speak freely, Lord General. There is nothing you cannot say before my sister or the chamberlain."

"I have come to give you this." He placed a scroll into the King's waiting hand. "My letter of resignation, Sire, and my recommendation of General Agis as my replacement."

The princess pursed her lips in displeasure. "Resignation? On the heels of our father's death? What is this, Lord General?"

Having anticipated that his action might be viewed as a lack of confidence in the new king, the general shook his head. "This has nothing to do with Prince…with you, My King. I am an old man who has served as general for many years. I have been contemplating this action for months and intended to seek the same of your father. I would like to be able to enjoy my final days in my home with my wife, children, and grandchildren. There are many men competent to replace me, of whom I believe General Agis is the best suited."

"This is dishonorable…" the princess started, not one to hide feelings most of the time, especially when protecting her little brother.

Flushing, aghast that she would not allow him to speak for himself, Hagan said, "Enough, Diona. Lord General, you have indeed served Enesfel and my father well and long. It is reasonable of you to ask for peace in your twilight days. However, before I grant such a request, I ask that you attend a meeting tomorrow; I need to be informed of recent events, to know everything that is going on in order to make proper decisions. If you will do that, meet with me after and tell me everything you know, and make sure your replacement is settled and ready to serve in your stead, I shall grant your request."

Relieved that the young king was not going to deny him or make the transition difficult, Ternce bowed and retreated with a murmured, "Thank you, Milord."

"How could you…?"

Hagan shook his head and glared at his sister but did not speak until the general was gone. "He is right, Diona. He is an old man. If his heart is no longer in his duty, I should have someone in the position who is willing to serve. Doesn't that seem logical to you, Lord Cáner?"

The chamberlain had been silent during the exchange, listening but not interfering. Hagan had to find his way as king, make his place. He was no longer a little boy. "I think your decision is a sound one," he said with a bow. "I will speak with the others of our meeting."

But Princess Diona was not convinced or soothed. "I still think his timing is questionable and dishonorable."

Faith buoyed by Bhríd's opinion, Hagan grunted. Inside the castle, the new King found dedhá Claide waiting in the library, where Hagan and Diona retreated for privacy. The King was only mildly surprised to see him; though Claide rarely came to the palace alone as he had this time, he had missed the ceremony in the back garden, and it was likely he had come to express his condolences and wishes. Diona skewed her face at her brother but left him to the gdhededhá, not interested in overhearing anything Claide had to say.

"Welcome, dedhá Claide," said the King. "What might I do for you tonight?" He did not feel up to receiving visitors, but a holy dedhá he would make exceptions for.

The older man bowed. "I did not have the chance to express regret for your father's death. He was a great leader; He will be missed."

King Hagan tried to smile but the effort fell short. He was glad his assumption had been correct and that Claide had not come on some matter of business. Business would have to wait until some later time. "I appreciate your sentiments, dedhá."

"I also wish to share a recommendation with you, if I may. You do not need my advice, of course, as you are a wise man, but I do have an observation that might make the birth of your reign easier."

Anything that might make the future easier for the young man who was unsure of himself was worth at least a listen. And the flattery, while not believed, made Hagan feel good about himself. "What is it?"

Claide gave a thin-lipped smile, grateful to be heard. "I'm sure you have noticed the increasing amount of violence and negative incidents surrounding the Elyri in your father's employment. Not caused by them, you understand…and they have certainly served your father efficiently…but might it not benefit the kingdom if you removed them from your staff?"

"Removed them? They were my father's friends…" The notion of sending the Elyri away had not occurred to Hagan. The Elyri were family, had been there all of his life. The dedhá must be mad.

The area between his eyes began to throb.

"You are the king; you may take any advisors you wish. You do not need to keep one because your father trusted them. I made the same suggestion to your father, but he could not see the harm being…"

King Hagan rubbed the bridge of his nose and shook his head. "There are few Elyri in this house, dedhá. Lord Cáner is the most qualified man to be my Chamberlain and the only other Elyri are healers."

"And the bard," Claide reminded him.

"He has left Rhidam; you know that. We need healers; Teren doctors are good but Elyri healers are irreplaceable. The rest of the staff are Teren and will remain as they are. I will keep your words in mind, but I shall replace none of them unless they request permission to resign. They are causing no harm and I like them. They're family."

Claide bristled and backed away. "Do not be surprised if the controversy surrounding them continues. I will do as I can to support you, My Liege, but I cannot change what people think. You will find your reign more peaceful if you heed my warning."

Hagan wondered, grateful now to be alone, what the disappearing gdhededhá meant by that.

❧Chapter 12❧

"I admit I also considered resignation," Caol said with a shrug, aware the princess was glowering at him. "I dedicated my life to your father and it is difficult to conceive of things without him. However, I am in the midst of several investigations, and I cannot imagine leaving tasks unfinished or leaving in the middle of our current crisis. Besides, I like my job…it gives me something to do, most of my family and friends are here, and my apprentice is not yet proficient enough to replace me. I have a home here. I intend to stay as long as I can be useful."

The princess folded her arms across her chest with a sour scowl. "At least someone is thinking of his predicament," she grumbled.

"It has little to do with him. It is for myself and for Enesfel…and maybe for your father. You have little faith in your brother."

His observation made her appear more offended. "I love Hagan. He is intelligent and has the capacity to rule. He can do it if he trusts himself. He does not always look ahead to what consequences his actions might cause, but that should come in time."

"That sounds like more than one Lachlan I've known."

She opened her mouth to protest and then allowed some of the tension to leave her shoulders. "I know I am guilty of it, as was my father. Even Bertram. I support Hagan, and I will assist him as I can…but I worry.”

“You support General Agis' appointment?”

It was that appointment, or rather General Wyndham's resignation that had gotten beneath her skin to begin with. Her face darkened but she said, “Considering his part in the Neth war, I do not see how Hagan could appoint anyone else. The others qualified, General Zarkosta, Sir Gabersdon, and Lord Cáner, do not want the position, and Captain Delamo is not here and probably would not take it if it was offered. Agis is best suited to the post, from what I know, and I think he will be as successful as Lord McHador.”

“That is praise I am sure he would be pleased to hear,” the inquisitor said. “Have Cordash and Hatu been notified of…?”

Narrowly avoiding shuffling her feet, knowing she could no longer behave as a girl but had to be the adult in the family, the oldest living Lachlan, Diona sighed. “I sent Prince Espen word yesterday. He may not be pleased to hear from me, but at least he will know the state of Enesfel. Hagan was drafting a letter to King Renfrid last night; I assume it was sent. He wanted it sent the day of the coronation, to make it more official. He has had one day between funeral and coronation to adjust to the idea of being king. I hope it is enough.”

In the open doorway to the side, someone stopped and cleared his throat, causing Caol and Diona to look. “Yes, Denyan?” asked Caol, assuming the man was looking for him and not the princess.

“This arrived for you.” The soldier offered the inquisitor a scroll. “Thank you. That will be all.” He recognized Wilred's seal as he broke it and read the letter hastily, his frown deepening with each passing moment. “This explains it then,” he finally grunted with annoyance.

“What?” asked Diona.

“Wilred sent people to Rhidam for questioning. They should have arrived by now, but the team transporting them was waylaid and the prisoners escaped in the company of the brigands. This supports the claim that they set the fire and are guilty of murder. I must speak to the King about this."

"One more thing before you go…dedhá Claide…" The inquisitor waited, curious about her concern for a man of Faith. "Hagan confided that dedhá Claide encouraged him last night to release the Elyri from employment before irreversible harm is done. Hagan first thought it a threat and came to me, but by the time he bid me goodnight, he concluded he had misinterpreted Claide's intent. Perhaps so, but I am a believer in first impressions. If you have opportunity, perhaps you might investigate him. For me."

Caol cocked one eyebrow. "I don't know what negative information you expect to find about a dedhá, but if it will reassure you, I'll set people on him. Any potential threat should be examined, however preposterous it seems." He considered her concern absurd, but he also knew her not to be one to jump to conclusions. If there was a reason she was worried, beyond the man's suggestion to remove the Elyri from the Lachlan household, it was worth investigation. "Now, I must speak with Hagan before the coronation takes his attention."

The princess waved him off, closed the book she had been half-heartedly perusing, and stared absently out the window. What a way to start his reign, she thought with a sigh, trying to think of ways she might help her brother.

❧*❧

As the small group of men approached the city of Avarrou, the terrain became increasingly barren, the altitude higher. It took getting used to, especially for Wortham and Kavan as neither had been this deep into Hatu and were traveling on foot. Urian rode the mule most of the time, whittling what would be his fourth small figurine since Kavan met him. The figures were all saints, Bhenádíctus, Mátán, and Bhílycá. Wortham assumed this one would also be a saint.

Eridel was humming gaily, unaware that Kavan lagged further behind. Wortham could feel the bard's depression deepening and seemed to be the only one to notice his growing bitterness since Arlan's death. It did not help that Eridel was unable to grasp the burden the King's loss had on Kavan, and his repeated efforts to cheer his idol caused Kavan to retreat deeper into himself.

Last night out of desperation and concern that if he did not intervene, Eridel would drive Kavan away, the captain took the youngster aside and tried to explain the bond between the White Bard and the Lachlan King. Eridel listened, his expression rapt, and in the end came away not with an understanding of Kavan's pain but rather a head full of grand tales of friendship. In a second attempt to solve the dilemma, Wortham spoke to Eridel again but threw up his hands in frustration, confiding to Kavan that he was trying to help but may have made matters worse.

Kavan absolved him of guilt in a way that deepened Wortham's remorse. Kavan's complete forgiveness and understanding usually did that to him and he wished again that Kavan would be angry with him when he felt he deserved it.

The other thing Wortham noticed was the tension Eridel's constant music created. It was a persistent reminder of Kavan's loss. While the Elyri valiantly endured every song, Wortham could see the toll it was taking. That pain, coupled with Arlan's death, was becoming more than Kavan could tolerate. Wortham was surprised the bard had not broken already, and he wondered, with each passing night, how much more the Elyri could shoulder.

◈ * ◈

The morning of the twelfth day of the twelfth month, six days after King Arlan's passing, Gabrielle and Muir left for Káliel, while Owain and Piran began the long overland journey to Fiara. Ternce Wyndham departed for his country estate near Talladegah, leaving Agis in his place as Lord High General of Enesfel. Once Madalyn and Tayte left for Levonne, the Lachlan palace reverted to its normal state of affairs. Normal, that was, except for the absence of the Elyri bard and Arlan Lachlan. There were no pressing emergencies and no underlying tension within those walls or within Rhidam. It was peace of sorts, which gave Hagan a chance to acclimatize to the notion of being king.

It was a different matter in the Hatu city of Avarrou when Kavan and his companions arrived late in the afternoon. As they came out of the inn in which they had taken a room, they encountered a group of women near the city well. The women were content to let them pass unhindered, paying no heed to the strangers, until one of them unexpectedly shouted, "The White Bard of Bhryell!"

Kavan spun towards the cry with blinding panic. How could they recognize him, covered as he was? He had not expected anyone to know him this far south, in a region where he had never been. "I am not…" he croaked, trying to back away as the women surged around him. They clung to him, touching his face and hair after someone pulled the hood of his cloak away. He cringed and struggled to escape, searching frantically for Wortham in the rapidly accumulating crowd. He could not see him.

"Play for us!" someone called, a man's voice now as people poured out of shops and houses to investigate the commotion.

Kavan pulled free of a hand clutching at his cloak. The brooch Wortham had given him broke free and was lost underfoot as the garment fell. "I cannot…" he gasped, realizing as he struggled that he had not tried this hard to escape his attackers the two separate times he had been beaten.

Another voice rose up out of the crowd, an unwelcome one calling, "I shall play for you…" that made Kavan feel sick. But the crowd had taken up the chant, drowning out Eridel's offer so that Kavan alone seemed to hear it.

"Play for us!" Such a fervent response was new; none of the cities and towns he had traveled through in Enesfel had responded this way. Here in this place where he had never been, he had found a larger audience than he had dreamed; but he could not listen to their pleas without feeling dismayed and frightened. He was a sham, not the man they thought, and he could not bear the begging for something he could not give. He was unable to break free, but he did make it to a stone bench upon which he climbed to stand above the heads of the crowd as they threatened to pull him into their midst.

In desperation, he pulled his newest gloves off and held up one twisted hand for all to see. "I cannot play!" he cried. "I cannot play for you ever!"

A stomach-turning silence fell as the crowd froze, staring at the deformed hand of the Elyri harper. Shocked murmurs ran through their midst. Some at the rear of the gathering were already falling away.

"I am not what you want, am I?" Kavan shouted bitterly. "Flee from me…you who cannot bear to see what I have become…who shun me because I have nothing to give…" The crowd drew back before his vehemence, enabling him to drop down on the bench where he pressed his face to his hands and let misery wash unchecked, refusing to look at the retreating faces. Voices dwindled, shuffling feet receding through the dusty streets, Eridel speaking from far away, songbirds gradually filling the silence, and then a hand on his shoulder, firmly reassuring in its grip. When Kavan felt strong enough to lift his head, it was to see the last of the crowd following Eridel away and Wortham squatting before him, his large hand on the bard's shoulder, the other holding both the torn cloak and the brooch.

Kavan choked and sobbed harder at the sight of those things. Once people would have done anything to obtain a small piece of him and it had made him uncomfortable to feel like a commodity. Now they discarded such things and he found he hated being abandoned as much as he hated being worshiped. "They did not…" he sniffed, "even my cloak…it is as she claimed…I am less than nothing…"

"Milord…" Wortham began to protest. But Kavan rose from the bench and pushed past, seeking an escape from the one thing he could not escape. Himself. The captain was torn between pursuing him and giving the Elyri the solitude he normally sought when upset. However, when he saw that Kavan was not seeking solitude but instead was following in the direction Eridel had gone, the Captain hurried after him. If there was to be a confrontation between the two men, it was Wortham's responsibility to lessen the damage to them both.

They found the young man in the tavern, singing a tune as he strummed the gut-strung harp. His brown hair hung in his face and his dark eyes sparkled with mirth as he performed several bawdy numbers in succession, songs of a sort Kavan never sang. At a table near the bar, the monk was engrossed in conversation with three young men, displaying the figures he had carved during their journey. Kavan, however, did not enter, but remained outside the door, listening where he could not be seen, the look on his face sullen, mournful and devastated. Wortham stayed in the doorway where he could watch both men, poised for the unpleasantness destined to erupt.

It seemed, however, that the Elyri was content to listen, to wallow in misery, until Eridel broke into a song about a great king and the bard who had befriended him. Wortham tensed with a sick feeling in his stomach, wondering how Eridel could turn Kavan's private sorrow into a song for these people who had never known either man. In the darkness near the door, Kavan trembled enough that the captain could see it, and Wortham felt sure the bard would break. Yet he stayed through the end of the song and Wortham grunted. Perhaps the song had not offended Kavan as expected; Wortham could accept that.

But when Eridel began a gloomy allegorical ballad of a bard who lost his music, however, a song Wortham believed referred to Kavan without naming him, the Elyri bolted. One instant he was there, the next when Wortham recovered from his shock and looked back, he was gone. He was unable to follow, having no idea where Kavan would go.

Furious, the captain slammed his fist into the doorframe, which did little except gain him a sore hand full of splinters. He pushed through the crowd, his heavy footsteps and large frame causing people to move out of his way. He stopped short of hauling Eridel out of the tavern mid-song, but glared at the man with disgust and rage. The young bard recognized anger on the man's face, though he naively seemed not to realize he was the cause. Rather than risk a brawl, he finished his song and indicated to the gathering that he was going to step outside for a breath of air. Wortham grabbed his arm and pulled him along until they stood in the darkness, glad that no one stopped them though he would have gladly fought anyone who tried.

"How could you?" he barked. "Are you so insensitive…?"

"Insensitive? What do you mean, milord? I was playing for…"

"You stole the crowd from Kavan!"

Fear on his face, as he was quite sure the larger man was going to strike him, Eridel said, "He cannot play…"

"He can sing. Given a chance, he might have…might realize that his musical career is not over. He might have regained his confidence. Instead, you mock his pain by singing of it, trample his losses in the dust, make him feel more alone and worthless." He spat on the ground in frustration. "I hope you are proud of what you have done."

Eridel's mouth began to quiver and there was visible wetness upon his cheeks. "I did not mean to…"

"You have turned his pain into songs to entertain the crowd who was reaching out to him!"

"Many men are immortalized in song…"

Wortham leaned closer until his face was inches away from Eridel's. "After they are dead perhaps," he snarled. "Did you not stop to think that he would hear those songs tonight and be reminded that he is…I warn you, sir. Watch yourself. I do not have the patience or the depth of forgiveness he has…and he is the world to me. The more you hurt him, the more you try me. Do not test me." He spun and stalked into the night to look for Kavan, leaving a confused, frightened, and upset Eridel gawking after him.

Kavan wound his way through the city streets, feeling whispers as if they were stares, feeling gazes as if they were daggers pricking his skin. They knew who he was. Everyone knew. Waves of pity, curiosity, amazement washed over him, bombarding him until he felt more vulnerable and raw than he could ever remember feeling. He thought he knew how it would be when people who once worshiped him as almost divine discovered the truth of his failure. He thought he knew, but he had not anticipated it being so painful. They turned away, shunned and renounced him, because he could not give the one service they wanted. Music.

They had instead turned to Eridel, a harper with less experience and, to Kavan's ear, middling talent. They drank his music as if it were the nectar that Kavan had once offered. They feasted upon Eridel with eyes and ears, giving praise as if he was the heir to what Kavan had once lauded over. There were none of those praises left for him. He wondered if this was how Owain felt when he lost the crown to Arlan.

Outside the southern gate of the walled town, a scatter of tents was erected, interspersed with colorful wagons, skinny wandering cattle, and round-bellied goats. Sun-browned people gathered around fires, dining on roasted meat and skins of wine and water. Many wore tattered clothing; some wore little, as the weather in this region was warm and pleasant. Near one wagon, a group of men played crude instruments, pipes and drums and a battered, square-bodied stringed instrument Kavan did not recognize. Their hearty voices and songs accompanied several women dancing barefoot like wild nymphs in long skirts of brightly patterned cloth. One of the women swung a tambourine, slapping it upon her plump hip to the pulse of the music. Kavan hesitantly drew closer, mesmerized by this new and unfamiliar sound, these bronzed people different from any he had met before. They were not natives of Hatu, he guessed, and he wondered if they would welcome him, a stranger and not a known musician, or at least not question his presence if he sat in their circle.

His movement forward halted when another song, familiar and sweet, reached his ears, a humming from somewhere nearby. The sound drew him to a tent where a fire burned beyond the canvas wall, silhouetting the form of a woman. She was the one humming. Now that he saw her, now that he was near enough, he realized that not only did he recognize her hypnotic song, he knew her voice. She was the one Kóráhm had sent, the woman leading his quest…the one of whom he dreamt.

She appeared to be bathing, casual languid motions moistening a cloth in a basin at her feet and then drawing it over her silhouetted form. Her back was to him. When she straightened, her hands fumbled at the top of her head until her hair fell free around her shoulders. Still humming, she picked up a brush and began to run it through her hair. Kavan was mesmerized, trapped by the sight of her. He had never been this intimately aware of a woman's curves before, the narrowness of her waist, the roundness of her hips. With a swing of her head, she turned sideways where he could view the shape of her there as well, lush, not too thin, and inviting, from the curve of her calves up to the swell of her bosom. The smoke of the fire behind her rose into the air and wrapped around her as if caressing the skin he knew had to be hot…and soft. And moist. Propping her foot upon a crate, she bent, picked up a larger cloth, and began to dry herself.

With a stifled moan, unable to look away from the roundness of her breasts, Kavan straightened, made aware of what he was doing by the longing forming in his belly. Mortified, he fled, not aware that the woman turned towards the canvas wall as if detecting his presence.

He made it to his rented room, glad none of the others were there, and threw himself upon the bed, weeping, cursing, moaning, unable to find the words he wanted for prayer. Never in his life had he seen a woman that way, never had he imagined spying upon one as she bathed, and now that he had, the images would not leave his head. That it had been her silhouette and not her actual body he had seen did little to appease his conscience. He knew she had been undressed and the knowledge was enough to fill him with shame.

His anguish passed into sleep, his sleep into dreams. Tortured, ambiguous, intangible dreams. The memory of their substance left when he woke before sunrise, but the pain in his wrists and in his ankles persisted as a reminder. There was no sign of physical damage to his body, and he ruled out having run into, or knocked against, anything that might have bruised him; there was residual pain and mental distress but no injuries. What connection the pain might have to last night's events or dreams, he did not know, but he was grateful when Wortham came for him, as it meant he did not have to be alone with those tormenting thoughts.

There was another three-day journey from Avarrou, three days of strain in the party because Eridel insisted on continuing with them, with the intention of making up for his boorish behavior. Thinking it might help, and not understanding how fragile Kavan was, he constantly asked for his opinion of songs, of his performance technique, or about the way he sang, as if showing Kavan he could teach even if he could not play, as if that would be enough. And it appeared, Wortham decided as he watched Kavan give the younger bard musical advice, that perhaps Eridel had indeed found the key to helping Kavan find peace. At times the captain caught Kavan humming an unfamiliar tune when he thought no one was listening, and he hoped it meant there was a change ahead for Kavan. His mood, however, did not appear to be better.

Despite Eridel's efforts, the captain believed it would be best if they parted company with the young bard in Enda. The gdhededhá concurred as Eridel's excessive, continual drinking and disrespect for the Faith were grating on the holy man's nerves. The gdhededhá had tried to convince Eridel to stay in Avarrou, but the young man refused, not yet ready to go his way when there were such interesting travel companions to be had. Once they reached Enda and settled in for the duration of Kavan's search for information about Saint Kóráhm, perhaps it would be easier to be free of Eridel. The young bard was likely to grow bored being in one place for too long. At least, Wortham hoped that would be the case, for the sake of Kavan's sanity.

Each night as they made camp, Kavan asked Eridel to play, and then stared at him with an intensity Wortham found disconcerting and frightening. And Kavan knew it. Yet he felt he had to hear anything Eridel could play, over and over, to drive the woman's tune, her voice, out of his head. The image of her bathing silhouette was festering on top of every other burden he carried. He brooded over it by day unless he was actively engaged in conversation, and he dreamed about it at night. The lure of her body and that song were powerful enough that they managed to keep the thoughts of disfigurement at bay. Since he could not make music to drive the negativity away as he once had, and he could not shake the frustration he felt, he hoped desperately that listening to Eridel's music would have the same effect.

❧Chapter 13❧

Enda was situated less than ten miles from Hatu's southern-most border; its location resulting in the city being overrun or destroyed every time the people living beyond the mountains pushed north in a quest for territory, water, or usable resources. Most of the sun-dried brick and clay structures were a single story and as simple in design as they could be to allow for easy rebuilding, as the residents knew reconstruction was inevitable. Why they remained, with the constant threat of destruction looming, Wortham did not understand. The countryside was not fertile enough to make most agriculture profitable except during the brief rainy season and the period of snowmelt from the mountains, but there were herds of sheep and goats dotting the scrubby landscape, giving rise to wool and cheese production, Hatu's two largest exports. Enda looked to be the hub of trade in both commodities.

He supposed if the city-dwellers relocated north, there would be less resistance to the periodic invasions, allowing the foreigners to gain an easy foothold within Hatu's borders. Enda's residents were some of the kingdom's first line of defense, a duty they persistently took to heart.

The city was atop a plateau, overlooking fields of small livestock on two sides, forest to the east, and the rolling Margotha Mountains to the south. It no longer had walls surrounding it as many of Hatu's southern cities had, which left it open to invasions and to the rushing winds that squeezed through the mountain passes. The rise up the plateau was the most protection the city had. Walls failed to protect Enda from anything, and the garrison of soldiers perpetually stationed there had as well. There seemed little reason to expend energy to rebuild the walls but the soldiers stayed.

Yet the frequent contributions of outsiders also had a positive influence, creating a diverse panorama of houses and shops and customs unlike anywhere else in the Sovereignties. The streets were lined with vendors bartering their wares, and the pungent aromas of food and drink wafting from the carts were unique to Enda. The brass pots and vases etched with intricate geometric carvings, the variety of exotically flavored foodstuffs, and the kaleidoscope of colors in the cloth for sale and in people's clothing overwhelmed the senses, encouraging Kavan to set aside his troubles long enough to take in his surroundings.

They discovered a place of worship on the western edge of the city soon after their arrival, a squat, plain building with a single tower that ended in a bulbous dome decorated with gold and blue tiles. The tower was the one structure in the city taller than a single story and within it was housed a heavy metal bell that peeled once every hour. The clerics welcomed Urian and his companions with gentility and offered housing for the duration of their stay. Fascinated by the dialect of these people and believing he could learn something from, and teach something to, the holy men there, Urian chose to remain at the náós for the remainder of the day.

Eridel declined the accommodations, separating himself from the group as soon as they reached the city. He had not said where he was going or what he was doing, though it was assumed he sought drink and female company. Wortham knew he was not alone in the hopes that the youngster decided to leave them. The captain neither accepted nor rejected the gdhededhá's offer; he would stay wherever Kavan chose to stay, even if it meant sleeping in the street. The Elyri was vague in his intentions, and as his sole goal was knowledge, he felt unable to plan anything until he had it.

But after the pair wandered the streets for several hours, Kavan bid Wortham go his way, to see what he wished of Enda, as they would likely be leaving for yet another destination within days and the opportunity to drink, to shop, to rest would be lost. Knowing that Kavan had yet to find what he sought, that pronouncement of imminent departure confused the captain, and though he hesitated to leave Kavan alone, he sensed no threats in Enda and so did as his friend asked.

Kavan wanted information from these people, and Wortham's intimidating size, even when not suited in armor, seemed a barrier in gaining the trust of anyone who might be able to help Kavan reach his goal. Encouraging the captain to explore on his own was less hurtful, he believed, then telling him he frightened people. Continuing his search alone meant that Kavan could attribute failure to no one else.

Near a cloth merchant's cart, an elderly woman spun wool into thread and curiously watched the bard approach. Her wheel stopped as he neared and she called, "Are you seeking something, young one?"

Kavan paid little attention to her until she spoke, and once she did, he realized she had been watching his approach. As she was the first to speak to him voluntarily, he squatted before her and tried to smile. "I seek information, dhábhyne. Perhaps you can help me?" He knew from experience that elders were often the best source of knowledge.

"Elyri," she cackled softly. "There have been no Elyri here in more years than I care to recall. What do you seek that brings you so far from home?"

He bowed his head, feeling unexpectedly humbled. "I recently obtained a journal which makes references to several places with which I am familiar. It was written during the days of the Great

Persecution and makes mention of a man in Enda, a man named Bhóité, who was given something of great importance…an object or knowledge, I know not which. It has been many centuries since it was written; I will not find this man, but I am interested in details about him, or directions to where I might be able to find such information." Such details might be found in the náós, but Kavan wanted to exhaust other possibilities first. It would keep him out of a place where he felt he did not belong.

"Old Bhóité? I know him, have known him for many, many years. Everyone in Enda does."

Kavan stared at her. "There is a man by this name? Surely not the same man?" Even if the original individual had been Elyri, the Persecution had occurred too many centuries ago for a man alive now to be the same man.

"No, not likely. A namesake, perhaps…or a descendant. I do not know. I see him rarely; he is older than I and does not come into the city often. He is…what is the word…a collector. Stories, artifacts, trinkets…good wine…" She laughed, a more guttural sound than her speaking voice was. "If anyone knows about this man you seek, he would likely be the source."

"Particularly if he is of the same family," Kavan said with interest. "Is it a common name?"

She shook her head. "I have heard of no other by that name; it is not a name that originates locally."

Kavan clasped her hands as best he could within his gloved ones. Though he had left his first set of gloves in Rhidam and did not need them in this warm climate, Wortham replaced them as soon as he was able. Wearing them made Kavan feel less self-conscious. "Where might I find the man, dhábhyne?"

Looking at his hands with a tender expression, she raised them to her withered lips before answering. "East, about half a day's hike from town, near the edge of the plateau. You can see his hovel from the edge of town on a clear day, and particularly on nights when he builds a bonfire.”

Quirking one eyebrow, wondering what use any man would have for a bonfire in these warm lands, Kavan nodded and murmured, “Thank you. How may I repay your aid?”

“There is no need; information is free. And for a handsome face, I could be tempted to reveal much.” She gave a nearly toothless smile. “There is urgency in you that deserves answers. However, I will tell you one more thing. Bring him a gift. Wine, an artifact, some interesting trinket. He will be more likely to receive you if you do.”

Already planning to offer something in exchange for what he needed, after her description of the man as a collector, Kavan rose and bowed. “I appreciate the advice, dhábhyne. I shall do as you suggest.”

He returned to the náós after buying a flask of the most expensive wine he could afford with the coins Wortham had given him. He could think of no trinket of those he passed that might make a suitable gift in exchange for what he sought, until the sight of Urian seated on the ground in front of the náós whittling as usual, with Wortham in a chair beside him sipping something from a ceramic jug, gave Kavan an idea.

Wortham rose to greet him with a smile and offered the jug to Kavan as the bard approached. “A drink, my lord? I am relieved to see you have returned,” he admitted sheepishly.

Assuming the jug contained wine, and wondering why Wortham offered it, Kavan scowled, waved the offer away, muttering. “I said I would. Whatever failings I have, whatever I might be, I am not a liar.”

“Milord!” Wortham’s face lost color. If this was the mood the bard was in, he would not mention he had sent a letter to Ártur. “I would never accuse you of such a thing! I was merely concerned for your…”

“I…” Kavan realized he had been unfair in his hasty words and bowed his head. He had no cause for irritability, no reason to make negative assumptions about a man who had been nothing but loyal, “Forgive me, Wortham…my judgment is unfair.”

The captain, though still concerned, gave a long breath of relief. "Forgiven, milord. Have you had success?" He thought not, as that would account for any darkness lingering over the bard's mood.

"The man I must speak to lives outside of Enda, about half a day to the east at the edge of the plateau. I will journey there in the morning. gdhededhá…I have been instructed to bring a gift in exchange for his knowledge. I can think of nothing more worthy than one of your carvings. I shall pay you for it, of course…"

"No you shall not!" the blind man exclaimed, setting aside his current work to fumble in his pack. "My work is not for pay but for the love of it alone. You share your meals, your company, and your mule with me. I think one tiny block of wood is less than a fair exchange. I shall be happy to give you one. Will this one do?"

The one he presented was a záryph with a long herald's trumpet, a messenger to k'Ádhá, carved of a soft white wood in detail that no blind man should be able to produce. His wings swept upwards as though he was hovering above the ground, and in his other hand was the Sword of Honesty. Given that Kavan was seeking a message, and the truth, the symbolism was ideally suited.

"Thank you, gdhededhá. I am sure he will admire this, especially when he learns that the artist is a devout man of the Faith."

Wortham touched Kavan's arm. "Would I presume too much if I asked to accompany you tomorrow?" The man Kavan sought might be harmless, as scholars often were, but these were strange lands and the captain was uncomfortable about allowing the bard to travel so far out of his company alone.

The captain's question brought a surge of joy that made Kavan want to embrace the man, but he did not. Even after the insulting presumptions Kavan had made, Wortham still desired to be at his side. Instead of an embrace, he bowed his head and murmured, "I would be pleased with your company, Wortham."

"I shall remain here if you do not object," said Urian. "A few days of stability sound divine to me. I will use the opportunity to learn whether Eridel has left us, and if he has not I will make every effort to encourage him."

Kavan's jaw twitched. As much as he agreed with Urian's desire, it was against his nature to push people away. "There is no need to…"

Wortham snorted. Though Kavan did not say it, it had to cause great vexation to tolerate and encourage Eridel's pursuit of music when denied that pursuit himself. "Milord, there is no need for you to suffer when he has no reason to continue with us. We are on a mission; he is not." Nor, for that matter, was Urian, but at least the gdhededhá helped around the camp and was not a constant source of irritation.

"It would be in his best interest to leave us," added the blind man. "Too much studying under a master can bury one's uniqueness. He needs freedom to grow."

Kavan rubbed his temples, knowing they were right but feeling awkward about the situation. "Speak with him if you must, gdhededhá, but do not be cruel. To endure hardship is part of my atonement, and I will accept him as long as I must. If he does not wish to go his way…we will accept his company."

Urian began to speak, but Wortham cut him off with a hand on his arm. As far as he was concerned, the matter was put to rest. With an arm around Kavan's shoulders in a brotherly fashion, he said, "Come inside. The gdhededhá are preparing the meal; I am hungry for more than travel rations tonight and you should eat as well."

❧*❧

As the old woman claimed, the home belonging to the man named Bhóité was indeed a hovel, constructed mostly of sun-bleached wooden planks, deteriorating badly in spots so that the sun, wind, and rain pushed through to the inside. Many places where the wood had rotted away were patched with thatched reeds, pieces of canvas, flattened sheets of metal that had once been breastplates and shields, or in one case, a wagon tipped on end. The wagon Kóráhm had used, Kavan wondered with curiosity as he studied the clutter around the outside of the dwelling. Something about the collection of oddities reminded him of Tíbhyan's home, and of the dwellings of other bhydáni Kavan had visited. Eclectic, disorganized, but each item served a purpose, held a memory or a tale or a bit of information only a learned individual of great age would appreciate.

There was a large charred circle in front of the hovel, far enough away that the building was in no danger from fires built there unless the frequent wind storms the area was prone to carried embers to it. The man who lived here was likely wise enough not to light his fire on nights of extreme danger. There was no fire burning, though an accumulation of sticks, logs, lumber scraps and miscellaneous broken items indicated that once night fell, there might be a fire. Around the house were scattered pieces of other wagons and furniture, the skull of a large animal, a great mound of dirt, a fallow garden plot, and other unidentifiable items. Wortham refrained from mentioning the clutter; if the disarray did not bother Kavan, the captain would resist making judgments about what he saw.

A tanned, gnarled stick of a man balanced on an unstable ladder, hunched over a task on the roof of his home. He swiped the back of his hand across his narrow nose, glanced at the mid-afternoon sun, and saw the two approaching men. He continued working until his visitors stopped at the foot of his ladder, at which time he looked down with a twisted expression that might have been normal for his ancient features. "I have no time for dawdling. There is work to be done. What do you want?"

"Are you the one known as Bhóité?" asked Kavan.

The old man climbed from his perch and tried to see inside of Kavan's hood. Hesitantly lowering it, Kavan noted the way the man's skin seemed to sag as if sliding off his skeletal frame. He truly was an ancient individual, and not Teren either. He was Elyri, which opened a wide range of possibilities about the information Kavan sought. The elder, recognizing Elyri in Kavan as well, did not hide his surprise as he studied the bard's face.

"That depends on who is asking."

An anxious tremor rolled through him. Logic told him this could not be the man spoken of in the journal, but something else suggested that it could be the same man. If that was so, had he known Kóráhm firsthand? How old was he? "I am Kavan Cliáth," he said, "and this is my dearest friend, Wortham Delamo. I come seeking knowledge."

"Cliáth." He spoke the word as if it held meaning, but his expression did not change. "Knowledge is not free," the old man muttered, in direct contradiction to what the elderly woman had said the day before.

"We brought you these in exchange." Wortham held forth the gifts when Kavan bid, as the bard had not wanted to carry them and risk dropping either from useless hands. There was a childlike grin on the man's face as he took the wine and tucked it in the crook of his arm against his body. What an Elyri wanted with wine, Kavan could not imagine; the thought of drinking it made him feel ill. The grin on the man's face turned to awe as he studied the carved záryph in his hand.

"You got this from the blind brother?"

"I…" Kavan exchanged a surprised glance with Wortham. "The gdhededhá who carved it is blind, yes. Are you familiar with him and his work?" Urian had not indicated he had been in Enda before or knew Bhóité, but then again, Kavan had not shared the man's name with the gdhededhá and had never asked him about his travels.

"Never seen him. Never seen his work. But I know." He tottered to the stoop to set his treasures on a rickety table. "Lovely gifts. Thank you. Been out of wine for a while; haven't' made it to town for more.

Still, there is much to do. If I stop to talk to everyone who comes to call, I will not get the hole in my roof patched before it rains."

"Pardon my ignorance, sir," Wortham interrupted, reasonably sure this man did not get many guests, "but it does not appear to have rained in this region in many months. Nor does it appear it will anytime soon. Why be concerned with rain? We need but a few minutes; what harm could there be in sparing them?"

Bhóité squinted and shook a bony finger in the captain's face. "Think you what he wishes to know is a simple answer to be given in a matter of minutes? Think you I do not know the weather better than you, foreigner? I have lived here most of my days. If I say it will rain, it will. And if you think I work as fast as you can…" He paused long enough to look at Kavan. "You," he pointed, "Come, assist me. Then we shall talk."

Kavan hung his head. "I would be of little use, bhydáni." He did not know if the man had ever held that title, but it seemed to Kavan he should. "My hands render me useless in most daily matters. I could not even make it up your ladder…"

An odd look crossed the old man's face and Wortham thought he was about to send them away. Apparently, Kavan thought the same, since the sadness in his green eyes deepened. "Sir," the captain quickly interjected, determined to salvage their quest and make up for any perceived rudeness. "I will be honored to repair your roof if you will supply the materials and speak with milord about the matters for which he seeks answers. Your roof will be repaired, we will have what we came for, and no time will be lost. Is that an acceptable trade?"

Smiling, Bhóité hooked his arm through Kavan's. "It is as I was told to expect. Everything you need is there," he pointed to a pile of wooden shingles and a pail of sticky substance resting near the base of the ladder. "Come inside, Cliáth. You shall assist in preparing dinner and we shall speak.

Kavan followed after a quick glance at Wortham. He had no idea if the captain had experience in repairing roofs, but he was not about to ask. As Wortham worked, the bard strove to do likewise inside. It was no easy task to assist in the meal preparations, though he did succeed in cutting several slices of bread from the loaf the man produced. A stew pot bubbled over the fire. Bhóité did not speak other than to give instructions and to mention how long it had been since he had shared a meal with guests. By the time Wortham declared his task complete, had cleaned his hands and face, and their host had returned from inspecting that work, the table was set with a fine spread of stew, wine, cheese, bread, tiny sweet cakes, and a pale orange fruit covered with a paper-thin, fuzzy skin. It seemed he was eager to impress his unexpected visitors.

"Wine?" he asked as he settled on his stool. There was not enough seating to go around, thus they improvised, taking a sturdy crate from outdoors for one seat, and a large chunk of log for another.

Kavan shook his head. "I cannot, thank you."

"One too many bad experiences, eh?" he chuckled as he filled Wortham's glass. "You must learn to consume it properly. Eat the right thing with it and you will not notice you have been drinking alcohol. Try one of these." He passed the bowl of fruit across the table.

He questioned them about their journey, questions Wortham answered since it seemed that Kavan was either distracted by the clutter around the room or was slipping into another bout of non-communicative melancholy. The meal passed slowly, with the bard's face periodically revealing despair and annoyance as it seemed Bhóité would not answer questions as promised. Once the meal was over and the table cleared, the old man went outside, ignoring his guests until his bonfire burned to his satisfaction. It gave off a bitter, pungent smell, something unrecognizable, a smell that wafted towards the house upon the evening breeze. He settled next to the fire, staring at the sparks in the air, lost in his thoughts. Kavan watched from inside, despairing that the man was mad and would not have answers, even if he agreed to talk. At length, nearing the end of his patience, he joined the ancient man beside the fire.

Wortham followed but stopped on the front step, giving Kavan the privacy he thought the two men wanted.

"Do you like the aroma?" Bhóité asked. "Oleander…difficult to come by here, but worth the expense. Don't burn it indoors though; the smoke's enough to kill a man. Deadly as they come." He grew quiet and poked at the fire with a metal rod in one hand, a smoking pipe in the other.

"Milord…" Kavan started, his voice stretched thin as he watched the apparently poisonous smoke rise into the sky.

Bhóité laughed. "You have more patience than I expected, my friend," he said, offering his pipe; Kavan rejected it. "Some would have pushed for answers long ago; others would have left or responded in anger. I admire that you have done neither. You are as I thought you should be when you came. What is it you wish to know? Mind you, I may not have your answers…and you may not like the ones I do have."

"Chances a man must take for knowledge and understanding. I was told you would be the best source for the knowledge I seek, thus I was willing to wait for it…though I admit my patience grew thin."

"Any man's would," Bhóité said. "Tell me what you seek."

Kavan stared into the fire, wondering where to begin. "I recently obtained two journals written during the Great Persecution. One was by a woman, the other by her suitor. He seemed to be a man of tremendous wisdom, charisma, and fortitude. He discovered a náós below the Enesfel palace…a holy place I have stood in myself. I knew when I discovered it that something was not right within its walls…but until I read this man's journal, I had never imagined it had been…"

"Defiled?"

Kavan nodded, wondering how this man knew as much as he seemed to or if he was merely well-adept at leaps of logic. "The defiler was the brother of the male author…a man responsible for a number of sacrifices upon the altar in that place. The author wanted to right the wrong, to cleanse the temple, but claimed he could not, that it would be up to his descendants to complete the task. I have no knowledge who this man was, or how to find any descendants he might have, but I feel compelled to undertake this cleansing, both for my own redemption and for Enesfel to have peace. The author implied he had imparted instructions, or tools, for the cleansing with a man in Enda, a man bearing your name, a man named Bhóité."

"And you think I am that man?"

"You cannot be that man. The journal and those events occurred over two thousand years ago. The Bhóité of the journal would be long dead. But you bear his name and I hope you are heir to the information I need as well as to the name. I have no recourse but to hope."

The old man squinted, a shift in the night breeze causing the smoke to blow towards them, making his eyes water. Kavan also blinked away the sting but as he was holding his breath, waiting for a reply, he was spared the burn of smoke in his lungs. With a sneeze, the ancient fellow nodded and patted Kavan's knee. "I have what you seek, or at least part of it. I was beginning to believe no one would ever come for it."

"Will you share it with me?" Kavan asked eagerly, the first spark of light coming into his eyes in weeks.

"Only a blood relative of the defiler may cleanse that space," Bhóité cautioned him.

Kavan nodded solemnly, understanding that condition, despite the disappointment it carried. "Then perhaps, if you will tell me what there is to know, I can find the man or woman who must do this. I am convinced I must try. Please…tell me what you know. Direct me that I may complete this quest and find redemption."

The man's hand upon his knee squeezed with surprising strength. "You are determined. That is good. Determination you will need if you are to see this to its fruition. If I share my knowledge with you, you must swear you will do everything that needs to be done."

Kavan met Wortham's gaze as the soldier finally joined them at the fire. To accept this task would mean returning to Rhidam sooner than expected. It might mean his death. But he did not feel he had a choice. Events had brought him thus far for a reason. Wortham nodded, accepting the quest as well, willing to follow Kavan through this as he had everything else. That support made Kavan square his shoulders before looking again at Bhóité. "I swear on my life, for what that is worth, I will not rest until it is finished."

The look that crossed Bhóité's face spoke of disappointment, or perhaps pity, before he sighed and said, "Very well. There are items you will need…Diwi…Orec…water from a newly purified spring or well." He wiped his eyes of the smoke and explained. "Diwi is a spice common enough in the southern lands, used in cooking occasionally but most frequently in embalming and the preparation of the dead. It comes into Hatu via traders, but the majority is purchased by the royalty and nobility for funerary rites. To buy it here would take a great deal of money and royal approval, if you are lucky enough to find it. To buy it at its source would be much simpler."

Kavan nodded, wondering if he could obtain it from Prince Espen in Natrona. That, however, might lead back to Princess Diona, and he was in no way ready to face her. "Go on," he murmured.

"Orec oil is derived from a desert plant, something you have already encountered as it is the poison associated with the daggers you call Coryllien."

Wortham had been paying marginal attention to the details presented, not believing the conversation applied to him, but his head snapped around at the mention of the Coryllien daggers and a chill raked up his spine. This man knew entirely too much about Kavan and it made the captain nervous. Memories of the events surrounding the Coryllien dagger were still painful for both soldier and bard. However,

Kavan's face revealed none of the trepidation Wortham felt, so the captain did his best to be calm and listen more closely.

"Where can it be obtained?" the bard asked.

"It comes also from the south. As you can imagine, it is illegal to possess it here, for obvious reasons, though if one goes through the proper…or rather improper…channels, it can be found." The sage grinned. "Again, it will probably be cheaper and easier for you to obtain nearer to its source. As for the water…I cannot tell you where to find that, as I am not privy to what water sources k'Ádhá chooses to purify and when."

"Is there more? What do I do when I have obtained them?"

"Most of what you need," Bhóité said enigmatically, "you already possess…and you will know when it is time. In order to perform the rite originally used to bless the room, you will require all three pieces of the staff and the chalice. These items were dispersed after the initial blessing to keep them safe."

Assuming that the mentioned staff referred to further pieces of the one Kavan had found clutched in Dawid Coryllien's hands, he asked, "Dispersed? To where? What chalice do you speak of?"

The old man shrugged his shoulders. "No one living knows where they were taken. It is said that the staff and chalice were constructed by the phae k'kairá and that they are the ones who consecrated the sites. Some claim that to possess all four items will give a man a powerful hold over those who created them, thus the reason they were dispersed. The k'kairá alone know if this is true. I have heard the one called Coryllien obtained a piece or two of the staff…"

Kavan's breath caught as Wortham asked, "A gold staff?" It seemed impossible that Kavan might already possess part of the puzzle.

"I have not seen it, but so says the tales."

"We found the resting place of Coryllien…I knew it was him upon contact," Kavan said in a low tone. "He had the bottom portion of a gold staff clenched in his hands, but not its upper portion. I secured it, and the dagger he held, in a place of safekeeping. No one else knows where they are. I know he is rumored to have participated in the sacrifices of men, women, and children, and the negative energy in his resting place was similar to that of the náós beneath the castle. I have wondered if there was a connection. I…his thoughts were strong even in death. He called me brother. Traitor. Was he the defiler? Did he have a brother?"

Bhóité grinned as his eyes glazed over for several minutes. It was a look Kavan was told he wore when the Sight came over him and he wondered what the man was seeing. In a faraway, singsong voice, with no change of expression, he said, "The náós may be cleansed on a single night of the year, the night of its original cleansing; I do not know what night that is. Miss it and it will be another year before you may try again. That you possess the dagger will strengthen the cleansing, if you are able to proceed that far. As for the chalice and the rest of the staff, I do not know where they might be."

Disappointed, but undaunted, feeling confident he would not have been brought this far without being able to proceed, Kavan asked, "Is there anyone who might? Anywhere you would suggest I look?"

"Go south. South is your best chance of finding the items you seek. Speak to the locals. Ask for the whereabouts of k'ílshwythnec."

"k'ílshwythnec?" The word was High Elyri, and it surprised him that any outside of Elyriá might speak the language, or that any of the words might exist in the lands his ancient ancestors had once journeyed through. The word meant female prophet, and if such a person existed in those distant lands, she must surely be Elyri. That peaked Kavan's interest.

"Among the people of the south, she is reported to possess the knowledge of the ages, a great seeress and fount of great power. I have not met her. Not many have. She entertains few but dispenses wisdom via messengers. From the tales I hear, if anyone can point you in the direction you must go, it will be she. I do not know where to find her, but beseech her people and they may. Even if you do find her, she may not see fit to tell you." He grinned impishly. "Those with great knowledge are like that, burdened to know that there are some things they must keep hidden, even from those who seek to know."

Kavan knew that from experience and suspected he was confronting that now with Bhóité, else the man would tell him many more details than he was sharing. How many times had Kavan learned something via the Sight or otherwise and needed to keep it hidden to protect others? He prayed it would not be the case this time, however. He felt his cause was just and righteous and he did not believe he needed protection.

It was quiet at the campfire. There was a look of purpose on Kavan's face, a glimmer of hope in his eyes that Wortham was pleased to see. Knowing where their next destination would be, a town or city somewhere beyond the Margotha Mountains, meant more travel ahead but the captain did not mind.

"It is too late tonight for you to start back," Bhóité finally said. "I have no spare rooms, but you may stay if you do not mind hard floors."

"After repairing a roof, I can sleep anywhere there is shelter over my head. Milord?" Wortham was already getting to his feet.

"I will follow shortly," Kavan said. He had one more question for the man beside him, one that would not allow him to rest until he had an answer. He was grateful Wortham did not feel the need to loiter or wait for him. After he heard the creak of the door hinges, he focused on the sage and asked, "May I ask how you came by this information?"

The old man stretched his thin legs with a mysterious smile. "It was given to me many decades ago; I was told to keep it until the one who needed it came for it."

Perplexed, Kavan asked, "You knew that someone would be me?"

"I knew what to look for in the person seeking it. I did not know who it would be, but you fit the requirements in every possible way."

Kavan thought it best not to ask what those requirements were. Men who met the requirements of prophecy were better off not knowing. "Who gave you this information? The original Bhóité?"

"I received it from he who was first to know. Kóráhm di Curnydhá."

"Kór…" Kavan stammered. The rest of the name was unfamiliar, but he doubted there could be more than one man with that name. No one in Elyriá gave that name to their children, and to his knowledge, he was the only one to carry that name as his second. "The man who was first to…that would make you…it is not…Saint Kóráhm?"

The possibilities that presented made no sense.

But Bhóité had risen, a satisfied cat expression upon his face that indicated he would speak no more on the subject. He entered the hovel, his movement that of a man whose burden was lighter, content to leave the fire burning. Kavan remained where he was, too stunned for coherent thought, until long after the fire had burned itself out.

❧Chapter 14❧

"How could a whole family be abducted?" King Hagan asked with vexation, aware that behind him, his sister was staring at gdhededhá Claide who had been present when the letter from Wexel arrived.

"This says nothing about abduction…" the gdhededhá started.

Diona cut him off. "How else would you explain it, dedhá? A peasant family would not have the means to move their home, and if it was their intent to relocate, they would take their few possessions with them. Possessions are important to those who have little. They would not leave everything they own behind; it does not make sense."

"Precisely why Duke Ethelwyn brought this to our attention," agreed the inquisitor, his sideways glance at the princess telling her he was investigating the dedhá as requested, now that he witnessed firsthand a glimpse of why she thought the man suspect. "Shall I look into it?" The man's attitude might be innocent. It also might not be.

The young King looked skeptical. "Can you do that without pulling resources from your other endeavors? I mean…the family was missing for five days before the Duke sent the letter. How likely is it you can find anything now? Perhaps they have returned home…"

"Or are dead," his sister snorted, giving Caol no chance to reply.

"Diona! That is unnecessary. Of course they aren't dead. Lord Dugan, do what you must. I am curious to learn what has happened."

Rather than speak, Caol bowed and retreated from the room. Claide looked about to say something, locked eyes with the princess, and changed his mind before following the inquisitor. The King groaned and sank into the nearest chair with an expression of frustration. "Maybe they did not like Duke Ethelwyn and left for another estate…" he said hopefully.

"Or maybe the Duke killed them and we're sending Caol on a fruitless expedition."

Hagan scowled. "Always with death. You do not believe that."

"No, I don't," his sister admitted, "Ethelwyn has been a good and loyal subject, known to be kind but firm with his people. But nor do I believe they abandoned everything they owned and walked away from their home. Neither do you, otherwise you would have asked Lord McGrannis to run a census of landowner holdings to find where they went…rather than have Lord Dugan look into it."

"What more can I do? We have to know. If there were a way to prevent these crimes, I would do it, but there isn't. We seem able to do nothing more than punish people after the fact, death for death, and I don't like it. We're not solving anything."

She took his hand and sighed. It was mildly reassuring that Hagan at least recognized the possibility of a crime having been committed in the peasants' disappearance. "No…we're not…but we're trying. It's all we can do. Like you said, this has to stop."

Hagan nodded, more uncertain that he was up to the task of ruling, of deciding the fate of the people, of issuing commands to his staff. "How?" he asked with fearful eyes.

Unlike many other times in his life, Diona had no answers for him.

❧*❦

Kavan and Wortham returned to Enda late in the afternoon, their travel hindered by a heavy downpour that swept out of the mountains with little warning. The air had been oppressive as they left Bhóité's company, a heaviness that had little to do with impending rain. Kavan departed the old Elyri's presence with the certainty he would not see the man again, and he wondered if he should remain longer to learn as much as this sage could teach him. But he could not stay. There were tasks he had to complete, and Bhóité commanded him to go.

They arrived at the náós, cold and wet, to find that Eridel was seen briefly with a young woman on his arm. He left after learning Kavan was not at the náós and had not been seen since. When Kavan revealed his intention to continue south through the stony mountain passes, it was with the hopes of dissuading the gdhededhá from joining them too. He and Wortham would travel faster alone. But the prospect of traveling into unexplored territory and making new converts excited the blind man and he was eager to continue with them.

Since what money they possessed would be useless once they passed outside of the Five Sovereignties, Wortham used what remained to purchase a second mule and as much food and supplies as the animal would carry. The gdhededhá giving them shelter would provide water before their departure in the morning. Once they left Enda, they would be on their own for provisions.

After the rain stopped and he was dry again, Kavan took the opportunity to spend his final hours exploring Enda's streets, protecting his identity but speaking to anyone who cared to approach as he sought items of interest or tidbits that might offer direction or healing. There was no pity here for his hands because no one knew him. No one had reason to think of him as anything other than a traveler, albeit an unusual looking one.

"A word, milord?"

He did not recognize the woman who fell into step beside him; she was nearly his height and dressed in well-fitted armor. Taken aback by her attire, as no woman in Enesfel wore armor to his knowledge, he stopped to look at her more closely. Her hair was pulled out of sight beneath her visorless helm, but her face was visible. Her gray-blue eyes were a little large for her otherwise noble features and the sword she carried on her hip appeared larger than she would be expected to wield. Upon her back was slung a longbow and a quiver of arrows. Though he did not recognize her, there was something about her, perhaps her strange attire, which Kavan found alarmingly attractive.

But she had approached him with a question, and he saw no reason to be rude, despite his impulse to flee. "How may I aid you, milady."

She smiled, liking the neutral timbre of his voice. "It is more a matter of how I might aid you. I heard someone near the náós discussing a journey into the southlands in search of k'ílshwythnec. You are part of that expedition, are you not?"

"I have spoken to no one…" he started, his guard immediately up because someone might know his business. He quickly realized, however, that Wortham and Urian might have been discussing the trip, and thus anyone could have overheard them. He nodded and replied, "That is my intent."

With no change in mien, she said, "I desire to join your quest."

That appeal caught him off guard. "Why? It might be unsafe."

"For a woman or for you?" she asked with a light laugh. "Do you think I am dressed thus in jest? I wield this sword better than many men. I do not fear trouble. I do not fear you."

Perhaps you should, he thought as his eyes inadvertently traveled down over her armor. "I do not think…" he choked, forcing himself to look back into her face, "it would be wise…"

She lifted her chin defiantly. "Do not judge me hastily. I hunt as well as cook. I am familiar with the lands through which you will travel; I know what is safe to eat and what is not. I know the people, their languages, and their customs. If you allow, I can lead you to k'ílshwythnec and assist in finding whatever you seek. I shall keep myself apart if the presence of a woman is distasteful." She relaxed her shoulders a little before she continued, some of the steam having gone out of her words, "I know little of your customs, but I will do my utmost to be inoffensive. You shall not need to be concerned about protecting me. I am not afraid to defend myself."

Head cocked, he looked into her eyes before beginning to walk, partially with the hopes of escaping the tingle of familiarity in the back of his mind that he could not place but which made every nerve in his body prickle. He had no doubts her words were true, that she would be an asset to the party, but it was her effect on him he was worried about. He liked this woman. He knew that already. He liked everything about her…perhaps too much.

She fell into step beside him.

"We have no provisions for anyone else…" he said lamely, knowing it was a poor excuse, also feeling that she could surely sense he was on the verge of giving in despite his protests.

"I shall bring my own supplies, as well as any I think might be needed with the people we meet." She smiled, still beside him, matching his strides with ease. "Is this a pact then, milord?"

Kavan groaned, certain he was going to regret this decision, and asked, "What is it you hope to gain from traveling with us?"

"Your acquaintance," she said with a warm expression that made him shiver with unusual expectation. "And a little adventure. It has been many years since I have had something of this nature to do. I think this journey is precisely what I seek."

"What you offer is logical, and if you can provide for yourself…" He let his voice trail off as his distracted thoughts followed in a direction he did not want to go. Shaking his head, he added, "We will depart at dawn from the náos. If you do not change your mind, be there. We will not wait."

She grinned and offered her hand to seal the deal, but he did not take it. "I will be there, probably before you are ready to depart." Her hand dropped to her side and she turned down a side street towards her destination. When he could not see her any longer, Kavan realized he had not asked her name.

As promised, she was waiting at the náós door with a sturdy dappled gray horse and wooly burro loaded with an assortment of supplies when Kavan, Wortham, and Urian emerged before the sun broke over the horizon. Dressed in the same helmet and armor, she smiled at Kavan in welcome, a look that made Wortham glance at the bard curiously. Kavan ignored him. "This is gdhededhá Urian…and my dearest friend, Captain Wortham Delamo." He had mentioned to them that he had found a guide who spoke the languages of the people of the south. He had not mentioned that the guide was a woman.

"Of the Káliel guard. I have heard of you, Captain. Your stature matches your reputation." She shook his hand and smiled wider at his surprise. He had not expected anyone here to know of him. "And it is a pleasure to make the acquaintance of a man of Faith, gdhededhá."

"A lady," the monk said as he gave a partial bow from the back of his mule. "It will be a pleasure to have you amongst us."

"Not just a lady," Wortham said with a smile nearly as wide as hers, "A lady with a sword. Can you use that?"

"Please, call me Orynn." Kavan latched on to her name and locked it in his memory to never forget it…or her. "Would you care to put me to the test, Captain?" she challenged.

Laughing, he shook his head. "I think not. I would like to proceed with this journey uninjured…and I would not like it to be said I have harmed, or been harmed by, a lady. I will do you the courtesy and honor of taking you at your word."

"Has there been no sign of Eridel?" asked Urian.

"None," replied the captain; Kavan gave a long sigh of relief.

"He cannot accuse us of leaving him if he does not let us know where to find him and is not here when we leave. Shall we be off?"

"Yes," Kavan said hastily. He had a mission to complete, and he made no efforts to hide that he wanted to be rid of the young bard.

They began climbing the Margotha Mountains within two hours of leaving Enda's plateau. Orynn asked for no special treatment and refused to ride when Urian bid her to, despite the fact that Kavan believed her armor to be cumbrous and heavy, not to mention hot and uncomfortable. Her horse, a gentle beast despite its size, served as a pack animal, and since Kavan and Wortham were both on foot, she saw fit to travel likewise. Her strides matched Wortham's with whom she spent much of the morning chatting about combat styles and experience. Kavan watched and listened with a mixture of irritation and interest, wanting to know more about her yet unwilling to ask questions. He was certain he would make a fool of himself. He could not shake the growing certainty that he should know her, but no matter how he tried, he could not place her face or voice.

When they made camp that evening, Orynn erected a tent away from the others, a means of providing privacy from her male companions, especially the one most uncomfortable with her company. She disappeared into it while Wortham built a fire and helped Urian prepare their meal. Kavan was brushing down the animals, the one task he had mastered this far with an extraordinary amount of effort, when Orynn emerged from her tent and joined him.

"Have you cause to regret my company yet, milord?"

A shiver raced through him at her tone; when he turned his head to look at her, he dropped the brush and stumbled backward until he tripped over a large stone and lay on the ground, staring with undisguised panic. Her auburn hair was loose about her shoulders, not as dark of shade as he had thought, and instead of armor, she wore a pale blue tunic-like gown. Her gray eyes did not appear quite as large with her hair framing her heart-shaped face, a face he recognized with the helmet no longer serving as a mask. The sweet huskiness of her voice was intimate, familiar, and made the blood run hot in his veins.

By the heavens, he thought with a mixture of horror and amazement. She was more breathtaking than he had imagined. "You…"

She smiled, thankfully not laughing at his predicament, and retrieved the fallen curry brush. "It has taken you this long to recognize me?" she asked, offering her empty hand to help him to his feet. "Should I take exception to that?"

He crabbed away from her. "I…when you have shown yourself before…it has not been in armor…" he croaked, recalling without wanting to that one of those times she had been wearing no clothing at all. "And your face has always been…vague in form…hidden…" Except in that dream of coupling at the foot of Kóráhm's shrine, another rush of memories that came unbidden and caused his skin to flush. "You are the one to lead…"

Dropping her hand, she laughed with affectionate warmth rather than ridicule. "You know I am. You also know the injury to your hands does not offend me, milord, but if you do not desire help to rise…"

Once she moved away, he managed to struggle to his feet with audible relief. "Why did you not reveal yourself when you asked to accompany us?"

"A test of sorts," she shrugged. "It was necessary that you include me because you wanted to, not because I have been leading you. If I had revealed myself and then asked, you would have felt compelled to bring me. It is more fun this way."

For whom, he wanted to ask, examining her aura, completely perplexed by it. "You are not…Teren?" She was certainly not full Elyri. He would know if she was.

She smiled, her expression vague. "So many questions. I am alive, if that is what you are asking. I am neither spirit nor záryph. I carry Teren and Elyri blood…I do not know precisely what that makes me."

That did not explain her ability to manifest in his dreams, and as he was afraid of that knowledge, of letting her know he felt her there, he chose to let the matter drop. "Why come now…and not before?"

"To assist you, as I said. It has been a great undertaking on my part to be allowed to do this, but I know it is the right thing to do. It took much effort to join you, any sooner would have been impossible. Time is of the essence, and without my aid, I fear you may fail. And my investment…well…they had no recourse. They had to allow this."

"They? Who? What investment?" He did not doubt that he could not succeed without her; Kóráhm had sent her for a reason, because he believed Kavan needed her assistance. That was good enough.

Again, she smiled and Kavan noticed at that moment the way the moonlight glinted in her eyes. Urian called them to dine before she could answer and Orynn joined the men at the fire, glancing impishly over her shoulder to where Kavan remained, his expression puzzled and unsettled.

He could not make his feet budge to follow. His entire body, from head to foot and particularly in the middle where she affected him most, was engulfed in the fire of one realization after another. Orynn was the woman who had led him here, the woman on the bow of the boat, on the beach, the woman he dreamed of holding and loving as a man should love a woman…the woman he had watched bathing behind a canvas tent wall. Being near her now, he knew the truth was more intoxicating than any alcohol he had ever consumed, or any dream he had known, and possibly as deadly as either, he thought with a moan. Knowing her identity explained why he was drawn to her when they met the day before. As he watched, memories of his dream filled him again, accompanying the throbbing in his belly, the recollections of how he had imagined it would be to touch and smell her, the passion and joy she inspired in a single dream. She may have been a dream then, but the smell of her was the same, and she was here, flesh and blood, radiance and sweetness…and he wanted her.

That realization had him drowning in physical sensations he did not believe he had the willpower to suppress. He could not bring himself to be near her, to go to the fire; instead, he hastened further into the darkness to wrestle the emotions and desires that threatened to control him.

"Milord?" Wortham, a bowl of broth and hunk of bread in hand, followed Kavan away from the camp. "What has happened? Did the lady say something…?" He assumed it had to be her since it had been a conversation between the two that led to the bard's abrupt retreat.

"Yes…no…" Kavan shook his head, obviously conflicted. "It is nothing she has said or done."

Then it was because she is a lovely woman, the Captain deduced, having seen similar reactions in men and recalling what Ártur had told them about Kavan and Gabrielle. "If you would prefer she not travel with us, I will see to it that she is taken care of in the next village."

"That will not be necessary," Kavan added perhaps too hastily. As much as she made him uncomfortable, he also could not imagine leaving her, now that she was here. And Kóráhm had sent her.

"Good. I suspect she would not be easy to be rid of," the captain said with a laugh. "Besides, I like her, milord. She has an unusual aura…and I think she will prove helpful…"

"Yes," the bard conceded, casting a side-glance towards the fire where Orynn admired Urian's figurines and laughed at something he said. Kavan wondered if her cheer would be contagious, if it might likewise affect him.

"Are you coming to the fire to sleep?" Wortham asked with a stifled yawn as he gave Kavan his meal.

"I…think not…" he muttered. The thought of sleeping anywhere near that woman was frightening. "Unless you think I should."

Wortham shook his head. "Yours is the first watch; you may keep it where you wish. I trust you." He started towards the fire and added over his shoulder, "I will do what I can to see that the lady does not disturb you."

The variety of things the captain might mean by that made Kavan shiver and blush. He was grateful it was dark.

❧Chapter 15❧

Princess Diona gaped at gdhededhá Claide from the rear of Hes á Redh Náós. Normally she sat in the front, in the area reserved for the king, his family, visiting guests, and dignitaries. It was situated to the left of the altar, slightly elevated to allow the faithful to see their monarch and his family in attendance. The princess was the sole member of the royal house here tonight and she had not wanted to call attention to herself by sitting alone in that place. Hagan was hosting a Dhágdhuán Feast Eve ball, his first official event as king. His advisors were in attendance, as were several Lords and Ladies of the realm. The mood had been too festive for the princess, and after watching Hagan and Gaelán vie for Asta's attention, Diona felt it necessary to leave the castle. Her brother's maneuverings looked too much like her own, a painful reminder of her words to Kavan and the devastation on his face before he fled Rhidam.

Dhágdhuán's Feast Eve did not feel the same without Kavan's music to mark the occasion. He composed new pieces to celebrate the birth of the founder of their Faith each year, music more uplifting than anything heard in any other Gathering. This year, for the first time in her life, his music was not heard and she was the one to blame.

Arriving late to the Gathering was another reason she remained at the rear of the náós. Denyan and Belda were with her; she did not fear for her safety but she knew that having attendants was the proper course for one of her station, particularly at this hour of the evening. Those around her whispered, and soon she knew the whole congregation would be aware she was here as one of them rather than separated from them by an impenetrable divide of steel and stone. Without intending to, she realized she might have committed a savvy political maneuver. Allowing a small smile, she settled onto the bench, to enjoy the Gathering as much as the uncomfortable wood and memories of Kavan allowed.

gdhededhá Claide, however, remained unaware of her. If he had known that one of the Lachlans was listening to his sermonizing, she doubted he would speak so ferociously against magic and sorcery. Or perhaps he would have, but he might have tempered the undertones of anti-Elyri sentiment that fired his words. Not that he mentioned the Elyri specifically, and to those not paying close attention, it might not have been noticeable. But Diona noticed. As did the k'gdhededhá, she realized, and gdhededhá Tusánt and Rankin, all three of whom were behind the altar, behind Claide with paling faces as the man they thought they knew continued to speak. gdhededhá Valgis, in the front pew, had his back to her. Did he notice, she wondered? Did anyone else hear the hatred? Did they care?

No one would be able to prove Claide's anti-Elyri sentiments, of course. His wording was too vague to offer solid evidence of such beliefs, and surely he knew that such a position would put him on the outs with his fellow gdhededhá and the Lachlan house. But after recent events in Enesfel, and Rhidam in particular, anyone with interest could twist his words to imply that Elyri were demons in earthly form, waiting for the opportunity to destroy every Teren with whom they interacted. If the princess, who did not believe those notions to be true, heard such implications in his speech, how could those whose beliefs leaned in that direction fail to hear it?

She had been suspicious enough before to ask Caol to watch him. She was more mistrustful of his motives now. Words were not deeds, but they could, and often did, precipitate action, and if he was inclined to utter such hatred publically, even in a couched manner, what were the odds that there was suspicious behavior to support them?

As the procession to end the Gathering passed down the aisle, Diona pulled back amongst the common folk, hiding behind her escorts' bulk, determined that Claide should not know she had heard his words. She hoped he would reveal his intentions without her manipulations. The k'gdhededhá, however, did notice her loose ebony tresses amongst the covered heads of the common folk in their shawls, winter hats, and bonnets, and he nodded to her. He understood why she hid.

Claide, Valgis, and Rankin blessed the parishioners as they left for the night. Jermyn slid away, unnoticed by the others as he often retreated into the thóres to attend other Faith business, and he beckoned the princess to follow. Her escorts went with her; if their group movement attracted Claide's attention, Diona did not see it. In his private room, Jermyn closed the door and paced as furiously as his bulk and the small space allowed.

"Tell me I was not the only one to hear that," he demanded.

Diona clenched her fists at her sides. "That depends on what you believe you heard. I will say, I believe Rhidam will see a dramatic increase in anti-Elyri incidents in the weeks ahead."

"I can't believe I…that he would…such slander…from a man of the Faith…on this night. Claide can assuage his guilt by claiming that people will take his words out of context…but I won't believe that for a moment. That's exactly what I heard…but how to prove it…"

"We were not the only ones to interpret his message this way. I am certain dedhá Tusánt and dedhá Rankin both did. The problem will not be finding people who heard it but finding people who would willingly admit it to you or to the King. He must be prevented from speaking thus again."

"Yes, he must. I will speak to him immediately," Jermyn growled. There were no laws, ecclesiastical or otherwise, to prevent one from voicing an opinion, but there was common practice, there was moral justice to consider, and Claide, in Jermyn's view, had undermined all manner of decency and every tenant of the Faith with his slander. His sermon had been but a twisting of the written word, the accepted teaching of the Faith, and such misrepresentation and misleading speech could not be condoned.

"Is it wise?" she asked, though it was precisely what she wanted. "As you said, he will deny malicious intent…and what good will an admonition do?"

The k'gdhededhá swallowed the tirade meant for Claide and continued pacing. He had always liked this woman, who seemed to have the heart of a leader, despite the mistakes she had made of late. When the answer presented itself to him, he suspected she had already thought of it. "I will confer with k'gdhededhá Dórímyr and ask for his recommendation, and request that Claide be defrocked if it is possible. I hate to consider such a measure for a first offense, but I think I've known it was coming to this. Something has brewed within him for a long time…but I never expected this. It may be the best way to prevent the innocent from being hurt. I will need a letter from you and from the other gdhededhá present tonight, concerning his inappropriate words. It may do no good, but I think we must try."

"I will get it to you at once," she agreed readily.

"I must still speak to him…give him opportunity to recant, to let him know that if this attitude does not change, action will be taken."

Diona frowned. "That would let him know we…"

"It would let him know that I do not condone his speech, nothing more. I do not need to mention anything else, nor suggest that anyone else interpreted his lesson as I did. As his superior, it is my duty to keep him on the path; to suspect him and say nothing is to accept his errors as truths. Speaking to him is the proper thing to do. If he is to face the stripping of status before the Faith and k'Ádhá, he must know why he is being punished, must be given the opportunity to reform. Otherwise, there is nothing even k'gdhededhá Dórímyr can do."

The princess understood the way political wheels worked, even within the Faith, but she did not like the delay it would cause in resolving a situation that had yet to reach fruition. "May I discuss this with Lord Dugan? He has been investigating the anti-Elyri incidents and might find this information helpful." She decided not to mention that the inquisitor was already investigating Claide at her request.

Jermyn rubbed his temples. It was difficult to accept or believe that one of his subordinates could be the root of such acts or beliefs, and he hoped that Claide's words were not mirrored by equally appalling acts. "By all means, tell him. If Claide is connected to any of these deeds, or k'Ádhá forbid, responsible for the attack on Lord Cliáth or anyone else, I want him punished. Regardless of what form that punishment takes."

❧*❧

The marble hall of Owain Lachlan's home was garnished with evergreen boughs, dozens of white tapers, and a single wreath of needle branches suspended over the red sun inlaid in the center of the floor. As was his custom, Owain invited as many people as would fit in his hall to attend the feast spread in the room. Merchants, peasants, farmers, and beggars: everyone was allowed to enter and dine until the food was no more, an opportunity that few in Fiara passed up. Piran was currently in the crowd playing with a group of children and Owain made no effort to restrain him, though he made certain the boy was watched over by guards at all times. He wanted his son to have contact with those beneath his station, particularly other children. Both were things Owain had been deprived of as a boy, and he was aware of how that had influenced his choices and actions over the years. He wanted Piran to suffer none of his prejudices.

That also extended to prejudices against Elyri, but thus far Owain had been unable to persuade any to enter his employment. Whether that was due to something about him personally or because his estate lay in an area that had once been part of Neth…a notorious hot spot of Elyri hatred…Owain could not say. Since Piran could not be exposed to them here, Owain took every opportunity to take the boy to Rhidam, the best source of Elyri exposure Owain could think of outside of Elyriá itself.

Watching his people revel in gaiety, he sighed and rubbed the ridge between his eyes. As Fiara grew, this event became more expensive. He considered not hosting it this year, considered finding a different gift for his people. After weeks of thought, however, he decided to host the banquet one more time. They might forgive him for finding a different way to celebrate this occasion, but this affair was as much for his benefit as it was for theirs. It was the best way he knew to ensure he would not be alone for Dhágdhuán's Feast Eve.

It had been especially vital in those years when Piran spent the feast days with his mother on Káliel, or in the years before Piran was born when Muir had not been with him. Perhaps because he had been forced out of Enesfel twice, perhaps because he had been dethroned and lost esteem in the eyes of the people he had ruled, perhaps because he had few people he felt comfortable enough with to call friends. Whatever the case, he had developed an intense dislike for solitude and tried to keep as many people around him as he could.

Whenever Kavan and Wortham came to Fiara, Owain did not feel that loneliness. His sons eased that burden as well. But Muir now lived on Káliel with his wife, Kavan and Wortham were on a pilgrimage in lands far away, and Owain felt isolation creeping in again. This celebration, with its feasting, music, and dancing, was necessary this year; he did not think he could face the turn of this year alone.

❧*❧

He awoke in agony, a scream forming but unable to pass from his lips. Struggling to rise revealed what he already knew; his wrists were pinned to the ground by a crushing unseen force, the source of the pain that speared through his body like bolts of flame. He might have believed it a result of his injury and disfigurement, or at least residual memories of the attack that had stolen the use of his hands, if not for the identical spearing pain in his ankles. A glance from side to side at his hands showed nothing except that his arms were stretched above his head. Struggling to arch back to see more, trying to get free and finding he could not, he choked back a strangled, frustrated cry.

"Milord Cliáth?"

Orynn knelt near him, her hair in her face, her lips pursed in a pout as she examined him for injury. The pale tunic she wore pooled around her knees, near enough to his head that Kavan felt as if he would drown in it. He would escape her if he could, but he was unable to move.

He had not talked with her since learning who she was, though he had, at least, been civil. Closing his eyes, trying to avoid the longing her proximity birthed, he groaned as the phantom pains reached their pinnacle. Her fingers brushed hair from his forehead before stroking gently over his cheek and a shiver ran through him, chased by the memories of Diona's touch that rushed to fill the void the pain created. Orynn's touch diverted his focus from the pain in his arms and legs, however, until gradually it lessened to a dull throb and then ceased. As soon as he was certain the pain had passed, he turned his face away from her touch and attempted to flex his limbs. Successful, he inched away, rubbing his wrists to feel for damage.

"You appear uninjured," she said in a tone too neutral to reveal what she thought or felt.

"It is a bad omen. Perhaps," he looked into the darkness, "Ártur has been injured. Or King Hagan." He did not know if that peculiar link that had caused him to feel Arlan's injuries had passed to his son, but the repeating nature of these pains led him to suspect it had no connection to the Lachlans. This was dreamborn, and a thing dreamborn had no earthly cause. Not knowing for certain, however, his thoughts wandered into speculations of the most horrific sort.

"It was a dream, milord. Nothing more."

He refused to believe that. "Dreams do not cause physical pain…and even my dreams I have learned to heed. This has come to me before during recent weeks…though it was not this intense."

He had not spoken of it, had not shown any indication of nightmares or any traces of lingering physical pain, but as he seemed adept at masking discomfort, his hiding it did not surprise her. "Can you recall it? The dream?"

Kavan shook his head. He did not want to talk about it, especially with her. "I awake with nothing but pain. There are no memories of images or emotions…only pain."

"Sometimes intense dreams cause physical symptoms. You should know that, milord." She smiled as his expression changed from one of confusion to one of mortification. "Something troubles you. I have known it since I was first sent to you. Once that has passed, perhaps the dreams will cease."

She could not possibly know of his dreams, he thought in panic. Could she? "Can you be certain?" he stammered, pushing his thoughts to the more worrying matters of his hands and his soul's damnation. He wondered if she knew of that too. He wanted to believe the pain would pass when his soul was free and his hands were healed, but experience had taught him differently. Troubles never left so easily.

"When you confront what haunts you, put it behind you, you will be amazed at how the world will change. Sleep, milord. Dhágdhuán's Feast is not many hours away."

❧*❧

It fell to gdhededhá Tusánt to perform the first Gathering at dawn in celebration of Dhágdhuán's Feast. He rose early to prepare the sanctuary by lighting candles at the stations and around the altar. As Lord Cliáth had taught him years ago, there was power, an aura, within the confines of a holy place, its intensity and quality dependent upon the use of the location and, perhaps, the amount of faith displayed within. Feeling it, relishing those moments of holiness when he was alone, was the first act Tusánt took whenever he entered the náós. Yet when he stepped from the thóres into the náós this morning, he knew immediately that something was wrong.

The aura and power in the náós this morning gave him shivers of dismay and pain. Someone had defiled the space. It filled his senses with a crush of negativity. Doing as the bard had taught, he closed his eyes, trying to pinpoint the origin of the dark power, tracing a definite path he could see better with his eyes closed. He followed it slowly until his leg hit something hard and bruising. The impact was painful and sent a shock through him that left him temporarily psychically blind. When the accompanying nausea of that blindness passed, he opened his eyes, dreading what he might see.

Bile rose in his throat but he squelched it back. For a few moments, he was unable to look away from the sight or to move from the step on which he stood. He wanted the k'gdhededhá to see this but did not dare leave it while he fetched the man for fear it would be gone when they returned or that someone else might see it and begin the spread of horrific rumors. Instead, he relied again on Lord Cliáth's teachings; he reached with his thoughts, nudged the consciousness of the sleeping k'gdhededhá, and planted within him the need to come to the altar as quickly as he could.

Within minutes, Jermyn was stumbling through the thóres door, muttering to himself, still in his nightshirt and rubbing the sleep from his face. He saw Tusánt, cocked his head curiously, and approached, only to stop in shock at what he saw lying at the Elyri's feet. There, upon the top step, at the foot of the altar, lay a dead infant, its body unclothed, its face purple, its neck bearing the marks of strangulation. Jermyn's knees buckled and Tusánt reached to steady him.

"I am sorry for waking you this way, Your Grace," the Elyri gdhededhá said. "I found…this…and was not sure what to do. At the very least I thought you should see it, be aware of it."

"Fetch a cloth, a towel…something…and blessed water. Hurry."

Tusánt rushed to obey and watched Jermyn bless the tiny body before wrapping it in the altar cloth he had brought. He could have done those things himself, but it seemed wisest to avoid accusations by allowing someone else to see his discovery first. "It is not Elyri…is it?" he asked, wondering if it had been killed here or left on the steps.

"I don't know. When we are born, our peoples look the same. I cannot tell the difference. Regardless, this is not good. Even if its mother could not care for it, there is no reason to murder it and leave it like this. No…this was a message…a warning…and I pray you were not the one meant to find it. The last thing you need is to be accused of murdering a child on the altar steps." Tusánt's face grew ashen at the insinuations that could be drawn from such a charge. "This is to go no further. Only you and I…and Lord Dugan since it may be part of his investigations, are to know of this. I'll hide the child until we can bury it; you finish preparations for the Gathering. People will arrive soon and I want them to suspect nothing."

Tusánt, his head full of images of what might be done to him if he was accused of such a crime, could not agree with his superior more.

❧*❦

Being in Bhryell amongst family for Dhágdhuán's Feast was a luxury Ártur had not had since Arlan Lachlan made his push for the Enesfel throne. The healer had not realized how much he missed it. His family had changed in the years he had been away; his mother and father were showing minute signs of age, as was his brother Sámel. Aleski and Bhen had grown to adulthood and Aleski had married a lovely young woman named Chátá. They had no children yet, but Llucás' rambunctiousness compensated for the lack of other children in the MacLyr household.

Though it had not been long since he had seen her, the healer thought his wife looked rounder than when she left Rhidam. More at peace. A pang of guilt filled him when he realized that perhaps she missed Bhryell more than she admitted. Perhaps he should make some other arrangements for the future of his family. But what? He could not bear the thought of leaving Rhidam; his life since becoming a healer was intertwined with the Lachlan House and he could not fathom leaving it, even with the possibility of death looming. Could he expect her to stay there if she did not wish it? Could they live separated by too many miles, even though the Gates afforded immediate access to each other? It was something he knew he needed to discuss with her soon.

Not today, however. It was the first day in a long while that he felt free of care and stress. There was no mention of Kavan; Tám would not allow it. Other than Ártur's brief conversation with Syl and Bhen to inform them that there had been no news, the topic of his cousin had not been mentioned. It was as if the sole remaining Cliáth, the last of that ancient bloodline, had ceased to exist. It was painful to endure, but better, Ártur knew, than sparking a feud on a day he would rather enjoy with his family.

Llucás had begun attending Bhen in the shop, cleaning up wood shavings, fetching tools and supplies from the shelves for his cousin while learning his way around the trade. He did not mind the menial tasks, was learning the names and qualities of various sorts of wood and the names of tools, and was becoming marginally interested in the art of harp making. By the time he was old enough to begin a proper apprenticeship, Ártur suspected his son would either resent the trade chosen for him or love it as much as Bhen did. He hoped it would be the latter since he knew it would please Tám to have at least one of Ártur's children carrying on the family business.

There came a scratching sound at the door, an unexpected visitor at this late hour. Being closest to it, Ártur rose to answer and was surprised to find bhydáni Tíbhyan leaning there on his walking stick. As his legs continued to fail, the ancient sage rarely went visiting. People normally went to him. In the room behind, the healer sensed the mixed reactions of his family, especially his father's annoyance.

"bhydáni…would you like to come in?" It was polite to ask, even though his father did not welcome the sage in his home.

"No…I came for a word with you when I learned you were in Bhryell." He inclined his head to the porch bench and Ártur followed, closing the door before helping the man to sit and settling beside him.

"I have little news about Kavan," the healer admitted. If there had been news, he would have gone to the bhydáni straight away. "He traveled to Kílyn and returned briefly the night King Arlan died…"

"Yes…he would have had to…to break the binding…"

"Binding?" Ártur did not like the sound of that.

"I have seen the medallion he wears and was told King Arlan possessed the other half. There is an ancient legend, from the earliest days in these lands, about a binding ritual, about two halves of the circle shared between men, the ties to be severed if one was to die. I suspected that was what he had acquired in that medallion, though we did not discuss it. He knows the legends, however. Not to have gone back for the other half might have meant his death. Do you know what he has done with it?"

"King Hagan has it," Ártur grunted. "It appears Kavan bestowed it upon him that same night."

Tíbhyan shook his head with a frown. "Continuing the binding. I hope he knows what he is doing."

"Could it be…dangerous…for him? For King Hagan?" The healer's palms grew cold.

"I do not know. When the k'kairá are involved, for that is likely where this binding originated, who can say what is dangerous and what is not? Kavan has the capacity to make the best of it, yet like you," the old man sighed, "I worry. I recently became aware of an ancient force departing this world. Though I do not know what it has to do with your cousin, I feel certain it is connected to him…like a prophecy come to pass. Men who fulfill prophecy often die too soon. I hoped you would know something."

The lines around the healer's mouth deepened. "I wish I did. When…if…I learn anything, I shall keep you and Bhen informed. It is the best I can do."

Tíbhyan nodded. Kavan had always been one to act without telling others where he was going or what he was doing. This was little different, except for the circumstances of the bard's departure and the condition he had been in when he left. "I hear from your wife that her brother's son is a healer? The one born to his Teren wife?"

"The youngest son, yes. It is so," Ártur replied. "I have undertaken his training."

"As you should," agreed the sage. "Might I meet him? Read him? Perhaps offer a little training? There would be no charge for this. It would be as much for my own benefit as his, as I would like to know what potential he has. I have never known any of mixed blood to carry our gifts. Will you ask his parents if that is acceptable?"

The healer smiled. "I shall. He asks about Elyriá and I do not think Bhríd will object."

"Thank you, Ártur." He smiled too as the healer helped him up.

Surprised by the change in address, Ártur asked, "Not MacLyr? Or Healer MacLyr?"

The sage shrugged. "You and I have known each other long enough, to progress beyond simple friendship. I think, too, I have taken you away from your family too long this evening. aesíthaen át aemárdhesi dhi."

"aesíthaen át aemárdhesi dhi, bhydáni."

Llucás' laughter drew Ártur back into the house after the old man hobbled out of sight, pulling Ártur's thoughts away from his cousin.

❧*❦

"Why didn't you wait for me?"

Eridel's normally pale face was red with anger and betrayal. He had ridden hard to find those he had traveled with, his single clue to their whereabouts being that they had traveled south along the main mountain road. That the day was Dhágdhuán's Feast meant they remained camped and was the reason the young harper finally caught up with them.

"I did not undertake this pilgrimage to cater to your needs," Kavan's voice was clipped, his hopes to be rid of the young bard dashed. "We could have lingered indefinitely waiting; for all we knew you were no longer in Enda."

"Of course I was in Enda! Where else would I have been?"

Urian cuffed the young man on the back of the head as one might a disrespectful child. Eridel pouted and moved beyond his reach. "You departed without word. You did not bother to learn our plans. This is Lord Cliáth's expedition; we go where and when he dictates. If you do not wish to abide by those guidelines, you would do best to go your way. It would be a benefit if you made up your mind."

Orynn chose that moment to emerge from her tent, causing Eridel to forget the argument and his upset at being left behind. "Milady?" he asked with a charming smile plastered across his still red face, and an offered hand that had been, until that moment, clenched tight at his side. "How have you come to be in our company?"

"I asked," she replied, her expression friendly though unamused. She did not take his hand. "I offered my services to…"

"Indeed?" Not liking what his tone implied, nor how Kavan would likely interpret the insinuation, Wortham cast Eridel a sharp glance. Having been threatened by the captain before, the young bard heeded that look and refrained from continuing his sentence.

"As a guide," the woman clarified. The mannerisms of some men never changed. "I know these lands and people. If Lord Cliáth is to find what he seeks, he requires guidance and a translator. What, may I ask, is your purpose in traveling with them?"

"I am a bard, a harper. I am here to…" He stopped, realizing he had no purpose beyond that. Defensively he finished, "I provide entertainment. Isn't that enough?"

Sensing the discord when she emerged from her tent and hoping to help resolve it, she asked, "Was your company requested?"

"I…no…but…"

Kavan interrupted, weary of the tension and wanting it over. "I bid him join us."

The look Orynn gave him suggested she knew that was not true, but rather than call Kavan on his half-truth, she offered a greeting hand to Eridel. "That is cause enough for me to welcome you. I am Orynn."

"Eridel." He held her hand briefly to his smiling lips. Convinced that the tension was behind them, that he was welcomed now, and no longer concerned about why he had been left behind, he settled nearest Urian, the least threatening member of the group. "Any particular reason you are not traveling today if you were not waiting for me? It is nearly noon."

Wortham rolled his eyes and dropped down beside Kavan with his hand on the bard's arm to keep the Elyri from speaking. "It is Dhágdhuán's Feast. There are those among us who revere…"

"Dhágdhu…why yes, it is! I forget what day it is sometimes. When you travel as much as I, one day becomes like the rest. I often forget feasts and celebration days. It is a good reason to take rest. Shall I offer music for the occasion?"

"No music," Wortham and Urian said simultaneously, hoping to spare Kavan the awkwardness. Orynn and Wortham exchanged glances, hers in questions, his an explanative reply.

But in a small voice, Kavan contradicted them. "Hymns for the day are appropriate and I cannot provide them. Let him play."

Eridel scrambled to take out his harp while Orynn sat on Kavan's other side, her knee pressing against his. "You could sing, could you not?" Someone had to suggest the obvious, propose what Kavan needed to hear.

It was the first time anyone had suggested singing, and he realized he had not given thought to that option before. He might have considered it now if not for the contact between them that brought up a conflicting surge of emotions and physical sensations. Standing abruptly, he growled and said, "Without my harp, there is no music."

He thought to flee her, but she pursued him beyond the edge of their campsite, leaving Wortham to restrain Eridel and discourage him from making the situation worse. "I have sensed a change, milord," she said. Behind them, Eridel gave in to Wortham's instruction but began to strum a popular hymn as Kavan had requested, causing the bard to tremble at the sound of an instrument he could no longer play. Urian, in his off-key voice, began to sing. "Did I say something last night to offend you?"

"No." It was the truth, and the most he wanted to say about the matter.

"Then I have done something…"

He drew his arms to his chest as a shield. "It is…when you touch me…" If he admitted it, she might cease doing it and he would be spared the torment of that pulsing tightness in his lower body. It terrified him more that he did not want her to stop, did not want to lose that distressingly pleasant sensation.

"Touch is wrong? I am your friend…or at least I wish to be your friend. You do not flee from Wortham's…" She hesitated, trying to read his face, and when he refused to look her in the eye, she added, "or is it because I am a woman?"

Kavan did not reply but a spark of panic on his face and tension in his body affirmatively answered her question.

But to Kavan, it was not that she was a woman. The problem was, she was the only woman he felt a craving for that was almost too intense to control.

Her head hung and her voice was tinged with disappointment. "I have no unseemly intentions, milord. I want nothing from you that you are not able to give. Friendship is all I seek. Please…do not fear me."

What if I want you to have unseemly intentions, he thought, while aloud he said, "Fear? That may be the most accurate description there is." He watched Eridel grimly, trying to focus on the music to forget what her nearness was doing to him.

Aware of his discomfort, and sad that he feared her, if only in this one way, she stepped back and changed the subject. "You miss it? The music?"

He nodded, relieved for that small distance between them. "More than I thought I could. Until it was gone, I did not understand how fundamental it is to my sense of who I am. I am a musician…a harper. Without my hands, without the music, I am nothing."

"You can sing," she reiterated. "Give yourself the opportunity."

Stubbornly, Kavan shook his head. "I cannot…without my harp."

With a reluctant sigh and a tender squeeze of his hand, ignoring the panic that spurred him to reject her, though this time he did not, Orynn started back towards the others. "Remember what I said last night, milord. Until you confront what is tormenting you, do not expect to find peace," she said over her shoulder.

Kavan did not believe he would ever find peace again.

<h1 style="text-align:center">❧Chapter 16❧</h1>

Caol Dugan, Lord High Inquisitor of Enesfel, was originally chosen for the position because the tale of his siege on the Rhidam castle lent itself to the belief that he was the best man for the job and no one else would accept it. Later, when King Arlan learned of Caol's family history, about their connections to the infamous collection of thieves and criminals known as the Association, the King opted to put his friend's extensive collection of questionable acquaintances to use. It was normally a simple task for Caol to find the right man or woman for any given assignment and his family's entanglement with the Association afforded him information that even the best royal spies could not consistently obtain.

That they were falling short of providing useful information this time was both disturbing and irritating. It meant one of two things. Either the Association had become involved in the anti-Elyri campaign, an idea Caol found incomprehensible given their code, or there was no clear leader for this random upsurge in violence. The other, more distasteful idea was that the individual or group of individuals behind the upsurge of violence was craftier than any foe Caol had ever pursued.

No matter. He was confident he would ferret them out eventually. He always did. No one, short of another member of the Association, would have the extensive resource of informants he had. Given enough time, Caol believed he would find what he needed.

But at what price, he was beginning to wonder. How many Elyri would be killed? How many more of Enesfel's subjects would be added to the twenty-one reported missing since the peasant family in Wexel had disappeared? If this was part of the anti-Elyri threat, why were the missing all Teren? Or was it, as King Hagan feared, the work of a foreign agent? Neth had been unusually docile since being stripped of a third of her kingdom; perhaps King Merkar had decided to take action against Enesfel at last. That would be difficult to prove, but it was the answer Caol was beginning to suspect he would find at the end of his efforts.

He removed the crudely scrawled anti-Elyri symbol posted on a scrap of tanned leather from the signpost over the tavern door, shoved it into his pocket, and strode inside. Words with the owner looked to be in order.

His letter complete, Jermyn watched the pool of wax form before pressing his seal into it. He was not pleased about sending such a letter and knew k'gdhededhá Dórímyr would be less pleased to receive it. The news of the upsurge in anti-Elyri violence and the spread of prejudice would be proof enough to the patriarch that he had been right not to travel to Rhidam, although Jermyn believed that the upsurge was due in part to the man ignoring Teren branches of the Faith for so long. It would undoubtedly be disturbing to the Faithful in Elyriá that an appointed gdhededhá was a suspected leading voice within that dissidence. The k'gdhededhá wondered if Dórímyr would choose to deal directly with Claide, as was the customary thing to do, or if he would force the task of reprimanding Claide onto Jermyn.

The k'gdhededhá did not want that responsibility. He hoped he could avoid it. Yet, as expected, Claide claimed innocence in his Dhágdhuán's Eve Gathering sermon. There was no intent, he swore, of speaking against the Elyri and he was certainly not espousing violence against anyone. His plea for mercy sounded sincere, his tone apologetic, but Jermyn had felt a cold prickle up his spine when Claide left the room. It could not be proven without subjecting Claide to an Elyri reading, but he believed Claide was lying. That such vile sentiments would be repeated, Jermyn had no doubt.

He sent a summons to Dórímyr. If it became necessary, he should be prepared to act the next time Claide crossed the bounds of Faith and decency.

After he sent it, Jermyn regretfully reconsidered k'gdhededhá Dórímyr coming to Enesfel. It might not be the best choice, given the unsettled state of things. What if Claide's sermon was part of a plot to lure the Elyri Patriarch out of Elyriá to his death? It was difficult to fathom the idea, but the fact that it occurred to Jermyn meant it was plausible. Jermyn groaned. It looked as if he was going to be left to deal with Claide on his own, one way or another.

❧*❧

Pitching himself on top of Urian, Kavan felt the flight of an arrow stir the air above his head. Had he been slower, the arrow would have killed the blind man. Elyri senses told him there were five assailants. Nearby, Eridel sang gaily as he jabbed his new rapier at his opponent, becoming winded from the effort already and at risk of losing his battle though he seemed unaware of it or too stubborn to doubt himself. To the far side of the trail, Wortham dispatched the first brigand to emerge from the scrub at the roadside and was dancing around the second, avoiding the arrows that continued to fly from the brush.

Orynn toyed with a mountain of a man who thought to have his way with a weaker female opponent. She left several cuts on his face and arms while sustaining no damage herself. There was a precision to her technique that hinted at rigorous training, and a playfulness that looked like a cat toying with its prey before devouring it. Kavan wondered, in those moments watching her, where a woman had received such training.

The younger bard screamed when an arrow caught his shoulder and pitched him into the dust. No longer playing, Orynn thrust her sword into her opponent's torso, letting him fall before turning her attention to the rogue tormenting Eridel and taking him down as well.

It was happening too fast. The archer concerned Kavan as he rolled off Urian, seeking the bowman in the scrub. He could sense the knocking of another arrow, the tightening of the string in preparation to fire, targeting Orynn. Her armor would afford protection, but she wore no helm today and the thought of even the smallest wound upon her twisted Kavan's stomach into knots. Taking a breath, he reached with as much power as he could harness; the archer leaped from his cover with a scream onto the packed clay road, dropping the bow as it burst into flames.

"I am pleased to see you have not lost those skills," said Wortham with a grin as he pinned his opponent to the ground. The flames sputtered out, leaving nothing of the bow remaining.

"Power can be manipulated without hands," Kavan explained as he rolled to his feet and fetched rope from the side of the mule. As he said the words, it occurred to him that, until that moment, he had made little use of the power since the crippling attack. How much, he mused, might it allow him to do? How much of his irritable, disagreeable mood stemmed from pent-up energy in need of release?

"No need to bind him," said Orynn. "With three dead and the fourth fleeing with burned hands, he will not cross us." She glared at the man beneath Wortham's sword and spoke to him in a terse, rough language that none of the others understood. It sounded vaguely Hatuish, vaguely akin to the infrequently heard tongue of the desert nomads, but despite an occasional word that sounded as if it carried Elyri roots, it sounded like no language Kavan had ever heard. The captive nodded emphatically and sat up, heedful of the sword point.

She continued her tirade, asking questions that the rogue answered quickly. His face revealed growing awe and fear as the conversation progressed. Kavan made out the word k'ílshwythnec and determined she was seeking the location of the prophetess. Urian, meanwhile, tended Eridel's wound. When Orynn motioned to Wortham to withdraw his sword, the brigand scurried to the side of the road, from where he did not move as the people he intended to rob regrouped and continued along the mountain trail.

"What did he tell you?" asked Urian, who was walking while the pitifully moaning Eridel rode the mule. The youngster's face was flushed, though it was more embarrassment at his failure to drop an opponent than due to his injury.

Wortham believed he was not the only one to think those moans were a play for sympathy from the woman in their midst.

Orynn, untangling her damp hair with her fingers and braiding it behind her head to control it should they find themselves in another skirmish, glanced at Kavan before replying, "He knew nothing of use. I extracted an oath that he would leave us alone…and see that his fellows do likewise. He also," she chuckled, "made an oath to give up thievery as a way of life."

"What makes you think he will keep it?" Wortham asked. "In my experience, ruffians will say anything to save their hides."

"In these lands, an oath is binding. Breaking one is a mortal sin…and breaking one to me invites my wrath." She grinned and nudged Wortham lightly. "When people find out who I am, they seldom wish to do that."

From his awkward perch upon the mule, Eridel asked, "Then you are known in these parts? You should be after fighting like that."

She shrugged with that mysterious smile that Kavan had seen before and replied, "Many are familiar with me here and elsewhere, though not because of my swordsmanship."

Invited by her playfulness, the captain grinned and said, "We should pit you against Bhríd. That is a match I would pay to see." Unlike Kavan, he did not appear to suspect she had anything to hide.

Still grinning, ignoring Kavan's trailing gaze, Orynn said, "I would be honored to accept any challengers."

❧*❧

"Milord Prince," the page bowed to cover his smirk. "This has arrived for you from Rhidam."

Espen groaned inwardly and knew his cheeks flushed brilliant red, finding himself again at the butt of teasing about the Enesfel princess who continued to evade his marriage proposal. It had been too long since her last letter thus he suspected this would be from her now. He should have written, and felt guilty about not having done so, but he was trying to stay true to his pledge. He would pursue the woman no longer. If she desired to marry him, the next step would be hers.

It was indeed her handwriting, though it was shaky and uneven. Regret? He could hope. Breaking the seal, he read the message quickly and then strode from the room. His brother, King Noreis, was in his private garden at this hour, drinking a glass of strong ale, and beckoned Espen to him when he saw him in the archway.

"What is wrong, brother?"

The prince cleared his throat, finding the words harder to say than expected. "I have received word from Princess Diona…King Arlan has passed. Hagan is King of Enesfel."

Noreis said nothing as his eyes took on a faraway look. He had little firsthand contact with King Arlan, had met him but a single time on the day Noreis had become king, when Arlan had traveled to Natrona to renew the established treaties between their kingdoms. He had no knowledge of what sort of man Hagan was, other than the anecdotal stories Espen shared. Still, Arlan had been a successful ruler, well-liked and powerful, and the peace he fostered between Hatu and Enesfel benefited both sides. "Does she say how it happened?"

"He fell ill and died peacefully in his bed."

"Do you desire leave to travel?"

Espen thought about the question, weighing the pros and cons and the necessity of it against his personal feelings. Part of him felt he should go to Rhidam, show Hatu's support of the new King, but that duty should be up to Noreis, and he trusted his brother to take care of it. What he said, however, was, "I shall convey my sentiments and any you wish to send. If you wish it, I will extend the invitation to renew our treaties with King Hagan. However, I see no need to go to Rhidam, unless the family expresses need of me or you wish me to deliver your messages. There is little I can do except mourn their loss…" And because she did not say it, he assumed that Diona did not desire him there to mourn with her.

Noreis drained his ale and got up from the bench. "I will prepare a statement to send with yours and extend the treaties to him. Do you think he will be the king his father was?"

Having known the new King since infancy, Prince Espen was inclined to say no. Instead, he replied, "I do not know. I pray so."

❧*❧

A single rider left Rhidam mid-morning, his pace swift but steady. His destination was the city of Chantel, a few days ride at best, but he got no further than a few hours outside of Rhidam before being waylaid by bandits. Alone, he was outnumbered and easily beaten.

His belongings were searched, his valuables confiscated, his body dumped on the side of the road in a ditch thick with muddy winter water. His mission would remain unfulfilled.

☙*☙

The inner courtyard of Saint Kóráhm's Abbey was bathed in a soothing pink-orange glow at this same time every day when the sun was sinking low in the western sky. It was the hour Khwílen enjoyed most, tending the shrubs planted there, clearing away dirt and debris from the marble Kílyn cross Lord Cliáth had erected in the courtyard's center. Unlike other parts of the facility, this shrine was unpretentious, and, with the onset of winter, it looked barren, neglected, as the shrubs waited for spring to bloom. Come spring, when the roses budded and the almond trees flowered, the courtyard would be a wonder to behold.

Khwílen had thought of Lord Cliáth as a man with simple tastes when they first met. Kavan wore a plain robe, his personal room in Rhidam was adorned with nothing except the Kóráhm tapestry, and his home in Bhryell called no attention to itself. Khwílen had visited that home once when Llucás MacLyr was born, but he had been to Rhidam many times as the bard plied him with religious questions and lay down the foundation for the work done at the chellé. The Alberni estate, which Khwílen visited often since his appointment to Saint Kóráhm's was more elaborate, decorated with marble, velvet, and silver. It was regal and stately, beautiful without the flaunting of wealth many nobles and religious establishments displayed. It was beautiful enough to belong to a man of wealth and simple enough to belong to a straightforward man like Kavan.

Yet to see Saint Kóráhm's was to see a much different side of the chellé's benefactor. Khwílen knew of no instance where expense had been spared, or a shortcut taken. It lacked the ostentatious flaunting of wealth found in Clarys, Rhidam, or elsewhere, but was no less beautiful for it. He relished his fortune to serve as k'gdhededhá of this place. Even though it might, someday, carry a terrible price.

gdhededhá Tusánt saw fit to keep him abreast of the political and social climate in Rhidam since Lord Cliáth's attack, and Khwílen had already led three Elyri through the secret tunnels that connected Saint Kóráhm's to Lord Cliáth's estate, and thus to the Gate which would take them safely to Elyriá. He and three others in the chellé knew about those tunnels, knew their way through them, and one of those four was to be available at all times to aid any in need of safe passage. There was, to his knowledge, no Gate within Saint Kóráhm's walls. The gdhededhá knew, from what Tusánt had written, that there might be many more Elyri fleeing to safety soon. Not because they knew there was a Gate, or that there was access to one, but because Saint Kóráhm's was lauded across the kingdom as a safe haven for anyone who felt threatened.

Would it be truly safe was Khwílen's concern. There were sentries, men who had taken oaths to protect those residing within the chellé's walls, men trained by Wortham Delamo, Owain Lachlan, and Bhríd Cáner, three of the best fighting men in Enesfel. But the sixty soldiers stationed here would be no match for a full-scale military assault, should one ever come. They might, however, be able to keep others out until those within could escape to safer ground. Die to protect the others.

There were to be other measures taken, measures Lord Cliáth was going to install. What those were, Khwílen did not know, but having heard of the bard's access to abilities few Elyri dreamed of, Khwílen expected them to be purely Elyri measures that could not be thwarted by any Teren. With the bard absent from Enesfel, there was no telling when or if, those measures would be invoked. Khwílen had to proceed on the belief that he had every protection he was going to get.

He knew, however, that there were many who felt as he did, that to abandon this magnificent sanctuary to marauders without a fight would be a sin against their benefactor, their patron, and k'Ádhá. They would not flee in the face of adversity. They would stay and they would fight. And they would probably die if that day ever came.

❧*☙

The four wagons in the caravan were similar to those Kavan had wandered between outside of Avarrou's southern wall. Colorful mosaics were painted on their sides, symbols he did not recognize but assumed were of import to the owners. A small group of goats was herded between the wagons, and he counted at least six dogs running in and out of the clattering, painted, wheels. Small, dirty faces peered from behind dusty curtains, staring with the curiosity he expected from children. His complexion was a novelty to children and adults alike.

He abandoned the cloak when they left Hatu because, in these lands, no one knew who he was. These people did not know his music, did not know his name, and did not know any of the legends and stories that had sprung up surrounding his life. If they did, none had spoken of it. They could not pity him for what he lost, though as soon as someone noticed his hands he felt the flash of their sympathy. There was a new emotion from these people towards him, a respect for his strength in suffering that bolstered him. Each time they encountered a group of these foreigners it was the same, and each time Kavan was aware of the disconsolate way Orynn stared at him with large sad eyes as if he were doing something wrong.

She conversed with a man on the lead wagon while Eridel strolled about strumming his harp and singing, hoping for a handout of coins, food, or drink. The injury to his shoulder had not curbed his enthusiasm for entertaining. When the younger bard strolled past

Orynn, he eyed her with a hungry, playful leer, a look she ignored but one Kavan found irritating and insulting.

Eventually, the wagons rolled north, taking the dirty-faced children away. It was evening by then and Wortham had taken the liberty of making camp while the dialogue with the strangers ensued.

"They carried nothing of value to us, no Diwi or Orec, but they did direct us to Fikahr," Orynn said, stretching out beside the fire, disinclined to erect her tent this warm night.

"We will find what we need there?"

"At least the Diwi, captain. It is a bi-yearly crop in Fikahr and we have chosen the month when it is most plentiful. We should be able to barter for as much as is required."

"How much further to Fikahr?" asked Eridel who was irritated at losing his audience without recompense for his performance and was skipping rocks down the road in the direction the wagons had gone.

"If we travel at a steady pace," she replied, "ten days."

"Ten days?" Kavan's deflated expression mirrored Eridel's verbal dismay.

"Fikahr is on the coast, a port. We will pass through several smaller villages between here and there and it is possible we will find Diwi at any of them. But Fikahr is our best chance of obtaining both commodities at once."

The bard nodded and curled up to sleep. He felt more exhausted today than he had since leaving Natrona, and the prospect of ten more days' travel before seeing success was disappointing. Perhaps he was falling ill. Or perhaps it was a result of his fear of sleeping lest he endure that peculiar, painful dream again. Fear kept him awake at night more than was healthy and he knew he could not go on without it much longer. He had to sleep. "Then that is where we go," he murmured. "I am traveling to Fikahr."

Wortham drew off his boots and rubbed his aching feet. "You know I am with you, milord."

"I have no plans, and the lady is leading the way," added Urian around a mouthful of unleavened bread they obtained from the wagoneers. He looked expectantly at Eridel, though he could not see him, challenging him to reply.

Looking from one person to another, Eridel's gaze lingered on Kavan the longest though he said nothing for many minutes. When he did look away it was to smile at Orynn and speak. "I am not staying here alone. And a lady as beautiful as you needs a protector. I offer my services."

"I think," snorted Wortham, taking the water skin from Urian when Kavan refused it, "you need the lady's protection more than she needs yours. In Lord Cliáth's company, there is little need of protection."

Eridel rolled his eyes. "He did not keep us safe yesterday. He can wield no sword or bow…"

Orynn laid her hand tenderly on Kavan's shoulder before he could defend himself. He flinched but did not pull away. "He has been sorely distracted, with a great personal burden you fail to comprehend…and one does not need a sword to offer defense. If you recall, Eridel, he was the one who told us to take cover and pulled gdhededhá Urian from the mule before the first shot was fired."

"Moments before," the young bard sneered.

"With enough time to avoid harm to most of us. It is not his fault you chose to sing your way to injury rather than fight your adversary in earnest. Be kind, Eridel. He did what he was able. That is all any man can do."

Kavan opened his eyes, met Orynn's gaze, and swallowed uneasily. This lovely, enigmatic woman, whom he continued to push away, called him a man, and it had nothing to do with the act of carnal consummation. She graced him with a smile, and in that smile, he found enough peace to close his eyes and relax into hoped for sleep.

Tired of the talk, he murmured, "Are you going to play for us?"

"Do you wish it?" Eridel asked.

Kavan nodded once though he did not open his eyes and did not think the motion would be seen. "Would I ask it if I did not?"

Wortham sighed and toyed with the stopper of the now empty water skin. Yes, Kavan would ask for music to avoid deafening silence or conversation he did not want to hear. In the end, Eridel's music was a stinging salve the Elyri felt forced to endure, though Wortham could not see it making the bard's situation any better.

❧*↭

As Orynn claimed it was a ten-day journey to the outskirts of Fikahr, ten days' travel over arid, dusty hardened clay roads that proved an ever-increasing test to Kavan's endurance. He watched Eridel's increasing attention to Orynn, as if her saving his life meant she had a great interest in his survival and well-being. Generally, she ignored his advances or brushed them off with laughter, but there were evenings when she asked him to help hunt or took him aside to teach him points of swordsmanship. Eridel devoured her attention and constantly demanded more while Kavan watched in envy.

It was not envy of the activity; he had once been proficient in both, and though he could no longer hunt or swing a sword, he did not miss either. Eridel needed to learn to do both if he was to survive on his own. Nor did Kavan believe his feelings to be envy of the time Orynn spent with the other man. After all, Kavan strove to stay as far from her as he could without appearing rude; he had no right to be envious of whomever she chose to spend time with. Orynn respected his wish to be left alone and interacted with him only when he allowed it.

But he craved her attention constantly; even something as casual as a glance would start him trembling, start his blood pounding, though he could not admit that to anyone. It was easier, in some ways, to keep distance between them. He definitely felt it was safer. In the back of his mind, where he was beginning to admit he wanted her with him, his thoughts were beginning to circle the possibility that he was in love with a woman he knew too little about. It was the only explanation for what he felt and the thought of love frightened him.

Every night before sleeping, he asked Eridel to play, though the more he fought to endure the notes of the harp the more difficult the effort became. It made him increasingly irritable and he hated himself for it. But this was the right choice, he believed, to force himself to become accustomed to sounds he would never again create. Urian discouraged Eridel from his constant efforts to push music on Kavan, and Wortham tried to dissuade Kavan from what seemed to be pointless self-torture, but the Elyri would not be swayed and Eridel would not stop as long as Kavan encouraged him. The effort would succeed. It was going to take much longer than anticipated, but he believed it would succeed. It had to.

❧Chapter 17❧

Jermyn grew more concerned with every passing hour. His envoy had been sent to Chantel, where he was to pass the missive to a second messenger to take the remainder of its way. Thus far, the courier had failed to return to report success. It was possible he had remained a few extra days in Chantel due to weather or illness, even possible he had encountered reasons to take the letter to Clarys himself. But no word came and the k'gdhededhá did not think this was the case, not when he noticed how helpful and well-mannered Claide was behaving while still sporting a cold glint in his eyes that he may or may not intend Jermyn to see, a glint that fueled the k'gdhededhá's fear that something bad was fast approaching.

"Your Grace?"

Jermyn looked up from his desk work with a sigh. "Yes, Rankin?"

The man looked nervous and ill as he wiped his brow and said, "I think you should see this, sir."

The k'gdhededhá pushed to his feet. Not another dead infant, he prayed. Ártur MacLyr had identified the strangled child as Teren and further research indicated that it had been a member of the peasant family that had disappeared from Wexel weeks earlier. It had provided Caol drawings of the family, even a sketch of the last face the child had seen as he had given up his life. The inquisitor had a suspect, though at a terrible price, and Justice Corbin was scouring Rhidam for further information.

What Rankin showed the k'gdhededhá, however, made Jermyn wish it was something as terrible as a strangled infant. Atop the sign pole in the náós yard was the head of a man. An Elyri man, Jermyn was fairly certain. Sweet záryph, he thought as he choked on the bitter taste in his throat. What was the world coming to? There was a piece of parchment tacked below the severed head, but Jermyn had no desire to go closer to read it, particularly since the blood on it appeared fresh.

"We should summon Lord Dugan and Justice Corbin at once…"

"Yes, sir," murmured Rankin, "Tusánt is already fetching them. Unfortunately, the new altar attendants have already seen this, and who knows how many others before we found it. Why would someone leave this here?"

Jermyn could think of but one reason. "A message, one that could not be left at the keep. This is the next best place." A sudden flash of worry consumed him and he asked, "Have you seen Claide? Or Valgis?"

"Valgis is inside with the attendants, but I have not seen Claide."

That concerned Jermyn. "Find him. At once. If he has not already seen this, I want him to be aware of what he's done." He had no doubts that Claide's words had inspired this.

Rankin bowed and departed hastily, not asking why the k'gdhededhá thought this was Claide's doing, leaving Jermyn alone with the grizzly sight, aware of the gathering at the náós gates, people ogling the face whose blue eyes unflinchingly faced the horror of death. Jermyn wanted to say something but there were no words appropriate for such an atrocity. When the front door of the náós reopened, he expected it to be Rankin, with Claide at his side.

Instead, it was Ártur, who stopped mid-step and gaped. Even from this distance, he knew the head upon the signpost was Elyri.

"I wish you had not seen this, Lord MacLyr…no man should be exposed to this, particularly one of your people. It makes me sick…"

The healer came to the gdhededhá's side, his expression unreadable as the initial shock passed. Having served both Kings Innis and Arlan on the battlefield, Ártur was no stranger to such horrors, a fact many often forgot. "May I?"

"You wish to touch that thing?" Jermyn croaked.

"That thing was once a man…one of my people. I want to know what manner of monster did this. His eyes are open. He saw his killer. It is the best way to identify them both."

"Not until I examine it first, Lord MacLyr." Caol pushed through the crowd with Justice Corbin behind him, past the two men there, showing little aversion in removing the head from the pole and studying it before grunting and placing it in the healer's hands. Caol took the parchment from the post, noting the still tacky blood.

"Looks like he was killed nearby, doesn't it, Darius?"

The justice, circling the area to examine the ground for blood or footsteps, nodded in agreement.

"Here? On consecrated ground?" The portly k'gdhededhá looked more ill than before.

"The blood upon the parchment, the pole, and the ground indicate the victim was killed not long before his head was left here…not more than fifteen minutes I would say," Darius said. "There are scuff marks around the pole which look as if someone was trying to rub out evidence…possibly footprints or more blood. May I look around, Your Grace?"

"Do," was the emphatic response. "It is bad enough this is here to desecrate holy ground. I do not want a murder to go undiscovered."

"Lord Dugan?" the justice asked with a gesture, to see if the man would accompany him.

"One moment." Caol faced the healer, who was trembling and allowing tears to trickle down his cheeks. "Lord MacLyr?" he asked.

"He was…a minstrel…he heard about Kavan's injury…came to express remorse…offer support." His fingers twisted in the man's blonde hair.

"The murderer?" the inquisitor encouraged, not wanting to make light of the healer's grief but hoping for information he could use.

"Three of them. He was taken…from the home of peasants who gave him refuge…two held him…the third…"

"Where did this happen? Can you tell? And can you provide sketches of the three?"

Ártur nodded. "I can. And Caol…Your Grace…he was murdered here…in the yard." He glanced around, studying the collection of grave markers new and old and pointed. "There."

Caol and Darius strode in the direction he pointed, stopping at a freshly turned patch of earth at the edge of the burial ground with no marker near it. They glanced at one another.

"Who is buried here?" Caol asked, pushing dirt around with the toe of his boot.

"No one," Jermyn assured him. "There is no marker; there should be no one there."

Pushing up his sleeves, Caol grimaced. "I think there's someone here now. Do I have permission to dig?"

Jermyn snorted, "You think the body is here?"

"Sloppy work, I agree; they had to know this would be noticed. And if this was the typical anti-Elyri nonsense, it's not logical that they would bury the 'evil' on náós ground…"

"Unless they were rushed," agreed Darius.

"Or are suggesting there is nothing holy here…because of the Faith's support of Elyri," Caol concluded. "If, as Lord MacLyr says, this is where he died, it's likely this upturned earth marks the disposal site of the corpse."

"Nothing was heard! I would have known…"

Caol clasped the k'gdhededhá's shoulder. "We will determine what happened and let you know. Do we have permission to dig?"

"Allow my men to do this," offered Darius. "You and I should examine the rest of the grounds and speak to the dedhá. Someone must have seen or heard something."

"I will stay…identify the body if that is what is unearthed," the healer said grimly.

"And help me give him a proper burial, I hope," muttered Jermyn.

Ártur nodded. "I will. Caol? What did the parchment say?"

The inquisitor looked at the healer with a dour expression, fingering the scroll he had yet to relinquish. "Just three words. 'From the Corylliens.'"

❧*❧

"An Elyri head…on the náós signpost?"

Tusánt nodded to the King's distress, wishing he had better news. Beside Hagan, his sister's face was twisted with indignation and disgust. "Rankin was the first to find it."

"Is anyone…"

"Lord Dugan and Justice Corbin are investigating, My Liege."

King Hagan dabbed his mouth with his napkin, no longer interested in the breakfast he had been eating. "Good."

"No, it isn't good," Diona snorted. "Any Elyri not under our direct protection is a target…and Lord Cliáth is out there somewhere."

The King put his napkin down. "Captain Delamo is with him, Diona, and he is far away from here. Lord Cliáth will be safe."

"What of Ártur? He called upon the gdhededhá at the náós …he's out there alone."

"If he is at the náós, with Lord Dugan and Lord Corbin, he will be safe…but I will send Denyan and Avner to bring him home. No Elyri will leave this house without protection. Ethenae…" He groaned and hung his head. "Think of what this will do to commerce. Already trade with Cordash has decreased; no one wants to travel from abroad…or within the kingdom. It is hurting the treasury…not to mention what this will do to the Faith."

"If we are fortunate, Lord Dugan will find answers today…and this will be an isolated incident." The Elyri gdhededhá did not sound confident in his own words. If the name Coryllien was now attached to the atrocities, there was no reason he should be.

⮡*⮢

As anticipated, the headless corpse of the Elyri man was unearthed in the cemetery where the upturned soil was found. It was cut, twisted, splattered with blood, a sight the k'gdhededhá thought never to see. Caol and Darius found nothing more, although gdhededhá Hazen recalled the sound of a wagon stopping in the streets during the early morning hours, and then starting again several minutes later. Her recollections confirmed what they already knew. Caol left in search of his contacts with the rough sketches Ártur provided, hoping at least one of the suspects was still in Rhidam. After that, he planned to pay a visit to the home where the Elyri man had stayed. Darius, meanwhile, began a sweep of the city's inns and taverns, hoping for the same results, armed with a similar set of sketches. Rankin reported that, according to Valgis, Claide was visiting the faithful elsewhere in Rhidam, and thus he was nowhere to be found. Jermyn did not believe it; the excuse for his absence was too convenient and he had not scheduled such duties for Claide today.

Once the body was properly buried with its head, Ártur was no longer needed on the náós grounds. The soldiers sent to escort him had been drafted into service by the justice, and Ártur insisted he would be safe enough returning to the castle alone. It was not far to walk. His steps were depressingly slow. That man had died for no other reason than he was Elyri and had come to Rhidam regarding Kavan. Reaching out the best he could, the healer tried to find Kavan's mind but could not. He was not adept enough to reach wherever Kavan was. *Come home*, he thought. *I need you here.*

Selfish, he immediately chastised himself. Deplorable. Despite what he knew Kavan was enduring, Ártur wanted him home for his own benefit. Everyone missed the bard, wanted him back, but only, it sometimes seemed, for what he gave them, strength, peace, stability, faith, and hope. Yet what, the healer wondered, did they give in return? What had they ever given to make Kavan want to stay? The healer hung his head. *I need you here*, he sighed, *but it might be best, especially for you, if you do not come back. It is time we relearn to rely on ourselves. And you must find peace.*

His inward focused thoughts were interrupted by shouts of monster, demon, and defiler. Rocks pummeled him from behind. He turned in amazement to confront his assailants and found four young boys tagging along behind him. Not knowing what he could do to stop them, short of having a discourse they were not old enough to understand, he continued, bracing himself and trying not to flinch or cower whenever a stone struck a sensitive area, regretting now that he had not waited for escorts. If he ignored the boys, they might stop. He did not think they were even old enough to understand what they said and did. But his efforts to ignore them failed to discourage them and it was not until he was within sight of the castle gates that they fell back, wanting to avoid being seen by the palace guard.

There was blood on his skull; he could feel it. Deciding it would be wise to tend to it before encountering the royal family, his wife, or anyone else, he hastened to his room. Compared to the matters facing Enesfel and Rhidam, a few cuts on his scalp were a minor thing.

❧*❧

Fikahr was a cluttered, filth-ridden maze of constricted streets and narrow, pushed together buildings of gray clay brick that twisted about in no organized pattern until they arrived at the two wooden piers which served as its port. The boats moored there were small, meant to carry perhaps six individuals with a large cabin in the center for the goods they ferried up and down the coast. It was early in the first month of the year and the weather here was mild compared to what most in the group were accustomed to; the mid-afternoon sun provided enough warmth that Urian, who had complained about cool temperatures for much of the journey, finally shed his cloak. Other than the garbage along the base of the buildings, which gave off a continual greasy stench, and the clothes dangling from windows to dry in the open air, there were few visible signs of inhabitation. In the distance, a pulsing drumbeat shook the air, echoing through the empty streets like a call.

But beneath the odor of refuse there was another. A sweet, musky, pungent smell, tantalizing in its exoticness, similar to the incense used most frequently in the Gathering, but different in a way Kavan could not pinpoint. It almost overpowered the stench of decaying waste, for which they were grateful. Without it, the smell of rot would be unbearable.

"Diwi," Orynn explained quietly, as if not to break the silence. "It appears we have arrived during a religious festival." Wortham looked over his shoulder and she continued, "These people take festivals seriously…they do not conduct business on festival days, and they may not even speak with us depending on which festival we've encountered. We may not find assistance until it is over."

"Is there any way to know which festival…?" the captain asked, rubbing his hand over his brow.

"Unfortunately, the Fikahrs adopt and discard holidays as rapidly as some people change clothing," she chuckled. "We may know more soon enough if we follow the drum."

Eridel muttered, "Do you think we will at least be able to find a room? Somewhere to eat and drink?"

"With what payment?" Wortham smirked, prepared for another night of outdoor sleep.

Orynn smiled sympathetically. "I will see to it, if any rooms or taverns are willing to do business. I brought goods to barter. I will do what I can."

With Orynn leading, they followed the rhythmic pounding to the front of what seemed to be a holy place, a building wider than most before which was gathered what appeared to be the town's entire population. A man in dark brown robes paced the length of the platform, waving an uncharacteristically green leafy branch over the heads of the gathering to the cadence the drummer beside him pounded. Every fourth trip he took, he stopped in the middle of the stage, chanted the same phrase in an ominous tone, to which the gathering gave a shout in response before he continued pacing.

"He is asking the gods to lift the curse from their town," Orynn translated, "and the people are shouting in supplication."

"Curse?" asked an uneasy-looking Eridel as Urian said, "Gods?"

A man in a tattered tunic cast them an annoyed glance. Orynn said something to the fellow in his language, with her right arm crossed over her chest as she bowed. He nodded and turned his attention back to their holy man. Orynn motioned for her companions to stay silent.

The ritual continued until the sun was below the horizon, at which time the priest gave a more elaborate chant in a monotone voice before dismissing his flock. The man who had silenced them spoke tersely to Orynn, apparently unsatisfied with her earlier apology or else wanting an explanation for why she risked the wrath of the gods by speaking out of turn during their rite. Kavan longed to know what words passed between them, but assumed, after the initial clipped exchange, that they must be peaceful, for the man led them to an inn and provided rooms and a meal. It was impossible not to notice the preferential treatment Orynn received, particularly when it was given by other men, and though he should not care, it made Kavan's stomach tighten into bitter, annoyed knots.

"gdhededhá Urian," Orynn began as they picked an empty table and waited for their meal to be served, "our host will arrange for you to meet with the local gdhededhá. It seems their 'curse' has been a string of bad trades with their neighbors, and he believes advice from a missionary will be welcome. They do not have men of Faith here often, thus your arrival is viewed as a fortuitous omen. Be careful what you say, however; though they worship many gods here, and welcome others, they will not take kindly to criticism."

Urian nodded and asked, "How shall I communicate with them?"

"Some of the gdhededhá speak the Trade tongue of the Sovereignties. It is a necessity for trading with Hatu."

"If they have had bad trades of late, perhaps it will be to our advantage."

She nodded. "My hope as well, captain. I have several bottles of Káliel wine that will be a fair trade for supplies, and silk that should gain us Diwi. He gave me the name of a merchant to contact, but we will be forced to wait until the day after tomorrow…days like this are followed by feasting; I suggest we take the opportunity to enjoy it."

Wortham lifted his mug with a grin. "After so many days on the road, and the food we have eaten, a feast and bed will be welcome."

The bard arched his brow at the pair but did not speak. He was often interested in sampling new customs and traditions, but he did not want to waste time. Bhóité had said there was a single night each year he could act and Kavan did not intend to miss it. There seemed little to be done, however, short of traveling to some other village and hoping for success there, and his companions were eager for this unexpected diversion. Since three were indulging in heavy drink, something Wortham had not done since they had left Levonne, Kavan excused himself, retreated to the room he would share with Wortham, and fell asleep almost immediately.

Their night would pass without him and he preferred to be alone.

When he awoke the following morning it was to the sound of musicians outside his window. There were eight of them, nomadic female dancers with tambourines, rattles, and the same sort of stringed instrument he had seen amongst the wagon folk in southern Hatu. They swirled through the streets, their voluminous skirts and shirts of red, blue, and yellow flashing a kaleidoscope of color. He watched them draw people from the houses they passed, forming a writhing procession that wound towards the open square before the temple. Such gaiety to lift a curse, he wondered? Though the idea struck him as odd, perhaps even blasphemous, it was also a compelling one given his personal circumstances.

Was something like that expected of him?

Across the street below a canvas awning, within sight of his window, Orynn waved. She was outfitted in a pale cream dress in the local style and gestured for him to join her. He was hesitant, but his desire to experience the local customs, combined with her encouraging smile, convinced him to pull on his boots and join her in the street.

"I thought you had chosen to sleep the day away," she teased. "It is midmorning and Captain Delamo and Eridel are already enjoying themselves. Will you accompany me?"

"Mid-morning?" He had not expected to sleep late after turning in so early.

"A bed will do wonders for the quality of rest…and you have had little of late. The Captain and I saw no reason to rouse you earlier…but I admit I've been waiting for you."

Squirming beneath the effects of her smile as he felt his body temperature climb, Kavan said, "gdhededhá…?" in a tone that begged to be let off the hook. If he kept his focus on his quest, she might take pity on him and not force him into a compromising position.

Orynn would have none of it, however, and shook her head. "Is at the temple, as I said last night. I think he went there after dinner and has been there all night. Do you have any further excuses to put forth for not joining me, milord?"

He looked away, embarrassed, and pretended to admire the architecture they passed. "I suppose I am making excuses. I am not comfortable at festivals…"

"Unless you are playing at one. Well…this time you are allowed to enjoy it from the spectator's side." She extended her arm with a timid smile. After staring at her for several moments, he hesitantly followed her towards the square without accepting her arm.

If she was disappointed, he did not see it.

This festival was different than ones he was accustomed to. His ears were bombarded with music from no less than eight groups of performers scattered across the square, each playing different pieces. Local delicacies were everywhere, both to eat and drink, and to one side of the yard, a group of men had gathered to kick a round stuffed bladder from one line to a hole across a second line some ten yards away. Not far from the men, a group of women chatted as they watched the game and oversaw the welfare of a horde of children. The only other activities to partake of, other than gambling games or debates, were eating, drinking and dancing, and as the food and drink were offered at no cost, there was an overabundance of both. Kavan's stomach rumbled in response to the aromas, or perhaps, he mused as Orynn stopped and he caught up with her, it was a symptom of anxiety.

She pointed out several local treats and explained what each was made from, in case there were foods Kavan could not eat for physical or religious reasons. They eventually settled on bread, goat's milk, a plate of spicy roast pork, and a green, elongated fruit that tasted like mulled honey. The meal was shared between them, but Kavan kept his focus on the crowd, unable to look at the woman beside him. This was the closest he had been to her in weeks, and as he felt his body's response to her intensify, he was reminded why that was. The sunlight in her hair drew out the gold in its red tone and her skin was creamy and dark. He knew it without staring, knew that she was exquisite. He wanted to touch her but could not. His physical response to her might not be a sin, but doing anything about it most certainly had to be.

"Will you dance, milord?" she asked, noticing that his eyes had locked on to a group of children who had joined the dance nearby.

He looked at her with trepidation and quickly said, "I do not know these dances." Another excuse, but also an honest reason.

"I do…or would you be uncomfortable following me?"

She was teasing, he knew, but it did not prevent the sudden tension from settling between his shoulders and eyes. "I would be uncomfortable dancing. With anyone." Although when he watched Eridel swing past with his arms around two different girls and a third following, he wondered what it would be like to hold Orynn close, not merely in his dreams, but here…now. He pushed off the surging shivers and shook his head. No, it was best not to dance with her.

If she was disappointed, she did not show it. "Then you will not object if I do?" she asked, licking her fingers clean as she stood.

Kavan shook his head. "You are free to do as you please, milady. I am in no position to make demands of you."

"Not even if I allow it?" She grinned at his expression and was soon lost amidst the crowd. He tried to follow her movements but there were too many people and he quickly lost sight of her. When he did spy her, she was still dancing, a different partner each time, sometimes with a man, sometimes with a woman, sometimes with young children. Orynn's beauty was such that it took effort for Kavan to refrain from tearing her away from other partners to hoard her for himself. She was smiles and grace, courteous and playful, a flirtatiousness quite similar to Princess Diona's displays without the forceful undertones that demanded a response from her partners.

He never saw Wortham among them.

As the day wore on and she did not tire, Kavan wrestled more and more with his conscience and his faith. It was dancing, nothing more. There was nothing immoral about a dance. Holy texts often referred to dancing, in merriment, and in worship. It was celebrated, not condemned. What harm could there be?

In the end, as the sun sank lower and Eridel had vanished long ago, Kavan gave in to the losing battle fought throughout the day. He suspected that once his quest was complete he would not see Orynn again. As she had hinted many times, she had a life elsewhere and his place was in Rhidam, no matter how much he dreaded going back. What could be the harm in a single dance?

It took time to locate her in the push of the crowd, and Kavan found that the press and touch of bodies around him made his already heightened senses tingle uncomfortably. When he did find her, it was to stop and stare with a surge of longing that went deeper than the physical. It rooted him in place until she turned in her dance, saw him, and smiled. He took one step as she spoke a few words to her dance partner, and then stepped away from him to allow Kavan to approach. When the bard did not, she closed the gap between them, smiling.

"Is something wrong, milord?"

He shook his head no. "Only if you think a dance with me would be improper?"

She fell against him with a laugh of abandon. "Hardly improper," was her happy response.

Her enthusiasm almost made him drop her hand and flee.

With her hands on his shoulders, she directed him to put his on her waist and began to dance. It was a simple thing, five steps, in time to the music, spinning them around in the crowd. As a musician, he quickly picked up the rhythm, and once he grew comfortable with it and the feel of her beneath his hands, he could not stop. He was lost in her gray eyes, to the warmth and softness of her curves beneath his twisted hands, in the scent of her that seemed stronger than any meal, perfume, or incense could be. The rhythm controlled him; she controlled him. He would have done anything she asked, as he was beyond thinking, only feeling and absorbing what she had to give.

It was much later, after the sky had grown dark and many of the revelers had departed, that someone jolted into him, an elbow in the small of his back, making him aware of his surroundings.

The realization that night had fallen, the awareness of how much time had passed in her arms, caused him to halt in panic. "Milady…how could this…?" He knew how it had happened and the loss of control frightened him.

The joy on Orynn's face faded. "You object to a few hours lost to innocent diversion, milord?"

He stared at her. This had been no innocent diversion for him, not innocent at all. Surely, she must know that. "I should not have…"

"Do you regret the dance?" She looked as if she might cry as she waited for his answer, and the thought of hurting her tore at his chest like claws.

"Yes…no…I…we should not have…I should not…" He reached for her face, wanting to take away that sorrow, but she drew back from his touch before it happened and disappeared into the remaining group of dancers. Kavan tried to follow but lost sight of her as quickly as he had on the beach in Natrona.

He had lost her. The claws in his chest dug more deeply into his heart. He had not meant to hurt her, but he could not lie. It was not in his nature to lie. Now that she was gone, leaving him stumbling through dark streets in search of her, his thoughts scrambled for some logic that might resolve the confusing situation he was in.

What had been so wrong with an afternoon of dance? Had he injured anyone, offended anyone, or caused anyone to fall away from their Faith? Not that he knew. Dancing had taken his mind off his hands, his lost music, and his misery, more completely than anything else had to date. If anything, it seemed that dancing had been the best thing he could have done for a reprieve from his troubles, and he was confident, after what Kóráhm had said to him, that the Saint would have made the same choice as a mortal man.

He decided he would watch for her return from the window of his room, at which time he would apologize for his insensitivity and awkwardness. Once there, he discovered Wortham lying face down on his bed, snoring loudly, smelling strongly of alcohol as if he had spilled as much upon himself as he had consumed. The captain rarely got drunk; it was too much of an effort for a man who held his liquor so well. Rather than wake him, Kavan removed the man's boots and shifted him into a more comfortable position on the mattress to let him sleep. He pulled the room's single chair to the window and settled there to meditate and wait for Orynn.

A low groan woke him sometime later from the midst of a dream. Not a dream he decided, since the image did not fade from his memory as those of dreams did. The Sight. He did not recognize the structure or the elderly woman tending it, but he felt a strong urgency to go to her. It was an odd occurrence. The Sight had not come to him since Muir's wedding, and it rarely showed him anything pertaining directly to himself. Those two facts made the need to find this woman, this place, all the more important.

"Where am I?" the captain muttered in a thick voice.

Sitting on the bed beside Wortham, Kavan offered a tin mug of water. "Do you mean which city? Or which room? Or something else?"

"Milord Kavan? I'm…" He sat, expecting to apologize, but the spinning room made him squeeze his eyes closed and grasp his head with a groan.

"You're on my bed. I found you here when I came in."

Once the pain had passed, Wortham cracked his eyes open and accepted the water. "How long?"

"A few hours, I believe, at least since I have been here."

"I apologize for my condition..."

"Why?" Kavan asked. "Because you used alcohol to soothe your troubles? I am in no position to judge you. I have done so myself."

Wondering when that had been, since Wortham knew Elyri did not drink as a rule and he had never seen Kavan imbibe, the captain shrugged and put the mug down. "I have no troubles, milord."

The bard sighed. "You have been with me for many weeks, shouldering the brunt of my anguish and bitterness, defending me against Eridel, protecting both my body and my self-esteem. While I have not asked you to do this, I appreciate your loyalty and friendship more than you know. Still, it cannot be easy for you. Your endurance had to reach its end at some time."

"Has yours?" Kavan cocked his head, his eyes bidding Wortham to explain. "Have you reached the end of your endurance…at least with Eridel and the pain you cause yourself by welcoming him? The rest…your pain and frustration with your injury…I can withstand, but I find it difficult to bear the torment you inflict upon yourself to impress others with long-suffering tolerance."

The captain's words struck an unexpected nerve and Kavan's eyes narrowed. "You know nothing of what I face…"

Wortham staggered to his feet, not intimidated by the bard's sudden change in mood as the alcohol haze bolstered him. Towering over Kavan he grunted, "You think not? Do you think I do not have eyes and ears? That I do not see what I see every day I am with you? You judge me harshly to think me a fool, milord. I know what I witness. Perhaps someday you will see it as I do. Do not expect me to tolerate your self-flagellation forever. I love you more than my own life, but I cannot bear to watch what you continue to do to yourself in the name of penance."

The bard made no attempt to stop him as Wortham stumbled from the room without his boots. It had been many years since Kavan had felt this sort of anger and he could not recall a time when he had felt betrayed and condemned by his best friend. Let Wortham sleep in the street. Waiting for Orynn forgotten, Kavan was going to bed.

❧*❦

The peasant family with whom the murdered Elyri had stayed would tell the inquisitor nothing. They refused to open their door to an agent of the king and would not speak through the cracks. Not that Caol expected them to. Peasants were easily intimidated by thugs; they had little and what little they had could be easily taken. Fear was a useful tool. Nothing the inquisitor could say reassured them; even the promise of payment was not enough for them to risk their lives and he did not have the stomach to bully them as they had already been bullied. He came away knowing they had witnessed something, but nothing more. It would be hard for them not to have, when the Elyri minstrel had been forcibly removed from their home.

A quick tour of the small settlement revealed nothing. If anyone else had seen or heard anything, they were not speaking either. Not for the first time, Caol wondered how he and Justice Corbin were to do their jobs when the people they sought to protect would not cooperate.

"Sir?

The urchin looked at him with round blue-gray eyes as she tugged upon his trousers. Glancing around to see where she might have come from, he squatted to her level, something he always did with children, and asked, "What is it, child?"

"Those pictures…I could tell you something…if you help my Fa."

Caol suppressed a grin, not wanting to scare her with his excitement. Her sincere expression was frightened, but she was willing to part with her information for a price. From his pocket, he pulled five gold Crowns, more money than most peasants would see in a year or more, and said, "There is more if what you tell me turns out to be true."

❧320❦

For several moments the child stared at the coins with an expression of disbelief. Then she closed her tiny fist around them and said, "There was a bard here, staying with the Delins. It was overnight and he played for us. He was good…and friendly…" She motioned for the pictures and Caol held them for her to see. "This man was listening, but he left before the rest. There was a lot of noise after I was asleep. All I could see from the window, before father made me lay down, was a wagon going towards the city."

"Was this man on that wagon?" he encouraged.

She shrugged. "It was too dark. There was one person driving, and two in the back, but I could see no more."

Every little bit of information was helpful, but he was no closer to catching the killers than he had been. "Think hard. This man…have you seen him before? Does he live here?"

Her dirty blonde hair swung from side to side as she shook her head. "He does not live here. He comes with a wagon of pots."

A potter with a wagon. His first useful clue. He almost hugged her for that helpful hint. Giving her another Crown, he stood and smiled. "If this is true, and if it helps find these others, I will bring you more. I promise. Thank you, child. The King owes you his gratitude."

The thought of the King owing her anything made the child giddy with excitement. "Thank you!" she exclaimed as she scurried away to show her father what she had gotten for her family.

A potter. This made the next step in the investigation a job for the new Chancellor. Flannery McGrannis was about to get his first taste of what he had gotten into.

❧*❦

Kavan waited at a table in the lower level of the inn for Orynn to join him so he could gain the items he had come to Fikahr for. She had not yet arrived. Nor had he seen Wortham since last night's argument.

In one night he had wronged two people, one intentionally, the other not, and he was sick with shame. He wanted to rectify his wrongs, or at least apologize, but he was not sure how.

Would the captain forgive him? Kavan believed he would, as the man was the most resolute friend the bard had. But every man had a breaking point and he worried that he had finally pushed Wortham past his. And Orynn? What if, as he feared she had abandoned his cause? Unable to speak the language of these people, would he be able to obtain what he needed to cleanse the náós and redeem his soul. The bitterness was creeping back, sinking deeper than before, and this time he did not think he would be able to dispel it if it took hold.

When Orynn appeared in the doorway, she did not speak only beckoned him to follow with a motion of her hand. Her face was impassive. In her arms, she carried a large pack, the five bolts of Káliel silk, and though he asked, she would not allow him to carry it. He supposed it was because they could not risk the fabric being damaged if his crippled hands should drop it in the dust and muck of the city streets, but the refusal felt like rejection. He said no more as she led through the streets until she finally stopped before a closed door.

"The merchant we need is here. He will not do business with me because I am a woman; you must deal with him directly. I will translate and he will make the trade, but that is all I can do."

Her words sounded peculiar after she had repeatedly demonstrated how much influence she had with these foreigners, but Kavan was given no chance to speak or question her before she opened the door into a room filled with spices, incense, oils, and exotic plants. The strong aromas assaulted his senses, causing his eyes to burn and water, but he followed her inside.

The man behind the counter looked at them with red, puffy eyes and wiped his nose with a cloth. It seemed he was as affected by the vapors of the environment he worked in as Kavan was. "Foreigners. Rare in this place. What do you seek? How might I help you?"

Orynn translated and Kavan nodded his head. "We have journeyed here in search of commodities rare to our land. We were told you might be able to assist with what we seek."

"Merchants?" he laughed. "Trading in rare commodities?"

"Not merchants merely a man on a…quest. I am in need of Diwi and Orec."

Expression flattening, the merchant wiped his nose and then his eyes. "I have no Orec. To sell it to you would be a mistake…a fatal one for you."

Kavan nodded to show he understood. "I am aware of the hazards and risks, sir. I know its history, have seen it work…but I am in need of it nonetheless."

"What could you possibly need Orec for that you would be willing to risk your life to possess it?"

Listening to Orynn speak, the bard wondered if she was translating or having a private conversation with the merchant. The question caught him off guard but he tried his best to answer without giving personal details. "They are needed for the purification of a defiled náós. If it is not done, I fear great evil will befall my people and lands."

The man crossed his arms and leaned back upon the stool. These people, with their host of gods, festivals, customs, and beliefs, surely understood the desire to purify that which had been defiled, to rectify past evils for the sake of the present and the future. "Diwi is not free."

"I am prepared to trade. We have silk from the islands of Káliel, the finest they produce." With Orynn's aid, he spread one bolt upon the table for the merchant to examine. A flash of excitement on his round face was quickly extinguished, leaving a more business-like expression in its place.

"One bolt of cloth will not purchase much Diwi. How much do you require?"

Kavan could not answer that. He did not know; Bhóité had not mentioned quantities, only items. "Milady…I was not told…"

"You could request as much as five bolts will buy," she suggested.

"Will we need the cloth to trade for Orec?"

"I do not know, milord." She was speaking to him but her voice and features were unanimated. "It depends on where we must go to find the oil. But it would be better to have too much of what you need than not enough. I think you must take the chance. We can get by, if we must, with some other form of trade."

Turning back to the merchant who watched the exchange without interrupting, Kavan replied, "We have five bolts of silk. We could carry no more. We will trade them for as much Diwi as would be fair."

Sliding the stool back, the merchant went to the end of the counter and produced a clay jug the size of two fists, and a large clay container of a fine amber powder peppered with small gray crystals and dark green flecks. With a spoon, he scooped three times from the larger jar, deposited it into the smaller one, and was about to close the jug when Orynn snapped angrily. He jolted, nearly dropping the large container, and then his eyes crinkled as if in amusement as she continued her tirade. He barked something, an insult perhaps to put her in her place, but Orynn began to gather up the bolts of cloth. Kavan did not attempt to stop her, although there was a tight pain in his chest at the thought of not getting what they had come for. The merchant cried out and began hurriedly scooping the powder into the smaller jar until it was full. He corked it, sealed it with wax, and offered it to Kavan.

"Thank you for your business," the fellow said, bowing, gesturing, and smiling with apologetic gratitude.

Kavan nodded and bowed. "I thank you; k'Ádhá bless you for your aid."

In the street, Diwi secured safely in her pouch, Orynn grunted and muttered, "He already has. Three spoons for five bolts of Káliel's finest silk? He meant to cheat us. I may not know the exchange rate for Diwi, but that cloth should have gained us more than we got. I should have pushed for…"

"Trade for them has been poor," Kavan murmured, interrupting in a gentle tone. "It is not surprising he expected to recoup previous losses by bilking travelers. But I think we have enough; the weight of it feels right to me." He was not sure what right should be, but it felt that way to him. "Please, do not be angry with him…or with me."

"You?" If she had any inkling what he meant, she did not show it.

"I was needlessly unkind last night without meaning to be. I do not know my own mind on some matters, and unexpected emotional occurrences confuse me. It might not be much, but it is the sole claim I can make in my defense. I ask forgiveness…if you will grant it."

She was silent. People passed on the street without looking at them, people in robes, long tunics or baggy trousers, sandals on their feet and shawls around their shoulders with which to shield their heads from the sun and their faces from the wind. "I have already forgiven you," she said, "but knowing why does not make the pain less."

He closed his eyes and nodded. No, he did not expect his words to take the pain away. Words rarely did. "I understand. And apologize again. I would not blame you if you choose to abandon this cause and stop speaking to me…but I sincerely pray you do not."

The need for her colored his words enough that she stopped and stared until he awkwardly turned from her gaze. "I pledged my aid to find k'ílshwythnec; I cannot in good conscience leave before that is done. There are many who would be angry if I abandoned this, especially after the time and effort I've invested. Besides," her gaze softened a little, "I have no desire to part ways with you yet, milord."

With a sigh of relief and a giddy rush of warmth that filled him with unfamiliar joy, Kavan changed the subject, wanting to put last night as far behind him as he could and not risk making the same mistake again. "Do you know of a place of ruins…a shrine perhaps…a small building with an octagonal stone floor, attended by an ancient woman? Is there such a place within this land?"

She seemed to bounce in place with a smile of what looked more like relief than happiness. "Ergoth! The shrine! Yes, that is a logical place for you to begin."

"Begin?"

"The city of Ergoth was destroyed many centuries ago, but its history is something you should know, if you do not already. Any quest begins with knowledge; don't you agree?"

He nodded but said, "I know nothing of a place called Ergoth." If it was an important piece of history, be it his or Elyri history, he wondered why he had not heard of the place before. "Will we find Orec there? Or the chalice or staff crown?"

"Not likely…at least not in a usable form. There is little there that looters have not taken. But you may find answers to other questions…and Walga may know where to find Orec."

Wondering what questions she meant, as his life seemed to be full of questions and not many answers, Kavan nodded. His next destination was at hand, but he did not expect the others to be pleased with more travel. And Wortham, he thought with an ache, might refuse to follow him any longer.

❧Chapter 18❧

"Where are we going?"

The inquisitor's daughter held her finger to her lips but did not release his hand as she led Gaelán through the streets of Rhidam.

"If my father learns I am out here…" Of course, such rules had not stopped Gaelán before. He often snuck out of his parents' home to visit girls in Levonne. But this time, with the growing threat of anti-Elyri violence, he knew such an escapade could be dangerous. His trust in Asta allowed him to take this chance, but he was still afraid.

"He won't," she promised. "And if he does…you can claim I ordered it." She grinned and continued through the alley.

Gaelán rolled his eyes. Her words offered no assurance of safety or escape from punishment. "It will mean nothing if we get killed."

"Killed? Gaelán, don't be maudlin. No one is going to die. I want to…look…there it is."

She pulled him against the wall of the building the alley ran beside and pointed to a house across the street, one unspectacular in any way other than its newness. "That's the house father's been watching."

"Why?"

"I don't know. That is why I wanted to see it…to learn why…"

"And you brought along your own personal healer in case something goes wrong?"

"My own personal…?" She grinned and kissed his cheek. "I brought you because I trust you and wanted to share the adventure. No one else would be bold enough to come."

He did not consider himself bold. At the moment, as he silenced her with a rough tug on her arm when the door of the house opened, he considered himself a fool for undertaking this venture. She insisted he wear nondescript clothing so that they were less likely to be recognized and snuck past the palace guards with an ease that made him nervous.

A man emerged onto the stone step and turned for parting words with someone within. Asta's hand in his was trembling and he wondered if she was afraid or excited.

Though the clothes he wore in no way resembled holy robes, the hawkish features of the man at the door were recognizable to many in Rhidam. "dedhá Claide?" whispered Gaelán, finding nothing unusual about a dedhá visiting the Faithful except for his plain manner of dress.

"No…the other man." The doorframe obscured him and Gaelán could not see him clearly. "We must get closer. Come on."

"How…?"

"Do what I do," she interrupted, before running from the alley, screaming with delight and a look over her shoulder that indicated she wanted Gaelán to chase her. It seemed a dangerous risk, but as he could not let her face peril or harm alone, he followed. Asta plowed headlong into the gdhededhá, who looked down with stern annoyance.

"Be gone, urchins," he snapped coolly, barely glancing at them, his harsh gaze not lingering long enough to recognize those to whom he spoke.

"I apologize, dedhá," she said with a curtsey, using the opportunity to study the man inside out of the corner of her eye. "I was not watching where I was going."

"No, you were not. Off with you. Watch where you play in the future…and young man, you are old enough to know better than to chase a young woman thus."

Not trusting his voice, Gaelán bowed and followed Asta away from the house into a different alley. But she did not stop there. She ran back to the keep and Gaelán was challenged to keep up with her.

"Are you going to tell me what that was about?" he asked breathlessly when they finally stopped within the castle gates. He did not look at the attending sentries in case they noticed their return and were prompted to ask questions about how, and why, they had been out of the castle in the first place.

"Do you think dedhá Claide recognized us?" she countered, looking around to see if they were safe, though she knew they were.

"He did not seem to. What was that about?"

"I need to tell my father about this."

"Asta…" Gaelán protested. It was too late; Asta was already running inside. Gaelán had no choice but to follow and try to protect himself.

The pattern in the accounts before him seemed obvious to Caol and he could not believe he had missed it before. The number of missing individuals had risen to twenty-seven, probably more since he suspected many disappearances were unreported. For every report there was one common thread, one incident in the time immediately preceding the abductions, which seemed notable. In each location, an Elyri had either stopped at the house of the disappeared or else had recently settled nearby. In each case, while the people abducted were missed, and the abductions could be accredited to the Elyri, their loss to the community would not be a great burden, making their absence less likely to be questioned by anyone of import. The abductors had chosen their victims with care.

As inquisitor, Caol was obligated to look at the incidents objectively. It was possible, however much he could not imagine it, that Elyri were responsible for the abductions. But for what purpose? Elyriá never sought violent confrontation and this was a decidedly concerted, and aggressive, effort for them to make. It was equally possible that this vile trio of pranksters calling themselves Corylliens was coordinating the abductions to cause the Elyri to appear guilty, and even if the Elyri were innocent, the fear that they were not would be enough to create hysteria and violence as soon as anyone else noticed the pattern.

But for the Corylliens, whoever they were, to mastermind a kingdom-wide series of acts would have required years of planning to coordinate. They would need to have members spread throughout the realm, ready for a signal, members who had probably been in place for years. Possibly even decades, or centuries, he mused, wondering if Enesfel's earlier historical brush with Dawid Coryllien had left seeds to germinate in the years between the Persecution and the present. Was Enesfel dealing with a monster too large to behead or a monster with more heads than Caol could realistically confront?

"Father! You will not believe what I saw!"

The inquisitor caught his daughter in his arms as she burst into the day room, not wanting her to scatter his documents out of order. "Easy, Asta. Catch your breath. Hello, Gaelán. Now…what is important enough that you have burst in without a polite entry?"

Ignoring that subtle chastisement, she backed out of his arms. "The house you have been watching…"

Caol leaned his elbows on his knees, his eyes narrowing as he worried about what his daughter might know. "What about it?"

"dedhá Claide was there…"

"How do you know?"

Knowing she had overstepped the rules by going there without permission, she did not reply immediately, but she did notice her father's interest at the mention of the gdhededhá's name, which confirmed the importance of the conversation she had overheard between Princess Diona and her father. She swallowed and continued. "We saw him! I heard you talking about it with Diona and I wanted to know why it was important to keep a house under surveillance. dedhá Claide was coming out when we arrived. He wasn't wearing robes, and was talking to the man in the drawing, the potter you discussed with Lord Flannery."

"Are you certain of what you saw?" He trusted his daughter's eye and did not think she would lie about something like this, but this news, if it was accurate, was too important to take lightly. It was obvious, however, that he would need to be more careful with his conversations.

"I wasn't at first, but I got close enough to get a better look," she said proudly. "I am certain it was the same man."

Caol gathered the reports from the table. "I must look into this. Do not think this will cancel out punishment, however. I will speak to you soon." She dropped her gaze but the smile on her face did not fade. Helping her father do his job, proving that she could do it too, was more important than punishment. Thankfully, it did not appear that her father meant to give away Gaelán's part in her exploits. The youngest healer was safe.

❧*❦

Across the table, Ártur felt Syl's eyes boring into him. He could not look at her when she stared at him like that. With a sad shiver, he recalled a similar conversation with Elys the day that woman had told him she would not marry him. Both women accused him of loving Teren more than he did them, of loving Kavan more. While he could not deny that his love for his cousin bordered on obsessive, he did deny that he loved the Lachlans more than his wife and child.

How then could he explain the need he felt to stay in Rhidam after the death of the bard whose head had been crudely displayed upon the náós' signpost? He could not, and that is what hurt his wife the most.

"What of our children if their father is killed, kyá? What do I tell them?"

He shook his head stubbornly. "I will not die. Hagan will not allow Bhríd or me out of the keep without guards. I will make frequent visits to Bhryell to see you, every day if I can, and I will be with you for the birth of our child. If my life is in danger, I will come home."

Her eyes narrowed. "This decapitated bard does not make you think you are in danger?"

"He was alone. I suspect he had no idea what the political and social situation was like here. He had no protection. There is no need to be concerned about me."

She crossed to the window where she watched the snow fall outside. "You will stay regardless of what I say." It was not a question. She already knew what he would do.

"I…" Watching her, and then looking at his hands, he said, "If you demand it, I will stay in Bhryell. You know I will."

"You will be unhappy…frustrated. You will resent me."

"And you will resent me if I do not go."

"Ártur," she murmured, perching upon his lap and wrapping her arms around his neck. "I will be sad, I will be lonely, and I will worry about you every moment we are apart, but I will not resent you. Unless you use the Lachlans as an excuse to miss the birth of your child. Do what you must, but please remember you have children and a wife who need you too."

Hugging her with his face pressed into her neck, he breathed in the sweet scent of her and whispered, "I could never forget."

❧*❧

Everyone was present when Kavan departed Fikahr for the ruins of Ergoth. Wortham was surly and gruff and avoided Kavan when he could, keeping company with Orynn instead who, though she claimed to have forgiven him, could look Kavan in the eye no longer. The way they avoided him, coupled with the fact that a staggering drunk Eridel slowed their first day of travel, did little for Kavan's mood. Darkness sank its teeth into him deeper. There was no escaping it. Though he had a new goal and continuing purpose, the depression, jealousy, and anger were consuming him.

When they stopped to camp that first evening, Kavan withdrew from their company while remaining in sight of the camp. No one made an effort to approach him as his foul temper pushed even Eridel and Urian away; that, in turn, fueled the bitterness further. k'Ádhá, he thought. If he could leave them and proceed alone, it would be preferable to the torment.

Eridel picked up his harp and began to strum, though in his stupor the noise he produced was sickening to Kavan's ears. Urian tried to sound jovial about the result, and Kavan moved further away. The song stopped. Kavan did not look back to see why.

Hearing footsteps in the leaves, he stopped and growled but did not look back to see who was following. He already knew.

"It was rude of you to walk away."

"I was already away…"

"You know what I mean," Orynn snapped.

"I could not bear to hear that clamor. The harp is an instrument of beauty. He has turned it into a mockery."

"Eridel is young. He wants to please you."

Kavan glared, resentful that she took Eridel's side. "He wants to be me. And he is failing."

Her voice clipped, Orynn shook her head. "No one can be you. No one will ever take your place. You and your music are unique."

"Were unique," he reminded her bitterly. "Now I am nothing."

"Stop it! I will hear no more of this self-loathing foolishness."

"So go back to Wortham. You and he seem to be of the same mind." He left her, stalking angrily into the night, seeking solitude.

"Then perhaps you should heed what we say!" she called after him in an equally harsh tone. There was no indication that he heard her.

❧*❦

"There was nothing to find, My Liege." Caol sank into a chair, exhausted and frustrated after a day of unproductive effort.

King Hagan chewed his finger, a nervous habit from childhood he was trying unsuccessfully to break. "But the fellow was there?"

"I do not doubt my source. The inhabitants did not deny there was a potter there; they even showed me three new copper pots they had bought. It might explain why he was there, but not why gdhededhá Claide was talking to him."

"dedhá Claide? What has he to do with this?"

The inquisitor rubbed his eyes, wondering whether the King knew of his sister's suspicions. Deciding not to risk it, in case Hagan did not share Diona's doubts, he muttered. "Possibly nothing, but he was likely not buying pots."

"Perhaps he was offering advisement…that is his duty. Or visiting the sick. Or perhaps he was encouraging the fellow to turn himself in, if it was who you say."

"None of the dedhá have seen the sketches…except for k'dedhá Jermyn. Claide could not be encouraging a man to turn himself in unless he knew the man has done something wrong…which, in my opinion, would implicate Claide in something none of us want his involvement in."

The King crossed his arms. "Yes, I could see where that would be the case…but the man could have confessed, which would have made it a private matter between them." Hagan looked weary then as he closed his eyes and asked, "What next?"

"Chancellor McGrannis is examining census records to learn who this potter is. Potters do not generally roam far from home; their peddling range tends to be small. That means he should be from the area surrounding Rhidam. We will find him, which will lead us to the others. I am also investigating the possibility that the Elyri are abducting Enesfel's people."

King Hagan drew back his shoulders as his eyes flew open. "You do not believe that to be the case…do you?"

"No, but it is a lead I must pursue to its conclusion in order to rule it out. I need to know if we are dealing with two separate issues…Elyri abducting Teren and Teren killing Elyri…or if this is a completely Teren driven phenomenon as it was during the years of the Persecution."

"Persecution? As in Teren and Elyri sacrifices? As in Coryllien?"

Caol nodded. He had not yet mentioned the bloody message left upon the náós signpost to the King. It had not seemed prudent to worry him. Now, however, it might be time. "There is no evidence of sacrifices, but we do know that the Teren deaths and disappearances during those years were conducted by other Teren. The message left with the head suggests that, if nothing else, there is someone who has equated these times with those."

"How much longer before we see tensions explode?" The King did not ask about the message. Perhaps someone had already spoken of it to him.

"My Liege, I think we are seeing it already. Conflict will continue to escalate until whoever is behind this is caught or the Elyri are driven out of Enesfel. Justice Corbin is conducting a kingdom-wide inquiry of Elyri travels and the abductions, and we are spreading the word to get all Elyri in Enesfel to safety. It will be at least a week before we begin to get information. Meanwhile, there is also the possibility of

Neth's involvement, of which I have only speculation. If a foreign force is behind this, it would likely be King Merkar. And I will continue the search for this potter of course."

The King nodded. "Keep me informed of your progress, Lord Dugan. If Neth is involved, even indirectly, I want to know." If war was to be the outcome, Hagan did not want to be the last to find out.

It was two days later when Chancellor McGrannis learned the names of three different potters, all within Rhidam's radius, all with wagons used to service surrounding villages and homesteads. Caol and Darius visited each one. The first potter was too old to be the man they sought, but he did recognize the drawing as a rival potter named Gernadus Farley. That ruled out the third potter on the list, but they chose to investigate to be sure. When the third merchant turned out to be an Elyri woman, they knew their first contact's information had to be accurate.

The inquisitor felt compelled to give the woman a warning, alerting her to the recent violence against her people of which she knew little. He examined her wares as they talked and in the end regretted that she chose to return to Elyriá. She was an excellent craftswoman. The likes of her wares would be missed.

He was not surprised to find that the final home, a few miles outside of Rhidam, was empty. If the potter was selling his wares, it would explain his absence. And if he suspected he was being hunted, having either been warned by his rival or by some carelessness on Caol's part, he would seek to lie low somewhere far from the place he was most likely to be sought. Lie low somewhere, Caol wondered, like that house in Rhidam? Caol's Association contacts were watching it more closely, and gdhededhá Claide's tail was being more diligent. They wanted more money for the job and though the inquisitor had gotten a bit more out of the chancellor, he could not approach the King on this matter. Caol knew that, unlike Arlan and Diona, King Hagan was uncomfortable with the involvement of the Association. In situations like this, however, the inquisitor believed it was a necessity. Having been an insider to the Association once, having worked hard to regain some level of trust, who else would supply him with what he needed when he could not do the work alone?

❧*❦

The crystal decanter shattered against the wall, causing both Belda and Flannery to jump. The serving woman cast her mistress a wary look of disquiet before hurrying to clean the glass and wine from the carpet. The chancellor was quiet but also looked at the princess with concern. His new status had lifted his confidence in dealing with the woman, but he had seen her angry more than once and did not want to be involved in her problems.

Still, the polite course was to inquire, and when Belda did not, he finally cleared his throat and asked, "Milady?" not expecting her to answer or confide in him.

"Prince Espen sends regrets about father but cannot be bothered to comfort me in my grief," she exclaimed. There was no reason for her to tell him, but in her anger, she wanted someone to listen to her grievances.

"Did you ask him to come?"

She stared at the chancellor as if he wore a second head. "Why should I do that? Would it not be the proper thing for him to…?"

"If you had told me the same, I would send my regrets…but without an invitation, I would not presume to think I was invited to intrude on your grief. It is not polite for a man to invite himself to a woman's home."

"Yet he would visit Hagan…because Hagan is the King? And a man?"

The chancellor shrugged, doubting he would ever understand women, particularly this one. "It is the way it is…especially in Hatu. Women there do not enjoy the status they have here."

"Hmmph…men!" She paced the length of the library and then leaned across the table in front of Flannery. He found it difficult to divert his eyes from her pale, bare throat. "He might not come if I asked…but if I asked him to bring men to support Hagan, do you think he would come?"

"Possibly. If Hatu has troops to spare. What interest do you have in his coming…if I might ask? You have not accepted his marriage proposal…"

Her face twisted into almost a snarl. "What do you know of that?"

Flannery pushed his chair back and shrugged, a gesture that seemed to further incense her since she stepped around the table closer to him. "His proposal is no secret. If you had accepted, you would be wed. That is no secret either. It is no wonder he is reluctant to…"

"I did not ask your advice on my private affairs, Lord McGrannis," she snipped. "You can inform General Agis of my intent to invite the prince and his troops, to allow him to make preparations for their housing should the Harcourts agree to lend support."

"As you wish," he replied, grateful she left the library, and him, intact.

❧*❧

Eridel had not attempted to make music again since the night after leaving Fikahr. Watching Kavan stalk away had heightened his awareness at last to the Elyri's misery. The young bard was quiet, well mannered, helpful, and at Wortham's suggestion, he stopped pursuing Orynn's attention. The captain, however, did not attempt to cheer his friend. He would travel with Kavan, protect him, and make camp for him, but he had endured enough of the bard's self-imposed misery. He was doing everything he could to ignore the man's pain, not an easy task when he felt as if it were his own.

However, he and Orynn agreed. Kavan was allowing the darkness to grow unchecked, letting it control him. He appeared to relish the respect and sympathy from people they encountered, as he relished Urian's remarks about bravery and steadfastness in accepting suffering; it struck Wortham as perversely against Kavan's usual nature. Together, he and Orynn bolstered each other's decisions to let the Elyri succeed or fail, with every intention of being there to assist him back to his feet when he hit bottom.

That time was coming; Wortham could feel it. Irritants Kavan had previously taken in stride, minor annoyances and small setbacks made him snappish. He wore a permanent frown and slept little. His eyes were filled with smoldering pain and anger. Not anger at those with him but rather anger at k'Ádhá for testing him, for causing this suffering, and for leading him on a quest for which he could foresee no resolution. There was also, the captain believed, anger for being unable to rein in the despair that consumed him. Kavan hated failure and was failing himself.

After a particularly tense day of climbing rocky terrain in the pouring rain, it gave Wortham an uneasy shiver when Eridel finally chose to take out his harp. At first, he was merely cleaning it, wiping the red wood with an oiled cloth and checking the strings for damage. The bard lay near the fire, attempting to shut out the voices to sleep. With his back to them, he did not see what Eridel was doing and did not seem to hear the opening of the instrument case. As the first notes on those animal gut strings were plucked when Eridel began to tune it, however, Kavan lurched up and snarled at the man across the fire.

"I do not want to hear that thing ever again. No music. If I do…k'Ádhá help me, I will not be responsible for my actions."

Startled and fearful, Eridel dropped the harp. It hit Urian's foot and the gdhededhá squawked and jerked away. There was silence, broken by the crackle of the fire and the dripping of rain from leaves where it had pooled. The others stared, uncertain what to say or do.

"Milord…" Orynn started, the first to dare to speak, hoping to calm Kavan's jangled nerves.

He did not want to hear her. "I want no music around me. If I am deprived the right to play, I do not want to hear it. I will destroy that harp if I do."

Dumbstruck like the others, Wortham got to his feet but did not follow as he watched Kavan stride away.

"I thought he was asleep…" Eridel stammered. "I meant only to tune…"

Urian fumbled at his feet for the harp and gave it back to Eridel, pausing to pat the young man's knee. "He does not mean…"

Wortham grunted and tugged at his beard. "I think he does, dedhá. I know him well; he would not have said it if he did not mean it. It may be a temporary state, one that might pass quickly," he added with reluctant hopefulness, "but he does mean it. If you wish to keep the harp undamaged, Eridel…and you wish to escape injury…I suggest you be careful."

Eridel's hazel eyes blinked sadly at the captain. "He would not hurt me…would he?"

The captain wished he knew. "He has done and said many things of late that he would not normally do. I regret to say it, but I would not rule out the possibility of violence." Orynn looked about to speak, to contradict him, but hung her head instead. "You know it is true, milady. He is not himself."

The harp was wrapped in its case and held tightly to Eridel's chest. "If I cannot entertain you, of what use am I? If music is not welcome, I shall go my way at the next village or town."

"That," Wortham said with a sigh, "might be the wisest decision you have ever made."

❧Chapter 19❧

"Onea!" Caol had not been so pleased to see anyone in years. Onea Pantel, the Association leader in Fiara, was still one of the most beautiful women he had met. She had changed little; her black locks were longer than they had been when he had last seen her and there were creases at the corners of her mouth and eyes that spoke of the years in between meetings but they did not mar her beauty. They had kept in touch since fate had crossed their paths, their letters becoming more frequent after Deidre's death. He had not traveled to see her, however, as duty kept him in Rhidam, and he had not anticipated she would ever come to him.

"Surprised, Lord Dugan?" she said with a laugh. "Your informants aren't very good if they did not know I was coming."

He grinned and offered his hand. "My informants also work for you. They might have known you were coming, but if they were instructed not to tell me, they probably wouldn't…at least not without significant incentive. Have you come on business or for pleasure?"

"Business is pleasure…and pleasure is business for some." She smirked as he pointed to a chair. "Actually, I have come with information."

As she expected, Caol grew more attentive and after locking the solar door, he drew closer to hear what she had to say. If Onea felt it necessary to bring information herself, rather than entrust it to a subordinate, it must be significant. Caol was not going to flatter himself by believing she had come to see him.

"Some habits don't die, do they, Dugan?"

"Caol. Please. Here, perhaps more than in the streets, privacy can be a rare commodity. I have never adjusted to it."

She traced her nails over the back of his hand. "Have you considered coming back to the life?"

Smiling at the shiver her gesture produced, he replied, "Not seriously. There are benefits here you cannot find elsewhere; I like it fine where I am. Someday, perhaps, I will retire to the life of a simple landowner, but that will not be for many more years. Now…what is it you have come to tell me?"

Though she did not remove her hand, she did take on a more business-like demeanor. "It came to my attention, and I have gotten several confirming reports, that there has been increased traffic near the Elyri-Neth border."

That concerned the inquisitor enough to make him lean forward with a sharp intake of breath. "What type of traffic?"

"Nethites trying to get through…small units of soldiers. Thus far they have been turned back at mountain passes, some have been killed. They are unusually persistent. Elyriá is not taking these advances kindly and I have heard speculation that they have small military units now guarding the passes more persistently, to keep invaders out."

Caol ran his hand through his hair, wondering if the deaths were caused by the Elyri units or by the dangerous mountain passes. "Troops? Spies? Traders? There's not much Elyri-Neth border left…and what there is, is near impossible to cross. Has there been mention of what they hope to gain or accomplish?"

"Not that I have heard. But I know King Merkar is sponsoring the efforts, trying to send spies into Enesfel. To my knowledge, they've all been captured, even those who attempt detours through Cordash.

Some may have gotten through, however; you might have Nethite spies circulating as we speak. Merkar seems very interested in what is happening here."

"Which means he either hopes to take advantage of our difficulties or has his hand in them." His hunch about Neth's involvement seemed less far-fetched, and he decided to have Darius investigate any possible Neth connections amongst the people who were missing. "It occurred to me that stirring up anti-Elyri prejudice might suggest an effort to regain the territory he lost, but I have yet to find anything that implies Neth's involvement. This doesn't prove it, of course, but it does look suspicious."

She nodded. "None of my people want to see Merkar regain a hold in the north. Not that we have been any more or less profitable under the Lachlan Crown, but our life expectancy has risen dramatically. A fair trade, I think," she added with a grin.

There was a rattle at the door, a clink, and it opened slowly, a crack, without making a sound. The inquisitor rolled his eyes and shook his head with a grin at Onea. "If you wish to pick a lock, Asta, you will need to learn to do it quietly."

The door opened and the girl entered, her face blank as if she were innocent of offense. That, at least, was one skill she had mastered. "You heard."

"It was difficult not to," her father chuckled. "What do you want?"

She shrugged. "The door was closed…and locked…which meant you had to be in here. If it was locked, it meant there was something to hide. I want to know what."

"Did it occur to you that I locked the door to keep from being disturbed?"

She grinned and replied, "Did it occur to you that if you wanted to exclude me, you should have gone elsewhere? Either that or you should not have taught me to pick locks?"

Onea laughed with delight. "Your daughter?"

As Asta scrutinized the woman whose hand was still on her father's, Caol said, "Yes. Asta, this is Onea Pantel from Fiara."

"The Association woman you correspond with."

The look of surprise on Caol's face made Onea laugh. Caol, not having realized his daughter knew about that correspondence, wondered what else Asta knew and what effect this would have on his relationship with Onea and the Association. Perhaps he was training her too effectively.

"Any youngster with such talent and boldness has to be a Dugan. It is a privilege to meet you." Onea offered her hand, and after staring at it cautiously, the girl shook it.

"Now, Asta, please. We are discussing matters of importance. Will you find some other way to amuse yourself?"

"Oh, very well," she sighed melodramatically, closing and locking the door behind her as she left.

"And no eavesdropping," he added, remaining at the door until he heard her footsteps retreat. To his guest, he said, "I apologize for that. I was not aware of how far her training had progressed…" He had known she was learning quickly, knew she spent many of her waking hours practicing the skills he taught, but she had, it seemed, hidden her adeptness from him.

"Which means she is a credit to her teacher, to be able to hide her skills. No need to apologize. It is a treasure to find a gifted child…but surely the Lachlans…"

He held up his hand to silence her, and with his other hand slowly unlatched the lock and pulled the door open. Asta looked at him with wide eyes. "How did you know…?"

"Instinct. Now run along or I shall banish you to a lesson in embroidery for the remainder of the day."

Asta skewed her face, indicating a distaste for such domestic female endeavors, and ran down the corridor. When Caol felt sure she was gone, he returned to his chair. "The Lachlans do not know about this…although I think Princess Diona believes Asta is too much like her father. Yet she and I regard the Kingdom the same. She would agree that grooming an heir is in the kingdom's best interest."

"You expect to leave your daughter as Inquisitor?" Onea found this both amusing and surprising.

Caol nodded. "King Arlan once said my background and connection to the Association make me uniquely qualified for this position; I agree. My son has no interest, for which I cannot blame him. His experience with such things was not endearing, to say the least. Asta has been interested for a long time; she was the one to approach me about learning the craft. I was reluctant but decided it would be for the best. I have too much knowledge to let it waste. I want her to know everything I can teach. I want her to gain the respect of the Association so that she can carry on without missing a step. She might not have the direct experience with the Association I have had…as far as the criminal activities and the need of hiding from the authorities, but she will have as much instruction as I can give."

"A hereditary connection between the monarchy and the Association? It is an intriguing idea, but I do not know how feasible. After all," she smiled," the position is traditionally Lord Inquisitor, not Lady Inquisitor."

Caol snorted. "Then Asta will be the first…as long as the Association and King Hagan will work with me, of course."

"Yes…there is that…" Onea stared at the closed door then said, "I would be willing to take her aside, teach her a few tricks while I am here if you wish…and will put in a good word for her in the future."

Having Onea's backing would prove beneficial, and for that, Caol was grateful. "Thank you, the opportunity is appreciated. Now, back to Merkar."

"I know little else," she replied with a shrug. "The atmosphere in Glevum is strained; the generals do not, apparently, approve of whatever is going on. My people tell me the army backs Prince Kjell."

Such unrest in Neth's royal house was not unusual, but keeping abreast of the interplay was too good an opportunity to pass. "I've not heard much about him. What is he like?"

"Handsome…the most dashing member of a royal family I have ever seen," the woman said, and then laughed at Caol's rolling eyes. "He looks nothing like the de Corrmicks, which has led to gossip as you can imagine. And he is clever. He would have to be to stay alive as he has. Either clever or a simpleton. Somehow, he stays out of the spotlight and has gained the military's backing at the same time. I don't think they would back a fool unless they intend to manipulate him. If Merkar knows Kjell has military support, he must fear retaliation if he has Kjell killed, because he has not tried to do so yet. Maybe Kjell is shrewd, too shrewd for Merkar to suspect he is a threat. I'm not alone in thinking Prince Kjell could be the best thing to happen to Neth, if he gained the throne without resorting to the treachery that often precedes a change in leadership there…as long as he's not some military puppet."

Caol nodded thoughtfully. "Perhaps Enesfel could lend him a hand in taking down Merkar. Even if he is a simpleton, it would be better than the typical de Corrmick leadership."

"A tempting idea. One to keep in mind if conditions turn foul. I'm watching the situation; I want to know what Merkar is doing before he does something irreversible."

Propping his feet on a stool, the inquisitor asked, "Have you considered setting up a contact with this prince? Might he make a good ally? Or connecting with someone in the military who has an in?"

"I am pursuing the military angle. Direct contact with the prince is the last option, I think. A man as shrewd, or foolish, as he is, is not one to approach lightly. I want to know as much as possible before I consider using him…"

"Or being used by him?" Caol asked cheekily, making her laugh.

"Precisely. Though being used by him could be enjoyable." The humor on her face dropped away quickly, however, as she asked, "Is it true about King Arlan?"

Countenance darkening, the inquisitor nodded. "Yes. His son Hagan is faring well thus far, given the state of the kingdom."

"I hope it stays that way. I finally adjusted to King Arlan's way of business; I would hate for something else unfortunate to happen."

"Aye…we feel the same. Is that all you came to discuss? It hardly seems necessary for you to have come so far…" The part of him that hoped she had come to see him persistently demanded attention.

This time when she smiled, it was different. "I needed to get away from Fiara for a time. A change of scenery, a chance to get a fresh perspective." That could mean she was skirting a brush with the law or that she was contemplating getting out of the business. Whatever it was, Caol did not need to know. "And I thought it was time to see you, thus I decided to bring the news myself. Objections?"

That sounded like she had a definite interest in him, which made him smile. "No. No objections. Shall I secure you a room?"

She shook her head. "I have lodgings. No offense, but I do not think I would be comfortable in a palace not of my own making…nor would I want to be blamed should anything turn up missing."

They both chuckled and he helped her to her feet. "Stay for the evening meal. You can meet the king, make your own judgments, and get a taste of what I endure every day. You might even learn something I can use."

Eyebrows raised in interest, she said, "I might indeed."

❧*❧

With the known body count of abductees up to thirty-four, Justice Corbin believed they might never gain the upper hand on the violence. Other issues he had dealt with during his tenure as Justice seemed petty compared to this. But he agreed with every point the inquisitor made, which made both of their jobs easier. When Minos Cornell was Justice, he had been determined not to rely on Caol's information network, believing that criminals would not spy on other criminals. Darius believed that, given enough incentive, a criminal would do anything, and Caol's contacts usually provided information that, while not always producing quick results, provided a framework within which to work. For now, as he strode out of the inquisitor's chambers, newest sketches and notes he had made during their conversation in hand that would hopefully produce further results, it was enough.

❧*❧

Ternce Wyndham had expected his retirement to be peaceful. He had not counted on the events preceding his retirement to explode into a full-scale, kingdom-wide epidemic. If he had thought Talladegah would be spared the upheaval, he was now disavowed of that notion. He came to the tavern, as he did once or twice a week, to keep abreast of local gossip. To Ternce, it was the best way to discover his subjects' needs.

When he came in out of the sun and wind, there was an argument in bloom at the bar between two small clusters of men. Sides had already been taken, with some declaring Elyri as the root cause of the problems facing Enesfel who should be driven out or exterminated. The rest argued for restraint and an end to mayhem because the anti-Elyri violence was keeping out not only the Elyri but also traders from other kingdoms, and discouraging people from traveling further than their own neighborhoods.

An argument that Ternce had heard before, and one he steered clear of when he could. It was not new; even in times of peace, there were the same two sides to be heard. Ternce had no problems with Elyri being in Enesfel, as long as they followed the rules like everyone else. Rules were meant to be obeyed, and that included not murdering someone simply because you did not like them. He chose to stay out of this argument as well, though he continued to listen as he ordered his drink and found an empty table.

His back was to the argument for a second too long; one moment he was listening, the next there was a crash and a stool flying over his head as he picked up his tankard in one hand. Someone shouted obscenities and another chair sailed through the air. A brawl ensued as punches flew, and Ternce was caught in the middle of it.

If he were younger, he would have fought his way to the door and let the brawl play itself out. These sorts of confrontations normally ended on their own or with the intervention of the establishment's owner and the local sheriff. If he felt particularly feisty or belligerent, he might have joined. But he was not in the physical condition to make an easy escape or to make participation wise. He picked up a chair, wielded it as a shield, and began to make his way to the door.

A tin mug struck the back of his head and the man who threw it realized quickly what he had done. There were at least two dozen men fighting, breaking chairs and tables, spilling ale, destroying the establishment, and Ternce was incapable of stopping it.

"Enough!" He shouted, but his demand was unheard. It did not surprise him. Something else struck him in the side, a chair or stool he guessed without turning. He finally got his back against the wall where he could see everything and protect himself from the majority of airborne objects and swinging fists. The tavern door crashed open, nearly hitting him when several members of the town patrol pushed into the room. They could not easily enter past the doorway without dragging those closest out into the street, but they hit whomever they could with fists or wooden sticks to incapacitate or stun them enough to get them out of the fight.

Their arrival gave Ternce an idea. Swinging his chair, he knocked a man through the doorway into the arms of the patrol who quickly restrained him. One by one, or in pairs, the retired general maneuvered several more brawlers to the door where the patrol could reach them, subdue them, and pull them outside. Eventually, the room was emptied enough that some of the patrols could get in to break up the heart of the fight.

The exertion had taken its toll on Ternce. He sank down on the chair he had been using, wobbly now that its legs and back were cracked in several places, and tried to catch his breath. He would reconsider coming to the tavern if this sort of thing was likely to happen often.

"Milord Wyndham! What are you doing here?"

Ternce liked the constable, a man whose father he had known since childhood. He shook the offered hand with a groan. "Hoping to enjoy a drink…not a brawl."

"Do you know what happened? Who started it?"

"The stool that almost hit me in the head started it," he chuckled. "No, I don't know who threw it. It was the same old argument, should the Elyri stay or go? I don't know anything more about it."

"We'll talk to them, sir, and get to the bottom of it. You should go home and take care of that gash on your forehead."

"Gash?" Ternce fingered the top of his brow and stared at his wet, sticky fingers. That unexpectedly made him grin. "Maybe I'm not quite the old man I thought…but I think I will have my drink at home."

The officer helped him up. "Aye, it might be better tonight, sir."

∾*∾

"Lord Dugan? Justice Corbin is in the stateroom with the King and Healer MacLyr; they request you join them at once."

In the midst of overseeing the training Asta was undergoing with Onea Pantel that day, Caol frowned. He did not want interruptions. It was not that he did not trust Onea; given his daughter's recently proven resourcefulness, he wanted to know what Asta was learning. However, the King's summon could not be ignored. "Of course, Denyan," he said as he stood. "Asta, please do as Lady Pantel asks…and stay out of trouble."

"I thought that was the whole purpose of studying with her, father," Asta said with an innocent expression, "to learn to get into trouble properly."

A vein in the side of Caol's neck began to throb and he opened his mouth to argue, but Onea cut him short with her laughter. "Do not worry, Caol, I will take care of her."

"I'm sure you will…" the inquisitor muttered before leaving the room.

Asta liked Onea. She was the first woman, other than Diona, Syl, and Madalyn to treat the youngest princess with adult respect. She was of an age to need a woman in her life because there were things he could not teach her. He wondered, as he strode through the corridors, if he should make a permanent arrangement with Onea or another woman for his daughter's sake.

"Lord Dugan, we have a gift," Darius said with a grin, indicating the bound man beside him as the inquisitor entered the stateroom.

Introductions were unnecessary; Caol recognized the man's face at once. He stepped closer, looking the man up and down, judging visible strengths and weaknesses. "Potter Farley…or shall I call you Gernadus? How pleased I am you could come. I've been waiting to make your acquaintance."

"What is the charge?" the man asked sourly. "Why have I been brought here bound like a criminal?"

Elbowing him in the side, making the man buckle and grimace, Darius barked, "Because you are a criminal."

"Enough, Lord Corbin. That isn't necessary." King Hagan stood, not feeling confident in this situation, in a room of his elders where he should be the dominant voice. He wished his sister were here. She would know how to handle this. "Do you deny," he asked the captive, "that on the night of the fourth day of the first month, you and two others abducted an Elyri from the home of a family near Rhidam? That you transported him in a wagon to Hes á Redh Náós, where you executed and beheaded him, displayed his head on the signpost and improperly buried his body in the náós grounds?"

The stout man chewed his cheek, eyes shifting around the room to determine what they knew and what they did not. Finally, he sighed. "I told them where he was…and agreed to let them use the wagon. I was there…I drove it…but I did not expect a killing. I was told to hold his arm, but I did not think he would kill him…"

"Who?"

The potter did not answer the inquisitor's question.

The King looked at the healer. "Lord MacLyr?"

Ártur nodded grimly. "His story coincides with the images I received from the victim. He is not the murderer."

Relieved, the potter almost tried to smile. "Then I am free to go?"

Caol scoffed and shoved a finger into the man's sternum with enough force to make him cough and gasp for air. "Hardly free. You did not wield the sword, but you participated in the abduction and are an accomplice. You did not turn in those who did the killing. All of that is punishable by death. Tell me…who are the others?"

Farley did not respond, his face paling as he faced possible execution. The King sighed, finding what he had to do next particularly distasteful. "Lord MacLyr? Can you gain the names?"

It was not, however, as distasteful to ask as Ártur found the prospect of reading the unwilling man. He grimaced but replied, "If you wish…"

The King nodded.

Ártur stepped forward reluctantly.

"He will not touch me!" Farley shouted, but despite his struggle, Caol and Darius held him fast. He fought, screaming curses as the

Elyri cautiously placed his hand upon the man's flushed face. Farley hated his sovereign for subjecting him to this. He screamed as if in pain for many seconds after the healer withdrew. When he realized those in the room were staring at him, that Ártur was again beside the King, Farley stopped struggling. He smiled smugly, convinced that since nothing had happened, no painful devices used, no expected Elyri torture, only a hand touching his face, the healer had learned nothing. Everyone knew Elyri inflicted pain.

"Lord MacLyr?" the King asked, hoping the healer had gotten what he needed.

Ártur cleared his throat, with his eyes closed as he sorted the images in his head. "He does not know the name of one…the other accomplice. But the man who did the killing…this man…" He opened his eyes and pointed to one of the sketches on the nearby table, "is called Hugh. He knows little about him, except that he was told that if any Elyri were seen in Rhidam, he was to leave word for Hugh at the Black Dog Tavern."

Farley's face turned a peculiar shade of gray. The Elyri had extracted information without pain…and he had not known it. He began to quake and pant. The story of pain infliction was a lie, but it would have been preferable. How much more fearful was it that thoughts could be read, by touch, without the victim knowing?

"There is an inn next to the Black Dog; I will see what I can learn." Darius relinquished the prisoner to Caol. "Will you see to his incarceration?"

The inquisitor grinned wickedly. "I would be happy to. And then, I shall seek out my contacts and see if they can assist in identifying and locating this fellow named Hugh…if that is even his real name. If he's the one giving orders, then he is the one to reckon with. Find him and we may find he's responsible for much more."

The King, and all in the room except Farley, hoped it was true.

⮾Chapter 20⮿

There was something amiss in the village; Caol felt it as he arrived, before dismounting his horse. The villagers shied away from him, avoiding eye contact, skirting him as though he were a plague carrier. Those he approached hurried away and barred themselves behind their doors. He had enough experience to guess why, and it galled him that he had not considered the consequences of his actions sooner. Perhaps, as Onea suggested, he had been away from his roots too long.

He finally found someone who did not flee, perhaps because she was too infirm or because she desired the confrontation. She stared with venom in her eyes as he approached, and though hesitant to speak to her, knowing what to expect, he cleared his throat and began.

"I am seeking a child…a girl…about this tall, with blonde hair…"

"She is not here," the woman spat.

Swallowing back the emotions those words gave birth to, he asked, "Where is she?"

"Taken away."

"By who?"

The woman's already squinted eyes narrowed. "You know who. You bribed one who knew no better; now she is gone."

"I did not bribe anyone," he protested. It was a reward for information, he told himself, which was still a bribe to the very poor, and he knew it. "When was she taken?"

She scowled. "I'll tell you no more. You invite death. Be gone."

He started to speak but decided against it. There was no point in pushing the issue and he knew no one would help now unless he resorted to force. He did not want that. The coins he carried as he rode back to the city felt twice as heavy. He would donate them, try to assuage his conscience of blood money. He did not think it would help, but keeping it would eat at him and make him ill.

He should have expected his suspects to retaliate and should have offered these people protection. He could have brought the child and her family to the keep until arrests were made. It had not mattered to such men that they punished a child. Her sole crime had been speaking without knowing the consequences. Caol's experience should have prevented her involvement. But he had learned two important details from these unfortunate events. Given the Associations code against harming children, Hugh and his cohorts were not likely to be part of the organization. And at least one of his suspects was still near Rhidam.

ȣ*ȣ

For the four days following his outburst, Kavan made every effort to be polite and considerate to those around him. Success was tenuous, as the darkness was always right below the surface, coloring even his most heartfelt acts of kindness. He spent evenings at the campfire, listening to the reserved banter rather than fleeing to solitude, and he endured Eridel's wounded gaze that begged for forgiveness, begged without words for permission to pick up his harp. The young harper understood now how it felt to be denied a musical outlet, and at least until their paths separated, Kavan was the only one who could give his music back.

Eridel stared across the fire with an intensity most would find embarrassing and uncomfortable. Kavan, however, was used to it. People had stared at him for as long as he could remember. Urian was whittling, as usual, this time a figure he said would be for Kavan, and Orynn was in her tent where she had been the last four nights. There was a change coming, one Kavan could feel. She laughed less, smiled less, though she did not seem to be in despair as Kavan was. Wortham was not speaking to anyone unless it was necessary; even the banter he had shared with Urian was gone. With no sign of Kóráhm and none of his companions for comfort or distraction, Kavan was reminded how it felt to be isolated and abandoned. He was nearer the point of continuing his journey alone than he had been a few days ago. These people did not need him; he was causing nothing but pain. He would be no more alone on his own than he was already.

Feeling useless, Eridel mimicked Kavan's morose behavior as hours crept past. That he understood was good, but Kavan could not stomach what he saw. It reflected too closely on him as he saw his own behavior in that man. An attempted conversation with Orynn about their destination was aborted when she excused herself for solitude and Urian's focus was on the malleable wood. In desperation, wanting to give kindness another try before turning his back and traveling alone, Kavan swallowed his anxiety and spoke.

"Eridel?"

"Milord?" It was clear he was afraid to speak, but he did not refuse to answer.

"Do you know any of my works?"

Eridel nodded warily. "I know some. They were the first pieces I learned to play. I try, but I cannot make them sound the way they should." He hoped admitting that failing would excuse misplayed notes if the Elyri ever heard him play them.

Kavan almost lost his nerve. Hearing music would be difficult enough. Hearing Eridel attempt Kavan's creations would be harder. The thought of those songs misplayed was almost unbearable. But he was determined to try, and thus with a clenched jaw asked, "Would you play something for me?"

Orynn emerged from her tent with a flicker of hope on her face and Wortham looked at her expectantly. Urian stopped whittling. Eridel stared at Kavan. "Do you mean it, milord? You would like me to play for you?"

The cumulative attention of every party member made Kavan's skin prickle and crawl. "I have asked, haven't I?" he replied, praying Eridel was not going to argue or protest until Kavan changed his mind.

"But you said…"

"I know what I said. There is no need to remind me. I was not…" he glanced at Wortham before using the captain's words, "myself."

Wortham's head bobbed once in acknowledgment.

The younger harper fumbled to produce the harp quickly. "I understand," he commented apologetically. "I understand, a little, how you must feel. I do not want to cause further…"

"Pain is something I must learn to live with," Kavan interrupted quietly. "It should not be cause for any of you to suffer. It is selfish. Please; I want to hear the legacy I leave behind, want to know that, regardless of what becomes of me, I leave something worthwhile."

Eridel's nervousness was evident in that, while the first song he played was flawless, it was flat, impassive, even dull, and Kavan could not imagine it had anything to do with how it had been written. He had never heard another bard play it in such a way, and Kavan knew it did not sound like that when he played it. The second song he attempted became quickly muddled and several key notes were missed.

"No…not like that." Kavan hummed the bar twice, slowly and clearly, not noticing the way Wortham shivered at the sound, or the way Orynn's eyes teared, or the way Urian's jaw fell slack. Kavan gestured for Eridel to play; though he played the fragment flawlessly, when he started the piece from the beginning, he timidly misplayed the same section.

The mistakes made Kavan grimace. "Did you not listen?" he hissed, trying to keep his annoyance in check. Teaching music had never occurred to him; the bards who came to Enesfel's court took the songs with them in their heads without having their author drill the music into them. He heard none of those minstrels play his compositions; he had no idea how true the reproductions were. With his nerves paper thin from weeks of distress, he could not understand how Eridel could make the same mistake after playing it properly. "There is no downward progression to the first five notes." He hummed it again, beckoning Eridel to hum it with him, and then to play it as Kavan hummed.

Again, Eridel played the measure alone, but when he tried to incorporate it into the song, the notes came out jumbled.

"I am sorry," he squeaked. "I guess I need to hear it played properly first, hear how it is done…"

Wortham closed his eyes and groaned. Those were the worst possible words Eridel could have said.

Exasperated, Kavan snatched the instrument from him. "Humming is not enough?" He set the harp upon his knee and attempted to pluck the section, but the deformity of his hands made it impossible. The sound he created was worse to his ears then Eridel's misplaying had been. He tried again. And again. Each time Eridel's face grew whiter. Each time brought Wortham a half step closer, as if he could save Kavan from himself. Each time brought a ragged hitch in Orynn's breathing. Each failed attempt made Kavan angrier, more desperate to succeed, but when it was clear he would not, he growled and shoved the instrument back into Eridel's hands and turned away.

Wortham stood firm. Orynn released her breath in a long hiss.

It was over. Kavan was suffering, but he was still with them.

"I will try once more," Eridel said meekly. Wortham tried to stop him, aware of the brewing storm in his best friend, but Eridel did not see, or did not understand, the captain's gestures. He restarted the song. He made it flawlessly to the same section, hesitated, and plunged ahead with bated breath. And failed. Furious at himself and the cruel fate thrust upon him, Kavan spun, inadvertently knocking the instrument from Eridel's hands into the fringe of the campfire.

Orynn grabbed at it as Eridel screamed, "You are a pitiful excuse for a man! Horrible, despicable! I hate you!" With tears running down his cheeks, he ran into the low scrub forest, into the night and out of sight of the others around the fire.

"Fool," hissed Wortham, possibly referring to Eridel, possibly to Kavan, as Kavan stared at what he had done before fleeing in the opposite direction. Orynn clasped the captain's arm, restraining him.

"Let him go. It had to come to this. We knew it would. Perhaps the worst is over."

"I pray you are right," the captain grunted, brusquely wiping tears away, angry with himself for what he had said. The days since leaving Fikahr had been torture, knowing he was unable to do anything for Kavan, that if any progress was going to come, Kavan had to find it on his own. Wortham hated being helpless, especially when it came to his best friend's pain.

In the twilight, Kavan stumbled over a fallen tree and lay face down upon it, sobbing tearlessly in frustration, pummeling the rotten wood with his fists, tearing rotting bark from it with misshapen fingers. The strangling anger metamorphosed into consuming despair, washing over him in wave after wave of raw, powerful emotion. He could not stop it, and with the images of Eridel's hatred and the echo of his words fresh in mind, Kavan would not have stopped if he could. It was the sight of the harp in the fire, however, that was the final straw, the jolt from anger to despair, as if his heart was burning as the flames licked the wood. A Cliáthan in flames. He did not even know if Orynn's attempt to rescue it had been successful.

He hated himself. He wanted to die. He wanted out, some way to escape the hell his life had become. He had abandoned the inner quest to discover what faults denied him healing, convinced he would not find them and was doomed to live as a cripple. Having abandoned that quest, he found his transgressions piling up so that he could not see beyond them to what his life had once been. It seemed his existence had always been hopelessness and despair. Mired in self-deprecation, he could see no way to extricate himself from it.

Rolling over, head thrown back against the log, he stared at the stars in the cloudless sky. Kóráhm, he pleaded. Give me a sign. Am I fated to misery forever? What must I do to gain forgiveness and peace?

He fell asleep that way, staring at the sky, and awakened sometime later to a thrust of pain in his wrists and ankles. His arms were stretched above him in an awkward position that added to his discomfort. It was an identifiable pain, evoking vivid memories of a dagger ripping into flesh. Waiting for the pain to subside caused it to linger. He felt wetness gathering inside his boots, and the attempt to move a hand to take them off caused greater agony. He could not flex his hands from where they were pinned to the fallen tree behind him. Inevitably, he arched his neck to look at his hands. And shrieked.

This could not be. He had heard of this; it appeared in many stories of the saints. But the rósádhá …the wounds of the god…could not happen to him. Not to Kavan Cliáth.

But unless this was a dream, it was happening. It was real. Both wrists showed injury, a single puncture through both, from which blood flowed down his arms to stain his sleeves and drip into his hair. He blinked to clear his vision, hoping it was a dream or manifestation of the Sight. When it became clear that the wounds were genuine, not a nightmare, he screamed, unable to suppress his terror and confusion.

Wortham sat up. He was supposed to be the one on watch but exhaustion had made him nod off. Eridel had not returned, nor, it appeared, had Kavan. The sound that roused him returned, the cry of some terrified beast echoing through the darkness that made him shudder. Not knowing what animals lived in this wilderness, there was something unnaturally terrifying and yet familiar about the sound. It did not, however, disturb either Urian or Orynn, and since it sounded far away, Wortham did not think it a threat. Unable to shut the echoes of it out of his head, he stared into the fire and forced himself to hum. When the cry dwindled away in a final, desperate shrill hiss, Wortham realized he had been humming one of Kavan's songs. The first one he had ever heard the bard play.

Come sunrise, there was no sign of Eridel as Kavan limped back into camp. The rósádhá was gone, leaving blood staining his boots, his sleeves, his hair. Fortunately, he was not wearing his white robe; the stains on his clothes were barely noticeable upon the darker material. What was in his hair, however, would be seen, making his return to camp more uncomfortable than it might be otherwise. Three heads turned to look at him, even Urian, but if they noticed the discoloration in his hair across the distance, they did not address it. He wanted to beg forgiveness but did not feel he deserved it. Instead, he remained silent, apart from the others as best he could be, packing the mules with his near-useless hands while the others ate. He felt Wortham's gaze burning through him, following everything he did. That man would leave him soon; his truest friend would abandon him. Kavan sighed with resignation, raking his hand back through the blood in his hair, hopeful it would make the stain less noticeable. There was no reason to mourn Wortham's impending departure when Kavan's anger and folly were the forces pushing him away.

"Should we await Eridel?" Urian asked to break the silence.

Orynn straightened, her hand resting on her stomach as if she had eaten something unsettling. "I do not think we can afford to if Lord Cliáth plans to complete the purification of the náos. Besides, Ergoth is not far; we might reach it tonight…or at least early tomorrow morning. Eridel might have already reached it on his own."

Rather than speak, Kavan started in the direction of Ergoth, leaving the packed mules behind. By the time Wortham finished consuming breakfast and they had the horse, mules, and themselves ready to go, Kavan was long out of sight. The captain swore and hurried after him. Kavan might think his company unwanted, might believe he was unloved and abandoned, but Wortham did not intend to prove him correct.

❧*❧

Gabrielle cast a glance at Muir. "What do you mean people were sighted on Pháne?" She and her son by marriage were the only two on Káliel who understood why that tiny island had been declared off limits. There was little there of value…rocks, scrubby trees, no source of drinkable water except after a rain, and no viable place for homes or crops. All that was there was an ancient cave, a room housing an evil almost as old as the island itself.

The man who brought the news continued. "We were running our trawler through the channel when we noticed a moored boat. We didn't see anyone and had no means of boarding her, thus we came to report to you. It wasn't an island boat. It bore no markings, but I'd wager it was an Enesfel or Cordashian craft rather than a Hatuish one."

Another glance passed from the Magistrate to Muir before she dismissed the messenger with instructions that anyone spotting such a vessel again was to come to her at once. "Do you think it was Kavan?"

Muir shrugged as he paced. "Perhaps…but I think he would inform us…if only so you would know it was not one of your people or foreigners trespassing."

"If he did not want us to know he was there, to get in without anyone's knowledge…?"

"He would have Gated in or something, not left a boat that would raise suspicion. And he hates sea travel. Besides, I think he would need the Serpents to gain entry…and they're still here. Do I have permission to investigate? Lord Cliáth made it clear no one should go there…at least no one who isn't prepared for what they'll find."

The woman nodded, her expression grave. She did not know what danger lurked there, but after Prince Bertram's death in that place, it had been easy to take Kavan at his word, and easy to convince the Council of the precautionary measure as well. "Take as many men as you need. But please be careful. Kavan's warning was as much for you as for any strangers."

Remembering that place, the death that had occurred there and those that had almost occurred, Muir replied, "I will not enter unless I must…perhaps it is time to issue a stricter ordinance…"

Gabrielle sighed in agreement. "I think you may be right."

❧ * ❧

There was little left of the once thriving city of Ergoth, nothing more than charred stone husks abandoned centuries ago and left to crumble under nature's assault. The grass, the trees, the shrubs, were as dry and dead as the buildings, awaiting the next rain. There were no visible or audible signs of birds or beasts beyond the constant buzz of insects, and the well he located failed to produce water when Kavan attempted to draw from it. He wondered if the Sight had misled him, or if he had misread what those visions had told him, as there seemed no way for anyone to live in these partial structures, no reason anyone would want to, merely to tend to a shrine he had not yet located.

He reached the ruins before the sun crested the horizon, having not camped with the others during the night. They were far behind him and would not likely arrive for several more hours. Part of him admitted he preferred this solitary travel. If he found what he needed here, it might change the way things currently were. If not, he would continue to find his way without being a burden to others any longer.

It took more exploring through one building after another, and opening up to the power that such ancient places held, before he located an edifice on the far side of the abandoned city that fit what his vision had revealed. Unlike the ruined stretch he had combed to get here, there were green shrubs surrounding this small thatched roof shelter and he could hear the bubbling water from a source he was determined to find. Whomever this shrine had been built for, it seemed they had not been abandoned as the rest of the city had been.

Abandoned the way Kavan had been.

Despite the foliage, the running water, and the thatched roof, the structure did not appear to be an inhabitable place, but at least it was more inviting than the rest of the city, and as he sensed no one around, he decided it was safe to enter. The water he heard bubbled out of the earth and formed a small pool within, encircled by carved rocks that kept it from spreading across the rest of the earthen floor. It tasted cold and clean, a rare thing on their journey through these dry lands, and refreshed both his body and spirit. He wondered if this was the blessed water he needed to rededicate the náós. He could not be sure, but he suspected that, when he found that source, he would know.

At the rear of the shrine was an open-aired octagonal area surrounded on each corner by the remnants of crumbling stone pillars upon which flowering vines clung in their quest to be nearer the sun. The same vines nearly obscured the front of another small building on the opposite side of this terrace, but someone had cleared them away from a square of white stone inlaid next to the doorway. Everything about this place, down to the web like pattern of sunlight and shadow the rising sun cast upon the terrace, was exactly the way he had seen it in his vision, and in the depths of his withering soul he felt as if some part of him had been here before, as if, perhaps, he was home.

After a quick search to verify that he was alone, Kavan crossed the terrace with careful steps, both out of reverence for what felt to be a place of great significance and out of concern that there could be unseen danger. He approached the marble plate, brushed the dust from it with the side of his hand, and stepped back in surprise. He had not expected the words upon it to be written in High Elyri.

"aelás Khweltz Córíllyén ibh it aepháló, dó chellé
phaen gaethaelás nuáth íth k'málneag aelás rásaï"

Coryllien? What saint, Kavan wondered could possibly be connected to that name? He rubbed the letters harder as if to change what was written, or to clarify it, but all the effort did was hurt his hand. He knew his people were said to have passed through these lands long ago on their journey to the place they now called home. Finding the old language in such places should not surprise him, but it did.

"Are you here to remember the dead or commune with Kóráhm di Curnydhá?"

It was the second time Kavan had heard that name, but when he turned to address whoever was beside him, he paused. The ancient woman who spoke reminded him of someone, but he could not recall whom. The crescent pendant he wore around his neck, the symbol that bound him to the Lachlan House, tingled against his skin. k'kairá, he wondered, as she eased down upon the stone bench beneath the plaque. Recognizing her as the woman the Sight had shown him, he assumed this was the woman Walga of whom Orynn had spoken, and that it was the reason she seemed familiar.

"Kóráhm di…you mean Saint Kóráhm? Saint Kóráhm was born here? I thought he was…?"

"Elyri, like you," she said with what might have been a smile on her toothless face. "Though he lived much of his life here, calling it home, he was not born on this spot, any more than he was born in your great Clarys. Aye, that be the truth…as you have expected."

She was right in that. From his first reading of Kóráhm's writings, Kavan had suspected that they were not the thoughts of a man raised in the metropolitan bustle of Elyriá's largest, and best-known, city. And when the Saint began appearing to him, Kavan had detected a trace of accent unlike any he had heard in Elyriá. But there were no manuscripts or clues to reveal his origins or birthplace. It was accepted dogma that Clarys had been his home.

But how did Walga know of Clarys?

"And Khweltz Coryllien?" he whispered as a shiver passed through him.

"The father of the one you call Dawid Coryllien. You know this."

Again true. The name was not a common one in any language Kavan knew. Two men with the same name had to be related by blood or marriage. "Then…" His heart, his head, his very soul began to rebel at the realization taking root there. Connections that had always been there began to reveal a picture too obvious to be anything but the truth. "How can this be? How can they be…Coryllien was Teren."

"Half Teren. And half Elyri," she replied. "They share a mother."

For a long time after that remarkable statement, Kavan was quiet, staring at the marble in shock. Such a revelation would rock the foundations of the Faith, as it did his own, but Kavan wanted to know more. Needed to know more. The true importance of this fact had yet to be heard, he suspected, and he desired to hear it. Finally, he looked at her with heartfelt clarity of purpose and said, "You know their story, dhábhyne. I do not know how this could be true, but I must learn it. Please tell me, that I may understand how these things came to pass into my history. Much has been lost to my people…and for their sake, as well as my own…I must know what has brought us to where we are. Will you speak of these things to me?"

She gestured for him to take a place on the bench beside her, but instead of sitting, he knelt at her feet, feeling close to some earth-shattering revelation at the feet of his Faith. Sitting as her equal felt wrong. He could never be that.

"If I speak, you must not interrupt. Few care for the truth; it frightens them…as it does you. But your heart seeks even what it fears; if you wish to know, stay. Listen and learn."

He nodded solemnly. "I will hear you, dhábhyne. I will hear whatever you are willing to reveal."

Her violet eyes took on a faraway glazed look, as if she were falling into a trance or perhaps on the verge of sleeping. He held his breath, waiting impatiently, mindful of her admonition not to interrupt. When she did finally speak, her voice was quiet, almost monotone, and it seemed to Kavan as if she were seeing the events of which she spoke.

"There was a woman called Sósáná, lovelier than any that lived. She was as you, Elyri, come from across the sea, the consort of a prince of those lands. She conceived a son before her prince returned to the place from which they had come. Alone, unable to care for the child she bore, she abandoned hope of her prince coming back to her. In time, she agreed to marry Ergoth's governor, Khweltz Coryllien, a wealthy, compassionate man in search of a wife. He knew her heart belonged to another, but he worshiped her and gave her everything she could want, caring for her and her son Kóráhm di Curnydhá as if he were his own. She, in return for his generosity and kindness, remained faithful and compassionate unto him.

"Years passed for the family in the peace and prosperity of their thriving town. Kóráhm was a bright child, as gifted as his mother was beautiful. Before his fifteenth birthday, his mother gave birth to a second son, given the name Dhábhiyhá at birth. Kóráhm loved his half-kind brother, and young Dhábhiyhá worshiped him as if he were k'Ádhá himself. It was not long after that Sósáná disappeared, and it was believed by many that her prince returned, found her, and took her back across the sea. Kóráhm did not see his mother again.

"The boys pursued different paths as they grew to adulthood. Dhábhiyhá became a successful trader, following in his father's footsteps, and eventually married a local Elyri girl. He had the prospect of the governorship before him, and as a powerful and convincing spokesman, he was well-liked and respected in the community. Kóráhm did not wed but devoted his life to the study and teaching of the powers he had been born with, as well as the study of history, faith, medicine, music, and languages. His crippled foot, something he had been born with, did not lend itself to a life of trading and hard labor, though he did often tend flocks in exchange for favors from the locals. He was not a strong man in body, but the strength of his mind and faith made up for that. He was handsome, loved by women in Ergoth and beyond.

"There came a day when Dhábhiyhá grew to suspect that his bride had married him to be near his brother, an assertion that many believe correct. Dhábhiyhá's worship distorted into loathing and then hatred as he coveted his brother's fine face and potent gifts, particularly the ability to use the means of travel which Kóráhm called k'rylag…the Gate. Kóráhm tried to keep peace with his brother but to no avail.

"On a trading excursion to the city of Yashir, Dhábhiyhá discovered and brought home a sweet-smelling oil he believed would be profitable as a wood treatment. His bride put it to use and became ill at once. Knowing of his brother's skill in medicine, Dhábhiyhá hastened to Kóráhm, pleading with his learned brother to heal his wife. Kóráhm did what could be done, but there was no cure. None of those antidotes normally applied to poisons had effect. She grew sicker and weaker despite their efforts. Nothing helped, thus he left Dhábhiyhá with detailed instructions for her care, took the k'rylag to the destination he believed to be the most promising, vowing he would return with the means of saving her life.

"Within three days, the woman passed in violent throws of agony. Dhábhiyhá lost reason and set fire to his home, killing his father and many townspeople when the village burned. He attempted to poison himself with the oil he had found, but it failed to have the same effect on him; it made him ill but did not kill him, and cost him what remained of his sanity. Since he could not operate the k'rylag, he rode north, seeking his brother, wishing to exact revenge for allowing his wife to die. In his madness, he vowed to destroy both his brother and any who shared the gifts that he had been denied by birth.

"The k'rylag had taken Kóráhm to the city of Clarys. While he did not find the cure, he did discover a healer, one with talents outside of his experience, as there were no healers in Ergoth or the surrounding territories. He brought the healer to Ergoth to discover his home razed and his brother gone. With the healer's aid, he determined what had happened and cursed himself for not having brought his brother and his wife with him. His despair over the death of his brother's wife lent credence to the question of their love. None of those still lingering in the remains of Ergoth knew where Dhábhiyhá had gone; they could only say that he had traveled north in search of his brother. Kóráhm followed, seeking to stop his kinsman at any cost.

"And the rest…" she smiled wistfully at him, her eyes clear again, and continued, "is history as you know it."

Kavan was quaking, overwhelmed by a story he could never have imagined. "I…there is a náós in Rhidam, Enesfel, below the castle that has been the home of the Lachlan dynasty for decades. I deduced that Coryllien was the man to defile it from the entries in a journal by his…" His jaw fell slack and his eyes widened. "Kóráhm's journal!"

Walga's response was to stare silently at him.

He had Kóráhm's journal. Not a religious text re-copied by gdhededhá over the centuries, but a personal piece of the man's life, written by his hand, held by him, a book that absorbed the Saint's tears as he wrote. Kavan clutched his pack in protective reverence, knowing what a blessed relic he possessed and wondering who had bestowed it in that crypt to be found so many centuries later. "I was told by a man named Bhóité that a descendant or blood relative of the keeper or defiler…of Kóráhm or Coryllien…" his voice dropped in growing awe, "is needed for the cleansing and to rededicate it to its holy purpose. None of our legends bear testimony to Kóráhm fathering children…and indeed you say he never married. Were there other family members…however remotely related?"

She shook her head. "Khweltz had no siblings and a single blood heir in Dhábhiyhá. Sósáná had no living family in these lands at the time of her disappearance, save for Kóráhm. As for the people of Kóráhm's father, no one knows where they can be found. Neither Kóráhm nor Dhábhiyhá fathered children in Ergoth, but I do not know what may have happened in their lives once they departed for the kingdoms of the north."

"Then how…" But Walga, seemingly finished with her tale, got to her feet and shuffled away, leaving Kavan alone at the door of what had once been, he realized, the home of Saint Kóráhm.

It was disturbing to realize how right Kóráhm had been. There was much Kavan had not known about his patron, though the language of the journals, its time of authorship, and many other details in its pages should have given Kavan clues enough to suspect this in advance. It explained how Kóráhm had come to Clarys, and why the Faith leaders assumed he was born there. It was likely, knowing what Kavan knew now, that Kóráhm had fostered that belief in an effort to hide a past he was not proud of. It explained Coryllien's dark need to destroy the Elyri as his wife had been destroyed, and if he had, in time, learned to use the Gates, it would explain how the Teren gained entrance into the náos and how the Elyri High Family had been killed. It also told Kavan why Kóráhm had been dedicated to bringing peace between the two peoples, an attempt to counter the hatred his brother fueled.

But it did not tell Kavan how he was to find a descendant of Kóráhm's or Coryllien's. He thought of Yhsábhel, the woman in the second journal. Had she carried any child of Kóráhm's? Or, if Kóráhm had been as enamored with the lure of women as he claimed, might he have fathered any number of children throughout his lifetime? Were there records anywhere that might contain the answer? Would it be necessary to scour the records in Clarys, or to return to the final resting place of Coryllien once more to determine if that man had fathered offspring? He prayed not.

Yhsábhel. Of course. Kavan berated himself then for his lapse of memory of the old histories he had learned. Yhsábhel, the adopted sister of the Kyne, whose family was butchered within the walls of the Rhidam palace…by the Corylliens. Yhsábhel, whose body was never found when the slaughter was later discovered.

But if Kóráhm's Yhsábhel was this same one, who was her family that had fled behind the mountains, into Elyriá, into safety. And why had she not gone with them? Why had she stayed?

Kavan knew why. She had stayed for Kóráhm. She had stayed because she loved him. And she had died for that love.

Kavan hung his head as his thoughts turned to the patron who had been a friend for many decades. As Kóráhm had said, he had been no more than a man. One of great knowledge, compassion, and wisdom, perhaps, but still a man. One thrust into the middle of history's most powerful events by the tragic death of a woman by the same poison Coryllien used successfully against Elyri in the years that came after. And he had loved her. He had loved his brother's wife. Walga had not said it in clear terms, but Kavan knew the truth because Kóráhm had hinted at it in the past. He might or might not have touched her, but he had loved her. He had done what he could to save her, but in the end, it had not been enough. Kóráhm could not heal her, could not stop his brother, any more than he could later prevent the Faith from canonizing him and then declaring him a heretic.

There were some things in life man could not change. Things happened and men could but react according to integrity and abilities. Was that, Kavan wondered, what Kóráhm had sent him here to learn?

The new insight, and a renewed surge of faith and kinship with Kóráhm, gave Kavan purpose and potentially another destination. Orec had come from Yashir. If it was where Coryllien had found it, the bard believed he would find it there as well. And somewhere the staff piece, the crown, the chalice, and the heir awaited him. k'ílshwythnec, if she existed, would know where at least one of those items was. He was convinced of it.

Kavan rose from his stiff knees, noting by the light in the sky that it was past noon. If the others had arrived, he would join them. As long as he had a purpose, he had hope. That should be enough to prevent him from causing his companions further grief and pain. He paused to place his hands upon the plaque, offering a brief sincere prayer of thanks, a prayer that sought forgiveness for his transgressions and one that asked for help in controlling the darkness within and finding the way to restore his hands.

His vision clouded as he turned, and the ground before him seemed to open into a great yawning pit, black and hot, reeking of death and rot. He stretched out his arms to steady himself, but there was nothing to support him and the sensation of falling wrapped itself around his ankles and pulled him forward. He stumbled and fell.

"Milord!" Wortham caught him as he collapsed, lifting the pale man in his arms as Kavan sagged, weeping and broken.

He sought forgiveness, and was, instead, further from it. That had to be the explanation of this vision.

"Forgive me, Wortham," Kavan wept, his arms around the man's shoulders, his face pressed into the big man's neck. "I have wronged you…wronged so many…I am beyond redemption…"

"Never, milord. No man is beyond that." He shivered at the Elyri's nearness, the intimacy of holding him. If he had ever thought he could abandon this man, this moment of tenderness proved him wrong.

"You do not despise me?"

"You know I could not. No amount of torment could make me do that." He helped the bard to his feet since it seemed Kavan wanted it but kept his arms out to steady him. "What has happened?"

Not prepared to speak of it, overwhelmed by the recent revelations and convinced of his own damnation, Kavan shook his head and murmured chokingly, "Is Eridel with you? I must make amends…"

The captain shrugged. "We have not seen him but hoped he is here…or will be."

"Then we wait. Are the others with you? I must remain…until morning…leave an offering. Then I must journey to Yashir?"

"Yashir, milord?"

"The city where Dhábhiyhá…Coryllien…first obtained Orec. If it can be found anywhere, it will be there. Hopefully, Orynn knows the way. Is she with you? And Urian?"

"Of course. They have been as worried about you as I. It will be good to have you back with us."

Those words almost prompted a relieved smile. They might have, if not for that vision of doom stuck in his head. "We make camp. But Wortham, do not mention what you have seen to anyone. I do not know the meaning of what I have witnessed, what caused me to fall…and I would rather not discuss it with anyone."

"I will say nothing if that is your wish. But will you tell me what you learned here that has pointed us to Yashir?"

"In time, Wortham. In time I will tell you everything."

Satisfied with that, and with being back on speaking terms with the bard, the captain nodded and led Kavan to where the others waited.

❧*❧

The small boat was still moored on Pháne's coast, though an initial inspection of the cliffs showed no sign of people. Muir took a dozen men from the ship he commanded and boarded the other before examining the shore. There was nothing in the boat except a stash of food and drink that suggested whoever had come here planned to stay for a long time or had a lengthy journey to return home. Leaving sailors to guard it, Muir lowered a sloop and rowed towards the cave, armed for a clash. Without the Káliel Serpents, the brooches possessed by the ruling family of Káliel, which Gabrielle had retired from use and hidden away, no one would get past the second door. Muir expected to find whoever was here trying.

As it turned out, there were five men in the outer cave with picks and chisels, balancing on the ledge that would be the only dry ground at high tide. Muir heard them before he saw them.

"Need to rethink this, Anri. We'll never get in there this way…"

"There must be a key or…

It appeared they had been trying to open the door for some time, a day or more at least, and were failing. That made Muir grin. He grinned wider at their surprise at being discovered as Muir and his men closed in behind them.

"Well, gentleman…don't you know it is illegal to be here?"

One of them, possibly the leader though it was difficult to tell as they wore similar wet clothes, asked, "Illegal? We're explorers…"

Not wanting to expose his connection to the Prime Magistrate, Muir grunted, "Something the Prime Magistrate said about protecting the island from looters. You will have the chance to ask her yourself."

"We will? Who are you to threaten us?" The speaker's tone put a sparkle in Muir's eyes, tempting him to reveal himself. A twitch of his head had the other six in the sloop aiming crossbows at the intruders.

"Who I am isn't important. I'm the one sent to protect this place. Drop your weapons and tools and come peacefully if you wish to save yourself injury and embarrassment. The Magistrate may be lenient if you cooperate but she hates to be kept waiting."

He was pleased they chose to cooperate and more pleased that they had failed to find a way into the passage. The last time Muir had been here, his brother had died. That memory haunted him, as it was the first time he had killed a man. The only time, if the truth were known.

❧Chapter 21❧

Sir Balint Gabersdon of Nelori was once the youngest knight in Enesfel. The passage of years stripped away that distinction but he was still one of the best, second to none but Chamberlain Bhríd Cáner. Knowing Elyri had advantages meant that Balint was the top-ranked Teren knight in the land, a distinction he did not take lightly. To his credit, outside the arena of war and tournament, he had resurrected Nelori's struggling economy and brought the territory into the position of the third most prosperous city in Enesfel. It had become more of a struggle to maintain that distinction since the day Lord Cliáth assumed leadership in Alberni, increasing their production of ink, manuscripts, parchment and other writing necessities. Alberni was becoming Enesfel's center of learning with the construction of Saint Kóráhm's, and Nelori, with its pearls, glass, and cattle products found it a challenge to compete.

But the kingdom needed all of those commodities, and Balint was a realist. There was no point in worrying about the financial position of Nelori in comparison to other cities, as long as his lands turned a profit for the Crown, himself, and his people. He admired the Elyri Duke for what he had done in such a short time. He also liked him as a man, though he could not claim to know him as well as some. Balint did not begrudge him success because he was a competitor or because he was Elyri.

"Milord Gabersdon. Please…a word…"

The Duke reigned in his brown gelding and waited for the man running behind him. He recognized his sheriff despite his strained and breathless voice. "What is it, Reynold?"

"I must speak with you, but away from here." He looked around at the street full of people. "What I must say is confidential."

"Where is your horse?"

"At home. I was in the cobbler's when I saw you.

That ruled out riding away. "There aren't many private places. Can't you lower your voice and speak here? The street is quiet…"

Reynold snorted. "Precisely… many people and too much quiet. We can speak here if you wish…"

To accommodate his sheriff as much as he could where they were, the Duke dismounted and strolled beside him to speak at his level. "Speak freely, please."

"You are aware of the Elyri brother and sister, jewelers, who set business on the waterfront?"

The Duke nodded. "I have not met them, but I have seen the gentleman a time or two and have heard great praise of their craft."

"Sir…the young woman's brother has been missing since yesterday morning. She claims he left before dawn but said nothing to her of travel, and with the rumors of recent events throughout Enesfel, she is concerned for his welfare. I placed her under the protection of my best men, but she is unconvinced of her safety and thinks my men suspect." There was a touch of insult in the man's tone but he continued, "She has petitioned to speak with you directly, as soon as you can spare the time."

Dark eyes creased with concern, the Duke said, "I shall see her at once, today if I can manage it"

"Also…there has been unrest…no acts yet but there is talk, rumors that the old mill is used for Elyri to gather and perform evil practices."

"The old mill?" Balint asked, unable to stifle his laughter. The mill in question had been empty all of his life after a landslide had diverted the flow of the creek that had run it. The childless couple had been unable to maintain it, or correct the water issue, and after the woman's death, her husband lost all interest in trying. Balint was surprised the place still stood. "What sort of evil practices?"

"Sorcery…though I agree, it is nonsense. I investigated but saw no hint that anyone has been there to warrant this fear. However, it is not the rumors that concern me. I know no one, Elyri or Teren, is practicing sorcery there. What worries me is the talk about doing something about it…marching on the place…putting a stop to it. What if this fear of sorcery has bearing on the disappearance of the jeweler?"

Rolling his head from side to side to ease the stiffness in his neck, Balint grunted. "Yes, I can see where that would give cause for speculation. You searched the mill, you say?"

"Not the inside, but I have men combing the outside still and have increased patrols in the area. I want permission before entering, seeing as the mill falls under your ownership since its abandonment."

"I will ride out with you and your men this evening; patrol the road to the mill, and we will investigate the inside together to put an end to these rumors. Right now," he smiled and straightened his tunic before getting back on his horse, "I must make myself presentable for the lady jeweler. Please let her know I shall see her and bring her to me straight away."

❧*❧

King Hagan felt indisposed that morning and left his sister to conduct the affairs of state. Diona relished the chance to show the men of Enesfel she was as capable as her brother and their father before them. There was a dispute between merchants to settle, two other men who claimed ownership of the same wagon, and the usual gaggle of people petitioning for tax reductions and waivers, tariffs or the reductions of tariffs, or other special favors of the Crown. As expected, the morning began as a rowdy, disgruntled affair when the people learned that the princess, rather than the King, would hear their requests. The presence of Chamberlain Cáner and Chancellor McGrannis, however, kept the uproar to a minimum and lent credibility to her right to oversee the day's affairs.

It was not only the subjects present who were surprised by her ability to judge wisely and fairly. The King came from his room and watched the proceedings from a hidden place until he could no longer tolerate either the illness in his stomach or the sight of his sister gracefully conducting court business. For him, it was frequently an uncomfortable duty. He disliked making decisions over people's lives while they stared at him with pleading or angry eyes. It was difficult to think when others watched him, which frequently led him to make the judgments he thought were expected rather than the one that should, perhaps, be made.

He needed self-confidence; that was what Diona often told him. But it had been a difficult thing to develop when his father had treated him as if he was the cause for whatever was wrong in life. Diona explained that it was the death of their mother, shortly after Hagan's birth, that caused their father to behave as he had, and that it was in no way a reflection on Hagan as a person. As Hagan had not asked to be conceived or born, he knew he was not the cause of his mother's death, but it did not keep him from feeling guilty and inadequate. He would rule Enesfel because it was his destiny, but if given the choice, he would much rather have been somewhere else.

What he also needed, he was beginning to realize, was an heir. It seemed strange to consider the prospect of children and the future of the kingdom when he felt like a child. He had little interest in marrying, particularly when the first person that came to mind when he pondered the subject was more of a child than he was. While watching Diona finesse the people of Enesfel with her wit and intelligence was belittling, it also assured him that, should something happen before he had an heir, or should he not marry, his sister would be able to rule Enesfel quite capably.

❧*❧

It was raining and cold under the dim light of the hidden full moon by the time Duke Gabersdon, his squire, and two of his personal retainers joined forces with the sheriff and the fifteen road guards selected for the night's job. They slogged towards the mill through the viscous mud, listening to the raindrops bounce off their helmets. Hearing was difficult enough within a helmet without the echoing ping of rain. It made Balint grateful he had chosen not to wear his, even though it meant that his dark brown hair was plastered to his skull and the water ran down his forehead into his eyes. Sight or hearing. When he had his choice, Balint chose to hear. That sense had seemed more trustworthy to him in battle than his eyes.

His thoughts shifted away from the rain to the Elyri woman he had spoken with earlier. Unlike other Elyri women he had met, she was tall and her hair was a darker shade of brown than he had seen in most Elyri. Her coloring was more like that of Bhríd Cáner. He found her beautiful and spirited when she was not talking about her missing brother. Her name was Dhybhé. He promised to do everything in his power to find her brother and offered her shelter within his keep until it was deemed safe. To his surprise, she accepted the proposal, although with reluctance. Appearing to have the favoritism of the nobility was possibly more dangerous for an Elyri than anonymity. Balint sent his people to collect her belongings and bring them into the walled stronghold he called home; he gave her an unused portion of the barracks as her residence where she would have space to continue her craft and be surrounded by men who could protect her.

He would have shared dinner with her, if not for this impending matter of the mill that called him out of the keep before the meal was served. Perhaps, he mused now, they would dine upon his return.

There were no lights in the abandoned structure, as Balint expected. There was no reason for anyone to be here. Behind him, the Duke could feel the edginess in many of the men the sheriff had selected for duty; they knew why there were here and it seemed they believed the rumors to be true. More determined than before to prove them wrong, Balint slid down the side of his wet horse, tethered the animal out of the rain as best he could, and entered the mill with three escorts, leaving Reynold and his men to patrol the road and surrounding land.

The Duke found nothing within except dust and mud, rotting timbers, and a family of foxes nestled into a mound of moldy flour bags. There was no evidence that anyone had come here for any purpose in a long time. As far as he could see, no one had disturbed the layers of dust but himself, his men, the foxes, mice, and birds, and the wind and falling rain. Grunting, he turned to leave as a commotion outside caught his attention.

"Look!" someone shouted angrily. "It is as we feared! See how the light dances. It's sorcery…"

The speaker quieted and drew his sword as the door opened and the Duke stepped into the rain. He held up his lantern and his squire did likewise. "Lights moving on their own? I see no such specter, sir."

The lead man of the torch and tool-wielding rabble stepped closer. "Milord Gabersdon! You have come to aid in purging the evil?"

"Evil? There is no evil here, unless a fox counts," he snorted.

"A…" Murmurs and grumbles swept through the disappointed crowd. The burly leader snapped, "Of course you would find nothing. It is illusion meant to blind the ignorant!"

Balint stepped forward until his face was inches away from the man who had spoken. "You are calling me ignorant, sir?"

Realizing his error, the man mumbled, "No, milord, I meant…"

"That I can be more easily fooled than you, perhaps? I have searched every corner of the mill and found nothing suspicious except for the presence of all of you. Please explain. Why trouble yourselves with this abandoned building?"

"Those who practice sorcery must be exterminated," he stammered defensively.

"Unless foxes practice sorcery, there is no one here to do so. I do not know who you plan to exterminate, but I hope it was not the poor animals…and if you have designs on me and my men, I suggest you rethink your plan. It is my understanding that sorcery is practiced under a full moon. No one is here; there are no practitioners. Also, it would not seem wise to confront them on a night when their powers would be at their strongest." He glanced at the barely visible full moon behind the storm clouds. "Nor is it profitable to assault an abandoned building when it belongs to me. I suggest, if you suspect someone of wrongdoing, you bring the matter to Reynold or me. It is our responsibility to see justice done, to see that everyone is protected, not yours. Justice is not to be meted out by a torch-bearing mob."

"You call harboring an Elyri justice?" someone shrieked. An uneasy sound ran through the mob.

Hand resting on his sword hilt, the Duke straightened his shoulders and growled. How dare these people question his actions and authority? "The lady has come to me for safety, as a guest, until her brother returns. Nothing more. And what I do…who I do it with, is my own affair."

"You harbor her because she is Elyri!"

His voice lowered into an angry rumble that made the crowd back away. "If there were not people like you determined to kill everyone different from yourselves, it would not be necessary to offer protection. It is the position of the Crown that all are welcome in Enesfel, Elyri included, and it is my duty to uphold the law. Anything else would be an ignoble injustice. I expect my subjects to uphold the King's law as well. Go home. There is no one here. This ends now."

Many hours later, after the last of the crowd dispersed and the rain slowed to a drizzle, Balint felt confident enough that there would be no incidents, that he could go home. He departed after giving instructions to Reynold that the mill and surrounding area, and other such empty structures, were to be watched from now on. The trouble was passed, but he knew better than to expect his words to have a lasting effect on an apprehensive crowd. Unfortunately, fear and superstition often won when pitted against logic and rational thought. Balint had gotten a taste of the ugliness festering elsewhere and hoped he could head it off before it grew worse.

❧*❧

"What do you mean by such a question?" Asta's expression was calm but her voice revealed astonishment. She was eager for an interruption, Gaelán, Ártur, her father, anyone else, but she knew she could not count on that. Her wits alone would have to suffice against the proposal of her cousin and King.

"Precisely what I asked," replied Hagan. "I know you are young; I think I am too. But betrothal would be acceptable; I thought it best to ask you before going to your father with my intent."

"We are cousins, Milord," she said. "Your father was my mother's brother. The Faith does not permit…"

"But a dispensation can be granted, I think. It has been done in Enesfel's history." The King knew he was losing this battle, not that he had expected to win it. He was almost hoping she would deny the request, and then he would not need to dwell upon her anymore. However, the question of an heir had thrust itself into his mind and would not relinquish its hold. She might deny him, but at least she would know he had presented the offer to her first, in case she was ever ready to consider such a future with him.

Asta resisted shuffling her feet. "I do not know. I do not think I can make such a decision. You may approach my father if you want…it is your prerogative. If he tells me to marry you, I shall."

"But not because you want to." He had doubts that her father would approve the union and suspected she knew that too.

Smiling playfully, she replied, "I do not know what I want from one minute to the next. It is the nature of being a woman I am told."

"If you desire time to consider it, you will have it. I will not speak to your father until you decide."

"Thank you," she curtseyed, hoping this would be the end of the discussion. "Would you care to join Gaelán and me for lunch in the solar? He has some new skills to show me, that Healer MacLyr taught him. It is the most amazing feat I have ever seen, to watch what he is learning. I wish I could do things like that."

Hagan chewed the inside of his lip. "No, I must meet with Lords Cáner and McGrannis. Please, give Gaelán my regrets."

She nodded and skipped from the room in an unladylike manner, which reminded him, as she intended, that she was still a girl. The King sighed. Asta would consider his proposal as she said, but her regard for the sons of Bhríd Cáner was too deep, and her fascination with Gaelán's newfound gifts spelled disaster for any possible union between the King and his cousin. Not even the idea of being Queen could tempt her, which Hagan grudgingly admitted was one of the traits he admired most about her. Things such as grandeur and wealth could not sway her.

It did not solve his dilemma, however. Perhaps, as Diona suggested, he should host a ball and invite all of the eligible young women he knew…and many he did not. There must be at least one who would be interested in marrying Enesfel's King. It would be more difficult to find one he liked.

❧*❧

"Mother?"

Tayte looked much like his grandfather as he waited in the doorway dressed in a simple blue tunic and breeches. He was big for his age, taller and heavier than his King though they were a year apart in age, Tayte being the younger. When Madalyn watched him working alongside those who tended the vineyards or watched him shoeing horses, he reminded her of her father, the grandfather he closely resembled. His interest in the vineyards and winery pleased her as it meant the continuation of the work her family had pursued for generations and it meant that her lands would be cared for when she was gone.

"Good morning, Tayte. What is it?" she asked.

"Sheriff Everard is here with two others. They have prisoners. The sheriff wants to speak with you."

Rather than ask questions, Madalyn followed him to the front hall where men she did not recognize were guarding two others, bound and tied to prevent escape. Her sheriff, Everard, stood apart, looking as though he trusted neither his prisoners nor the two guarding them.

"Lady Cáner." Everard bowed. "I am to place these two men in your custody."

"My custody?" she asked, aware that Tayte lingered behind her. She was not accustomed to taking custody of prisoners. Her home did not have adequate facilities to detain anyone for more than a few days.

"They are part of a royal investigation, milady. These two," he indicated the guards, "are in the Lord High Inquisitor's employ. With their help, we have seized the remaining men responsible for the attack on Duke Cliáth."

The Duchess was torn between praising the sheriff and his assistants for the arrests and launching a tirade against those who seemed unconcerned for their fate. She took several breaths to calm herself, smoothing the front of her gown to give her hands something to do before speaking.

"Lord Everard, thank you for your efforts. And I thank both of you for your cooperation and aid in this matter. But I cannot keep them here. My instructions were specific. If any suspects or information is found, it is to be sent directly to the king. Can the three of you escort these men to Rhidam?"

Everard shuffled his feet. "I would need to set some matters in order; it would take a few hours."

"We would be pleased to escort them," one of the Association men grinned. "I think we should pay Lord Dugan a visit."

And demand a handsome reward, no doubt. They deserved it, in her opinion. "Then set your affairs in order, Lord Everard. I will detain these two while you do so. Be ready to leave before noon; I will send men with you."

"May I accompany them?" Madalyn looked at her son with surprise and shivered at the indescribable expression on his face. Seeing his mother's concern, Tayte continued, "Lord Cliáth is my cousin. What these men did was vicious and uncalled for. I want to see that they make it to Rhidam and receive punishment."

One of the prisoners lowered his gaze; the other glared at this young lord he knew carried Elyri blood. He might have spoken, regardless of the Duchess's cool gaze, but the dagger at his back kept him quiet.

Proud of her son, though apprehensive about sending him on a potentially dangerous mission at a time like this, Madalyn finally nodded and replied, "Very well, Tayte. You are old enough for this and your father will be happy to see you. I will leave you and Sheriff

Everard in command of this trip, but I expect you to listen to what he says. You are old enough but…"

"But I am inexperienced. I know, mother; I shall do as you wish."

"And you," Madalyn turned her attention to the captives, "I pray to k'Ádhá I do not see your faces again. You are responsible for one of the greatest crimes ever committed. Even if the King imparts leniency, I doubt k'Ádhá will be as forgiving."

❧*❧

To Muir's dismay, Gabrielle had no option but to set free the men found on Pháne. They claimed to be from Enesfel, most from Rhidam and Levonne, men in search of adventure who had heard about a secret cave and felt compelled to investigate. As foreigners, they had not known the island was off-limits. Muir was not convinced their tale was true, particularly since the man called Hugh spoke with an accent that suggested he was from Neth, not Enesfel as he proclaimed.

But part of Enesfel had once been Neth, thus the matter of accent carried little weight with the Káliel Council, before whom the matter was presented. The Council saw no reason to punish or fine the trespassers, instead, they extracted a promise that they would stay away from the island and released them. The Council did agree with the Magistrate's suggestion of establishing a small outpost upon Pháne to warn off potential trespassers, and to Muir's pleasure, he was placed in charge of its staffing and construction. His own little place in the world, and tiny fleet, to rule.

That unexpected victory did not overshadow the nagging belief that the apprehended men were not adventurers but had been in that cave for a nefarious purpose. The Káliel Council did not place faith in his gut reactions, but his experience and time with Kavan had taught Muir when to pay attention to what his instincts were telling him. As a precaution, he wrote a letter regarding the matter, made three modified copies, and sent them addressed to his father, his sister, the King of Enesfel, and the Lord High Inquisitor. The Council was willing to dismiss the matter but Muir Lachlan was not.

❧*❧

"The old mill's on fire!"

Balint's head snapped up, the evening of conversation with Dhybhé abruptly halted. The news of a fire was a surprise but when given the opportunity to think about it, he would realize it was expected. Perhaps not so soon after warning his subjects to leave the place alone, but such an act was preordained by the delusions of men.

"May I assist?" the woman beside him asked.

"It would not be safe for you, milady." He was already pulling his cloak around his shoulders. "This is the direct result of the fear of your people. For you to be there will incite further unrest and I do not think that is wise. Stay where you are safe. In fact, stay in this room. No one will harm you in my home. I will come to you when I return."

"I hope so," she smiled with a sigh of resignation. This seemed to be the safest place in Nelori. "Be careful."

"I will be," he nodded and started for the door. As an afterthought, he turned back and kissed her hand. "I will return as quickly as I can."

He hastened to the mill that was fully engulfed by the time of his arrival. The old structure was far enough from the edge of the city that the blaze posed no threat to Nelori, but the citizenry had come in force to battle the flames to limit the fire's spread. Balint was not above lending his strength to carry water, yet it was many hours later, when the sky passed from dark to light and was nearing noon, before the last of the flames were extinguished. And it was near evening before the charred remains were cold enough to search, a task left to Balint, Sheriff Reynold, and three of Reynold's men.

Little remained to comb through since any part of the structure not made of stone was reduced to ashes. It seemed unusual to Balint considering how wet the wood had been after the rain of a few days before. From the size of the mob when he arrived to put out the fire, Balint knew it unlikely he and his men would ever learn who had set the blaze. He was tempted to write the incident off as a loss until he found the body.

Twisted, charred beyond recognition, nothing else could be told except that the body had been a person. Male or female, Teren or Elyri, it was impossible to tell. But from the location and the position of the body, he knew it had been in the middle of the blaze, unable to react or escape. Whoever it was had been bound and unconscious, left to die or dead already, murdered; Balint would stake his life on it.

Perhaps, he thought, Dhybhé could identify the body in the same way Healer MacLyr could. Not that she would want to, as the thought of touching the charred remains was revolting, but he thought it worth asking. If it was her brother, she would want to know.

But Dhybhé was not in his day room where he had left her. The servants he questioned could not recall seeing her after he left. Thinking she might have gone to her barrack housing, as waiting for him all night in the dayroom had not been expected, Balint went there to discover that everything within her two rooms had been destroyed. The bed in which she had slept was broken, the table and chair smashed to splinters. Pieces of jewelry and tools were scattered across the floor; the tiny gems, stones, and glass jewels left behind. Not a robbery then, but a malicious act of vandalism.

Balint feared for the woman's life. It would not have been her in the fire; that victim had been there when the blaze was set. But she had been under his protection, in his care, and he thought she should be safe within the walls of his fortress home. The taint of anti-Elyri sentiment seemed to have reached within his household too.

He knew he had a temper and had long ago learned to control it. A successful knight would not live long if ruled by negative passions. To curb it now, Balint set about cleaning the rooms, gathering the valuables that had been dispersed, piling the broken items outside the door, taking his anger out on the already destroyed furniture. Many of his staff saw him and eyed him curiously, but did not attempt to help or question his activities.

They knew. They had all been part of it. He could not prove it, but he suspected it. By the time his task was complete, he knew what he would do. He would dismiss each of his servants, every member of his guard and staff. If they felt compelled to turn on him after his loyalty to them and their families, he would leave them unemployed and homeless. None would get anything more from him.

"Milord?"

Though he thought his anger and indignation were under control, he turned and snapped, "What?" The older man and woman cringed from his wrath. Recognizing his squire and the man's wife did not give Balint cause to apologize.

"This has been…a terrible injustice." The squire looked at the mountain of broken furniture with a shake of his head.

"Where is she, Izbin? Where is Dhybhé?"

"The Elyri woman?" he asked.

"Who else?"

The older man stared wide-eyed. "You did not send for her?"

"I have been at the mill since last night," the Duke exclaimed. "Why would I send for her?"

"k'Ádhá…" the squire swore. "Sir Jorges asked her to accompany him, said you wanted her to join him here. No one thought anything of it, nor apparently did she since she followed. That was last night. I saw them to the door, watched them come here…but that is all."

"Then you did not know about this? You are not in on this treasonous…?"

Izbin looked like he was in pain. "I would not betray you, milord. You know I wish no ill to Elyri."

The Duke growled and smashed another bit of broken furniture with the heel of his boot. "Do I? I thought I knew all of you. I thought she would be safest in my home, and now k'Ádhá alone knows where she is or what has become of her."

Hoping to soothe his lord, Izbin murmured, "There does not appear to be blood, milord. I will ask if anyone saw her leave. Perhaps she has merely gone walking…"

"No," the Duke shook his head. "From this moment, the House of Gabersdon is closed. No one…not one of those here will remain…"

The squire and his wife looked faint and distressed. "You cannot mean to…dismiss me…" Izbin said in a weak voice.

Balint studied his squire who, while distraught by the thought of being dismissed in disgrace, showed no indication of having been involved in whatever had happened here. He grunted. Izbin and his wife had been with Balint since his boyhood. Experience and instinct told him they were innocent. Reluctantly he swallowed back some of his ire and said, "You two will remain to manage the estate, Izbin. Everyone else goes; the gates will be locked. There is enough food and water stored here to last the two of you for more than a year."

After a look exchanged with his wife, the squire hesitantly asked, "Where will you go? What is to become of us?"

"I am going to Rhidam, to beg pardon from the King for what has transpired under my watch, to atone for it I shall pledge myself to bring this violence to an end. I shall not abandon you, dear friend. I will make sure you have what you need, and hopefully return as soon as this is behind us. Only then will we see to the rebuilding of the House of Gabersdon."

The squire bowed. "Your honor is admirable, milord, but surely not everyone was involved. Some might know about this…but to have willingly collaborated against you? Would it not be wiser to question everyone, find out what there is to know, and dismiss those who are in the wrong? Why punish the innocent, milord?"

Leaning against the building, Balint sighed. He watched members of his household staff crisscross the courtyard, some looking in his direction, others ignoring whatever business the Lord was involved in. Some had lived here since their birth, some since his or before. Some had come later. Punishing all for the sake of the guilty was wrong, and he was grateful to his squire for subverting his fury and standing up for the innocent. "Your duty has always been to keep me from being hasty and I bow to your wisdom. Very well. Assemble the staff in the dining hall, and then the cooks, and finally the guards. I will have the truth, and anyone who…" He coughed, covering his rising annoyance, and added, "Do it, Izbin. I am waiting."

"Yes, milord. I shall at once."

❧*❧

There was chaos and dust around him as Tayte picked himself up off the ground where his mount had dumped him during the melee. The horses were stamping and skittering and he could hear groaning. He examined himself for injury but found none as he rubbed his head.

"Master Tayte? Are you injured?"

He could not see the sheriff but sounds behind him made him crawl to the edge of the road where he found the man pulling a stranger from the ditch. "I am well," said the young man. "Did we…?"

"Three who attacked us have fled with injuries and we caught one of the two who tried to escape. Thanks to your excellent swordsmanship, the other will no longer give us any problems."

"I killed him?" Tayte was shocked, not having expected to kill anyone during his first adult duty. When the caravan was ambushed, the prisoners they escorted tried to escape. Tayte was nearest to them and not directly engaged by the rogues who attacked, possibly because they saw him as a child rather than a young man capable of fighting. But Tayte's father was the best knight in the land and spent as much time as he could ensuring that his sons knew how to handle a sword. The opponent he chose had not been armed, and Tayte made a point of hitting him with the flat of his sword, enough to stop him, not anticipating the blow might kill him.

Everard shrugged with a pleased grin. "I do not know if you did it or if the credit belongs to the rock on which he fell. Either way, there won't be any need to question him. We will bring his body for the sake of allowing Lord Dugan to identify him and hope that is enough."

Tayte helped secure the body on one of the horses and then mounted his own while the others took care of the surviving prisoner. The body of the third man was already secured. "Perhaps we should be more diligent on our watch?" he suggested nervously. "Rhidam is a few hours away, but whoever they were, they could come back."

The sheriff patted his back. "I doubt they will return, milord, but we will be mindful. It would be wiser to be prepared and have nothing happen than to be unprepared and ambushed again."

❧*❧

By early evening, the house of Gabersdon was emptied of two-thirds of its staff. Most of those remaining were cooks and servants, a few were groundskeepers, twenty-three were guards. Balint was ruthless in his questioning and at the slightest hint of anti-Elyri sentiment, or apathy to their plight, he dismissed those who had, he felt, failed to serve him and their king. Those who shared what they knew confirmed what Izbin said; during the night of the fire, Sir Jorges, Balint's Captain of the Guard, escorted Dhybhé to her rooms. Sometime later, with no evidence of a struggle, she followed Jorges through the gate of Balint's stronghold. It had not been until afterward that the sound of furniture breaking from within the rooms she had used was heard. None of those who heard had bothered to investigate.

At least Balint knew that she had not been injured while on his estate. That she had left of her own volition. But where she had gone and why was a mystery. The single clue he had was that one groundskeeper mentioned hearing Jorges say something to the lady about her brother. Perhaps his captain had found her brother and took her to him. Equally likely, however, was the threat of harm to her or her brother if she did not cooperate, an indicator that his man was involved in this matter.

Leaving strict instructions with Izbin for the upkeep of the estates and what he should do if Dhybhé returned, and leaving orders for his sheriff to continue searching for her and Jorges throughout Nelori and its surrounding territories, Balint prepared for departure at dawn. He was going to Rhidam to seek the King's pardon; it seemed the most honorable action he could take.

Ártur was not expecting an audience with the King and his advisors tonight; when Flannery found him painting in the library and summoned him to the stateroom, the healer was surprised. Perhaps someone was unwell. Or perhaps, he thought, heart skipping a beat, word had come from Kavan. He hastened after the chancellor with a hopeful bounce in his step. There were many people in the stateroom, the King and his sister, Caol and Bhríd, Tayte Cáner, General Agis, Justice Corbin, and three others. The lone bound figure in the room glowered at them, his head of greasy black hair thrown back defiantly at the sight of the Elyri Healer entering the room.

"You sent for me, Milord?"

King Hagan cast a quick glance at Bhríd who nodded. "I want you to read this man, Lord Healer, and tell me what you learn."

Ártur came forward. "You would like me to confirm what you already know?" It was not an unusual request, he did not need to ask, but the captive's countenance made him warily want validation of his duty.

"Yes," replied the King.

Bracing for contact with a hostile mind, the King's uneasy, strained tone echoing in his head, Ártur waited until the three surrounding the prisoner held him secure. Ártur trembled as he placed his hands upon the man's chest and opened his thoughts.

Trepidation morphed into outrage as foreign thoughts filled him. "How dare you!" he hissed. Anger blinded him as he forced energy through his hands into the cavity beneath his palms, an act he knew but was forbidden to use by the healer's oath.

The prisoner's face began to turn dark as he gasped for air. Bhríd rushed to pull Ártur away, though apparently, direct contact was unnecessary since the prisoner slumped in his guards' arms even after the healer's hands were removed. A small touch in Ártur's mind, a whisper of something he thought beyond his grasp, snapped the healer's head up, breaking his psychic hold on the man he had tried to kill. Ártur collapsed against Bhríd, sobbing and shaking.

"He tried to kill…sínréc…his hands…"

The King rose with the first truly cold look that any in the room had ever seen upon his face. "You attacked, maimed, and almost killed the Duke of Alberni, the royal court bard…"

"He is Elyri."

"He is the White Bard of Bhryell!" exclaimed Diona. "He is the last man in the Sovereignties to deserve such brutality. He has caused harm to no man."

Hagan waved his hand to silence her. Perhaps he should chastise her for the interruption, but he understood her feelings and did not begrudge her the outburst. "Enough. Words are wasted on men such as this. We have the proof we need to pass judgment: the statements of these two gentlemen, two patrons, and the keeper of the Merry Sow, and the word of Sheriff Everard of Levonne. Both Bhríd and Ártur have read him and confirmed it."

"You should have let Ártur kill him," the princess spat.

"Let him break his oath?" the chamberlain asked, his arms still around his cousin. The healer was more shaken than Bhríd expected him to be, and hearing the princess's words distressed him further.

"No," King Hagan said in a firm voice. "He will be an example. An attack on an Elyri, any Elyri, because he is Elyri, will not be tolerated, and an attack on Lord Cliáth cannot be forgiven." The King looked at his sister, at the others in the room, and back to their prisoner. "I sentence you to death."

Everyone in the room was shocked. No one expected King Hagan to pass a death sentence. No one believed he had it in him.

Justice Corbin bowed and was the first to speak. "How should the sentence be carried out, Milord? Shall I ready the gallows?"

"Burn him!"

The prisoner's face grew pale at the suggestion.

"Diona!" croaked the King. He was prepared to have the man killed but he was not prepared to endure the stench of burning flesh.

She met her brother's gaze with flashing eyes. "Common criminals are hung. He is no common criminal. If he is to be an example, make it one that means something."

Looking around him, the King read in each of his advisors' eyes that, while they thought Princess Diona's suggestion extreme, they also agreed with her judgment and would support such a death if Hagan decreed it. But burning at the stake was messy, and the King knew he did not have the stomach for it. He needed something more memorable than the gallows, and he knew what it should be.

"Behead him."

"Milord?" The justice wanted certainty that he heard the pronouncement correctly. Beheading was reserved for traitors or enemies to the Crown. Using it to punish a man for anti-Elyri violence was sending a message that such was a crime against the Crown, a precedent no one expected.

"Tomorrow, at sunset, sir, you shall die by beheading. That allows you time to consider what you have done and what your actions have cost. I will send a dedhá to you that you may seek absolution, but I do not think even k'Ádhá will listen. Lord Dugan, take him to a cell and see he has no visitors without my consent. Lord Corbin, select an executioner and prepare the square. The rest of you are dismissed."

The King waited until the room was cleared of all except the two Elyri and his sister. It looked as if the healer did not have the strength to do anything other than weep against the chamberlain's shoulder and Bhríd was not going to move until his kinsman was prepared to do so.

"Lord Healer?" asked the King, his hand on the man's back. "I am sorry for asking that of you. Bhríd had already confirmed it but…"

"You wished me to know," the healer croaked. "He tried to kill Kavan. He ruined his hands. And because of…I nearly broke my…"

"But you did not," his cousin gently reminded him.

"I would kill him without remorse if Kavan had not stopped me.

Sure that the healer had misspoken, the princess said, "It was Bhríd who…"

"No. Bhríd pulled me away, but it was Kavan who broke my concentration. He knew…if he had not stopped me…" he sobbed, "he did not want me to…break oaths on his account."

The King beckoned his sister to follow, and the princess for once had the good sense to remain silent and do as her brother asked. Neither knew how Kavan could have intervened, but this was not the moment to inquire. The King looked back. "Ártur, go to Bhryell for a few days. Visit Syl and Llucás. It will do you good. I will send Bhríd for you if you are needed. I, for one, would not have held you responsible for killing that man after what he did. I understand if you would like to take some time away."

The healer bowed his head. "Thank you, Milord." He wished he could say that his cousin had left some message, but all the bard had done in that contact was keep Ártur from making an irreversible mistake, for which the healer would be forever grateful.

❧*❧

When the Sight had shown him the image of Ártur trying to kill someone, Kavan had not understood why nor wanted to believe it could happen. His cousin was the most steadfast healer he knew. But the Sight was never wrong, only his interpretation of it inaccurate, and Kavan knew he could not take a chance on it being wrong now. He hesitated to contact Ártur when he had indicated he would not reach out until he found his answers, but this was an emergency. Regardless of his personal wishes, he could not turn his back on his cousin. Ártur must not break his healer's oaths. No one around him, as they paused their travel for a noon meal, noticed as he closed his eyes, pulled lightly upon the well of energy within, and reached with his thoughts across the miles separating him from Rhidam.

He was successful in that reach, his touch to Ártur's thoughts coming in time to distract the healer from what he was doing, disrupting his link to power and halting any further damage he might have caused. In that brief second of contact, however, for Kavan allowed no more, he learned what it was that filled his cousin with bloodlust. His intended victim was the man who had smashed Kavan's hands. Doubling over with the spasm of pain that memory created, his hands clenched to his chest, caused Wortham to look at him with a worried expression but nothing more.

The days since leaving Ergoth had been serene despite the eerie strain plaguing them. Eridel had not returned. Both Urian and Wortham were satisfied and grateful for his departure, thinking little of it beyond the lamentable way it had come to pass, but Kavan was less comfortable with the situation. He had offended the younger harper, destroyed his harp, both of which would be more than sufficient causes for Eridel to leave them, it was true. But there was something more to the young man's absence. Kavan felt it in the depths of his soul, the only thing he felt there other than the ever-present despair.

Little else had changed. Though his hands remained useless, he made an effort to take on new skills. He gathered kindling for their fires, tended the animals, and spread the bedrolls. It was not much but it was progress, but it did little to regain Orynn's favor or ease his internal suffering.

Tonight as with every night since Ergoth, she remained quiet across the fire, vacantly staring at the stars or studying Kavan with a sad, wistful expression, her arms wrapped around herself as if she were a child with a stomach ache. She spoke to no one about her troubles and come dawn it seemed her melancholy passed. She began to ride her horse now that its stores were running low, and often she hummed the same tune that Kavan had first heard her sing. What he wanted as he watched her, almost as much as he wanted his hands and his music restored, was for her to smile, to laugh, for her to forgive his folly. But he could not ask that of her. He did not feel he deserved it and believed that if she refused when he asked, it would kill him.

❧Chapter 22❧

News of the proposed beheading swept through Rhidam like a wildfire; by the time the construction of the execution platform was complete there was a large gathering of townspeople in the square. Justice Corbin thought they would disperse come nightfall, or that the rain that fell during the night would drive them home. Instead, by the following dawn, the crowd was larger and a few individuals carried wooden signboards declaring outrage over the violence against Elyri or the violence against Kavan. The justice was content to allow peaceful demonstrators to remain in the rain, keeping their vigil, if it meant an end to the events destroying Enesfel.

As a precaution, however, several of Agis' soldiers patrolled the square looking for trouble. It came as expected, with squabbles erupting when the pro-Elyri segment came into conflict with the anti-Elyri faction. The skirmishes were minor, however, the show of military strength enough to keep the crowd in check throughout the night and early morning.

About mid-day, the justice's men escorted the k'gdhededhá to the castle, elbowing through the crowd to be sure he reached his destination safely. The portly clergyman did not seem to notice the rain, nor did he notice much else as he sloshed through the mud in the streets. His expression was grim. He hated hearing the final concession of the condemned, and this time he did not know if he would be able to absolve the prisoner, even if the man wanted it. k'Ádhá might be able to forgive, and Dhágdhuán too, but the k'gdhededhá would be hard-pressed to do likewise.

Within the keep, the mood was no less grim. Diona and Caol derived perverse satisfaction from the scheduled execution. Everyone knew the inquisitor was callous to such things, but few understood the princess's eagerness to see this man suffer. Few knew how desperately she wished to transfer her guilt for wronging Kavan onto this man and execute it with him. The King knew. He saw it in her eyes every time he looked at her.

"You will not talk me into witnessing this, Diona," he said as he finished his midday meal. "There is no law that says a sovereign must attend an execution he has pronounced."

"No law, but you know this is the first beheading in decades…and it was your decision…"

"You were the one who pushed for some end other than hanging. I can barely endure that."

She shrugged. "You did not need to listen to me. I am not…I am your sister, not one of your advisors. You are the King. It is your words that stand, not mine."

The King snapped indignantly, "Then why do my advisors go to you before they come to me?"

"I…" Diona stepped back. "They wouldn't…" She had suspected it was happening on occasion, but she had not thought it happened often enough for Hagan to notice.

"I have ears and eyes," Hagan pouted, crossing his arms over his chest. "I notice details even when people think I don't."

"I have never asked them to…I did not think they…I thought they were…I will point out this error to them at once," she offered apologetically.

Shrugging, the young King sighed and looked away. She might not have known his advisors were seeking her input before going to the king. If true, it was their wrongdoing, not hers, and perhaps his own if they felt his sister was the kingdom's decision maker. If he could not convince them to bring matters of state to him first, why should he expect her to change their behavior?

"I made the proclamation for beheading because it is the right thing to do. I could not tolerate suffering for suffering's sake, and in the end, what would be the point? He would still die and still not recant what he has done. And you're right; hanging would not suffice. You knew it. Even Ártur knew it, though he detests violence more than I do. That does not mean, however, that I must watch it."

Diona knelt at his feet, hoping her gesture made him feel better. "It would do much for your public image, Hagan. I will be there; I must for my own sake. I will go in your stead if you refuse to attend. But think on this; the people may think you weak if you make these declarations and do not follow them through to their conclusions."

"The sentence will follow through. I will not change my mind. I think my fainting or becoming sick from watching a man lose his head would be worse for my image than not attending. dedhá Claide." The King stood as the man entered. "What brings you here today?"

"I have come to see the condemned, Milord, and hoped I could have a word with you." Claide ignored the princess' presence.

She, however, did not ignore him. "k'dedhá Jermyn has seen him," she said coolly as she rose with her brother's help. "What he has done is heinous, but it does not take two dedhá to hear his concession."

Unruffled beyond an annoyed glance in her direction, Claide replied, "His family asked me to speak with him, to learn why he did these things. The k'gdhededhá must have told you he is repentant, My Liege; he was drinking at the time and you know drunken men often say and do things they do not mean. I plead leniency…"

"Drunkenness is no ex…"

The King cut his sister off mid-sentence. "He knew what he was doing, drunk or not. Lord Cáner read him, as did Healer MacLyr…"

"Begging forgiveness." Claide bowed, hiding his face, but not before Diona noticed the twitch at the corner of his mouth and the dark flash of bitterness in his eyes. "Those men are related to the victim; their testimonies would be biased. I believe you should seek a neutral third party…someone not Elyri…to learn the truth."

The King grunted. "The men who turned him in gave sworn testimony that he was not drunk at the time of the attack, and five witnesses place him in the Merry Sow minutes before the assault. Each of the accounts concurred that he was the mastermind of the attack, which is what the Elyri have testified to. It was a premeditated assault. I trust my chamberlain, and though I would expect Lord MacLyr to react harshly, I do not believe he would lie to encourage execution."

Still in his bow, Claide murmured, "I hope you are correct." He straightened, his face neutral once more. "But please be lenient, your highness. A man cannot learn from mistakes if he is dead."

Diona thought she detected a note of desperation in the clergyman's voice, but her brother appeared not to notice. She wished Caol were here to confirm her perceptions. "Others can learn from it, dedhá," she said. "It is a lesson Enesfel is in sore need of learning."

"I am sorry, dedhá," the King said, agreeing with his sister. "It is either beheading or," he cast a glance at Diona, "burning at the stake. Beheading is more merciful. If k'Ádhá thinks the sentence unfair and unjust, I will seek forgiveness for my decision…but I will not change it. The execution will be carried out this evening as proclaimed."

Claide bowed in defeat and retreated without further word, his sour expression causing Diona to shudder. "I don't like this."

"What?"

"His pleading leniency for that man."

"It is a dedhá's duty…"

"k'gdhededhá Jermyn did not see fit to put in such a plea…"

Hagan started towards the door. "The k'dedhá likes Lord Cliáth."

Princess Diona's jaw twitched and her eyes narrowed at what those words implied. "That should make no difference. If a dedhá's responsibility is to plead leniency for criminals, k'dedhá would have done it too. They are supposed to seek repentance from the condemned, but this is the first time to my knowledge that any of them have begged mercy for one."

"As you said, it's the first time I'm beheading a man…"

"Death is death, be it hanging or beheading. It should not matter. And you should be there…"

"No. That is final, Diona," the King growled.

❧*❧

The worn path that wove up the hill into the forest behind the MacLyr house, overgrown with shrubs and grass much of the way, had been untrodden for decades. It had been a favorite place of Kavan's when the bard was a child, before he discovered shapechanging and flight, and Ártur found treading in the footsteps of his absent cousin comforting. Beside him, Bhen was silent, his arm around his uncle's shoulders. Until now, Ártur had not noticed that Bhen was taller than he was, nearly as tall as Bhríd.

They stopped at the edge of a clearing where an underground spring bubbled to the surface and created a pond. At the water's edge, the healer picked up a pebble, testing its weight in his hand.

"Have you seen Kavan create moonlight…or sunlight…in his hands?" he murmured to no one in particular as he remembered bits and flashes of his time with Kavan.

Bhen settled beside him and stared at the water. "I have seen very little of k'aendhá or what he can do. Only when he brought Mílne home…but I did not have a chance to spend time with him. I could tell he was…different. Special. But few talk about him and I know little. I should like to get to know him. How does he do it?"

The healer shrugged. "I do not know. I am afraid to ask."

"Afraid?"

"It is not something anyone else I know can do. He first did it when he was six, before most children even become aware of the power. He says it is a simple thing, but simple for him is not necessarily simple for anyone else. Shapechanging is simple for him too, second nature. To be honest, the power he wields is intimidating."

"People say he is the most powerful ágdháni to ever live…I have been loath to believe them, thinking their claims inflated out of fear. Is it true then?"

"Maybe. I hesitate to say most powerful…but when you witness it firsthand…" Ártur shook his head. "Certainly the strongest I will ever see. He restrains himself around everyone, even me, displays very little. Sometimes that restraint makes him irritable. I think bhydáni Tíbhyan is the only one who has a hint of his potential. To see it…to feel it…it is something you can only understand when you experience it yourself."

The thought excited Bhen and he nodded wistfully, "I hope I will. Power does not frighten me. I am not as trained as I could be because I devoted my early attention to harp-making rather than training…but I seek to learn more when I can. Is it true…there have been miracles?"

Knowing that was a sore spot with his cousin, Ártur struggled with how best to answer. "There have been miracles attributed to him. I have witnessed some of them," he admitted. "There have been none in several years, perhaps because there has been no need, but I don't think we have seen the last…unless he does not come back to us."

"He will come back." Bhen felt sure of it as Ártur's stone skipped across the pond. "If he is bound to the Lachlans as you say, he must."

"But to what end, if his hands…?"

"Do not wish trouble upon him, k'aendhá. You do not know what the future holds for him. Or for us." When the healer sighed, Bhen put his hand on the man's back. "There is something more that brought you home, is there not? Something more than a wish to talk about how you miss him, more than the wish to see your wife and son?"

If that had been Kavan asking, the healer would not have been surprised. Kavan's knack for feeling someone else's turmoil was frightening at times. But Ártur had not expected it from Bhen. He stared at him for a moment and then hung his head. "They arrested the last of the men who attacked Kavan, the one who destroyed his hands; they actually arrested two men, but one was killed in an escape attempt…and I nearly killed the other."

If he thought his nephew would be appalled or would chastise him, he discovered he was wrong. Instead, the younger man lowered his hand, rested his elbows on his knees, and muttered. "I think it would have been for the best. It would have been justice."

"Justice?" It was the healer's turn to stare. "I nearly killed a man."

"Which is against your oaths. I know, and I am sorry if my opinion sounds callous, or if it sounds as if I take your calling lightly. But it would have been justice for him to die at the hands of his victim…or at least someone close to his victim. I do not think I would have restrained myself, oath or not. I do not have the puritanical views of many of our people, Ártur. Sometimes violence is necessary to accomplish an end. I hope he will be punished for his crime."

Dumbstruck by Bhen's point of view, wondering how much the death of his sister had influenced Bhen, the healer murmured, "King Hagan has sentenced him to death. He will be executed at sunset today. I thought to stay, to see it done for Kavan's sake, but I felt more in need of my family then in need of watching justice served. It will happen without me there. That is enough.

Bhen scratched the back of his head. "Maybe I should go, be there in your stead, show support for k'aendhá. But Syl will be happy to see you. She and Llucás are staying with me, but today she is visiting her parents. Do you plan to see her?"

"I will when she returns. I think I will stay here longer, and then visit bhydáni Tíbhyan."

"He will be pleased to know that Kavan's attackers have received their due. I know the tragedy has upset him as deeply as it has you."

❧*❧

Despite the continuing rain, a large crowd remained near the platform as dusk approached, and it appeared to the princess that it had grown larger throughout the day. It had divided into two factions, and to her relief, the pro-Elyri, pro-Kavan, anti-violence group appeared to be the larger. The anti-Elyri faction was more vocal, however, shouting threats at others, catcalls at Justice Corbin and the palace guard, and once the princess, chamberlain, and inquisitor arrived, they began taunting them as well. Onea Pantel, still in Rhidam, joined them on the platform. With them were Asta, Tayte, and Gaelán; Bhríd had tried to discourage his sons from attending, but Tayte felt that, because he had brought the man to Rhidam, it was his duty to attend the execution. Gaelán came partially because Asta was here, and partially, he admitted, because he wanted Kavan to have retribution. That, and perhaps because he could not allow his brother to outdo him.

"Where's the King?" someone shouted."

Similar calls were made, questioning the monarch's fortitude, but when Diona stepped up to address the crowd, the inquisitor stopped her. "Do not give them cause for derision, Milady. When they see you cannot be baited, they will stop."

"What of Hagan? Should I not defend him?"

"Do you think they will believe he is conveniently indisposed?"

The princess knew the inquisitor was right, but she was not pleased with making concessions to the crowd. When the vocal members of the throng got no response from her, however, they resumed taunting their rivals as Caol had intimated they would. That was no easier to hear, however, and she almost preferred their derision of her brother to their derision of Kavan and his kind.

Before long, there was a roar of indignation from the gathering as the condemned was escorted to the platform, Justice Corbin, and General Agis. Some were outraged by the prisoner's crimes. Some were outraged that he was a prisoner. Shouts of "Free him!" intermingled with cries of "Murderer," and "Death to you," were heard over the booing and hissing. It was touching to realize how beloved Kavan was, both by her and by many others as well. Perhaps, she mused, her love for him was no different from the way these people loved him. And, she realized, as stones, rotten fruit, and other debris pummeled the platform and bounced off the box where she and the others waited, marrying him would be the worst possible end for Enesfel, as her father had warned.

Even Kavan had said it more than once, that a marriage union between the Lachlans and Elyri would spell disaster. Many could abide advisors, bards, and healers at court, but mixing Elyri blood in the royal lineage would be more than they could stomach. You are a wise man, she thought as if Kavan could hear her. You knew it would come to this.

Justice Corbin and the executioner, a muscular man in a black hood, mounted the platform with the prisoner. A hush fell over the crowd and a scatter of murmurs followed as a large group of individuals pushed their way into the box where Diona waited. It was King Hagan and his attendants.

The princess resisted the urge to embrace him, settling instead for a proud smile in his direction.

He nodded but did not speak. He had given consideration to her words since that morning, and hearing the crowd's derision from inside had made him realize how right she was. As he studied the man on the platform, he decided that if he could not stomach what was to come, he could close his eyes. None of the crowd was near enough to see him.

It would not, however, dampen the crunch of the ax.

"Coward!"

The King's eyes swept the crowd, knowing the word was directed at him and feeling insulted after he had dared to come out for this. He also knew that many, including the condemned, did not expect him to carry out the sentence now that he was there. They believed his arrival meant a stay of execution.

"Do you have any final statement?"

The sound of the King's voice, slightly tremulous but loud and firm, echoed through the square, bringing silence in its wake. King Hagan had addressed the prisoner. Perhaps there would be a beheading after all.

"Free him!" someone cried.

The condemned man had nothing to lose. Those words from the king meant it likely he would die regardless of what he chose to say. Standing defiant, he shouted, "Death to Elyri!"

The cry was returned, accompanied by a surge forward by part of the crowd towards the prisoner and the royal box, but the palace guard pushed them back.

Caol scanned the gathering as a prickle ran up the back of his neck. Something was not right. He could see pushing and some sort of conflict at the back of the crowd. With a flick of the King's hand, Justice Corbin and General Agis forced the prisoner to his knees, thrust his head into an eyeless hood, and placed his neck into the carved groove on the executioner's block. The general held him there. That uneasy prickle up the back of Caol's neck intensified.

"Onea, take the children into the keep."

"Father," Asta began to protest. The others in the box eyed him. The King opened his mouth to speak.

"Do not argue, go. My King, My Princess, you too. Now."

Onea hustled the children towards the castle gates, trusting Caol's instincts enough to have no need to question him.

The princess planted her feet and willfully growled, "I will not…"

The thumping snap of ax against wood silenced them and drew their eyes to the platform. The King's knees grew weak and he turned his head from the sight of the headless, bloody stump; now he was willing to let his retainers usher him back to the castle. Diona, however, continued to stare, eyes wide with wonder that General Agis could calmly hold the victim and watch the blood spurt from the torso. Few had believed this would happen, that King Hagan, little more than a boy, would carry this through. But he had. The deed was done. Kavan's torturer was dead.

"Death to Elyri!"

The cry rose again and pandemonium erupted. It was no longer rocks being thrown, but punches, arrows, and a few daggers. Burning torches were next. Bhríd pushed the princess down and stood over her, his sword already in hand as Caol leaped into the fray after Onea and the children. On the platform, Justice Corbin wrestled the basket containing the head away from someone who thought to take it and passed it to the executioner for safe keeping. The corpse was collected by several soldiers and pulled out of the melee. No one was making this man into a martyr.

Diona struggled to rise, found she could not with the chamberlain above her, and then buried her face against her arm as Bhríd thrust his blade through a man who thought to challenge him; the body fell inches away from the princess's head. She shuddered but did not panic. She did not feel fear but rather exhilaration.

A handful of palace guards made their way to where Bhríd fought. He pulled Diona up, held her to him with one arm, and with the guards surrounding them, retreated slowly towards the outer gate.

"Where is Hagan?" she cried, but her words were lost amidst the shouts and clash of weapons. Flinching and nearly fainting, she clamped her mouth shut as a sword slashed past her face. That attacker also fell under Bhríd's blade.

The palace gates were closed, the drawbridge raised to keep the rioters from crossing to reach the closed inner gate. Bhríd's only recourse was to pull the princess into the nearest gate tower and push her towards the stairs before jumping back into the fight. Diona, realizing it was best to seek safety, ran up the stairs to the top of the tower, her wet and soiled gown catching and tearing as she ran. She barely noticed, beyond the delay it cost her to pull free. Few guards remained in the towers, enough to defend the bridge but no more; the others had gone out to break up the riot. The princess found an out-of-the-way niche with a small window that allowed her to watch what was transpiring below.

With the crowd ever-shifting in the light of torches and burning debris, it was difficult to see where the execution platform was. Nor could she see Justice Corbin in the crowd, and General Agis was spotted only once as he hoisted two men by their tunics and shoved them into a group of soldiers. Nor was there any sign of Bhríd. Her brother and the children she could not see and she could but pray they had made it safely inside before the gates closed. She shivered, though whether at the thought of Bhríd's arm around her, carrying her with a strength she had not known he possessed, the cold dampness of the rain and mud that soaked her hair and dress, or the realization that she could have been killed and that perhaps harm had come to her brother, she did not know. She longed for a shoulder to cry on, but none of those within the tower took notice of her. Even if they had, she knew she would have waved away their aid to keep up appearances. No one would ever accuse her of weakness. She had decided that long ago.

The evening dragged into night, the crowd thinning as those not interested in fighting broke free and retreated to their homes. The remainder were gradually subdued, apprehended, or killed, and still the rain fell. There was little remaining light, as the rain had extinguished most of the torches and small fires that had started across the square. The lessening of the noise below indicated that the situation was being brought under control.

Then the night was quiet except for a few hoarse voices barking orders. Diona could not see who was speaking. Before long, the gates opened, yet she remained where she was. She did not know if it was safe to move, or what would happen to her trembling legs if she tried.

"My Princess…it is safe."

Throwing herself against the muddy, bloody, rain-soaked chamberlain, Diona's resolve to be strong shattered. She had never felt as grateful to hear anyone's voice, not even Kavan's or Espen's. Bhríd held her as she wept, knowing he smelled of blood and exertion; he was weary to the bone but he also knew she needed to regain her composure in this safe place before they did anything else. Someone in the room lit a torch, then another, until at last Diona pulled back from the chamberlain, forcing herself to more seemly behavior as she became aware that there were other men in the small area to see them.

"I am happy you are unharmed, Lord Chamberlain," she said in a rough whisper as if his safety had been her greatest fear and the reason for her tears.

"Did you expect anything less of the King's Champion, Milady?" he asked with a weary grin.

"The justice and general? Lord Dugan? The children…Hagan?"

Guiding her by the elbow, they descended the spiral stairs as he replied, "The children made it inside with Lady Pantel, as did the King, but Lord Dugan did not. Do not fear, Milady; he is safe. As for Justice Corbin, he kept his wits and got the body out of the ruckus. Agis…" he chuckled, "I think he enjoyed himself a little too much. Everything is under control now."

"Praise be. Will you report to Hagan? Let him know that…"

"As soon as I escort you safely inside. There should be no further problems, but an escort is advisable." They reached the door at the base of the tower where he paused to look at her. "May I say, milady, you handled that admirably. I am sure few others in your situation would have remained so composed."

She blushed and curtseyed, realizing then how filthy she was. "Thank you, Lord Cáner, but please do not mention this…crying…to my brother."

Bhríd laughed. "Your secret will not pass my lips," he assured her.

Relieved, she chuckled too. It felt good to laugh. She suspected that, if her father had been here, once he finished railing at her for being in the middle of such a dangerous situation, he would have been proud of her. She certainly felt proud of herself.

❧Chapter 23❧

The huge orange ball hung low in the sky, giving the last warmth of the day to the already parched land. There were few trees this far south; small scrub patches, low bushes, and yellow grass thirsty for rain dotted the empty land as far as could be seen. Even the road they traveled, if it could be called a road, was cracked and blistered from the heat. They saw few animals, small rodents, owls, snakes and lizards, and a furry creature that resembled a cross between a fox and a cat that hunted the rodents in the coolness of the night and sometimes crept near enough to the fire, in their curiosity, so that the reflections of their eyes could be seen.

It felt more like late summer to those from the north, and Wortham's face and hands had long ago become dark from constant exposure. He could not be comfortable day after day in his heavy breastplate, but he did not protest. A better man than I, Kavan admitted often, using the desolate landscape as an excuse not to look at those he traveled with. He did not complain either, since he could moderate his body temperature no matter what the weather, but his ill-tempered behavior more than made of for the absence of such complaints.

The most prominent scrubby bush, with its blue-gray tinted dusty leaves, small and bud-like as if withered by the sun, gave off a bittersweet stench. It offered little shade, and most of the animals seemed to give it a wide berth, drawing near only to drink from the puddles of water that often pooled at its base. It was from the oil-thick sap that seeped from broken branches that Orec was made, or so Orynn claimed when warning the party not to brush against it or eat any animal found dead nearby. Finding such animals, as it turned out, was rare, as if they too knew the dangers of the shrub.

How, Kavan mused, was the toxin ever reaped? Why take the risk?

It was in the midst of the tall dry grass to the side of the road that Kavan, far ahead of the others today in an eagerness to reach their destination, first saw boots protruding behind the low, poisonous scrub. He halted mid-step at the shiver that ran up his spine. No one took immediate notice of his departure from the trail until Wortham saw him kneel beside the brush.

"Milord?" Concerned for the bard's safety, he left the path to see what Kavan had found, and though he motioned for Orynn to stay back, she had already come close enough to see what the men saw.

"It appears wild animals have done this…" she murmured. "Or he may have ingested the sap while seeking water…"

Kavan shook his head, letting his white hair fall into his face to hide eyes devoid of expression. "No, milady. I have done this to him."

Wortham touched his shoulder. "You had nothing to do with this."

"I drove him away. He was unarmed. There was no way for him to defend himself against men, wild animals…or against me."

"He could have come back to us…" the captain said, but let his voice trail off into silence, the thought unfinished.

Kavan looked at him sadly. "And suffer more abuse? I would not wish that on anyone, not even those of you who continue to endure it. I am as guilty of this as if I had taken his life with my own hands."

He began to tremble beneath the touch of Orynn's hand on his other shoulder and dared to press his cheek to it. For once, her touch did not fill him with panic. "You cannot be guilty of all injustices in life, Kavan," she said. "As much as you wish to be. You cannot atone for the wrongs of the world, nor can you be accountable for something you could not control. Do not be a martyr, milord. It does not suit you."

He did not want to be a martyr, and he had no desire to atone for the sins of the world, but he still felt this was his doing, and when he looked at her, unable to retort, it was with a largely blank expression.

On his mule, still on the road, Urian called, "We should afford him a proper burial."

Assuming the monk had overheard them, as they had not been speaking in whispers, the captain said, "There is little left to bury…but yes, that would be fitting…"

"I will do it," murmured the bard.

"Milord…not here…" Wortham indicated the bushes beside them, where one sun-bleached arm stretched into the shade.

"I will use gloves…and burn them after…"

"Your hands…"

"I know. But I must do this. Make camp across the road; it is near sunset and we should rest. This place is good enough. Please…let me do this, Wortham. For my own sake."

The captain sighed, understanding why Kavan wished to undertake this alone, and knowing that it would be a more difficult task than the bard anticipated. Perhaps the usual small collection of groundwater would lend a softness to the parched dirt, but the task would still not be an easy one. "Very well, but let me point out…even with the water…this soil is hard and dry. You will not be able to dig a grave without a spade. The best you can hope to do is cover him with loose soil, rock, and grass." Not branches. Wortham prayed Kavan had no intention of ingesting the poison or getting it on his skin to suffer a prolonged, lingering death.

Kavan looked away. "There are ways, Wortham. I will make do." When Orynn did not follow the captain, he added, "Go, milady. Rest. You look weary. There is nothing you can do. I will be careful."

"Can I not stay and offer companionship?"

It seemed to Kavan that she desired his company at that moment more than he desired hers, and since she had sought it so little recently, he said, "I would prefer to do this alone, but if you wish to stay…I will not object." He shrugged, leaving the choice in her hands.

She nodded sorrowfully and sat a few feet away to watch him awkwardly scoop handfuls of soil and spread them over what remained of the unrecognizable corpse. Even the fabric that remained, shredded and faded, offered few clues, but it did not deter Kavan from his certainty that Eridel had met his fate here. He could touch him to know for sure, but he did not dare. That was a sickening certainty he did not desire.

He did not speak as he worked, and when Wortham announced the meal prepared, Orynn rose, brushed her hand over Kavan's head, and joined the others at the fire. She did not return.

Until far into the night, Kavan gathered rocks and dirt, crawling about, covering the body until his hands were raw and bleeding within the gloves, his back, shoulders, and arms stiff and sore. Everyone else slept, but still, the covering was not to his satisfaction. Eridel deserved better, no matter how he had died. Certain that no one would see him, Kavan knelt at the man's side, removed his gloves, closed his eyes, and placed his hands on the layer of soil covering the remains, pouring energy into the dirt, into the body, into the ground below. Beneath his hands, he felt the mound gradually shift and sink as the earth opened to take Eridel into its embrace.

When he was confident that no more animals would further desecrate the remains, save those in the soil that brought each man's corpse to its end, Kavan sighed, lay face down on that fresh grave, and began to pray. He wanted peace. Either the restoration of his hands or the knowledge that he was forever denied that blessing and the ability to come to terms with that. He had lived long enough with anger and pain. He had reached the point where he was ready to accept any outcome as long as it gave him peace. He did not want what had happened to Eridel to happen to any others because of him.

Eridel. A young man, selfish and foolish perhaps, who had not wished Kavan harm but rather had emulated him as a master and mentor. A young man cast out to die alone, the way Kavan felt he had been cast out and longed to die. The Elyri had suspected for days that Eridel had met his end, but it had not been until seeing this that Kavan felt the full weight of remorse. But there were no tears; he had spent too many on himself and had none left for mourning anyone else.

Lying there, he stretched his arms up above his head to ease the ache in his shoulders. The hurt within was crushing; he did not notice any unusual pain, but when he eventually realized he could not lower his arms, he became aware of the trail of wetness that ran from his wrists onto the earth below. He could feel it in his boots as well, and when he lifted his head, he could see the dark stain on his skin beneath the light of the moon. Blood. Now aware of it, his wrists and ankles began to throb and ache while his blood flowed onto Eridel's grave.

Dhágdhuán and Kóráhm, he thought frantically. He was not worthy of this. It was said the saints and those of great faith welcomed the rósádhá, the marks of Dhágdhuán's martyrdom, the wounds of the death that sparked the birth of the Faith in his people in days long forgotten by living man. But Kavan did not welcome this. He was not a saint, only a man, and not a good one. To what end must he endure this? What was k'Ádhá trying to tell him? That he too would die?

Panic-stricken, he struggled, but it was in the midst of that terror that an idea came, more like a small voice from the depths of his soul than a conscious thought. Orynn's touch had once provided a diversion from this pain. He did not dare call to her, but there must be another distraction to which he could turn. Something else that would divert his focus from agony and terror. But what? Prayer had proven unsuccessful, as it seemed to focus his mind more on what he was trying to ignore. The only other thing that had ever distracted him from the world, the one act that gave him peace, was making music.

Music. That was his answer. But he had no harp upon which to play, and even if he had, even if his hands were functional, he could not have played with his wrists pinned to the ground by an invisible spike. How then could he offer up music if he had none?

It struck, suddenly, jolting him out of the haze he had been in for far too long. He could sing. It might not be as grand an effort without his harp; it might even be quite bad. But it would be music, and if, by concentrating on notes rather than pain, he could be free of this torment, he might discover an answer to the peace he sought.

He sang, softly, a wordless hymn absorbed into the grave beneath him. The notes were difficult to find at first; he had to direct them to his lips instead of his hands as he typically did. As his confidence in the song grew, its volume increased. And other than that peculiar soprano register he had never outgrown, the song did not sound bad. He could do this. There was a glimmer of hope. While he did not know what any of those who had once loved his music would think, the simple tune pleased him and he knew he was his own harshest critic. The tone of the notes, the purity of sound, both were enough to drive misery from his thoughts and body until it ceased to trouble him.

❦*❦

For the first time since he was a small child, Gaelán wanted to curl up beside his father and mother and drift to sleep in the security of their presence. Of course, that was out of the question. If he wanted to be treated like a man, he could not behave like a child. But he did not want to be alone. What he wanted most was Kavan.

He did not, however, understand why. He had always been in awe of the man, always felt a deep love for him that seemed rooted in nothing but the fact that Kavan was his uncle…though he knew it was not the same as the love he felt for Ártur. He loved him, but he barely knew him.

Why then, when faced with this unexplainable pain, were his thoughts on Kavan? Why did he desire nothing more than to be with the man, as if that would somehow make this pain stop, or at least make it bearable?

The door of his room opened; the sound made him jump and made his heart thump wildly in his chest.

"Gaelán? Are you alright?"

"Asta?" he squeaked, recognizing her voice though he could not see her clearly.

"Who else?" The door closed behind her and her voice drew closer as she came into the room. "I heard you shout. Are you hurt?"

"It was a nightmare I think…" he whispered. He was not going to tell her he felt physical pain. She would think him out of his mind.

She reached the settee by the window and perched there with her bare feet dangling. "It must be hard to be Elyri…everyone wants to hurt you," she murmured. "And after the execution…what people were saying. I'd have nightmares too if I were you. When I'm Inquisitor, this will stop."

"You? Inquisitor?" He found it easier to look at her feet then her face. And speaking of anything other than the dreadful pain helped clear his head.

"Of course. Do you think I can't do it because I'm a girl?"

She did not sound angry, as she knew Gaelán better than that, but there was a challenge in her question. He shook his head earnestly. "I think you would be a good inquisitor. Like your father. I did not know you wanted to do it." The room was quiet for a long while, Asta thinking about her life goal and Gaelán trying to think of anything other than the pain he still felt. "Asta?"

"What?" she muttered, turning her face to look at him, the pale light of the stars shining upon her skin.

"Do you think Kavan will come back?"

Asta shrugged. "I don't know. I hope so. He was the best tutor I've had and I miss his music. Nothing feels right with him gone." Reluctantly she stood. "If everything is alright, I should return to my room before father notices I am missing."

She looked at him as though expecting him to say something. Did she want him to stop her? He was tempted; he wanted her to stay because he was afraid to be alone. He felt better with her in the room. But he could not ask that of her. His father would not forgive him, and nor, it seemed likely, would hers. Nodding as if she read his thoughts, Asta left, closing the door behind her. Gaelán pulled the blanket from his bed, crawled beneath the settee, and hoped to fall asleep again.

❧*❧

Kavan awoke in the morning to Wortham leaning over him with a look of horrified concern. It was not yet dawn but sounds across the road indicated the others were preparing to set off for the day. His arms had remained stretched over his head in that position throughout the night; now they were stiff and numb. Sitting up made the bard dizzy and he remembered what he already knew, that his entire body ached from the night's exertion, both the grave preparation and the bloodletting. When he saw what Wortham was staring at, he doubled over weakly and groaned, clutching his hands in his lap where they could not be seen. The wounds themselves were gone but there was dried crimson on his skin. He had shed a tremendous amount of blood, enough that it might have killed any other man. The stains on Eridel's grave were extensive, still fresh and wet.

"Your hands, milord?" Wortham knelt, his face creased with worry as he tried to pry Kavan's hands out into view. If this was some effect of the poisonous plants nearby, the captain felt obliged to know.

"No...yes..."

He tried to resist Wortham's pulling but quickly gave in. He held his hands forth, and though they were scraped and bruised from the digging, there was no trace of the rósádhá and no trace of any sort of poisonous intrusion. His sleeves were stained and there were dark smears of something other than this dry dusty soil upon his skin. As a man of battle, Wortham had seen blood, fresh and old, and he knew what he was seeing. It took a few moments more to realize that while he did not know what this meant, something had occurred last night, something of miraculous proportions. Something that had caused Kavan to sing. Wortham had heard it and listened with tears of joy until the sound was heard no longer.

"Let me help you." He bore the bard's weight as they got to their feet. "You are weak, milord. Blood loss does that to a man. Come. Eat and drink. I think Urian will agree to you riding for the day."

"Wortham," the bard objected, not wanting preferential treatment.

The captain silenced him with s scolding sound. "You know he prefers to stretch his legs periodically, and the lady says we shall reach Yashir later today. One day, milord. It is either that or we do not travel. You are in no condition for exertion, and while I would not object to carrying you, I know you would object to being carried." He grinned though his eyes still expressed concern. "As close as we are to Yashir, I cannot imagine you wish to remain here for the day."

Though he tried to stand on his own, his legs were too weak, on ankles that still ached in his sticky boots, to support him. Kavan leaned heavily upon the captain's arm. "Your point is made, Wortham. I shall do as you ask if you will mention to no one what you have seen."

"I will do better than that." Using his foot, the captain rubbed through the stains until they were no longer obvious. However it had been removed, the corpse was no longer seen. "Is that acceptable?"

Kavan graced Wortham with the faintest expression of gratitude. The captain felt his stomach tighten giddily and his heart rose into his throat. "It will do very well."

❧*❦

Leaning against the wall, Caol watched Onea gather her things, regretting she lived so far away. "Too bad you can't stay longer," he remarked. "Life has been much more interesting with you here."

She grinned with playful curiosity. "Should I take that as a compliment?"

"Take it however you wish. It is the truth. Things here have been livelier…" It was not the word he wanted, but it would suffice.

"Yesterday was certainly lively," she agreed. "Are all executions in Rhidam that exciting?"

The inquisitor snorted. "We haven't had an execution in quite a while, and there hasn't been a beheading in more years than that. It was King Hagan's first. Given the political state at the moment…"

"It went remarkably smoothly." She had to agree on that point. If they had been in Neth, such a riot would have turned into a full-scale slaughter. "At least your family is unharmed."

"Thanks in part to your swiftness in getting the children to safety and in knifing that fool who thought to harm the King. I think he will be more favorably inclined towards the Association now."

With a warm laugh, Onea swung her bag over her shoulder and glanced around the dingy room she had rented while in Rhidam. "Not likely," she said. "He probably believes I did it for what I could get out of it. I doubt he thinks me capable of acts of charity and he is not likely to judge the entire Association on one woman's deeds. Nor should he. Besides, your observation and quick action alerted us in time. The credit is yours. Now," she leaned in and kissed his mouth, a gesture that might have been merely friendly or might have been something more, "it is time for me to go home and find out what Prince Kjell, King Merkar, and the Neth army have been up to during my absence. No good, I'm sure, but I want to know specifics. As should you. Staying here isn't a viable option if you want news of the north."

"Asta will miss your company." As would he, but he did not say that. She could not stay in Rhidam; she had business to take care of. And as tempting as the idea was, marrying her was not an option either. For now, this was the best solution.

"I will come to Rhidam again, I promise. And I will be in touch."

He nodded. "You will see that Lord Lachlan gets the princess's letter?"

"I will deliver it to him personally if his guards will allow it. I will send a messenger back as soon as it is done."

He offered his hand, though what he wanted was another kiss. "Good luck, Onea. Watch your back."

"You watch yours, Caol. You've got a more daunting task here, and I want to see your back again…along with the rest of you."

Grinning, his face flushed with the implications of those words, he escorted her to her horse. Sometimes he hated duty.

❧*❧

Jermyn had looked everywhere he could think of on the náos grounds, but neither gdhededhá Claide nor gdhededhá Valgis were found. Rankin had seen Valgis leave earlier in the day dressed in his robes, apparently going out on Faith business, though of what nature the k'gdhededhá did not know. Claide's absence was another in a long line of them, and thus less surprising or perplexing. It was the fact that both were absent simultaneously that Jermyn found unnerving.

Scratching his nearly bald head, the k'gdhededhá directed his attention back to the documents before him but was again distracted. He was convinced his message and the princess's letter had not reached Clarys, that his messenger had probably not made it out of Rhidam. Without telling anyone he was doing it, he made two more drafts of that message, including the details of more recent events. One he sent on the same route the first messenger had taken. The second he would send to gdhededhá Khwílen at Saint Kóráhm's. If the message made it as far as the gdhededhá, it would make it to Clarys, and Jermyn was counting on it getting there.

❧*❧

Once they reached the port city of Yashir, a more metropolitan conglomerate of buildings than any they had passed through thus far, its air heavy with the warm stench of fish and salt, Orynn bartered four expensive obsidian Hatu brooches for the best rooms the port had to offer. The rooms were not elaborate compared to those Kavan and Wortham were accustomed to in Rhidam, but covered beds in ventilated rooms, with meals available when they wanted them, made the rooms worth the price. She left the remainder of her trade goods…three bottles of Dubuais Sherry, a set of gold and amber earrings from Cordash, and a jade vial of perfume from Elyriá, for Kavan to utilize as he found necessary. Her instructions were to try trading the perfume first, in his quest for Orec, and then she left the room Kavan was to use and disappeared.

He had not seen her since. He slept upon arrival and devoured the breakfast Wortham brought him, making up for the weeks when he had eaten almost nothing. Though his legs were still unsteady, the bard made his rounds of the city with the captain's aid, seeking an outlet for the Orec he needed. It was reassuring to learn that, despite Wortham's inability to master the Elyri language, his hours spent on the road speaking with Orynn had taught him enough of the local language to allow bartering. But it was to no avail. Few would speak with them once they learned what commodity they sought, and of those who did, none were willing to direct them to a reliable source. When they were eventually directed to the local religious establishment, they were belligerently informed that the gdhededhá would not trade with either of them.

Despite Kavan's pleas and Wortham's exhaustive arguments, that information turned out to be true. They learned from the short man who served as the leader of the local faith that Orec was consecrated oil, used to bless holy items and anoint the dead for burial. Those not pure enough would die when exposed to it, it was believed, and thus they would only supply it to another priest or to someone whom a priest had blessed specifically for transporting it. No amount of persuasion could convince them Kavan was a holy man, and they returned to the boarding house empty-handed to find Urian at a table downstairs, eating roast meat and gruel, drinking a large tankard of something alcoholic, and conversing merrily with the inn's patrons.

"No success?" the blind monk asked.

"None," Wortham muttered as Kavan took a seat near the open window and stared forlornly at the sunset. It was not like the bard to give up easily, but given what was at stake, the captain felt his frustration was justified. "We found a source, but apparently, milord is not pure enough to warrant parting with any amount of the oil. They will only share it with another religious…"

"I can try," the monk offered. "Though not of their faith, perhaps it will be enough that I am gdhededhá. It could not hurt to try?"

Kavan looked at him intently. If the Elyri had not known the monk was blind, he would have sworn their gazes met. He thought back through their journey, of the opportunities there had been for Urian to go his way. Yet he had not, and Kavan had felt no compulsion to force him to go. Perhaps this was the reason Urian had been sent to him. Perhaps the gdhededhá had been needed all along and Kóráhm, Orynn, or some divine providence, had seen fit to offer him for this purpose.

"gdhededhá," he murmured, reaching across the table to grasp the blind man's hands between his as best he could, "Your assistance may be precisely what we need. Tomorrow we shall try again, and I pray you will succeed."

Across the room near the fire pit, a young girl began to sing, clapping wooden castanets in her fingers, dancing to the tune she made. Kavan watched her while Wortham brought food to the table. When her song was complete, another patron took the floor, and then another. It was a competition of sorts, which they were asked to participate in when one of the patrons handed the castanets to Urian. The gdhededhá accepted the challenge though he could not dance, his singing voice was weak, and the only songs he knew well enough to sing were hymns. The castanets were then passed to a little boy.

"Will you sing, milord?" Wortham whispered. Kavan looked at him with what the captain knew to be fear. "I heard you the other eve. It was not your harp, I confess, but yours is the most beautiful voice I have ever heard."

The bard lowered his gaze, flushing at the unexpected praise, and muttered, "I have no songs to sing." Others had complimented him before, but it had been a long time since he had sung in public.

"You have written songs with lyrics, milord. I have heard them. You could sing one of them without accompaniment…"

"No," Kavan shook his head. "Without my harp…I will fail."

The captain shrugged, knowing no way to convince Kavan that was untrue. "I doubt that. I doubt you have ever failed at music. If a simple song without words can compel me to tears, how much more could you do for them?"

"But you love me." The green eyes seared through the captain sadly. "That is the only reason…"

Wortham chuckled and covered Kavan's hand with his. "I love your music because I love you? Is that why you think I listen? Even those who hate you because you are Elyri acknowledge that your talent is superior to any other. Why judge yourself harshly? It is not justified."

"Because no one else does." He broke from the captain's touch and hastened up to his room, avoiding the young boy who was about to place the castanets into his twisted hand. Inside his room with the door closed, Kavan leaned heavily against it and closed his eyes, relieved to be alone. There had been some inkling of joy when he realized he could still make music last night, but his fear of failure, his fear of being unloved, his fear of mockery, kept the fullness of that joy at bay. He knew he had to overcome it, but how? How could he stand before people with his ruined hands and sing when they would know the truth of what he was?

But these people did not know what he had once been; there was no comparison to make. If the first step was to be taken, it would need to be here in this foreign land. If he did not overcome his fears, he knew his music would be forever silent. He would not have the courage to begin in Enesfel.

❧*❧

"Did we expect the violence and kidnappings to stop with the execution of a single man?" Bhríd asked. His head hurt this morning, after arguing with his sons over their heredity and the need to cooperate with one another the night before; he was not looking forward to two days on the road with Tayte. He did not know when or how it had happened, but there was bitterness and anger in his oldest son that had gone unnoticed before. Some of it was directed at Gaelán, possibly due to jealousy over the newly emerged healing abilities, but most of it appeared directed at Bhríd, a man who barely used his Elyri gifts. This was something he needed to discuss with Madalyn, and he prayed it would not erupt into an argument. It was the most common result of their discussions about the boys. He rubbed his eyes and looked at the King. "Word of the execution may have made it as far as Levonne but I doubt anyone else knows."

"We can hope it will have the desired effect," said the King. He was content with this audience. His attendance at what turned out to be a not quite typical execution had caused many of his advisors to view him in a new light. They treated him with more respect and had begun approaching him with matters they had previously taken to his sister. Diona was not involved in the briefing, which gave the King the undivided attention of the other men.

Caol leaned back in his chair. "We can hope for a lot of changes, but that doesn't mean they will come. Thus far, all I have managed to prove is that the Elyri are not involved in these disappearances. If they were, they would not be turning up dead soon afterward and the families would reappear. Someone is going to a great amount of effort to stir trouble and keep it stirred. Almost as if Coryllien has returned from the dead."

The King grimaced. "I wish we would stop using that name."

"Considering that our adversaries have taken it as their epitaph, it does not seem we can, Sire. I do agree it is repulsive." Taking a long sip of water, the chamberlain continued, "Anything else, Caol?"

The inquisitor rubbed the back of his neck. "I wasn't going to mention this until I had more to reveal…but perhaps I should. King Merkar has been making an effort to cross into Enesfel, via our borders, and through Cordash. He has gone as far as to try to cross Elyri borders, provoking them into erecting a temporary militia…"

Bhríd's body tensed. "Nethites? In Elyriá? Milord…"

"According to my source, Merkar's forces aren't efficient. Elyriá has killed or driven off every attempted incursion. Whatever is driving him, his militia is against it. They seem to be supporting Prince Kjell."

"What do you think this means?" asked the King. He might have survived his first declared execution, but Hagan was not ready to contemplate war.

"My guess is Merkar is interested in the current state of affairs here either as a precursor to hostilities, likely with the intent of regaining his former territories, or because he has a hand in what is happening. We are working on infiltrating his forces, perhaps even approaching Prince Kjell…"

"Is that wise?" Agis asked, speaking for the first time.

"We won't attempt it unless it appears a safe or necessary risk…and you approve, of course, Milord. I'm told he might be the best thing to happen to Neth, at least from the viewpoint of his people. If the military backs him, if they don't like Merkar playing with our politics, and he is willing and able, Prince Kjell could be our most accurate and valuable resource. Alliance would have to be arranged carefully, of course, as we wouldn't want to put anyone in danger."

The King grumbled. "Why did you not speak to me before nosing around in the de Corrmick court?"

"I did not seek this information, My Liege; it was brought to me by people already there. I have given no orders to do anything other than learn more about what is going on, which is precisely what I am supposed to do. Would you prefer me to recall…?"

"They are Association, aren't they?"

Caol did not like the accusing tone of the King's voice, but he saw no point in denying it. "Some of them. Some are informants. I do not know who exactly…"

"You do not know?" The King's chair slid back and Caol thought he would rise.

"Most are people employed by those I employ. A pyramid of sorts. The further down the chain you go, the less they know about why they are looking for whatever they are looking for. Nor are they aware of who will ultimately line their pockets with coin and favors. The information is more reliable if they think they are working for their bosses rather than the Crown."

King Hagan folded his arms across his chest with a growl. "I do not like the way you do business, Lord Dugan. I would prefer some other method."

Having known this argument would come did not make Caol any happier about it. "It is the best way I know, My Liege, and it works. It has worked since before you were born. If you have some other suggestion as to how to conduct successful espionage, I would be pleased to hear it."

The King did not have any other suggestions. Espionage was something he knew nothing about. He knew that he asked questions and his uncle found the answers. But he did not like relying on a criminal organization to supply the Crown with facts. "I have none, Lord Dugan, but be advised I do not like it. If this network of yours causes trouble or proves to be an intelligence leak, you will be responsible." Caol nodded curtly but said nothing; the King continued, "I want you to keep me informed about every report that comes in, every detail you uncover. Lord Cáner, take special care on the way to Levonne. You will have men going with you, both yours and some of mine. Make use of them if you must, but return safely."

◈*◈

Kavan had hoped to go to the local temple as soon as he awoke, but Urian was too drunk on the local beverages from the night before, and though it was a weak alcohol according to Wortham, it was strong enough to keep the gdhededhá from rising until nearly noon. The bard had to be content with re-reading Kóráhm's journal for the fifth time, paying closer attention to the choice of words and the handwriting as he sought clues he might need for what lay ahead. Each reading made him feel closer to his patron, though Kóráhm had not revealed himself since Kílyn. The bard stopped asking why; there had been other lengthy periods of absence, and if Kóráhm was gone, there was nothing Kavan could do to bring him back. He had no control over the Heretic-Saint.

Finally, after a hearty lunch, the monk was steady enough to accompany Kavan and Wortham to the local center of faith. Once there, the celebrants allowed Urian to enter their temple with sour looks at Kavan, with the captain as his barely tolerated escort since the gdhededhá was blind. If this exclusion had occurred a few days earlier, Kavan would have felt angry, slighted, and betrayed. But Eridel's death had brought a change. Kavan vowed to do his best to fight against the darkness. He would not begrudge Urian this attempt, succeed or fail. If Orec was to be found here, k'Ádhá would deliver it.

As he waited, he watched the local people in the street and wondered what had become of Orynn. She had not been in her room this morning, and if she had returned during the night, it had been long after Kavan was asleep. He suspected she had not come back and that soon she would depart and he would never see her again. That thought made him sad and left him wondering if there was some way he could keep her from leaving.

"We have it, Kavan!" Wortham was so excited as he burst from the náós; he did not notice he had called the bard by name. Beside him, Urian wore a wide smile and held up a large, sealed metal bottle.

"Orec!" exclaimed the gdhededhá. "As much as they would part with. I did not even need to trade for it!" Pleased at their good fortune, if less than happy about being snubbed the day before, the bard reached to take it, but Urian shook his head and kept it out of Kavan's reach, as though he could see what Kavan was doing. In a low voice, almost a whisper, he said, "I shall give it to you later. To give it to you here, where they can see us, may be taken as an insult."

Kavan sighed and fell into step with his companions, feeling the priests' eyes watching them until they were no longer in sight of the temple. Urian clutched the precious metal bottle to his chest, beaming proudly as they walked.

"May I ask how you convinced them, gdhededhá?" Was it really a mere matter of his being gdhededhá?

The monk smiled. "We discussed the Faith, and I told them of an altar in desperate need of consecration that has been unused for many years because of the horrific tales of sacrifices associated with it. I explained that Saint Kóráhm sent us here, which is very close to the truth, and though they may not share the details of the Faith, at the mention of Kóráhm, they could not wait to assist me."

"Kóráhm is known here?" Though the Saint had lived and traded in these lands, that had been centuries ago. He was not a saint here, to Kavan's knowledge, so what was he to these people?

"There was no time to share stories," Urian said with a hint of regret. "Perhaps when your undertaking is complete, we may return and learn more."

Kavan nodded. "I should like that, gdhededhá." If there was more to Kóráhm's tale to be heard, it would be valuable to hear it.

"When they asked why I did not come yesterday instead of sending others to do my work," Urian continued, "I told them I was weary from my journey and that as you are a student in the order of Saint Kóráhm, I believed you to be a suitable representative on my behalf. You are accompanying me as my aid since I am a weak, old, blind man. They apologized profusely for not cooperating with you and were most eager, then, to grant my request."

The enthusiasm with which he spoke made Kavan chuckle darkly. "Your…creative…version of our mission and relationship was successful, if not entirely truthful."

"Truth is in the eye of the beholder, Lord Cliáth. To me, you are a student of Kóráhm's…and you have aided me on this journey. They think I am the leader, not you, but even that could be debated. In the end, who have I hurt?"

No one that Kavan could see, and Urian might have saved countless lives if the purification of the náós could be accomplished in a timely manner, which seemed more likely now that the Orec was in their possession. It appeared even more probable when, to Kavan's relief, they reached the boarding house to find Orynn waiting for them, dressed not in her armor but in her pale blue robe. She had been wearing the armor when he had last seen her. She was flushed and her hair was disheveled as if she had just arrived. When she saw Kavan's face light up at the sight of her, she smiled. It was a strained smile, however, with a forced quality that Kavan did not find reassuring. Still, it was a smile, and it brought with it unexpected hope. Not as much hope, however, as the words that followed.

"I have found k'ílshwythnec."

He was glad he was not carrying the bottle, as his quaking hands would have dropped it. "Where? Can you take me there? Now?"

"Calm, milord," she chuckled, warming under his enthusiasm. "There is a village, Zabin, some six or seven days from here, near the mountains. She has made recent pronouncements from that region. She does not stay in one location for long, but I think our chances of meeting her there are good if we depart soon."

"What harm is there in a few more days of travel," Wortham shrugged with a grin. "I am sure she will send us somewhere else which will require even more traveling before our journey is ended. I am prepared for it, milord. You know I am."

Orynn indicated the vial. "You have the Orec?"

"Thanks to gdhededhá Urian; we would not have succeeded without him," Kavan said, words that caused the monk to grin.

"Then you are half way to your objective. Congratulations. I pray the rest of your journey is as successful."

"Are you not…?" Kavan's voice caught and he had to lock his knees to avoid collapse. "You are not continuing with us?"

"My purpose is to assist you in finding Diwi and Orec, and in locating k'ílshwythnec." She sounded sad. "I have done my part, but I shall continue with you a little longer. k'ílshwythnec may not be in Zabin by the time we arrive; I should at least see that you find her there." She took Kavan's hand; he flushed beneath her touch and the captain's bemused look. He did not, however, pull away. Soon he would lose her. He could not afford a rift between them now. "I am not quite ready to leave you yet. I have grown to enjoy your company. And yours, Captain, dedhá."

Forcing his voice to work, Kavan said, "Then we shall leave as early in the morning as we are able. I think, since we did not need to trade for the Orec, we have something to trade for supplies. Will you see to it, Wortham?"

The captain bowed. "Of course, milord."

They left before daybreak, as Kavan wished, traveling deeper into the heart of this foreign land. It was difficult to fathom these people coming together into any cohesive unit capable of invasion against Hatu. This was not a single kingdom but a collection of self-ruling cities and villages. The countryside was poor, agriculturally speaking, and seemed depleted of tangible resources. It was every person for himself here, every family for themselves, and in times of severe hardship, Kavan imagined they pushed each other to breaking, spilling their unsupportable population into Hatu with the hopes of finding somewhere more hospitable to reside. Except for those cities on the sea, Kavan was not sure how these clusters of people survived. But for the mission behind and ahead of him, it was fortunate that they had.

⚞*⚜

Prince Espen stared at the letter in his hands, debating what course of action he should undertake. Princess Diona had asked him back to Rhidam, though this time not for her own sake. Instead, she requested that he bring troops in support of King Hagan to assist in putting down the unrest plaguing Rhidam. There was no word of her feelings, no requests for herself, and he found her choice of words to be stilted, formal, and severe. It meant one of two things. She had either decided against marrying him or was afraid to ask him back because he had told her he would not return. A show of force in support of the new King would be acceptable, however, and he could, on behalf of his brother, the Hatu King, renew their treaties while there.

And going would allow him to see Diona one more time. He missed her, no matter how much he pretended he did not. Either she would accept his proposal or it would be the final time he would see her. Her tone suggested it and Espen feared it to be true. One final trip to Enesfel to put the matter to rest. As he sought out his brother for permission to make the journey, he prayed that this would not be the last time.

❧Chapter 24❦

"I have invited Lady McPhelan to visit for a few days."

The King eyed his sister suspiciously as the woman sashayed into the library and pulled a seemingly random book from the shelf. Jilletta McPhelan was many years younger than Diona, little older than Hagan. While his sister kept an open communication with the youngest daughter of General McPhelan, as she did with many of the daughters of the noble families, Hagan did not consider them to be close enough for his sister to want to spend time with her.

"Why?"

The book was replaced on the shelf without her looking at it. That too suggested his sister was up to something.

"I'm bored," she said with a shrug as she pulled down another book. "It is not safe to ride, and looking at the castle walls is growing dull. I cannot even convince Prince Espen to come to Rhidam."

"To entertain you? I would think he has better things to do." He ignored the face she made. "What makes you think Lady McPhelan will amuse you? You have little in common."

"We both like a good story, and she does like to play dice. Also, she has asked repeatedly to needlepoint together. I have put it off for a long while, but now…she is the closest person…no one else is near enough to risk coming to Rhidam."

That truth made King Hagan sigh. The castle was beginning to feel like a prison, and he was less of a free spirit than his sister. He knew she hated confinement. Still, he suspected there was something more; perhaps it was his sister's attempt to find him a potential queen after he had offhandedly brought up the notion in conversation with her over dinner. He started to speak but movement at the door drew his eye instead. He reached the doorway before Caol got far in passing.

"Lord Dugan, what is the count today?"

The inquisitor frowned. "Fifty-seven…thus far. That is subject to change; the day is still young. I'm on my way to get an update from Justice Corbin and am expecting a few messengers today. I will let you know if that figure changes."

"Fifty-seven…" The King looked grimly at his sister. "Fifty-seven people gone with no trace. No bodies…nothing. Where did they go?"

Diona frowned too and put the second book back on the shelf, her interest in reading gone. "If we knew that, they would not be missing." Perhaps it would not be safe for Lady McPhelan to come after all.

∽*∽

A message from Rhidam bearing the princess's seal was waiting when Owain came down for his morning meal. Rarely hearing from anyone in Rhidam, now that Wortham and Kavan were not there, he was not surprised the letter was from her, however. He doubted anyone else except Ártur would take the time or make the effort. He sank into the nearest chair and read the letter hastily. The last of Kavan's attackers had been found and executed. It was the first good news he had heard since Arlan's death. He regretted missing the execution, as Diona's account, however embellished, was nearly as exhilarating as attending must have been. He was grateful she and the others had been unharmed during the riot. In a way, he was also grateful he had not been there. He had presided over more than his share of death. If he could avoid witnessing anymore, he gladly would.

From his window, he could see Piran attempting to sail his wooden boats on the ice in the fountain. Today was the first snowfall of the winter, likely the only snowfall since it came late in the season. It hinted at a dry year ahead, not a good portent for crops. Drought would make the already tense population in Enesfel more restless.

Perhaps, he mused, he should take Piran to Káliel. The boy enjoyed his father's company and was learning quickly the skills Owain was teaching, but he yearned for the boats in the harbor. And after recent events in Enesfel, Owain felt the boy might be safer with his mother. It did not appear conditions in Enesfel were going to improve soon; Owain had dealt with his share of unrest already. He had disarmed two disturbances, imprisoned five men for killing an Elyri sympathizer, staved off a murder by happening into a tavern as a small group of men was harassing an Elyri merchant in the establishment. None of his people had disappeared, as far as he knew, but he did not expect to remain lucky for long. And he suspected that the few Elyri who dared trade this far north would soon cease coming.

The woman who had left the message had been quite beautiful, someone Owain could not recall seeing before even though she assured him she lived and did business in Fiara. After complimenting his methods of ruling, she gave him no name, claiming only to be a friend of Caol's. It explained much. Association. The woman had nerve to make herself known and reveal her connection to the inquisitor for surely she knew Owain would figure out her business. He had no interest in arresting or questioning her, however. She was guilty of no crime he was aware of, and if she was a friend of Caol's she was likely to be working for him. Owain did not want to knowingly disrupt the information network the inquisitor had in place. Caol was doing the majority of the work to put an end to the madness of anti-Elyri violence, as far as Owain was concerned. Without him, things might be beyond improvement.

∾*∾

"Balint!" General Agis was one of the few who called the knight by his given name. To most, he was Duke Gabersdon, Sir Gabersdon, Milord Gabersdon, or simply Sir. He preferred his name to the titles, and thus smiled at the towering dark-skinned man and offered a hand in greeting.

"Agis. I heard you are Lord High General now."

"I am." His eyes gleamed as he smiled. "The King feels I am the man for the duty since you and Lord Cáner will not take it…for which I thank you both. And with Captain Delamo out of the service…"

Handing the reins of his horse to a stable hand, Balint glanced at Agis with surprise. "What has become of Captain Delamo? He has not been killed in this unholy anti-Elyri business, has he?"

"You have not heard about the attack on Duke Cliáth?"

"No. News takes a long time to reach Nelori, I fear. When was this? What happened?"

"Then you have also not heard about King Arlan's death?"

The knight blanched. "No…I have not…" Why, he wondered, had news about Agis' advancement reached him and none of this other news had?

"We tried to get messengers out…but given the state of things, we cannot be sure they are reaching their destinations. I am sorry you have to learn of these matters this way."

Agis slowly crossed the courtyard with Balint, relaying the full news of the King's death along with the tale of Kavan's attack as he knew it and any other news in Rhidam he thought the man should hear. It was many moments after he stopped speaking, when the horse had been turned over to the stable staff and they had reached one of the rear entrances to the keep, before Balint found his voice. "I thought my problems were bad. It is fortunate I have come to Rhidam to pledge my services to the King."

"You are having the same problems?"

Balint nodded. "A mob burned down a mill because they believed Elyri were performing sorcery there. There was a body in the middle of the fire, though whether it belonged to an Elyri jeweler recently reported missing or someone else, we couldn't tell. The jeweler's sister was under my protection when my own people abducted her…or killed her, perhaps," he added with a reluctant sigh. "It sounds to be the same all over Enesfel."

The nomad nodded in agreement. "It is. Lord Dugan is heading the investigation; I will let him know you are here as he will want to hear of these events. And the King will be grateful for your support. Come, I will secure you a room."

❧*❧

Enda? It took Bhríd several minutes and the study of a territorial map of Hatu to recall where that city was, and when he did, he felt a sinking in his stomach. Enda was the largest city farthest south from Rhidam in the Five Sovereignties. And Kavan was going further away still, into the heart of barbarian lands, unmapped, reportedly hostile territory. What could the bard possibly hope to find there? An escape from those who knew his face and name, or something else? Wortham's letter did not say; the letter only stated that they traveled in pursuit of Saint Kóráhm and that he had every faith that when Kavan found what he sought, they would return home.

Creasing the letter, the chamberlain held it to his face. Yes, the smell and sensations in the parchment were Wortham's. The impressions were strong enough that Bhríd could almost see Kavan through the captain's eyes. He was curious to know why that was.

First, however, he was going to write of this to k'gdhededhá Jermyn, Owain, and Prince Muir, to let them know, as Wortham requested, that Kavan was safe. And he would not speak of Kavan's location to either King Hagan or Diona as asked. He respected his cousin too much. Then, as soon as he could get away, Bhríd would take the letter to whom it was addressed, Ártur MacLyr.

ॐ*ॐ

By evening, Caol had a few more pieces of the puzzle to play with but was no closer to solving it than he had been that morning. He pushed Chancellor McGrannis for answers when the message arrived from Prince Muir claiming that Anri Heward, also called Hugh, had been arrested on Káliel for attempting to enter the caverns on Pháne. Though there was no sketch to compare, how likely was it, Caol mused, that there were two Hughs involved at the heart of this Coryllien scheme? It was possible…but was it likely? Was this, as he believed, the same man, the third suspect in the death of the decapitated Elyri minstrel? That he might be the same, had possibly been on Káliel trying to enter what Kavan believed to be the final resting place of Coryllien…at a time when someone was terrorizing the kingdom using that name, sent up a warning to the inquisitor.

There was a connection. As Muir suspected, the man had not been on Pháne by accident. Those calling themselves Corylliens wanted something. Caol wondered what it was, other than mayhem and the death of any Elyri who crossed their paths. The chancellor's study supported what Muir and Caol both suspected. There was no Anri Heward in the census records. Perhaps, as feared, he was a Nethite. Caol sent a letter to Onea, asking her to investigate.

While Balint's story offered nothing new, it was the first report of violence and unrest so far south. Would it spill into Hatu, he wondered? Had it already? And what of Cordash? What would happen if every kingdom bought into this anti-Elyri doctrine and marched against Elyriá? It looked as if it was Caol's duty to prevent a war and he would. If he could.

❧*❦

It was uncommon for k'gdhededhá Tythilius to have a restless night. Normally he slept soundly enough that people found it difficult to wake him. Not even the náós bells roused him. That he had tossed and tried to sleep for half the night concerned him. Was he unwell, he wondered, or simply worried about his messengers, about Claide, and about the events in history through which he was passing?

He had entered the thóres earlier in the day, interrupting a conversation between Claide, Valgis, and a third gentleman he did not know. Jermyn might have thought nothing of it if it had not been for the instant silence that accompanied his arrival and Valgis' momentary expression of panic. Excusing his intrusion, Jermyn got what he had come for and left the room, though he stopped outside the door out of their sight. The conversation resumed, but their three voices were low and muffled, as if they knew he was listening. The tones of men with something to hide. Perhaps it was innocent; perhaps it was not. The k'gdhededhá had no way of knowing. But he jumped to the worst possible conclusion, and that had the unfortunate effect of keeping him awake as he tried to decide what to do about Claide.

Sensing that someone had entered his room, Jermyn rolled onto his back and sat. There was someone at the window; he could see the shape but not make out who it was. The window and door were closed. An assassin, he wondered, suddenly afraid as the figure came closer.

"No need to fear me, Jermyn."

The k'gdhededhá did not know the voice or recognize the speaker until the man lowered the hood of his cloak to reveal thick waves of hair that glinted auburn in the moonlight. "Saint Kóráhm!"

"You recognize me. I am pleased." Kóráhm came to the bedside with a melancholy smile.

"For what purpose have you come…shown yourself. You never have before." He knew Kavan communed often with the Heretic-Saint, but until this night, Jermyn had experienced little direct interaction with the divine.

The saint nodded. "That is not completely true."

"Aye…yes…" Once, long ago, a ghostly visitation had sent Jermyn on a path of discovery that led him back to Kavan and to Prince Arlan. Until tonight, he had never been certain who had visited him. "You bring some further word or revelation?"

Voice heavy with regret, Kóráhm murmured, "I have come to prepare you for a great trial and beseech you to be strong."

Jermyn held the saint's gaze for many seconds as he let the gravity of those words settle over him. Then he sighed. "I am going to die."

It was not a question, but Kóráhm felt obliged to respond. "Yes."

"Soon?"

Again the answer was yes, though this time given by a nod of the Saint's head. Speaking the word seemed unnecessarily cruel. "I may tell you no more, unfortunately. I am sorry…"

The k'gdhededhá sank against the headboard of his pallet. "I am not afraid of death, milord. I fear pain, yes, but death is not something to fear. But I sense in your demeanor that I shall face both. Pray…stay this sentence a little, if it is in your power, that I may lay eyes on Lord Cliáth again. I must know he is well, for if this land has any hope for the future, faith tells me he is it."

"I cannot stay the inevitable, though for your sake I wish I could. Kavan will not return to Rhidam in time, but I can tell you he is on a personal mission, a spiritual quest. He is physically well, except for his hands, and is growing emotionally stronger."

For Jermyn, that was not enough. "But may I see him? With my own eyes? To see his fair face…see that he is as you claim?"

"Because you do not believe me?" Kóráhm's question was gently amused, not accusing, but the k'gdhededhá hung his head. Understanding it was the great love many held for the bard that fueled Jermyn's wish rather than disbelief, Kóráhm waved his hand and murmured, "Look."

At the foot of Jermyn's pallet, a pale blue-white mist formed and spread, rolling like a cloud of steam, opening to reveal a campfire at its center as clear as if Jermyn were standing before it. There were three mules and a large horse tethered nearby, and close to the campfire, three sleeping figures. One was a monk in the brown habit of a Bhenádíctuan missionary. Another was a woman who seemed almost familiar though he did not think he had ever seen her. The third with the head of dark curly hair was recognized easily as Captain Delamo. With a smile, Jermyn continued to search the image for what he wanted to see. The territory was unfamiliar, barren and dry, nearly a desert, and Jermyn wondered where they were.

"Lord Cliáth is not with them, milord."

"Look further."

The image shifted to the right to where Kavan knelt in prayer, the only one of the party awake. His watch, perhaps, since he paused periodically to scan the area as if for danger before resuming his vigil. Feeling a stab in his breast, Jermyn whispered, "His hands…"

"Yes," said Kóráhm with palpable grief. "It was a debilitating injury, one he allowed to go untended in his belief that he was being punished."

"Punished? What could he have possibly done to deserve such punishment?" Kóráhm shook his head, not willing to discuss Kavan's plight. Jermyn shifted as if to get a better view of the Elyri harper he missed the same as everyone else. "Will they be restored?"

"That is up to him. As I said, he is making progress; he is growing and facing issues he has avoided his whole life. If I had the benefit of a saint's wisdom," Kóráhm chuckled, "I would have been a much better man." The image faded as Kóráhm stepped back into the shadows near the window. "Be strong, Jermyn. When it is time, I will be there; I will come for you. On that, you have my word."

The room grew darker, the light of the moon no longer enough to brighten it, and Jermyn knew he was alone.

The k'gdhededhá was too awake to sleep and he knew that if he did there would be dreams he would rather not have. He groaned and rubbed his face. "I am not reassured, but I will be grateful for that."

Hunched upon his pallet, he stared absently until the night gave birth to the day. He had not been thinking in any conscious manner but as dawn came, he knew what he had to do. Dressing in his old monk's habit, a robe he had not worn in years and which barely fit any longer, he hustled from the room in search of Tusánt, whom he found already finishing his morning meal. It was fortunate for the k'gdhededhá that the Elyri was an early riser.

"Tusánt, I have a favor to ask. Is there a Gate in Alberni?"

"A…" Tusánt looked up in surprise. "I know of one in Saint Maicel's…"

"That will do. Will you take me there today? Now, if possible? I must seek immediate audience with k'gdhededhá Khwílen."

"Of course." Breakfast was pushed away and Tusánt pulled his cloak from the hook behind the door. "Shall I wait there until you are ready to return?"

"No," Jermyn said with a shake of his head. "I do not know how long I shall be required to be away. I want you to come back here and watch Claide. And Valgis. If anyone asks for me, tell them I have gone into seclusion and may not be disturbed."

Tusánt did as instructed, asking no further questions. He knew enough. The matter involved Claide, and in some roundabout way involved k'gdhededhá Khwílen. The Elyri gdhededhá suspected it was more involved than that but he knew his place. He parted with his superior outside the door of St. Maicel's and returned to Rhidam.

k'gdhededhá Jermyn had no difficulty finding his way to Saint Kóráhm's abbey. Having spent many years in Alberni, he knew his way to every place of import in the city. Borrowing a horse from the gdhededhá of St. Maicel's, he rode with four attendants to the chellé, a structure whose sprawling stone façade commanded attention even from a distance. Much of it was a single story; the only sections taller than that were the two housing dormitories, the dome of the náós, and a single tower set away from the others with windows on every side. The scriptorium, if he recalled Tusánt's description correctly. From the outside, it looked to be a spacious circular area with enough natural light throughout the day to keep the room brightly lit. He wanted to see that room, to see where the texts, both holy and secular, would be copied and illuminated. He hoped he would live to see their first product complete.

No thoughts of dying today, he scolded himself as he dismounted and allowed the guards to escort him inside where he was to await the k'gdhededhá. His attendants returned with the horse to St. Maicel's. Alone save for residents who came and went from the room, Jermyn slowly circled the expanse, studying the frescos and murals, the way sunlight sources played into the splendor of the place. Tusánt's claimed had been accurate; no one could precisely describe this beauty. *Ah, milord Cliáth,* he thought, weeping freely, *you have created a masterpiece.* And he was blessed to see it before he confronted whatever lay ahead.

Footsteps stopped beside him and someone handed him a handkerchief. "k'gdhededhá Tythilius. I am surprised to see you. There was no word you were coming to visit our humble chellé."

"Humble?" Jermyn wiped his face and nose and looked at the Elyri beside him. "I think not, Khwílen. This is…a miracle of a place. Tusánt told me I must see it for myself to understand; I am pleased he did not exaggerate. As for my arrival, it was a last minute necessity; I had Tusánt bring me."

By Gate, Khwílen understood though it was not said, "What urgent matter has brought you to me, k'gdhededhá."

"You will likely receive a letter today or tomorrow on these matters, unless this messenger goes missing too…but it has become imperative that I share such things myself. First, however, I would like to see the rest of this splendor."

"You are welcome to roam as you please," the blond man said. "I have duties I should attend if you wish me to be free for discussion, after the noon meal perhaps?"

Jermyn nodded. "That would be acceptable."

"Shall I have one of the gdhededhá escort you?"

"I can show myself around; I shall not get lost. But I tell you, free up your schedule for tomorrow."

"Why?"

"Because once you hear what I have to say, I want you to take me to Clarys. I intend an audience with k'gdhededhá Dórímyr."

ھ۶*‑ھ

Tíbhyan hunched upon the wrought iron bench on his back porch, watching Bhen and Llucás till his little plot of a garden. Nothing had grown there in years, since the last time Kavan had been here to tend it. Since crossing paths with one another during Kóráhm's Feast, Bhen had come to the bhydáni's home at least once a week. He repaired broken or deteriorating items around the man's house or merely came to talk. With spring not far off, Bhen decided to ready the plot for planting. And because it was Ártur's wish that Llucás be exposed to Elyri teachings, learn as much as he could, Bhen brought Llucás every time he came. Ártur wanted no fear of the power in his son and he wanted Llucás to be free to explore it if he desired.

Coming here was also an opportunity for Bhen to dabble and experiment with his underdeveloped power. Hearing about the range of Kavan's abilities gave the harp-maker incentive to see how much he could learn. Not that his trade allowed much time to pursue study, but he would take advantage of what time he could afford and spend the rest of his life learning.

The bhydáni enjoyed the company. He did not say it, and there were times when the old sage knew his gruffness was interpreted as annoyance. But he had few social visitors and if Bhen felt like coming to his home, lending his strong back, discussing anything and everything that came to mind, the sage was willing to return the favor with a few lessons.

In some ways, it was like having Kavan in his home again. Bhen was bright, thoughtful, and even a little more gifted than his untrained status should allow. It seemed that Power was coming to ground more and more in Kavan's family, though none of them mirrored what Kavan possessed. And the harp maker wanted to talk about his cousin, learn more about the man he did not know, then he could learn at home. It made Tíbhyan happy to talk about his favorite student, especially to members of the bard's family.

Today, Ártur was here too. The bhydáni had already heard the tale of Ártur's attempt to kill Kavan's attacker. He lightly scolded the healer for almost breaking his oath and then consoled him with his own wisdom: oaths were meant to keep one from wrong behavior, but sometimes breaking them was unavoidable, even allowed or expected. Ártur was not sure he believed that, but here he was not judged. What he wanted was time to heal inside and the chance to miss the cousin he dearly loved and he found that in the bhydáni's home.

"I intend to bring Gaelán the next time I come. This was not a planned visit. My second child is due soon and I will be here for the birth. I will endeavor to bring Gaelán then. He has had a difficult time lately; he seems to miss Kavan more than most."

"Then it would do him good to come, to see Kavan's home."

"I hope so. This distraction is not conducive to study."

Tíbhyan chuckled. "Children and young men are prone to distraction…and it seems as though Rhidam is a distracting place these days. When will you go back to Rhidam?"

"Tonight. I have been gone too long; I worry when I am away and no one summons me."

"I would think that would be a good thing; at least you know no one is in need of services."

"Either that," the healer grunted, "or Bhríd is the one who has been injured or killed. Besides…I want to be there on the day Kavan returns. I cannot stay away long until I know he is safe. And I cannot keep you informed of news if I am not there to learn anything."

"I hope you are careful."

"You sound like my wife, bhydáni," the healer chuckled.

The old man grinned. "Wives usually know their husbands best, Ártur. Listen to her."

∽*∽

The first daily Gathering in Hes Dhágdhuán Náós had already begun when Jermyn and Khwílen entered. At this hour, most of the attendants were gdhededhá, as they were plentiful in Clarys and frequently the earliest risers. Every order of the Faith had adherents in Clarys, both as spies and representatives of each group's interests, or merely as pilgrims come to worship in the largest náós in the lands. In some ways, the Faith in Clarys was more of a political venture than a spiritual one, making Jermyn glad he had escaped it. Had it always been thus, he wondered as if seeing the machinations for the first time, or had it developed unchecked after his departure for Enesfel?

He remembered dwelling in one of the many wings of the k'gdhededhá's palace which was directly linked to the náós by several halls and walkways, more than one underground passage, and at least two Gates. It was a posh life, one he abandoned when he chose to follow Kavan and Prince Arlan to Enesfel. His position as k'gdhededhá now offered him a few of these luxuries, but because his post was in Teren territory, the Elyri k'gdhededhá feared sending resources there and more often than not, the Faithful outside of Elyriá were left to supply their own needs.

Unfounded or not, it was a fear Jermyn could see more clearly now. The belief in peace and diplomatic resolutions, of avoiding violence and bloodshed, was too ingrained in most Elyri to seriously consider self-defense. Some, such as the Cáner's, the MacLyrs, and Lord Cliáth, were not willing to die passively, but even they showed a reluctance to violence that most Teren rarely exhibited. That philosophy made Elyri vulnerable anywhere on the other side of the Llaethlágárá Mountains.

But if the Elyri banded together and threw off the cloak of non-violence, Jermyn had little doubt the Teren kingdoms would be subdued or obliterated swiftly enough that they would never know how it happened. Surely, it meant something that as a people Elyri would rather suffer the indignities of periodic persecution than obtain peace with conquest.

Following the halls of the k'gdhededhá's palace, after the Gathering was complete, Jermyn found the man's rooms but was turned away by his attendants. He stressed the urgency of his visit, made a formal request to see the k'gdhededhá as soon as possible, and was assured that when the k'gdhededhá was free he would be allowed to see him. Yet the day passed with no indication that Jermyn would get his audience. Finally, as evening approached, a smallish fellow with curly red hair entered the chamber where Jermyn and Khwílen had been asked to wait.

"k'gdhededhá Tythilius?"

"Praise be," the man said, getting to his feet expectantly. "I was beginning to think…"

The little man shook his head. "I am sorry, Your Grace, but the k'gdhededhá will not be able to see you today; there were unexpected matters he was forced to attend. If you wish to stay overnight, you will be provided a room and he will gladly endeavor to see you tomorrow."

"Endeavor?" Jermyn threw his hands up in disgust. "Tomorrow, and the day after, just as he has endeavored to visit my náós and has yet to do it! I must speak to him now; it is a matter of great urgency."

"I am sorry. He understands that of course but was unable to clear his day. If you would prefer to leave your request in writing…"

Jermyn shook his head. "Oh no! It will get lost in a mountain of other such requests and disappear for months. I understand bureaucracy, you see. I am quite good at it myself when the need arises, and I use to live here. I cannot stay; I am expected in Rhidam."

"I see." The man sounded contrite but his expression was relieved.

Khwílen tugged at Jermyn's sleeve. "I can stay and await an audience, Your Grace. Saint Kóráhm's can manage without me for a time, and I do not think the k'gdhededhá can put me off forever." He cast a sly look at the attendant. "Unless, of course, he wishes me to reveal his secrets."

Face flushed with dismay, the attendant squeaked, "He knows you?" He had done his best to keep these men from the k'gdhededhá, knowing his dislike of Teren, something he might not have done if he had known this Elyri knew the k'gdhededhá personally.

"Let us say that I too spent several years here as one of his personal aides, the same position you hold. I do not need to point out the advantage that offers; I saw and heard many political and personal details I doubt he wishes to make public."

"I might have seen him already!" Jermyn groaned in further annoyance upon learning this.

With an apologetic expression, Khwílen said, "I don't like to use blackmail. It is messy and embarrassing. I hoped he would agree to see you without resorting to less attractive coercion. Since Dórímyr chooses to avoid us, he leaves us no choice but to force his hand. Your cause is too important and many lives depend upon him hearing you. If you cannot stay, write the details or allow me to read you so that your words are imprinted in my mind. I will take this up with him; you have my word."

Jermyn did not like it, wanted to do this himself, but he had little choice. With his days numbered, he needed to seek every advantage he could find. "Very well."

"And you, sir," Khwílen smiled innocently at the attendant. "I know it is late and that Dórímyr does not take business after dinner. Nevertheless, would you inform him that Khwílen Kesábhá is interested in an audience first thing tomorrow? If he is inclined to reject my request, please remind him that I was here at the dinner given in honor of Kyne Mórne's two hundred and fiftieth birthday…"

What the significance of that event had been, Jermyn did not know, but the attendant blushed furiously, apparently knowing what the man referred to, and hastened out of the room. Jermyn almost hoped, as he was delivered home to Rhidam, for Dórímyr to refuse, in order to learn the man's secrets.

❧*❧

The healer was not sure which surprised him more, the riot that had broken out after the execution of his cousin's attacker, or Diona and Hagan's involvement in it. Having known the two since infancy, Ártur had expected neither of them to behave in the manner they had, but he had also not imagined Prince Arlan needing to battle to assume his birthright. Sometimes, the events he had lived through and been a part of astonished him. He was beginning to think he should write everything down. It made sense that many histories were written by Elyri. No one else lived long enough to see what effect one event had on subsequent generations.

He had not expected word from Kavan either and was delighted that Bhríd had a letter from Wortham waiting for him. He was as confused over his cousin's destination and actions as the chamberlain, but at least he knew that at the time this message was sent, Kavan was alive. There had been periods before when Kavan was absent from his life, particularly when they were both younger and Ártur had served Kings Innis and Donal. But the possibility of his cousin's eternal absence had gone unimagined, as had the chance that if he did come home, Kavan would not be the man Ártur knew.

The healer went every day to clean Kavan's room, though most of the time it was an unnecessary gesture and he ended up staring at the wooden case housing the black kestrel harp, wondering if it would ever produce music again. Once or twice, he opened the case and plucked the strings unskillfully, trying to imagine that the sounds came from Kavan's hands and not his. The effort failed. In the end, he would sink to the floor with the harp clasped to his chest and try not to weep.

❧*❧

"He knows too much."

Valgis twisted his hair and rubbed his fingers over his earlobe. "Are you certain? He did not overhear us; you said it yourself."

"But he knows. I can see it on his face. His time with Elyri has tuned him to the thoughts of others."

The young gdhededhá did not believe it. "He cannot read minds. If he could, he would have scolded me for drinking the serbháló."

"Believe me, he knows," scowled the older man. "He allows compassion, and his belief in the goodness of men, to hinder his actions, but it will not last. In time he will strike unless he is stopped."

"How? You have already said he cannot be swayed to our cause…"

gdhededhá Claide folded his arms and stared at the wall, the glint in his eyes cold, his smile calculating. "Leave it to me. The less you know, the safer you will be. It may require me leaving Rhidam for a few days. I have friends who wish me to call upon them. We will deal with him when I return."

❧Chapter 25❦

It was the second month of the year. Kavan did not know how he knew it, but when they broke camp that morning he realized it was the fourth day of the second month, almost four months since leaving Rhidam. It was the day of Ártur's birth. It was the first time in all of those months, other than the night of Arlan's death, that Kavan wished he were home. As the day wore on, he gave more and more thought to what he had left behind and how much he was missing. Ártur's child would be born soon. Gaelán was likely receiving training, and Asta, no doubt, was continuing hers. Had Diona accepted Prince Espen's proposal? How was Hagan faring as King without Kavan to guide him as he had the boy's father? Was he still King or had the crown passed to Diona?

No, Kavan concluded with a glance at the haze-hidden sun. If that had happened, he would have known, in the same way he had known Arlan was dying. The connection afforded by the medallions he shared with the King would have broken if Hagan had died, and that had not happened. It led Kavan to believe that the King was alive and safe and that life in Rhidam was passing without Kavan being part of it.

Not many weeks ago, such a thought would have filled him with debilitating depression, to think he was not needed by those whose lives he once shared. It was a comfort now to feel that their lives continued without his constant presence. Not having to be responsible for such weight was gradually bolstering his mood and outlook.

Orynn's disposition, on the other hand, was faltering. She spoke little and her eyes grew sadder as each day passed. She rode, walked, or sat as near to Kavan as he would allow but said little and rarely looked at him. Last night she had slept near him while he kept watch, but he retreated from her proximity when it came time to sleep. He was slowly accepting her nearness, growing accustomed to the fire she flamed within, but he was not prepared to sleep beside her. Today as they traveled, she stared at him continuously and he wanted to hope her behavior was due to the impending moment when they would bid the other farewell. That it might make her as sad as it made him, however, was something he had difficulty believing.

Tonight, she had stepped away from the camp, claiming to hear a band of gypsies nearby with whom she wanted to speak about the whereabouts of k'ílshwythnec. No one else heard them, and Kavan could detect no one close enough to be noticeable, but knowing she possessed gifts of her own, Kavan did not rule out the possibility that she spoke the truth. She had not yet returned though the hour grew late, and he was concerned for her safety.

In his hands this night was the figure Urian had finally finished for him. It was a three-inch cedar figure of King Arlan. The detail was perfect in every way; staring into its tiny eyes was like looking into the eyes of the late King. The resemblance was uncanny for a man who could not have laid eyes upon the King of Enesfel; Kavan believed that somewhere in that blind man was a touch of the Sight. The figure felt warm and smooth in Kavan's twisted hand, and as he stroked the wood with his thumb, he imagined stroking the late king's hand that last night together. Missing Arlan, missing the talks and arguments they had shared, made the bard sad. Being in the same room with him one more time would have been a comfort.

An unexpected jolt of pain in his wrists and ankles made him yelp and drop the figurine into the dust at his bare feet as his arms were yanked up above his body. He had two simultaneous reactions. The first was to reach for the figure to retrieve it from the ground, which immediately resulted in the second, to hide the blood he could feel upon his wrists. It was too late for that, however; he could not lower his arms. The captain leaped to his feet at the cry and unexpected movement, and watched in amazement as the red flow, which was certainly blood, coursed down the bard's arms, dripped onto his head, and began to pool on the ground around Kavan's feet.

Kavan looked at him with misery. To date, none of the miracles, none of Kavan's powerful abilities had adversely affected the captain, at least not for long. But things such as sparing Owain's life had been something any healer could have done. The rósádhá was another matter. Wortham had enough experience that he could tell the difference between the use of power and a miracle, and he would recognize the positioning of the bard's arms and the locations of the wounds. He would know what this was. The captain stared, unmoving, at the blood, until he was finally able to tear his gaze away and meet Kavan's eyes. There was no revulsion, no disgust, and most reassuringly, none of the blind worship with which many responded to the miracles that passed through the bard's hands. What Kavan saw on Wortham's face was the same love he was accustomed to seeing and it brought tears to the Elyri's eyes.

"Are you injured, Lord Cliáth? I smell blood?"

"I…"

Wortham answered the monk as he hastily retrieved a water skin and cloth from his pack. "His hand is cut, dedhá. I am tending to it."

"It must be a very large cut."

"It is." The captain knelt beside Kavan but the bard shook his head. There would be no washing the wounds until the bleeding stopped. He could but wait and endure.

Urian nodded, accepting the explanation as he shuffled to where his bedding waited. Wortham did not watch him, focusing instead on Kavan and the need to reassure his friend. He touched the bard's fingertips, the corners of his trembling mouth, and wiped the traces of tears from his cheeks but he did not speak in order not to reveal anything to the blind man. It was sometime later, long after the gdhededhá's snoring indicated he was asleep, that the bleeding ceased, the wounds closed, and Kavan's arms dropped to his sides. Wortham immediately began the tender task of cleansing away the stains from his friend's skin and hair.

"This has…the last time?" Wortham suspected the truth, that this had been the extraordinary event that had given Kavan back his voice, but he felt that speaking about it would be more useful than pretending it had never happened.

"Yes, it has occurred before," Kavan timidly admitted, watching the tenderness with which Wortham worked. "Does it offend you?"

"Offend? If it offended me, it would be an offense at k'Ádhá, not you…as you did not cause this. Besides, it confirms what I have always known."

Kavan cocked his head, almost afraid to hear what the man would say, but still, he asked, "That is?"

"That regardless of the state you believe your soul to be in, you are, and always have been, a man most blessed. Do not deny it, Kavan. You would not receive this gift if you were not blessed."

The bard did not speak but shook beneath the tenderness of the man's touch. Wortham's words were unexpected, not those he anticipated, and left him speechless. Was he blessed? How could he be, after what he had done? And if he was blessed, why then had the use of his hands been taken and not yet restored? Perhaps they would never be restored and he was meant to seek blessings beyond his hands.

"This also explains your weakness the last time. There is enough blood loss to kill most men. But there, you are clean. Would you care for food?" Kavan shook his head no as Wortham rubbed out the bloodstains in the sandy soil with his boot. "At least water. You need to keep your strength. Take this." He gave him the water flask and debated tossing the stained cloth into the fire. In the end, he chose not to, and instead folded it and pushed it into his pocket. This was his friend's blood. The blood of a miracle. Such a treasure should be preserved.

"You should sleep. We are not far from Zabin. Two days. My opinion, though I do not presume to know k'Ádhá's thoughts or intentions, is that you are being cleansed. Purified. Perhaps in Zabin, or soon after, you will find the answers you seek. Afterward, this will likely leave you."

The bard laid a twisted hand on Wortham's wrist. The captain did not shudder or retreat. "Wortham, if your words prove accurate, I will believe that I am truly not alone in the Lachlan court. That you are a wiser man than any one of us knows."

He dropped his hand and lay down to sleep to the big man's warm chuckle. "I speak what I see, milord…and I have long thought I was underestimated."

His attempt at humor brought faint amusement to the bard's face. "I agree, Wortham. You are. You will not speak of this?"

"You know I shall not."

"Thank you. No man has ever had a truer friend."

Wortham looked at the pale man who sometimes seemed strong and sometimes incredibly frail, and murmured, "Not so, milord. For I have you."

Orynn was there when Kavan awoke near dawn, but he judged from her attire, the dark circles under her eyes, and the way Wortham catered to her, that she had been away most of the night. Kavan had wanted to stay awake until her return but the loss of blood had drained him. She did not speak but smiled sadly at Kavan and nodded as if to suggest they were on the right path. Tomorrow, perhaps, if his luck held, he would find k'ílshwythnec. Kavan did not dare consider what might come after that.

❧*❧

The healer watched the k'gdhededhá depart, a man he had known for decades, and shivered. "Did you feel that?"

Caol stared at him from the chair. "Hmm?" He was too distracted by his private worries to notice someone else's, but now that the healer mentioned it, he had to concur. Something was not right.

"He seemed…sad. Distant…almost as if he…I don't know." Ártur shrugged. "Like he was going to be going away for a long time."

"I don't think I would say that," Diona said with a shrug. "He seems sad, but I think we are all so since Lord Cliáth's departure."

The healer held up the letter in his hand. "Then why give me this to give to Kavan? He knows Kavan's not here, knows I do not know where he is or when he will return. Why not keep it, give it to Kavan himself?"

With a glance at the letter that none of them had read, the princess replied, "He was afraid he would forget it if it was not written down…and afraid he would lose it if he did not give it to you?"

Caol slouched back with his hands steepled beneath his chin. "He has grumbled of forgetfulness in the past. Still…" his eyes looked to be gazing far away, "he is doing the same thing Arlan did before he… he called upon the King, on Bhríd, had words with the children…"

"And he told me to give Syl his love and blessing when I saw her," the healer added as if making his point was some sort of minor victory.

With resolve creasing the corners of his mouth and eyes, Caol got to his feet. "I do not think asking is going to reveal anything, but I will keep an eye on him. If he expects trouble, thinks his life is in danger, perhaps I can prevent it before it comes to pass. With the vanishings of late, he might merely be cautious. Please, excuse me."

He bowed to both and hurried from the room. Princess Diona stood, a scowl on her face that seemed too permanent of late. "I do wish Espen would get here," she muttered.

Being the sole person in the room, Ártur was unsure if she was speaking to him or to herself. Not wanting to appear rude if she were talking to him, he asked, "You have sent for him?"

"I asked him to bring troops in support of Hagan…and offered to extend the Hatu-Enesfel treaties. I thought he would be here."

Heavens forbid, the healer thought, that Hatu turns its back on Enesfel. Aloud he said, "The winter storms sometimes make travel difficult, by land or by sea. If he is coming, he should be here soon. And if he is not, he will send a messenger with his regrets."

Diona wanted to believe it, but after her abysmal treatment of the men in her life, she had little hope that this one would stay true to her. With her hand on the latch, watching in the direction her uncle had gone, she asked, "Lord Healer, what will happen if something happens to the k'dedhá?" She knew little about the religious hierarchy of the Faith; in her lifetime there had been only one k'gdhededhá.

"No one says he is going to die. Perhaps he is considering retiring to a more peaceful, less hectic life. Many gdhededhá do. He is an elderly man who has given his life to the Faith…"

"But if he does…or if he retires?" she pushed.

"If it follows as in Elyriá, a new k'gdhededhá will either be chosen by k'gdhededhá Dórímyr or elected by the gdhededhá in Enesfel."

Her face grew dark. "Do you think…could Claide be elected?"

Ártur's expression was curious. "You dislike Claide?"

"You do not?" The thought surprised her.

"I deal mostly with k'gdhededhá Jermyn or gdhededhá Tusánt. I do not know Claide well."

"That is a good thing," she snorted. "I have no proof…but even k'dedhá Jermyn believes he is anti-Elyri and has been inciting violence against your people. He gave the most abysmal sermon on the eve of Dhágdhuán's Feast…be grateful you did not hear it. Uncle is probing his activities, but other than agreeing they seem suspicious, he has not been able to prove anything. Please, Lord Healer, stay away from dedhá Claide. I do not think I can bear to lose you too."

The healer bowed his head. "I did not know my life means anything to you, Milady."

Despite wanting to embrace him, the princess refrained. She was struggling to control less seemly behavior now that she was more than King Arlan's daughter. "Of course you do. You have always supported Hagan and me. You are part of our family, an uncle of sorts. I have lost enough family in one lifetime. I do not want to lose more. After what I did, you are justified in thinking I despise you." She met his gaze. "Are you still angry with me?"

Though his eyes were sad, the healer managed a miserable smile. "I should be, but it is difficult to be angry when my thoughts are on Kavan. I am not sure I have forgiven you, but I am no longer angry."

Suspecting that full forgiveness would not likely come until the day Kavan returned, or the day the bard forgave her too, the princess curtseyed with an understanding bow of her head. "That is a start, Lord Healer. It is more than I deserve. I must find Lady McPhelan before she embarrasses my brother too much." This time when she grinned it was wide and playful.

❧*❦

"Rankin, have you seen Claide?" Part of the k'gdhededhá hoped he had not.

"I cannot say I have," replied the other man. "I have not seen him since last night. Valgis has done most of his duties today. Perhaps he knows where Claide is."

Jermyn scowled. "Probably…but it is just as well he is not here. I have too many duties to attend today to worry about where he is or what he is doing. As long as his duties are tended, that is good enough. Have you started preparations for St. Mátán's Feast?"

"The preliminaries, yes. But it is still over two months away, and with recent events, there has been an increase in parishioners to soothe and council. They are uneasy, afraid they will be the next victims."

The k'gdhededhá knew how they felt, as Kóráhm's warning lay ever-present on his mind. "We cannot fault them for that…nor can we realistically assure them they will be safe. I suppose we reassure them the Crown is spending every waking moment, and probably many sleeping ones, dealing with the problem. Sir Gabersdon has come to assist. We encourage them to protect and support their neighbors, to keep each other safe, show love and kindness instead of suspicion and hatred. Peace will be restored. We must have faith and work together for that end."

"I am not the one that needs that sermon," Rankin said warmly. "Perhaps you should give a Gathering for Peace to address them."

That idea made the older man smile. "A grand High Gathering; yes, that is a splendid idea, Rankin. Find Tusánt and see to the preparations at once. The mid-morning Gathering at week's end. Tell everyone. And please try not to disturb me. I have a lesson to prepare."

❧*❦

Ártur ran his hand through his hair and tried not to panic. No one had seen Gaelán in several hours. Not Bhríd, not Asta. His bed was slept in, but it was empty when the servants arrived to tidy the room. The boy had missed every meal, every lesson, and in an atmosphere of danger to those with Elyri blood, it was difficult for the healer not to fear for the boy's safety. He believed this to be his fault. He had known for weeks of Gaelán's disquiet, mood swings, and his inability to concentrate. Ártur thought it would pass, thought it a phase his nephew was going through as he learned to accept that he was different from his brother. But this had gone on too many days, meaning there was something more to Gaelán's episodes than met the eye.

Looking one more time in the boy's room, not ready to give up as the rest of the staff combed every nook and cranny of the castle, he prayed this was no turn of foul play. Not finding him there, he went to the oratory to pray in the hopes that some form of divine inspiration would tell him where to find the young man.

As with every night since Kavan had gone, there was nothing there. Ártur felt nothing in those walls but an empty void that nothing would fill. He groaned, the sound masking the hiss of the k'dhín bhólibh curtain parting; when the light footfalls came behind him, he spun, startled. He was more startled, and then relieved, to see Gaelán looking wan and weary but at least safe and unharmed.

"Gaelán! Where have you been? We have been searching for you!" He swooped off the steps and pulled the boy into his arms.

"I am sorry. I did not mean to worry anyone. I wanted to be alone. I have been in the k'dhín bhólibh."

"All day?" the healer asked in surprise.

"Most of it," he replied with shuffling feet and hands clasped.

"Why? With the state of things…Kavan missing is enough…"

"I don't know. It seemed like the best place. But he's not missing, k'aendhá. He is out there."

Ártur pulled him to sit on the altar steps. "Of course he is…"

"No…I mean it, k'aendhá. These nightmares…when I have them I feel…very close to him."

"Nightmares? When did you start having nightmares? Tell me about them." He did not think Gaelán had the Sight, but he also had not thought Gaelán could be a healer. Ártur was intrigued and concerned about why there had been no mention of them before.

Gaelán fumbled with the edge of his tunic as he sat beside the healer. "There is not much to tell, k'aendhá. I do not recall images from the dreams when I wake…but I wake up feeling terrified and alone. No…" he shook his head, "not alone. It feels like he is here, as if he needs me, but I cannot help him. Sometimes my hands hurt…and my feet…but not every time. Every time I have it though, my head hurts terribly when I wake. It's like I have been trying to gather energy together…but did too much too fast."

"Too much too fast…?" The healer bit his lip as he stared at the boy. "This only happens with this dream? When you feel Kavan's presence?" Gaelán nodded, afraid to speak. "It could mean…I don't know how but…how would you feel about sleeping in my room? Or me sleeping in yours?"

"Why?" He could imagine what his brother would say if he thought Gaelán was afraid to sleep alone.

Ártur patted his knee. "The best way to determine what you are experiencing is to be there when it happens, to read you the moment it occurs. If I am with you when the nightmares come, I can do this."

"Do you think…am I losing the ability to heal?" he whispered.

"I don't think that has anything to do with it. I have a hypothesis, but I want to test it before I say anything. Can we do this?"

Gaelán hesitated and then shook his head. "You come to my room. If I go to yours, Tayte will call me a baby. If you come to mine, it will look like I am unwell and you are caring for me."

That rationale made the healer chuckle. "Very well, Gaelán. But promise me, no more hiding. No more shirking your lessons."

"Yes, sir. I will do anything to make these dreams stop."

"I don't know if I can make them stop, but I will see what I can do to help with them. Come, off to bed with you. I will let your father know you are safe and be with you shortly."

❧*❦

He had given his sheriff strict orders that should any vanishings be reported, any murders occur, he wanted immediate notification; he wanted to be involved in the investigation from the beginning. Owain had not expected much to come of the order; he was further north than Rhidam and thus far his small city had been relatively tranquil and his sheriff did not always follow requests. To arrive before what appeared to be an abandoned hovel at the edge of Fiara seemed ludicrous. But he was here with his sheriff looking at him expectantly, wondering what Owain was going to do.

Not a coward and not expecting a trap, Owain pushed open the door of the two-room structure with the tip of his sword. The main room was vacant, layered thinly with dust as if empty for a week or more. He could almost believe, due to the lack of personal items in the room, that the family who lived here had picked up and left. But there was a stench filling the place, a smell he recognized, that turned his stomach. There would be no danger here. Coughing to clear his throat, he sheathed his sword and crept towards the back room, motioning for the others to remain outside.

Despite his exposure to his Nethite relatives and their customary way of life, despite going to war against King Bowen, despite his years as a fairly unyielding monarch, Owain had never experienced death as brutally as he did now. He had even presided over executions, but they had all been hangings. What he saw here was butchery. It was impossible to tell at a glance how many bodies were in the room; they were mutilated, decapitated, and in varying stages of decomposition. Dried blood and entrails were everywhere. One of the victims had been a child, one of its hands clenched forever in a tiny fist of rage on the end of a severed arm; another, the head closest to him with her green eyes open in shock and horror, he was sure had been Elyri.

Owain fled the sight, stopping outside the front door to retch while his sheriff and those men with him looked past with curiosity. He could not stop; his stomach had its own agenda and each flash of the woman's cloudy eyes that crossed his mind started it lurching. Not quite as green, but he saw Kavan's eyes, and the thought of Kavan similarly dying twisted his gut more. It gnawed at him to think that such a thing could happen in Fiara. She was one of but a few Elyri to travel here, and her daring had been met with death. When he could speak, he wiped his mouth on his sleeve. "Get someone to clean this up. Count the bodies; I want to know if they are all accounted for…who they are. Did anyone hear anything? See anything? Did anyone know the Elyri…?"

"Elyri?" his sheriff gasped. "Elyri did this?"

Unable to restrain himself, Owain struck his sheriff in the face as his disgust blossomed into rage. "Never! She was the victim in this as much as anyone. No Elyri would have committed such a barbarous act…and then dismembered herself. I will not tolerate anti-Elyri sentiment…from you or anyone else." He knew none of those around him could claim to know a single Elyri personally. Owain knew several. "What is in there is the act of madmen. k'Ádhá help them when I find out who they are. Their fate will be exactly the same!"

The sheriff rubbed his aching jaw as he entered the house to learn what had upset his lord, and returned moments later to add his stomach's contents to Owain's at the side of the house. "I…agree with your assessment, milord. There was no struggle…or not much of one; it was a slaughter. I will find the guilty and see them punished."

Owain shook his fist. "You find the criminals…I will do the punishing. Is that clear?"

Bowing apologetically, not wishing to be on the receiving end of that fist again, the sheriff said, "Of course, milord. As you wish."

❧Chapter 26❦

Overwhelming doom. That was the most accurate way Kavan could describe the crushing sensation plaguing him since he awoke. It was connected to the dreams; he knew it. So many in succession, surreal recollections of torture and pain, meant something. He relived Owain's sanctioned weeks of beatings, the stoning by people in Neth, and finally, the attack that nearly killed him in Levonne. If it stopped there, he might have written off troubling dreams as a product of too many weeks of depression. But upon waking, Kavan had felt as though he was falling into the noxious black chasm of infinite torment he faced in Ergoth. Because Orynn, who was unexpectedly sleeping near him, shifted closer in her sleep and rested her head against his shoulder he was able to refrain from bolting in panic but the memories did not leave him.

It was almost the same feeling he felt before Arlan died, except there was more terror and torment involved in this experience. Was Hagan facing torture and execution? Why? But the Sight, if that was what these dreams were, showed him nothing more. He wondered if he should find a Gate, return to Rhidam, be sure the young king was alive and safe. With that fear in mind, as the day wore on, he kept his senses attuned for any faint energy signature that would suggest a Gate, although he did not expect to find one this far south of the

Sovereignties. While it was known his ancestors had passed through these lands, and he had been told the Heretic-Saint had used one to journey to Clarys, that did not mean Kavan would find one. Likely, he mused, if King Hagan was dying, he would soon die too and the mission he was undertaking was for naught.

Because of those dreams and the morbid focus on death and failure, there was a reversal in roles that day, with Kavan withdrawing into himself, silent and moody, and Orynn trying diligently to cheer him. She had made a small pouch of black velvet for the figure Urian had given him, a figure now stained with Kavan's blood, and presented it to him as they journeyed. She attempted repeatedly to engage him in conversation, but nothing worked and by mid-day, she stopped trying.

Zabin was not much further by her calculations and the increase in the scatter of farming plots supported her assessment. Some of the fields were filled with a knee-high grain plant, while others contained what Kavan assessed to be a short, scrubby form of cotton as was grown in southern Enesfel and northern Hatu. How anything could grow in this climate with little moisture was a mystery, as was why there seemed to be no people tending their crops. Perhaps, given the brown, faded nature of the plants, the crop was dead, already harvested or failed. Being unfamiliar with it, Kavan could not tell. He looked forward to the sight of people, for people meant the chance of success in his mission. Seeing no one was troublesome.

Yet in spite of that eagerness, he came to an abrupt halt as the others pulled ahead and he made no effort to stop them. There, on that road, for reasons he could not fathom, he was engulfed in a shower of warmth and light, a sensation of purity he had not felt in a long time. As he swayed unsteadily, alone and afraid of this unexpected feeling, the warmth ebbed, leaving a prickling static in its wake. Gradually, the prickle made its way along his spine, coming up from his feet and down from his head, until it gathered in his core and came to rest in his crippled hands. Unmistakable, that tingle, and one he thought to never experience again. k'Ádhá and Dhágdhuán, he thought with a moan. Not this. I am unworthy. More than anything else, I am not worthy of this distinction.

Loud chatter and running footsteps erupted to his left where a group of men emerged from the collection of scrubby trees at the far side of the grain field. Between them, carried upon a large canvas, was another man, bleeding profusely from his chest. Kavan looked at his hands and groaned a second time. No, please. Take this from me, he begged. I do not think I can do this.

By then, Wortham and the others had heard the voices and turned to see the men, lumbermen they appeared to be judging by the tools slung over their backs, reach the road between them and Kavan. The men were running in the direction of Kavan's companions in their haste to seek help.

"Wait!" Kavan called.

The men halted and turned towards the speaker, not understanding the command but recognizing the authority of tone. Unable to be rid of the sensation in his hands and knowing he did not have the courage to deny what he was permitted to offer, Kavan hesitantly came forward, aware that Wortham must surely recognize his expression, or perhaps the change in the air, because the captain ran to join him.

The Elyri looked at the wounded man as he approached, struggling with himself and with his Faith. The puncture wound in the middle of the man's abdomen appeared to have been created by a large stick or spike. The object was already removed, leaving a hideous lesion and broken ribs that should have killed him. How he had lived this long was in itself a miracle; if he did not receive immediate care, he would die. Too much blood had been lost and too much of his insides were exposed. If the blood loss did not kill him, infection soon would. Kavan did not want to touch him, did not want to do what needed to be done, but he could not do otherwise. If he ignored this, he would be further damned, possibly eliminating any hope of restoring the use of his hands. It was his choice to make, but not much of a choice at all. He could not condemn a man to die when he had the opportunity to allow him to live. The choice between life and death was not Kavan's; k'Ádhá had already made it.

With a surge of resolve, the bard lay his hands on the man's chest and felt the swift discharge of energy, the awesome pouring forth of divine healing through his body and from his hands. At one time, he had been able to tolerate the sensation; now it drove him to his knees in shame. Added to that sense of unworthiness, as his hands touched the dying man, Kavan saw, within his mind's eye, himself naked, alone, bound as Dhágdhuán had been, though the pyre itself was invisible, and felt the strike of nails through his wrists and ankles. He bit back the scream, closed his eyes in hopes of dispelling the image, knowing he was bleeding, that his blood mingled with that of the man beneath his hands and that everyone around him could see it. That image in his head filled him with terror, but it was knowing that he was a public spectacle that frightened him most. Another sharp pain ripped through his body, centered low on his back; he was thrown away from the injured man with a screech and collapsed.

Gaelán caught Asta's wrist as he stumbled from the pain exploding in his head, blinding him. Asta tried to catch him but his weight, and the unexpected nature of his fall, was too much and they ended up in a heap on the ground. "k'aendhá," he cried in a strangled voice. There were tears on his cheeks that scared her; she had not seen him cry since they were much younger children. Asta looked around for aid, amazed that, with the large number of people in the keep, none of them were nearby. Not a servant, not a guard, not any one of the

King's advisors. Drawing out her kerchief, she wiped Gaelán's face, wishing she could wipe away whatever was hurting him.

"Gaelán? What is it? Shall I fetch Lord MacLyr?"

He rolled away, clutching his head for several agonizing moments, and then it was over. As if it had never been there, the pain passed and he felt nothing beyond a lingering throbbing inside his skull. He looked at her with worried eyes, wondering if she thought him mad. "There is nothing he can…I thought this was a dream…but dreams do not happen like this, when you are awake." He looked around as if seeking something and asked, "Did you feel anything? Was he here?"

Worried for him, Asta shook her head. "I felt nothing…except fear for you. No one's been here but us. Are you certain Lord MacLyr should not know about this? What if something is wrong with you?"

Gaelán did not want to think about that. Nor did he want her to worry. "I'll be alright. I will tell him when I see him. He was with the King the last I knew, and there's nothing he can do unless he sees it happen. I'm sure it has something to do with k'aendhá Kavan."

Eyes wide with awe she asked, "Do you have the Sight?"

He grimaced as he stared at her. "I do not know…but I hope not." If Asta was curious about his reasons, she did not ask as she helped him to his feet. "Do you still want to play with the puppies?"

"After you, milord!" She was still worried, but she was relieved that he seemed unharmed. She intended to keep a closer eye on him and report this incident to the healer whether Gaelán did or not.

❧*❧

When he regained consciousness, Kavan discovered he was in a small, drafty wooden building, in the dark, alone and covered with a coarse, scratchy blanket that smelled of dust and sweat. His limbs were weak and shaky but otherwise uninjured, his head was heavy, and the large amount of blood on the sleeves of his robe and across his lower back caused the fabric to stick uncomfortably. The memory of what had transpired came back in its horror and magnificence, making him roll onto his side and curl into a ball, wishing he could hide from his thoughts. He wanted to understand why he had been given that gift of a miracle, and wanted to know what the associated vision meant, to know if he had seen his death or if the vision had some other import, but he was too afraid of the truth in this instance to seek it.

He felt restless and lying alone allowed him to dwell on negativity. Frustrated, he sat and waited for the dizziness and disorientation to clear before trying to rise from the rickety pallet. His companions must be nearby; he hoped seeing them would take his mind off his troublesome thoughts.

"You are awake, milord!" Urian exclaimed as he bustled into the room; Kavan wondered if the creaking of the pallet had let the gdhededhá know he was awake or if his arrival at that moment was coincidental. "That man! He is alive! The people are proclaiming the miracle…"

Kavan shuddered at the word and closed his eyes. "gdhededhá…"

But the excited man ignored the interruption, having never been witness to anything of such significance in all of his years in the Faith. "They have an ancient myth of a man with skin like clouds coming to them, a prophet and saint, a man who performs miracles!"

"Please, gdhededhá…do not continue…" Kavan struggled to his feet; the room swayed but righted itself quickly. He did not want to be the subject of legends, a prophet, or a saint.

"They believe you are that man! You have fulfilled the prophecy. They await your words."

Kavan shook his head, though the blind man could not see it or the alarm on his face. Prophecy or not, he steadfastly denied being what they claimed. He could not be. "I have no words, gdhededhá. Tell them. I am not a holy man; I am not the one they seek."

"But what of the rósádhá, milord? Only holy men…"

Realizing that someone must have told Urian about the rósádhá, Kavan stopped listening, troubled by those words, and pushed his way out of that room in the hopes of escaping, only to emerge into a more awkward situation at the center of a cluster of poorly constructed homes. The sky in the west burned pink and orange and the aromas of a cooking meal hung in the dusty air. Most of the residents appeared to have gathered here, waiting for him, and many dropped to their knees when they saw him in his bloody robe, prostrating themselves before him. Some cheered, others chanted, while others surged forward to touch him in a suppliant manner, the manner of people petitioning for miracles he could not give. He had experienced this before, more times than he cared to recall, and it still frightened him.

"I have no miracles," he called, shrugging the hands away as gently as he could. "There is no great wisdom I can bestow; no blessings I can give." Yet the harder he tried to turn them away, the more persistent the villagers grew. He could not see Wortham, but Orynn was at the rear of the gathering, too far away, obscured by the crowd, to accurately read her expression.

The people began to chant. "málneag! málneag!" Sickened by that word, Kavan tried to back away and bumped into the gdhededhá as he emerged from the building.

"What are they saying?" asked the blind man as he clutched onto Kavan to steady himself.

"málneag," the bard whispered. "High Elyri…saint." He pulled free of the blind man's hands, not noticing him stumble under the force of it. "No!" he cried, edging sideways towards the corner of the building, hoping there would be somewhere to flee. "Not málneag!"

They did not hear, did not understand, or chose to ignore his plea and, focusing on that one word, pressed around him more fervently. He heard Wortham's voice as the captain attempted to break up the mob and make his way to Kavan's side, but he had little success getting through the crowd.

"málneag!"

"Stop!" Kavan made it to the edge of the building, and as he hoped, the empty passage there provided an escape route. Kavan tore free of beseeching hands and fled into the surrounding forest of short, scraggly trees and large, sharp rocks that jutted from the earth like fangs. The villagers' shouts of disappointment and the sounds of a few attempted followers died out quickly as he fled. One Elyri gift he had not used in years was the ability to throw off pursuers, something he had used often as the White Hart but never as a man. Right now, it made sense to use it, as he wanted to be free of everyone.

málneag. He had heard the word saint whispered about him while growing up in Bhryell and had disliked it even then. It had been a relief that no one had ever said it to his face. To him, málneag was something sacred, a person perfected by years of dedicated service to the Faith and k'Ádhá, who lived purely, whom k'Ádhá had blessed with some sort of divine, special quality. He was none of those things. No one who spoke High Elyri had ever called him málneag; hearing the esteemed High Elyri title used to refer to him was more painful and frightening than hearing the Teren word saint had ever been, though in translation they meant the same thing.

These people…they knew about the miracle on the road. In such a small village, it was impossible for them not to. And they knew about the rósádhá, and revered it, even if it was not a cornerstone of their beliefs. He could not hide it, could not deny it had happened, could not pretend it had not. Years ago, when he had seen the cloth gdhededhá Bhílári used to wipe the miraculous blood from the sacramental chalice, it had become impossible to deny such miracles. He still had that cloth in his trunk of treasured belongings in Rhidam. There was nothing tangible to offer proof this time, nothing except what he had seen and felt, and what these foreigners had witnessed, but that was proof enough. Proof enough for them, and for him.

With a burst of anguish, he cried to the stars, "I am not málneag! It cannot be! I will not allow it."

"Kavan?"

The hands that reached to comfort him were eluded as he lurched sideways, trying to hide his tear-stained face. He had spent hours running and had not expected anyone to find him. Particularly not Orynn.

In that moment, she looked more stunning than ever. Her auburn hair fell in waves around her pale blue robed shoulders. Her eyes were large and dark in the shadows of the scrub forest and her full lips were set in a sad pout of concern. It took effort not to touch her, not to throw her to the forest floor and drown his pain in her kisses. The fire within flared more brightly as she tenderly touched his arm, and while it was remotely comforting to know that his flesh had proven the princess wrong, that he was a man, he did not trust himself to allow that touch. In his current state, it was too tempting to do something he would later regret. He pulled away and retreated as far as the clearing allowed. "Leave me. I am not fit company. I may say or do something hurtful or offensive and I have no wish to do either."

"You have not driven me away thus far with your melancholy bitterness," she reminded him. "Do not think you can be rid of me so easily." She sat with her back against a tree, appearing weary and frayed. "What has happened that you find distressing?"

"They call me málneag."

"Saint. I know. I speak the language."

"Then you know it is a lie. I am not a saint. I am nothing." He kept his back to her, too distraught to consider how she knew High Elyri.

"You are the nearest to a saint these people will ever see, and you do fit their legends of a prophet. You have saved the life of their leader's son, as their legends claimed you would."

With a low hiss, almost angry for not realizing that injured man's importance, he said, "That does not mean I am málneag. I have erred against k'Ádhá and…I have killed…"

"Wild animals, or perhaps poison, killed that young man; that is not your fault, however much you wish it. And the others…there were reasons. Those are behind you, and you know it. Every man and woman has transgressed. It is the nature of living."

As if not hearing her words, or at least without letting them sink in and take root, he protested, "I am nowhere near perfect…"

"No," Orynn agreed, watching him flinch as she said it, "you are not. I have yet, in all my years, to meet anyone who was. No man nor woman is required to be perfect before being accepted into the Faith or before the gdhededhá declare them to be a saint. Perfection is a prerequisite only if you have aspirations of divinity."

Kavan spun towards her, horrified at that suggestion as her implications hit home. "I would never presume to want…"

"I hope not. Those who think themselves divine are usually quite intolerable." She paused as Kavan blanched and turned away again. She knew he was considering how insufferable he had been throughout their journey, knew he was evaluating his behavior. It was as it should be.

Studying his profile in the moonlight, etching his záryph-like features into her mind, she gave him brief moments to think before continuing, "But sainthood, or perfection, is not the true issue, is it? There is something more. What is it, Kavan? Speak your thoughts."

He hesitated to do so, his heart, soul, and mind waging an internal war against doing as she asked. Finally, defeated by his need for the peace he prayed she could give, he squatted, his head hanging as if ashamed to admit what weighed most heavily on his soul. "What pains me most is that…it seems I am a worthy catalyst for a miracle…and yet k'Ádhá has rejected me and I have nothing left to offer with which to gain redemption."

She leaned forward as if to encourage him to lift his head but she did not touch him. "Nothing you can do will gain redemption; don't you know that, Kavan? Dhágdhuán died to bridge the gap between mortality and divinity, showed us what it was to have true Faith, and it is in believing we find redemption. Our actions reflect our faith…they do not redeem us. If it were true that you are rejected, as you say, then why were you deemed worthy to be used for a miracle?"

"I do not know," the bitterness in his voice cut her off. "I wish I did. I only know I had one true talent…and because of my iniquities, k'Ádhá has stripped me of that and I do not know how to get it back."

"There. That is it. I was wondering how long it would be before you got to the heart of the matter." She got up, paced for a few minutes as he continued to squat there, and finally stopped with her back to him. Kavan did not watch her but listened as he stared at the ground, unable to find his voice. "He wanted you to learn these things on your own," she muttered, more to herself than to him, "but you are as strong-willed and obstinate as he is. I can no longer bear to see you miserable, knowing what I…and my time with you is too short." She stared at the defeated curve of his back. "What is the one thing you want most, Kavan?"

"Forgiveness." The answer came out too quickly, but he did not look at her as he said it.

"You know you have that. You know that it only takes asking for k'Ádhá to give it. You were forgiven long ago. There is something else. The one thing, Kavan."

It took the bard slightly longer to provide her an answer. "To play, to feel a harp in my hands, hear the notes, feel the music…find that peace. My hands restored. I would give up anything…"

Looking at him squarely, a touch of steel present in her gray eyes, Orynn said, "Give up your pride."

"Pride?" Kavan was sincerely baffled and it showed on his face. "I prostrate myself before k'Ádhá daily. I pray. I weep. I give to others.

There is no pride in that. People tell me constantly…you have heard them…that my humility is greater than…"

"And you are proud of that humility, of your piety, are you not?" Before he could protest or reply, she took a step forward, a menacing step, and continued, "You are proud of how you suffer on behalf of your faith, your race, your singularity. You suffer brilliantly, milord, and delight in others praise of your steadfastness through adversity. Given the choice, you would sooner accept suffering and travail than know peace and joy…"

"It was foretold at my birth…"

Again, she cut him off. "…that you would know little of the joy you bring to others. I know the prophecy. But prophecy is often the art of taking what you know and projecting it into the future to derive the most probable outcome. Knowing what he did of the personality he saw manifest in you, it was natural for Kóráhm to conclude you would deprive yourself of joy if it meant that others could be happy and would remember you as the one who suffered on their behalf. Is this not true, milord?"

Kavan shrank away from her barrage of words as if they were the assault of a sword. Try as he did, he could not look at her. Indignantly he muttered, "My hands…"

Her tone grew a little colder, a little angrier and more frustrated. "No one deprived you of their use but you. You convinced yourself you were attacked as punishment for not being a man, for drinking, and for trying to bed a whore." Recoiling, he choked on a sob and covered his face. No one knew about that; he had told no one except Kóráhm; how could she know? "You were attacked because you are Elyri, nothing more."

"Things happen for a reason," he wept, wishing she would withdraw the sword of condemnation she had set loose upon him.

"Perhaps the reason was to teach you onyhéc…a little honest humility. Not every man who has gotten drunk, who has slept with a whore, has been beaten nearly to death. Many men do those things regularly and are not beaten, or punished, in their lifetime. Or do you think all who do such things should be beaten as you were…?"

"No…" he admitted in a whisper, "none deserves…"

"Exactly. You are a man, milord; in the end that is all you are. A man like any other. What makes you more worthy of such brutal punishment if others are not?"

When he did not speak, she continued in a softer voice. "If the attack had been meant as punishment, you could have been left to die. If you had been meant to die, to be a cripple, to never make music, you could have been stripped of your voice and k'Ádhá would not have presented you with an immediate source of healing."

"Gaelán could not…"

"You do not know that! You did not know what he was capable of because you did not permit him to try. I know, you see. I was there. The cat that saved your life, the woman who brought Gaelán to you, told him he could heal you with his own hands. It was I. He did not know he could heal…and you did not give him the opportunity to attempt it. And you know Ártur could have healed your hands if you had allowed Gaelán to send for him."

"It was a test…to see if I would accept punishment though it would cost me that which is most precious to me, or if I would be weak and seek the quickest way out…"

Kavan grasped for some explanation, anything to refute her words, but she threw his arguments back at him. "Even now you are proud that you had the strength to suffer in order that everyone could look at you with pity and awe and find some nobleness in your suffering. You were testing yourself…"

"I did it for…"

"…yourself. It was a selfish act meant to make you feel as if you were suffering on k'Ádhá's behalf, as if you could prove yourself more worthy than any other man. Self-flagellation to purify yourself for wrongs only you perceived. k'Ádhá is the purifier. Your acts to justify yourself are in vain. Don't you think that a melody born of your joy at being whole would be more pleasing to him than these past four months of brooding, angst, and endless pleading over what is unmitigated suffering? Don't you think that perhaps suffering is not what k'Ádhá wants of you, but what you want? Perchance what you think you need or deserve for what you see as the curse of being the most powerful ágdhání that has ever lived? It is your selfish choice to suffer, and your pride in it, which has cost you your vocation, your passion, and has made you miserable. You cannot even see beyond this to acknowledge that you possess other talents…"

Angrily sweeping his hair from his face, he snapped, "Why do you speak to me thus? I am not proud…"

She did not shrink from the flash of resentment in his eyes. It was better that, she thought, then misery. "You think you know the mind of k'Ádhá, that you are privy to the divine's wishes for your life in a way that borders on sacrilegious. If you are as unworthy, as forsaken, such a terrible offender, as you proclaim, why would k'Ádhá make known his every wish to you? Thinking you know as much as the divine is its own wickedness, milord, one that Kóráhm tried to point out to you but which you have failed to see because you believe yourself to be wise. Until you assess your life, see yourself as you truly are, admit your shortcomings and step down from the pedestal upon which you have placed yourself, I am powerless to do anything more for you. There is nothing more I, or Kóráhm, can do. Your quest is complete. We part company here."

"Then go!" he cried in fury, only to instantly regret his words and shout, "Orynn! Wait! Come back! I did not mean…I must know…"

He grasped for her but came up empty-handed. She was gone, disappeared into the night like an intangible mist. He stared at his empty, twisted hand. Gone from his life forever if her words were true, and there was no reason they should not be. He had not known her to lie. Angrily he dropped to the ground, tearing at his ruined robe, crying to the sky with everything he was, praying for answers and probing the recesses of his soul for any truth Orynn's words might hold.

Hours spent in contemplation upon the hot, rocky ground, time spent searching his soul and asking himself questions that had not been asked in far too long, revealed that Orynn's words and accusations, however distasteful, were true. Utterly, completely, true. It was not that he believed she was correct for the sake of regaining her company and aid, or to gain k'Ádhá's favor; he knew in every fiber of his being that her assessment of him was accurate. These were the very faults Kóráhm had tried to point out but Kavan had not been ready to hear. It had taken months of agony and suffering to reach the place where his heart and soul could hear and understand such truths, and he knew he might still be stumbling blindly about in moral darkness if not for Orynn, but what had that time wasted cost now that she was gone? How could he continue his quest without her? Was there even a quest any longer, if he was not right with himself and k'Ádhá?

How many times in his life had he chosen pain over joy when he could have as easily accepted joy? He could not recall, but he knew it happened more frequently than his memories would ever admit. His choices had been made with knowledge of that prophecy ever-present, something to blame misery on, when he could have made a conscious choice to prove that prophecy wrong. And how often, when those choices had to be made, had he heard the words of praise from others, felt the awe and pity and respect they held for his suffering and strength. He knew without a doubt that such responses pleased him, that they made him feel…holier…to accept suffering without question…even when it was unnecessary.

But it had been different this time. He had brought this suffering on himself and blamed k'Ádhá for it. As Kóráhm had said, k'Ádhá's sole part in those events had been to allow the beating; he could not be blamed for any of Kavan's choices before or after that. Kavan had put himself to the ultimate test for his impotent, selfish reasons, thinking it would draw him closer to the divine, and he had come up lacking. His suffering had driven him further away from his Faith, until Kavan was forced to admit he had failed. Failed…and yet k'Ádhá kept him near, loved enough to use him to give the miracle of life to a stranger. k'Ádhá had not turned his back or failed him. The failures were Kavan's.

Once the realization came, he wept for hours, a repentant purging cry that left him feeling empty, fulfilled, and at peace for the first time since he realized Gabrielle's kiss was not the affront to k'Ádhá he had believed it to be. That was so many years ago it felt like another lifetime. Someone else's lifetime.

No, he realized, pulling up from the ground to see that dawn had come and gone. His lifetime alone. This was the most peace he had ever felt. He could err, he could fall from his own pedestal, but in the end, he was a man, accepted by k'Ádhá, still alive with the chance to try again, and still a man who possessed much to offer. Let others say what they would of him, saint or demon, man or monster. He knew his own truths. He knew and was content.

Agony spent, he wiped the dirt from his face and looked at his hands. Twisted, mostly useless, but they were his hands. He still had them and they still had some functionality. In time, he might learn to write again. Their loss did not cause as much anguish this morning as it had in the previous weeks; a spasm of regret that he had been foolish enough to let them go unhealed was what he felt. Would k'Ádhá see fit to restore them or had Kavan taken too long to learn the truth? Had he failed because he had not found his own way but had needed someone else to point him to it? Did it matter?

He decided it did not. He accepted himself as he was.

A gong sounded in the village; the sun was at its zenith. Noon already. Wortham would be looking for him if he had not chosen to leave Zabin. Not without him, as Kavan doubted Wortham would willingly leave him. There was one way to know, one way to make it up to Wortham, and one way to find k'ílshwythnec. He must return to the village and face the people he had fled from the night before.

The short hike back revealed he had not fled as far from Zabin as he believed, an hour's distance at most. He must have spent a great deal of time fleeing blindly in circles in his efforts to elude his pursuers. An effort to elude himself. But he had done neither. Orynn had found him and brought him face to face with the harsh reality of his failings.

He arrived to find the villagers gathered at the town's center sharing their meal. They bowed respectfully but none spoke. Perhaps, he realized, he had offended them, or perhaps his companions had left to continue the quest, if there was one, on his behalf, and these people felt pity for him. Before he could take someone aside to question, however, Wortham emerged from the hut Kavan had been in the day before. His smile was the warmest and sincerest Kavan had ever seen.

"Milord!" The big man clasped Kavan's crippled hands between his. "I thought perhaps you left us…"

"I thought the same when I did not see you or the mules," the bard admitted. "I would not have blamed you if you had. I think, after what I have subjected you to, you would each be justified to go your ways."

Wortham smiled. "I could never do that, milord. You know I could not. I made a promise…"

"Yes, I think I do know it at last." He looked around him at the crowd and asked, "What of gdhededhá Urian…and Orynn?"

"The dedhá is here; he has been tending to the sick and trying to preach to the villagers. I have not seen Lady Orynn since she followed you last night. Did she find you? Have you seen her?"

Kavan's expression darkened a little as his gaze fell. "We talked. Or rather she talked and I listened. She had a great deal to say…and may not be rejoining us." It was painful to admit, but it had to be done.

"Why, milord? What has happened?"

He shrugged. "It is as she said in Yashir…that she would lead us to k'ílshwythnec and then be bound to depart. I think that time has come." It was an easier explanation than providing lengthy details about the discussion they had shared.

"Aye," Wortham admitted. "She did say it. I would have thought she would say farewell first." A peasant passed, bowing and mumbling something Kavan did not understand. At the bard's baffled expression, the captain asked, "Would you rather they repeat last night's display?"

That memory made the Elyri shudder. "No. Definitely not."

"dedhá Urian and I convinced them that adulation and praise, no matter how deserved or justified, makes you uncomfortable. I told them that if they wished for you to return, to look favorably upon them, they would need to temper their displays and treat you with respect. And dedhá Urian did what he could to make them understand that no one has canonized you yet."

Kavan shivered but refused to ponder the thought of sainthood. "Thank you, Wortham. I do not deserve such loyalty. I wish to speak with gdhededhá Urian; I need him to hear my concession before we go further. Will you bring him to me?"

"Certainly."

"And Wortham?"

The captain turned to do Kavan's will but looked back. "Milord?"

"I would like you to be there. You are not a gdhededhá, but I feel the need to make this concession before you as well."

It was an unusual request, one that surprised Wortham. "Why?"

Kavan glanced at his hands. "Because you, more than any other person, will hear the truth in what I say and will correct me if I am in error. Because your love for me is pure and I fear that it is you I have wronged the most. And, after I have said what I must, you may be able to keep me from making the same mistakes in the future. Will you do this for me?"

Wortham clasped Kavan's hands with an affectionate squeeze. "If it is your wish, I shall be there."

❧*❧

Khwílen grimaced as he stepped out of St. Maicel's. It was raining in Alberni when there had been sunshine in Clarys. It was almost enough to make him turn around and go back.

But to what end, he sighed in disgust. He had gotten his audience with k'gdhededhá Dórímyr, as he had known he would, but despite the saga he put forth and the numerous good reasons for removing gdhededhá Claide from the bosom of the Faith, Dórímyr seemed disturbingly ambivalent. Not that he failed to see the threat the man could present. Rather, the k'gdhededhá indicated that it might be setting a bad precedent to remove a Teren gdhededhá for anti-Elyri sentiments when he had never removed an Elyri gdhededhá for anti-Teren ones. Khwílen pointed out that no Elyri gdhededhá, regardless of the extent of their anti-Teren feelings, supported their extermination, whereas gdhededhá Claide seemed quite content to allow the butchery to continue and had, in fact, encouraged it.

Speculation, Dórímyr touted. Even if such were the case, the k'gdhededhá preferred to keep Claide under the banner of the Faith where others could keep an eye on him. Few had ever been barred from the Faith and there were few precedents for such punishment. If Claide were expelled, who would be able to keep him in line?

Who was able to keep him in line now, Khwílen argued, when the k'gdhededhá's words were unheeded and the k'gdhededhá failed to take interest in what occurred in the sees beyond Elyriá's borders. That accusation made Dórímyr angry enough to eject Khwílen from his chambers. It had been the end of their dialogue.

It appeared that k'gdhededhá Jermyn must take action on his own. Khwílen would make a brief stop at Saint Kóráhm's to gain an update and see if he was needed, and then he was going to Rhidam for an audience with Jermyn. The man deserved to know that the Elyri k'gdhededhá cared little about his people's lives, or the Faithful, outside of Elyriá; as well as the Elyri who traveled abroad. Khwílen had every intention of making known how little the k'gdhededhá thought of the Elyri who left the safety of their homeland. He would not be opposed to seeing Dórímyr taken down. He felt confident, after leaving Clarys, that there were others who would feel the same way.

❧*❧

Wortham had not wept so sincerely since he had been a small boy; if he had, he could not recall it. He felt the depth of honesty in Kavan's confession, as well as the truth of what the bard said, and he could see that, because of this unburdening, the Elyri had found new peace. If Wortham could do anything to keep Kavan from falling back into suffering, if he could find a way to protect Kavan from unmitigated pain and torment, Wortham knew he would. There was no longer lingering agony in Kavan's eyes, except for a sporadic spark when some movement of his hands troubled him, but that was something the bard had to learn to endure, a link to the past Wortham could not take away. He could only look to the future and help Kavan do likewise.

"What now?" he asked quietly as they sat side by side in that small room. Urian had gone out nearly thirty minutes earlier to leave Kavan alone with his thoughts, but Wortham stayed. "Lady Orynn was to help us locate the seeress but you say she has left us. How do you propose to find this woman, to find the items you need?"

Kavan closed his aching eyes, glad the last tears were shed. "Orynn brought us here because k'ílshwythnec is supposed to be in this region. You and Urian speak the language of these people…at least effectively enough to convince them to give me peace. Will you ask where she might be?"

The dark head of curly hair bobbed once. "Aye. I think the least they owe their 'prophet' is information. I will…"

The door pushed open and a fearful, middle-aged man leaning on Urian's arm entered bowing, trembling, and speaking rapidly. Urian said something to him that made him stop, bow low, and begin again more slowly. A smile crept across Wortham's face and when the speaker finished, Urian patted his back.

"I asked them about the seeress," the gdhededhá said, having anticipated what they must do next. Or perhaps, thought Kavan, this was k'Ádhá's intervention. "He says she is near, up the mountain. If you will be ready at daybreak, he will take you to her. The trail is treacherous and will take nearly two days to reach where she is. I will remain here, I think; I would hinder you in such a climb, milord…and this is your quest. You do not need me for this."

Kavan exchanged an excited, worried glance with Wortham. To be near to what he hoped was the end was both exhilarating and terrifying. What if Orynn was right and the night's revelations had come too late? "You may both wait here since I do not know…"

The captain shook his head stubbornly. "You might need my assistance. And I keep telling you, I am with you until the end…even if that means climbing a mountain."

Kavan smiled weakly. "Tomorrow then?"

"Daybreak, milord. We will be that much nearer success."

❧*❧

k'gdhededhá Jermyn Tythilius' High Gathering was the most densely attended Gathering Hes á Redh Náós had seen since officially re-opening its doors for use. The entire Lachlan household, family retainers, advisors, and servants, were in attendance. Citizens of Rhidam and the surrounding territory filled the aisles, crammed in at the rear and sides of the thóres and spilled through the doorway into the yard beyond. The only person of importance the k'gdhededhá did not see in attendance was Claide, but Valgis had told him Claide was called to visit a dying parishioner and would return when his services were no longer needed. His absence might have been for the greater good, given that Jermyn was convinced that, if the man heard his fiery pro-Elyri, pro-peace, sermon, he would have reacted badly.

The King had also chosen to stand before the attendees to add words of encouragement and reassurance to those Jermyn shared. In King Hagan's words, Jermyn heard the makings of a kindhearted king. The people of the parish left the Gathering uplifted, reassured, and, he hoped, ready to abandon the violence that gripped the kingdom.

Lying in bed, the k'gdhededhá stared at the ceiling. He was hungry from a day of prayer and fasting but determined not to eat until morning. With a contented sigh, he smiled. His life had been fuller than most, taking him from the post of lowly monk in the order of Saint Kóráhm to a missionary in the service of Prince Arlan, and finally to k'gdhededhá of the restored Faith in Enesfel. He had been part of that restoration, part of the reconstruction of the náós in Enesfel, and he had made the acquaintance of the White Bard of Bhryell, the Bhryell Prophet. He could, he believed, consider the man his friend. Few people could claim that; few people could claim to have seen the miracles. He had done everything he intended to do with his life. If it had to be, if Kóráhm's prediction was unavoidable, Jermyn felt ready to face it.

He must have dozed since he was suddenly brought wide-awake as if roused by a frightening dream. He sat abruptly, aware of noises in his bedchamber, moments before several hands closed upon him and pulled him from his bed. Struggling, he tried to break free, his sheet clenched in his fist, but his attackers were bigger, stronger and larger in number. There was no chance of escape. I was not serious about being ready to die, he thought with one last attempt to break free. Something struck the back of his skull and he lost consciousness.

❧Chapter 27❦

"Whoever these Corylliens are, they are more widespread than we anticipated," Caol grunted. "There has been reported activity from as far as Seres and Durham. Wilred caught a fellow who claimed to be a Coryllien, but interrogation produced only his death. I think I need to school my son in more non-lethal forms of interrogation."

Darius leaned against the stable door, watching the blacksmith shoe his horse. "Is it possible there is one group of actual Corylliens, and the others have borrowed the name to label their acts of violence?"

"I'm sure it is. There is simply no way to prove it. I think we must act on the theory that there is one extensive group and seek its leader."

"If people are foolish enough to borrow that name to justify their actions, they must be prepared to accept the punishment." General Agis glowered, wiping his dusty hands on his trousers. This meeting was a break from his early morning routine, but also a necessity. "I suggest we show no leniency to any of these…"

"I don't intend to," the inquisitor reassured him.

Darius chuckled, "You want more riots."

"I admit I found that stimulating," grunted the general.

Footsteps upon the gravel outside made the three men turn their heads. gdhededhá Tusánt appeared, his face lined with deep crags of worry. "Good morning, dedhá. What may we do for you?"

The Elyri shuffled his feet. "Lord Dugan…I know of no other way to say this…I think k'gdhededhá Jermyn has been abducted."

His words brought the men to attention. Even the blacksmith paused his work to listen with a look of alarm. "How on earth…?"

"Nearly an hour ago, while it was dark…I awakened to noises, a struggle in his room. I woke Rankin and Valgis and we hurried there; the door was open, the room ransacked. There is no sign of him. We searched the grounds, spoke to the other gdhededhá, but we have been unable to find a trace of him. Valgis was hesitant about bringing this to you since it might be nothing, but we overruled his objection. We know nothing about investigations. Perhaps you can come…"

Caol was already striding away before the Elyri finished speaking. He swore under his breath, wondering why his spies had not reported this to him sooner. The Association appeared to be less useful every day. It was an effort for the others to catch up to him, but they did before he reached the palace gates. People cleared from their paths; the sight of the justice, inquisitor, and general going anywhere together with purposeful steps meant there could be trouble and many soldiers and townsfolk tagged along, hoping for a glimpse of the excitement. Many turned back, however, when they saw the four men going into the náós where there were no visible signs of a problem.

The justice questioned everyone who lived within the náós' walls, the general searched the buildings, and the soldiers who had followed searched the grounds for signs of disturbance. It left the dubious task of exploring Jermyn's rooms to the inquisitor's expertise.

There was, as Tusánt claimed, conflicting evidence within that room. The sheets had been pulled halfway from the bed and hung upon the floor; the candle holder, Jermyn's prayer beads, a carafe and two wine glasses had been knocked to the floor when the nightstand fell.

There was no blood, no sign of anything other than the quick rising from bed and, perhaps, the subduing of the k'gdhededhá. There was also his obvious absence. Caol spun with his dagger drawn when a noise in the doorway startled him, but he secretly hoped in that brief moment that the noise belonged to Jermyn.

"I did not mean to…I…oh my…what has happened? Where is k'gdhededhá Tythilius?"

"Why don't you start by telling me who you are?" Though the man wore religious raiment, Caol did not recognize him and that made him suspect.

"gdhededhá Khwílen Kesábhá, rector of St. Kóráhm's Abbey in Alberni. I was conducting an errand for the k'gdhededhá and came to report…but he does not appear to be here…"

"You must be Elyri," Caol snorted, knowing from the man's name that he was. There was no need for sarcasm, but he was not in the mood to debate the obvious with a stranger.

"You cannot tell by looking at me?" the blond man asked.

"I have more important matters on my mind. It appears a crime has been committed. If you are what you claim, can you confirm it?"

If this man was that familiar with Elyri, then he was likely part of the Lachlan court, as the inquisitor's badge on his lapel suggested. Still, Khwílen was nervous, given the violence currently directed at his people. One look at the state of the room, however, and he decided he was not nervous enough to keep from helping the man he had come to see. "Anything in particular? The sheet perhaps?"

Caol grunted, his mood no better for having found a willing assistant. "Whatever you think will give the most information."

Khwílen squatted and pressed his hand flat upon the sheet where it lay on the floor. The images, murky as they were in the predawn light, played before his eyes and then passed. He repeated the action with the upturned night table. "Five…larger than him…strong men.

They came while he slept…pulled him up…knocked him out. It was too dark to see faces. They wore dark clothing. None appeared armed."

"Then what was used to knock him unconscious?"

"Unknown…something in the room perhaps…or one of them carried an object he did not see." He stood, sheet clutched in his hand, and something clattered to the floor. Caol stayed the gdhededhá's hand and retrieved the fallen object. A brooch, a pin of the sort that some men wore in their caps, something that did not belong to the k'gdhededhá. The inquisitor's face broke into an evil grin.

"I think I may have found my answer. You would not object to helping again, would you, dedhá?"

"I will, gladly…if you will do me the courtesy of your name, sir."

Caol sniffed, a little embarrassed he had not given it already, and replied, "Caol Dugan, Lord High Inquisitor."

"Well then, milord, allow me to follow you, for you might be interested to know that the errand I was on could have a direct bearing on your investigation."

❧*❧

It was almost sundown two days after leaving Zabin before their guide stopped on a wide ledge outside of a foreboding cavern. In truth, they had not traveled far, as there were times when Kavan could hear voices below or see the light of the fire in the village square as they struggled over the rocky, rutted terrain. What had been a clear path at one time was washed away in places, covered with boulders and debris that slid from further up the mountain, or was narrow enough that they could only pass slowly one at a time. It was the deterioration and the steepness that slowed their progress, not any matter of great distance. Wortham grumbled about their path good-naturedly, but he understood that those individuals with a reputation like k'ílshwythnec rarely made getting to them an easy thing. If people had to work harder to see her, they would make certain what they sought was worth the effort it took to reach her.

Their bodies were aching, sore and bruised from slipping, clawing, and bumping into rocks and each other, by the time their guide settled cross-legged in front of the cavern's opening. He said something in a quiet, reverent tone and pointed into the cave; Wortham scowled and started to speak, but the man shook his head and repeated the admonition.

Kavan understood a single word. Wishing he could dispel that title, he murmured, "What did he say?"

"You alone may enter. He and I must remain here. He says the rest is up to you. But I cannot allow you to go in alone. You do not know what is in there and you are unarmed. You could be hurt or killed."

Kavan did his best to grasp Wortham's hand. "I would think he knows of what he speaks. And we do know what…or rather who…is in there. I doubt I would have been led this far to die." He looked into the cave, trying to see anything, hearing a low, snarling growl from somewhere deep within, but the shadows were impenetrable and the source of the sound impossible to identify. "If you come, she may not agree to see me. You knew it could come to this, Wortham. Please…wait for me here. I will be well."

The captain's grim expression indicated he did not believe that to be true, but he took up a post on the opposite side of the cave entrance, drew his sword, and prepared for what might be an extended vigil. None of them had any idea how long this might take. "Be careful, milord. No quest is worth your life."

Kavan, in turn, murmured, "My life is worth nothing if I am not willing to lose it to restore Enesfel. I will do nothing foolish. You have my word." A tongue of flame sprung up in his hand and the guide instantly jabbered something with a persistent shaking of his head.

"No light," Wortham translated. "You have to let faith guide you or you will not find her."

The light sputtered out as Kavan extinguished his reluctance at the same time. He did not fear the dark, and he had other senses available, but he had not anticipated being tested again so close to his objective. He approached the entranceway and looked back at his friend.

"I will return, Wortham. Have faith."

The captain nodded. "Because you ask it, milord."

With one final glance and smile at Wortham, conveying in the action, if not his expression, that he was anxious about this undertaking, Kavan stepped into the shadow and was engulfed by an oppressive wave of powerful energy undetectable from outside. It emanated from the rocks around him, filled him, drowning his senses in a way that rendered his Elyri abilities useless. Faith indeed. If being psychically blind was a condition to find this woman and retrieve what he needed, so be it. Going back was not an option. He feared the loss of his music, but the loss of his abilities made him the same as any other man and that he did not fear nearly as much.

One step. Two steps. Perhaps faith should allow him to tread a quick pace, to proceed at a normal stride, but common sense forced him to proceed with caution. If there were pitfalls here, he would not reach his objective by being imprudent. Faith did not necessarily require foolishness, and there was no need to hurry. He would tempt k'Ádhá with his folly no more. His foot hit a rock, sending it skittering ahead, and then it dropped. Unmoving, he listened but did not hear it hit bottom. Either the sound was muffled by the power of the place, or else there was a great chasm before him.

What he did hear, that snarl again, came from somewhere ahead.

Pleased with his foresight and choice to proceed with caution, though not eager to face the beast that waited, he dropped to his hands and knees and began to crawl, using twisted fingers to judge what lay in his path. Crawling with his robe was awkward, so he paused long enough to remove it. Leaving it behind, he began again to inch forward carefully, realizing as he did, that the deformity of his hands and the need for caution made travel no less slow.

Without the robe and without any other means to warm himself, it was colder here than outside. He shivered at the unfamiliar sensation and paused to rub his arms, not use to such a temperature change. Focused on that peculiarity, when he started again he almost failed to notice when his damaged fingers found the lip of the chasm that split the room. Wondering how to cross, or if he was meant to drop into it, he felt to the left and right, judging the distances from the side walls. His probing proved that the cavern had narrowed considerably, as he could easily reach each side without much lateral movement. The probing of walls and the floor located a narrower outcropping of stone extending forward, but he could not tell if it reached across the chasm, nor how wide the chasm was. Not knowing if it would support his weight, Kavan knew it was either make that attempt, fall into the pit, or turn back. Of the three choices, trying to cross was the only possibility if he was to succeed.

He continued to crawl, determining as he did that this was not a natural path but a bridge made of hewn stone blocks. Several more rocks skittered as he crawled, falling when they reached the edge of the footbridge; each time he stopped to listen but there was only silence. The fissure surely reached into the bowels of the earth. If he fell, he wondered if he would live if he hit the bottom.

The echoes of growling were beneath him now; perhaps the animal he feared was down there and would devour him before any wounds from the fall could kill him.

The thought of plunging to his death, of being ripped apart by fangs and claws, threatened his equilibrium, so he banished such musings from his mind. He could not afford negativity. Once he felt steady again, he continued to crawl until his aching hands found the flatness that indicated the opposite side of the bridge had been reached. Gingerly, he made it off the narrow path, but when he tried to rise, his head bumped the ceiling, the impact nearly causing him to stumble back into the ravine.

Chest aching at the thundering within, he leaned against the wall, fighting to regain both his balance and his sense of calm and focus. When he could breathe normally, he dropped back to his knees, but after a single shuffling step, the path gave way beneath him. There was an involuntary squawk as he fell down the incline, bumping into the walls as he rolled, unable to stop despite his efforts.

He landed with a thud upon stony ground littered with sharp rock and rubble. Every inch of his body felt bruised and cut and a hasty inspection with his hands revealed wet spots upon his skin that meant bleeding. He was numb from the frigid temperature and felt little pain; he hoped that none of those scrapes or gashes were enough to kill him.

Brushing away the dirt and debris, he looked around, able to survey his location for the first time. There was light here, a glow far up the wall of what appeared to be a naturally rounded cave. The glow, occasionally obscured as if something was pacing between the opening and the light source, was of a size and shape to suggest a door, but there appeared no easy way to reach it.

Kavan rose slowly, shook his head clear of the dizziness he felt after that fall, and began circling the room, running his hands over the walls, examining everything he could see. Some of what was on the floor appeared to be bones, and the thought of them being the bones of men made him shudder with distaste. How many had come seeking k'ílshwythnec and died in the attempt? Or were these the bones of animals that had gotten in and were unable to escape? His search located the way he had come into this place, a path high enough off the floor and steep enough that many animals, particularly those injured by the fall, would have found it difficult to get out.

And though he had not heard the growling again, and found no trapped animal here, it was possible these bones had been left by the predator that seemed to live within this cavern.

His path, if he was to find the seeress, was to seek some way to reach the light. His first choice was flight, but the power here was as strong as in the outer cavern, meaning that a shapechange was impossible. There had to be another way.

He made three passes around the room, each time with his hands at different levels along the wall, until he found a protruding edge of stone, lined up below the light source, which seemed wide and deep enough to serve as potential footing. Further investigation up and down the rough surface revealed a series of similar protrusions, a rock ladder of sorts. He believed he could climb them, but they were slippery with age and he suspected his boots would hinder him, as their soles were worn smooth from months of foot travel. Reluctantly, convinced that climbing was his only way out, he removed his boots, dropped them upon the floor and looked towards the light. Wearing only thin, gauzy trousers, he began his ascent, wondering if it was going to be necessary to go before the seeress completely unclothed.

The climb felt to take hours, and several near falls almost ended his efforts. His hands did not allow for a sure and steady grip. Now and then, a soft, warning growl echoed, and the nearer he got to the opening, the more noticeable became the shadowing in front of the light, the padding of footfalls upon rock, the snarls that warned him to come no closer. By the time he reached the four-foot wide opening, however, the growling, the pacing, and the movement in front of the light had ceased.

Uncertain whether that meant the threat was gone or if the beast was waiting in ambush, Kavan took a deep breath and hoisted himself through into a tunnel barely big enough to crawl through. If there was a predator here, it was not a very large one.

His feet were as scraped and raw as his hands, and judging by the width and length of the tunnel he would need to snake through on his stomach, the skin of his torso was going to fare no better. At least there was light and warmth ahead; he could see it and feel it in the air, and those two reassurances were enough to compel him warily forward. He wondered, as he crawled, how many people successfully made this journey and what, if anything, had been the results of their efforts.

As his body slowly warmed, he began to recognize the power surrounding him. It was power he had experienced before in the presence of those he believed to be k'kairá. It did not surprise him that k'ílshwythnec, whoever she was, might be one of that elusive race, yet it was astonishing that they had made themselves known to him more than once. Few could claim to have encountered them; many did not believe they existed. Yet for some reason, the k'kairá continually confronted him, or allowed him to see them, or gave him knowledge of their presence. Connecting this energy to them caused him to look forward to this meeting with greater anticipation.

At the end of the tunnel, another ledge that dropped him onto the floor of yet another cavern. A blazing fire in the center lit the room and provided warmth he desperately needed. His limbs felt numb. The smoke of the fire, fragrant and sweet, curled its white limbs up to where the half moon and three bright stars shown through an opening in the ceiling. There was nothing else there.

He was alone. There was no beast here unless it was hidden in the fringe shadows, perhaps in a crevice he could not see. Exhausted, aching, and bemused, he crawled nearer to the fire and rubbed his skin. Such a being would make her appearance when she was ready; one did not make demands of the k'kairá. What would he say when she came? She had known he was coming; Kavan believed that. Hence, it seemed likely she knew what he sought, knew what he hoped to learn. But for that knowing, would she have the information he needed? Would she willingly give him answers?

Staring at the half moon, watching it pass gradually from the left of the opening to the right as time crept by, Kavan was tuned to his thoughts and the warmth of the fire, paying no attention to the empty room until he abruptly realized he was no longer alone. He met the woman's gaze with a start, his eyes wide and his breath catching in his throat at the sight of her.

"Orynn…what are you…?"

Where she had come from he was not certain; there did not appear to be any way in or out of the room except the way he had come and the opening to the sky above. She gave him a ghost of a smile and settled beside him, tucking her bare feet beneath her and arranging the thin folds of the white fabric she wore about her modestly.

"You were expecting someone else?" she asked with amusement.

"k'ílshwythnec…"

"You have found her."

"But this place is…you said you are both Teren and Elyri…"

"I am. I am also, in large part, that which you call phae k'kairá. Does that surprise you?"

He shook his head yes, though he realized he should not be surprised. "I anticipated k'kairá…the power in this place is great…and it would explain a vast accumulation of knowledge. I was not, however, expecting you."

He thought then about the growling, and her revelation of having been the cat that had saved his life in the Levonne alley many months ago. Had she been the one to guide him to a Gate…to Arlan on the night of his death? Had she been the source of the growls and snarls heard as he had crept through the passages of this cavern?

Had she been with him all along?

"Then I have done my duty." He could tell that pleased her.

"How could you…you are no older than…" He bit his tongue and, embarrassed, studied the bruises and bleeding cuts upon his arms and hands instead of looking at her. As the fire revived his senses, he grew sorely aware of every injury received to reach this room.

"How old do you think I am, milord?" When Kavan lowered his head to further hide the blush on his cheeks, she smiled. "You will not even hazard a guess. Suffice it to say I am old enough to hold this station, and to have firsthand experience of a great deal of what I know. In reality, I am the thirty-fourth to hold this duty; it was passed from my mother to me, and will someday pass to my daughter when I have one.”

For a moment, the bard looked betrayed. “Then you know where I must seek the chalice and the staff pieces, and find the heir to perform the cleansing. It was not necessary to lead me here…”

“It was necessary, milord. I rarely do anything that is not. I am not free to dispense knowledge on a whim. There are rules I must obey, qualifications that must be met. Kóráhm begged me to watch over you as much as I was able in your time of need…and I chose to take his request literally, as participant rather than observer.” She stared into the fire, watching it flare. “Passive I am not. I like what I see in you and gladly invested much to ensure your future. Your success is important to many. I broke rules to guarantee you would have it; it is in my best interest to see that you do.”

Her words made no sense, as she referred to others he did not know, conditions he was unaware of. Blinking smoke from his eyes, Kavan asked, “What is my success or failure to you?”

Orynn shook her head, cutting him short. “Some things you are not meant to know, milord. Leave it with this: I have been with you with the hopes of being there when you completed self-discovery in order to give the knowledge you need. Normally such tests are not required, but Kóráhm demanded it. It was his condition, his wrong to rectify, my promise to keep. As much as it saddens me, there is nothing I may do until you acknowledge your shortcomings. Kóráhm has decreed it; it cannot be undone.”

“I believe I have done so,” he said quietly, pondering the oddity of Kóráhm’s wishes. A condition to purify the temple, he wondered, or a personal desire for Kavan. Perhaps both. “You were more accurate in your accusations than I wished to acknowledge, but I see it and I have admitted, and accepted, that what you said is true.” There was a long, awkward pause. "I am weaker than I sometimes think, but my faults are no worse than those of other men. They are, however, possibly more damning because I have refused to acknowledge them."

He swallowed hard, stood, and began to pace with stumbling, shuffling steps in order to be away from her. The cave was not big enough to pace more than a dozen steps in any one direction, which meant he could not escape. "I am not the man I thought I was, hoped I was, wanted others to think I was…but I am a man. Once, Ártur asked me if I was trying to be holier than Dhágdhuán…perhaps not consciously, but I see that I was taking the emulation of his traits too far…by refusing to see that I could not be as he is. No matter how perfect I molded myself to be, how perfect others think or say I am…I am as mortal, as damned, as imperfect as anyone else without my faith…and my faith means I am not damned. It changes neither my mortality nor my imperfection…and I have accepted that."

When she did not speak, he continued, "I have admitted before k'Ádhá, Kóráhm, gdhededhá Urian, and Wortham. I do not know if Kóráhm heard or accepted my plea, but Wortham did and I accept that gdhededhá Urian and k'Ádhá did as well. That must suffice. I have not considered myself a proud man, but the fact that I tried desperately to deny the allegations convinced me that it was…is…true. While I have not knowingly committed myself to suffering to gain the praise of others, self-analysis reveals that I have, indeed, done so. I know myself enough to know that words of praise are something I have sought my whole life…in any way I could have them."

The smile she gave him was comforting and understanding. "Because you received little of it as a child. I know this, milord… as I know many other moments of your life. You crave security, the welcome you have never felt. However, what you seek…men can offer just so much. In the end, you need to love and accept yourself. You must start there. The acceptance and welcome others offer, the love they give you…is it enough for you?"

Ashamed of his answer, he sank to the floor, careful not to sit too near. "It seems nothing is ever enough…and I do not know how to make it be. Wortham alone accepts me unreservedly, and even his love and devotion I sometimes doubt. For the same reasons, I sometimes doubt k'Ádhá and thus strive harder to prove myself worthy…"

"You know you are worthy without trying…?" she asked gently.

"I know it in my head," he groaned, wrapping his arms around his torso, "but I wrestle with my heart. I may not know peace because of it, but I accept that failing and know I must struggle to accept the rest."

Though her eyes showed sympathy for the plight that Kavan had to resolve on his own, she did smile and say, "It sounds as if your journey has been a profitable one. You do not know how pleased I am to hear it, how happy I am that you are on the path to peace. I was afraid you would be forever miserable…and I am sure Kóráhm is satisfied. It means I may answer your questions, at least some of them. You do realize there may be things I cannot tell you?"

Trembling, his breath caught in his throat as he whispered, "Yes." Knowledge was close, attainable at last, and he prayed that the answers he needed were not those she would withhold.

"Then ask what you wish, Kavan. Let me help you one last time."

"One last…" He shook his head, not wanting to ponder the implications of those words. Nor did he want to think about the warm shiver that the sound of his name on her lips sent sliding along his spine. "You do not already know my questions?"

"After our time together, of course I know. But it is required that you ask them, as it will prevent me from volunteering information you either do not want or do not need to know. This places upon you the burden of the questions, for if you later fail due to lack of knowledge, that responsibility is upon your head. Can you accept this?"

He nodded gravely. "I would never seek to place blame on anyone other than myself. Even now, after what I have learned, that is one habit I shall always retain, I suspect. I accept your conditions…and ask where I might find the sacred chalice and the staff pieces of which Bhóité spoke. Where do I look? How do I gain them?"

"I appreciate your directness," she chuckled. Scratching at one bare foot she replied, "Very well. Two pieces of the staff you already possess. The chalice and third staff piece reside in a cloister near the town of Gorbesh where they have been guarded for many centuries."

"Third piece?" Another reference made to two pieces he was said to own, but he could not think of anything he possessed that resembled the golden portion of staff he had taken from Coryllien's tomb.

"You will know it when you see it…the base and the crown." Kavan's scowl did not lessen, but as she seemed disinclined to describe the pieces to him, or perhaps did not know what they looked like, he did not press for answers. When he did not speak again, she continued. "The residents of the cloister have a series of tests you must pass before you will be given what you seek…and only then if you agree to do with them exactly as instructed."

"What are these tests?" he asked with a small frustrated sound. He felt he had endured more tests since leaving Rhidam than he had in the rest of his life. These items, and the náós he sought to purify, must be more important than imagined given the number of tests on his character he was required to fulfill.

"You will learn that when you arrive. No one may assist you, you must pass them alone. But I have no doubt about your success, as I have no doubt the altar will soon be blessed once more."

"Do you know what night this must be done? What signs I must watch for to know when to act?"

Again, she shook her head. "That knowledge will be bestowed after you have the chalice and staff, when the time is at hand. You must think me limited, to be unable to impart such details, but the limits are on what I may tell you, not on what I know. I can tell you that the time is nearing, that the day is not yet passed."

That was a relief to hear. "How is this to be accomplished? Both Kóráhm's journal and Bhóité made reference to a descendant or other blood relative of either Kóráhm or Coryllien, that such a relative is necessary to perform the ritual. Do you know where to find this person? Does one exist?"

"There are two," she answered as she produced a small book from the folds of her robe. Its leather cover was creased, cracked, and smudged, faded with age and use, but Kavan was able to make out the tiny High Elyri script upon it.

"A genealogy?" he asked as he took it. He was not sure why he hesitated, except that it felt he was facing one of the most important discoveries of his life. He thumbed carefully through the pages, noticing that the handwriting changed many times and that the pages grew less faded and worn as he neared the middle of the book. Coryllien's lineage stopped with a blank line and Kavan looked at Orynn with confusion.

"There is an heir…but the identity is unknown to us for the child disappeared on the day it was born. That it lives, we have no doubt; the signs and portents tell us they are there. In time, I am sure that heir will be revealed."

Due to the memories of Coryllien's final resting place and what that corpse had said to him, that thought was frightening. After an uncomfortable shiver, Kavan turned several more pages until he found Kóráhm's name, and then skimmed his family tree without paying close attention to the names written there. As frightening as it was that Coryllien could have had an heir, it was reassuring that Kóráhm's bloodline had continued. Reassuring, that was, until he came to the final few entries, at which time the book tumbled from his hands as he looked at Orynn in shock.

"This cannot be," he choked with a shake of his head. "How…it cannot…is this true?"

"You have always suspected it… as you have suspected that you are the one meant to purify the náos. None of it is chance, Kavan."

"But how…?"

"Once you have read it, you will see. You must read it all. Learn the names, for it is necessary for you to know the truth. I think you will find many answers in those pages before you must return it to us."

"What is he?" he murmured as he read and reread that final page. "Spirit? Mortal?"

Again, Orynn shook her head. "I cannot answer that. It is Kóráhm's place to tell you if he desires you to know. I have broken confidence enough by demanding you see the truth about yourself. Someday, perhaps, you may learn all there is to know about him, but it must not be from me."

Kavan was not surprised by her answer, though he was frustrated. There was no certainty that Kóráhm would ever return to him, though what Kavan had learned tonight suggested he would. He stared at those pages for many silent minutes without seeing them, thoughts sifting through memories for new and special meanings, until finally, he suspected his host was growing tired of waiting.

"How will I be able to return this…if I do not see you…?"

Orynn sighed. "Do not concern yourself with that. When you are done with it, we will know…and we will reclaim what is ours."

Scowling at the mysteriousness of that brush off answer, he asked instead, "What of the blessed water? Where might I find…?"

"Any gdhededhá may bless water for your needs."

"I was told it must be from a newly purified…"

She cut him off with a wave of her hand. "Newly purified water, that is all. Newly as in recent to your acquisition, not necessarily recent to the date of the rite. You may ask Urian to bless it for you, or one of your gdhededhá in Rhidam. I would recommend, however, that you find what you seek in Gorbesh…which will gain you water of such strength and purity as cannot be found elsewhere."

That seemed the preferable alternative. Surely, the more blessed the water, the more complete the ritual would be. What wonders, he mused, awaited in Gorbesh? "What must I do?" he asked in a low voice. "How will I know?"

"You will know…trust yourself. You will know when it is done."

"When what is done?" Her hint spoke of power and the miraculous, matters Kavan had experience with. He preferred not to be the hand through which another miracle flowed, and hoped there might be some other way.

She gave him a metal flask, also from the folds in her robe, though Kavan could not explain how she could have hidden items of such bulk upon her. It shone of the same silvery metal his half-moon pendant was made from. "This has been blessed for your purpose; use it. Guard it well." She smiled as he took the flask, his fingers brushing over her skin, the flask surprisingly light. "It is up to you to choose."

He studied her gray eyes, and for the first time reached and tenderly touched her hair, her face. Her eyes closed and Kavan felt peace in the soft sigh that escaped her, the gentle tremor that ran through her body. It ignited passion, the desire to crush her to him forever, and he realized that this was how he was meant to feel. There was something right in those brief touches that he had not felt with either Gabrielle or Princess Diona. He believed that he loved her.

As if hearing his unspoken thoughts, Orynn drew away and reluctantly rose. "I fear, milord, that what I must do now will cause us both pain, but I may no longer travel with you. We part ways here."

Hand falling to his side, Kavan resisted hanging his head. He had known this moment would come, despite the bond that had developed between them. He studied her face, seeking some reason, and when he found none he asked, "May I ask why? After this long, I feel I am entitled to that much."

He thought for a moment she would not answer him, as her expression grew sadder before she looked away. "My people were reluctant to allow me to interfere, but when they realized they had no choice, they allowed it. I have done too many things I should not have, the worst of which was forcing you to see your way to redemption to enable you to proceed when I should have allowed you to find the path on your own, even if it meant failure and left the naós unclean for many more generations. I saw no reason to allow that, considering the number of people who have already died by that taint of evil."

She held out her hand to assist Kavan to his feet. "It is difficult to watch someone suffer, knowing you can help…particularly when you love them."

"You…?" He could not have finished the sentence if he tried, both because his voice and words failed him and because Orynn chose that moment to interrupt with a kiss. Ardent, sensuous, the meeting of lips and probing tongues, devouring the familiar taste that came back to him from his dreams. But this was no dream. The press of her supple curves against his firm body, her fingers stroking the hair at the nape of his neck, brushing against his skin with feather light touches, and the thundering in his veins like a thousand horses running, were real. He wound his twisted hand in the thick waves of her hair, pulling her closer, seeking to merge into her body to avoid letting her go.

But reality was a cruel herald and he knew if he did not release her he was going to lose whatever control he had on his passions. Perhaps she would not regret it if he did, but he was confident he would. It took a great force of will to put distance between their bodies, but it was Orynn who broke the kiss, allowing him to move away from her.

"It is good to know you have learned at least this much from your suffering," she said, her eyes brimming with unshed tears. "Do not be afraid of love, Kavan. It is the one thing in life that is truly good."

"Orynn…"

She pressed her fingers to his lips. "You must go. I pray we meet again…in the flesh…not as dreams and memories. But I cannot go with you, and you may not go where I must go now. There are differences between us that cannot be overcome, and we both have duties. I will remember you always; you will live in my heart."

"Likewise," he whispered, choking on the word and the emotion behind it. There seemed much more he should say, but it was as if his brain had ceased functioning.

"Come." With his hand in hers, making sure he had both the flask and the book, she led him to the side of the cavern opposite where he had come in. As they approached the wall, the power in the room dissipated until all Kavan could feel was the power in her touch and that in the ground at his feet. He looked at her in surprise.

"Yes, it is a Gate. It has one point of exit, inside the mouth of the cave where you came in. It will save you the effort of repeating the work it took to get to me."

He let his gaze travel down to their joined hands, and then back up to her eyes, drawing those hands up with the action. "Thank you," he murmured in a voice that cracked and broke. "For everything."

She nodded and kissed his hand, seeming to Kavan as if she did not trust her voice either. "Go, milord. It is time…" The tears in her eyes broke free and he leaned forward one last time to kiss them away. With their salty moisture upon his lips, he let her go, drawing energy together to make the transfer. He might have kissed her again, but as he opened his eyes to bid her farewell, she was gone. The connection to the other Gate was completed as his heart broke in two.

As she claimed, he emerged on the inner side of the cave entrance, where he immediately dropped to his knees, gasping for breath in a fight against the pain in his chest. He understood now what Arlan had felt upon Brenna's death, too late to share that understanding with his friend. Yet there was something else in that pain, something that left a faint smile as he struggled to his feet. Yes, he loved her, and this pain of parting was vast. But knowing he could love, that he could feel passion as any other man without self-condemnation, that another could love him as well, was a heavy burden lifted. The pain would pass in time; he would heal. Even if he never saw her again, he would remember. And if he was twice blessed, he might love once more.

His boots and robe lay at his feet, collected, he presumed, by Orynn and left for him, and he hurried to dress. Outside, Wortham paced the ledge while their guide dozed against the stony mountainside. Kavan wiped his face of any traces of tears, took a long, calming breath, and then squared his shoulders before stepping out of the cave into the cool, fresh, air.

"Milord!" Wortham grasped him roughly, pulling him into a crushing hug, and then drew back enough to look the man over. Even in the dimness, he could see evidence of scrapes and small cuts upon the bard's white skin. "What happened? It has been hours; I was growing concerned for your safety." Their guide, awakened by Wortham's cry, scrambled to his feet.

Kavan smiled at the captain in a way the man had never seen him smile before. "You were concerned for my safety before I went in, if my memory is correct," the bard teased. "It was a challenge to reach O…k'ílshwythnec, but I did, and I know what I must do next. Return to Zabin, obtain directions to a town called Gorbesh, and secure supplies to get us there if you can. Inform gdhededhá Urian of our destination and ask if he intends to join us."

The vexed man pouted. "Are you not returning with me, milord?"

"I will return," Kavan assured him. "I wish to remain here to pray, that is all." He admitted to himself that there was a pull to re-enter the cave, to find Orynn one more time, but he knew she would not be there. "After what I have learned…what I have endured…I do not mean to exclude you…and you know there may be things I need to do on my own to complete this quest, but for now…I desire time alone."

The bard's pleading expression prompted Wortham to hug him again. He felt something had changed in his friend, but it was too soon to tell what that was. Kavan was a man prone to periods of seclusion, for solitary prayer and reflection, and privacy was something he had experienced little of since this journey had begun. The request was reasonable, even if Wortham worried for the bard's safety on this mountain and when traveling back down by himself.

"I could forgive you anything, Kavan…I will do as you ask. Come back to me and everything will be right."

Kavan gave the book to Wortham with instructions to take care of the near-sacred item, and then waited until the captain and their guide disappeared down the eastern slope of the mountain. Once he felt confident that Wortham would do as he asked and not come back for him, Kavan found an overgrown, precarious hold that took him to a ledge he had noticed above the cave's opening. Back to the stone for the warmth it would give, he sat cross-legged, facing north, and sank into meditative, healing prayer.

He felt the heat of dawn crawl across his body as the sun rose over the village, listened to the chirp and hum and buzz of insects, and a distant sound that reminded him of water churning and bubbling in a fountain or perhaps a waterfall tumbling over the rocky mountain facade. He fought the compulsion to investigate, to collect water from a source that was surely precious in this dry land, thus nearly sacred in its own way, and closer to him than Gorbesh. What would it hurt to gather water now and be one step nearer to the completion of his quest? When his resistance was nearly worn through, when his legs and buttocks were numb from his stationary perch and the urge to rise, to find water to satiate his thirst and fill the flask was too great a temptation, a strong wind arose, pushing through the narrow canyon, its whistle sounding like the wailing of a thousand souls. It did not physically prevent him from rising, but the crying of souls brought with it an image of people suffering, birthing that sound…and pricked his conscience with the guilt of not waiting for the blessed source Orynn had encouraged him to seek.

Chastised and humbled, he hung his head and settled back into his meditations. He would wait until he reached Gorbesh as bidden.

His submission to destiny brought a dying of the wind, and in its place, the sweet, plaintive notes of birdsong, some lone nightbird bidding farewell to the setting sun and greeting the rising moon. Kavan listened as the lonely notes rose and fell, with the distinct impression that the creature was seeking a reply, perhaps from a lost mate or in search of a new one. In the gathering dark, Kavan sang the notes back, tone for tone, pitch for pitch.

The bird trilled the song back to him with what sounded to Kavan like a new note of excitement.

After several exchanged phrases, however, the bird ceased to reply. The night was quiet again.

In those notes, however, notes that now lodged within Kavan's head and would not leave him, Kavan heard something else. His own voice. Orynn had said it. Wortham had said it. But Kavan, behind the long-lingering veil of self-deprecation, self-loathing, and pride, had not heard them. Even his voice given to Eridel's grave had not given him what he needed.

Whatever that bird, if indeed it had been a bird, had been sent for, Kavan had heard the reassuring revelation once again. He could sing.

He knew peace, he knew love, and he knew the direction his life must turn.

Why should he not sing for the blessings he had and be proud of the voice and talent he was given?

Chapter 28

Princess Diona encouraged Lady McPhelan to return home to safety as soon as they learned k'gdhededhá Jermyn was missing, seemingly taken by force from the náós. She was bored of the young woman, and Lady McPhelan was more interested in the pursuit of the King than in time spent with the princess. To Diona, it was just as well that the young woman was sent away.

She half listened to Caol and gdhededhá Khwílen brief the King on their progress, or rather lack of progress, in the search for Jermyn. What Caol knew for certain was that the discovered brooch belonged to the man called Anri Heward. Ártur had sketched the image from what Khwílen had obtained from the object, and it was an exact likeness of the previous drawing, apart from the man's attire. And in the first drawing, the found pin adorned the man's cap.

Ah, Mr. Heward, the inquisitor thought smugly. You are getting careless.

The princess had already had her audience with the inquisitor and gdhededhá on the matter. Of the King's advisors, Caol continued to come to her first, both because of the investigation of gdhededhá Claide and because he knew she did not harbor the bias against his methods that her brother did. Both were aware that, before his disappearance, Jermyn had taken the matter of Claide to k'gdhededhá

Dórímyr, a duty Khwílen undertook when Jermyn failed to gain audience. If Claide had gotten wind of any plan to reprimand or defrock him, which was likely if Jermyn had verbally rebuked him as he had said he must, it was not a far leap to make to think that Claide, or someone else, was working to put a stop to that effort.

There was no proof of this, however, beyond Khwílen's story, and Caol was left with no tangible clues he could use against Claide. Both he and the princess knew better than to present their suspicions to the King without evidence, particularly since the King was holding out hope that what evidence they did have was wrong. Hagan persisted in the belief that the k'gdhededhá had merely gone back into seclusion and that the mess found in his room was an indication of robbery, not abduction. Many wanted to believe the King was right. Few could.

As she listened to Khwílen's voice, having heard the information before, she daydreamed, wondering if she could lure this beautiful man away from his vocation. When she realized what she was doing, however, she sighed wistfully. Obviously, regardless of her realization that marriage to an Elyri would be the undoing of the Lachlan House, they held a powerful attraction for her. Escaping it would require continual effort. *Espen*, she thought as she excused herself from the meeting, *hurry. Provide me with the proof and reason to forget that Elyri are some of the most attractive men in Enesfel. Provide me with reason one more time to marry you.*

❧*❧

Circling the three men his sheriff and Caol's ebony haired female associate had brought to him, Owain barely suppressed the urge to beat each one to death. Four sworn written affidavits and two other eyewitnesses placed these three in town around the time the two Elyri women had died, in the house where the murders had occurred. The trio arrived in Fiara that morning, merchants from the north, and had immediately taken notice of the Elyri seamstresses. They followed the women much of the day, between their work, taunting them with rude, suggestive remarks and crude behavior. When the women entered the home where they had gained lodging, witnesses claimed to have heard and seen the men banging on the door, demanding that the women be thrown into the streets so the three could entertain themselves. The family refused, barred their door, and did their best to ignore the pounding. Eventually, the frustrated merchants left.

Why no one reported the disturbance, Owain could not guess. Fear of involvement perhaps, or the belief that the fellows were drunk and not an actual threat. Yet according to a neighbor, the three returned later that night to resume their banging and catcalls. Despite this, it seemed that no one heard the door open, or heard screaming, or had any idea when the murders took place…except that the second round of banging had ceased before the midnight bells. If the witnesses and neighbors knew more, they would not admit it.

The men before him stared straight ahead, not answering questions, not volunteering information. Their stance and bearing were familiar to the prince. They did not seem to be merchants. He circled again and stopped behind them to inspect something he had not noticed before. A tattoo behind the bald middle individual's left ear. Careful inspection of the others revealed the same mark. Eyes narrowing, Owain grinned. Could it be? If his cousin held true to custom, there was one way to find out.

"Rousset!" he barked. The center man snapped to attention, amazement on his face and an obvious desire to turn his head to stare at the speaker. "Rousset!" Owain demanded again. He had no way of knowing what the proper response code was this time but his prisoners did not know that. From the look on the man's face, he had not realized beforehand whom he was dealing with or had rightfully believed that there was no reason the traitor bastard prince would be privy to the customs of the de Corrmick military.

"Backstab." He held his breath with an expectant expression.

Fitting password for a de Corrmick spy, Owain mused, grinning coldly. "Isn't this a surprise? What, may I ask, are you doing here?"

That exchange of passwords seemed to open up their willingness to talk. "Journeying to Enesfel, Your Lordship, to determine the state of affairs and…"

"…and you stopped to kill a few Elyri along the way?" he asked with a sick shiver.

"It is what we swore to do if we found…"

"…and you had to kill everyone else with them?"

The spokesman realized perhaps he had made an error but replied defensively, "They are not citizens of the Crown. Their fate does not…"

One of his fellows elbowed him in the ribs. The man questioning them might know the proper password, but he was not a citizen of Neth. Not anymore. Owain pulled the speaker up by the front of his tunic with an angry glance at the others and growled.

"They are my citizens, his no longer, but obviously my cousin has forgotten that." The man dropped his gaze. "Not that I expect Merkar to care about anyone else. You may think our kinship will temper your punishment, but it is the Lachlan name I bear and the Enesfel Crown I serve. You," he dropped the man to the floor and then stared at the others, "are trespassing. Spying."

"We are merchants, milord…not spies…" said one of them. "We did not know he was…we just met…"

Owain grabbed the second man by his tattooed ear and yanked him to his feet, making sure the others saw the mark. "This tells me you are lying. I am not foolish enough to forget living in the de Corrmick house, the way of things. I understand how de Corrmick spies work." He let this man go with a rough shove that landed him on the floor by the first and stepped back. "Do you know what we do to spies in Enesfel? Generally, they are hung…but I think that is not good enough for you. You are not simply spies, you are murderers."

The dark-haired woman beside him wore a decidedly wicked grin, taking a perverse pleasure in this interrogation.

"The Elyri were not Enesfel subjects, but as travelers here they were under the protection of the laws of this land. Those laws state that anyone who intentionally, without cause or provocation, kills foreigners passing through Enesfel, can be executed for their crimes. You have violated those mandates with flagrant disregard. What is more, you have brutally butchered Enesfel citizens, my citizens, people who were once your countrymen. Both are crimes that shall not remain unpunished."

One of the men on the floor, his voice even and flat as any well-trained de Corrmick spy's voice would be, said, "You will hang us." Accept death before dishonor. Because they had been exposed and provided Owain with details of their mission, however vague, they could not return to King Merkar. They would be killed, their families dishonored and stripped of anything they owned. For anyone in the employment of the Neth crown, the best they could hope for if they were captured was a swift death at the hands of their captors.

Owain's voice lowered to a deadly purr. "Oh no. Hanging is too good for you. It might suffice were I a more benevolent man…but if you knew anything about me, you would know that benign I am not."

"Then what are you going to…?"

"I do not know yet," he said with a malicious expression. "First, I must inform the King of your existence, your plan, the things you have done. And I should ask your King if he wants you back." Their faces paled at the suggestion. They doubted that any fate Owain could dole out would be as horrifying as what their King could give. Neth rulers were well known for their proficiency and preference for torture. While the de Corrmicks trained their spies and soldiers to be fearless and resist pain, that training never quite erased the fear of their king's wrath. "After that, we shall see. In the meantime, I have some less than pleasant facilities for you to occupy. I suggest you make yourselves comfortable, for it could be several days, several weeks, or several months before I hear anything from either king."

He signaled for them to be taken away and waited until they were removed from the room before bursting into laughter. The woman remained and chuckled at his mirth. "You enjoyed that, didn't you?"

"I will admit I find it entertaining and satisfying to prove Merkar a fool. If Kjell had sent them…"

"If they worked for Prince Kjell, I suspect they would not have been on this ill-advised mission," she said.

"True. My young cousin is a better man than that," agreed Owain, wiping his face of the traces of laughter. While it had been a long time without communication from the younger prince, Owain could not imagine Kjell turning into the sort of man Merkar was, or their father had been. "It appears, milady, that you and I may have more than casual contact. Is there something I may call you since you know my name and I do not know yours?"

She smiled. "Onea…and that is all you will get. Do not expect anyone to tell you more when you start asking questions. They won't."

With a smirk, he said, "I never imagined they would. Lord Dugan picks his associates wisely; I would expect nothing less. Have you been in touch with him recently?"

Onea settled upon the empty seat in the hall, having no qualms about sitting when the Lord of the House remained standing. In her world, she was royalty, and being a woman, she felt she had certain privileges, whether she actually did or not. "No…but I will share something with you, since you have given me proof of something I was trying to verify. I have heard about King Merkar's spies trying to push into Enesfel by any means, through Cordash and with small battalions through Elyriá. To my knowledge, none have succeeded, but it appears these three almost did."

Unbothered by her actions as he paced, Owain murmured, "A few more miles and they would have been in Enesfel's heart. It was our fortune, and their misfortune, that they chose to stick around Fiara long enough to be captured."

"It does not appear King Merkar chooses efficient employees."

"There are always bad ones, the ones who slip up. When you force men to serve you, there always are. Merkar will ignore them, claim no knowledge of their existence or activities as he usually does, and replace them with others." He looked down as he stopped in front of her. "Should I reward you for your part in their capture?"

"Not this time," the woman replied. "That family…those people were friends of mine. I want to see their murderers punished. Besides, I have been looking for a way to infiltrate Neth's ranks, to learn what Caol wishes to know. Perhaps if you will tell me about this password and tattoo, we can consider our scores settled?"

Owain smirked. "I should not trust you; I know what you are. However, I believe you are being upfront with me, and infiltrating Merkar's troops could mean an end to Enesfel's troubles; I am willing to do what I can to see that it happens. But I can tell you only as much as I know. The most elite forces in Neth bear the tattoo behind their ear, no one else. The symbol varies depending upon the branch they serve and what year they were initiated into service. Anyone not in the services found with such a tattoo, imitating one of the King's agents, will be executed. I know little about the actual training they endure thus I could not advise you on how to proceed with imitations…nor do I know how they determine the tattoo each time. I was not privy to that in my years at the de Corrmick court. As for the passwords, it has been…Rousset is Merkar's middle name. The first code is usually a middle name or a nickname of the king…or occasionally a favored hunting dog. The second codeword is changed when the king thinks it is time for a new one. Knowing Merkar, I'm not surprised he has not changed passwords since becoming king. He has always been an overconfident, arrogant bastard."

"Backstab is certainly an appropriate choice. When you send your message to the King, may I include one for Lord Dugan? He will be pleased to hear of this."

Owain bowed and offered his hand. "By all means. I will send it at first light; have your message here and it will be delivered. It has been a pleasure to make your acquaintance, Lady Onea."

"And I yours," she replied. She had a feeling they would work well together. It was a feeling he shared.

☙*☙

"Where is Duke Cliáth?"

His tormentor, a face hidden beneath a black hood, had asked him the same question so many times that Jermyn lost count. He was no longer hearing the voice, only the words; his ears were ringing and his head throbbed hotly. His wrists and ankles were shackled to the wall; he was hanging more than standing and his hands had long ago lost feeling from the loss of circulation. It was just as well, since one of the first tortures his captors had subjected him to was dislocating one finger after another until all ten were broken. It was best he could no longer feel that pain.

There was enough pain elsewhere as it was. He had not eaten or drunk anything since his abduction, causing his tongue to swell and his stomach to churn constantly as if it was devouring itself. There were few places on his body where he was not burned, whipped, beaten or cut. Even the soles of his feet had been charred with a red-hot rod, making him grateful they did not support his weight. Hanging thus might be unpleasant and uncomfortable, but at least it would not burst the blisters on his feet.

His captors seemed to want to know only three things. Had he been successful in contacting k'gdhededhá Dórímyr? To that, the answer had been a resounding no, and as he had no way of knowing if Khwílen had spoken with the k'gdhededhá, his conscience was clear of any lie. They asked the question sporadically, as if repeating it would change the answer, but for the most part, they seemed satisfied with his response. They asked where Kavan was, that one Elyri they feared most because he had more influence upon the Lachlan House than any other single person. Jermyn had no idea where the bard was, except outside of Enesfel, and told them so, but they persisted in repeating that question, pushing for a more specific answer with every new torture they introduced.

The other question was broader, a request for details on what sort of tortures Elyri could inflict with their sorcery. The k'gdhededhá steadfastly refused to answer that question, at least when he was conscious, and he prayed he had given these men nothing of use against Elyri in the moments when reason left him and he babbled incoherently in pain. Pain had always been his greatest fear. His tolerance was low; it meant he spent a great deal of time unconscious, which he hoped meant they got little information out of him. One could not question an unconscious man. Kóráhm, he groaned, I hope you do not mean for me to endure much more of this.

"Where is Lord Cliáth?" the shadow shouted from the darkness as the heated end of a pointed metal rod punctured Jermyn's shoulder. The k'gdhededhá's gurgled scream was the only reply.

❧*❧

He did not realize he had slept. When Kavan opened his eyes, he was bewildered by his cross-legged position upon the smooth surface of the mountain ledge. He stretched his sore limbs as last night's memories returned, every moment within the cavern, and when that final parting kiss sifted through his mind and settled low in his belly, he moaned and closed his eyes again in the hopes that he could shut out the longing and remorse. The inevitability of losing Orynn, the ache of it, hindered his desire to leave this mountain, rejoin Wortham and Urian, and travel towards whatever awaited in Gorbesh. But the practicality of it, the illogical nature of surrendering to the elements, to hunger and thirst, versus the destiny that demanded his return to Rhidam to right a centuries-old wrong, meant he had no choice. He stared at his crippled hands as he shifted positions often enough to regain feeling in his legs.

Orynn had not restored them, offered no indication that their use would ever be restored, an unfortunate reality he grimly accepted. He had done this to himself. Anger, despair, and regret were of no use. Crippled or not, Kavan had a purpose. He could let nothing prevent him from fulfilling it, not even embarrassment and shame.

Easing to his feet, muscles screaming about the abuse he had put them through both in the cavern and here on the ridge, he picked his way down the mountain. Climbing it with Wortham's help had taken the better part of two days; alone, without the captain's support, Kavan expected the descent to take considerably longer.

But it was time. Wortham, and Rhidam, were waiting for him.

☙*❧

Gaelán should not have been beyond the castle walls, but he had grown tired of staying put, either ignored by those around him or watched too closely as if he was still a child. Perhaps he was not yet considered an adult, but he did not feel like a child, particularly now that he possessed the art of healing. It garnered him greater respect from the entire household, except his father and his uncle.

Ártur had told him this morning that, considering his late start on the path to healing, and his lack of full attention of late, he was nearly as proficient as full-blooded Elyri children of his age with the same gifts. If he continued training, by the time he was sixteen or seventeen he might be ready to take on the mantle of apprentice healer. There was one obstacle he found difficult to overcome, however. It was hard to concentrate on that source of power within, supplementing it with external energy to increase the strength and duration of his healing. As it was, the entire well was often depleted within a matter of a few minutes or less. The older healer assured him that control would come with practice and maturity, but Gaelán had little patience, a short attention span, and felt that this failing was more due to his mixed parentage than any shortfall on his part.

After his lessons today, feeling the need for adventure, he found his way out of the keep without anyone trying to stop him, just as he had done not long ago with Asta. Maybe it was because he looked as if he had a purpose, permission to go out alone, rather than looking guilty for sneaking away. Or maybe it was because no one paid attention to the Duke's youngest son. He made it out but then was not sure where he wanted to go. He wandered through the streets, peering in shop windows and at vendors' wares, passed by the house Asta had shown him previously, and then turned back into the bustle until he arrived at the livestock yards where he spent a long while watching the horse sales, dreaming of being a knight, wondering if he might convince Sir Balint to help improve his horsemanship.

Not that he would ever be a knight, nor did he long to be one any longer. His swordsmanship was average and he had yet to be able to carry a lance properly. He was better with a bow, but even that skill was lacking compared to his older brother. A healer, at least in Elyriá, was required to take oaths against purposely and knowingly taking life, and while Gaelán was not living there, he chose to accept that rule and train in the manner in which Elyri healers trained. He did not need to be a knight for that.

But he liked to ride and horsemanship was something he excelled at. He also knew a great deal about the animals, what points made one more fit for riding, for labor, for breeding or for battle. He would like to ride like a knight to impress the girls.

He was stirred from his daydreams by a skirmish on the far side of the corral between two men, one a seller and the other, presumably, a buyer. An angry buyer from the sounds of it, though the horse they argued over appeared to be a beautiful specimen, the best in the run. Gaelán knew, however, that some of the worst animals could be made to look spectacular in the right groom's hands, and he guessed that the animal had some flaw that could not be seen from a distance.

A few of the nearby men watched the argument but made no effort to arbitrate until the buyer pulled a knife from his belt and thrust it into the other's belly. Someone yanked the attacker back while someone else caught the injured man as he fell. Without considering what he was doing, Gaelán leaped over the wooden fence, startling horses as he ran, and squeezed through the fence on the other side.

"Someone get a physician!" a man cried.

Kneeling beside the injured man, Gaelán replied, "I am a healer."

"You are a boy."

Gaelán had already ripped the man's tunic open and placed his hands over the gash. There was internal bleeding. He had dealt with that sort of serious injury one other time, with Kavan, and though he was not sure he could repeat his efforts, he was determined to try. He felt he must. This man was Elyri.

Behind him, the attacker broke free, grasped the reins of the horse, about to make off with it until two other men stopped him. The wound was healing under Gaelán's hands, though as usual, his supply of energy was spent in the moment of initial contact and it was difficult to complete the process beneath the gaze of both curious and hostile onlookers. He had told them he was a healer and they expected success, not failure by a student. The internal damage was repaired, his belly no longer filling with blood and Gaelán knew the man was in no danger of bleeding to death, but the external area was still open and bled more than he liked.

"Someone fetch water or wine to cleanse the wound." It was an unnecessary action for most Elyri healers, as a fully trained one could fend off infection from dirt in the wound. But these people might not know that, might not know how quickly a trained healer could close a wound, and would accept that a wound had to be cleaned first. Gaelán hoped the few extra moments would give him the energy he needed to complete the healing.

A flask of wine came sooner than anticipated; he took his time in cleaning the area, the unconscious man flinching and writhing at the alcohol burn. Afterward, Gaelán had just enough energy to close the gash, leaving him none to stand. He had not realized how exhausting working under external pressure would be.

He lifted his head to look at the attacker and asked, "What was the meaning of this attack, sir?"

The man growled and lunged, but was held back by the strong arms around his. "I will not answer you, demon-spawn," he spat.

Gaelán swallowed his first remark and the tears that stung his eyes. Men did not cry when insulted. "You are a criminal, an almost murderer, and a horse thief. You might not talk to me, but you will talk to my father. You will suffer the consequences of your insolence."

"And who is your father that I should quake in his presence?"

The young man pushed up, locking his knees to remain standing against the dizziness he felt. Collapsing would detract from his threat. "Chamberlain Bhríd, Cáner, Duke of Levonne. You have heard of the King's Champion, have you not?" He was pleased to see that the man did know of his father. He looked at the men holding the attacker and said, "Escort this man to the castle." He did not ask. Nobility did not ask for obedience. They made demands. Then he looked at the man at his feet who was awake and staring with wide, grateful eyes. "Sir, are you able to come with me? My father will wish to speak with you."

"I do not want him near me!" the attacker called over his shoulder. "He thought to cheat me! Go home to play with your toys, boy! You have no jurisdiction…"

Gaelán threw back his shoulders. "I do not…if you care to try me, I challenge you to…"

"What is going on here?"

Startled, Gaelán spun to face Justice Corbin. The once-injured Elyri sat up, and with the help of others in the crowd, got to his feet, but no one seemed inclined to speak.

Gaelán did. "I was examining the horses when these two men engaged in argument. I know nothing of the disagreement, Lord Corbin, but I did see him," he pointed, "stab this man. I am bringing both to the keep to speak with my father."

The justice frowned. "I will take care of this, Master Cáner. Thank you for detaining them until I arrived and," he glanced at the Elyri's bloody tunic, "for saving a life. You will be favored in my reports."

The young man swallowed hard, realizing that one way or another, his father would know his son had been out of the keep alone. Gaelán could beg to be kept out of them, but he would not do that in front of the many adults around him. He would face the penalties for his actions like any other man. "I will accompany you to the keep. My business here is done." But it was going to be a long, shaky walk back to the castle. Rather, he decided, like a man facing the gallows.

∾*∾

The sun was setting as he reached the outskirts of inhabitation. As was their habit, the community was gathered in the center of the village around the fire for their meal, meaning Kavan had to pass them to find Wortham and Urian. The villagers looked up when they saw him, smiling with welcome as they bowed and murmured words of respect. The meal appeared to be nearing completion and there was no sign of either of the men he sought; Kavan concluded they had already retired for the night, though Urian was normally inclined to remain in the company of strangers, drinking, conversing, learning their ways.

But the hut they were given to use was empty, Wortham's satchel lay beside one pallet and Urian's whittling tools were scattered across the crudely formed table. Wondering where the men were, Kavan took another opportunity to study his hands and to glance at the packs that belonged to Orynn, feeling the pang of losing her all over again. He could stay in the hut and await his comrades' return, or he could go into the midst of the villagers and take his chances with their greeting. Perhaps they would praise him again.

It did not matter.

He opted for the latter, hunger outweighing anxiety. He knew what they might say, the words he might hear, but he would be a coward no more. The villagers looked up as he returned, bowed their heads and smiled, and though the meal was ending, a boy filled a bowl with some form of grain gruel flavored with fat and meat scraps and offered it to Kavan. With an uneasy shiver, the Elyri bowed his head in gratitude and began to eat, aware of their quiet, reverent but polite stares. It was not a large meal but he found it satisfying after the time spent upon the mountain without food or water. He had fasted before, but this time he felt different in body and soul without knowing why.

A hand on his shoulder interrupted his final mouthful, and Kavan looked into the eyes of the man whose life he had restored. The fellow, healthy now though gaunt of face and body, was quaking, his eyes worshipful and afraid as he knelt with hands outstretched in a gesture of supplication. "málneag," he started in an uneasy voice. The word made Kavan's breath catch, but he resisted the eruption of panic, sensing it was important for this man to speak. Though he could not understand the phrases, Kavan could probe the edges of his thoughts, something he had not had the presence of mind to do in months. He learned that the fellow wanted him to take the leather-bound object he held. Kavan took it reluctantly and upon peeling back the covering, he found a polished, seemingly never-used knife. It was small, the blade no more than four inches long and gleamed of the same unusual alloy the Coryllien daggers were made of. In its hilt was the same smooth, smoky gray crystallized stone.

Kavan looked up from his examination determined to return the item. He barely knew how to use it except for mundane, everyday purposes, and it was undoubtedly one of the village's few items of wealth. The eyes of every individual were upon him, however, waiting for his next act, pleading with him to accept their gift. And the gaze of this man's father, the village elder and leader, studied him with a look that demanded Kavan accept the only gift he could offer in exchange for his son's life. That, and the power Kavan felt in the blade, helped him make his choice. He had no desire to offend his hosts and his interest in the blade's power and origins was too tempting.

"I should not take this," he finally said, clasping the healed man's hands, allowing his intentions to pass through that physical contact so that his words were understood. "Is there anything I can do to repay you? You have been more than generous to my friends and have tolerated my insufferable behavior. There must be something…"

The night bird's song echoed through the surrounding forest, drawing memories of the mountain with it. He knew what to do.

He had one gift he could trade for food, lodging, and assistance in his travels. His stomach lurched at the thought, his throat tightened, and his hands began to shake, causing the knife to drop into the dust. The other man scrambled to retrieve it, returning it to Kavan's hands with a look of fear that suggested he thought he had angered their prophet. Kavan tried to smile to reassure him but knew that the expression looked forced.

Most of the songs he knew with lyrics were hymns and cradlesongs. Uneasy about his unusual voice, he had written few vocal works. It would not matter to these people what the words were, however, as they would not understand them. All that would matter would be the sound, the purity, the passion in song, qualities he knew he could give if he conquered his nerves.

Placing one hand on the man's head to soothe him, Kavan gave. He began with a gentle hymn, a prayer of Saint Kóráhm's in lullaby form he had learned in childhood. His clear, warm voice was barely audible at first, and though his eyes were closed, as they often were when he played, he felt the rapt attention and adoration of his audience as if it was hands upon his skin. They approved. They approved and were in awe. Even without his harp, he could perform, as both Wortham and Orynn had argued he could; he could please others with music still. Discovering it added an element of exultation to his next song, and more to the next, until the long silent bard could no longer contain the emotion and let it erupt into one ecstatic song after another.

The berries they shared at the noon meal had been the most savory treat Wortham had tasted since the onset of their journey, and with the aid of several village children, he and Urian had set out on a gathering expedition that lasted most of the afternoon. The crop would not last many more days before the heat and wildlife stripped the bushes until the next year's harvest. A basket of berries would be a nice supplement, he felt, to their diet. The village had little to offer to sustain them for their travels, beyond water and a sack of milled grain which, on the road, would be good only for the mash or gruel these people often ate. Wortham had not turned down the offering, knowing that some portion of it could be traded for other commodities later or used to feed the horse and mules along the way. It, along with the berries, would have to do.

When the dinner gong sounded, the children scampered back to the village, taking most of their harvest with them, but Urian had consumed his fill of berries as the day passed, and Wortham, in his anxiety over Kavan's safe return, was not hungry. They continued gathering berries until darkness fell. Ready for a night's rest, hoping Kavan would be there so they could be on their way at dawn, Wortham carried one basket and led the gdhededhá, who carried the smaller one, back towards the light of the village fire.

They had not yet reached the outer buildings when Wortham first heard it, and he stopped abruptly, causing Urian to trip and nearly spill the fruit he carried. The captain held his breath and absorbed a sound he had nearly given up hearing again.

Hearing it too, afraid to speak as if it might break the spell, the gdhededhá whispered, "Such unearthly beauty…"

"Milord Cliáth," was Wortham's rough-voiced response.

He could barely believe it but knew that sound was not his imagination. Dragging the gdhededhá along, not caring if the berries spilled, he hurried towards the source, needing to see this marvel. He did not pause to deposit the baskets in their hut but instead pushed through the crowd, straight for the fire, straight for Kavan.

The bard turned his head towards his friend, his song trailing into silence as he met the captain's gaze. What Kavan saw there was not revulsion, but rather tears and quivering lips, an expression of ecstasy that looked out of place on the large bear-like man.

"Milord!" The basket was set down before Wortham rushed to the bard, clasping him to his chest, kissing his head and face in a manner that would have embarrassed Kavan if it was anyone else doing it.

"Wortham." The man was trembling as though he had been afraid he would never see his friend again. Kavan, a hand on each side of the man's face, gently drew him back to look into his eyes. "Wortham, please…I am here. I told you I would be."

Wortham seized the bard's hands as if his life depended on never letting go. He had hoped that something might transpire during the bard's time alone that would restore his hands. Kavan had endured enough; in the captain's eyes, he deserved to be whole again. But such was not the case, and his chest ached with regret.

Something, however, had given Kavan his voice, and for that, Wortham was glad. "Praise k'Ádhá for your return, and your voice."

"Enough, my friend," the bard said with an awkward smile. "They are only words…"

"And they are beautiful, Kavan. Sing for me…for them. I could ask for nothing better." Wortham smiled and kissed the bard's forehead. "Please, Kavan…sing."

❧*❦

The endurance of his physical body was near an end. His arms and legs were broken in more places than he knew. His skin, what remained of it, was raw, bloody, and blistered, barely clinging to the muscle beneath it. In a way that struck him as morbid and perverse, he knew it was a blessing his captives had taken his eyes, as it meant he did not see the thing of horror he had become. But he felt it, every tiny prickle of pain. Coherent thought was no longer possible. No longer did he fear pain; he no longer felt any emotion. If it were not for the unceasing agony, he would believe he was dead already.

He was surprised he was not. Such anguish as he had endured would have killed many men long ago, and he was the first to admit he was weaker than most. When his tormentors blinded him sometime earlier, he had screamed for what felt like an eternity and then lost consciousness. But he had not died. It might have been his misfortune that his body refused to let go of life, or perhaps it was his soul and will that forced him to endure, clinging to the distant sound of an angelic voice that fed his soul's hope. Saint Kóráhm had promised to be with him at the end. The Saint had not yet come, or if he had, the Jermyn had not sensed it. He knew he could not endure much more, however. Whether the Saint came or not, he would die soon. There was no way he could tolerate another day of this degree of suffering.

"Jermyn."

The voice came from the silence, carried on the gentle waves of melody, faint and soft and calming. The k'gdhededhá of Enesfel lifted his head as much as he was able, towards whoever was speaking. What he did know was that this was not the voice of his abductors.

"Yes?" he rasped through his toothless mouth.

A hand rested gently on his dislocated shoulder. There should have been great pain at the touch, but instead, there was comfort.

"It is time, Jermyn. There is no need to endure any longer."

"Time…Kóráhm…have you come…for me…?"

"I have. Are you ready?" Rather than answer, Jermyn allowed his head to droop forward with a sigh of relief. "Give yourself to me."

In the next second, the dank room littered with instruments of torture, blood, and bits of flesh, was quiet. The body of k'gdhededhá Jermyn of Enesfel hung limply in the shackles upon the wall and ceased to move.

❧*❧

Music filled the village until Kavan's strained voice gave way beneath the exuberance of his effort. When he bid the villagers to retire, he was delightedly drained yet too excited to sleep. Such elation did not dissipate easily, nor did he want it too. He wanted to revel in the first wholly positive experience he had enjoyed since Muir's wedding. He watched each person depart and remained by the fire where Wortham had dozed with his strong arms wrapped around Kavan's ankles, as if to disallow the bard to stand, to walk, to leave him again. Not that Kavan intended to. He was content where he was.

"You know peace, átaelá haeles. You cannot know the delight I take in that, how I have lamented at your travail. Your happiness warms my heart."

Kavan sensed that comforting, long-absent presence moments before the man spoke, and though he hung his head in shame at first, he lifted it when the saint settled on the log at his side. "I thank you for what you tried to do…to lead me to this place, though I refused to listen. I was blinded by arrogance and ignorance, but you did not give up. It is a wonder you endured my conceit as long as you did. If it had not been for you and Orynn, I…"

"You would still be bumbling around in your own self-made torment. I knew, though I told her to allow you to find your own way, that she would do everything in her power to lead you to deliverance. It is her nature. It has caused her…difficulty…but she would have it no other way. Nor would I, since I prefer your joy to your sorrow and suffering. It is good you have found your way, for what I have come to tell you, to show you, would have sent you into deeper despair."

"What must you tell me?" Kavan asked in alarm, disliking Kóráhm's tone. "Am I too late? Is the náós beyond redemption? Has something happened to Ártur? Kóráhm, please. Tell me what you have come to say; do not spare me unpleasant news when you have come to deliver it."

Kóráhm laid his hand upon Kavan's, calming his panic despite the unexpected throbbing it awoke in his crippled joints. "I have come to tell you Jermyn has died. I delivered him personally to his rest."

Swallowing the lump in his throat, Kavan looked into the embers of the dying fire. He did not try to hold back the tears that gathered on his lashes. Of those he knew in Rhidam, other than his own family members, he had known Jermyn the longest. The man had been a lowly monk serving the Order of Saint Kóráhm's in Clarys when Kavan made his first journey there to play publically. That had been a fateful day for both of them, setting each on paths that took them into Enesfel in the service of Arlan Lachlan.

The k'gdhededhá was not a young man; his death should be neither a shock nor surprise. Yet it hurt, and it seemed that the Saint would not have come to him if the k'gdhededhá had died naturally.

Kóráhm nodded, his expression grim. "It was not natural, you are correct. It was, by far, the most unnatural death I have been forced to endure for many centuries. Knowing you thought highly of him, I came to tell you, to offer the chance to witness his passing if you choose. But be forewarned; what you see will not be pleasant."

Though the warning troubled him, Kavan offered his hands and whispered, "Show me, Kóráhm, that I may know."

Kóráhm's scarred hands on his were as warm and real as any living man's could be, a mystery Kavan still did not understand. Every excruciating moment of the k'gdhededhá's ordeal passed through that link of minds in a matter of seconds, the sights, the sounds, the smells, the agony, overwhelming the bard with the sheer sum of its brutality and horror. In the background of the man's torment, when the moment of death came, Kavan could hear his own voice faintly singing.

Jermyn had heard him at the end and the song had given him peace.

Kavan convulsed in response to Jermyn's suffering and fell forward from the log on which he had been sitting, waking Wortham.

Kóráhm was gone.

"Milord?" yawned the sleepy captain with worry.

"Go back to sleep, Wortham." The bard's eyes were closed against the ghastly images, and he tried not to choke on his own bile, his own scream, the emotional distress birthed from another man's hell. What Jermyn had endured burned through him, leaving traces of each moment of torture in every muscle and nerve in Kavan's body.

But the captain saw the distress on his friend's face and sat beside him. "What has happened. Your face reveals great pain. Your hands?"

Kavan shook his head, fighting as he did so to bury that suffering rather than succumb to it. "Please, Wortham…you do not want to know what I know. It is too great a burden for any man to carry…"

Wortham grasped his hand to steady him. Kavan's skin felt hot to the touch as if exposed to a fire rather than a fever within. "If it is such a great burden, do not bear it alone. Allow me to share it."

Kavan was reluctant, but he also felt obliged to let his best friend know what had happened to a man they both respected. Perhaps if he shared this pain, it would lessen the terror of it. In a choking voice, he finally said, "In Rhidam…the k'gdhededhá has been tortured, martyred, in the name of peace between Teren and Elyri."

The captain's face fell. "Jermyn is…dead?"

"Tonight," Kavan replied, choosing not to share the images of that death with his friend. Talking about the event had not helped ease his own reaction to it, and he did not want Wortham to suffer as he did. "Kóráhm saw to his repose and saw fit to reveal it to me."

"Kóráhm was here?"

With a nod, the bard helped Wortham to his feet, or perhaps the captain helped him. "I think we should rest. Enesfel awaits healing and we are that source. We leave for Gorbesh in the morning and pray we acquire what we seek swiftly. I hesitate to wait much longer. Enough lives have been lost. I do not want Ártur to be next."

He did not, however, think he would sleep tonight.

❧Chapter 29❧

The Elyri healer rode behind Caol, close enough that anyone watching would know they were traveling together, yet far enough back that he could not be accused of eavesdropping on the conversation between the inquisitor and justice. The healer had been asked to join them to identify a body found before dawn in a fallow field west of Rhidam. From what Ártur heard, there was little left to identify, as if animals had gotten to it. Not for the first time he wished there were others in the Lachlan employ called upon for such unpleasant tasks. No one asked Syl as if she were too sensitive for such things, unless Ártur was unavailable, and no one ever seemed to consider calling Bhríd to the task, as if being a healer and dealing with death were the qualifications necessary to identify the dead.

If Kavan was here, he would do it. Not because he was more at ease with the distastefulness; such occasions gave the bard legitimate excuses to use his power and he welcomed them. But Kavan was not here, and Ártur was left to face whatever grisly form they found.

There was a gaggle of peasants at one side of the road who scattered as the riders drew near. Caol dismounted before his horse stopped and was already circling the body, shooing back those who lingered with an unreadable expression before the healer reached him.

The report had been truthful, if not entirely accurate. The corpse was mutilated, broken, and bloody; they were lucky it was even recognizable as a person. It lay in a crumpled heap, face down in the moist soil, arms beneath its naked torso. It had every appearance of having been pushed from a wagon and abandoned.

"Teren?"

Ártur was circling as well, dreading touching this poor soul to learn what hell it had endured before finding peace in death. "I am not sure. I believe so…" Few Elyri were as heavy as this individual had been, which made it likely to be Teren. "I can confirm it was male."

The inquisitor started to turn it over with the toe of his boot but hesitated. "I hate to do this," he muttered. With one delicate shove, the body rolled until it was sprawled upon its back. Many of the peasants still in the vicinity fled. The eyeless skull, its mouth open in a toothless gasp, was bloody, hairless, and blistered. There was no visual way to identify this man and the healer was but one in the group to nearly lose their stomach's contents over the sight.

"If it is the same to you," he choked as he inched closer to better examine the corpse, "I should like to read him somewhere more private." Whatever he learned would be traumatizing. He would rather not have an audience. Squatting, he noticed something on the man's left hand, something it appeared no one else had seen. A ring hung loosely upon one dislocated finger. Using every ability he had, Elyri or otherwise, Ártur closed his eyes and senses to push emotion away as he pulled that ring free. The contact with the object, however, was enough to confirm what he had already guessed. They knew this man.

Justice Corbin caught his eye, assuming that the healer had learned more than he cared to, wondering what the man had removed from the dead man's hand. He helped the healer to his feet and asked, "Do we take him back or shall we bury him here?"

"k'Ádhá no!" the healer cried with more force than he meant to. Struggling to restrain his first impulses, he continued, "I would like to take him back to Rhidam for a thorough examination. This is by far the worst incident Enesfel has seen."

"You think it was torture then?" the justice grunted.

"There is no other explanation," Caol said in a schooled, neutral voice. "No one gets like this naturally…after what he must have suffered, I think the poor man deserves a decent burial. We should learn what we can of how this happened and see he is put to rest."

Two of the soldiers who had ridden with them were called to assist as Caol and Darius maneuvered the corpse onto a large canvas, which was then bound tightly to keep the body inside and intact before heaving it up onto the back of the inquisitor's gray charger. During the entire effort, the healer looked dazed, wearing a sick expression Caol knew he was not going to like.

It was a silent trip back to Rhidam, except for a short discussion about where to take the body for analysis. It was decided he would be taken to a place Caol knew, where they would be less likely to be disturbed. It also seemed wisest to not let word get out until after the King learned of the latest death. Secrecy seemed wisest for now.

"Especially," sighed the healer as the body was placed on a table for examination, "since this has the potential to be extremely volatile."

"Why?" asked the inquisitor as he began to untie the bindings.

"This man," Ártur said in a broken voice as he dug in the pocket of his tunic and placed the ring in the inquisitor's palm, "was, until very recently, the k'gdhededhá of Enesfel."

⮞*⮜

"You thought to challenge that man to a duel?" Bhríd did not know if he should be amused, proud, or horrified at his youngest son for the risk he had taken in leaving the keep without word to anyone, breaking up a fight, healing a man publically, and nearly threatening a duel to an older, and likely more skilled, opponent.

Gaelán shrugged, trying not to stare at the floor or shuffle his feet. "It was the first thought that came into my head."

"And a foolish one! You are lucky Justice Corbin arrived when he did…not that accepting a duel from a child would be…"

"I am not a child!"

"Oh no?" asked the chamberlain, staring at his son with annoyance. "What miracle has brought about such an abrupt change and when did it occur? Gaelán, you are becoming a man; it will happen soon enough. But you are, for another seven months at least, a boy. Not a child in the true sense, but you are not legally an adult. You know that. You have great intelligence and drive, I know, but being a man is more than age or wielding a sword. It is also about wisdom, wisdom you do not yet have, the wisdom, for example, to know better than to challenge a much older, larger opponent to a duel when you know you cannot win. Also, this rashness of late is unnerving and not adult-like. I admire your tenacity, but please, for your mother's sake and my own, do not seek out trouble. Do as you are told by people who know the risks of the world. Times are dangerous for us; I would not want to lose you prematurely to such recklessness."

Gaelán saw none of the expected disapproval in his father's face, but rather honesty, love, and concern. There was also a connection there, one he did not share with his mother and certainly did not have with Tayte. It was a matter of Elyri power, realizing that he was his father's son, that his father considered him to be Elyri in a way he did not with Tayte. "I will do as you ask, father. I did not mean to…"

Diona's voice interrupted his apology moments before the princess entered the room with Tusánt and Khwílen at her sides. The Elyri gdhededhá had spent much of his time in Rhidam with either the princess or gdhededhá Tusánt, and occasionally with Ártur or Caol. Something was going on, some secret the four of them shared to which Bhríd had not yet been initiated. He suspected that when it was important for him to know, he would be told. Her laughter stopped abruptly as she realized the dayroom was occupied.

"Are we interrupting you, Lord Cáner?" Tusánt asked.

The chamberlain looked at his son and said, "I think we are done." His expression suggested that if they needed to repeat this discussion, Gaelán would not get off unpunished.

"Stay, Lord Cáner," said the princess. "Lord Dugan and Justice Corbin have asked us here; they and Ártur should arrive shortly to brief us on a body found this morning."

Understanding he was not welcome in this discussion, but fearing, after hearing who would be involved, that the body in question belonged to Kavan, Gaelán skulked out of the room. He had no desire to hear any more about dead bodies, and if it did belong to Kavan, he would rather never hear of it at all. Bhríd, however, frowned and asked, "Another one?"

"I do not have details, but we will, soon enough. I beseech you, however, to keep what is discussed in this room between those here. It is not to be uttered to anyone, including Hagan."

"The King's chamberlain must hide something from him?" Bhríd crossed his arms, leaning back in his chair with a skeptical expression.

"If you find the idea distasteful, you are under no obligation to stay and hear this. The choice is yours. It is my opinion, and Lord Dugan's, that Hagan gaining knowledge of this investigation would jeopardize its success."

It was at that moment that the trio they awaited entered the room. Of the three, none but the healer's face bore any expression; he looked pale, shocked, and sad. Bhríd studied his cousin and knew that this would be no ordinary tale. He nodded to the princess, making his choice to agree to her terms.

"Do you have any objections to allowing Lord Cáner in on this discussion, Lord Dugan?" the princess asked.

Caol shook his head, taking a chair but immediately rising again. He paced when he was troubled; all in the room knew it except Khwílen. "I think he should be included. This could directly influence his life and the welfare of his family. Have you told him anything?"

"There was no time before your arrival," she admitted, "and I think you are the best person to explain this."

With a shrug and a sigh, knowing he had the most information of any in the room, Caol made sure the door was closed and locked before beginning in a rough, subdued voice. "Suspicion began the day Arlan was buried. dedhá Claide called upon Hagan and asked that he dismiss the Elyri employed by the Crown. Not that there are many, but when the King pointed that out to him and refused to comply, Claide made inferences that, while he would do everything he could to support the King, he would not be responsible for anything that might go wrong because of that choice. The King at first thought it was a threat and said as much to Milady, but he later decided he had misinterpreted the dedhá's words.

"At Milady's insistence, I set people to follow Claide to see if there was reason to believe he had threatened the King. He frequents a house at the edge of the city, a house that has seen much unusual activity in the short time it has been inhabited. The man we captured who was responsible for the head upon the náós signpost was seen at this house talking with Claide.

"Then there was the lesson he gave on Dhágdhuán's Eve at the Gathering, when much of Rhidam, including the other dedhá and Milady, heard his anti-Elyri rhetoric condoning slaughter without actually uttering the word Elyri. The k'dedhá was concerned and took action; he reprimanded Claide, informed him there would be penalties if he spoke that way again, and sent a messenger to Clarys, asking for the k'dedhá's aid. The messenger did not arrive, has not been seen since his departure. Jermyn spoke to k'dedhá Khwílen and the two traveled to Clarys. It seems the k'dedhá has little concern for the Elyri outside Elyria, which is distressing on its own. Within days of that trip, k'dedhá Jermyn was abducted while Claide is conveniently out of town where no one, not even his fellow dedhá, knows where he is or how to contact him to tell him what has happened."

The inquisitor scratched his cheek. "I admit that each of these is circumstantial and subjective, particularly when taken alone. But taken together, when including his frequent absences from, and evasion of, religious duties, it does look suspicious. It is our opinion, both Diona's and mine, that while he may not have direct involvement in the resurgence of anti-Elyri activity in Rhidam, he may be working behind the scenes encouraging it. I mean to catch him at it, if it is true, because no man of suspicious morals should be allowed in a position with the amount of influence he has. Neth is a prime example of what happens when such a man is in power."

"Why keep this from the King?" the chamberlain asked.

"Think, Bhríd," Caol said, sounding exasperated as if the man should already know the answer. "The King demands concrete proof of everything. His faith in the infallibility of the dedhá is such that, without something more tangible, he would either call off the investigation or say something to Claide that might tip him to our inquiry. I think it is our responsibility to be certain that Claide's first words to the King were not a threat to his life."

The chamberlain studied his cousin who had not yet spoken and appeared not to be listening. A brief psychic touch indicated that the healer was seeking contact with Kavan, but Bhríd's interference broke Ártur's concentration. The healer's bloodshot eyes closed.

"What has this to do with the body discovered this morning," asked Tusánt. "Was it another Elyri? What has happened?"

Ártur shook his head. "No, he was not Elyri…though I almost wish he were. The individual was freshly deceased, no more than six hours before he was dumped and found. All fingers were broken, as were several other bones…arms, legs, ribs, pelvis. The entire body was covered with bruises, welts, cuts, blistered burns, lacerations and more blood than…" He shook his head with a shiver of distaste. "The skull was fractured in a few places from the blows of a blunt object. It appeared that the hair had been ripped from the skull, all of the teeth…some extracted, some knocked loose, skin peeled away, and his eyes had been gouged from his head."

"My word…" It was Khwílen's voice but it was the sentiment reflected on every face in the room. The princess's face was the whitest it had ever been.

"Who did this? Who was he to deserve such…?"

"We do not know who did it," Ártur said. "His torturers were hooded, in dark robes, their faces hidden. I could not see them when I read him. Even the voices came as distorted and unnatural, due to injuries he received early in the ordeal…and much of the time, he was blindfolded or sightless; there was little to see. And he was in too much pain to process information accurately. Wherever he was held was not familiar to him…or me. The worst part is that it does bear directly upon Lord Dugan's investigation." His gaze dropped and he wrapped his arms around his middle. He did not want to finish, did not want to speak the inevitable, but they needed to know.

Everyone held their breath. Ártur stood at the window, not wanting to utter the name. Admitting this aloud would make it undeniable. Kavan, his mind screamed. Come home.

"For k'Ádhá's sake, Lord MacLyr, please finish," said Tusánt, twisting his hands nervously.

With a reluctant sigh and without looking back, Ártur croaked, "It is k'gdhededhá Jermyn."

Silence. He wanted to leave, unable to bear the shock in the room. When the silence was finally broken, it was the princess who spoke. "I will personally see that Claide rots on a spike for this."

"Milady!"

She glared at the man who dared to chastise her. "No one will stop me, Lord Justice. I know he is behind this. I need no proof or account."

"What of the Corylliens? It might be them and not..."

"You do not believe that, Lord Justice, I see it in your eyes. This was retaliation, the act of a man desperate to protect himself. A man who hopes to see the Elyri in Enesfel murdered...a man who..." She looked abruptly at Caol. "Where is the body?"

The inquisitor was not going to give in, regardless of her demands. "In a place I have rented under guard by Denyan and Avner. We can trust them; I thought it best not to show anyone else the...ugliness."

"Good." It was the princess's turn to pace. "I want word of the k'dedhá 's death to go no further than this room."

"Milady?"

"There will be no argument. Do you remember when I asked what would happen if the k'dedhá died, Lord Healer? From what dedhá Khwílen has said, it is unlikely k'dedhá Dórímyr will come to appoint someone, particularly when he learns that the last k'gdhededhá was tortured to death. That will mean an election, one dedhá Claide might win. We cannot take that risk. As long as everyone believes k'dedhá Jermyn is missing, not dead, he cannot force an election...can he?"

"Not initially," Tusánt agreed. "But it will eventually become obvious that the k'gdhededhá is not coming back..."

"And if," remarked Darius, "as you suspect, dedhá Claide knows the k'dedhá is dead..."

Caol smirked, seeing what the princess was suggesting. "But he cannot claim the k'dedhá is dead without raising questions about how he knows it to be true. If we wait too long to reveal his death, however, it will look like the Crown has something to hide...possibly being interpreted as protecting the murderers. If Claide puts that idea into anyone's head and convinces people that the Elyri are responsible for the k'dedhá 's death...and the Crown knows..."

"It would be a disaster for Hagan's reign, for everyone," the princess whispered. "But I do not think we have a choice. If we can keep his passing from the public for a week or two, it is that much longer we can keep Claide on a leash. If we are fortunate, it may be long enough to learn something with which to condemn him."

Tusánt spoke. "But he must be buried. How do we…?

"Saint Kóráhm's," replied Khwílen. "It would be, by necessity, an unmarked site until you choose to acknowledge his death, and his burial will not receive the attendance he deserves, I'm afraid. The absence of too many of you from Rhidam will look suspect, especially if Claide starts seeking answers. I can give reason to take Tusánt with me overnight and the two of us can bury him. Is that acceptable?"

"Acceptable, no…but it will have to do," said the inquisitor. "We can't store his corpse somewhere and hope it is not found in the meantime…and explaining a secret burial later may be tricky…but it is the best we can work with for now. The rest of us will need to continue as usual as if nothing has changed."

Ártur shuddered. "Bring the…bring him here, Caol. Using the Gate in the lower oratory will be the safest…"

"And I will see to it that your path is clear for getting here undetected," offered the Justice.

"I will make certain Hagan and the servants will not interfere," the princess promised.

"I have already preserved the body to prevent decay, but the sooner we take him somewhere else…"

"The less chance there is that someone will find him," agreed the inquisitor. "We should take a message to dedhá Rankin regarding Tusánt's visit to Saint Kóráhm's."

gdhededhá Khwílen stood. "Once the formality of burial is over, I shall make a second call upon k'gdhededhá Dórímyr and let him know what has occurred because of his apathy. I will also press upon him the necessity of not speaking of this to Claide…not that I think he would come to speak to anyone."

"Then you might want this." Placing the k'gdhededhá's ring in the gdhededhá's hand, Caol continued. "Please, pray for the k'dedhá for us. And pray that both he and k'Ádhá understand what we are doing."

With a grimace caused by the images the ring gave him, Khwílen replied, "I think we are doing exactly what they would have us do."

❧*❧

There had been music all day in an effort to erase from his mind the horrific images he had been shown, humming mostly since the bard's throat was raw and hoarse from hours of singing the night before. But it had been music, and the sound, the pleasure Kavan found in the simple act of humming, had an uplifting effect on each of them. It did not ease his inner turmoil but it offered a distraction he felt sorely in need of.

Though he had no proof, Wortham was sure they traveled further in that one day than they normally did, bolstered on the wings of song.

Across the fire they had built at the end of their day's sojourn, Urian was whittling a figure made of fragrant rosewood. Kavan focused on the sound as he tried to will his overactive mind to put those gruesome images to rest. Wortham had the first watch.

"Milord?"

Kavan rolled towards the captain and looked at him. "Yes?"

The captain glanced at the gdhededhá who kept whittling and seemed not to have heard the exchange. "The death…was it terrible?"

Propping up on one elbow, Kavan hesitated to answer, thinking about the horrific implications of such a death. He wanted to drive those thoughts from his mind, but obviously the nature of Jermyn's death weighed heavy on Wortham as well and demanded answers.

Such memories made Kavan feel ashamed about how he had endured his own trials when Jermyn's ordeal had been much worse.

"Do you wish to see? I can show you…but, be warned. I will spare you the physical sensations, but what you will see is bad enough." He held forth his hand and waited to see if Wortham would take it.

There was no hesitancy. Wortham clutched his hand around Kavan's and closed his eyes, tensing in preparation for the unpleasantness to come. Rather than flash the images through the connection, the bard allowed them to fade in, stay clear long enough for Wortham to take in the detail, and then it was abruptly taken away. Kavan lay back, though after dredging up that imagery, he knew sleep would elude him. Instead, he watched Wortham stare glassy-eyed into the fire as he tried to assimilate what he had been shown.

"Do you know who has done this?" the soldier finally whispered. He looked and sounded as if he would be sick.

"I know no more than you; I would rather not dwell on it. It was a horrific way to die." Compared to the k'gdhededhá's travail, Kavan's own was nothing. He felt humiliated.

Wortham's response was a nod as he continued to stare at the fire. Sensing Kavan's shift of mood, however, he put his hand reassuringly upon the bard's shoulder, seeking comfort for himself as well.

The captain's reassuring, loving touch allowed Kavan to sleep.

❧*❧

Khwílen and Tusánt made it from Caol's safe house to the oratory Gate, and then to Saint Kóráhm's chellé, without incident. The gdhededhá were called together to witness the solemn burial and told that, for their safety, they could not be told the identity of the first man to be interred in the chellé's cemetery. When the time came, they would learn the truth. There were no hymns for this one, no words of praise or remembrance for the unnamed soul they had taken as one of their own. For the time being, Khwílen solicited prayers for the peaceful repose of a martyr, whose brutal, torturous execution would bring changes in the Faith and in the politics of Elyriá and Enesfel. He bid them pray that these changes were for the good, because if they were not, many more people, Teren and Elyri, would endure the same sort of end. It was a death the k'gdhededhá wished on no one. No one, perhaps, except the ones responsible for this deed.

❧*❧

Princess Diona had not left the day room since learning of the k'gdhededhá's death. Her initial outrage, while still present, had faded to be eclipsed by deep grief. So many people had died recently, several of whom she had loved and respected. And Kavan was gone. Her world was shrinking, losing its foundation, and she was more afraid than she had ever been. Afraid, with no one to comfort and reassure her as her father would have done, or as Kavan had done when she was younger, before her pursuit of his affection drove him away.

She leaned against the sill, looking over the courtyard, having noticed the large group of men who came to the palace gates. Reinforcements, she presumed, since she knew her brother had called for men from around the kingdom as supplemental city patrol. She doubted it would do little more than offer the citizens peace of mind. She hoped that was enough.

"Milady?"

The princess did not turn to look at the woman behind her. "What is it, Belda? I told you I do not want dinner…"

"There is someone to see you."

The serving woman stepped aside, allowing heavy male footfalls to enter the room. Diona turned as the man said "Greetings, milady…"

"Espen!"

Not caring how he might take the gesture, the princess threw herself against him and wept, grieving for her father and Jermyn simultaneously. She had never been happier to see the Harcourt prince, and as he enfolded her in his arms and allowed her to cry, she knew she would marry this man. Regardless of what she felt for anyone else, Espen was the one person she could not imagine living without. Not to marry him meant losing him forever, and that she could not risk.

Holding her, Prince Espen wanted to kiss her tears, take the burdens she carried and make them his own. He could not recall her ever showing this sort of weakness; whatever had happened, perhaps the death of her father, had shaken her more than he thought possible. He did not want to release her and was thus content to keep her close for as long as she allowed. If it was to be their last time together, at least he would have this memory to savor.

When she drew away from him, he could see she was embarrassed by her outburst and struggling to regain composure. "What is it, Diona?" he asked, his hands dropping as she moved beyond his grasp. She did not go far, and when she stopped, she turned and came back to him. "You cannot be so pleased to see me that you weep…?"

He almost kicked himself for saying it, particularly when she stared with wide eyes and declared, "Of course I am pleased to see you! I thought you would not come…you would not believe how that thought hurt." She paused to wipe her face on the kerchief he handed to her. "I have learned something terrible today and it…can you keep a secret, even from my brother?"

Hearing that she had missed him, that the possibility of perpetual separation was as painful to her as it was to him, gave the prince the courage to say, "For you, I can do anything," without stopping to think about the implications of such a statement. He guided her to the nearby settee and pulled her gently down beside him.

"k'dedhá Jermyn was found this morning, after being recently abducted. He was tortured…mutilated from what I was told though I did not see him. I could not bear to. First my mother, then Bertram. Captain Cornell, my father...now this. When will it stop? Must everyone I love die before it ends?"

She started to cry again and Espen drew her close. She did not resist. "I will do what I can to see that no one else you love dies, Diona. I swear it."

❧*❧

For the first time in his life, Khwílen Kesábhá wished he could do what many Teren did when they found themselves overwhelmed, depressed, and frustrated; he wanted to get staggering, blindingly drunk. It might have helped him feel better, or at the very least, he would have been unable to feel anything, particularly if his body rejected the alcohol and it killed him.

The room he was in, with its red velvet drapes and canopied bed, was one of the most sumptuous rooms the k'gdhededhá had to offer in Clarys. Even the meal he was given was more elaborate than most he recalled from his years of service within these walls. *Consolation for my sorrow,* he muttered as he lifted the lid from a tray to reveal the roast fowl within. *Or perhaps an attempt at appeasement.*

While k'gdhededhá Dórímyr had seemed honestly saddened by the news of k'gdhededhá Jermyn's death, and appalled by the manner in which it occurred, he brushed off Khwílen's requests with the excuse that he had too many duties to attend in Clarys, making a trip to Rhidam impossible. *And he quite rightly feared for his safety.* Also, he argued, not knowing any gdhededhá in Enesfel, he was not qualified to choose Jermyn's successor. A poor excuse, as Khwílen knew that the standard procedure was to interview candidates without the need of knowing them. Nor would he justify choosing another from those in Elyriá and sending him to Enesfel, be he Teren or Elyri.

Enesfel was simply too dangerous. Enesfel would have to select their k'gdhededhá from the Faith leaders they had on hand.

Was that not a risk of the Faith, to go amongst others and serve, whether safe or not? And what, Khwílen asked, if the successor chosen was gdhededhá Claide or someone worse? That would be the worst error the k'gdhededhá could commit, sanctioning the deaths of his people and countless others by refusing to intercede.

Rather than respond with the argument Khwílen expected, or throwing him out for his rudeness, Dórímyr developed a sudden headache and asked to resume their discussion later. That had been early this morning, over nine hours ago. Gauging by the others going in and out of the k'gdhededhá's chambers, Khwílen knew he was dismissed, that the discussion was closed, even if this token of goodwill was meant to make him believe otherwise.

He was faced with a difficult choice. He saw no option but to expose the k'gdhededhá's shortfall to other gdhededhá throughout Elyriá. Any man who could allow his people to travel into dangerous lands without support, without being willing to intervene when it was another member of the Faith sanctioning the slaughter, did not deserve to serve as the highest officiate in the Faith. Khwílen wanted nothing more than to drag the pompous man from his post, strip him of any honor he might have, and replace him with someone more caring and less politically inclined.

Yet Saint Kóráhm's had recently opened and Lord Cliáth had personally selected Khwílen for the post of k'gdhededhá there. Could he abandon that post so soon after accepting it? What would the Duke want him to do? It took little thought to come up with an answer based solidly on the Duke's own life choices. Kavan would tell him to follow his heart and faith, to do what needed to be done for the greater good of the people. If Khwílen succeeded, while it might not save the lives of those Elyri already in Enesfel, it might prevent future losses. If he failed, he would be defrocked, losing any chance to serve at Saint Kóráhm's as anything other than a common man.

But that was an acceptable risk. Being a common man in the service of k'Ádhá and Saint Kóráhm was nothing to be ashamed of. After all, that was what Kavan was. Khwílen knew he was the one man, of those who knew the k'gdhededhá's stance, who could expose him. He also knew no one else was willing to take the risk.

Tonight, after eating as much of this meal as he could stomach and writing a flowery letter of apology for the upset he had caused and his hasty departure, he would return to the chellé. He would set his affairs in order and arrange for someone to take up his duties during his temporary leave. As soon as that was done, he would return to Elyriá. No k'gdhededhá had ever been challenged in Elyriá's history. War would be declared on Dórímyr, a war that Khwílen had every intention of winning.

❧Chapter 30❧

"What do you mean k'gdhededhá is missing?"

Tusánt could not believe it, knowing what he knew, but it almost seemed true that Claide had no knowledge of Jermyn's absence. Almost. If not for the seeds of doubt planted by the princess and Caol about Claide's involvement in this unseemly anti-Elyri business, Tusánt might have accepted the man's story about visiting his ailing sister. Tusánt knew Claide had a sister in Chantel; she was not a strong woman and it was possible that the gdhededhá's story was valid. He had left hastily, without word, and claimed she had died while he was with her.

With a sigh, barely managing to maintain eye contact, Tusánt answered, "He was abducted the same night that you…you were not here and could not be found. Lord Dugan and Justice Corbin are investigating the matter."

"Do they have suspects? Is there any way I can assist?"

To himself, the Elyri thought, 'Turn yourself in.' Aloud he replied, "I do not know if there is anything you can do, or if they have suspects. You will have to ask them. But if I may…you are the senior gdhededhá by three months, you should remain in Rhidam until the issue is resolved."

"Resolved? Do you mean until we receive word of his death?"

The Elyri took notice of the remark and of Claide's not quite hidden regret at having said it. But because he did not want to tip the man off, Tusánt shrugged and replied, "There is no reason to assume his abductors plan to kill him. Lord Justice says it is early; they might seek a ransom."

Claide snorted. "Is there reason to believe the abductors want a ransom?"

"You will have to ask the Inquisitor. I am not given the details. But I would think, if his death was their intent, they would have killed him in his bed rather than take him. I was the one to find him missing, his room pillaged, but that is all I know. k'gdhededhá Kesábhá of Saint Kóráhm's was here, involved I think in the investigation, and took the news to k'gdhededhá Dórímyr, but we have heard nothing from Clarys. It could take weeks for the k'gdhededhá to gain an audience."

He was careful not to give Claide details of the investigation, not the Elyri reading the room, not the discovered hat pin, and definitely not the discovery of Jermyn's body. He hated mentioning Khwílen's name, but Claide had to know that the news had been taken to Clarys in the hopes that he did not attempt to do it himself, if he even would. Tusánt doubted Claide could tell he knew more than he was sharing.

"I suppose there are things to do, duties to perform, speaking with the King and the inquisitor. There are no gdhededhá to fill our ranks; we will be required to do more. If you will inform the others, I would like to meet this evening to discuss…"

He did not finish the sentence as he left the room, assuming Tusánt would know what he meant because he was Elyri. Such a test was galling, particularly since it seemed to Tusánt that it was some sort of effort to incriminate him, some means of getting the Elyri gdhededhá out of Rhidam, either for failure to do his duties, should he pretend he had not heard his instruction, or because he was Elyri. Let Claide hate him, he decided. Tusánt was not going to be accused of shirking his responsibilities. He was not going to show fear of this man.

❧*❧

"A message from Owain? For me?" The King rarely conversed with that particular member of his family; if there was news from Fiara, it usually reached him through his sister.

"Rather official looking." Caol did not mention that he already knew the general contents of the letter; Onea's message had outlined it for him. While the King broke the seal and read it, Caol eyed Prince Espen and Princess Diona. Since the Hatu prince's arrival, Caol had yet to see the two of them look at each other at the same time. There were stolen glances, the sort shared between people who were courting and did not want the world to know, but the inquisitor had no idea what had passed between them upon the Prince's arrival. Espen's gaze seemed intense and confused to Caol, and Diona's reminded him of the same devouring looks of longing his wife had once given him. What they needed, he thought, was time alone in a locked room with no political crisis to distract them.

"Lord Dugan," said the King in a reluctant tone, "it appears your source was correct. Neth is interested in our affairs, or at least King Merkar is."

"What does he say?" Princess Diona asked while Caol gave a shrug to the hesitant compliment from his nephew-king.

"He captured three spies; they were arrested for murdering two Elyri women and the family with whom they were staying. He asks if I want to question them. He also wants permission to execute them. He sounds angry."

The strength of darker emotion restored some of Diona's spark and color. "I would hope so. Uncle has never been one to take affronts lightly. I hope you are going to allow the execution."

"Will you question them?" asked Espen.

The King shook his head as he replaced the message into its leather travel tube. "There is little point. He says these are three of Merkar's elite; they will not likely break under torture. They told him what they did because they mistakenly believed he was an ally. And the risk to transport them here…or for me to travel there…is too great. If they would rather die than talk, then we should grant their wish. Diona, have you sent him word about k'gdhededhá…"

"Two days ago, with instructions to the messenger to travel as quickly as possible. Owain will receive it within the next few days."

"Then I will draft a second letter and grant his request for execution. Excuse me, Prince Espen. I would like to do this quickly in order that we may resume our discussion."

The prince nodded. "Of course. I am here to assist, not keep you from duty."

The King left the stateroom but Caol lingered, waiting until he felt sure they were alone. "Onea is seeking the identity of Mr. Heward, but it may be some time before she finds anything; she does not have access to a census record or anything like that. I think we should enlist Owain's aid in this; he can look where she cannot. If Merkar's men are killing in the same way as the Corylliens here, it seems certain there is a connection. And from what I just learned…you might want to be extra vigilant in the days ahead. Claide has returned to Rhidam."

"He left before the k'dedhá disappeared and returns after the body is dumped…" murmured the princess.

Espen leaned his elbows on the table. "Coincidence?"

When a nod from the princess indicated that Espen had been included in the particulars of Rhidam's dark events, the inquisitor replied. "Possibly, but I rarely believe in happenstance. I do have someone confirming his alibi and will let you know what I learn."

❧*❧

Kicking the edge of the bed upon which he sat, Gaelán watched Ártur pack a few articles of clothing in his leather satchel. "What if I'm not ready for this," the young man whined. "I am not fully trained…you've said it yourself. I'm not even an apprentice yet. What if someone needs more help than I can give them? What if this dream…or whatever it is…comes back?"

Ártur smiled to reassure him and patted his thigh. "Then your father will fetch me. It should not be many more days before your newest cousin is born and once I am certain the baby and Syl are strong, I will return. But it is likely Syl will wish to remain in Bhryell where the children are safe, which means I will travel back and forth frequently. The welfare of the Lachlan house is going to be more and more on your shoulders, Gaelán, until Syl believes it is safe enough to bring the children to Rhidam. Do you understand?"

"Yes," he pouted, "But I do not like it. Besides, you said you were going to take me to meet bhydáni Tíbhyan the next time you go."

"I will take you; I promise. I have not been able to get away; the King doesn't want me going as it is. He allows it because Syl is like a mother to him and he knows she will be angry if I am not there when the baby comes. Besides," he buckled the satchel and slung it over his shoulder, "I need someone here in case Kavan returns, or in case there is word from him. I left word with everyone that messages for me are to be given to you or your father. Will you guard them for me?"

That particular duty made the young man draw his shoulders back in pride. "For k'aendhá Kavan I can do it," he agreed.

Tousling Gaelán's hair, the healer smiled. "You want to be treated like a man. This is your opportunity to prove you deserve to be treated that way. Live up to your responsibilities, do not shirk them, and you may be quite pleased with the results. I will leave tonight. After I leave this in the oratory, is there anything else you want to talk about?"

"No. Just, teach me to heal the way you do. I want to be the best healer in the world while you're gone."

❧ * ❧

It was the middle of the second month, with little snow and less rain. Prince Owain chewed his knuckle as he looked over his books, trying to project the earnings for the upcoming year by studying the previous ones. It would be low, he suspected. The soil surrounding his city was not agriculturally profitable. It fed his people, but that was all. Fiara had to content itself with the production of lumber and livestock. As he had long ago established methods for maintaining resources without cutting down every tree on his lands, the lumber industry would not be harmed much by the lack of moisture…unless there was fire. But livestock and what little farming there was needed water, and the rains had not been kind to them this year. He hoped to develop some other means of income to supplement the deficit ahead.

Piran was still with him, as Owain had been unable to find a good opportunity to travel to Rhidam and then Káliel. He would not dream of sending his young son on such a journey with only retainers to protect him; if anything happened to Piran, Gabrielle would not forgive him. He would never forgive himself.

When he returned from the survey of his lands, he found two messages waiting. One was from Princess Diona, the other from Muir. Since he had not expected a prompt reply to his letter, Owain guessed that she was writing about some other matter. He had not heard from Muir since the wedding thus he set aside Diona's letter in favor of reading his son's.

Muir was well and happy, enjoying his newly married life and settling into Káliel's customs. But his purpose for writing was more business than pleasure and had nothing to do with his marriage. He wrote of events on Pháne, of the outpost being constructed and manned there to discourage trespassers. That someone thought to obtain entry was unsettling, but to learn that the man who led them, one Anri Heward, spoke with a Nethite accent was cause for concern, particularly after having apprehended those three spies. If this man was one of Merkar's agents, and if the Nethite King was interested in Coryllien's resting place, that could not be good.

Four months, he thought, memories of Pháne turning his thought toward Kavan. He had the feeling that most had begun to give up hope for the bard's return. If Kavan ever did return from self-exile, it would not be safe for him in Enesfel. Owain knew he would be lucky to ever see the bard again. All because of this uncontrollable rash of violence and the princess.

Feeling uncharacteristic annoyance with her, he picked up her letter. It was not as casual as expected. k'gdhededhá Jermyn had been abducted, and later found tortured and murdered, though this was news she bid him reveal to no one as the security of the kingdom and the King's life were at stake. She bid him stay in Fiara and control the lands there, saying she would summon him when he was needed, or as soon as the news about Jermyn's death was made public.

He held the page to the heat of the sputtering candle, watching Diona's words turn to flame and ash. He would stay as asked, because he had other matters, such as his prisoners, to tend to. By burning her letter, no one would suspect he knew of the k'gdhededhá's death, though he wondered what the secret had to do with national security.

Another friend dead. His generation was falling away one by one. Brenna, Deidre, Minos, Arlan, and now Jermyn. Other than the Elyri, there were few left in positions of power who would remember the years before Arlan had assumed the throne. Few who could recall that Owain Lachlan had once been king, had once been a man feared and loathed. Soon the passage of years would take him too, leaving the Elyri in the Lachlan court to tell his tale. He wondered often if any of them viewed it as a tale worth telling.

To stave off encroaching morbid depression, Owain took out a quill and parchment. He would write a letter to his wife. Soon he would go to her and take Piran with him. With her was the one place he most longed to be.

❱*❱

His father glared across the table; Ártur did not need to see it to feel the triumph in the elder man's eyes. Early in life, when he realized his natural gifts would take him in a direction different than his father or brother, Ártur had been forced to accept that his father would be forever disappointed. Perhaps that had been the deciding factor that compelled him to seek employ in Enesfel, to offer his services to the Lachlan House. Every village, town, or city in Elyriá boasted at least two healers; most places had more. In Enesfel, in fact, anywhere outside of Elyriá, there were few Elyri healers available. Teren doctors were adequate, but in some instances, such as the battlefield or life-threatening injuries, only an Elyri healer could save a life.

Tám MacLyr approved even less of his son's choice of employers than of his career. If a child was born with healing gifts, he or she was trained to use them. It was expected, required by centuries of custom. It was believed that not to train a healer child was to do irreparable damage to that child and to society. With healers common in Dháná's family, the harp maker had resigned himself to that path for his youngest son, grateful that of his three children, only one had been born a healer. But at the time Ártur accepted the post of healer to King Innis Lachlan's court, few Elyri took service abroad. It was considered too dangerous by any but the most adventurous individuals. Ártur did not consider himself adventurous…but he had gone anyhow.

There had been little anti-Elyri violence during Ártur's tenure in Enesfel. Bowen Lachlan had persecuted them, but he had persecuted everyone and his reign had been mercifully short. Ártur had returned home during the years between King Donal's death and Prince Arlan's bid for the throne and was spared that brief, treacherous time. Of course, he had gone back to Enesfel with Prince Arlan and took Kavan with him, despite his father's wishes. Or more precisely, Kavan had sworn himself to the prince's cause and the healer agreed to join him, wanting more than anything to keep his cousin safe.

Most knew there was little love shared between Tám MacLyr and his half-brother's sole child. Tám resented and feared the boy's differences, his abilities, his spirituality, and the fact that Kavan had no interest in the family trade had not helped. As the last of the Cliáth bloodline, Kavan should, in Tám's eyes, continued to make harps as generations of Cliáths had done. As it turned out, Kavan had little aptitude for making them; his passion was the music he could create with his family's instrument.

That had been marginally useful to Tám, as it provided an immediate means of testing the quality of any instrument he crafted. But then Kavan was expelled from the house over religious differences and an embarrassing, to Tám, confrontation between Kavan and the leader of the Faith that caused the two to cease speaking to one another. Kavan had adapted to life as a performer, turning his back on his uncle, and at the first opportunity fled Elyriá to escape Tám's resentment, as Ártur had done many years before.

The man's attitude now was no surprise to Ártur, but it did sting.

"I did not suggest my return to Bhryell was permanent…"

"But Ártur…the stories…"

"aene," he sighed, looking from his mother to his wife, who turned her gaze away. "I am in no immediate danger. The palace is well-guarded and Bhríd, Gaelán, and I are allowed nowhere outside the keep without attendants. None of us have received threats. It would be suicide for anyone to attempt…"

Dháná shuddered. There was none of her husband's indifference to her son's life choices in her heart. "What of Chancellor Cornell? Is it true he was part Elyri? That he was killed because of it?"

"He was killed for backing an unpopular ruling and because he was not careful. I have no illusions about needing protection. Besides, I have access to the Gates and will be here as often as I am able."

Syl pushed wearily out of her chair and left the room; Ártur listened to the knocking of the front door as it closed. Sensing her son's need to be with his wife, Dháná nodded and let him go; his father said nothing, only glowered as he left the room. Ártur found Syl on the porch with her shawl tight around her narrow shoulders, staring at the starry sky. He stopped beside her but did not touch her or speak. He doubted she wanted to hear what he had to say.

"You think you are safe, kyá. You did not tell them about the k'gdhededhá," the woman said softly in a strained voice.

"I saw no reason to," Ártur admitted.

She shook her head. "Of course not. It would be counterproductive to your argument. You believe you are untouchable, yet even he…"

"Jermyn hated using guards; he always has. He would not use them to guard his sleeping quarters. I don't think he had reason to believe he was in danger…"

"You said that he seemed to know something was happening, that he tied up his affairs…"

Ártur offered a weak shrug. "He might have planned to retire, might have chosen to accept a threat rather than post guards and stay his fate. I do not know. There's been no indication that he was threatened. What I know from my contact with him, was that while he suffered greatly, he died in peace. I do not know what else to say. I do not feel I am in danger, and you know I rarely leave the grounds unless I am coming here or going to the náós. The princess has screened the palace staff to avoid incidences in the keep. And Agis is…well, none of the guards in the keep would dare raise his wrath. Discipline under Agis is the tightest it has ever been."

"You tell me what I want to hear but it makes me feel no better. Every night I pray you are safe, that you will come back to me one more time and love me." She looked into his pale green eyes. "Take me home, Ártur. By now, Bhen has Llucás asleep and I want no more arguments with your father tonight. I am tired. I want to go home."

With a squeeze of her hand, Ártur went inside long enough to bid his mother goodnight. This was a simple thing Syl asked of him, the least he could do to make up for the worry he caused.

❧*❧

In the darkness of what had been his father's room, the young king hovered at the window watching Balint and Agis outside of the soldier's barracks, deeply involved in whatever they were discussing. Something Hagan had little doubt he would hear about soon enough. It was quiet tonight, both inside the castle and out, the sort of crushing silence that led him to dark thoughts. He wondered why he found silence to be frightening. The quiet before a thunderstorm broke, the silence that filled the air before an execution, the way his father had been silent before exploding in anger. They were good reasons, but Hagan suspected there was some deeper meaning in it for him.

He had watched his sister when dedhá Claide called earlier in the evening. The acting-k'dedhá expressed concern over Jermyn's disappearance and was pushing for a quick resolution for the sake of the kingdom. Were they sure Jermyn had received no threats? Were there clues? Had there been a ransom demand? King Hagan assured him that they knew nothing yet but that everyone was diligently working on the matter. Claide hinted less than subtly that in his opinion, the inquisitor and justice could not find a field if they were standing in it. He obviously did not trust them to resolve anything and no amount of reassurance from Hagan helped. His unflattering remarks were dismissed as the result of agitation and fear, though Hagan noticed his sister seemed to see it as something else.

gdhededhá Claide asked again if keeping the Elyri employed by the Crown was worth the trouble they were inspiring throughout the land. Rankled, Diona declared that thus far it was not the Elyri causing problems. The gdhededhá assured her he meant no affront and wished the Elyri no ill, but surely, allowing Elyri to come into Enesfel left them open to torture and abuse. Neither they nor King Hagan could continue to afford such violent attacks.

With Diona's gaze searing into the back of his bald head, Claide left, as Hagan watched his sister curiously. She turned to stare at him, and then, with an exasperated look, stalked out of the room before he asked what was wrong.

Was the gdhededhá right, he wondered. Was expelling the Elyri from his kingdom and closing Enesfel's borders the best way to keep them safe? Many had already fled; he doubted there were many left in Enesfel. But should he keep them out, forbid them to return? If such a law was made, what about those Elyri who served him? Where would he find a more suitable chamberlain? What would he do for a healer? How could he deprive Gaelán and Tayte of their father, and Madalyn of her husband, or would they be required to leave too? What about their lands, those two Elyri who served as Dukes within the kingdom? And wherever Lord Cliáth was, how could word reach him, how would he know he was no longer welcome in the House he served, should he ever journey back?

The King was not ready to make that decision.

❧*❧

"Hagan's going to expel you from Enesfel!"

Caol looked up from the manuscript he was reading. Bhríd and Gaelán stopped their game of dice and stared at the princess with a trace of alarm. "Who is being expelled?" asked the inquisitor.

"All Elyri. He was talking with gdhededhá Claide, who suggested it might be in the Elyri's best interest if they were to leave Enesfel…"

The chamberlain nodded with a sigh. "That is likely true, but that does not mean…"

"But to be thrown out? Outlawed?" She was near hysterical, though she knew her brother had not specifically said he would take action. "Leaving of your own accord, or not coming by choice, is any man's right. Even during the Persecution, and the years after, there was no writ controlling the movement of Elyri in Enesfel. Not allowed in by royal proclamation is…"

"…his prerogative."

"Uncle!" Diona cried. "You cannot believe this is for the best."

"It does not matter what any of us believe," Caol reminded her. "If he asks our opinions, we will, of course, give them, but he will do what he thinks he should. Did he say when he would do this?"

She shook her head. "No. He did not…but I know the look on his face. He is considering it! If gdhededhá Claide continues to reinforce the idea, if the violence does not stop or we do not do something, it will be a brief matter of time before he does."

Caol placed the manuscript on the side table and stood. "Then I suggest we keep him busy, keep his mind off of such notions…and do our utmost to stop the violence. Otherwise, we prepare for the inevitable day when our friends are no longer welcome."

<h1 style="text-align:center">❧Chapter 31❧</h1>

As they neared the town of Gorbesh, the terrain grew gradually greener, more fertile, and supported a wider range of crops than Kavan had seen since leaving northern Hatu. The days were warm and summer-like, and Kavan shed his dark robe in favor of simple gray breeches, new suede boots, and a grey tunic he acquired in the last village they passed through.

The white robes he had worn since childhood, indeed any robe, felt like part of his old life, a part of the man he had been. He was no longer that man, and such attire was no longer appropriate. When he returned to Rhidam he might take it up again, but robes in his mind were equated with gdhededhá, and he was certain now that he was nothing but a man. Robes might be reserved for times of devotion or high holy days, but for the rest of his life, Kavan decided he would dress the part he was born to.

Despite the stops in the villages and towns they passed through, villages suffering from poor harvests and drought, the trio was running lower on supplies, enabling each to ride now, Urian on a mule, Wortham and Kavan upon the horse Orynn left behind. The remaining two pack mules carried little weight, their water, the bundles of food they obtained along the way, and the balance of Orynn's belongings which she had yet to reclaim. Wortham suggested selling one of the mules and the horse in exchange for those needed supplies, but Kavan would not hear of it, clinging to the hope that Orynn would return for her belongings and her horse, that he would see her one more time.

They would make do with what they had until they learned what future Gorbesh held for them.

Their destination sprouted from the midst of the fields, appearing beyond the rows of tall grains they passed through. The structures in the distance looked nearly identical, brick of yellowish pink, the same colors as the heads of grain, with thatched roofs likely of the same material. They passed people in those fields, either stooped with baskets or swinging sickles and scythes to cut and gather those plants that had already dried and were ready for harvest. It meant that the village streets were largely empty when they reached the town, giving it a forsaken appearance, though sounds to the southwest heralded activity there. Like so many of the smaller villages they had found, there appeared to be no inn, suggesting that Gorbesh rarely saw traders or travelers. Kavan and his companions decided to erect their camp near the water source on the southwest rim of the town where women were gathered around a communal grain-grinding wheel.

As he had done since leaving Zabin, Kavan began unloading the mules, pushing through the awkward discomfort in his hands in his conviction that his disability had hindered him long enough. No more. He would learn to make do with what he had. He might never play the harp again, but he would be useful. He would not allow others to care for and pity him for what he had done to himself. Some tasks came easier now, while others continued to frustrate him, but he was determined to succeed.

As the first bedroll dropped to Kavan's feet, he realized Wortham had stopped short of lifting the saddle from the horse. Following the captain's gaze towards the well, a natural direction of interest since both they and the horses needed water, Kavan inhaled with an uncomfortable shiver.

The woman arranging several clay jugs and pots on the stone lip of the well was barely more than a girl, or at least she was small enough to be that young. Her fawn brown hair hung in a loose jumble of curls, hiding her face as she drew water with the pail that hung over the well on a rope. Saddle forgotten, Wortham took their own water skins and went to her aid as she had more containers than she would be able to carry when they were full. She hung her head self-consciously when he spoke, and though Kavan could not hear what Wortham said and would have been unable to understand the language, he saw her smile as she gestured into the village. She laughed as he filled one container after another until he pointed to his companions and returned to where Kavan and Urian were. She remained near the well, watching him.

"Milord, if I may be allowed to assist her…"

"You already are," the bard reminded him, recognizing the flicker of attraction in the captain's eyes. Kavan had seen it often enough in others', though never before on Wortham's face. It made him uneasy.

"I mean," the captain chuckled, not sensing anything unusual in Kavan's response, "if you will allow me to carry water for her, she offers lodging within her home and a meal. It is the custom of these people to take in travelers…and it would be better than sleeping outdoors, would it not?"

Urian nodded, his features wan and weary. "I would love nothing more than a meal cooked by a woman who knows what she is doing. No offense, but none of us can be considered good cooks."

Struggling to gather what he had already unloaded from the first mule, Kavan said quietly, "Go then. Quickly."

Wortham hesitated, this time hearing something unidentifiable in his friend's voice, but when Kavan did not look up or speak again, he hurried off to gain them shelter for the night.

The time spent waiting for Wortham to return allowed Kavan opportunity to reflect on the source of his irritation, though it did not require much thought. It stemmed from fear, fear that at long last the man truest to him would abandon him for another. The possibility of it had never occurred to Kavan; he had taken the captain's fidelity as a steadfast, immutable fact, even in his lowest moments of doubt. He lost Arlan to the duties of ruling a kingdom and to Brenna and finally to death; lost Ártur to Syl, Owain to Gabrielle, and Muir to Clianthe. Each except Arlan was still accessible, and thus not truly lost, yet their relationships changed when other people came between them. Wortham was the one individual to whom Kavan felt he could confide everything, whom he could expect to be there when he needed him. To realize their relationship could change was an unexpected blow.

The captain returned and beckoned them to follow, grabbing up what Kavan could not carry and tugging the reins of the horse and one mule to lead the way. There was no need to point out their destination, for the woman, whom Wortham called Zelenka, waited before the doorway to her home not so far from the well, though not in sight of it. At closer inspection, the bard saw that she was closer to Princess Diona in age than he had thought, perhaps a few years older, though she was no taller than Kavan's shoulder. Her round face lit when she saw Wortham, but changed quickly when her gaze settled on Kavan's face. Likely, thought the bard, he looked different close up than she expected. Timidly, she spoke, her brown eyes studying him curiously before darting back to Wortham. Kavan had long ago grown resigned to scrutiny; the white of his skin and hair were not a common sight, and the fact that this woman had likely never encountered an Elyri did not escape him. But it was his eyes that appeared to fascinate her; she stared with such intent that when he gave a reassuring smile and blinked, she jumped back, startled. She said something to Wortham in a tone of amazement.

"She wants to know if all of your people have eyes of the same color," Wortham laughed, relieved she had not questioned the bard's complexion or the injury to his hands. "Nearly everyone here has brown or hazel eyes. Any other color is an indication of divine favor."

Not again, Kavan thought with an inward grimace. Why did people automatically equate him with the divine? He shook his head in denial of her question, and Wortham spoke. Introductions, Kavan guessed, hearing his name and Urian's in the dialogue.

"Zelenka," she gestured to herself before taking the reins of a mule and leading them to the rear of the small building. The back building was little more than a shed that housed three goats, but there was room enough for the mules and the horse to share tight quarters. She was about to refuse help in unpacking and currying them, but a discourse with Wortham made her relinquish the pack she had picked up.

Wortham glanced at Kavan who was pouring grain into the trough. "She seems to believe she must cater to us," he said in a low voice.

"It would be consistent with what we have encountered; women are treated as inferior here…which explains how Hatu came by their customs," Urian remarked. He was given a pack to carry, and with the animals fed and watered, and their belongings in hand, they followed Zelenka into her home.

It was cooler within the clay brick structure, causing a shiver at the abrupt change of temperature. There appeared to be no bed beyond the cot on one side of the room near the fire, upon which an elderly woman rested. There were two rickety wooden tables, one of which held a rusty metal water basin. Two chairs were beside the other table, and in the corner nearest the door lay a wooden storage box, a straw broom, and a collection of tools for stirring the fire and other home maintenance tasks. Above the old woman's cot, a curtain hung the length of the bed though Kavan had not noticed a window there to be covered, and to the side of the cot, one of the same faded fabric hung from floor to ceiling, concealing something beyond, the chamber pot perhaps, since there was none visible in the room. It was a tidy enough place, except for the scatter of elongated husk-covered vegetables upon the table. It looked like a variety of corn, though the husks were of a different color than was grown in Hatu and southern Enesfel and the ears were shorter and rounder than what Kavan was familiar with. Again, Zelenka spoke, pointing at the curtain.

"There is a loft behind the drape, milord, which will hold two people. She has a straw mat that can serve as a third bed, and she will sleep with her mother as she normally does. All she asks in return is help with her duties."

"How may we assist?" Kavan directed his question to her, though she would not understand. Wortham translated between them.

"More water will be needed. The corn must be husked and boiled and sausage fetched from the cellar. The goats must be milked and dinner prepared."

"I can shuck corn," Urian offered, grinning. "That would be ideal for my nimble hands and sightless eyes."

"It has been many years since I have milked, but it something I am familiar with. I believe I can do this…unless you would rather I fetch water with…"

"Zelenka and I can do it…" Wortham caught what might have been hurt in Kavan's eyes but the look was extinguished before the captain was sure of what he saw. But the bard's abrupt exit through the rear door left little doubt that he had offended him, perhaps by being so quick to cut him off.

When he finished milking the goats, a mindless task that helped clear his head despite being more difficult than he remembered it being, Kavan refilled the water trough from pails left for the animals, then went back inside to find that Urian had dozed at the table with his head on his arms. The gdhededhá had tired quickly of late; he was a traveler by the nature of his order, but no doubt he was finding the rigors of Kavan's relentless pace from one locale to another to be less to his liking. Since Wortham and Zelenka had not yet returned, Kavan took up the task of shucking the remainder of the corn, hoping, not only for Urian's sake, that his quest was nearing completion. If, as Orynn said, the náós of Gorbesh held both the chalice and the third staff piece, and if Kavan could pass the necessary tests to acquire them, they should be able to return to Enesfel soon. Perhaps if he were not lucky enough to locate a Gate, he could convince Urian to take his rest here in this land, serving as the missionary he was, rather than continue to exhaust himself.

Not for the first time he wondered about the other piece of the staff it was said he had. If it was so, he hoped he could identify it in time.

He was unaware he was humming until a dry voice rasped something from across the room. The only word Kavan understood was Zelenka. The old woman on the cot had pushed up on one elbow and was looking in Kavan's direction with rheumy eyes, one arm outstretched to him. Leaving the corn, Kavan knelt beside the cot and watched her eyes focus on the face she studied with frail fingers.

"You cannot understand me, dhábhyne, but I mean no harm," he murmured, laying a reassuring hand on her bony shoulder.

"dhábhyne? dhe ibh k'elyryhánag?"

Inhaling sharply, Kavan drew back with wide eyes. Though he could not translate the last word, the rest had been spoken in High Elyri. k'elyryhánag? It seemed the word shared some root with Elyri, and thus he wondered if that was what he was. When, in his confusion and surprise, he did not reply to her question, she sank back onto the straw mat with a groan.

"bhánys."

Sing. Or, in High Elyri, make music. He felt he must oblige a woman of such age and infirmity, and he hoped music would prompt her into a conversation that might explain how she could speak High Elyri when no one else in this region seemed capable of it. He began a quiet hymn in the language they shared; she clasped his hand on her shoulder beneath her frail one with what strength she could. One song after another he sang, more comfortable with his voice in this setting than he had been in Zabin.

Movement behind told him Urian was awake, his face turned towards Kavan's voice, and in the doorway, when she entered, Zelenka halted with an expression of delight. The captain pushed past, setting down his water jugs, and then took those she carried. Their arrival did not interrupt his song, yet when it was over, the bedridden woman tightened her grip on Kavan's hand and said something to her daughter in their tongue. There was that word again. k'elyryhánag. Zelenka knelt at the bard's feet, kissing his dusty boots.

In the distance, the deep bass echo of a tolling bell shook the air.

"Please," he squeaked, trying to pull away without accidentally hurting the old woman or Zelenka. "What is…I have done nothing?"

Wortham spoke quickly to Zelenka, hoping to subvert the panic he heard around the edges of the Elyri's voice, fumbling for the correct words to use to make the women understand. When at last he spoke to Kavan, it was in between Zelenka's excited words. "It has been many centuries since one of your kind has been here, she says. They left long ago and exist as myths. They were musicians, artists, and healers, kind and gentle people…the stories claim that great wonders would happen when one returned to sing."

Not yet realizing the implications of what Wortham said, Kavan croaked, "I am not a saint! I am only a man!"

Wortham grasped Kavan's hand. "Not a saint or holy man, she says, rather a positive omen for Gorbesh. It has been centuries since anyone has seen one of your kind; they had come to believe Elyri were a mythical fable."

"Like the phae k'kairá…" Kavan whispered, finding peace in the captain's touch, enough of it to hear what had been said. His people were taught that they had come to the Sovereignties first, with only the k'kairá preceding them. If what this woman said was true, then the

Teren had been here far longer…at least in this part of the world. What, Kavan wondered, did that mean?

The captain nodded. "Very much like, yes. Since you have gifted them with your voice…"

"I am the first to return to sing for them." He freed his hand to sweep his hair from his face as he swallowed another nervous flutter. "Tell them I hope my arrival brings good fortune…and that it will benefit us as well. Will you ask about the náós? Where it is? How I may get to it?"

There was an anxious pause as Wortham posed the question to the women. Dark eyes dancing, Zelenka nodded and spoke for Wortham to translate.

"There is an ancient order in the hills. The village trades with them but they have little interaction otherwise. The people there are ascetics who do not leave their home. She does not know the way and has not seen the place, but she says most of the village men can provide direction. She thinks if you sing they will agree to take you. She will announce you after we eat, if you are willing, and they will come."

"Then k'Ádhá willing, we may be able to depart at dawn for the náós. Tell her thank you, Wortham."

The bard did not fail to note the sad exchange between Zelenka and Wortham as the captain relayed the bard's words. Zelenka began the meal preparations and Wortham followed as it occurred to Kavan that departing Gorbesh might be more difficult than he hoped.

❧*❧

It was no surprise that King Merkar disavowed his spies, claimed no knowledge of them, or their movements and activities, and went to great lengths to show support for whatever Owain chose to do to them in the name of peace between Neth and Enesfel. Knowing his kinsman would take perverse pleasure in whatever form of execution the three received, it was enough to cause Owain to consider, briefly, letting them go simply to frustrate and annoy Merkar. Merkar would kill them himself, or have one of his generals do it, but returning home as traitors would bring hardship to their families. It was compassion for the wives and children, if these three had any, and the knowledge that they might still find their way into Enesfel if he released them, that kept Owain from letting the three go.

The wording of the King's message was precisely what Owain expected and he wondered if Nethite kings had a stock of formulated letters used in situations like this.

"Father?"

Rarely objecting to being interrupted by his son, Owain opened his arms and said, "Yes, Piran?"

The child climbed onto his lap and stared at him with a disconcerting expression that Owain had seen before but had yet to define. "Is it true there are prisoners you are going to execute?"

He had not spoken about them to anyone since the day he had thrown the three into the dungeon, but it was possible a servant could have overheard his threat and servants, being servants, tended to talk too much. "I have prisoners, yes. They are spies who have killed people. Their fate has not been determined." But Merkar's apathy, and the expediency of the situation, pushed that decision closer.

"Spies for Neth?"

"Yes."

"Doesn't their King want them back?"

"King Merkar cannot…"

And then he had an idea, an unexpected, splendid idea, and marveled he had not thought of it before. He would have to be extremely cautious in what he asked for and what he revealed, for if he was wrong, Enesfel's integrity could be in jeopardy. If his hunch was correct, however, if his plan worked, he might be able to forge a more positive bond with Neth. "He cannot acknowledge them without admitting he sent them. Not a wise political choice."

"When will you do it? How? May I watch?"

Owain shook his head. "You are too young, Piran. And I have made no decision about them. Run along. See to your fleet, my little sailor. I have important duties to attend to."

Piran got down without questioning his father's choices. He was a well-behaved child, of whom Owain grew daily more proud. His toy boats were his favorite thing, the best-guaranteed distraction Owain could find. Retrieving a quill, inkwell, and parchment, Owain began to draft his letter and his plan.

❧*❧

gdhededhá Claide had indeed gone to visit his sister in the village of Rolstecher near the city of Chantel. Caol felt it was about time his Association contacts provided him with something useful, even if it was not the news he wanted to hear. The gdhededhá's sister had been ill and died while Claide was there. He stayed for the burial after which he returned to Rhidam. Innocent enough, though it hardly meant the man was guiltless, and his contact's tale gave credence to Caol's suspicions.

Though Claide had been there on the pretense of visiting her, he spent little time at her home. He spent most of it at two other establishments. Claide had brought his horse for re-shoeing, and as he was the village's only local blacksmith there was nothing suspicious about it, but there was no apparent reason for the other three visits that Caol's contacts could find.

The second location was more suspect and made the inquisitor's stomach tighten with giddy anxiety. It was the home of a notorious gambler and drinker, a man known by his neighbors to be bitterly anti-Elyri. It was a promising lead, one that deserved further inquiry, and

Caol made arrangements for it, wanting to know as much as he could about that man and his movements as well as those of the blacksmith.

The other splinter of festering doubt came from the deceased woman's daughter, who claimed her mother seemed to improve at first with Claide's arrival. She managed to get out of bed to prepare dinner for Claide and this same blacksmith. Quite unexpectedly, she was dead the following morning. A local physician found no unnatural causes and attributed the woman's death to her illness. No one in the village suspected foul play, except the woman's daughter. But Caol did. There was no way to prove it, however, now that the body had been buried. It left the inquisitor wondering if Claide would kill his sister, or would allow or request someone else to do it, in order to protect something. Or someone. After what Caol had witnessed in recent weeks, he was not about to put such an act past any man.

The remainder of gdhededhá Claide's activities of late could be viewed in the same fashion. His outings in Rhidam could have been for the purpose of visiting the sick and dying, but a short interrogation of each household might prove otherwise. Three of his haunts seemed suspicious, three Caol deemed worthy of further investigation. The home of a tanner's widow on the north edge of the city lent itself to easy speculation, particularly since Claide was seen there at no other times except early in the morning or late in the evening. By all reports, the widow had a striking face and sizable fortune; perhaps Claide hoped to get his hands on her money. Or their assignations could be more intimate in nature. They were never seen together in public and she rarely left her home so it was difficult to know the truth.

Each time Claide was seen at the Boar's Garden Tavern, he was with someone different or he went alone. He did not drink and was cordial to the Teren who approached him. Many nights he stayed late, occasionally joined by gdhededhá Valgis, until either the tavern closed or an Elyri traveler entered. Afterward, Claide returned to the náós, with or without stopping at the widow's home. Claide did not seem the sort of man to mingle with people in such a fashion unless he hoped to gain something. Caol suspected he was meeting nefarious contacts in this public place, perhaps thinking it would draw less suspicion, but he did not know the inquisitor well enough if he thought Caol would let any hint go uninvestigated.

Yet it was that one house that drove Caol to distraction, that one place Claide frequented most which made no sense. Caol had verified that the two men who owned that recently built home were the youngest sons of Duke Charles Gottfrid. Young men with money and nothing to do with their time except sponge off their father's fortune and idle away their days. The elderly Duke catered to his young sons, while his oldest ran the estate in Erleta. Neither the Duke nor his eldest son had much contact with the younger two except when they sent requests for money.

But for what purpose had Idal and Kent Gottfrid come to Rhidam? Not for audience or proximity to the throne or for political gain since neither had called upon the King nor shown any interest in courting the princess. They did not seem to be building any sort of occupation and the structure itself was not the sort one expected wealthy young men to call home. They were clearly there for a purpose, something that brought gdhededhá Claide to them on a continuing basis, but there was, thus far, no information about what that business was.

To Caol, it seemed the Association must have an agenda with the Gottfrids because they seemed unable, or unwilling, to tell Caol anything he could use. He considered calling them off that particular duty, but he decided not to do so yet; the moment he did would be the moment he was likely to miss something important.

❧*❧

Despite his sore throat and nervousness, Kavan entertained late into the night on the eve of their arrival in Gorbesh and was pleased that the villagers reacted as he hoped. Whatever doubt about his voice he clung to dissipated a little more before their unabashed adoration. He was approached by a farmer who offered to take him to the náós if Kavan would assist in the repair and loading of his wagons. Kavan agreed, willing to do anything to obtain his goal, no matter how difficult due to the state of his hands, anything, perhaps, except watch Wortham's growing interest in Zelenka.

Urian took to bed with a fever, and Zelenka tended him while Kavan and the captain sought the farmer and his son the following morning. Between them, the wagons were repaired and loaded more quickly than the farmer expected, given Kavan's disability, leaving the bard with hours to spare. Kavan wanted to question him about the náós, the history of the village and the land, but the man chose other duties around his home over conversation, and Wortham returned to Zelenka's side, fetching more water and assisting in the care of both Urian and her mother and repairing things around the hovel that had been uncared for too long. The old woman wanted Kavan to sing again, but he could not. Or rather, he would not, as he preferred not to be in the confined space in such proximity to the intense emotions generated between her daughter and his dearest friend.

Feeling that longing in others created an ache he wished Orynn would take away. But she was gone, and the bond that had begun to grow between them could not be regained. Intellectually, he accepted it, and when he managed to keep his mind busy, it was not an issue. Emotionally, however, he was far from accepting the loss. He had witnessed how long some people took to recover from the pain of lost love. Others, like Arlan, never recovered. There, beside the well, watching the workers far off in the fields, he mourned silently as he clumsily began to transcribe the Kóráhm-Coryllien genealogy into a blank journal he obtained in the last village they had passed through, praying as he did that he would be forgiven for this relapse of melancholy. Progress was slow as the need to write legibly outweighed any haste, but it was a tremendous relief to know that, if he took his time, he was able to write again.

He was still there when the villagers gathered that evening and begged him to sing again. Knowing that music would soothe his heart better than any other remedy, he gave what they desired, seeing Wortham and Zelenka arrive, content to linger at the rear of the gathering rather than push to the front as Wortham would have done in the past. That painful difference was nearly enough to cause Kavan to fall silent.

'Do not begrudge your friend the happiness you seek for yourself.'

The voice was in Kavan's head as he sang. Kóráhm's voice. His presence was there, like a pair of comforting arms around the bard's shoulders, although the saint could not be seen. Though his song did not falter, Kavan's first silent reaction to the admonition was, 'As you did not begrudge your brother happiness with his wife?'

Kóráhm's aura pulsed and flashed, angry perhaps, or taken aback by Kavan's unusual vehemence. When the voice returned, it was low and sorrowful. 'I did not envy him. I loved her, it is true, and she loved me more than she should have, but our love remained chaste, though not for the lack of wanting. But this is different, phyl haeles; you do not love her. It is Wortham you do not want to lose. Yet think on this; if you force him to choose, what shall he do? Choose you and resent you for her loss? Or choose her and mourn forever that you are gone?'

'I lose him either way,' Kavan thought as his voice caught in a sorrowful crescendo of breathtaking clarity. Wortham's head snapped up at the note, his banter with Zelenka interrupted. That ache in the bard's voice he knew well, and though Kavan used no words, the captain understood.

'You will lose him only if you drive him away.'

Then Kóráhm was gone. Kavan's voice trailed mournfully after him, the song falling into silence. The adulation of the crowd lifted his spirits temporarily; he had yet to accept the power his voice could carry, the emotion he could convey with some instrument other than his harp. Yet elation waned as the villagers departed for their homes, leaving him alone. Alone except for Wortham who hung back tentatively, his manner that of a chastised child.

Kavan did not want to talk. He would likely regret any words that came out of his mouth. "Go, Wortham. You do not want to speak with me now. It may cause us to say things we will both lament."

"I have hurt you."

The bard clenched his jaw. "Wortham…"

"I do not know what I have done…"

"I do not want to speak of these things." Kavan brushed the dust from his trousers before picking up the books he had been working on.

Hoping he had a solution that would make Kavan happy, the captain said, "Allow me to travel with you tomorrow, milord…"

"You are not needed," Kavan said in a flat, slightly bitter tone, aware how his words stung. "This is my quest. I told you that when you found me on the ship. I must do this; you do not need to. Do what you wish, Wortham, and give me no further thought. Go your way."

The Elyri strode towards the fields, leaving the captain alone. He was still there when Kavan's circle of the village brought him back. Rather than approach, the bard watched from a distance as Wortham leaned on his elbows, staring into the depths of the village well. He was weeping, that much Kavan knew without getting closer. He could feel the man's grief and tears pricking his skin, a sensation that filled Kavan with guilt. Had he ever seen Wortham weep before? He could not recall it, and it hurt him now to witness it. But he did not have the strength for a confrontation. Instead, he returned to Zelenka's home, where the women already slept, and climbed into the loft.

He was still awake, though feigning sleep, when the captain came in. Zelenka spoke quietly and Wortham replied before climbing the ladder. Settling into the straw, he was quiet for many minutes, and then hesitantly fingered the silver-white hair at the back of Kavan's head. The bard fought against the tears spawned by the intimate gesture, but he remained as he was with his back to the soldier.

"I made you a promise, milord," Wortham whispered, his voice rough with emotion, "to follow wherever you lead, to stay with you. While you might forgive me for breaking such a promise, the pain I would inflict by abandoning you might not heal and I could never forgive myself for that. I will follow you tomorrow and always."

Unable to bear the following silence, Kavan rolled to face his friend. It was difficult to look into the big man's dark eyes, but Kavan forced himself to do so. "No. I am taking the choice from you this time, Wortham. What awaits me at the náós is something I must do alone. I was told this when I was sent here. You cannot help me. gdhededhá Urian needs care and it is unfair to expect Zelenka to tend him when she must see to her mother."

"Milord…"

Kavan shook his head, hoping Wortham could not see his face clearly in the darkness. "You are not abandoning me, Wortham. I admit I fear your loyalties are shifting, but perhaps that is as it should be. I do not know. I only ask that you…"

The captain grasped Kavan's hands and squeezed them earnestly, noticing how they trembled. "Anything, milord. I will do as you ask. My loyalty will never break from you."

A dozen thoughts raced through the bard's head, favors he could ask, some outrageous, some too embarrassing and personal for Kavan to utter. When he did finally speak, his forehead pressed to Wortham's, his voice broke. "Do not stop loving me, Wortham. Do not forget me. You are my truest friend. Do not deny me that."

"Never, Kavan," the bearded man said earnestly, eyes fixed on Kavan's as he kissed the white hands he held between his. "Anyone who could turn their back on you is a fool, and no one has ever called Wortham Delamo a fool."

⚘*⚘

"A daughter! Syl, we have a daughter!"

Ártur could not contain his joy at the sight of the pink, wriggling mass that had emerged into the world, and he thanked the stars he had been here to greet her. The child's hair was quite red, the same color Syl's brother Phaedr's had been. No doubt about it, this was their child. Wrapping her in a towel, he delivered the infant into the waiting arms of her mother.

"She looks like Phaedr," Syl said as she stroked the girl's cheek.

"I think so too. Syl…our daughter a healer. How do you think Llucás will feel about a sister?" His wife's response was an exhausted smile. "Chethá?" he asked.

She nodded and replied, "Chethá Llyárá."

That name, honoring Kavan's mother, made Ártur smile. "I think Kavan will be pleased with the choice."

The bard sat abruptly, his senses alert though he heard and sensed nothing in the room that should not be there. Kavan had not been sleeping, merely dozing, but it had been enough to allow night to give way to the faintest traces of dawn without his noticing. What he did notice, the thing that roused him, was that Ártur and Syl had brought a daughter into the world. The image of the infant, her pale blue eyes closed in contented infant sleep, was clear to him, as was the girl's name. Chethá Llyárá. Named after Syl's grandmother and Kavan's mother. Odd that they had chosen to honor the long-absent women in that way, but pleasing too. Also odd that they had chosen to name her so soon, rather than at the customary three-month anniversary of her birth. They expected, because Kavan had said she would be a healer, that the girl would live. Kavan prayed they were right.

Without disturbing Wortham, Kavan pulled free of the hands that still clung to him and climbed from the loft. Zelenka had already risen and placed bread and goat's milk upon the table for him before going to the well for water. He ate quickly, silently, but before he could make it to the door, the old woman's voice stopped him.

"Take care of my child, k'elyryhánag," she croaked in High Elyri. "I am all she has. When I am gone, she will be alone, and a woman her age, single, is not respected. Do not let calamity befall her."

There was an image in his head, a feeling of cold accompanied by Urian's singing and voices weeping, that told him she was likely not to be here when he returned. Clutching her hand, he kissed her forehead and murmured, "dhábhyne, dytae áti. síndóbhaene áti, átaelás haeles íd ghaies áti." It seemed, regardless of his feelings, Zelenka was to remain in his life.

He hastened out of the home to find the farmer, his son, and the two wagons waiting to begin the journey up the winding mountain trail. Perhaps Wortham would be angry that he did not say farewell, but after the intensity of last night's emotional display between them, Kavan knew he would not likely be able to talk Wortham into staying, or endure seeing his sad face, as they parted.

❧*❧

Draping his arm across the divan, watching the princess stare at Prince Espen, Caol muttered, "I am beginning to believe that if I am to gain any knowledge about the Corylliens I will need to infiltrate them myself. None of my people have been successful at learning anything, or they have not tried that approach…which means they think it too much of a risk."

"It would be dangerous?" Espen asked.

"Undeniably, but not more than anything else in Enesfel these days. I know how to achieve it, and other than my contacts and the Association, I usually keep to myself. I think even most of Enesfel's nobles would fail to recognize me if I changed the color of my hair. I believe I can do it."

The princess shook her head. "We can't take the risk, Uncle."

"We might not have a choice," the inquisitor said with a groan. "The terrorism is increasing; men storming through a farmhouse on horseback to kidnap six children…from a family that has had no connections to Elyri as far as we can tell. The kidnappers did not even try to disguise that they were Teren. Not that they could have. No Elyri would make such a show of force, and most of Enesfel knows it. But this is the sort of behavior Coryllien was known for, kidnapping children for sacrifices…"

Prince Espen unconsciously reached for Diona's hand for mutual comfort and she did not pull away. "Do you think that is what is being done to the people who are taken?" he asked. "Would someone sacrifice children? What of the missing adults?"

"Would men knowingly, willingly, butcher whole families because an Elyri slept in their house? There is no proof these criminals have resorted to sacrifice, but murder is murder, and men will do a lot in the name of terror. Bodies have turned up across Enesfel, though not enough to account for the number reported missing, and with no one to accurately identify them, we have no way of knowing who they are. We cannot send an Elyri from town to town to identify them…not without risking their lives. I know no Elyri willing to take that risk and I won't ask. Something more effective must be done."

"There is no further information about Claide?" asked Diona.

"He has been seen little since his return. Tusánt says he is settling into the k'dedhá's job, working to keep the day to day matters of Faith running smoothly. If he had a hand in the k'dedhá's death, he is, no doubt, wondering why no one has reported the body. Those peasants who found him have been paid enough that they will not talk unless threatened, and I have relocated them to lands far from Rhidam as a precaution, but he could find them if he is determined enough."

Prince Espen snorted. "That sort of determination would be an inference of guilt…and so long as he does not suspect the Crown of deceit, I don't believe he would have reason for that degree of effort."

"We will have to report something soon, at least to my brother. He questions what you and I talk about." There was a sparkle in her eyes that pleased him. She, at least, was beginning to act normal. There had been less mention of Kavan as the weeks had gone by, and less talk about her father. If not for the violence plaguing the kingdom, life in Rhidam would feel normal.

"I am sure you will think of a suitable explanation," the inquisitor chuckled. "But you're right; he has been asking Lord Corbin too many questions and is becoming increasingly annoyed that there has been little progress made in the case. If it comes down to me infiltrating the Corylliens to learn the truth though, you know the King will not allow it. If we decide it must be done, we will need to cover my absence."

"Wilred would do it." Diona was sure of it. "After all, you have not gone to see your granddaughter. Excuses are easy to fabricate."

He grinned. "Then I shall have you teach that ability to Asta…or perhaps I won't." He rose with a stretch and said, "I must speak to Bhríd and Darius; if you will both excuse me."

Once the inquisitor was gone, Espen spoke, anything to avoid the uncomfortable silence that filled a room whenever he was alone with Diona. "You are on good terms with your uncle."

She had yet to let go of his hand, and he had yet to try to take his back. Despite the awkwardness between them, there was also something genuine that they were closer to exploring. "We have needed to be, as insurance. Unlike my brother, I think my uncle's background is beneficial for what he does, necessary. At the very least, it makes him ideally suited for the position my father appointed him to. I have no qualms about what he does or how, as long as it succeeds and does not reflect badly on the Crown. I trust him, and he knows that in some matters, I am the one who can get things done. Hagan would have closed the investigation long ago and Claide would already have his victory."

"What if dedhá Claide is innocent?"

Diona scowled. "If it turns out to be true, so be it. But I know he is not innocent. Call it woman's intuition if you wish." She turned in the chair to face him. "I suppose my involvement appalls you?"

"Appalls me?" He chuckled and squeezed her hand. "I can think of few things you have ever done which have appalled me. Knowing you as I do, I am not even surprised. Witnessing the workings of your mind in serious matters, seeing you take command of such details is refreshing and reassuring."

"Reassuring? That is hardly a word expected from a man of your country when referring to a woman with power," she said with a smirk.

"I suppose not. But since meeting you, I have not exactly been a typical man of my country. It has caused me to wonder long and hard what any man would find attractive in the women of my land, beyond their faces. They have little spirit, little initiative, or if they do it has been too much harnessed as to be almost snuffed out. It is reassuring that my heart chose wisely in you."

At that slight hinting of a future between them, Princess Diona released his hand. He expected her to leave; it would give him the answer to his proposal he anticipated. He needed her answer, some final word. But instead of departing, she clasped her hands before her and looked into his face.

"You have not mentioned marriage once since your arrival. Is that because you no longer wish to pursue the topic?" She thought she knew the answer, but she wanted to hear him say it.

He shifted in his seat and cleared his throat. "I told you at our last parting that I would pursue you no longer. The final decision is yours to make; there is nothing more for me to do or say."

"Do you still wish it?"

Rising to stand eye to eye, feeling his heart catch in his throat, he asked, "Are you ready to give an answer?" Suddenly, he felt anxious and afraid of the answer she might give him.

She shook her head with the faintest hint of a coy smile. "Answer my question, Espen, and I shall answer yours."

He brushed her hair from her face with one hand and replied, "I have always wanted it. It has been my dream for more than ten years."

She turned towards the window, aware of the defeated sigh that escaped him. He thought she was saying no. She turned again and offered her hand. "I cannot say I have a final answer, Espen, but I can say I am giving the matter more serious consideration. There are only two men I have considered marrying, and I have recently realized and accepted that pursuit of one is a waste of energy as well as not in the best interest of Enesfel. That is a marriage that can never, will never, happen. And it is not the one I long for most. The other…pursues me with more fervent interest than I have admitted…"

Espen took her hand and stepped closer, finding hope in that gesture. "What are you saying, Diona? Speak candidly."

"Give me a reason to marry you, Espen. Convince me that what I want most is for the best. Court me as you once did, when I was younger and our relationship was not yet comfortable, and I will give you the attention you deserve. I suspect we will both be pleasantly surprised at the outcome."

Though he wanted to throw his arms around her, Prince Espen restrained himself. A proper courtship. Yes, that was something they had never shared, the sort of courtship any lord would offer a lady whose hand he wished to win. She had been too young for that when he had first proposed marriage, and by the time she was of age, their relationship had become, as she said, comfortable. Courtship was an appropriate step. "Tomorrow. Will you join me for the noon meal in the garden, Milady?" he asked with a bow.

She curtseyed with a smile. "I am honored to accept, milord."

⁊Chapter 32⁊

It still felt odd to Caol after so many weeks, to address his nephew, many years his junior, as king. Today it felt even stranger because he knew that the young King would not like the latest report. "I am afraid I bring bad news, Your Highness," he said after a bow.

"I assumed it would be bad when you asked for an audience. It would be too much to ask for this dreadful business to be behind us," the King snorted.

"There was a woman named Puncilla…"

"Puncilla? The madam?"

Caol stared at Hagan in surprise. King Hagan still seemed too innocent to know about such things as prostitutes. Seeing his uncle's expression, the King squirmed, blushed, and said quickly, "Dayly's mentioned her. I have not met or seen her…"

That embarrassment made Caol snort and shake his head. "She was murdered last night…"

"And…?" Hagan knew by the inquisitor's pause there was more.

"Unlike many ladies of that profession, she was not part of the Association. One of her…fellows, found her strangled in her bed, though she had taken no clients last night to anyone's knowledge. Indeed, as I've heard it, she has taken no clients in several weeks. Some found it odd that she stopped working, but her affairs and income were her personal business as she had no agent to answer to. The Association has no jurisdiction…"

The King snorted. "I do not care about the inner workings of the Association. I want to know why you interrupted my riding schedule to tell me a prostitute has been murdered."

Keeping his annoyance in check, the inquisitor replied, "During her period of unemployment, she was seeing a single man on a rigorous basis. Rumor is, she was giving up the profession to marry him. No one has given me his name yet, but I have heard from several sources that her suitor was Elyri."

Hagan started to speak, stopped, and then restarted but fell silent again. The inquisitor took the opportunity to continue. "This suggests either a client wished for her to continue working for his sake, or a member of the Corylliens discovered the affair and killed her…"

"What would the Association lose if she stopped working?"

Annoyed with the King's inferences and that he had not listened to his previous words, he replied, "As I said, the Association held no authority in her affairs. She was a free agent. Other than dues to remain free of their control, and whatever someone might steal from her clients, the Association loses nothing. In fact, they gain by her retiring, as it sends her clients to those the Association controls."

"They gain from her death," the King snorted, crossing his arms over his chest smugly.

"Not enough that it would be worth the risk of killing her, else they would have done it years ago," Caol snapped indignantly. "They lose her dues by killing her, and this brings an investigation by the Justice they do not want. They do not need the scrutiny and she was no threat to them."

"Would she know secrets about the Association that could have been a threat?" the monarch countered.

"She was on the outside. There's nothing she could have known that would endanger them. If they killed every threat, they would kill me, for I am more of a threat than any unbonded prostitute. I am in a position to cost them or make them more money than she ever could. Believe me when I tell you, her death was not at the hand of the Association. They would never sanction it."

The King's face was crimson at Caol's reproving tone. "So you say, Lord Inquisitor, but there is a chance I am correct and that you are being led by the nose like a mule. I think we should consider breaking connection with your friends," he coughed, 'before the Crown is implicated in something more repugnant than the death of a madam."

"Milord, that is not wise," Caol began. "You are not implicated…"

But the king would not be swayed. "I want no arguments. Look into some other way of doing your duties. I want a change. Soon."

The inquisitor stalked from the room, fuming, wondering why Princess Diona could comprehend what he did when her brother could not. The King had no idea what he was asking; to replace the network he had in place via the Association would take years and more resources than the Crown could afford. But Caol would investigate as instructed. If seeing the monetary cost and the period it would take to implement a change did not change Hagan's mind, Caol would be forced to view the King as more foolish than imagined. And he might be forced to resign, despite his promise to the princess. He could not endure petty shortsightedness. Either he would do his duty or, if denied that, he would leave it for some other poor fool to figure out and pray for those who died in the interim.

❧*❧

It was a massive stone construct, emerging directly from the mountain that surrounded it on three sides, gleaming near white beneath the brightness of the sun. Up close, however, the stone bore the faint pink and yellow cast that so much in this region bore. The outer walls were twice as high as those encircling the Lachlan keep, yet the structure the walls contained towered over it by several stories. From one of its many towers, some square, some round, a bell sounded, a single echoing tone, the same heard in the village each morning, each noon, and each evening. No doubt the inhabitants were at their noon meal; it accounted for the inactivity when the wagons pulled before the great wooden gates.

Depending on how deeply into the mountain it stretched, this place could house a small city's population, Kavan mused, as the sun-bleached wooden gates swung open, allowing them to enter the courtyard. Could, he realized, awed by the sheer size and the amount of time and effort that had gone into building it, if there was a readily available food source. He saw no garden inside those walls, no way to raise crops or graze livestock either there or upon the rocky mountainous terrain surrounding the building. There were chickens, geese, and a dozen or so natty sheep and goats running amok in the piazza, but it was hardly enough to feed a sizable population for long.

The gate attendants, veiled by their cowls, closed the entry behind the wagons and gestured into the shadows of the arched doorways. Three bare-chested young men darted forth to assist in unloading the goods. Each took as much as they could carry and disappeared into the building, while Kavan assisted the farmer and his son in separating the goods into piles upon the ground. No one spoke and none took any particular notice of him. Except for the cowls the gate attendants wore, these men did not look to be members of any religious order Kavan had encountered. Nor could he imagine an order of men existing for centuries without venturing into the outside world. Those whose faces he could see were Teren; without women, they would have no way to replenish their ranks. And with no way to feed themselves, they would have starved to death.

A tickle, like the brush of fingers traveling up the back of his neck, told Kavan he was being watched. Without making it obvious, he craned his neck from side to side until he caught sight of a dark-haired figure in a window far above the courtyard. The individual released the drape and disappeared from view before Kavan could determine if it was a man or woman. Several more trips were made until the goods were unloaded, and the figure did not reappear. There was a brief discussion between the farmer and the gate attendants, with several gestures at Kavan indicating he was the topic of discussion, and then two of the residents took the wagons down a path to the right while the third led Kavan, the farmer, and his son inside.

The farmer spoke in a matter of fact tone, but without probing his thoughts, Kavan did not know what he was saying. He guessed, given the hour, that the farmer and his wagons would not return to Gorbesh that night, as it would mean traveling the steep, rutted path long after dark. Though hungry, Kavan cared little for food. He wanted someone to talk to, someone he could present his business to. If they were to leave in the morning, he would have a long night of business ahead.

The trio was escorted through a series of long corridors with high ceilings and barren yellow-pink walls, ushered into a round reception room, and left there alone. The walls of the room were adorned with once elegant tapestries faded in a way that suggested great age. Kavan made a circle of the room, taking in the reverent images while the farmer and his son settled upon stools, content to relax as they waited, their demeanor suggesting they had been here before.

Kavan stopped before a tapestry that, though much larger than his, was a duplicate of it. It was the largest work in the room. The dark-winged záryph above Kavan were nearly as tall as he was. Reflexively, he touched the twisted foot of Saint Kóráhm that was as high as he could reach on this magnificent work, admiring the way the Saint stared at Dhágdhuán's radiant figure.

"You find this one compelling?"

The low, melodic voice startled him. The man who had joined him was tall, with the wiry muscular frame of an athlete. His face was handsome and gentle in expression though his black eyes glinted with merciless intensity. His brown hair, almost as black as his eyes, was long, pulled from his face and shoulders by a black cord and he was dressed in a mid-length white tunic cinched at the waist with another length of black cord. His legs were covered in trousers of the same light fabric and his feet wore simple cloth shoes. He spoke in perfect, if stilted, Elyri, the first other than Orynn and Zelenka's mother to communicate with Kavan in a language he understood. The bard took in every detail in the first few seconds after meeting him.

"It is very old?" Kavan countered, hoping for information.

"It was made within these walls centuries ago, long before I was born. I cannot give you a more detailed age I'm afraid."

That seemed logical since this man looked to be physically no older than Kavan appeared to be. "Has anyone from outside these walls seen this? Have any duplicates been made?"

The stranger smiled. "I am sure traders from the village have seen it. As for duplicates, I cannot guess. None have been made while I have lived, but before that, who can say. Why do you ask?"

"This is Kóráhm di Curnydhá."

"You know of Kóráhm?"

Kavan was not sure whose surprise was greater, his or this man to whom he spoke. Not knowing how much he should reveal, he replied, "He is my patron; I was born on the eve of his martyrdom; I bear his name. I possess a tapestry that could be this one…though it is smaller."

The other man's face lit up as he asked, "Was it Kóráhm who sent you to us? Is that why you are here?"

"Indirectly, yes, I suppose he did have much influence in my coming here. I have come in search of…"

A tinkling bell chimed in the distance and the stranger bowed. "Enough talk, friend. There will be time for talking later, after our Gathering and meal. I am Myreth. You will dine with us and stay tonight. I have many questions and I see you have many for me."

Disappointed that he must wait for the information he needed, Kavan replied, "I shall stay as long as I am able. My mission is one of great import and what I require is here. I do not intend to leave until I acquire what I came for." Unlike elsewhere in these foreign lands, Myreth was the first to call their religious service a Gathering, a fact Kavan interpreted as a fortuitous sign.

The other man smiled, an expression Kavan wanted to see more of. "Then allow me to give you a room. May I request your name or would you prefer formality?"

"Call me Kavan. I would prefer it."

"I have been appointed to attend you, Kavan, if you will allow it."

Myreth eyed him with the passion of a man long confined and hungry for adventure to interrupt routine. There was a contagious energy in his black eyes that made Kavan shiver. He knew he would stay to converse with this man even if he was denied the items he sought, and that for meeting him this trip was worth it. Myreth bore the same expression Wortham often did, one of knowing to whom he spoke, or at least a comprehension that he was about to experience something of profound, life-altering, significance. As Kavan had learned long ago with Wortham, that expression generally proved to be accurate. The bard knew he would quickly grow to like this man.

"I shall follow you, Myreth. I should be eternally grateful to find myself in a place of worship. It has been too long."

Myreth nodded. He made no notice or mention of Kavan's hands.

❧*❧

gdhededhá Kesábhá expected resistance. He was the first person to challenge a k'gdhededhá in Elyriá's history, and the fact that his jurisdiction placed him in Teren territory made him inevitably suspect. It also did not help his cause that he was of the order of Saint Kóráhm, the Heretic. But he chose to start in Ánásair, the agrarian community from which he hailed, where people knew him. He was known to be a brilliant scholar and artist, but not overly gifted as Elyri go. They would know he was not lying.

He presented his case to the clergy of the town. No one believed him initially; no one wanted to believe the leader of their Faith was condemning people to death with apathy. As they argued, heard Khwílen's accounts of death and brutality, heard the violent end of k'gdhededhá Tythilius to which their k'gdhededhá expressed indifference, they one by one began to concede that perhaps Khwílen had a valid grievance. After the eldest gdhededhá chose to read Khwílen to test the truth of his words, there was no further doubt. Dórímyr's words, the horrors in Enesfel, were there to witness. While many did not condone Elyri traveling outside of their homeland, they did believe that an ecclesiastical mandate should be issued, warning others of the dangers they faced if they chose to travel abroad. No one could condone ignoring the matter of safety.

Nor could they condone the slaughter of their countrymen that went unnoticed by those in Elyriá. There had been rumors before but no stories any could confirm. All of the people in Ánásair would be told. If the k'gdhededhá would not address the danger, it was up to the people to do so. This issue had to be taken before Kyne Mórne and the ecclesiastical lómesté in Clarys. Not until Khwílen completed his circuit of towns, however. To his relief, some of those gdhededhá he first served with, and some of the people he had grown up with, agreed to take the message across the country as well. Every Elyri must be told. Every man and woman had to know the truth. When they next met in Clarys, it would be to take k'gdhededhá Dórímyr to task.

∾*∾

Though the atmosphere and the words of the Gathering were familiar, there was much that was alien to every indoctrinated detail

Kavan learned growing up. The room, with its frescos and columns, was a large half circle hall, and while there was an unadorned cedar altar, it was not separated from the congregation like most he had seen. It was located on the flat wall of the room, an image of Dhágdhuán the Resurrected suspended on the wall behind and above it. The image was dressed in red robes, as he often was, with his arms outstretched in a welcoming manner. There was no pyre, no images of death or injury, anywhere Kavan could see.

Austerity was the custom here; the wooden benches were of a simple design and curled in towards the altar from the curved back wall, like ever-shrinking rings within the cut trunk of a tree. There was a single aisle that led from the rear door to the altar, tiled in red, and as the residents entered, they filled the pews from the outside edges in, leaving room for others to sit beside them. Unlike other religious orders, however, not one of these people, male or female, wore robes. Kavan had seen no one in robes except the attendants at the gate, and he deduced they had worn loose clothing more for protection from the elements, the sun and wind and rain, then out of religious piety. That this place housed both men and women answered his questions about how the order sustained itself, but he had not expected, after witnessing the segregation of the sexes in the outside cultures, that these people would gather together in the same náós for worship.

Noting his perplexed expression, Myreth smiled, a vaguely seductive smile though his eyes betrayed nothing. As the dark-haired man directed him to the front row in the worship room, Kavan concluded that everything about Myreth was seductive. The earthy timbre of his voice, the warm sun-browned coloring of his skin, the manner in which his mouth set in a pout when he was not speaking, the way he moved. Was Myreth deliberately baiting him, he wondered, or was the man unaware of his sensuous qualities. He appeared to be an innocent, though there were times when Kavan could feel those veiled hungry eyes watching him in a way that seemed anything but innocent, and it made Kavan shiver to feel and see it.

When the first person approached the altar to lead opening prayers, Kavan was astonished to see it be a woman. Women in Elyriá mingled with the men for the services, but only the young girls serving as altar aides could contribute directly. Not even the female gdhededhá performed in the Gathering except within their own orders. That separation was something Kavan had never been comfortable with, and after his initial surprise at seeing it here, he accepted it as the way it should be. Other members of the congregation participated too, men, women, and children, leading songs, sharing a story or testimony, reading from any holy book that suited them, of which there were many available. They spoke partially in the local dialect, occasionally in Elyri, and two of the songs were in High Elyri. Throughout the ceremony, Myreth did not sing or speak, perhaps out of deference to the man beside him since Kavan knew none of these songs or prayers.

There was no determined pattern to the progression of the Gathering; each participant did as they felt led to do until the tinkling chime tolled. The final man at the altar returned to his seat, and once the room settled into stillness, Myreth rose and approached the altar. He motioned for Kavan to join him, but the bard did not. Not knowing what was about to happen, he was too wary of potential humiliation to move. With no obvious reaction, Myreth beckoned two others forward instead, a young girl of perhaps ten, and a much older man. The three joined hands to encircle the altar and the congregation began to utter a more ritualistic, formalized prayer than they had used thus far.

Kavan listened to the sing-song chant rise and fall in the echoes of the stone room. The sound made his skin prickle as if chilled, and in those moments he sensed the power of the altar, rich and strong from centuries of continual use. Having spent months struggling to reestablish his faith, struggling to find peace, to feel such power now brought tears to his eyes.

The prayer complete, Myreth produced a large bottle and small metal cup from behind the altar. The cup was given to the girl, the bottle to the man, and then the two of them faced the congregation. The first row of people stepped forward, knelt in a line before the young server, and waited.

Kavan was engrossed in watching the proceedings, noting each subtle difference in what should have been a familiar ritual, with his attention turned away from Myreth. When the man opened his mouth to sing, however, he commanded the bard's attention.

Such a divine voice. Lower than Kavan's, a velvety tenor with a power and sound that matched his. Myreth stood with the skilled poise of a natural performer, or at least that of a man who knew where his talent lay and was comfortable displaying it. He sang in High Elyri, a prayer of Saint Kóráhm's, something Kavan recognized by the words though not by the music. He wondered, as he absorbed the sound through his skin and ears, what their voices would sound like in unison. How much could they accomplish together? He wanted to know, wanted access to the talent in this man with the tempter's face.

Myreth flashed him an amused look without seeming to change his expression. The bard suspected it was why Myreth had invited him forward, a desire for those same things, even though he knew nothing about Kavan that could have revealed he was a musician. Somehow, Kavan thought as he held that gaze, Myreth knew more than he should.

When those seated beside him rose, Kavan did likewise, although he was apprehensive about partaking in the holy gift after such a long time separated from it. It also concerned him that this could be, as was sometimes the case in Teren centers of worship, real wine, something most Elyri could not tolerate. The last time he had consumed wine had been a disaster. To drink it here, in a public setting, was to be open to further embarrassment or even illness or death. But he knelt as the others around him did, keeping his head bowed until Myreth, still singing as he stepped from one individual to another, stopped before him. Myreth had blessed each person with a hand upon their head, but with Kavan, he took the chalice from the girl and held it to the bard. It had to be a significant gesture but Kavan did not know what it meant.

What he did know was that when he took the cup and drank of a liquid that was sweeter and milder than any serbháló he had ever tasted, and when Myreth laid one gentle hand upon his head as any confessor or gdhededhá might, he was engulfed in an unexpected feeling of comfort and tenderness; he wondered if the others felt it too. Whatever Myreth was, he was no mere novice or apprentice.

When the last individual had partaken, the congregation uttered a final ritual prayer and filed silently from the náós towards a large hall containing several dozen tables filled with platters and bowls of food. Kavan looked for the farmer or his son, who had not participated in the Gathering, and wondered where he should sit as most people headed towards tables with a focus that suggested they were accustomed to a routine seating arrangement. There were people of all ages here, including the smallest of children, likely the entire population of the cloister, nearly two hundred people.

"Come." Myreth took his elbow and guided him to a table at the far side of the hall. Eight older members of the community were seated there, along with twin girls and their mother. They looked at Kavan with curiosity but none spoke until Myreth made the introductions.

"You are impressed with our Myreth?" the mother asked, passing a bowl of boiled eggs.

Kavan accepted the bowl with a thankful nod, careful not to drop it or spill its contents. None at the table took notice of his deformity. "How could I not be? To hear such a voice is…" He was stilled by the feeling of Myreth's gaze burning into him. "I know talent when I hear it. His voice is rare and precious. Anyone knowledgeable of music would recognize his quality."

"Are you knowledgeable? About music?" asked one of the elders.

Though he felt as if a trap had been sprung, Kavan replied with a reluctant sigh and pang of regret. "I was a harper by trade," he murmured with a glance at his hands, "but I do sing."

Another of the eight, called Valesce, leaned forward, nodded, and said, "We have a harp but it has no strings. It is quite ancient and I believe it is secured in the vault. It is unfortunate we cannot hear you play it, but perhaps you could sing while you are here."

He waited, making Kavan shift awkwardly in his chair. "I could not after what I have heard today. I fear Myreth out-masters my skill."

With a warm laugh, Myreth smiled. "It is not a contest, Kavan, but a sharing before k'Ádhá…"

"No contest perhaps, particularly if I do not participate. I will not say no…but rather we shall see. It depends on how long I am here."

"You are not of Gorbesh; you did not come to aid in today's delivery. May I ask why you are here? What is it you seek?"

Kavan released his breath slowly, feeling a stab of nervous tension claw at the base of his skull. "I am on a quest, a mission, and was sent here with the hope that you can help me. In the land I serve, there is an ancient náós below our King's keep. It was defiled by acts of the most barbarous kind and I am seeking the means to cleanse it. I was told by a woman known as k'ílshwythnec that the remaining articles I need are here; she bid me come and ask for them…"

At the mention of k'ílshwythnec, several heads around the table bobbed in unison. "The Chalice of Llyr and the Staff of Drebhoti," Valesce said. Again, many of those heads nodded.

Myreth turned with surprise. "I thought those to be mythical…"

"No, Myreth," the old man corrected, "they are real, guarded in secrecy since they came into our care. The k'gdhededhá has sole access, and only he can dispense them. You will need to ask him."

Though he did not intend to cut the man off, Kavan could not refrain from hastily asking, "Where is he? May I see him?"

Valesce chewed a bit of bread longer than Kavan thought he should before replying. "No one goes to him unless summoned. He is the oldest of us; he rarely leaves his chambers except for one Gathering a week. I will see that your request for audience is presented, but you will need to be patient. Three days hence he will attend the evening Gathering. You are welcome to abide with us until that time if he does not summon you first."

Three days. Kavan had come to this place feeling close to success, hopeful of reaching the end of his journey; three days felt like an eternity. If the need for this audience was not critical, or if Kavan was a less patient man, he would be tempted to decline or make his demands more forcefully. But he knew he was to be tested, and this request for patience might be one of those tests. Besides, three days gave him time to spend with Myreth, to discover what mystery made the man irresistible.

In the short length of his hesitation, the dark-haired man must have suspected rejection. "You will stay, Kavan? You will sing with us?"

Kavan could not deny the plea in Myreth's voice and eyes. He took a breath and nodded. "I cannot leave until I have what I came for. This purification is desperately needed. If you will accept me amongst you, I will be blessed to stay as long as necessary."

Valesce nodded with a smile and said, "It is allowed."

The meal progressed with little conversation and a great sense of relief for Kavan that he might be a mere three days away from obtaining the last of what he needed for the cleansing ritual. Little by little, the room cleared of diners, with even the farmer and his son heading away for the night until Kavan was alone with Myreth.

"I can take you to a room if you wish to sleep…but perhaps you would care to witness something miraculous first?"

Apprehensive but curious, feeling that perhaps it was Myreth's way of keeping company with him by presenting such a cryptic offering, the bard followed his host through several corridors, up several flights of stairs, until at the top of one of them Myreth opened a hatch in the ceiling. They emerged onto the flat roof of one of the cloister's many towers to a view of a tapestry of stars and clouds and moonlight above.

In its raw, natural beauty, the shadows of the peaks around him and the distant flatland across which he had recently traveled were an extraordinary vision to behold. Though unable to see this place from the village below, it was possible to make out the lights of Gorbesh from where they stood.

"I come here often," Myreth said as if admitting to a matter of personal embarrassment. He stared in the direction of the village wistfully. "I try to get here before the sun sets, but that is hard to do at this season of the year. This is the only place I know of where I can feel alone…where I can see the world I have never known and wonder what life must be like there."

The need for solitude was one Kavan knew well. "Alone? There seems more than adequate space…" He made note of Myreth's longing to see beyond these walls and recalled the villagers claim that these people never left their cloister. How frustrating that must be.

The dark-eyed man snorted. "Oh, there is space enough. Too much space. But when you spend your life within the confines of a single set of buildings, with the same small group of people, you cannot ever be considered alone. Everyone knows everything; privacy is lacking."

It was a feeling Kavan knew well from his years in the Lachlan court, and even in Bhryell. The smaller the group of people around, the closer the quarters, the harder it was to have secrets. "Are…how many live here?"

Leaning against the wall, staring across the rocky landscape, shadows darkening his features, Myreth shrugged. "At last census ten years ago there were two hundred and seventeen. I think there have been…fifteen children born since then and seven have died. There used to be many more; these walls were once entirely full I am told.

Over the centuries, disease, accidents, and age have taken their toll and the birthrate has declined; we are fortunate to have never suffered attack or invasion. Sometimes guests choose to remain with us, renewing our blood, replenishing our ranks. Though no one is permitted to leave without the k'gdhededhá's consent, some scale the walls and do not return. Perhaps," he muttered, looking over the edge to the steep mountainside at the bottom of the high wall, "they died."

"You are prisoners?" Kavan found that hard to believe.

"No, not prisoners." Myreth frowned as he tried to find the words to explain. "At one time this was an open place, sharing with the outside as any other order, I am told. But a plague swept through the land and the people decided to close the gates so that those here would be spared. Their gamble paid off, in as much as we have endured, our way of life preserved, but decades passed before anyone was brave enough to attempt to open the gates and leave. By then, I imagine, life on the outside had changed and none of those born here were comfortable outside. Thus was created a self-perpetuating order. It is a good life, I suppose, as we lack for nothing and the visitors from Gorbesh and the pilgrims we sometimes share our tables with, who join our order, tell us it is good here, but with nothing to compare it to, no experience of my own, I cannot say I agree."

"If you wished it, why don't you leave?"

"I haven't the courage," Myreth admitted sheepishly. "I have known nowhere else and would not have the first idea how to survive."

"Your voice would support you." Kavan was sure of it. "There are many who travel the lands performing for a living. Those with talent and appeal are in demand and rarely lack shelter, food, and coin."

Judging by Myreth's expression, that possibility was foreign to him. "Is that how you live?"

"I did for many years. And then…until recently, I was employed by a king…" Kavan looked wistfully across the landscape. "But he has died while I have been away and I do not know what that means for my future once my quest is complete. I may return to Rhidam, or I may resume wandering. But I do believe you could do it if you wished."

Going back would mean facing the princess, which he did not want to consider, but to Myreth, he could be honest about the possibilities of his future.

Myreth shrugged, not ready to seriously contemplate a life away from the home and family he had always known. "You are perplexed by our Gathering," he said, changing the subject.

Respecting the unspoken desire not to discuss an anxious topic, Kavan said, "Its informality was perhaps the biggest…difference. In my land, worship has become entrenched, with set patterns for everything down to the smallest prayer, the way one kneels or stands or sits. Despite the exalted status of women in my homeland, they are rarely allowed to participate in Gatherings and in some places outside of my country they are made to remain apart from the men. We have a system of gdhededhá…"

"I am gdhededhá. All adults here are. We serve k'Ádhá and one another."

For a moment Kavan hesitated. Having lived his life as though he were gdhededhá when he had not trained as such, Myreth's words made him feel awkward. "Ours," he murmured, "must go through specific, detailed, ritual training to gain their status. No one else may serve the gifts."

"Our practices offend you?"

"No…not at all. To be frank, I find it preferable for everyone to be involved if they choose. Faith as an institution feels sacrilegious to me, as it removes the power of k'Ádhá from the people and takes away our ability and right to communicate directly with him."

Myreth nodded in agreement. "You speak Kóráhm's words."

"Kóráhm has not spoken such things. If the k'gdhededhá heard such words they would be deemed…"

Heretical. He knew then, deep inside, a small part of why the leaders of his Faith condemned Kóráhm. He met Myreth's gaze with a start.

"He spoke of those things when he was with us many centuries ago. How could you not know? He wrote of them, intending to share his thoughts, beliefs…the things he witnessed here, with his people…"

The third volume. The book that had been banned by the leaders of the Faith. The writings that caused many in that organization who had declared him a saint, to later decry him as a heretic. How unknowingly was Kavan following in his patron's footsteps, even making the same judgments of faith without anyone guiding his knowledge? The shiver that ran up his spine was violent enough that Myreth saw it and he placed his hand over Kavan's. A large emerald ring glittered upon the middle finger of his hand but it was the power that Kavan noticed most. He marveled at its source.

"Are you cold?"

Tearing his gaze from that ring, Kavan replied. "No…I have just realized something I was not prepared for. Kóráhm was declared a saint, and later, when his third volume of writings came to light, his words were deemed blasphemous and copies of his writings confiscated by the k'gdhededhá were destroyed. Kóráhm was condemned by some as a heretic. No one has ever been able to tell me why, as few…or possibly no one, have read the third book. Few have read the first two. I have searched my whole life for that book, seeking to unlock the mystery, and while I possess copies of his other writings, the third volume remains beyond my grasp. A copy was finally found, but it was damaged by water, fire, and age, and is unreadable. I have wondered what he could possibly have written…"

"It is undoubtedly disconcerting to find that your beliefs parallel those of a heretic…or a saint."

"Exactly." Kavan was beginning to suspect that despite Myreth's apparent naiveté and innocence, he was older than he appeared. "Kóráhm's presence here would explain the likeness in the tapestry."

"It is an accurate representation? You have seen him?"

Baited again, trapped by this man into revealing more than he wished. Kavan suspected, however, that Myreth would believe the truth and not overreact. "I have seen him many times, in the flesh and as…something else. I long ago gave up trying to determine why he reveals himself to me, although I think I am beginning to understand."

A few strands of Myreth's straight hair pulled free of their restraint and fell around his face. He made no attempt to push them away and seemed to have no idea how alluring the effect was. The spark in his eyes bordered on fanatical though he showed remarkable control over any impulsive gesture he might want to make. "This is surely an auspicious sign. It has been a long while since anything of…since anyone of consequence has been here. I am sure the k'gdhededhá will be swayed when he learns this."

"Is it necessary to make it known?" If it helped him in his quest, it would be a good thing, but how many others need know? What might they think?

"It is nothing to be embarrassed or ashamed of, Kavan. You are honored and blessed, the way many of us wish we could be. I believe the k'gdhededhá will be more willing to see you and grant your requests if he knows you are favored by Kóráhm di Curnydhá." He gazed into the sky with a wistful sigh, and Kavan realized that his arrival was probably the most exciting thing that had ever happened to Myreth. "Can I convince you to sing with me tomorrow morning?"

Kavan shook his head. "I do not think I am ready for that. I have recently rediscovered my voice, and after hearing you…"

"Then you mean what you said? You spoke honestly?"

"I am always honest. Your voice is sublime. My faith in my own voice is not strong. Where I am from, my voice is a novelty; it is not like any other. I have avoided singing publicly most of my life, except on rare or special occasions. But…be patient and I may yet do it. Three days is a long time for me not to make music." Especially after the months he had been without.

The pout faded to reveal a faint smile. "Patience. I am patient because I must be, but I am not very good at it. Ask anyone here. Now…the hour grows late and the sun comes early. You are a guest and not required to partake in our routines, but I implore you to attend me on my duties. It will give us further opportunity to talk."

The idea pleased Kavan. He was not, as his cousin often told him, a very good guest, in that he insisted on doing the duties of servants and staff rather than allow others to serve him. "I would be honored," he said, determined to contribute as best he could. "I am eager to learn how you live in this place."

Myreth smiled as he lifted the hatch to the stairs that would take them inside. "Good. I will come for you at dawn. You will tell no one I brought you here? It was indulgent of me to occupy you, but though I have never shared it with another, I wanted to share it with you."

The smile was returned. It felt good to smile. "I will not break confidence with you, Myreth and I implore you to do likewise."

Myreth tucked the stray hair behind his ear and said. "After you?"

⧓Chapter 33⧓

Caol had done business with Leord Stold more times than he could count. Stold was one of his most reliable contacts and one man away from Rhidam's Association leader. The inquisitor had every reason not to trust Stold, yet every reason to believe that the tiny bald man was being honest. He knew in the recesses of his soul, as he had argued with the King, that the Association was not involved in Puncilla's death, but he had to be certain, hear the words from Stold. That Stold had come to him first on the matter, rather than having the inquisitor search him out, was enough for Caol to know his read on the situation was correct.

"You don't believe there were orders to dispatch dear Puncilla? There were no ill feelings between us…"

"Not even after she was rumored to be giving up the profession to marry an Elyri?"

Stold toyed with his ear absently. "Give up…no, I had not heard that. I knew she was seeing the Elyri…we all did. A handsome fellow with a full purse…and I knew she had stopped taking customers while he was in town."

Caol wondered if the rumor of marriage had been perpetrated simply to have an excuse to kill her. It was distasteful but possible. His more immediate concern was for the Elyri. "Was? Is he still here?"

"Dunno. No one considered telling him about Puncilla's death, though he must have found out by now. Maybe he's here; maybe he left town for somewhere safer now that its attraction is gone." Stold smiled slyly and the inquisitor ignored the look. Killing the woman to drive the man out of town was another possibility, but it seemed more likely that the Corylliens, or whoever they were, would kill him and allow her to live. Or perhaps the Elyri was lying dead somewhere, the Corylliens having killed them both. It was a grim thought. "He was staying at the Boar's Garden."

That name set off alarms in the inquisitor's head. As one of the places gdhededhá Claide frequented, any Elyri who stepped foot in that tavern would likely face an untimely death. "I'll look into that." He groaned and rubbed the back of his neck. "You know I have to ask this, even though I know the answer, but you or your partners haven't had a hand in this anti-Elyri propaganda and terrorism, have you?"

The small man broke into raucous laughter. "What would we gain? It makes no difference to a thief who his victim is; what matters is that they have something of value…and travelers generally have more on them, especially Elyri travelers. It behooves us to keep them alive and keep conditions favorable for itinerants. This violence is keeping people away, indoors…it has been lean for us since this started. We've been considering our own investigation…"

"I wish you would," Caol snorted, "since you do not seem to be finding much to assist mine. I'm sorry about your empty pockets, Stold. I am doing what I can, for everyone's best interest."

Stold nodded. "You can be assured my boss is looking into Puncilla's death. No one kills one of ours and gets away with it."

"She wasn't one of yours." Caol adjusted the hat on his head and shifted sideways in his chair. "Any suspects you find must be turned over to me promptly, is that understood, Stold? Before any harm is done to them."

Looking slightly insulted the man said, "This is not a matter…"

"If it is in any way connected to the terror running our lives, it certainly is a matter for the Crown. I will say this once more. Turn suspects over to me. I will question them. If it turns out some motive other than anti-Elyri prejudice triggered the killing, I will return the culprit to you for questioning and punishment. If they are connected to my investigation even remotely, there will be a reward in it for the person who apprehends the killer. And there will be a reward for you personally for seeing that my wishes are complied with. Is that clear?"

The man's narrow face wrinkled with a broad smile as he nodded. A reward from Caol Dugan was a sufficient motivator, as the inquisitor always made it worthwhile.

❧*❧

Was there any purpose for an outpost on Pháne? The twenty-six men chosen to staff it, thirteen one week, thirteen the next, had asked him that many times and each time Muir could tell that none believed the reason Gabrielle had given them. They had to accept that this was at Gabrielle's orders and with the Council's agreement. His men wanted to know what they were guarding, why it was necessary to keep trespassers from the island and protect the narrow channel of sea between Pháne and Káliel. What treasure or danger, natural or otherwise, could exist that the Prime Magistrate and Council felt it necessary to guard with this new outpost?

Even the Council was curious, but it was clear that Gabrielle was not going to reveal her reasons. They gave in to her demands since there seemed no reason anyone should want to go there, and anyone who was going there, invading Káliel's sovereign space, was likely to intend trouble. People landing there meant that they could be sneaking onto Káliel from that side of the island, unprotected by harbor patrol as it was, and as isolationist as the islanders were, the need to keep strangers away was acceptable enough.

Yet the longer they were stationed here, patrolling the channel with no activity, the more likely it seemed to Prince Muir that the Council might revoke the order and recall them. Was the visit of Anri Heward and his men some isolated incident that the prince had no cause to be concerned about?

In the pre-dawn darkness, Muir paced the length of the wall, watching the starlight play upon the water, occasionally glancing in the direction of home. He missed his wife tonight. Clianthe wanted to come with him and Gabrielle had been prepared to allow it, but Muir convinced them both that it was best for his new bride to remain home because there was no suitable place for her to sleep or spend her days. The outpost had been constructed with minimal effort and had a single room for sleeping, a room shared by the men stationed there. Having her near and being unable to sleep beside her would be intolerable. Moreover, he knew her presence would affect the morale of the men, and not necessarily in a positive way. He, like the others, remained here for their shifts and would return to their homes and families soon. For the time being, it was for the best.

The distinctive sound of a boat pushing through rough surf pulled him from his thoughts. It was still dark; he could see nothing at first. But soon a small ship drew close enough to be distinguished in the light of the outpost's lanterns. Not a Káliel ship; it ran without lights, too close to shore. Any closer and she would run aground, which was, perhaps, their intention. One of the night watchmen sounded the klaxon as extra torches were lit. It was as much an effort to tell the approaching ship she was in danger and warn her away from Pháne as it was to wake those men who slept.

Lights aboard the vessel began to glow and she drifted out to sea. There was no indication of passengers except for the lighting of the lamps and the shifting direction of the ship. It was not a trader, not a passenger ship, and not a military vessel. Possibly a personal frigate for some wealthy lord, but as Muir strained to find some identifying marker, there were none to be seen. Unmarked. Unlit. Perhaps the vessel had drifted off course, but the prince did not believe it. It looked suspicious enough that he felt more justified in being there. Whatever might still be in that cave, or had been there and since removed, was significant to someone. They were chased away easily this time, but if the cave was important enough for someone to make a second attempt, Muir was willing to wager they would make a third, and some of his men now believed it too. How soon they would come, no one could say. His concern was whether or not his small outpost could successfully repel attempts by larger, more determined vessels.

❧*❧

"I am pleased you found time to dine with me, dedhá. Please, sit."

gdhededhá Claide bowed hesitantly but sat across the table, eyeing the rich spread with gratitude. Being favored of the Faith did not mean meals such as this were served on any regular basis. In fact, it seemed to him that good meals should be one of the benefits of his office; he should not have to settle for eating the meager foods others ate.

"I am the one honored, Prince Espen, but I will admit I am confused by this invitation."

"There is no cause for confusion, dedhá, I assure you." Espen laughed cordially while the serving girl placed another platter, this one of bread, upon their table. "I have heard much about you; I thought it was time to meet. If I marry Princess Diona, my hand may be influential in the future of Enesfel, and men in power can share benefits if they know one another well. Dinner seemed an appropriate compensation for your time."

As expected, the mention of the words power and influence were the hooks with which to capture the gdhededhá's attention. Claide's eyes flashed with a spark of hope before he turned his attention to the meal. The Hatu prince continued. "Of course, I am also aware there may be theological differences between the Faith in Hatu and Enesfel and feel that it would be beneficial for me to learn those differences. There is no surer way to destroy a perspective marriage than by offending the woman you are courting or her family…particularly if that family happens to belong to the King. I wonder if perhaps there is some difference that has prevented the princess from accepting my offer, and so decided upon this audience with you."

The man arched a single eyebrow. "I had thought…you have pursued the princess for many years, or thus it has been said. Why these concerns?"

"Until recently she has not taken marriage offers seriously, but as she has expressed interest in opening a dialogue on the subject at last, it is time for me to prepare. Besides, I seem to have a great deal of unused time on my hands. Study seems an adequate way to fill time."

They talked as they ate, Espen posing questions mainly of an innocent or diverting nature. He watched the shifts of emotion in the gdhededhá's face, listened to the subtle nuances of his voice and words with the skill of a trained diplomat. He avoided asking questions relating directly to Elyri or the violence of recent months, knowing them to be touchy subjects and not wanting to raise ire or distrust. Still, by the time gdhededhá Claide excused himself, Prince Espen knew much of what he wanted to know about Enesfel's senior gdhededhá.

Claide was ambitious, with a well-buried ruthless streak, something almost unrecognized or at least ignored by the man himself. His convictions were strong, every movement weighed carefully against some internal measure that only he knew. There was resentment there, of a nature Espen could not determine; if Claide knew of its origins, he hid it expertly. Though the gdhededhá said nothing incriminating, Prince Espen no longer doubted Diona's convictions. gdhededhá Claide had the potential of being a dangerous man and he was hiding something.

Perhaps, Espen realized, women were better at reading emotions and motives than men were. At least, with gdhededhá Claide, Diona was certainly proving that to be true.

❧*❧

"Master Cáner?"

Gaelán pushed up in his bed to look at Lord McGrannis in the doorway. What he did not like about being left in the position of court healer was that duty frequently interfered with either his sleep or his personal life. There seemed to be no shortage of cuts and scrapes and broken bones in need of mending. Sometimes it felt like the palace staff was injuring themselves simply to try his patience.

"What is it?" he asked with a yawn. "Is someone hurt?"

"No, sir, not to my knowledge. I have come to deliver this. It was left at the gatehouse for Lord MacLyr but I have been told he has not yet returned and that all messages for him are to be given to you. You will see he gets this?"

A relieved sigh pushed through the boy's lips. "Please leave it on the table there. Thank you, Lord Chancellor."

Flannery bowed and did as he was asked, his actions indicating he was still not accustomed to his title.

When he was alone, Gaelán rose and dressed. There was no point in trying to go back to sleep. A letter for Ártur. From Captain Delamo or Kavan? Kavan's name was rarely spoken now, as if the bard had ceased to exist with his absence. It seemed to Gaelán that no one missed Kavan unless a royal function came at which he normally would have played. Irrationally, Gaelán felt it was an insult that his cousin's sole use, the one reason he was loved, was for music. Several times during Ártur's absence, the young healer had been tempted to utter hot-blooded rebukes or insults at those around him, but his father's admonition always came to mind. If you served the King, you learned to keep silent. But it did not seem fair to Gaelán, and without Ártur to share his feelings with, he wondered how much longer he could remain silent.

Thus the prospect of a letter from Kavan or Captain Delamo was uplifting and exciting. He reached for the message but recoiled as he touched it. A violent, hostile shock of anger and hatred shot through him. Never before had anything like this happened and he knew, though how he knew confused him, that this letter had nothing to do with Kavan, just as he knew that the dark emotions of the sender were directed at Ártur.

His first thought was to find his father and give him the letter for investigation. Yet he did not know how to explain what he had experienced, did not know if it had an explanation. Also, since the letter was not addressed to him, he felt that perhaps he should let Ártur read it and then tell the older healer what had happened. He opted for the second choice. A letter, a single bit of parchment, would harm no one, and if it was a threat, as Gaelán suspected, nothing could be done until the nature of the threat was known.

And Ártur was safe where he was.

Tucking the letter into a dresser drawer for safekeeping, Gaelán decided to seek out Asta, who was undoubtedly already awake at this too early hour. Of the people in the keep, she was the one he could talk to the easiest. She also knew how to keep a secret. He hoped she would have some suggestion for him of how to deal with this letter.

❧*❧

"He is irrefutably guilty of something; I stake my life on it."

The corners of Diona's eyes creased at that remark and she stared at the prince with concern. "I pray you do not have to, Espen."

"Did he tell you anything useful?"

Prince Espen shifted to face the inquisitor. "We discussed the religious differences between Hatu and Enesfel and spoke a little about his decision to become gdhededhá. He chose his path out of a desire to bring lasting peace and stability to Enesfel, to which he seems to think any means are justified as long as the end is obtained."

"Like ejecting Elyri," muttered Caol as Diona asked, "He said that?"

"His words were about how sometimes a person must go through torments to find peace…but it was his tone and air that revealed more about his intentions than his words. Particularly when I agreed that sometimes one must endure unpleasantness to reap rewards."

"Espen!"

He shrugged as he glanced at the woman beside him. "It is true, milady, in many matters. Wars must be waged to secure national interests. A man must endure the agony of several disgraces before he finds a wife. A woman must endure the pain of labor to produce a child. If a lasting peace with the Elyri can be formed from recent events, it will be to the good of all. But the course will not be painless."

She scowled, an expression which deepened when Caol said, "The prince has a point."

"Did he say anything about the missing children…or any of the absent?" she asked to direct the conversation back on course.

"No. dedhá Rankin is offering the families comfort and support. Claide says it is a truly appalling turn of events, but he seems to believe that a ransom demand will come for them, as it will for the k'dedhá."

"Is he getting suspicious?"

The prince shook his head. "He does not seem to be. He sees it as a matter of incompetence on your part, and the justice's. He did mention he was considering launching an ecclesiastical investigation, but this was said flippantly; I do not know how serious he is."

"We cannot let that happen, but it sounds as if we can wait a few more days before exposing the truth. At least, we should try." The inquisitor scratched his elbow. "Anything else worth mentioning?"

"On the subject of religion, his ideas are quite set. If I did not know it, I would think him from Hatu; perhaps his family is. He wants women separate and subservient…"

"Not if I can help it," the princess muttered under her breath.

Espen continued unruffled. "His belief in the sanctity of the dedhá and their duty to protect their congregations from all forms of evil stretches to include censorship of written materials and songs, the barring of known criminals from Gathering Houses unless they perform proper penance…or pay a significant fine. Wrongdoers should be punished to the fullest extent of the law, even for the smallest of crimes…"

The princess interrupted with a sneer. "Yet he demanded Hagan stay the execution of Kavan's attacker, that he let the man go free. Next, you will say he is against the Crown."

"That is one area," the prince agreed with a nod, "where he seems to be in the greatest conflict with himself. He believes in the divine right of kings, yet he finds himself at odds with certain policies."

"Such as retaining the Elyri…"

"Diona," Caol finally said, annoyed with his niece's interruptions and need to have a say.

Espen reached for her hand and squeezed it reassuringly to show there were no hard feelings. "While he did not say it, it would seem to hold true. Kings have divine right, but they cannot rule over the Faith and are, in fact, subservient to it, I think is how he described it. He does feel the Elyri are a threat on every level, and, as I said, he is hiding something."

There was a long pause before the inquisitor sighed and spoke. "My people will continue to watch him. This gets trickier as I have to convince the King we cannot possibly pull my people from their investigations. I need them, but how can I keep them without the means to pay them?" He stood and bowed. "Thank you for your aid, milord. I don't think any of us could have done what you did."

"I am happy to be of service," the prince said with a smile. "It is why I journeyed to Enesfel. And if I can aid in the retention of your contacts, please, do not hesitate to request it" He had financial resources of his own and believed his brother would assist them. His sidelong glance at the woman beside him indicated that helping Enesfel and King Hagan was not his only reason for being there.

❧*❧

Myreth's hair was not tied back tonight as it had been for most of the previous two days, and in the darkness under the cloudy sky, it appeared black. Much of it had been pushed over his shoulder, long and straight. It was smooth, not the tousled softness of Kavan's own white-silver locks. Stifling the urge to touch it, an urge which grew stronger as they spent more time together, Kavan stood beside him atop the tower, where they stared at what appeared to be storm clouds gathering in the distance. It would likely rain during the night, Myreth said, and the Elyri was inclined to agree.

After seeing the farmer and his son off yesterday morning, Kavan's day was spent in a series of routine tasks. He and Myreth cleaned chicken pens, scoured several large pots and pans, and finally gave both his room and Myreth's a thorough scrubbing. None of it had been particularly unpleasant work, though it had been challenging for his misshapen hands, and the time passed quickly with his focus on new skills and the dark haired man to converse with. Kavan learned what few details Myreth was willing to share, but the bard suspected there was much more to the man that Myreth did not know.

He had been a foundling, left outside the cloisters gates when less than a month old. The community took him in, raised him, and not having known anything else, Myreth was content to remain. He had a quick wit, a playful spirit, and an intelligent mind. He liked to read, enjoyed sculpting in both clay and stone, and had developed a deadly hand with a sword and bow. But his main passion was singing. When his talent became apparent in his middle teen years, he was thrust into the position of Sacramental Chanter, the single formal post in their Gatherings, although before Myreth there had apparently been no single person designated to that task.

As the years passed, however, Myreth had grown weary of the distinction and wanted nothing more than to participate in the Gathering as a humble worshipper. He beseeched the k'gdhededhá to be released from the position, but no one else was willing to fill it for fear of failing to live up to the example he set. He remained in place and more years passed. It was obvious to everyone, but especially Myreth, that he was not like those with whom he resided. He looked to be barely an adult, perhaps a man of twenty years, but he had served as Chanter for more than forty.

Elyri? Kavan could not tell. He had yet to touch the man's thoughts and there were none of the physical characteristics that he could see since Myreth's body, except for his hands and head, were kept covered. Nor could Kavan read any psychic activity or see any sign that Myreth was attuned to the energies around them. That would not be unheard of; Kavan had heard tales of Elyri born psychically blind, or with such low levels of power that it was inconsequential. Without touching him to read him, Kavan could but guess if that was the case, and he resisted it with every ounce of his will. With that sort of age, Myreth could not be Teren, or at least not full-blooded Teren. k'kairá? Possibly, but every member of that race Kavan had ever met had violet eyes, and Myreth's were black. Perhaps he, like Orynn, was part of all three races. Only a healer might be able to answer the mystery. Kavan did not believe that, despite Myreth's discontent with his life, growing restlessness, and unsatisfied curiosity, the man was prepared for that kind of knowledge.

Today had been filled with a series of dogmatic dialogs on topics ranging from the daily application of Holy Ordinances to the divinity of saints. The latter topic had sparked Kavan's interest and invoked much debate on the nature of a saint, the qualifications for sainthood, and finally on whether anyone had the authority and right to declare a man a saint…or a heretic, when the subject finally drifted to Kóráhm.

Myreth spoke without looking at him. "You were troubled. May I ask why? You call Kóráhm saint…"

Kavan did not look at him either. It was easier to speak his thoughts without the distraction of the man's beauty. "I believe there are men and women who have lived devout lives…have done tremendous good in the name of Dhágdhuán and k'Ádhá, in the cause of Faith, who lived in the service of others. These people deserve to be respected, and modeling ourselves after them seems an acceptable practice. Calling them saints sets them apart, but what is a saint other than a title applied to people? If it is nothing more than a title, why should the k'lómesté have the final word over who is a saint and who is not? And if minor differences in theology and practice are enough to condemn anyone as a heretic, then I suspect there are more heretics in the folds of the Faith then there are saints, gdhededhá, or followers."

Myreth nodded. "Your ideas are set…or seem to be. So what was the cause of your distress?"

"I…" He hung his head, ashamed to admit the cause as he listened to the words he had just spoken replay within his head. "People call me málneag. I deny it with every breath because I do not believe it. Do not want to believe it. But I look back over my life, how I have lived, how it must appear to others…" For several minutes he said was quiet. "It is no less devout than some who have been called saint. The Faith has not canonized me, and I pray fervently they do not…but for what purpose do I tremble and weep when I hear the word?"

"Because you are a humble man." Kavan's expression gave Myreth pause. "You do not want to be an example for others and yet you are. We all are. It is the calling of Dhágdhuán, to follow in faith and guide others. You cannot escape it. When we know ourselves, our weaknesses and faults, it is difficult for most to find themselves equated with those who live seemingly perfect…"

The bard shook his head. "Kóráhm was a man with faults like any other. He was not as flawless as I long believed. It seems likely that many of those we call saints were as imperfect as men and women as I am, and yet they have been revered, accepted by the Faith. It is one lesson I have learned with difficulty but I believe I have learned it well. I wonder how many of them would be appalled to know they have been dubbed a saint."

Myreth chuckled. "Likely all of them. Fortunately, it is a title bestowed when they can no longer protest. What is Kóráhm to you?"

Never having tried to define their relationship before, it took Kavan a moment to formulate an answer. "I think the best title for him is mentor. Or friend. He has been both when I have been in sore need of it. And yet I can no longer claim to want to live as he lived. I have my own faults to struggle with and do not desire his."

There was peace. To speak those words aloud made the matter clearer than it had been. It placed many things into perspective. Kóráhm was no longer a model upon a pedestal, but rather his friend. Dhágdhuán, the true model of Faith, was in place as he should be. Another fault exposed. With a sigh of relief, Kavan offered a prayer and gave heartfelt thanks to Kóráhm for leading him to Myreth and this revelation.

"I should like to see him someday." Turning his back to the view, Myreth crossed his arms and leaned against the short wall. "The elders were pleased with your knowledge of the holy writings, theology, and Faith tenants. The villagers and pilgrims who come know little about the Faith and such spirited discussions as what we shared today are rare…unless it is a matter of explaining the issues to argumentative children who are too young to grasp the meaning of things. To be challenged by a knowledgeable adult for some purpose other than to relieve boredom is stimulating. And I am sure your familiarity with, and knowledge of, Kóráhm, surprised them. It was true?"

"I was told the tale by a woman I consider to be a reliable source, and it confirms much of what I previously suspected. Since Kóráhm did not refute it when I confronted him…"

"Then it must be." Myreth's smile was wide and awe-struck. "How wonderful it must be to be on intimate terms with a saint."

On intimate terms with a saint. The back of Kavan's neck tingled with the soothing presence of Kóráhm's touch, as if his gentle fingers had brushed the hair from the nape of Kavan's neck. He was tempted to turn but knew Kóráhm would not be there. If he was, Myreth would see him. He wrapped his arms around his torso and sighed. "If the elders are…then why have I not received audience with the k'gdhededhá? I was told I would be tested, yet I have spent my time in labor and study. I must gain what I seek, and soon, as there is no other means by which I can do what I must." He ended the outburst when he felt how slighted Myreth was. "I should not take out my frustration on you. You know little more than I."

"I know k'gdhededhá will see you when he is ready, perhaps tomorrow when he comes for his weekly Gathering. As for tests, if there are any, it is likely he knows what they are and will direct you. I know Valesce reports everything you do; perhaps you are being tested and are unaware of it."

There was tightness around Kavan's eyes as he considered this. It would be a likely scenario, but the bard did not like the thought of being tested without his knowledge. How could he know if he was passing the tests if he did not know what those tests were?

Sensing Kavan's unease, when Myreth spoke it was with a hesitant voice. "Will you serve with us tomorrow?"

"I told Valesce I will sing in the morning. after that, I don't know."

"There is too much hesitation in you. If you want to do it, do it."

You would hesitate too, he thought, if you had seen what I have seen during a Gathering. Out loud, he twisted the man's words back around onto him. "The same could be said of your hesitancy to leave here and explore the world. As with you, my hesitation is not without justification, believe me."

"I shall have to," the taller man shrugged, "since you will not explain it. May I sing with you?"

That thought brought a wistful smile. "Hear me first. I am honest when I say my voice is…unique. If my voice and skill are to your liking, we will see what can be arranged for a later Gathering. I doubt we know the same songs; we would need to rehearse." Now that he was talking about it, his excitement for the idea increased.

"I learn songs fast. Allow me to hear it once and I can repeat it. It will be good to learn new music; it has been too long of singing the same. I will be patient a little longer, as you have my curiosity. I want to hear you sing."

The rumble of thunder traveled across the leaden sky, cutting off any reply Kavan might have made. "It looks as if your prediction of rain may come sooner than anticipated."

Myreth graced him with another seductive, hooded look and followed Kavan indoors.

⟫*⟪

In the upper oratory of Rhidam's castle, Ártur emerged from the k'dhín bhólibh and paused to extend his senses, in search of something he did not find. There was nothing in the aura of the room to indicate that Kavan had been there, which meant that the man had not come home. He had not expected his cousin back; if he had come he would have gone to Bhryell to meet his newest niece. But Ártur had hoped.

The healer was more reluctant to return to Enesfel than expected, the first time he could remember feeling out of place in his years of service here. He had settled into the easy and pleasant routine of caring for his children, of being with Syl and his family, and the idea of returning to Rhidam without them, to face the horrors plaguing the Teren kingdom, troubled him. He hid that fact from Syl, as doing his duty was a priority still, and when his wife convinced him that if he had to go, she could manage their family with Dháná and Bhen's help, Ártur gave in to the necessity of returning.

But he had come back to discover how little had changed. Kavan was still gone and there had been no crisis large enough to summon him that Gaelán had not been able to handle. He did not know yet if the violence had ceased or grown worse and it was too late tonight to seek answers. The entire grounds, except for the night watchmen, would be asleep or preparing for bed. Tomorrow would be soon enough to find answers. If he was fortunate, sleeping in his bed would be enough to convince him that returning had been the right choice…even if Syl was not beside him.

Rocking the woman gently in his large arms, Wortham looked across the room to where Urian was sightlessly examining the emaciated woman upon the bed. When he pulled the sheet over her face, the captain knew Zelenka's assessment was correct. She had climbed the loft and shaken him awake, her voice bordering on panic as she told him that her mother would not wake up, did not seem to be breathing, and was cold to the touch.

"I am sorry, Zelenka. If we had known she was ill…"

The woman shook her head. There were tears in her eyes, on her cheeks, soaked into Wortham's shirt, but she was no longer hysterical. The knowledge of the situation took away her shock and fear and with

Wortham's arms around her, she did not believe anything could harm her. "Not ill. Old. Doctors could not help. Her days were short. We knew this."

"Is there anything Wortham or I can do?" asked the monk as he found his way back to them and put his hand on Zelenka's head.

Looking at the blind man, she waited while Wortham translated words she did not know. "We must stay with her until daybreak, keep the spirits away. Leaving her unattended before burial means the spirits will consume her; it will bring bad luck to Gorbesh. Tomorrow we give her to the earth."

It was to the monk's credit that he did not ridicule her beliefs or seek to disavow her of her notions that the recently deceased could attract spirits. Or perhaps Urian believed it was true; Wortham did not know. The monk shuffled to the cot and knelt beside it to pray for the woman's repose. Wortham leaned against the wall, his arms around Zelenka, and hummed one of the hymns Kavan often played as she rested her head against his broad chest. It was a melody he found comforting, and since tonight there was no harp to soothe them, his rough deep voice would have to do.

❧Chapter 34❧

When Kavan awoke several hours before dawn it was the result of a series of dreams, or rather a single continuous, nightmarish dream of times he would rather forget. One by one, the Gatherings of his childhood came to him, reminding him of the reasons he should not go forth with his plan to assist these people in their celebrations. The first incident at his Initiation when Hes Índári filled with light and music, the burial of Phyóná Térari when he was sure he could have restored the woman's life if he had been able to move, and his final service as altar attendant when the serbháló in the chalice turned to blood. Those were the most significant moments, but there were others between and after when his music, or simply his attendance, filled Gathering Halls with a divine presence that many had witnessed but none could explain.

His singing might call forth whatever it was; there were many times when the harp in his hands had summoned it. It was possible his voice could do the same since he believed it was either the music or his faith that brought forth those presences and not the instrument itself. He was confident that, of these people here, some would feel it if it came; Myreth would be among them. What would they do? What would they say? If he did anything more than sing, what might occur? Fearing that they would shun him as others had done, refuse him what he had come here to obtain, Kavan could resist participating in any way beyond singing, as a way to protect himself from embarrassment, but his singing alone might be enough.

Perhaps those divine presences would be the final test to pass.

Donning another off-white, long-sleeved tunic and trousers as Myreth had procured for him yesterday, Kavan glanced at the metal flask on the nightstand, heedful of Orynn's words. Should he fill it with water and take it to the Gathering in the hopes that some blessing would be bestowed on it? How would he carry it…and how would he know if the blessing occurred? He would know, she said, but still he doubted. In the end, he opted to leave it where it was and went to the náós, arriving before anyone else. He was gazing at Dhágdhuán, a string of words forming a song in his mind to the fragment of tune the songbird had given him, when Myreth entered, his expression child-like and serene. "Did you sleep well?"

"Yes…and no. I will not participate in this morning's Gathering beyond singing, Myreth. I cannot."

Myreth nodded. "I suspected as much by your expression. But I ask that you take my place as Chanter…"

"Myreth…"

The dark head of hair shook. "I have asked Valesce to lead the prayers and dispense the sacrament, but I ask that you sing in my place. I want to hear you. I listen to you speak and am overwhelmed by the sound. I want to drink in your music without the distraction of attending to the others. I want to do it for my soul. I think I must. Is that too much to ask?"

He begged like a child, no, like a lover, pleading for something to remember his beloved by when they parted. Kavan reached to touch Myreth's face before he could resist the impulse, but the arrival of others stopped him from making contact. With a nod, he took a seat beside Myreth in the front row and tried to refocus on the song he had been composing, his eyes fixed on the figure above the altar to shut out the soft clamor of others taking seats behind him.

His song was still incomplete by the time Valesce summoned him to the altar. Legs shaky and weak, he needed Myreth's gentle support to rise. He could feel the gazes upon him and hear the silence of collectively baited breaths. They could not know what to expect, but after many years of having Myreth perform this duty, they assumed this change was significant. Their suspense added to Kavan's nervousness, but this had been his choice and he was not going to back out. With a great force of will, he joined Valesce at the altar.

Two young boys were chosen to offer the sacrament this morning; they came forward, their clean-scrubbed faces beaming as if serving with this stranger was an unusual honor. Valesce handed the flask to one, the empty chalice to the other and then they took their positions, one on either side of the bard.

Kavan was silent, his throat constricted around air and words as he struggled against one last battle of nerves. From the corner of his eye, he saw Myreth nod, signaling for him to proceed when he was ready; Kavan took strength from the gesture, closed his eyes to concentrate on the song he had prepared and took a deep breath.

Be with me, he prayed. I cannot do this alone.

At that moment when the first notes seeped forth, low and soft, it wove its way among the listeners and Myreth felt sure his heart stopped. He fought to breathe and could not remain standing. He dropped into his seat, dumbfounded. Never had he heard a man sing with such a voice. An alto, perhaps even soprano; it was difficult to tell from those first few sounds. Natural, he wondered, having never encountered any man singing such notes, or had he trained to sing that way? This was the first voice he had found, save his own, that contained that element of emotional and tonal clarity that others treasured in his voice. He did not recognize the words of the song, and as he listened he realized that Kavan was composing as he sang, something Myreth could not do. Rising slowly to his feet, he came forward two steps to stand face to face with Kavan as the bard opened his eyes and then closed them again. Humbled by the realization, Myreth bowed his head. This man was his equal, perhaps even his better. He now believed he was not alone in the world.

It was difficult for Kavan to keep the quaver from his voice when the first swell of energy built around him. Not since kneeling in prayer in the upper palace oratory before Princess Diona had brought his world crashing around him, had the presences joined him. It confirmed in his heart that he was restored to grace. Slowly, steadily, as his confidence increased, the energy did too, until it surrounded him, filled him. There was no need to look to know that the congregation experienced the energy too; he felt it in the surge of emotion that further fueled the anxiety warring with his self-confidence. Yet he did open his eyes, some part of him needing to see the effect this event was having on those uninitiated into the White Bard's gifts.

To his amazement, none of their faces were fearful or condemning. Nor did they exhibit the rapture that generally preceded someone dubbing him málneag. There were tears on some faces, ecstatic smiles on others, but most were simply pleased expressions calm with acceptance. Only Myreth's was different. He received the sacrament, and as he retreated, his dark eyes devoured Kavan one last time, eyes passionate with fulfillment.

The song died away after the last individual partook, taking the energy with it until there were no presences in the room except for the people who lived in this place and the guest who stood before them. Valesce spoke the closing prayer and everyone filed out without a backward glance. Everyone, that was, except Valesce, who smiled and bowed to Kavan before leaving, and Myreth, who waited until they were alone before rushing to Kavan and embracing him.

"I am complete. I have found a man who is my better in every sense that matters. Your modesty is unwarranted. You have the voice of a záryph."

Uncomfortable in that embrace, Kavan gingerly extracted himself from it. "záryph, málneag…I am just a man, Myreth."

"Did I say you were not? It is a figure of speech. Not having heard záryph sing, I cannot mean it literally of course." He smiled. "But I would think there must be záryph with voices much like yours."

"The presences…"

"Is that what you feared?" He put his arm around Kavan's shoulders and steered him towards the door.

Kavan shook his head. "I do not fear them; they have been with me for so long that I have no reason to be afraid.

Myreth nodded in understanding. "And yet others who experience them with you do fear…particularly when they experience it for the first time. You dreaded what we might do?"

"Might do…might think…might say…yes."

They reached the doorway and paused there with it still closed. "Would it comfort you to learn that similar things have happened here before? Not of this nature, it is true, but there have been miracles, speaking with the tongue of the záryph…that sort of thing."

"Have you ever witnessed…?"

Myreth sighed. "There have been no miracles in my time, save when I was small. There was a stranger among us, a woman. I am told that there was a fire in the kitchen that she put out without going near it, and that during one service she restored sight to a blind man. I do not remember it clearly, but Valesce does. Ask him. He may tell you."

Kavan wondered if the woman had been Elyri, a healer perhaps. He knew he could put out such a fire, and it made him happy that he had chosen not to display any Elyri use of power here. There was no need to mislead people with acts that were in no way miraculous.

"But these things," Myreth continued, "we expect them. They are signs of k'Ádhá's involvement in our world, and also signs that a change is due. The k'gdhededhá says we have seen nothing in many years because we are in preparation for an event of great magnitude; when miracles again occur within these walls, the event is at hand. Whether or not that is true, whether or not you are he who will herald this event, none of us will know until it happens. But I believe it."

"You welcome these miracles and signs and do not call me…?"

"What?"

Kavan shuddered and leaned against the door frame. "In my village, when these things began occurring…men have been healed at my hand; I have seen…things have come from my hands that no man can do but for the touch of k'Ádhá through him. For these things I have not asked for, my own people call me prophet…saint. I could not bear it before, when some part of me considered the miracles to somehow be mine when I know they are not." He was ashamed to admit it but knew it was true.

"You may one day be hailed a prophet if, as I said, your coming is the precursor for some great change in our lives." Myreth clasped his shoulder. "And I know little about what truly qualifies a man for sainthood, but I can assure you, none of us fear you."

The bard nodded, his eyes closed as he forced himself to be calm. Not to be feared or worshiped were precious gifts, the sort that made him think he could remain here for many years and be content but for his occasional need for freedom and flight.

Sensing there was more Myreth wanted to say and was hesitant to, he swallowed uneasily and said, "You wonder about my voice."

"How can you…?"

Kavan looked into the darker eyes fretfully. "It is a question I face whenever I sing. I am not a eunuch. It is my natural voice." Peoples interest, he realized, would now be compounded by the mutilation of his hands. Thankfully, no one here had asked about that.

"It did not change when you became an adult?"

"A little. My registers…my tone…broadened, but not much. I can no longer reach some of the highest notes I reached as a boy but I can reach most."

"And thus you fear ridicule." Myreth opened the door and stepped into the corridor. "I think you need not have fear, at least from us. People will think what they wish no matter what you say, but I believe that anyone hearing you sing will not care one way or another for the reason. They will be too enamored with the beauty."

The compliment was accepted with a bow of the bard's head. "They might not care, but they are curious. As you were. as all except…one…of my friends have been curious. It is the way it is and I should be used to it."

"Once you sing more often, allow people to experience the beauty, you will grow accustomed to your sound and to their reactions and curiosity. Your confidence will increase. Please. I think I speak for the others when I beg you to serve with us at noon. Sing for us. I will arrange for us to deliver the sacrament together if you are willing."

"I…" He wanted to refuse, but some small prompting in his soul would not allow it. Tonight the k'gdhededhá was due to attend, after which, if Kavan was lucky, he would have what he needed and be allowed to leave this place. He might not see Myreth again, and sharing this one small duty with him seemed the right decision, for Myreth's sake if not his own. "You, Myreth, have a gift for soothing a man's fear. You have no idea how much I treasure that. I will do it if you will grant me one request. Sing with me."

A delighted smile flashed upon the sun-browned face. "This evening we shall sing…when the k'gdhededhá is here. It gives us the afternoon to select something fitting. This morning I am called into conference with Valesce."

The muscles along Kavan's jaw twitched. "About me?"

With a shrug, Myreth replied, "I do not know, but I think, since I have had the most contact with you, that would be a likely assumption. Will you share the morning meal with me?"

Kavan nodded, relieved to have made it through one uneventful Gathering; he knew he would not have thought about a meal for several hours if Myreth had not suggested it. When it came time to leave, be it tonight or tomorrow, he knew he would be reluctant to say farewell to this man.

❧*❧

Awakened by screaming, Wortham's first impulse was to reach for the sword he usually kept nearby, but recalled, as he fumbled for it, that he was in Zelenka's home and had put his sword out of her sight beneath the straw in the loft. Zelenka was beside the cot, staring at her mother as her scream died into a terrified whimper. The reality of her mother's death might have finally sunk in with the morning's light and the visage of the dead. He groaned as he pushed to his feet, planning to comfort her, and noticed then that the covering had been pulled back to reveal the old woman's face. Her eyes were open.

It was into those unseeing cloudy eyes that Zelenka was staring. Wortham wanted to say something, but Zelenka was babbling, something about how they had fallen asleep, broken the vigil, and evil spirits had come into her mother. Why else would her eyes be open in death except to see the living and curse them? Why else were they now clouded over with a ghostly film? The captain wanted to say something reassuring but knew not what. He had not bothered to see if the woman's eyes were open or closed last night; it had been too dark to know that detail. Nor had Urian thought to check. They had assumed she had died in her sleep.

It was possible she had been awake when death had come, as men on the battlefield were. Her eyes would have remained open unless someone closed them. Urian would not have noticed that detail, and Wortham had not been near her long enough to check. Or some involuntary reaction of muscles as the body had grown cold had caused them to open. Wortham had seen that happen too. And no amount of assurance that the cloudiness of her eyes was a natural occurrence and not the result of an invasion of spirits was accepted. Zelenka would not hear him. In her mind, her mother had died while asleep with her eyes closed. Now her eyes were open. To Zelenka, there was a single possible explanation. Evil spirits had come.

"What do we do?" The ignorance and uncertainty of his question seemed to frighten her more. "I am sorry, Zelenka, but where I am from, we do not have ceremonies to deal with evil spirits. Only those gdhededhá Urian can perform. Our ways are different than yours. It is your ways we must follow. Tell us what will happen, what we can do."

His calm words and strong grasp around her slowly helped calm her enough to allow her to think and speak coherently. She wiped her face and turned away from her mother. "There is a cave in the mountains with a stone closing its. We must take her there and seal her within, with the appropriate offerings. If it is not done today, the spirits will escape during the night and more people will die. Once she is in the cave, the spirits will leave the body and be trapped."

"Wouldn't opening the cave release other spirits trapped there?" Wortham asked, having no idea how many bodies might have been laid to rest there in the centuries Gorbesh had existed.

"The offerings are food for the spirits containing poisons to kill them. There will be no spirits when we open it. After that," she sniffed and wiped her face, "I must leave."

Urian took her hand. "Leave? This is your home."

"I have allowed spirits into my house. Once a spirit has found a way into the world, others will follow. If I stay, more will come. If I take another home in Gorbesh, they will seek me, find their way. I must either leave on my own or be driven out by the elders to expel the spirits. I will sell what I own and go. Once I leave, I am safe, and Gorbesh will be safe. It is the best I can do."

"Where would you go?" the gdhededhá asked, suspecting Wortham was not speaking because he was calculating the logistics of travel without Kavan.

"Pa'aliaka…or any village between that would welcome me."

How did Gorbesh replenish their population if people were forced to leave for something as simple as this? Wortham did not understand. "Somewhere where you know no one? Who will care for you? How will you survive?" Wortham knew she had been surviving before, bartering goat's milk and working with the other women to mill and grind the grain. She did not need anyone to look after her. But he felt compelled to ask, concerned for her welfare and her future. "I will not hear of it." He turned her to face him. "You will come with me."

It was too much to expect a smile on this day, but he could see in her eyes that she was grateful for his offer. "What of your friend?"

"He…" Wortham sighed. What of Kavan? How would the bard feel about bringing this woman with them when he clearly felt threatened by her? "He may not be happy at first," he finally said, "but he will not want you to suffer. He will allow you to come with us."

"I do not want to cause discord…you should ask first, but I will not be able to wait until he returns…"

"Find out when the next group of merchants leaves for Pa'aliaka," the monk suggested. "We make plans to leave with them, and if Lord Cliáth has not returned we leave a message directing him to follow us and explain the reason for our departure. But first, I suggest we take care of your mother before the day passes. Give us instructions, my child, and we will set to work."

❧*❧

The first words out of Gaelán's mouth when he saw his uncle were, "A boy or a girl?"

Ártur's thoughts were otherwise occupied when the boy bounded into his room and it took a few moments to determine what Gaelán was asking. When he did, he gave a warm smile. "Hello to you, Gaelán. You are the first to realize I am back."

Rocking on his heels, the young healer replied, "I sensed you in the oratory last night; I was in k'aendhá room when you returned."

Heart skipping several beats, the healer dropped the papers he held. "Is Kavan back?" He had not felt or sensed him, but Kavan might have hidden from detection.

"No," Gaelán sighed. "I was…missing him…and I slept in his bed. I get angry sometimes that no one thinks about him anymore. I feel better when I am in his room."

Ártur opened his arms and embraced the boy tightly. So this was why he occasionally found Kavan's bed unmade. "We think about him, Gaelán, more than you know. But what good is talking? It will not make him return any faster nor will it ease our sadness."

"It makes me feel better to talk about him…to remember…even though I have little to remember…but if you prefer not to…"

"You can talk about him with me, Gaelán," the healer assured him.

"Thank you." That made him feel better. "So? A boy or girl?"

"Your newest cousin is a girl; her name is Chethá. Her hair is redder than your mother's, if you can believe that."

"And she will be a healer?"

"Someday, yes. Syl and I will train her. Has anything happened here while I was away?"

"Very little." Gaelán perched on the nearest chair and toyed with the hem of his tunic. "Bumps, bruises, scrapes, cuts…a couple of broken bones from a fight…a splinter in Asta's finger. The princess claims King Hagan wants to take gdhededhá's advice and expel us from Enesfel for our safety. There were six children kidnapped but I do not know much about that. Puncilla the madam was murdered, supposedly for planning to marry an Elyri gentleman. Prince Harcourt took a meal with dedhá Claide, and Lord Dugan is being pressured to sever his ties with the Association."

Ártur side-eyed him. "You are full of gossip, aren't you?"

"I overhear very little, but Asta tells me the important things. Those are things I thought you might want to know; if you want details, you'll have to ask someone else."

"Have you had any more dreams?"

"No…maybe that is why I felt…disconnected." As chilling as the dreams were, he missed the aftermath, the nearness he felt to Kavan.

"I should like to continue my vigil a while longer," Ártur said.

"You cannot stay in my room forever…" the boy groaned.

"But I can check on you throughout the night. If there is any connection to Kavan in these dreams, they may not stop until he returns. I would feel better keeping my eye on you."

"You can if you want." He pulled the slightly crumpled letter from his tunic pocket. With that unpleasant sensation coming through, he almost decided not to give it to Ártur. "There is…this came for you a few days ago. I thought it might be from Captain Delamo, but when I touched it, I knew it wasn't."

Taking the letter, Ártur felt the violent shock and almost dropped it. His expression told Gaelán that feeling impressions and emotions from objects was not unusual. The healer broke the wax seal with shaking hands and read the contents hastily. Mouth going dry, he stared at the letter as he folded it.

"aendhá?"

"It is nothing important," was the distracted reply as he shoved it into the pocket of his yellow tunic.

The boy was unconvinced. He knew what he felt from it and it was most certainly something important. "It was a threat, wasn't it?"

Hoping to distract them both from the letter, Ártur forced a smile and said, "You read items well, Gaelán. I am not surprised; reading thoughts will likely be next. I shall have to teach you how to block unwanted…"

"It was a threat. That is why you will not tell me what it says," Gaelán grunted with his arms across his chest.

Ártur glared at him, not happy with being pushed by his nephew. "I want you to say nothing of this to anyone, not even Asta. I will decide when and if this should be mentioned. You will learn that threats are a common experience for us and I am safe in the keep. No one can harm me. If you say anything, I will not take you to meet bhydáni Tíbhyan as promised."

Surprised by the anger in the healer's voice, Gaelán nodded. He rarely saw his uncle angry. "I will not say a word. I have not told anyone about the…sensations I got when I touched it, and no one except for Lord McGrannis, who brought it from the guards at the gate, and Asta, know there is a letter. He thinks it was from Captain Delamo…and Asta only knows that I had a bad feeling about it. I promise my silence, Ártur."

"Then the next time I visit Syl, in about a week, you will come with me. It will be a short stay, overnight at most, but we will go. Thank you for your discretion, Gaelán. It is a wise decision."

Wise or not, if anything happened to Ártur, Gaelán thought with a shrug, he was going to tell everyone he knew about that letter and hope he was not punished for his silence.

Prince Kjell de Corrmick had not had much contact with his cousin Owain since the southern portion of Neth became part of Enesfel, putting the two men in opposing kingdoms. Owain continued to send gifts in honor of Kjell's birthday and always included a long letter, but by necessity, the messages were veiled and formal. King Merkar insisted upon reading each one sent by their traitorous kinsmen and denied Kjell the courtesy of replying. The twenty-seven-year-old Nethite prince was surprised year after year that Owain did not halt the correspondence.

Merkar once asserted that this was because Owain stupidly believed that someday Kjell might confide state secrets to him. Of course, no good Nethite prince would be careless enough to do such a thing. Kjell was hardly careless. It was why he refused to marry, as he wanted no wife or heirs Merkar could turn against him. It was better to keep private counsel. But one might share such secrets intentionally, as the prince was often tempted to do. That a message had come to him through unofficial channels and had, to his knowledge, reached him without Merkar knowing, meant Owain sought something from him. It was a peculiar and notable occurrence. The letter read simply:

> *Kjell,*
>
> *In honor of the blood we share and for the sake of*
> *peace, I beseech you come to Fiara. There are*
> *things you alone can do. If you are willing, I will see*
> *to your safety and comfort. I await your arrival.*
> *Cordially,*
> *Owain Lachlan.*

Go to Fiara? The prince had wanted to do that for years. He missed when he and Owain use to hunt together. As he burned the letter in his fireplace, making certain it was destroyed and out of his brother's reach, Kjell pondered Owain's request and intentions. It would not be impossible for any good intelligence network to learn that Prince Kjell had the backing of his country's military leaders; such support was necessary for any ruler, or prince, to survive in Neth. Even Merkar had to be aware that the military held the prince in high esteem, but he did not seem to fear his younger brother. Though often fickle in nature, Kjell had won military support years ago and curried it despite his unwillingness to have his older brother assassinated. Kjell wanted power, but he did not want to follow his predecessors and kill to get it. His reluctance to act, and the simpleton persona he put forth, were likely the reasons Merkar allowed him to continue living.

Perhaps it was that military support Owain wished to make use of.

It was equally possible that Enesfel had learned of the people's and military's discontent with King Merkar. Not that it was an abnormal state of affairs; Kjell could not think of one king in Neth's history who had been liked. Most were fearfully tolerated, and as soon as a reasonable substitute was found, the military or a rival dispatched the ruler. No doubt the fact that he had not already deposed his brother intrigued people. Perhaps there was an interest in overthrowing Merkar from the outside of Neth, or in offering the prince assistance in doing it. Owain might be interested in taking the throne. That, Prince Kjell thought with amusement, would be interesting indeed.

There was also the possibility that Merkar had done something, unbeknownst to Kjell, that had awakened the wrath of either the King of Enesfel or Owain. It would not be surprising. It appeared he was going to need to probe a little deeper into the current political goings-on to learn what his brother had been up to recently.

But Prince Kjell had principles he would not compromise and Owain, at least, recognized that. Kjell did not consider himself a traitor, but there could be advantages to talking with his favorite kinsman, the best of which would be the pleasure of his company. And if Owain had learned something the prince could use against Merkar or had devised a plan that meant removing Merkar without the usual assassination, it would be worth Kjell's time to hear it.

Thus, visiting Fiara was a tempting idea. But doing it without anyone's knowledge, without raising suspicions or earning the distrust of his military allies would be tricky. However, Prince Kjell had not lived this long by being dull-witted. He knew he could do this. He could plan it carefully and go to Fiara. He was too curious not to.

No one in the town questioned them when Wortham carried the dead woman from the small home; Zelenka kept pace beside him, guiding him towards the mountain path. Perhaps this belief of inviting spirits in through the dead was more common in the region than he thought. The townsfolk glanced at them but did not offer assistance. She explained they would have, if she had been alone and unable to do this herself, in order to avoid the risk of evil spirits overtaking the town, but with strangers there to help, particularly a man of obvious strength like Wortham, it was better the villagers let him face the spirits. They had to protect themselves. The strangers would leave Gorbesh and take the spirits with them. The rest of them lived there.

It was raining when the two left the house, and they decided to leave Urian behind. The trail would be slippery and treacherous due to the rain, Zelenka said, and there was no need for the blind man to risk himself. That was before noon and it took nearly two hours to traverse the trail and reach the cave. It then took the captain another long while to push the boulder away from the opening. He did not know what he expected to find, but he did not expect a cavern full of bones and withering corpses, the overwhelming stench of which made him gag. Either there were more evil spirits in these parts than anywhere else, and the dead here prone to collect them, or it took longer than normal for bodies in the sealed cave to decay.

Zelenka showed little fear or disgust as she carried her offerings inside and beckoned Wortham to join her. She picked the spot she wanted, kicking bones callously aside, and waited for Wortham to place her mother's body there. The dead were not feared, it seemed, only the spirits, a conundrum the captain found confusing. When the corpse was positioned in a manner she deemed appropriate, curled as if a child asleep, she placed her offerings around it carefully. There were two small jars of bitter smelling ointment, a clay jug of water laced with poison berries, and a collection of foodstuffs, also laced with poison. In the woman's arms, she placed a cloth doll, her mother's most treasured possession from her childhood, something she had given Zelenka when she had been young enough to play with it too. Having no daughter of her own, she chose to give the doll back to her mother now.

Kissing the corpse's cheek, Zelenka left the cave without looking back. The wind blew harder and thunder rumbled from many miles away. As the captain struggled against the weather to reposition the boulder before the mouth of the cave, he wondered if they would make it back to the house before the storm grew worse. Behind him, Zelenka wrapped her arms around herself and paid little attention to the wet hair clinging to her face. It was impossible to tell if she was weeping; the rain washed away any trace of tears. Her eyes held sorrow, however, and she gladly accepted Wortham's arm about her shoulders as they started carefully down the mountain.

❧Chapter 35❧

Though Kavan sang at the noon Gathering, the presences did not return. That should have reassured him but as he sang the chosen song, a prayer of St. Kóráhm's he had long ago set to music, a young girl at the rear of the congregation, her face discolored with red blotches, her eyes swollen almost shut, caught his attention and refused to relinquish it. There was none of the usual showering of warmth that was the prelude to a miracle, only a tingling in Kavan's fingers that gave him certainty to act. He hesitated long enough to look over the congregation and determine that no one suspected anything. Rather than go to her on legs he knew would collapse before he reached her, Kavan lightly brushed Myreth's thoughts with his, prompting him to action. He dared not try with anyone else, and dared no more than that fleeting touch with Myreth. The temptation to do so much more was difficult to resist, but this was not the time for indulgence.

Myreth turned in the front pew and, without questioning either his notice of the child or the impulse to bring her to Kavan, gathered her in his arms, and brought her to the front. Her mother rose but did not come forward. Like everyone else, she trusted Myreth, and after the morning's service, that trust extended to the newcomer in their midst.

Closer scrutiny revealed the child's hands and feet were mottled and discolored as well and she shivered in spite of her thick robe. The prickling in Kavan's fingers grew stronger, almost painful. Showing no hint that he knew what would happen, Myreth watched expectantly.

Not stopping his song, Kavan took the girl into his arms and held her close, her tiny head resting on his shoulder, her legs wrapped around his waist and arms around his neck. The power within discharged when he put a twisted hand on the back of her head. She whimpered, convulsed, and grew still. The Elyri knew that the ailment afflicting her troubled her no more, but he continued to hold her until his song was complete, at which time he kissed her forehead and set her on the floor. She looked at Kavan with big brown eyes, tugged at his hand, showing no revulsion at touching his misshapen hand, and when he bent down to her, kissed his cheek.

There were murmurs as she took Myreth's hand and returned to her mother. Everyone saw. Everyone knew. A miracle had occurred and they had witnessed it. None fell in awe, none declared him a saint; the words Kavan heard were praises to k'Ádhá for the gift of healing, nothing more. He was relieved that no one attributed the miracle to him, though he also felt a pang of regret that his part had gone unmentioned. How right you were Orynn, he thought. He would sooner accept the praise and discomfort of being thanked for a miracle then have his part in it remain unacknowledged. Pride made him seek the attention, pride and the fear of being forgotten and abandoned the way he had been as a young boy. But this was how it should be, how he wanted it to be, and he must learn to accept it.

Myreth smiled at him then, a smile that seemed to confirm Kavan's inner musings without Myreth hearing them.

It began to rain early that morning and continued for the remainder of the day. Myreth did not speak of the healing as they watched the storm during their midday meal, and then they retreated to Kavan's room to select and rehearse two songs for the Gathering that evening.

They chose one that Myreth claimed was his favorite, and a second that Kavan composed specifically for the event. Myreth had never tried to compose a song. He had borrowed tunes from others and adapted different bits of holy text and prayers to them, but he had never created his own tunes or his own words.

He was awed at his new friend's gifts.

Later, they returned to the náós. These people's lives revolved around this place, but as much as Kavan treasured the spiritual calm he found here, he did not believe he could endure weeks unending of the sort of emotional tension he endured today. There were others there already, some seated, some standing, eagerly awaiting what might transpire tonight. The k'gdhededhá would attend, particularly if he had heard of the day's events. If this white-skinned man heralded a new age, the k'gdhededhá must see for himself, must confirm it. They might show little visible reaction to the day's events, but their anticipation and early arrival this night revealed how deeply it had touched them. Kavan did not want to sit in the front pew, did not want to be where everyone could see him, but Myreth insisted, and thus he settled beside the taller man again and tried to ignore the stares. He might not be the cause of the miracles, but he was the agent and that fact was enough to draw them.

Before long, the Gathering Hall was filled to capacity except for two empty seats on the opposite front pew. Rustling at the rear of the room brought everyone to their bare feet; Myreth drew Kavan up with him. Valesce was assisting an ancient man down the aisle, a man as grizzled and wizened as bhydáni Tíbhyan, but potentially much older. They paused long enough for the k'gdhededhá to lock eyes with Kavan, long enough for the bard to notice one important detail. The k'gdhededhá's eyes were violet.

Once the ancient man was seated, Valesce started the service, a more ritualized and somber affair than any thus far. Knowing he would not participate until later, the Elyri listened to the voices around him, particularly the crackling distinctive voice of the k'gdhededhá easily picked out above the rest. He avoided staring, as much as he longed to. If anyone else knew what they had in their midst, or suspected that their k'gdhededhá was not truly one of them, they showed no indication. He wondered why this man lived so long among Teren.

As arranged, Myreth went to the altar before the sacrament was to be served and sang a simple hymn alone, intentionally downplaying his voice's earthy tones. The k'gdhededhá looked to be asleep, or perhaps was shutting out the peripheral voices and the wail of the storm to focus on his inner musings. When the song was over, Myreth beckoned Kavan with an extended hand. Timidly, Kavan joined him, and side by side, they began Myreth's favorite hymn.

Kavan had acknowledged during rehearsal that their voices blended beautifully. One low and warm, the other high and pure, a complimentary fit. At times it was difficult to distinguish where one voice left off and the other began, who carried the melody and who carried the harmony. The harp was Kavan's preferred instrument, had always been his favorite though he considered his ear for other quality music to be good; yet he had not considered that vocal music could sound this way, that his voice, alone or with another, could produce sounds that made him tremble before the beauty as the harp strings did. Singing with Myreth, he could believe, as the other asserted, that somewhere there were záryph who sounded like this.

The k'gdhededhá leaned forward, eyes open and intent upon both singers. Refraining from looking at him, Kavan wanted to touch the man's mind, to know what he was thinking, but he did not try. If this man was k'kairá, the bard would fail. It did seem, at least on appearance, that the man was as hypnotized by the singers as the congregation. Emotion played across his ancient face as if he had no control over his expression and no reason or desire to contain it.

Their second melody was more intricate, a fugue of notes that wove in and out of one another on a single word, sóane, a word that served both as an exclamation of praise and a plea for redemption. Tears slid down Myreth's face as Kavan's voice pushed his to the edge of his range, not to a breaking point but to a point where the taller man had to strive harder for vocal control. Despite his proficiency, he found singing with this pale-haired man, whose power of improvisation and composition were highly developed, to be the most difficult thing he had ever done. Difficult because he was forced to test his limits if he were to succeed. Difficult because he had never challenged himself and would never be so challenged again. And he loved Kavan for it.

Once the song ended, the two remained where they were, neither showing any indication that their effort had been difficult. They had chosen to present the sacrament together, Myreth with more excitement than Kavan…who worried that he might drop whatever item he was given from his twisted hands. The congregation seemed to approve of their decision and watched with eagerness. Valesce helped the k'gdhededhá to his feet but the ancient man came forward unaided. Kavan would sing his solo number as soon as the k'gdhededhá completed what Myreth promised would be a long-winded prayer. As the service had proceeded smoothly thus far, nothing unusual occurring, Kavan felt relaxed and ready to sing.

The k'gdhededhá did not look at him when he finished, his prayer not as long as Myreth insinuated it would be. It was Kavan's turn. A single breath, gaze focused at a point beyond his audiences' heads as he had learned to do as a boy to give each guest the illusion he was singing to them, and he began.

His song soared into the highest registers he could achieve, reaching for the záphyric realms, striving to draw each soul with him into the heart of the divine. He had pushed Myreth before, now he pushed himself, growing ever more comfortable with his voice until he saw the ancient man place the chalice in Myreth's hands.

That meant Kavan would hold the decanter.

Outside the rain fell harder; a loud clap of thunder echoed through the room and reverberated in the stone walls, bringing with it a building of energy that produced a quaver in Kavan's throat. He closed his eyes long enough to rein in his nerves, and when he opened them, the k'gdhededhá was in front of him, offering the decanter for him to take. The ancient eyes revealed that he too felt what Kavan did but he was neither agitated nor unsettled. Kavan reached with one shaky, reverent hand, to take the bottle.

As his twisted fingers closed around its neck, his song was broken by an unexpected sharp cry. Energy discharged through his fingers and the bottle grew warm beneath his touch. Knowing without a doubt what the discharge of energy and piercing sting in his wrists meant, he clutched his empty hand to his stomach, hoping to hide it. He struggled not to drop or spill the contents of the bottle that he held so tightly in his other hand that the glass threatened to break. The sensation slit through his other wrist as well, however, and fortunately, the old man, his hand also around the neck of the bottle Kavan now released, kept it from crashing to the floor.

The pain was almost unbearable and Kavan's body instinctively doubled over, wanting to hide what he knew was happening or run from the room. But fleeing was impossible as the invisible spikes had gone through the sides of his ankles, through his feet, and into the stone floor which cracked and splintered beneath him. Without boots, the blood that pooled around his feet, seeping into the new fissures in the ancient stone, was there for those closest, especially the k'gdhededhá and Myreth to see, as was the crimson spreading over the fabric of his shirt and trousers.

Upon the wall behind him, though he could not see it, the figure of Dhágdhuán also bled from wounds identical to Kavan's, wounds the figure had not borne before. The bard knew this from the broadcasted thoughts of those in the congregation witnessing it. The room grew steadily brighter as light showered from above. There was terror at the back of the Elyri's throat; what if this drove the congregation into some uncontrollable frenzy? But a soothing tendril of calm wrapped itself around him from head to toe, a lifetime of familiar presences embracing him with feathered wings of assurance.

Kavan did the only thing he could. This had come to him, to these people, for some greater purpose, as much as he wished otherwise. Even if he continued to hide his hands, the spreading blood over his clothes, pooling around him, dripping onto the floor could not be hidden. Rather than continue to cower, he painfully straightened and dropped his clenched hands to his side, hoping this event would be treated as the others, with no more than a passing air of holy ecstasy.

As one body, the congregation dropped to their knees.

Unable to look at the k'gdhededhá, Kavan fleetingly sought a glance at his new friend; Myreth's face was a calm mask in which his eyes feverishly burned, making maintaining eye contact an awkward, painful thing. Myreth was unwilling to present the sacrament with anyone else, and realizing that something far more sacred was occurring, he chose to forgo the ritual sacrament altogether.

The bard grudgingly looked at the k'gdhededhá then with fearful tears rimming his eyes. The presences around them grew in number, accumulating thickly around the altar and the Elyri bard.

Two other congregation members came forward of their own volition and took the chalice and the decanter to present the gifts to the rest, although Kavan worried about what that bottle now contained. Myreth spoke low to them both, words Kavan could not hear as the k'gdhededhá took Kavan's face between his hands and pressed his forehead to the white one.

"It is as it should be," he murmured, his voice sounding to Kavan less ancient and forced than it had before. "You have come to lead us from confinement into the world. I would gladly do as the prophets would have of me, if you would do one thing."

"What would you have me do?" The question was woven into his song; everything transpiring around him had become the song.

Dropping to his knees, a difficult act for the elderly man, the k'gdhededhá said, "Lay your hands on me, hallowed one, that I may receive this blessing given to you to impart."

The urge to deny him, to refuse, to do anything other than what he was asked, was overpowering. Kavan could barely raise his arms. He was surprised they were not pinned above him in the true rósádhá stance. As his eyes sought the reactions of those in the room, he saw that each person there wanted him to do as the k'gdhededhá asked, that such a blessing was of great importance to them. What am I, he begged silently as he sang, that you should ask this of me? I am not gdhededhá to impart blessings to anyone.

To his left, there was a familiar shimmer of air, or perhaps it was the movement of someone in the room, accompanied by a second, closer peel of thunder. It was enough, however, to draw everyone's attention. Some looked away, seeing nothing; others appeared bewildered at the sudden appearance of the gray robed figure. Whether they recognized the individual or not, Kavan did, as the Heretic Saint stopped behind the kneeling k'gdhededhá, his back to the congregation, and lowered the hood of his robe.

Myreth cried out in astonishment and would have dropped the chalice if he still held it.

Kóráhm di Curnydhá smiled at Myreth before focusing attention on Kavan as if to ask, 'Why do you hesitate?'

"lásánai…" Kavan could form no other word in the midst of his song. The k'gdhededhá did not look up from his bowed position and Kavan wondered if he was aware of the man behind him.

Stretching a scarred hand forward, Kóráhm rested it upon the k'gdhededhá's head. The old man shuddered and Kavan understood. It was not a suggestion; it was a command. He had known Kóráhm long enough to know it. With an uneasy sigh of acceptance released between notes of the song, Kavan fought the pain and placed his bloody hands upon the k'gdhededhá's head where Kóráhm's had been, brushing the saint's hands accidentally. They were flesh.

And yet some did not see him.

The saint's image had already faded but he was not gone. Kavan felt him there, a hand beneath his…another coming to rest on top. That moment of secondary contact brought with it excruciating pain, the same pain he had felt the night he had been robbed of the use of his hands. He vaguely remembered screaming before, the night it had happened, but he had been too drunk and too devastated to feel the full impact of the injury. Now he was sober, and the fullness of pain, as joints dislodged and bones splintered, nearly made him black out from the shock. Myreth rushed to catch him, standing behind to hold him upright. Kavan was not aware of it happening, but felt the other man there, his arms and body supporting the Elyri's weight.

The k'gdhededhá rose and backed away without help, an expression of content and purpose on his face. Another individual did not hesitate to take his place, the flock forming a line to receive this unique measure of anointing they would never receive again.

"Please."

Eyes glazed with pain, blood thundering in his ears, Kavan could not tell who had spoken, who had dared come to him first.

Unable to deny that begging tone, Kavan wanted to consent, but he could not move his hands, the shocks of agony racing up and down his arms left him unable to move them. His head dropped back against Myreth's shoulder as image after image chased through his mind's eye, intertwined with his song, dragging memories back to the forefront in his head. He was shackled to a wall in the Enesfel dungeon, hearing the slap of a wooden stick against a man's hand. White as a virgin. Blow after blow. A recollection he dreamt of often and one that caused his body to flinch and recoil with each remembered strike. He felt welts rising on his back beneath fabric rent by unseen hands. He knew it was memory, but the blows, the whisper of tearing cloth against his skin, felt all too real.

Behind him, Myreth blinked in shock. He looked down between their bodies to see the unexpected, fabric torn away by an invisible force. This could not be real.

Kavan's head lolled forward.

The sound of the rod against his back changed to the rumble of an angry mob and the sensation of that beating morphed into the pain of pelting rocks, pounding fists, striking boots. Closing his eyes did nothing to dispel the visions, which now replaced everything in the room he should have seen. No one else seemed to hear the things he heard, feel what he felt. They did, however, witness the effects upon him. Uncertain how he remained able to sing, it was the only thing, he believed, keeping the developing ball of death in his core from breaking free and killing everyone around him. He felt a stone graze his forehead, felt the stickiness tickling over his brow; peeping out from behind slightly parted lids gave proof of a single red droplet falling from his lashes. He tipped his head to the side to keep the trickle out of his eye.

The images might be memory, but the damage was real.

The line of congregants continued to pass, mercifully shorter with each one. Myreth moved Kavan's limp, bloody hands from head to head before they stepped aside to accept the sacrament from the pair near the altar. Maybe he should stop, he mused, but how could he?

If they left the room after that, or remained, Kavan did not know. He prayed they had moved on. If he lost control of that sizzling glow within, they would surely all be killed.

Kavan's body grew gradually weaker from the loss of blood, and to his ears, the storm outside seemed louder. From the sounds upon the roof, the windows, and the walls, he suspected it was hailing. His vision continued to dim, fading from red to grey, and soon left him altogether, and his knees buckled. The once intense pain had become little more than a throbbing that left every muscle numb. He had no idea how long he stood there, singing his wordless song, bleeding, but with a total congregation of more than two hundred people, he knew it was too long.

He had come too far to die here.

Why did no one stop this? Why did Myreth let it go on?

The sheet fell from his naked body. Diona's voice in his head.

Dead. Coward. Not a man.

The ball of power burned hotter.

I am a man, his thoughts screamed, his voice, whatever words or sounds he produced, momentarily erased by a too close roar of thunder. I am not a coward…and I am not dead yet.

He could not think or concentrate, and when his voice faltered and failed, the Chanter continued the song, singing the notes as Kavan had done but in his lower register. Head dropping forward again, his strength waning, Kavan began speaking against his will, words he could not translate, the voice he heard, not his own.

One last person, the thought passed from Myreth to Kavan as the Chanter breathed in relief between notes of the song. One last person and me. He placed Kavan's limp hands upon the final woman's head, worried that his friend would die from exhaustion and blood loss and the multitude of unexplainable injuries he was receiving as if from the air itself. He had no idea how much blood a man could lose before dying, but it seemed there was twice that much upon the floor, the bard's clothes, and the heads of every member of the order. Surely the shock of so many injuries would kill him if the blood loss did not.

If he died, Myreth would blame himself.

Kavan's attackers, his would-be murderers, taunted him with the knife in his stomach, the breaking of his legs. Hands lifted from the last woman's head, Kavan felt spun around as his legs gave way, so that his wilted body was pressed to Myreth's. The dark-haired man could not support his weight and lift Kavan's hands to his head for that blessing, and there was no one nearby to do it for him, so he did the only thing he could think of.

He pressed his mouth to Kavan's.

One final explosion of sound at that moment, louder than the rest, shook the ancient structure to its foundation. Pain erupted within Kavan's hands again, pushing a spasm of convulsions throughout his body. Both were accompanied by a simultaneous searing flash that might have been lightning or might have been the release of a core of power unlike anything those within this place had ever felt before.

Kavan collapsed and lay unmoving upon the trembling stones, pulling Myreth down with him.

❧*❧

The sage, quaking, blinded and breathless, made no effort to pick himself up from the floor where he had been unexpectedly thrown by a ripple of power unlike any he had ever experienced. It wiped away each of his senses, and for a few moments robbed him of breath and reason as well. One hand seizing at his chest as he waited for his heart and lungs to resume the rhythm of life, he coughed to the empty air, "Kavan…what has happened to you?"

❧*❧

Until late into the night, Ártur held Gaelán's limp form, brushing his dark auburn hair from his sweat-drenched face. He had seen it at last. The boy had not been sleeping when it came; it had been just after dinner, and he and the healer were discussing diseases and cures when the boy crumbled and began to convulse. Ártur caught him as he fell, opening to read Gaelán, searching for some illness or poison that would explain this.

It took longer than anticipated, as for several moments his healing gifts refused to do his bidding, refused to be manipulated the way they should have been. It made no sense, that raw, vulnerable feeling that formed a void behind it, only to be filled, gradually, by the power that should have been there, that he had been taught to use from a very young age. When his senses came back, what he found within Gaelán was Kavan. Kavan's presence. Kavan's power. Projected, focused, manifested in the younger man. Something was happening to the bard, something painful and horrifying that caused him to project his anguish outward. But for reasons Ártur could not determine, Gaelán alone felt it. Why the boy and not his cousin? Once such projections had come to Ártur whenever Kavan had been injured or unwell, but no longer. Perhaps Kavan had closed himself off to his cousin to keep the healer from following him. Perhaps it was something else.

Kavan! His thoughts screamed back along the threads of power that bound Kavan to Gaelán but found nothing. It was some sort of traumatic reoccurring injury but it did not feel, to the healer to be a life-threatening one. Something he was unable or unwilling to tolerate alone. Torture, perhaps, which might mean the bard was a captive. Then why had word not come of it from Wortham? Had Wortham been killed? Whatever it was, he was unable to share it with Ártur, leading to a tangled jumble of emotions within the healer that was too painful to sort. He felt cut off, abandoned, and alone. But Kavan was alive. And he had contacted them, knowingly or not.

Come home, sínréc. Explain this. Both Gaelán and I have a right to know what this means. We want you home where you are safe. Where you belong.

❧Chapter 36❧

"Sir Gabersdon? A woman is at the gate; she is in a sorry state, milord, asking for you. Master Cáner is attending her."

Balint followed the soldier Denyan, curious about what woman might have sought him out here. He could think of no one, and yet when he saw the brown hair of the woman over whom Gaelán Cáner was bent, he knew instantly who she was. Dhybhé.

He knelt beside the young man with his hand upon Gaelán's back. Unlike some, he had little difficulty thinking of Gaelán as a healer and ignored the fact that he was not yet considered an adult. "Master Cáner? Is she alive? Will she live?"

"She's alive." The young healer's head bobbed as he spoke but he did not look up. "She's badly battered and seems not to have eaten in many days. I have sent for Ártur and am doing what I can." His voice trailed off as his concentration returned to his task. The knight gave no further interruption, preferring that she live rather than having Gaelán engage him in conversation.

He was too busy chastising himself for his folly for talk. He had given her up for dead, thought her lost. Rather than search for her as he should have, he had given up and left finding her to his sheriff. Not that he had any notion of where he could have looked, what he could have done differently. Thankfully, it seemed her will to live was great and she had found her way free of her captors and to him, here in Rhidam. But why would she look for him? How could she believe he could provide her safety when he had failed her before? How could she trust him when it had been his people to harm her? She was delirious, repeating his name until he took her hand. Her eyes fluttered open, focused on his face for a moment, and then closed, her body stilling as her breathing slowed. Something in his gesture, in his nearness, brought her peace.

Ártur arrived, but Balint did not notice. When the healer spoke, his voice strained, the knight looked up with a start. "She is healed but she needs rest, warmth, food. You know this woman, milord?"

"Her name is Dhybhé. She and her brother settled in Nelori as jewelers. When he disappeared, I gave her shelter, but my captain of the guard took her. I had no way of finding her…no idea where to look…I gave up…"

"Will you assume care for her? Gaelán will attend you to be certain she is settled and one of us will check on her periodically."

The knight nodded his head. "It is my duty; it is the sole way I might atone for the suffering she has endured." She should have been safe with me. "I will do my best to see to her welfare; whoever took her might have followed her here."

Ártur watched Balint lift the woman and carry her inside, nodding at Gaelán's puzzled expression before the boy bounded after the knight. Regardless of the danger to themselves, a healer would not abandon his patient, and it was good to see that Gaelán had that instinct. Later he would tell the boy that it was his hands that had healed the woman. He was learning.

Currently, there was something more unpleasant and pressing the healer needed to do. He felt for the letter in his pocket that he carried for reasons he had not yet deciphered. If he could have avoided telling anyone about it, he would have. However, what he had seen within the woman's mind told him it could be avoided no longer. Whoever the men were she overheard during her escape, they meant to do him harm. And they were in Rhidam, as Balint feared. They allowed her to escape rather than kill her, hoping she would collapse or die near enough to the keep to draw the healer out, but they had not anticipated her constitution to be strong enough to carry her to shelter.

He found the King, princess, and Prince Espen sharing their evening meal in the dayroom rather than in the Hall where other palace residents were dining. They halted their discussion when he entered and stared, making him want to leave rather than speak.

"Pardon the interruption, My Liege…but there is something I think you should know…" he started in a strained voice.

"What is it, Lord Healer?" asked the King.

Ártur cleared his throat. He had never imagined that speaking to this young man would be so difficult. "During my absence, a letter arrived for me; Gaelán kept it until I returned, with the hopes that it was from Kavan. I was not going to speak of it, but I have discovered that I must. It was a threat on my life, Milord."

"Ártur!" Diona stood, nearly knocking her chair over in her haste.

The healer tried to keep his voice calm, though he hardly felt that way. "Considering that threats are an expected part of an Elyri's life outside of our homeland, I was determined to ignore it. However, an Elyri woman has arrived at the keep, someone Sir Gabersdon knows, who was badly mistreated. From her, I have learned that whoever her abductors were, they are the ones who sent this letter, the ones who wish me harm. They are in Rhidam. I can give Lord Dugan and Lord Corbin their approximate location but I have no description. Though Sir Gabersdon implies that his captain of the guard was initially involved in her abduction, I do not know if he was one of them or not. Shall I report this to them?"

The King nodded and pushed back his plate. "At once. And I want you to consider going to Bhryell."

"My Liege," the healer bowed, "I cannot do that."

"Why not? Your life is in danger. Your family needs you."

"And you need me here. Gaelán is not sufficiently trained to replace me and you will find no other healer willing to come to court. I have access to the Gates that affords me easy escape, and the princess has seen to it that I can travel nowhere outside of the castle without guards. My place is here, My Liege…unless you order me elsewhere. Even then, I might be forced to disobey such an order to appease my conscience and you would need to remove me bodily. I plan to be here when Kavan returns. I am going nowhere until that day comes."

King Hagan thought to say something but instead looked at his sister. She nodded as if agreeing with his thoughts, and then he said, "Very well, Lord MacLyr; you have me in a stalemate. We do need you here, and since you do not want to leave…remember this discussion should something unpleasant happen. I do not want your wife blaming me should harm befall you."

"She would not. The blame will be mine, and she knows it."

Ș*ș

"Will he live?"

"I don't…"

"He's lost so much blood…and his hands…"

"Myreth…"

"But how can anyone…?"

"Hush now…let me work…"

The voices were not real. The stabbing, burning pains were not real. None of this was real. Let sleep return and erase the nightmare. Yes. That was the best thing to do. Sleep. It would be over soon.

Ș*ș

Hes á Redh Náós gave gdhededhá Tusánt the feeling of an abandoned child, sullen and withdrawn, after the final Gathering of the week. It was normally the least populated Gathering and the one he least minded presiding over. Officiating this Gathering gave him a sense of closure for the preceding week and a sense of preparation for the week to come. The náós was empty and he was in the process of snuffing out the candles when Sir Balint found him.

"Pardon the intrusion, gdhededhá, but I seek a favor."

Tusánt smiled at the well-mannered knight, sensing the man's disquiet. He gestured to a bench in case the man wanted to sit and talk. "No intrusion, Sir Gabersdon. What can I do for you?"

Balint remained standing and Tusánt did likewise. "Master Cáner told me Saint Kóráhm's in Alberni is a haven for Elyri. Is this true?"

The gdhededhá nodded. There was no fear in telling the knight this. He trusted the man. "All Elyri, indeed anyone who goes, are welcome there, and security is in place to prevent harm to the residents. Why do you ask?"

"There is an Elyri woman in my protection; she was kidnapped and abused and escaped and I want to be certain she remains safe. I want to take her far from her abductors. Master Cáner suggested Saint Kóráhm's. If you recommend it, I shall take her there tomorrow."

"If you fear for her immediate safety, I can take her tonight."

The knight balked at that, as the gdhededhá suspected he would. It seemed that Balint knew nothing of Gates since he said, "I do not want to put you or your men out. I would be more at ease traveling with her, seeing to her security myself. You would hardly be safe traveling with her; I could not put you at risk. I will speak with General Agis', take some of his best men, and take her. No offense is meant."

"None is taken. I know you to be a good and just man who will do all in his power to protect his charges. I shall write a letter of recommendation for you. k'gdhededhá Khwílen is not there at this time; I do not think they would turn you away, but a word from me could be helpful."

The knight bowed. "Thank you. I will wait, but I pray not long. Master Cáner is with the lady, but I do not wish to leave her longer than I must."

"Come into the thóres." Tusánt turned and thought he saw movement in the doorway at the rear of the nave. He felt nothing, thought it might be his mind playing tricks on him, but he still lowered his voice to add, "I urge you to be cautious when you travel, sir. Anyone in the company of Elyri is in danger, and since this woman might be able to identify her abductors, they may be looking for her."

"I think so as well," he nodded in agreement. "Anyone foolish enough to cross swords with me deserves whatever end they find."

❧*☙

A damp cloth dripping soft upon his skin. Gentle hands like a mother or a lover wiping away the sting, leaving throbbing in the water's wake. A flash of light outside of closed lids followed by a distant rumble seconds later.

Rain. That was what bathed his skin. A warm, blessed rain easing the drought within.

Splatters against glass sang him back to sleep. He did not want to be awake.

He did not want to be alive with this pain.

❧*☙

It was General Agis' habit to bathe once a week in the cold waters of the Tegid River. For his people, natives of the desert, any body of water more permanent than a puddle after a rainstorm was a holy thing. If one could be found it should be revered, preferably by immersing oneself in it, allowing the element of water to reclaim the element of earth from one's skin and return it into the natural cycle of the world. Because the Tegid was an ever-present source of water flowing through the outskirts of Rhidam, and since Agis lived within easy distance of it, he made a pilgrimage to the river before the sun rose on the first day of the week, no matter how cold the weather, unless the river was frozen. He did not swim, as such bodies of water made him uneasy, but bathing was acceptable so long as he remained near the shore. There at the river's edge, he would say his ritual prayers before stepping naked into the water. Many of Rhidam's inhabitants had seen him there, some coming to the river out of curiosity each week to watch the dark-skinned general at ritual.

Such was the case when he approached the Tegid in the pre-dawn hours this day. Others were already there, further down the riverbank from the location he usually chose. He paid little attention as he began to remove his tunic, but when the shirt was pulled nearly over his face, he caught sight of a half-submerged burlap bag a few yards upriver. He tugged the tunic back down and approached the bag, eyes scanning it, the muddy bank around it, the people further down the river, seeking anything out of place.

The bag was stained dark brown and was heavy with the river water it had absorbed and whatever it held. Its end was tied securely with a length of sturdy rope. While he could not tell if someone had tried to throw this deeper into the flow and missed their target, if it had washed here from further up river, or if it might have been left for him to find, a gentle nudge with the toe of his boot told him that there was something solid within. Pulling it out of the water, he pondered opening it here. Despite its weight, it was easy to lift and carry, and as he hefted it and let the weight settle upon his back, he became aware of a smell. Not the dark brown of mud or refuse upon the fabric then, but the stain and stench of blood.

It had been a wise choice to take it elsewhere to open, he decided. Whatever was within the sack was best left unseen by unprepared eyes. He had no idea what he might be carrying. For all he knew, it could be a dead animal, but it could also be something worse. He would look, ascertain the necessity of bringing it to the justice and inquisitor, and then take what action was required. Ignoring the disappointed stares of those along the river who had missed the spectacle of the Cíbhóló general and his weekly ritual, he started towards the keep with his soggy package.

❧*☙

Bloody sheets. Bloody towels. Bloody clothes.

Myreth watched the woman carry all of it away as a man took most of the bloody water in two pails to be discarded. One wash basin, the water tinted pink from the cloth hanging over its rim, remained, but Myreth would not allow them to take it. Not yet. The sight, the smell, of so much blood turned his stomach, but at least Kavan's white skin, mottled as it was, was now clean. The possibility of resumed bleeding, however, remained, and Myreth wanted that basin and cloth here in case they were needed.

The physician had come and gone again without speaking his diagnosis, and though he stopped in the corridor to speak to Valesce, Myreth could not hear them.

For now, at least, Kavan breathed, moaning often in his unconscious hell, his body twitching as if in response to continued invisible beatings. Myreth wanted to remain at Kavan's side until he opened his eyes, reassure himself that his friend would live and be none the worse for his suffering. But Valesce summoned him away to give Kavan solitude, and obedience was so ingrained in Myreth that after a few moments of resistance, Myreth capitulated.

Whatever had happened, it would be the talk of the community for decades to come. In this, Myreth did not envy Kavan at all.

❧*☙

"There is a caravan leaving for Pa'aliaka before dawn. My belongings are packed. I will go with them, for if I stay I invite spirits. I cannot do that. You can come with me or wait, but I must go."

Wortham caught her hand as Zelenka turned away. He had considered the notion of letting her go and then catching up with her in Pa'aliaka, but he knew he would have little chance of finding her in the bustle of a large, unfamiliar city. If he let her go tomorrow, it would be forever, and that idea was nearly as heartbreaking as the thought of never seeing Kavan again.

"You would depart me easily?" he asked in a gentle voice.

She shook her head and tried to disguise the sadness in her eyes. "In body, not in heart. No man has treated me with the courtesies you have. And your foreignness intrigues me…but I cannot stay."

Keeping her hand in his, he gathered a handful of straw from the empty goat pen as he contemplated his position. Allowing her to travel alone, even though she would be in the midst of countrymen she had known her whole life, was against his nature. But so was departing Gorbesh without Kavan. The bard would have the means to find them in Pa'aliaka, unless he felt slighted and abandoned, in which case he might start for his next destination, or start home, without Wortham. The captain had no doubt that the bard's attitude and outlook had improved, but he did not believe it was improved enough for the bard to feel no pain over being left behind by his best friend.

Still, Wortham also knew Kavan would forgive him, particularly when he learned why they had departed in such a manner. As long as they left a message, and Kavan received it, Wortham chose to believe all would be well.

"We will travel with you at dawn, Zelenka. Lord Cliáth will forgive us and welcome you."

She leaned against his side and murmured, "I hope you are right."

The captain sighed and thought to himself, 'So do I.'

❧*☙

If King Hagan's face could look any grayer without being dead, Ártur did not want to see it. Agis seemed unaffected by the news he bore, news deemed important enough that the King had called together his staff, along with his sister and Prince Espen. No one looked pleased, but the King looked the worst, sick to his soul, likely, the healer guessed, because he fancied himself a child despite his rank.

"You will not touch them, is that understood, Lord MacLyr?"

"Milord, they should be identified…"

The King shook his head. "I think we already know who they are, Lord Cáner. Child torsos, minus limbs and heads…not long after six children are kidnapped?" His face turned from dismayed gray to the green of disgust. "It speaks for itself."

Caol, however, disagreed. "With the number of children reported missing within the last three months, this could be the bodies of any of them, the fact that there happen to be six in the bag meant to lead us to believe it was those children most recently taken. Without proper identification, it is impossible to say who they are."

"And without heads, only an Elyri…"

The King cut Flannery short with a wave of his hand. "Enough, Lord Chancellor. I do not want to hear one more word about headless children. You will not touch them, Ártur, nor will you, Bhríd. Such a task should not be asked of anyone. Lord Justice, find out if anyone saw anything at the river. Other than that, there is little to do. Lord Chancellor, if you will summon one of the gdhededhá to the keep I would at least like to have these…anointed. Perhaps they can advise us on the proper means of burial." He stood. "Until someone learns something, I do not want to discuss this disgusting incident further."

He stalked from the room leaving his unsettled advisors behind.

❧Chapter 37❦

Kavan drifted in and out of awareness, in and out of delirium, long enough that when full waking came, he did not know where he was or how long he had been there. The aroma of roast chicken drew his attention to the bedside table; there was a tray upon it, either the noon or evening meal, he was not sure. No steam rose from it, suggesting it had been there for some time, but as the grumble in his stomach demanded placation, he did not care if the food was hot or not.

Movement was difficult when he reflexively reached for the tray, as though he was fighting through gauze or heavy cobwebs. As the memories of excruciating pain and massive blood loss returned, it occurred to him that he was fortunate to be able to move at all…

…moments before his reaching hand came into view.

Startled, he scrambled backward on the bed away from what had to be a vision, a dream, a cruel hoax played upon his senses by an overactive, pain-blurred imagination. In that movement, however, the use of his other hand as leverage to push against the thin mattress revealed the same unexpected surprise.

His hands, discolored though they were with wine and charcoal contusions, were no longer twisted beyond effectiveness. Warily, he wiggled his fingers. He clenched them into fists. He opened them flat again, brought them nearer his face, and stared.

He began to weep, his heart swelling with unmatched adulation.

His hands were healed.

But how?

That question carried a rush of memory, of the Gathering and the inundation of past sufferings that had each brought a renewal of physical damage from every attack or injustice he had ever endured.

It also brought back, as he threw off the blankets…expecting to see his legs shattered as his hands had been…the memories of Myreth's lips against his. His mouth parted, his throat went dry, and the door of the room opened to reveal the dark-haired siren.

The men stared at one another, one with embarrassment, confusion, and shock, the other with an innocent combination of relief and fear. For a moment, as each sought words to say, it appeared as if Myreth would race across the room and throw himself at the mercy of the bard's embrace. Though desperate to stave off such an emotional moment, Kavan was unable to will his mind, his throat, his mouth to form words, and could not lift his hands to dry his cheeks in order to hide the tears, but thankfully, whatever emotion played across his face was enough to temper Myreth's first impulses.

Instead, the black-haired man came to the bedside, filled a metal cup with water, and placed it into Kavan's hands, careful not to make contact with him. Maybe he was afraid to cause added pain. Maybe he was leery of embarrassing or upsetting Kavan with such contact. Maybe he thought such a touch might result in yet another miracle.

"Drink," he murmured.

Kavan nodded, grateful for Myreth's restrained but also slightly pained by what seemed like intentional reluctant avoidance.

"How do you feel?" The man's voice cracked, his pout more deeply ingrained than usual. He swiped a tear away from Kavan's cheek, and after another uncomfortable moment of staring into his green eyes, stared at the moisture on his fingertip instead.

"I…" The first word came out coarse and broken, but after several swallows of water, Kavan continued, "I don't know. I hurt but I'm better then I believe I should be. That was…was it real? It happened?"

Uneasily, Myreth took the cup, refilled it, but when Kavan refused to take it, he set it upon the food tray. "What do you remember?"

"Singing. Kóráhm." He hesitated long enough to dry his face on his sleeve. "Pain. Blood." He looked at his wrists, touching the points where the piercing of iron spikes had struck. "A lot of blood."

He blinked suddenly and met Myreth's gaze in panic. "And power. How many are dead? How many did I kill?"

"Kill?"

"The burst of power…at the end. It kills. How many?"

Hoping to ease the rising panic, he caught the bard's hand, watching closely for the slightest indication of pain. "None, Kavan. I swear it. The windows burst. The benches tipped. Some walls throughout the cloister have sustained cracks. Some of us were knocked off our feet or suffer from ringing ears and pain in our heads…but no one has died. Kóráhm protected us."

"Praise k'Ádhá." Knowing what that power could do, what it had done, it was unfathomable that none had been killed. Only some manifestation of the divine already present that night could have sheltered them…just as it had restored his hands. Perhaps, as Myreth claimed, it was Kóráhm's doing.

He stared at his fingers again, once more marveling at a sight he had given up hope of seeing.

Maybe the blast of power had not been his doing at all. Maybe it had healed him.

"Your hands…?"

Kavan shook his head. "I know no more than you…except that they move freely…if achingly…when I thought they would be useless until the end of my days."

Myreth shook his head too. "Never have I…you are a man favored…a man blessed. You are…"

"…a man. That is all."

If Myreth intended to say more, he did not try after being cut off. It left an uneasy quiet between them, one Kavan realized was more awkward than whatever Myreth had wanted to say might have been.

But when he opened his mouth to encourage Myreth to speak, to complete his thoughts, it was Myreth's turn to interrupt by asking, "Shall I bring a fresh meal?"

Though tempted to say yes, Kavan sat up in the bed, glancing at the tray and the wash basin with the bloody cloth hanging over its edge, and declined with a shake of his head. He had no idea how long he had been incapacitated and feared it had been too long, that his opportunity to speak with the k'gdhededhá had passed and he would have to await the turn of another week before the chance would come again. Outside, however, the storm still raged, giving him hope that he had not been unconscious too long.

"How long have I…?"

"Yesterday evening and today. It is evening now. Valesce bid me check on you before I sleep…asked me to let you know, if you were awake," he sighed sadly, "that k'gdhededhá will see you when you can stand and feel well enough to…"

"Then I should go to him." Myreth's words gave him hope, despite the initial dismay he felt at hearing how long he had slept and the unhappy note at the end. There was lingering numbness and the ache of abused muscles throughout his body, but he had endured worse and was determined to defeat any remaining weakness.

He carefully swung his bare feet over the edge of the bed, the crisp linen nightshirt catching and twisting awkwardly between his body and the mattress, and Myreth caught his arm as he attempted to stand.

"There is no need for haste…the bones of your legs were badly broken. You should rest until morning. Surely, you cannot…"

But even Myreth knew those bones had already knitted together, the gashes and open wounds closed, just as the deformity of Kavan's hands had been healed, without the need for a physician or extended period of recovery. Whatever miracle had given him back his hands had healed the rest of the damage as well. There was visible bruising anywhere injury had presented, but the injuries were gone. When Kavan's feet touched the floor and he stood, unsteady and weak but on his own, Myreth knew there would be no keeping the bard in bed.

No keeping him in Gorbesh.

"I cannot wait," Kavan murmured as the discomfort in his muscles sucked the breath from him. "I do not know how much longer I have to perform the duty I am sworn to undertake." As it was, he suspected his weakness would not allow him to walk the distance from this place to the village, in the dark and the rain, so even if he was successful in gaining what he needed tonight, he would have to wait until daybreak, or the next village trader's visit, to depart. "If the k'gdhededhá will instruct me on what I must do to obtain the chalice and staff…"

"Then you will have what you came for…and you will leave."

It was inevitable, they both knew. There was little point in making promises that could not be kept. "Let me hear what he will say…and we shall speak afterward."

"Here." As if ignoring the topic now, Myreth reached for Kavan's own tunic and trousers that hung over the headboard, the clothing he had arrived in, put there as further confirmation that his time with Myreth was drawing to a close. Doing so knocked the metal flask from the table and as Myreth bent to retrieve it, he said, "I brought you these since the others were…not functional. Allow me to assist you."

Kavan began to protest, but with so much of his energy focused on remaining upright, he found the assistance to dress to be much needed. His gaze, however, as he endured the help in dressing, moved from the metal flask to the washbasin. The inner edges were stained with his blood, the cloth that hung over it also bloody except for where the tip hung in the water it contained…water that was clear of any trace of the blood he knew it should have shown.

He shuddered and groaned. Orynn had said he would know when it was done…when the water he required was blessed…and he did.

Worried about Kavan's health, and hopeful that the sound was the precursor to a decision to get back into bed and remain a while longer, Myreth whispered, "Kavan?"

"Fill the flask…from the wash basin…for me. Please…"

"Fill it?" Though puzzled, Myreth helped Kavan sit on the edge of the bed and removed the stopper from the bottle, expecting to fill it with bloody water with no idea why Kavan made such a request. He was more surprised than Kavan to see that the water in the basin was pristine, clean, when all of the evidence, and his own recollections, told him it should be red with the pale man's blood. Seeing it was not, he glanced over his shoulder at Kavan with curious amazement.

Thinking better of trying to offer an explanation he did not have, Kavan kept his attention on his boots as he pulled them on. He did not look up until Myreth set the sealed flask, now full, on the meal tray. He accepted Myreth's help to get back on his feet, and pocketed the flask before Myreth brought the bard's hands to his lips and kissed each palm.

"I give thanks for this miracle," he whispered, ignoring the miracle of the water which Kavan clearly did not want to discuss. "I only wish I could hear you play."

Swallowing hard, overcome with the realization that he would, soon, play his beloved harp once more, Kavan nodded. "You shall, Myreth. I swear it."

Fully dressed, feeling unusual in his own clothes, he leaned on his taciturn guide for aid, protecting the flask as they trudged through rarely used corridors, the stone cracked as Myreth had claimed, up a winding flight of stairs to another stretch of hall that ended in a single, unassuming door. The effort sapped what strength sleep had given Kavan and left him breathless, sore, and shaky, barely able to stand when they reached the room. Valesce stood outside the door, apparently expecting their arrival; he signaled them to wait and went in. Moments later, he returned and motioned Kavan inside. The bard cast one look into Myreth's forlorn black eyes before shuffling, unaided, into the room.

The cavernous chamber was unadorned and housed a single chair, a desk with an oil lamp flickering near the window, and a cot, none of which appeared used with any frequency. There were no adornments, no utensils or other signs of inhabitation. Whoever the k'gdhededhá was, this was not his private room; Kavan wondered if the man spent only those hours here necessary to meet Valesce, or any others he needed to speak with and then went elsewhere, somewhere beyond the walls of this place. At the open window, watching hail bounce off the exposed sill, leaned the man Kavan had waited to see. He was unable, in his weakness and discomfort, to find his voice and speak to this man whom he was certain was much older than either Tíbhyan or Bhóité.

"I know not who these men are with whom you compare me, but I wager you are correct, Cliáth. Your perceptions are strengthening. I recall a time when you did not recognize what you saw."

Recall, thought Kavan curiously. He wondered if they had met at some other time, but he could remember no man who looked as this one did. "I was much younger then, less worldly. Travel, time, and experience are remarkable instructors."

"Indeed." He turned to face Kavan, smiling. "Please sit. I shall use the cot if I feel the need to rest. You are weak from your trials and I am much indebted to you for it."

"Indebted? I have done nothing, milord…"

"On the contrary. Your coming here is the most precious gift you could have given. Please, dispense with formalities. My name is Qol."

Kavan did as instructed, uncomfortable with the man's grateful, gracious words, and asked, "You are k'kairá?" It was either that or discuss the bloodletting he had endured and how that might leave this ancient man indebted to him. That was a discussion Kavan did not want to have.

"That is your word for it."

"And Myreth?"

Qol chuckled. "You suspect him? You are perceptive indeed. It is unknown who his parents were, but there is Teren and k'elyryhánag in him. And yes, he carries our blood. As do you."

Kavan blinked and stared at him. "Me?"

"You know it to be true. That is partially why you are attuned to us. Remember this, any of your kind with dark hair, such as your kinsman, carries our blood in his veins, just as any of us who carries k'elyryhánag in them will have blond hair. There are exceptions of course, and in some, the blood is stronger than in others. In some, it lies dormant. Some siblings will not share our blood."

Thinking that peculiar, that Bhríd could carry their blood but not Syl, Kavan cocked his head. "The harper…from the Feast of Llyr." He had known even then that the harper and his followers were k'kairá, but he had not thought about them much since that night. The old man nodded, deciding now to rest on the edge of the cot. Kavan thought there was more Qol was going to say but decided against revealing. But Kavan needed answers and he knew he could not be shy about getting them. "Are questions permitted?"

"That is the purpose of this evening, to learn of one another. I am sure you have more questions for me than I have for you. Ask what you wish."

Though he frowned, thinking the man wanted to talk and not give access to the Chalice and staff piece, that Qol was somehow accessing Kavan's deepest thoughts without his knowledge, he decided to make the most of this opportunity. There was a burning temptation to ask about the healing of his hands, but Kavan understood that was not Qol's doing. That miracle had come through k'Ádhá alone. "That word, k'elyryhánag, what does it mean? I recognize Elyri in it, but the term is unfamiliar in any language I know."

Qol nodded, his expression suggesting that it was a good place to start. "It is a very ancient term, one by which your ancestors were called and first called themselves long before they found their way to the land your people call home. So long, in fact, that even with as many years as you will live, you might not comprehend the time. As for its meaning, that is a question best left unanswered, a dangerous question best not pursued."

Kavan clasped his hands in his lap, his no longer twisted fingers fidgeting, feeling a sting of residual pain in his hands and wrists. He could see no trace of the event that caused either the blood loss or healing, but still it hurt. It was tempting to stare at them, to marvel at the miraculous that he did not yet believe, to weep again with relief, but he forced himself to focus on the mission before him. Wondering why the answer to his questions about the distant past was dangerous, disappointed that he could not have that answer, he looked up at Qol. "You do not seem surprised by what occurred…"

"No more than you. I have seen a great many events in my time, though this exceeds them in magnitude and significance. What we have seen…with our eyes and our hearts…is of a nature never to be unseen or surpassed. The prophets told me you would come; more specifically, Kóráhm told me you would come."

"Kóráhm? When was he here?" Kavan leaned forward.

"He came to us three times. The first was an accident, the first time he attempted to manipulate the k'rylag he had found. Fearful of what he had done, he did not stay long. When he came the second time, he was older and wiser…sadder. He told us what had happened with his brother, and having learned that we possessed two of the items originally used to consecrate that náos, he asked that we hold them until the person came who could undo what was done. He gave explicit details of what to expect from that person. The final time he came was after the fire meant to kill him."

The bard's eyes lit. "Did it? Kill him? I wonder often if he lives."

"That is a question Kóráhm must answer…or k'Ádhá if he chooses. For your purposes, he is no longer as he once was. Let that answer suffice, Cliáth. You will receive no other."

Thwarted once more in his quest for knowledge, Kavan swallowed his annoyance and changed the subject with another question. "He told you that would happen? The rósádhá?"

"He said that the blood of Dhágdhuán and the chosen would mingle before our altar, said that which was whole would be broken, and that which was broken would be mended."

Then there was a purpose to Kavan enduring such torment. Perhaps everything that had happened, even the injury to his hands, had been necessary to bring him to this place, if his hands were the 'broken' detail meant to be mended. Had Qol known his hands would be restored or had that event been as unexpected for him as it had been for Kavan? Had Kóráhm known? "That does not mean I am the man you seek."

Again Qol laughed. "That we seek? You are the seeker. We seek nothing. These people are content, following the holy laws and books their entire lives, their purpose to love and serve k'Ádhá with the hopes to one day be called into the world to share their Faith. That you have fulfilled the requirements, passed the tests put to you, given us your blessing, is as much to their benefit as it is to yours."

"I was told my worthiness would be tested, and yet…"

"And it has been," the old man assured him. "There were eight requirements. The first was your willingness to set aside your wishes and aid us, to participate as a member of our community. It was not above you to perform manual labor with strangers. Yet that was a simple test, I admit. Any man could have done as you did.

"The second test was passed first, by your advent at our cloister. Your race, your color, and your musical talents were each details we were told to expect. When Valesce first spoke of your arrival, I was prepared to grant your request at once, but was reminded of the other tests and persuaded to wait."

Kavan looked at his hands, turning them over to study them back and front, marveling that even his white skin and hair might have been pre-ordained, or that at least Kóráhm had known of his birth long before his grandparents had been born. His body began to tremble.

"You are theologically well-versed yet worldly, and you know truths about Kóráhm which only a man determined to learn could know. Your compassion for that child…compassion was the fifth test, you see…and your sixth test was the miracles…the healing."

Qol returned to the window and stared into the night. "Still raining. Inconvenient." He sighed. "Even so, I knew it could be a test for me, to see if I would remain steadfast. There was another once, one we thought…" He shook his head.

"The woman? Myreth spoke of a woman…"

Qol cocked his head. "I am surprised he remembers…or perhaps he does not and speaks only of what we so often relate…the need to beware of false prophets." He was averse to speak of her further, again leaving Kavan with more unanswered questions. "When the blood came…I was nearly convinced and had but to await the final answer."

"Which was?" Kavan was almost afraid to know. That another sought the relics before him was troublesome, and he tucked that bit of information away in his memory to explore another time.

"That Kóráhm gave you his approval. I knew he was there, that he lay his hands on me. He said you were the one; you gave us the blessing that will open our doors."

"To the outside? Forgive me if I seem insulting or ignorant, yet you are…are not these people suspicious? Your age? How will you convince them you can lead them out of here?"

"They are suspicious, but no more than they are of Myreth. They believe my great sanctity has granted longevity." Qol chuckled. "I have known I shall have to leave them; your arrival has provided the exit. I will pass the mantle to the next generation, someone who will lead them, and be able to depart knowing prophecy has been fulfilled."

Though Kavan wondered if Myreth would be that man to lead, he did not believe Qol would admit it. "You know what I seek?" he asked.

"The Chalice of Llyr and the crown of the Staff of Drebhoti. We do not know who possesses the bottom portion of the staff, or the base; they were lost many generations before Kóráhm came."

"One is in my possession," Kavan admitted, "as are the blessed water, the Diwi, and the Orec. But the base? I know nothing of…"

"A great crystal made of the clearest volcanic glass…"

The carafe stopper, Kavan wondered. He had been compelled to take it from Coryllien's tomb, had stored it with other relics of import, yet had never studied it to determine its value. Perhaps it had not been a carafe stopper at all. "I may have it…"

If not, another quest would be required, and Kavan did not want to dwell on that hindrance. He chose to have faith.

"Good…Kóráhm has fulfilled his pledge to guide and aid you."

"The others…may I…?"

"The items are yours with but a single condition, that you return them here, including the pieces you possess, when you have fulfilled your duty. They must not fall into the hands of incompetents, ignorants, or fools. Our faith is in you because Kóráhm calls you trustworthy. Do not fail us or prove him wrong."

Kavan would never dream of being untrustworthy, and that Kóráhm thought much of him was a high mark to live up to. "By our…you mean your people, not those living in this place?"

"Yes," the old man nodded. "My people. Do not give us cause to regret this decision. Our wrath is something you do not wish to face."

"I fear Kóráhm's disappointment more, milord…and my own shame more than that. I will return them, as you request, or die trying."

"You will not die." Kavan did not ask how Qol could be certain of that. The k'gdhededhá knew many things he should not and seemed not to know others. What was one more?

"I will stay until you return. Bring them to me; place them in my hands, no one else's. Not Valesce' or Myreth's. Do you understand?"

"Yes."

Qol turned from the window. "I will give them to you when you are prepared to depart. There is a k'rylag, if you wish to use it to take you to Gorbesh or to take you directly home, but I must prepare you; the power of these items, particularly the Chalice, is strong. Llyr was a mighty gdhededhá warrior and powerful ágdháni, as you would say. He did nothing part way, including creating a chalice potent enough to hold the blood of the gods if he chose. You may not be able to manipulate the k'rylag if the Chalice's power interferes. It may hinder or magnify your other abilities; it is difficult to say. Nevertheless, you may try. Such attempts, and any successes or failures, will not interfere with its function."

Kavan noted the use of the plurality of gods and wondered why Qol chose that word. The main point of interest in the man's words, for now at least, was the mention of a Gate. A Gate would mean he did not have to stumble weakly down the mountain alone, nor wait for villagers to travel here to trade. None of those here, of a people who never left this place, would be free to escort him. A Gate meant that, as long as he was strong enough to employ the power, he could begin his journey home tonight.

Despite his reluctance to part with Myreth, Kavan wanted to avoid interaction with the other residents here. Qol's reverence, Valesce's perpetual neutrality, and Myreth's restrained adoration were all Kavan felt capable of bearing. "I will attempt the k'rylag tonight, if that is not ungrateful. I appreciate your generosity and kindness more than I can express, but my friends are waiting and I must return to Rhidam to be prepared when the hour comes to…" He hesitated and asked, "How will I know when it is time for the ritual…and how will I know how to use these items…what I am to do?"

"Faith, Cliáth. It brought you this far. Follow your heart and you will know. Whether the details will come from the Chalice, from Kóráhm, or from elsewhere, you will know when you are meant to. Are there further questions before you depart? We may not have this opportunity again."

"I think I have asked what I need at this time. Anything more would be for curiosity sake…and I suspect those questions will not be answered." He could not help but smirk. Most of the man's answers had not been answers at all. "Perhaps when I return, when the purification is complete, there will be time for dialogue. But there is one favor more I feel compelled to ask." This time he hesitated because though he felt he knew the answer, the thought had to be voiced. "Allow me to take Myreth with me."

"I cannot."

"Cannot?" Kavan asked. "He is unsatisfied, discontent and unfulfilled. He wants more than this life gives him, though he does not know what that is. He has lived here more years than many men will live, and he is eager for something more. Now that he has touched the outside, he will be less happy than before. If you plan to open the gates, how shall you contain him? How will you keep him from fleeing if you forbid him to leave? At least if he is with me, I can guide him through the obstacles he will face…and he would be of great use to me while I regain my strength."

Qol studied the Elyri, his violet eyes seeking something in the bard's. Then he shook his head. "Strength you have, Cliáth. Strength you have always had. Myreth is unprepared for life outside and I intend other things for him."

Feeling surprisingly frustrated, Kavan said, "It is unrealistic to assume he will fill your expectations. A son rarely fulfills his father's wishes. He is his own man, not an extension of you. Give him freedom if you desire to keep his respect."

The k'gdhededhá's smile was mysterious and amused. "You are a wise man, a man Myreth is blessed to know. I promise to consider what you say, for his sake. For now, however, he remains here. He knows where the k'rylag is, though he does not know its function. I shall have him take you to it, give you time to say farewell, and I will join you with what you came for."

Kavan stood, feeling compelled to bow despite his dizziness. "Thank you, Qol. I shall not forget your generosity."

"More importantly," admonished the k'gdhededhá with a wag of his finger, "do not forget your instructions and your promise."

Myreth was still in the corridor with Valesce when Qol opened the door and allowed Kavan to pass. It did not appear he had overheard any of the conversation from within the room. The k'gdhededhá beckoned Valesce inside and said, "Myreth, please take Lord Cliáth to the k'rylag. Await me there." The door closed, leaving them alone.

Myreth, again supporting Kavan's weight, moved silently, his steps dragging. "You do not have…"

"The k'gdhededhá will bring them," said Kavan quietly, feeling that dragging as if it were pulling him under, trying to drown him.

"Then you leave tonight."

The bard sighed. "If I can. Otherwise, it will be in the morning." As if to justify his choice, he continued, "I must. The náós must be cleansed before my lands can know peace. Its defilement has brought centuries of death and despair; the time for it to end is at hand. It is my burden to see it done. My journey will take many weeks unless I am lucky, and my companions will be waiting for me in Gorbesh."

"Companions? You have spoken of no one else." Myreth sounded both disappointed and jealous as a frown replaced his pout.

"Wortham is my oldest, truest friend; he remains when everyone else abandons me, when I abandon myself. I could never leave him. Urian is a blind gdhededhá who travels with us. They have been my companions throughout this journey, though for a time there was…"

When his voice trailed into a lonely note and he did not continue, Myreth asked, "A woman?" Kavan looked at him with mild surprise. "It is obvious in your tone. I have yet to meet anyone who inspires that heartache in me…until you." There was a long awkward pause before he continued, "I would have you remain forever, but I know you would be unhappy here, and I do not want you to be unhappy."

Kavan nodded but kept his eyes straight ahead. Was that why Myreth had kissed him? He had thought it some manner of holy ecstasy, a means of gaining the ritual blood blessing bestowed on others but which had not, to his recollection, been bestowed on Myreth. "I would gladly spend my days with you, and I do not wish you sadness either. I asked the k'gdhededhá for permission to bring you with me…"

They entered a small room, a marble construct, empty except for a large red sunburst inlaid upon the floor. It was a duplicate of the one in Owain's home in Fiara and Kavan suspected that this Gate would be the same as that one, one of those which showed extra destinations that could only be accessed from these special Gates."

"He refused your request." Myreth did not sound surprised, but he did sound disappointed.

"I begged him to reconsider."

The taller man shrugged as he fingered the ring upon his hand. "It is just as well. As tempting as the idea is, and as much as I long to travel with you, I have not the courage to do it."

"Your life is about to change, Myreth; I know this to be true. You may yet have the opportunity to gain what you desire. Weigh your options before making decisions. Follow your heart. We will meet again, sooner than you think, as I must return the items I am borrowing when I finish with them. Wait for me here."

Without warning, Myreth pulled Kavan against him in an embrace, weeping, kissing his cheeks fervently. "If I never see you again, my heart shall burst and remain broken." When Kavan did not respond, uncomfortable with the display, the taller man released him, stepped away, and wiped his face. "Emotional displays disquiet you, but it is how I am. I can hide nothing; what I feel is there to be seen. I want you to have this."

The emerald ring was removed from his finger; he took Kavan's left hand, stared at its bruised flawlessness for several moments, the perfect newness of it despite the discoloration of injury, an amazing thing, and slid the silver band with its large green stone upon the bard's middle finger. It fit as though made for him.

Before the healing, the ring would never have fit his hand.

"It was Kóráhm's ring, or thus the k'gdhededhá told me when he gave it to me," Myreth mumbled.

"Kóráhm…?" Kavan began to protest and remove it. "I cannot…"

The darker skinned hands cupped the white ones and Myreth shook his head. "You must. I saw him. I know. As Kóráhm is always with you, it is fitting you have what was his. I believe your hand is where it belongs. When you return home, look closely at the tapestry, at Kóráhm's left hand. If it duplicates the one here, as you say, you will see it there. Until then, wear it and remember us, remember me."

"I have noth…" Kavan hesitated and then reached behind his neck. For the first time since he had purchased it, Kavan removed the Kílyn cross and slid it over Myreth's head. His hands lingered on the man's shoulders, Kavan awed by his ability to perform such a gesture again, before dropping shakily to his sides. "This has been one of my most treasured possessions. Since the day I acquired it, it has been ever near my heart. Keep it near yours, Myreth, to remember me."

Myreth managed to smile as he whispered, "I can never forget."

The curtain covering the doorway parted to reveal Qol and Valesce. Both men noticed the ring upon Kavan's hand and the thick chain Myreth now wore, yet neither questioned the exchange. Valesce carried a wooden chest that he offered to Kavan without speaking.

"What you require is within," Qol said, "but do not open it until you need them; to open it needlessly may forfeit your right to their use." Kavan took the long narrow chest, amazed at how heavy it was and at the strong vibrations of power emanating from it. The k'gdhededhá's admonition about it interfering with his use of the power made sense. "Are you ready, Cliáth?"

"I am." Kavan did not look at Myreth as he stepped into the center of the sun symbol without indecision. If he hesitated, he might not leave. He waited for a moment, to see if Qol would send Myreth away or allow him to witness the use of the k'rylag. When Qol said nothing, Kavan spoke. "Thank you for everything. I pray you will not be disappointed in me or regret your decision. Myreth…"

"Goodbye, friend Cliáth. I pray we meet again."

Kavan nodded. "We shall. I made a promise. Wait for me."

For the second time since Arlan's death, Kavan gathered the energy, feeling the conflict of power between his own and the objects within the oak box. Qol's hand rested on his arm long enough to show him the pathway that would take him to Gorbesh and then the hand fell away. Despite the difficulty in making contact, once the connection was made, the actual process of travel was easier than anticipated, easier than any such travel he had made before.

In the room known as the dhín k'rylag, Myreth watched the air shimmer, saw a mist swirl up from the ground like a tiny whirlwind and surround Kavan, and felt a tingle of static of a sort with which he was unfamiliar. He must have blinked because in the next second both the mist and Kavan were gone. So too, he noticed, were the k'gdhededhá and Valesce. He was alone.

The Gate deposited Kavan in the middle of a grain field in the light rainfall, an unanticipated oddity. The energy signature beneath his feet that indicated a Gate was almost too faint to be detected by any but the most powerful or astute individual. It explained why connecting to it had been difficult. He might have passed over it without noticing. Likely there had been a building here in ages past, unless this was an exception to every Gate he had ever found or some sort of natural Gate. It had been unused long enough that its energy had almost dissipated. He would not, he judged by the power contained within the chest, be able to use this Gate to reach Rhidam. He would have to travel some other way.

To the southeast lay the shadows of the village structures, dark at this hour of the night except for the glows of hearth fires shining through windows. He wondered if Wortham was awake…and what the man would do when he saw the miracle of restoration Kavan had been granted. Pausing long enough to be certain he had not lost the ring or the flask of holy water, that the chest was secure in his grasp, and that the healing of his hands was not some persistent hallucination, he sloshed weakly through gathered puddles to the heart of the village and from there to Zelenka's home. He could sense three individuals within, two of those were asleep. The third, Wortham, was brooding. Rather than probe his thoughts or knock on the door and risk waking the others, the bard called silently to the captain's mind as he had done many times before.

Wortham's head turned, his heart thumping in his chest as he recognized the touch of a mind within his. He hastened to the door to throw it open with a wide smile as he came eye to eye with Kavan.

"Praise k'Ádhá you have returned!" he exclaimed a little too loudly as he crushed the bard against him and edged him outdoors, in spite of the awkwardness of the chest between them. He did not want to wake the others with his exuberance. "I feared we would be forced to depart without you and despaired how you might react. Is this it?" He looked at the box between them. "Did you receive what you need? What was the náós like? Will we be starting for Rhidam?"

With a delighted smile, pleased with both his reception and seeing his friend, Kavan replied, "Wortham, please. So many questions. I cannot answer them now and I would prefer to get out of the rain."

It was at that moment that Wortham noticed the dark circles under Kavan's sunken eyes, a sure sign of physical weakness. He opened the door, took the chest, and placed it carefully on the table as Kavan came in and peeled off his wet tunic. As the bard settled before the fire for warmth, Wortham, still unaware of the change in his friend beyond the horrific bruises scattered across his body, closed the door after him and built up the fire, muttering in a whisper, "What in k'Ádhá's name were you forced to endure, milord? I hope what you received was worth the ordeal."

"Ordeal?" Kavan chuckled, feeling in remarkably good humor despite being cold, wet, weak, and weary. "That may well be the best word to describe it. It was worth every moment, for I have gained the items I need to proceed. We may return to Rhidam."

"Truly? You are prepared for that?" He glanced at Urian on the pallet and Zelenka on her mother's bed, surprised that, if they were awake, they had not stirred or spoken.

He took a cloth from a hook on the wall. and squatted beside Kavan as the bard's good humor faded. "I admit I am unsure I wish to face what I left behind, but I no longer have an excuse to stay away."

As he said those words, Wortham reached for his hand without looking, intent upon drying the bard's mottled arm. Only when his fingers entwined with Kavan's did the reality of change jar him, and he spun sideways in amazement, falling onto his backside as he stared.

"Kavan! Praise be…your hands!" He scrambled to his knees to reach for the other, which Kavan offered with embarrassment and joy.

"Yes…I don't know how…but…"

"Ordeal indeed…" Wortham, in his happiness for his beloved friend, added tears of joy to the rainwater which already glistened on Kavan's skin. Kavan turned one hand over and cupped Wortham's face. No further words needed to be spoken.

"I admit I am not sure I wish to face the past, but I must return," murmured Kavan, changing the subject. Not even the awkward shame that might linger between he and Princess Diona for years to come would stay him. "My hands are restored, as you can see" he whispered, deeply touched by Wortham's response. He wiggled his fingers, the emerald catching the firelight in its facets. "I have all that is required to purify the altar. It is time to go back." Twisting his neck from side to side and gently freeing his hands from Wortham's, he asked, "What did you mean you thought you would be forced to depart without me?"

Catching Kavan's hand again, Wortham studied the ring, his efforts to dry him forgotten as he spoke. "Zelenka's mother died. Zelenka believes that, because we fell asleep while keeping vigil over the body during the night, evil spirits entered the corpse. In order to prevent the spirits from permeating Gorbesh, she says she must leave here. An unusual local belief, I agree, but I could not persuade her differently. There is a caravan leaving in four hours for the coastal city of Pa'aliaka. We are to depart with them and would have left word for you to follow…to find us…but I was unhappy about doing either."

"I would have understood," Kavan whispered, despite the pang the thought of being left created, "but I am thankful fate allows us to continue together. Perhaps in Pa'aliaka we will find a ship north. It would save time, I think, to take advantage of it. Is everything ready?"

For Kavan to willingly suggest travel by sea was significant. "Yes. The goats were sold and I have transferred your belongings to a single trunk. Zelenka has few possessions to bring, mainly clothing. It and what Lady Orynn left will fit easily upon a mule, and we will not need to worry for the time being about food or water as the caravan will supply what we need. You do not mind if she joins us?"

Thoughts turning momentarily from Orynn to Myreth, and how Wortham might have felt if Kavan brought him along, he chastised himself for not considering Wortham's feelings before. "I promised her mother I would assume responsibility for Zelenka after her death. She may join us for as long as she likes, to Rhidam if she chooses."

"I was afraid that, after what happened…"

"We are the dearest of friends, Wortham. You are the steadfast rock beneath me. I need you too much; nothing will change what we share. However, I am beginning to understand that I cannot hold you back from what your future holds. That would be unfair and unjust."

"Does it have anything to do with this?" Wortham indicated the ring. "Who was she?"

"His name is Myreth…and this belonged to Kóráhm." He pressed his hand to the captain's cheek and smiled, longing to disavow the captain of any jealousy. "Nothing will ever come between us, Wortham. I will not allow it."

"Good," said the big man as he began drying Kavan's skin at last. "You must rest if you are to travel. The horse is yours for the duration, as Zelenka is afraid of him, and you will be unable to walk in your state, no matter how much rest four hours affords you. You do not need to share your tale tonight, but I expect you to tell me everything later. It is the least you can do for leaving without saying farewell."

"True," the bard murmured. "We will have many days on the road in which to talk. I look forward to sharing it with you." He curled up on the floor next to the fire, hands tucked under his chin to his chest as if a precious treasure, and Wortham covered him with a blanket to ward off any chill, offering his cloak from the wall as a cushion for Kavan's head. "I am happy to see you, Wortham."

"And I you," the captain said as he returned to the table. There would be little sleep; what rest he could get would be good enough. He would not climb to the loft; he did not want any more distance between them. "Goodnight, Kavan. Praise k'Ádhá you are healed."

❧Chapter 38❧

Of the problems Caol faced, he was unsure which was more disturbing: the locked trunk of children's arms and legs, that it was one of his Association contacts who found it in what had been considered an abandoned warehouse, or that the King clung stubbornly to his belief that the Association was involved in this murderous outrage and were trying to pass them off as someone else's crimes. The inquisitor was certain of one fact; those limbs belonged with the torsos that Agis had recovered days before. He also suspected that these grisly remains were deliberately left where they would be found so that they could be reported to the King to upset him.

That effort, at least, was succeeding.

On first glance, the building where the trunk was found looked like any other empty warehouse near the river, meant to temporarily store shipments and deliveries from the occasional boats that sailed to or from Levonne and other points up and down the Tegid. It had one shuddered window overlooking the river and was close enough to the water that the burlap sack could have been tossed from here to be found downstream by the Cíbhóló general. Caol had little doubt it had happened that way though he did not have proof. Outside, he could hear Darius questioning the neighbors about anything they might have seen or heard. If he found anything useful, Caol would be surprised.

Scuffs on the floor along the back wall drew his attention. The trunk had been there, the abrasions left behind when the justice's men had dragged it outside. The deed was already done by the time Caol arrived, but his source had told him what to expect, what had been found when the fellow opened the front door to show the space to a potential customer. What the man had not mentioned was what the inquisitor now uncovered. Perhaps, since the fellow had not come into the building once he found the trunk and smelled the inescapable stench of death that still lingered in the air, he had not known it was there. However, if he was the owner of this building, Caol felt certain the man knew the layout and features of his property. He might have hoped no one would notice and would have no reason to investigate if they did. The other less pleasant option was that the King was correct, that some member or members of the Association were working both sides of the Coryllien anti-Elyri business.

Either way, a cellar door demanded investigation from a man who was familiar with such details in the Association's world. Caol whistled for someone to join him and was already pulling back the recessed bolt to open the door before the Káliel guardsman named Waljan entered the building.

"Watch my back. I'm going down."

"Not without light, sir. One moment." The soldier shouted out the door for a torch, and in short order had one in hand.

Equipped with the smoky yellow light, Caol nodded his thanks and started down the wooden steps into blackness. It was cold, but that was to be expected of an underground storage. As the steps continued, deeper than a standard cellar would be, he concluded this was not a typical storage. A hiding place for illegal merchandise, he mused, expecting to find a collection of stolen goods when he reached the bottom. His father's shop had contained such a room. Not mentioning it was the proprietor's way of keeping his commodities secret.

The inquisitor might have been willing to let the matter rest since he was not currently interested in illegal merchandise or stolen goods, but at the bottom he found a door with a smell even more gruesome than what had permeated the floor above, seeping from behind it. Whatever this was, it was not to be ignored or forgotten. Awkwardly, he fumbled in his pocket for his picks and then struggled one handed with the lock on the door. Without the lock to hold it, the door swung open effortlessly, an indicator that the hinges were used often enough not to have rusted.

An empty room, empty except for a small fire-pan of burnt coals, open manacles upon the wall to his left, and a table cluttered with various items that Caol recognized upon closer inspection. Branding irons, knives, tongs, and pokers. Pliers, saws, and thumb screws. Instruments of torture. The amount of blood and offal below the manacles told the tale.

The room told Caol more than that as he looked back at the door. He was too far below ground for anyone to hear anything that transpired here, well insulated by earth and stone. Anyone could have used this room without the owner's knowledge…or with it for that matter. The unpleasant possibility that the King was correct tugged at him. It was possible the children had been dissected here. It was equally possible k'gdhededhá Jermyn had been tortured here as well. The thought made him sick and he tried not to retch as he backed out of the room without disturbing anything, locked the door, and returned to the room above.

"Anything, sir?" asked Waljan.

Unable to share this news because of the sensitive nature of the k'gdhededhá's capture and death, Caol skillfully lied. "A cellar. Nothing that concerns the King. I think I shall have a talk with the owner, however; this kind of cellar has limited uses and I think I need to discourage his current line of business. Tell the justice that no one is to be allowed down there until I return. I will not be gone long."

❧*❧

"I want it done today, Friid. I don't care how." Owain rubbed his aching forehead. "They deserve to suffer for what they did, especially the bald one. I'm sure he is the leader, in spite of his feigned ignorance. Make it painful; make them know suffering the way their victims did. I don't care to know the details. I have wearied of their stench. No one else wants them and they've taken up enough resources."

Friid, the captain of Owain's household guard, nodded. Ever since being forced to keep watch over those three northerners, Friid had wanted nothing more than to oversee their deaths. Particularly that bald one who spent his captivity taunting his jailers for their inability to harm him. On most days, Friid was a man who could scarcely be called friendly or benevolent; he was fair-minded, but gentle and patient he was not. He would love nothing more than to inflict the slowest death he could imagine upon that man.

Now that Owain had sanctioned execution, Friid took the first, the one who had not spoken during their entire captivity, without telling the others what he planned. It would be morbidly satisfying to let them wonder. Each was taken aside and questioned sporadically during their captivity, so they would expect nothing different this time. There was a side room in that dungeon, a room generations of Nethite lords had used to torture captives into confessions, often for crimes they had not committed, all in the name of power. But this first man was not questioned or tortured. By Nethite standards, his death was merciful and relatively painless. After binding him to a chair, Friid slit the man's wrists and then his throat and left him to bleed to death. It was a largely silent passing, one that, even with the door left open, the other prisoners could not witness.

But the blood upon the captain's hands and boots was its own testimony when he went back to the cell. Behind him, one of his men dragged the deceased and deposited the corpse inside the cell the three shared. Friid took the second man out, noticing the look between the two living spies. Friid smiled. Execution was much more interesting when the condemned did not know what was coming.

Since no public execution or display had been announced, the midday crowds passing the stockades were puzzled to see Friid locking his captive into the wooden device. One of his soldiers carried a basket of stones and announced that this man was one of those responsible for the murder of a local merchant's family. He was condemned to public stoning, by any who wished to participate, before his execution.

Most of Fiara had heard about the butchery, and several daring, bloodthirsty, or outraged individuals took the opportunity to make the murderer pay. Long before the man was dead, however, though certainly long enough for him to feel the effects of the projectiles that struck his face and body, Friid unlocked the stockades, bound his hands and feet, and dragged him by his wrists back to the dungeon. He was thrown roughly into the cell, face first onto the bare floor, thinking the worst of his sentence was behind him. Perhaps, despite the public decree of impending execution, he would be allowed to live.

With a flick of his wrist, Friid gestured to the guard with him, who brought a heavy mallet down upon the center of the man's back. The crack of spine and ribs was barely audible over the scream. The bald prisoner lunged, and the fellow with the mallet smashed it into his arm, driving him back against the wall. Friid left the man on the floor to suffocate in his own blood from punctured, collapsing lungs, the dead and dying the only company the remaining prisoner had.

"You cannot do this! I demand better treatment!"

Face blank, his hand on the cell door, Friid looked dispassionately at the bald man. "You are in no position to make demands. Your King has abandoned you and King Hagan has no interest in your fate. Lord Lachlan is weary of your presence, and frankly, so am I. It is my privilege to dispose of you in the manner I choose. Your friends have been entertaining, but not as much as watching you die will be. When I decide your fate, you will be the first to know. In the meantime, enjoy the company and consider if there is anything further you have to say which might stay your punishment."

ॐ*ॐ

Princess Diona closed the door behind her brother but did not turn to look at the others in the library. "It is insulting, particularly to you and Hagan, Uncle, that dedhá Claide refuses to bury these unfortunate children in the cemetery. He has to agree that these are the six…"

"But without proper identification, that is not definite, and the King has specifically forbidden me and Bhríd to touch them." The healer did not turn away from the window as he spoke.

"Foolish. They certainly did not dismember themselves." These were no deaths by suicide. There seemed no reason they should not be buried properly in the náós yard.

Espen agreed with Diona but knew that surrender to the King's wishes was their only choice. "Perhaps, but he is the King and his rule is to be obeyed, and it's Claide's right to deny burial on náós grounds."

"We might still be able to identify them." Caol fingered the dagger he carried concealed beneath his tunic. "The King decreed they will be buried in the royal vault. We ask dedhá Tusánt to bless them. I doubt Hagan will issue him a command against touching the corpses; he can identify them at the same time, if he is willing."

The princess nodded gratefully, appreciating that they were able to find a way to do what needed to be done without flaunting her brother's orders. "Thank you, Uncle. I will see to it at once."

"Wait," he called, stopping her before she could leave the room. "Closer examination of the building where the trunk was found revealed a cellar; it contained no merchandise or goods, but it does contain a table and instruments of torture."

"Instruments of torture…?" Diona croaked, face losing color.

"And manacles on one wall. From the looks of the place…it is possible the children were killed there, but I wager the one man we know to be tortured to death was also. There was no evidence of a specific individual being held, but there is a strong possibility…"

"I will gladly escort you there, now or in the morning, to learn the truth if you wish," said the chamberlain with narrowed eyes.

"Is there nothing I can do?" asked Ártur, turning around at last.

"You are not to leave the castle until whoever is threatening you is apprehended. Is that understood?" Ártur nodded at the princess's reminder though his disappointment at being unable to help was stamped on his face. "If this turns out to be true, the problem of breaking the k'gdhededhá's death to Claide and Hagan is solved, if we can make it appear the discovery of this room coincides with the discovery of his body."

Caol did not like it. His deep frown said as much. "I will try to think of some way to make it work, but it presents a serious dilemma, regardless. The owner of this building is Association…" Prince Espen was surprised to learn that the royal family of Enesfel had ties with the Association. The inquisitor shrugged off his expression. "A tale too long to tell, my prince. This man had to know that room was there. Maybe he never used it. Someone else could have been using it without his knowledge, or at least for purposes he knew nothing about. It is also possible that he knew what was being done there, which means I have a security problem. Not to mention, if the King learns of it, he will assume the owner, and perhaps the entire Association, was involved in the k'dedhá's death. We can't have that."

"Could we bring him to the keep for questioning?"

The emphasis on questioning told Caol what the chamberlain meant. "It might alert him to our suspicions, allow him to remove evidence…" suggested Prince Espen.

"But Caol has already seen the room, and you know what you saw. Even if everything is removed, including the manacles, there will be traces I can read and removing evidence will make him look guilty," Bhríd added.

The princess put her hand on the door latch. "Search it first thing tomorrow; we will worry about my brother after you learn the truth. If we need to question your contact, we will…but not here in the keep. I will have dedhá Tusánt brought in the morning to bless the children and identify them. Then we decide if notifying their families is worth the risk of angering Hagan. Goodnight, gentleman…tomorrow may be a very long day."

❧*❧

Friid's face was blank by this time, both the humor and the horror having gone out of the effort long ago. His final prisoner, slumped forward in the chair he was bound to, muttered incoherently. The chair was surrounded and covered in the blood of his cohort killed earlier that day, and now with his own. At least he was no longer screaming.

Not that he had screamed much. True to his training, the man had a high tolerance for pain; it was one of the many essential requirements for any military officer of the Nethite Crown. They were trained not to speak under torture and did their best to inspire that strength in the average soldier. But Friid had not been tormenting him for information; he had no reason to drag out the pain for anything other than sadistic amusement. Friid's training had been of that same school, having originally been Nethite, and thus he knew methods of exacting pain that were sure to produce results in most men. He also knew that, regardless of the amount of training given, there came a point in each man where the body could not tolerate anymore.

This fellow had remained remarkably composed when he lost both his feet and hands. Tourniquets were applied to keep him from bleeding to death prematurely, as well as to provide further torment when they were removed for the next phase…the severing of his arms at the elbow and the crushing of his kneecaps as the tingling of awakening nerves reached its peak. Though there had been a little more reaction that time, the brief screams were cut short by the captain's wicked grin.

Friid left then while his men reapplied the tourniquets. He hoped the prisoner was comparing his pain to that of the family and Elyri he had dismembered. The captain left for dinner and made certain that his men were brought their meals where they could eat in front of the victim. After having been denied food and water for two days, the simple act of being able to see and smell food without being able to consume it was another form of torture.

There was time for a brief nap afterward, and then Friid returned to the dungeon. The amount of blood, his hunger and thirst, and the sight of his limbs scattered around him brought the prisoner to the breaking point. He screamed as his arms were cut away at the shoulders, screamed until Friid left the room to await silence. When it came, he returned and slapped the man awake; it was time to end this. Groggily, the fellow looked at him with pain-glazed eyes.

Nodding at his assistant, the captain gestured at the prisoner's abdomen as he drew his sword. Bleary eyes showed no comprehension until the moment the blade cut through him. Eyes widening with clarity, he watched his insides fall onto the chair between his spread thighs, but was spared the necessity of screaming as the man behind him took his head from his shoulders in a single stroke.

The room was silent. Friid stared at the stump on the chair as if it were nothing more than a slab of meat from the butcher's.

"Get rid of this mess," he said, leaving the room for the final time that night. It was time to report to his lord that the order had been carried out. The spies were dead.

❧*❧

She had not expected gdhededhá Claide to arrive with Tusánt for the burial of the children's bodies, particularly after the man's hostile refusal to bury them in the náós cemetery. Still, despite her surprise, she knew she had to behave affably to keep him from suspecting anything. "Good morning dedhá Tusánt, dedhá Claide. Have you come to assist in the interment?"

With a dismissive wave of his hand, Claide shook his head. "No, I have no time for that today. I have come for an audience with the King. k'gdhededhá Tythilius planned to visit some of the parishes in the area surrounding Fiara this month. Since it does not appear he will be able to make the trip, I have made arrangements to go in his place and will leave Tusánt in charge until I return in a few weeks."

It was clear he found the thought of leaving the Elyri in charge of anything to be an unsatisfactory one, but Tusánt was the next most senior gdhededhá in Rhidam. There was no way he could leave someone else in charge without raising questions about his decision. "I last saw the King in the stateroom with Chamberlain Cáner." Diona thought she saw him bristle and tried not to smile. "He is probably still there discussing the day's business. Shall I announce you?"

"That is not necessary; there is no need to trouble yourself…"

But she believed she understood his weaknesses, and having a woman, especially a princess, cater to him was surely one of them. "Nonsense, k'dedhá," she said with a sweet smile. "I have to let him know dedhá Tusánt is here…"

The corners of Claide's eyes and mouth twitched. "No…I will do that. You must have more important duties to perform than to be the King's messenger."

He hastened from the room and Diona sighed gratefully, though she worried over why he wanted to keep her out of the room when he spoke to her brother. Perhaps Claide believed she had too much influence on the King and believed Hagan could be more easily manipulated if she was not present. "I suppose this is in our favor, as I'm sure he will detain Hagan long enough for you to identify the children. They are in a casket in the garden, where they have been under Lord Dugan's guard since morning. If you will go to him, I shall bring Healer MacLyr and Prince Espen."

gdhededhá Tusánt bowed. "Yes, I shall."

Ártur was easy to find as he was generally in the solar with Gaelán at this time every morning. Locating Prince Espen was more of a challenge, but she did soon spot him through the open door of the first-floor oratory, gazing at the stained glass window with a troubled expression. It was not a place she expected him to be, and she judged from the way his hands moved in front of him that he was playing with his turban, his habit when he was lost in agitated thought.

"Espen?"

"Yes?" he said without turning.

She did not speak at once, finding the distance in his voice disconcerting and painful. "dedhá Tusánt has arrived and gone to the garden. Claide is speaking with Hagen, which gives us time to do what needs to be done."

"Good." His voice trailed off. He did not move.

"You are weary of being here."

"I have not said…"

"You say nothing, but that is because you are a gentleman. You came to support Hagan and feel obliged to stay until he dismisses you…which may be a long time from now since he fears that the moment he sends you away he will have need of your men. You are a prince, not our subject, and can leave anytime; Hagan has no hold over you and the soldiers do not require your presence. Yet you are too attentive of his wishes and too bound by oath, to leave during such troubled times. You miss home. I am sorry I asked you to do this."

"You asked…" He turned to look at her. "Yes, it was your letter. This was not Hagan's idea?"

Twisting her hair around her fingers, she sighed. "It was my idea; I admit it. I missed you. I thought this would be simple. And because of my hesitation, you are tiring of me. I cannot blame you, but I beg you to be patient a little longer."

"I am trying," he said, positioning his turban upon his head. In truth, he felt more hopeful about a future with her as they traversed this new courtship phase of their relationship, but he wished she would make up her mind more quickly. He had promised proper courtship, which they were given little time for as recent events poured duty after duty upon her shoulders but they were trying. He should be more patient, should give her what he promised, but it was not as easy as he had believed it would be.

"I did think of something that might allow you to feel more useful during your stay… if that is your wish."

"What is it?"

"Come. I will tell you on our way to the garden. We should not keep everyone waiting."

❧*❧

Leaving Gorbesh was akin to tearing a hole in his soul. Kavan focused on the fact that at long last his quest was over, that he was now able to do what needed to be done in Rhidam and return without the shame of disfigurement hanging over him. That should be enough to shed light into the recesses of his heart. Instead, a single man named

Myreth, and the lingering pain of missing Orynn, foiled his contentment. Orynn was beyond reach, but Myreth…one day their paths would cross again and he looked forward with anticipation to what fate that day would bring.

His dark twin. That was how Kavan saw Myreth. They were alike in many ways, and yet profoundly different. If it had been possible, he would have returned to the cloister when he awoke that morning, but he knew Myreth would not have come and Kavan could never force him to do so. He missed the other man more than expected.

The caravan of mules, oxen, farmers, and merchants, with their carts of grain, vegetables, and crafted furnishings, left Gorbesh before daybreak. Urian was perched upon a mule, meticulously whittling despite the jostling pace. Behind him was Zelenka on another mule, with her trunk of clothing and belongings balanced precariously at her back. Wortham, on foot once again, led her mount and the third mule that currently carried their supplies, trade goods, and Kavan's trunk, which he would protect with his life. The bard, who rode Orynn's gray horse at the rear of the string, had no doubt that the captain would protect it if necessary, but prayed it would not come to that.

He looked again at the mountains shrinking behind them, singing to himself as he had done since they started east. Somewhere up there, Myreth bid him farewell, the alluring bow of his mouth quivering in an unhappy pout. We will meet again, my twin. I swear it.

The torsos and limbs were interred in the royal crypt as King Hagan ordered, though he was unaware that gdhededhá Tusánt had identified them as belonging to the six most recently kidnapped children, as expected. Prince Espen left Rhidam shortly after the service, telling the King he had been invited to visit Prince Owain, which was marginally close to the truth, though the invitation had come from Diona and not Owain. Caol and Bhríd left the princess with the duty of deciding if they should tell the children's family what they had learned and how to do it if they did. The inquisitor and chamberlain had their own priorities for the day.

The proprietor met them at the door of the warehouse, appearing unruffled as he unlocked the door to let them in. He did not react when Caol went to the hatch, slid back the bolt, and threw open the cellar door. His was not the behavior of a man with something to hide.

"Are you looking for something in particular, milord?" he asked.

"I don't know," Caol shrugged. "I will let you know if we find it." He started to light a torch but Bhríd shook his head with a grin.

"I won't need that." The chamberlain started down. "Why don't you stay here and keep an eye out for trouble."

"How do you expect to get in?" He frowned when he noticed that the building's owner had slipped away.

Bhríd chuckled. "You doubt my ingenuity?" he asked before disappearing from view.

Descending the stairs quickly, the chamberlain found the door at the bottom by the glow of his handlight. Years of living in proximity to Kavan had taught him that some abilities were harmless and generally useful. Handlights were one of those things. Beyond the door, he sensed no one; with one powerful thrust of his shoulder, the lock snapped and the door opened by brute strength alone.

He suspected those in the room above heard the sound.

Though there was an empty table in the room and the manacles hung on the wall where Caol said they would be, the room was clean. There was neither a trace of dust nor pools of blood. Maybe the man had thought it wise to clean it before showing it to prospective customers. Or perhaps whoever had used it came during the night to remove the evidence. Below the manacles, however, the stain of blood was still present, enough to confirm the inquisitor's claims, but contact with the manacles or the blood was needed for definitive confirmation.

Reading anything psychically, whether a person or object, was something Bhríd tried to avoid. To him, it seemed like the ultimate invasion of privacy; if he was meant to know something, he would find out by some less intrusive, means. In cases like this, however, or with the dead or uncooperative prisoners, he knew of no better way to learn the truth. It was better than torture, and it would be more accurate for determining what had happened in this room, and to whom, than any other method could be. With Ártur unable to leave the castle, only Bhríd was available to do this.

He closed his mind and eyes, took one manacle in each hand, and opened his senses slowly, far enough to gain information without being overwhelmed by the horror he expected had occurred here. It still amazed him that Kavan could approach this task so boldly.

The k'gdhededhá had been here, had suffered and died in these chains. The chamberlain backed away, having seen enough to make him sick and faint. As Ártur had learned from the man's disfigured corpse, there were no faces to be seen and what voices there were had been mostly too garbled to distinguish, except for one. He did not recognize the voice but found it non-threatening. Not having maintained contact with the shackles long enough to learn the fellow's identity, he started back up the stairs, wondering whom that final voice belonged to.

At the top of the steps, the door was closed. It was also locked, he learned, and not even a careful push with his shoulder would open it. There were at least nine men in the room, none of them the inquisitor. Where was Caol, and who were these men? Bhríd was not trained enough to read them without physical contact, but he could guess they were not friends. Waiting for him then, he decided, content to wait until Caol returned or until these fellows gave up.

It felt as if hours passed upon the steps in the dark, his sword ready in his hand. He could sense that, while the men above were prepared to wait for him to come out, they were not daring enough to go after him and were growing restless and inattentive with the passage of time. Another few hours and they would either give up or come looking for him despite their fears. But the chamberlain was hungry and concerned for Caol. The inquisitor would not have left Bhríd alone without a damn good reason; perhaps the man was hurt or dead.

If he planned it right, Bhríd thought he could take these nine by surprise, and even without his armor, he knew he stood a better than fair chance of living through a skirmish with nine assailants. He was stronger and faster, more experienced, and had senses none of them could match. With his sword ready, the chamberlain steeled himself for the charge.

A powerful thrust of his shoulder threw the hatch open. He leaped into the room, much to the surprise of those waiting. A scurvy bunch they were, unclean, unshaven, wielding a motley assortment of weapons that they scrambled to make ready in their rush to meet his attack. Three were struck down before they had the opportunity to draw arms, and the next two, though ready to strike with ill-maintained blades, were beheaded with one swipe of the chamberlain's sword.

From outside, they could hear the distinctive approach of a large group of armored men clattering through the streets. Two assailants thought to rush the door and make their escape, but they found it difficult to extricate themselves from combat with the larger than average Elyri. Another man fell, as his legs were cut out from under him, leaving Bhríd three foes, one of whom attacked with as much furor as he could muster. A wild swipe from one missed the intended target and disemboweled the seventh man instead, while the eighth freed himself to run for the door.

Two stocky Lachlan guardsmen blocked his route of escape; rather than allow himself to be captured, he fell upon his sword. The soldiers made no attempt to prevent his death.

The arrival of the guards and the cry made by the man who took his life was enough to distract the last man from his attack on Bhríd.

Dropping his sword, determined to take this one alive, the chamberlain rushed forward, pulled the man to the ground and knocked the sword from his hand. A knife was drawn and Bhríd struggled for it. In the tussle that followed, the blade bit deep into the Elyri's shoulder, causing him enough pain to jerk away reflexively. His assailant rolled, grabbed for a nearby sword, and followed the previous man into death by falling upon it.

Bhríd rushed to him, pulled the blade free, and tried to keep the man alive. Without a healer, there was nothing he could do but plop heavily upon the ground with his hand pressed against his injury and watch the life leave the other man's eyes. Seeing movement in the doorway, Bhríd looked up as Caol pushed his way into the building. "About time you got here," he grunted."

The inquisitor shrugged, his face apologetic but grim as he examined the bodies. "Looks like you had everything in hand."

"A little help would have been appreciated. We might have taken at least one of them alive. Where were you?"

"The proprietor left us too abruptly; I thought he should be followed. He went to the Boar's Garden where he spoke with a couple of men before departing. I came back, found these men here, and sought help. I also made a point of arresting our dear proprietor, since this man," he kicked the man without legs who groaned in his last moments of life, "is one of those he spoke with at the Boar's Garden."

"Sent to kill me?"

"Or me…or both of us. We will find out when we interrogate him. Either way…" He examined the dead men further. Three of them were Association, men Caol recognized, which meant his worst fears were being realized. He would have to talk to someone in authority, Stold if he could arrange it; if his money was not good enough to make the Association at least largely reliable and trustworthy, then he and they would find themselves at odds, and a man of Caol's knowledge in such a position to the Crown was an enemy the Association could not afford. "I'll have these men clean this mess up and keep an eye on this place. Logros will escort you back to the keep." He kicked at the cellar hatch door and grunted. "I wish you hadn't broken this."

"I didn't have a choice," Bhríd shrugged, mirroring Caol's earlier gesture. "If you like this, you should see the other one."

"Did you learn anything?" asked Caol as he helped the chamberlain to his feet.

"It is as you suspected…not good. I will tell the princess at once."

ക*ക

"And remember to get the choir up to the task of the Adhár Gathering. Without our usual musicians, you will need to be creative." Claide was packing for his trip, not looking at Tusánt as he gave the Elyri gdhededhá parting instruction.

We would have our usual musicians, Tusánt thought bitterly, if one of the two Teren musicians had not retired and the two Elyri had not left Rhidam in haste after the severed head appeared on the signpost. For that, Tusánt could not fault them. It left the flutist and the choir, which had also seen a dramatic decline in membership since the Udhár Gathering. Creativity was not what was needed. Tusánt needed a miracle.

"Will you be back by then?"

Claide glanced at him but continued to bustle about the room. There was no proof yet of Jermyn's death, but Claide had wasted no time in commandeering the man's private quarters. He, at least, seemed certain Jermyn was not coming back, and such certainty made him looked disgustingly guilty of complicity. "Oh, yes…of course. Nothing short of unanticipated disaster will keep me away. Without the k'dedhá …it is my duty to officiate if he is not back. You have no need to fear that I shall not return. I will be perfectly safe."

I wish you would not, Tusánt thought bitterly. It would make many people much happier. "What should I do if word comes of the k'gdhededhá? Or if he returns? How can I reach you? Is there somewhere to send word?"

"I do not know where I will be on any given day, unfortunately. There are many small náós around Fiara that require attention…but I will not be gone long and do not anticipate word…"

"Why?" Tusánt asked before he could stop himself. "Of course we could hear something."

As if regretting his remark, Claide replied, "It is possible, of course, but since the Lord Justice and Inquisitor have failed to turn up anything thus far, and there has been no demand for a ransom, I doubt they will turn up anything of use in the span of a few short weeks. Common sense, you see. Oh, and I am waiting for word from k'gdhededhá Dórímyr on this matter…"

Tusánt nodded, knowing better than to expect any reply from Dórímyr. If Claide had actually sent the Elyri k'gdhededhá a message, it had been simply for the formality of saying it was done. "I wish you a pleasant journey," he said politely while hoping that the man found his time away pleasant enough that he decided not to return.

Claide muttered something under his breath as he strapped his travel bag closed. "Thank you. I have a few more tasks to complete before I depart in the morning. Any further questions?"

The final words were demeaning in tone; the Elyri gdhededhá would not have replied even if he had thought of another question. He shook his head and left the room, feeling a prickle up his spine that told him Claide was watching him with thinly veiled hostility. Tusánt turned abruptly to catch the look. Claide tried to hide it but he was not quick enough. The Teren focused his attention on his bag, letting Tusánt depart unhindered.

❧*❧

Caol ranted and swore at Stold for an hour, hoping for information about the storage building and the attack on Bhríd but the bald man had none. If he knew anything, he was good at feigning shock and ignorance. He was vehement about the Association's lack of knowledge or involvement and promised to look into it. The inquisitor wanted so desperately to believe Stold that his head hurt. He demanded to speak with the local headman, and though Stold scurried off with his request, Caol was not surprised to be denied. No one in his position could make such a demand of the head of Rhidam's Association affiliate and expect to have it granted.

It left him with the unfortunate conclusion that the Association knew more than they were telling and could not be trusted any longer. He was beginning to regret setting up this network of informants whom he apparently could not rely on to keep their word. So much for the Association's code of ethics. They were that much closer to learning what angering Caol Dugan could do to them.

Stold's promise to look into those involved and into previous uses of the facility did little to make Caol feel better. He promised that no one would go near the building without Caol's permission, but Caol no longer trusted that promise. To enforce it, he posted sentries to watch the building, with no thoughts to discretion. He had little doubt that the moment his guard was down, someone would be there to dismantle or destroy as much of the building as they could and Caol did not intend to let that happen until they no longer needed it.

"Halt!"

Balint Gabersdon stopped his horse out of range of the four men in the wagon bed ahead of him, a wagon that straddled the road and prevented anyone from passing. Dhybhé clung to him, whimpering, still weak and frightened that harm was about to befall her again.

Behind Balint, the four soldiers General Agis chose to accompany him rested their hands upon their swords but did nothing, content to await the Duke's command.

"Who are you to order me to halt?" Balint called.

"No one travels this road without consent." The speaker sounded young and did not recognize Balint, who was traveling without standard or crest.

"Oh? At whose command? Pray tell, has Duke Cliáth returned to keep order? I am within the boundaries of his holdings, am I not?"

There was shuffling and muttering amongst the four before a second man spoke. "We have no Duke; we make our own law."

Balint snickered. "An absent Duke is no excuse for the misconduct of his vassals. King Hagan makes the laws ultimately, dear sirs, and the acts of highwaymen such as yourselves are expressly forbidden, unless, of course, you have a justifiable reason to stop travelers."

"We want no Elyri here," a third shouted.

"Your Duke is Elyri."

"He is not here, and we prefer he never come back!"

Balint shook his head. "Pity. He will be pained to hear such words from those he has favored and bettered. I have heard his return is imminent, though perhaps your actions will escape notice. Still, I demand to pass."

The four looked at each other indecisively. They were not looking for trouble from their Duke, but they also did not want more Elyri coming into Alberni. "You have no right to make demands, offal."

The knight pulled gingerly free from Dhybhé's arms, and after handing her the reins slid from the horse with sword in hand. "What is your name, sir, so that I may know who I am about to challenge?"

"A duel?" The other took a confident step and said, "Charles Nedcalf. And may I ask to whom I speak, who dares be so bold?"

"Sir Balint Gabersdon, Duke of Nelori."

Nedcalf quickly put away his sword and took a hasty step backward. "We have no quarrel with you, milord. Had we known it was you, we would have allowed passage."

The knight lowered his sword but did not sheath it. "That is better. I would be sorely grieved to sully my sword for such a petty thing as the right to pass. You will remove this wagon and return to your homes, or I shall be forced to report your activities to the King."

They hurried to turn the wagon and remove it from the road rather than respond vocally. When they stepped to the side of the path one of them asked, "What of the lady, milord?"

Eyes narrowing as Balint remounted his horse, he replied, "Does it matter? She is ill and under my protection until I reach a suitable physician. That is all you need to know."

"She is Elyri," another spat.

When Balint reached the wagon, he snagged the front of the speaker's tunic with his sword tip. "She is my sister. Go home and let me pass before I make good on my challenge. I do not think the King will look kindly upon you if you fail to comply or challenge me again."

The four let them by without further hindrance. None of them knew whether Duke Gabersdon had siblings, none knew if perhaps he had Elyri parentage, or if this woman was not Elyri as they assumed. They did, however, know Balint by reputation and were wise enough to have no desire to cross him.

It was not until many miles down the road, safely out of harm's way, when, content that those men were not following them, Dhybhé stopped trembling. "Milord? You lied to save my life…"

He chuckled. "The Faith teaches we are brothers and sisters. And I do have a sister in Alberni. I will speak to her while I am there and ask her to keep faith with me on this. Besides, saying you are my sister was the first thing I could think of to protect you that they might believe. I could have claimed you as my betrothed, possible but even less true, or I could have claimed you as my wife, though I believe nearly everyone knows Duke Gabersdon has yet to marry."

She was quiet and her grip on him tightened, something he found he liked. "Thank you, milord…for your aid…for everything…"

"I owe you much more, milady. I intend to support you until my debt is repaid, however long that takes."

Gradually, the manner in which she rested against his back with her arms settling loosely around him, told him she had fallen asleep. It gave him a small measure of contentment to know she trusted him enough to sleep after what she had endured. With a sigh, he kept his eyes focused on the road.

❧*❧

His son had done an admirable job of healing his shoulder, Bhríd acknowledged silently, his attention focused on Ártur and the man under interrogation. Not that the interrogation lasted long. No sooner had the healer placed his hands upon the man when the captive slumped backward into Justice Corbin's arms. The lines of Ártur's face drew tight and his expression changed, and for a moment the chamberlain thought the healer was trying to kill him. But a gesture to Gaelán for assistance suggested something else. After instructions of a more medical nature, Bhríd approached to ascertain what was happening but he, Asta, the king, and the princess could not see past the two healers.

Finally, Ártur stepped away with an unhappy frown. "Enough, Gaelán; there is nothing we can do. He is gone."

"Gone?" asked Hagan, white-faced after seeing a man die so near.

"Poison, My Liege. He had something in his mouth, likely to avoid interrogation." Why he had not used it before being dragged before the King, none knew, though Bhríd harbored suspicions that someone along their path, in the city streets or in the castle, had supplied the fellow with something he had not previously had.

With his hands bound, how had he put anything in his mouth?

The King threw up his hands in exasperation. "How will we learn anything if they keep killing themselves?"

"I did get a single name." Ártur looked at the justice to see if it meant anything and added, "Narn."

"Narn? What kind of a name is that?" snorted the monarch.

Ártur rubbed the back of his neck. "I do not know, Sire, but I do know it is a name. This man was often contacted by a nameless courier with orders from someone named Narn."

It was the princess's turn to snort in disgust. "Taking orders from someone he doesn't know? How pathetically…"

"Nevertheless," the healer said, "that is what he has been doing. His thoughts were well-hidden for a Teren…"

"Shall I tell Lord Dugan?" asked Bhríd, noticing that Asta had already slipped into the shadows and out of the room as if she had not been present. He could feel her there, however, beyond the door.

"No," commanded the King. "The Association is being pulled off all investigations, in case my inquisitor failed to mention that."

"Milord?" said the justice. "He said he was looking into it, but that it was not a viable short-term solution…"

King Hagan glared. "Lord Justice, I do not care what he said. Until I say otherwise, I want no further involvement of the Association. Do not take this to Lord Dugan. Is that understood?"

Bhríd's face darkened with concern. "He will wonder what we have learned since he did arrest this man and…"

"You shall tell him we learned nothing useful before he died.."

"Lie to him, milord…?"

The King was already leaving the room as Asta's presence faded rapidly. Very well, the chamberlain thought. I will not speak to Caol. But I cannot promise his daughter will do likewise.

Once the King was gone and the shock bled out of the room, the princess spoke. "What happened, Lord Cáner? Hagan believes your story about my uncle needing your advice on matters of policy, but I know the truth."

The chamberlain explained how they were allowed into the building, how the owner snuck away and Caol followed him, how Bhríd found nine men waiting in ambush as he came out of the cellar, nine men apparently sent by this same proprietor, contacted in the tavern dedhá Claide frequented.

"The cellar has been cleaned and emptied, but I can say this…the k'gdhededhá was tortured in that room and died there. There was nothing left to identify the guilty but I think we can assume that this fellow," he looked at the dead man on the floor, "was in on it. And so was this fellow Narn."

"Then we find him," said the princess, "using any means it takes. No matter what my brother says."

❧Chapter 39❧

K'gdhededhá Dórímyr waved his aide away without looking up. "I have no time for frivolity or interruption, Hwensen."

The other man, use to this from the k'gdhededhá, stood his ground. "Not frivolity, Your Grace, a letter from gdhededhá Claide, Hes á Redh Náós, Rhidam."

Dórímyr lifted his head, looked at the man on the other side of his desk, and snatched the parchment from him. It was read hastily, with much grunting and wiping of his eyes as he scanned the page, and when he finished, his head turned towards the window, his expression blank. His primary aide knew better than to interrupt the k'gdhededhá's thoughts, even to stoop to pick up the letter that slid from his hands and floated to the floor. The man's fingers drummed on the desktop, paused to play with the rings he wore, and then the k'gdhededhá crumpled a sheet of parchment beneath his hand.

Hwensen could make out a few words on the fallen letter; he could read the Teren languages but these words were upside down from where he stood and shadowed by the desk. He made out the name Jermyn Tythilius, the k'gdhededhá of Enesfel. Hwensen had not been at his post when gdhededhá Kesábhá was in Clarys, but he knew a little about the matter, unlike most in Clarys who were disallowed this morsel of gossip: Jermyn had been abducted. Had he been found? Alive? Was he still missing? Or worse, was he dead?

When Dórímyr turned back to the documents he was composing, it was without speaking. Nor did he retrieve the fallen letter. Hwensen could gain no insight from either the letter or the k'gdhededhá's thoughts, but it was clear the k'gdhededhá cared little about whatever the gdhededhá had written.

"Your Grace?" The k'gdhededhá grunted. After some hesitation, his aide asked, "The letter? Has k'gdhededhá Tythilius been found?"

"No, at least not when this was sent." He continued writing.

"Should something be done, Your Grace?"

Dórímyr's response was rising irritation that creased the folds around his mouth. "What can be done? Some say he lives…some say he has died. I do not know where he is, do not know which is the truth, and we cannot look into replacing him until we know his fate. gdhededhá Claide sounds as if he has everything in hand. Leave me; I will send for you when I need you."

If Hwensen wanted to make a comment, ask a question about gdhededhá Claide's loyalties and competence as he had already heard questioned, he refrained. As far as he could tell, only Claide was unaware of Jermyn's fate. Dórímyr knew it already. To make his point, however, before he left the room, he picked up the fallen letter and placed it on the desk directly upon the paper Dórímyr was writing on. Perturbed, the k'gdhededhá met his aide's gaze briefly before the man strode from the room. Hwensen knew his message was understood.

Diona knew what had to be done but she had no good idea how to accomplish it without raising her brother's suspicions. Normally, she got away with hiding things from him merely by being the older sister he trusted; Hagan had adored her since he was a small boy and took her word as truth no matter what she said. Now he was determined to grow up, to be independent, to be the King he was crowned to be, and Diona worried that if she did not pull off a plan successfully, her brother might choose to imprison her for treason.

"He is gone."

There in the garden, communing with her family's dead without hovering servants or the press of courtly lords and ladies, she turned towards the healer who sat beside her. "Who is gone?"

"gdhededhá Claide. He left the náós before dawn, stopped at a house briefly where he entered and came out with a traveling satchel a short time later, and then started north. Or so says Lord Dugan. As of nearly an hour ago, Rhidam is free of him, for now."

She snorted and clenched her hands in her lap. "Good. Without him to inflame hysteria, Rhidam might know peace. It is fortunate you came to me…I have been meaning to discuss something with you."

When she faced him, she noticed how much older he looked. Kavan's absence, separation from his family, the birth of his daughter, the events of recent months, and the threat on his life that led to his current confinement, all had the accumulative effect of making him appear several years older than he had before the start of the new year. Not that he looked to be his actual age, but it was enough of a difference to be noticeable. At least to her.

"You preserved the k'dedhá's body before it was buried? How does that work? What state would it be in now?"

"Preservation is still in effect and will be thus for several more weeks. He would appear no worse than he did when we found him," he sighed, "which was bad enough."

She nodded thoughtfully. "I think that, with the discovery of this cellar and dedhá Claide's absence from Rhidam, this may be the best time to 'find' him and make his death public. We cannot wait indefinitely, and dedhá Claide and Hagan are both suspicious. Not of us, perhaps, but I would rather not test our luck. Do you think it possible, using the Gates, to sneak his body into that room and arrange for…Lord Corbin perhaps…to discover it?"

Ártur looked puzzled. "I am not the person to ask about subterfuge, Milady. Lord Dugan is more knowledgeable in that area than I. But if the particulars can be worked out to your satisfaction, I am willing to do my part…if that is what you are asking. There was a time when such acts of secrecy from a king weighed heavily upon my conscience. Either I am growing old and amoral, or I am learning the ways of court at last."

The princess squeezed his hand. None of this was easy. On any of them. "Do you know where Lord Dugan is?"

"No…Princess Asta brought the news about gdhededhá Claide. I will find him for you if you wish."

"Thank you, Lord Healer."

◈*◈

He had not anticipated a place of such grandeur when he first heard about the chellé being built in Alberni. Even when rumors came of its magnificence he had been skeptical. The first stories of the restoration of Hes á Redh Náós had been of beauty beyond compare, impossible he had thought. When he saw that building for the first time, while he considered it beautiful, it had not met the expectations the rumors had built. Saint Kóráhm's, on the other hand, surpassed even the most elaborate rumors he had heard. Awed by its beauty, Balint was more ready than ever to accept the successes Lord Cliáth might have within his holdings. The vision behind the chellé would carry Alberni to the status of Enesfel's richest city, provided the fact that its duke was Elyri did not destroy it first.

The gdhededhá of the chellé welcomed Dhybhé with kindness and generosity, establishing her in a comfortable room and bringing their resident female Elyri healer to see to her well-being. The acting k'gdhededhá, a Teren named Garrett, offered Balint a tour while the women were given privacy. As much as he disliked leaving Dhybhé and worried for her safety, he trusted these people. And he was eager to see the rest of the grounds.

Despite his thoughts never straying far from the woman, he was glad to have this opportunity. The libraries of bountiful books, scrolls, and parchments, and the vast collection of artwork were a testimony of the truest kind to learning, to peace, and to the love of the divine, qualities many Teren denied Elyri possessed. Balint was tempted to recommend the tour to every man and woman who ever crossed him with anti-Elyri sentiment. Here there were Teren and Elyri, men and women, young and old. They lived and worked in harmony. Why could it not be the same elsewhere?

Later, k'gdhededhá Garrett invited him to share dinner, telling him that Dhybhé was asleep and that once the repast was over he would be given a room and be free to see her if she awoke. It was a simple meal, bread and broth, dried fruit and wine, but in spite of its simplicity, it tasted to the knight to be the most satisfying meal he had eaten in years. He attributed that to the days of travel, exhaustion, and the peace he found in this place.

Dhybhé was awake when he went to her; she was eating, dressed in the simple pale green gown the other men and women here wore. He was pleased to see she was improved.

He smiled, a smile that grew wider when she returned it. "I was hoping you would be awake."

"I feel better, milord; being in a place of safety has a miraculous effect on a person's state of being."

"I think being here would have a miraculous effect on anyone. I would not have thought such a place possible without seeing it myself, experiencing it for myself. I am confident you will be safe and cared for here, and I apologize you were not while in my care."

Her smile faded and she clasped his hand. "We had no reason to doubt your man. But I live and you have brought me safely here."

Balint settled on the edge of her bed. "Still, I feel I should do more to make amends for the wrongs done to you. Leaving you here feels like abandonment…betrayal. There must be something more…"

"There is nothing to do that you have not already done."

"Perhaps," he sighed as he looked at their hands, "we should marry."

"Milord…?"

Her choking sound made him realize he had spoken that thought aloud and he quickly withdrew his hand. He tried to find a way to take back those words, or at the very least disarm them, but he did not know how. "It would be honorable of me to do so…but I fear you would be no safer as Duchess Gabersdon than you were as my guest. You would likely be in greater danger. I do not want that. I want you safe. I was thinking out loud…I could follow through but at what cost to you?"

Dhybhé tilted her head and did not hide the misting of her eyes. "In another time and place, I might have accepted this proposal, such as it is. However, you are right; the danger to both of us would be great. You are a man of decency and integrity, a man Enesfel needs in its fight to extricate itself from darkness. Marriage to me, or any of my people, would encourage dissidence. Two Elyri in positions of nobility may be as many as Enesfel can tolerate. I thank you for the offer and consider it an honor you would think to present such an option, but the wisest course is to decline."

"Of course." He was not sure which was greater, his relief or his disappointment. "What will you do when you are healthy and rested?"

"I may remain here. I might return to Elyriá. I do not know. But I promise to let you know what I decide so you will not worry. I would like to keep in communication with you."

"I would appreciate that." He could not say he loved her, he did not think he had ever been in love with anyone, but he cared about her, cared for her welfare, and that was enough.

"Are you leaving tomorrow? Or will you stay for a few days?"

This time Balint offered his hand. "Would you like me to stay?"

When she smiled and placed her hand on his, he knew what he would do. "I would. We could forget, at least for a few days, that there is violence and death in the world, that there is a world beyond these walls, and imagine what life might have been like…"

He kissed the back of her fingers gently. Her proposal sounded like a good one to him.

❧*❧

"I am sorry bhydáni Tíbhyan is unable to see you today, Gaelán."

Ártur could tell his words were unheard; Gaelán gaped at the houses they passed, different in style from those in Enesfel, with wide-eyed wonder. It had been much the same expression on Kavan's face when Ártur took him to Rhidam the first time, but the healer had not imagined that Gaelán would feel the same about his first journey into Elyriá. If the boy was nervous about meeting his grandparents or any of his other Elyri kin, it was not obvious. Until they stopped outside the door of Ártur's childhood home, Gaelán was too engrossed in his surroundings to be nervous.

The house was quiet but there were sounds from the shop. The family should have just finished their noon meal and been gathered around the table; Ártur wondered where everyone was.

"Father?"

Ártur heard the small footfalls and turned towards the kitchen as the boy spoke. Scooping him up, careful not to spill the cup of water he carried, Ártur laughed in delight. "Llucás! How wonderful that you are the first person I see. I have brought Gaelán to meet everyone. Where is your mother?"

"Upstairs, making Chethá sleep," he replied as he hugged his father, relinquishing his cup to Gaelán. "She cries a lot."

Wondering if his son referred to his sister or his mother, the healer kissed his cheeks and put him back down. "I should go and see them. Will you introduce Gaelán to the others?"

"I can introduce myself," Gaelán muttered with rolling eyes.

Ártur chuckled. "I was not so bold at your age. Go on then."

Closing the door as the boys headed to the shop, Ártur crossed to the stairs to find Syl descending. The hug and the kiss she gave him were filled with the longing their living arrangement fostered.

"More of that, Ártur," she giggled, "and we will need to find a more private location." She buried her face in the crook of his neck.

He had to laugh too. "I think we would be pardoned either way. The wish to sleep alone is not the reason I married you."

She stiffened, but deciding that he was not making accusations, she relaxed and did not pull away. "But it is necessary. What brings you home?"

"Other than you?" he replied, making note of the fact that she referred to Bhryell as home when home had once been at his side. "Gaelán was begging to meet Tíbhyan. Of course, my timing is unfortunate, as the day I bring him, the Lómesté is in conference. Gaelán is in the shop with Llucás, meeting the men. It gives us a few minutes alone." He kissed her again and let his hands roam down her back. "What is this I hear about crying?"

Syl chuckled. "It is not as bad as Llucás makes it sound. He thinks that something is wrong because Chethá cries. I have not been able to convince him that she cries because she cannot talk. It upsets him."

"I'll talk to him," he promised. In some respects, Llucás had always been a sensitive child.

"It could not hurt. He misses his father."

That, to Ártur, was an accusation. Or it sounded that way because he felt guilty. "I will do what I can to come more frequently. I have had little luck gaining liberty from duty, though there is little I need to do most of the time. Perhaps you should discuss it with Hagan. He respects your opinion and advice more than he does anyone else's."

In a perfectly serious tone, she said, "I may do that. There is something else? What is it?"

Ártur drew away, knowing she would not like what he had to say and wishing he could hide such details from her. "Princess Diona has decided to bring Jermyn's body back to Rhidam; Hagan will learn of his death. Caol and Bhríd located the place where he was held and…"

He did not finish the sentence and she chose not to press him. "Is she requesting our attendance at his burial?"

"No. This must be done with the utmost care so that Hagan and those responsible for Jermyn's death…and gdhededhá Claide… believe his body has just been discovered. If you return too soon for the burial, it will appear suspicious. Bhríd will go to Levonne in the morning to be with his family, in order to cover his involvement. Prince Espen has gone to Fiara. That leaves few of us in Rhidam who know the truth. The body will be moved within the next few nights and Darius will discover it. I felt you should know."

"Why the need to hide this from dedhá Claide?" She rarely questioned political intrigue, as she did not comprehend it and did not want to. But this was a matter of Faith and something she did want to understand.

"The evidence is circumstantial at this point…and you must speak of it to no one. The princess and Caol believe Claide is partially responsible for the anti-Elyri violence, that he is connected to the Corylliens. They suspect he may have had a hand in Jermyn's death…and I am inclined to believe them."

"A gdhededhá…killing another…? Because of us?" She gripped his hand. "You may be in more danger than you realize…"

He swallowed uneasily, knowing the threat he received was still his secret. "I am aware of it, Syl. You know I am. Let's speak of it no more but see if Gaelán's charm has worn through my father's skin."

❧*❧

Prince Owain ushered his guest into his sitting room, dismissing the servant behind him. "This is an unexpected surprise, Prince Harcourt. Of all the callers to my home, I did not expect you."

"I am far from home, yes. But I often wonder where home is." Taking the glass of sherry his host offered, Espen smiled and removed his turban with his free hand, gratefully accepting the offered chair.

"I trust your journey was uneventful?"

"The way things have been lately, I would think that, if my journey had been eventful, I might not have arrived. In answer to your question then, yes, uneventful and a welcome change from tedium."

"I hardly call events of late tedious." Owain refilled his already empty glass and offered more to the prince. Espen declined. "Is Diona still playing games?"

The prince shook his head. "Playing? No, I do not think so. She has no concept, I think, of what she truly wants…and she seems genuinely afraid though I cannot say of what. She may hope I will force a decision or will make it for her. I do not understand how she can be indecisive in this matter and yet decisive in others."

"Has she sent you here? Or the King perhaps?"

Though no one else was in the room, Espen lowered his voice as if not to be overheard. "Diona sent me on a mission of which King Hagan has no knowledge. There is reason to believe dedhá Claide is in league with the anti-Elyri faction dividing the kingdom. He recently left Rhidam, claiming he was to visit the sees surrounding Fiara, as k'dedhá Jermyn intended. There is some doubt about the truth of this, and we feel he is here for some other purpose than business of Faith."

❧738❧

"Like meeting spies," Owain muttered over the rim of his glass. "Milord?"

"Call me Owain. Spies have been trying to come south for months; I captured a trio recently. They lingered too long after murdering some of my people, and I wondered why…perhaps they were waiting for a contact. For dedhá Claide. Not that they can meet with him now unless he has a talent for communing with the dead."

Not knowing Owain well, Prince Espen did not know how to interpret his words, whether they were serious or in jest, so he said nothing. "Diona wishes for you to contact the sees in your jurisdiction and learn if dedhá Claide is coming, or is here, or if the k'dedhá was scheduled to visit at this time. dedhá Tusánt and the others know nothing of any visits Jermyn had scheduled."

Owain scowled thoughtfully and set his glass on the mantle. "I would think k'dedhá Tythilius would have told me if he planned to be here, but I will do as the princess requests. Anything if it will further peace. I hope you will remain in Fiara until I have an answer, a few days at least. It will give us opportunity to learn more about each other. My house is open to you."

Accepting the offered hand, Prince Espen replied, "I accept your offer, Owain. As one prince to another, your hospitality is welcome."

"Then I will give you a room where you can rest from your journey and we shall meet again for dinner."

⟡Chapter 40⟡

It had been many years since gdhededhá Bhílári had anyone of importance come to his parish, and he could not imagine why gdhededhá Khwílen was in Bhryell. Bhílári knew the other man had been appointed k'gdhededhá of the newly constructed Saint Kóráhm's, a post Bhílári had desperately prayed for even though he feared living in Enesfel. Despite the number of years since he had served with young Cliáth, Bhílári remembered the holy air about him, the music that summoned záryph, the miracles that sometimes occurred when the younger man was present.

It was those memories and the compelling desire to experience those moments again that caused Bhílári to petition for the position. He had hoped his past with Kavan, the fact that he knew what was possible and yet did not reject or flatter him, would influence the decision. It had, but not in Bhílári's favor. Kavan wanted no part of those memories, no reminders of the town he felt had rejected him, no one to serve with the expectation of miracles. That and Bhílári's fear of leaving Elyriá had kept the post beyond his reach.

Without having met Khwílen, knowing him by no more than name and reputation, he did not know the man with the gentle handsome face who was calmly waiting for him in the first pew.

"Good morning, k'gdhededhá," he said with a bow, recognizing the man's position by the robes he wore and because he had been told who was waiting by the attendant who announced him. "I am honored to have you here, though I admit I find it puzzling. Has Lord Cliáth sent you? Is he well?"

Khwílen shook his head. "There has been no word from Lord Cliáth in many months, unless he has returned while I have been away. I have been in Elyriá on a matter of Faith business."

Intrigued, Bhílári joined him on the pew. "What sort of business takes you from the magnificence of Saint Kóráhm's and the duties you pledged yourself too?" Though he had never seen the abbey, he was confident of its splendor and could not deny the flash of hope that he might yet have a chance to serve there.

Not being one to hedge around the inevitable, at least not for long, the blonde man replied, "I mean to have k'gdhededhá Dórímyr defrocked and removed from his post."

Bhílári almost laughed until he noted the other man's serious expression. "On what grounds do you do this? Such a challenge has never been made."

"k'gdhededhá Jermyn of Rhidam was kidnapped and murdered and Dórímyr shows no interest or concern for his demise. He refuses to go to Rhidam to appoint a new k'gdhededhá …"

"One cannot blame him for that," Bhílári scoffed. "And I would think Rhidam capable of electing their leader…"

Use to that reaction now, the blonde man did not blink. "Even if the person likely to be chosen is vehemently anti-Elyri and suspected of being partially responsible for the violence against our kind? Acts of barbarism, I might add, that Dórímyr ignores. He has turned his back on those in the Teren kingdoms and does nothing to support our people or discourage others from following. His apathy ignites the outrage of many; if he does not see fit to protect us and the Faith, to try to quash this violence, and see to appropriate leadership in Enesfel, then he does not deserve loyalty. The Teren faithful are under his governance, as are we, and should be afforded the same rights and protections. He should be involved in this affair and should certainly show compassion for what is transpiring abroad."

Bhílári listened and did not speak until the other man fell silent. "Your conviction is great, k'gdhededhá, but on what grounds do you speak thus? I have heard of the deaths and violence in Enesfel of course; Ártur MacLyr was here yesterday and shared some of the most recent developments."

Khwílen held out his hand confidently. "Read me if you wish. I have already been to Ánásair, Sídhári, Turyn, and every village between to share this message. I am not seeking belief on blind faith; this is too important. All I ask is fair hearing and for each to make their decision accordingly. Can you do that, gdhededhá Bhílári?"

Looking the other man over, hearing him speak, Bhílári understood why Kavan chose Khwílen to lead the flock in Saint Kóráhm's. His beliefs and powers of persuasion were strong, perhaps rivaled only by those of the bard. "I can learn what you have to teach me, gdhededhá, and I will allow others to do likewise. But I cannot promise we will receive your message in the manner you hope."

~*~

"That ought to do it, sir." The nondescript fellow, badly dressed, unwashed and stoop-shouldered, allowed the trunk lid to slam and clicked the numerous latches and locks to keep it securely closed.

"Not too many locks. We want him to be able to open it. No point in sending it if he cannot enjoy our gift. Everything is included?"

"Yes. The spices you asked for are there. I do not think I could fit more inside if I tried, but I think what's there should be enough."

"It had better be. This is a very special delivery. I want our sovereign to be impressed. I want it to be an unforgettable gift. Any failure to make the proper impression and it will be you who pays the price. Am I understood?"

"Yes, sir. I understand. Shall I see to the delivery?"

"No. I will arrange it. I want it done right."

❦*❧

With luck, the caravan, lighter in load as goods were sold along the route, would reach Pa'aliaka by nightfall. Thus far the trip had been uneventful except that Kavan had difficulty sleeping much of the time and had thus yet to fully recover from the bloodletting in the cloister. Images, dreams, and shadows of things unrecognizable and vague plagued what rest he did get. The dreams were strongest and most disturbing when the emerald ring came in contact with the chest containing the Chalice and staff piece. He tried to avoid it, but he could not relax if the chest was not near him, and no matter what position he fell asleep in, he would stir later to find his hand upon the box. That contact created a constant dull throbbing in his joints that caused him to worry about residual, unhealed damage that might disallow him to play his harp again, but a silent vow to himself, repeated as necessary, pushed that negativity away.

It did not matter what pain remained, what damage might be unhealed. He could freely move his fingers and he would play his harp once more. Nothing short of death would keep him from it.

His sleep was also beset with dreams of Orynn and Myreth. He had been unable to get the woman out of his head until he met Myreth; then that man's presence drove most other thoughts from his mind. The memories of both were tightly intertwined; the bard often had to concentrate to untangle them.

An uncomfortable tingling clawed at the back of his neck, an indication of danger, making Kavan draw his horse up short. The ring on his finger made his hand pulse, and inside the saddlebag on his left there was a strong thrumming rhythm that ran up and down his leg. The horse snorted, shaking its head, its ears flattened against its skull as it took a few nervous sidesteps to escape the tremor. But it could not be escaped, and Kavan placed a calming palm upon the animal's neck as he tried to determine the source of peril.

The land here was open and flat except for low dense shrubs, mostly dry from months without rain. They were low enough that they offered little cover unless one was sitting, kneeling or squatting. As that thought formed, he saw them within his mind, at least two dozen, though his eyes saw nothing except yellowing brush. The rest of the caravan continued ahead, directly into danger of which they were unaware, and there was no time for Kavan to warn them.

Without closing his eyes, an unnecessary habit he used to help him focus, he cast energy outward, surrounding the caravan with an invisible shield as they pulled further ahead. Much further and they would be out of range of his reach. He was about to spur his horse into action when the first bandits broke cover.

And froze. To the amazement of those in the caravan, the attackers, and Kavan, every one of the twenty-eight men he could count was held in place. Surprised and terrified, they froze mid-run, posed in awkward positions from which they should have fallen but for Kavan holding them in place with unseen bonds. He knew he was capable of holding at least a dozen men this way; he had done it before. But holding this many so effortlessly, without conscious thought to the attempt, was unanticipated. The pulsation from the saddlebag was more intense, almost audible. Curious, Kavan shifted his leg away from the bag as Wortham scrambled for rope or anything he could find to bind the attackers. Kavan discovered that, without the aid of the chest, while he could hold the entire unit, it took more concentration and effort. As soon as he put his leg back against the box, the effort was reduced. This time, at least, the artifacts were magnifying his natural abilities.

The captain barked orders to the others, directing them to bind as many as they could with what material they found. It was his experience that Kavan could not sustain this ability indefinitely and he did not want to risk bloodshed should they fail to finish before Kavan released them. But a glance at the bard gained him one of the Elyri's rare smiles and Wortham relaxed. He did not slow his pace but he did recognize that they were in no danger of a fight.

"Thank you, milord," the captain called as he approached the rogue nearest Kavan. "We might be dead if it weren't for you."

"Dead? Nonsense. Do you think I have gone to so much trouble to be killed...or to let you be killed?" The bard laughed softly, the extra power in the artifacts making him light-headed.

"Still...it is fortunate that k'Ádhá is with you and you are with us." The leader of the caravan, a grizzled man with a patchy beard, took Wortham's arm and spoke hurriedly, gesturing at the men they had captured. "He says we can take them into Pa'aliaka, but it will slow our progress. He wants to know..." Wortham hesitated, worried about continuing, but eventually finished the sentence. "He asks what miracle prevented the caravan from being overtaken, what miracle caused those men to stop the way they did."

"Tell him..." Noting that the vibration against his leg had dwindled to a purr, Kavan looked around to see that the last of the bandits were bound. Wondering what both Orynn and Myreth would think of this, he shrugged with the smallest glimmer in his eyes. "Tell him what you wish, Wortham. Perhaps it was a miracle."

With another laugh, he dismounted to assist in stringing the prisoners behind one of the wagons in the middle of their caravan. Miracle or not, he thanked k'Ádhá they were safe and for the healing that allowed him to help his companions with such mundane duties as tying ropes.

❞*❝

She did not understand what she saw, or exactly how it pertained to her father's work, but her first thought was to scramble home to tell him. That the men detected and chased her fueled her impression that this was something her father needed to know. What she had seen was important. But first, she had to get to safety. They were bigger, with longer legs, and stronger than she without a doubt. But Asta Dugan had learned her lessons well and took every alley and shortcut she could, staying in the shadows, keeping a firm fix on her destination while leading her pursuers to think she was heading somewhere else.

Asta was surprised, therefore, to find the large, dark-skinned man ahead of her as she came within sight of the alley's end. If she judged correctly, she could dodge past him or take her chances in scaling the wall to the window not far above. Knowing he could reach the window, she opted to try to dodge past him, gambling on speed and agility. It was a gamble she lost as he caught her by one arm.

"Going somewhere, little urchin?"

Instead of panicking or screaming, she squirmed enough to allow her to draw the knife tucked in her shoe, and in one agile movement bit down on his hand as she raked the blade across his face. He cried out, dropping her, and when he reached for her again, she was gone.

"Let her go," said another who entered the alley from the direction where she had come from. "She is a child. She is no threat to us."

❧*❧

There was no recourse, the King knew. The need for an heir grew more pressing as the violence in his kingdom continued, though he knew little about raising children or producing them. And since Asta had rejected his proposal by dismissing it, never mentioning it again, he had few options left. He knew three available young women his age, or near enough to his age that he would not feel any more awkward considering a future with them than he already did.

But which of the three should he choose, he wondered? Jilletta McPhelan was certainly the most eager of the three; she pursued the young King relentlessly whenever she was in Rhidam. Yet Hagan found her shallow and boring, not someone he could imagine spending his life with. That left Ordelia Cornell, who was nice enough and the one he knew the best, and Sigrid Niall. He had met Sigrid only once when they had been children, despite the fact that her brother Dayly was his closest friend. She was also nearest to him in age, but as far as he knew, she could be a shrew. Or betrothed already, though Dayly had not said she was.

What he needed was a gala, an event to invite the women to, an event during which he could compare them discreetly and talk with them as much or as little as he wished, perhaps even dance with them. There would be other young women there as well, from other noble families, so perhaps one of them would catch his eye. None would know it of course, but he intended that by the end of such a ball, one of them would leave Rhidam as the chosen queen.

Grinning expectantly at the covert game he was to undertake, the King bounced off to find Chancellor Flannery to discuss how much they could afford to spend on a ball. He had the future queen of Enesfel to impress.

❦*❦

gdhededhá Valgis leaned against the back wall of the k'dhín bhólibh, his breathing labored and shallow in his nervousness.

"dedhá?" asked the voice opposite the opaque screen that separated them.

"That is all, my son. You know what you must do?"

"If I carry out this penance…I will be forgiven?"

Valgis nodded though he knew the gesture could not be seen. "I will do everything in my power to see your transgressions are dismissed and your soul is clean in the eyes of k'Ádhá. Do as I command, accept it as you would from a higher authority. It is the best way to earn forgiveness."

"Very well, dedhá. I will do as you say."

That parishioner left and Valgis let out a long groan of relief, fingering his collar anxiously as another entered the room.

"I have come to be cleansed of the errors of my ways…"

❧*❧

"Is my horse ready?" Caol asked, peering past Agis' shoulder to where the blacksmith pounded another nail into the animal's hoof.

"One more shoe, your lordship."

"You said that thirty minutes ago," the inquisitor muttered.

Agis grinned. "Patience, Lord Dugan. We must await our turn. I had…"

"Father!" Asta tumbled against him, shaking, her face ashen. She did not object to his arms around her as she usually did in public.

"What is it, Asta?" She shook her head and rolled her eyes in the direction of the blacksmith. In a fatherly manner, as if this was going to be a father-daughter talk, he kept an arm around her and led her a discreet distance away. He was surprised to find Agis behind him and assumed his daughter had beckoned the general to join them, which meant that, whatever else this was, it was business first. She was learning well.

He was surprised that her first question was presented to the general. "Who is Narn?" she asked.

"Where did you…?"

"He was the greatest warrior in the history of my people," replied the Cíbhóló, speaking simultaneously with Caol.

The inquisitor faced the nomad. "Was? What do you mean?"

"There are many tales recounting his heroism in our chronicles. He lived centuries ago when my people first came to the great desert."

Asta listened as intently as her father. "Is it a common name?"

The general nodded. "Many firstborn sons are named after him; it is said to make them stronger and more likely to survive. My first brother bears the name, as do two of my kinsmen."

"Then it could be anybody…" Asta frowned. "I went to the baker's to get Gaelán his favorite sweet cakes…since he cannot leave the keep to get them…you know, the baker near the Boar's Garden?"

Her mention of that place made Caol both excited and concerned for his daughter's welfare. "Go on," he encouraged.

"I had to pass it to come home…" Passing the tavern had not been necessary, but hearing the place mentioned by her father on multiple occasions, Asta had been unable to resist the opportunity to see it. "I glanced inside as I passed and saw two men talking. One was the fellow in the sketches…the one called Heward. He was talking to a big man…dark like you, Lord General. Heward called him Narn. They chased me, almost had me…" She shuddered and continued in a low voice. "I do not know how many nomads are in Rhidam, but this one should be easy to identify now."

She ran her tongue over her teeth as she gave her bloody knife to her father. "I marked him. Left cheek. Deep enough to scar I think. And I bit his right hand, drawing blood." She smiled, terror receding as the adventurer emerged and she realized she had survived her first street encounter.

Examining her knife, wanting to scold her but finding he did not have the heart for it, Caol asked, "What are the odds the Narn we have been looking for is Cíbhóló, Lord General?"

"Very high. There are not likely any but Cíbhóló with that name. If I had been told the name sooner, I would have suggested it."

"His Majesty has placed the investigation in Darius and Bhríd's hands. I am not supposed to know about it." The inquisitor's expression grew more angry than hurt as he said it. "Still…even I would not have thought to ask you. Someone with that name is spending time with our elusive Mr. Heward. I will talk to Darius and go to the Boar's Garden. Darius will be pleased to know I can still be useful to the investigation. Asta, come with me."

"Lord Dugan? What about your horse?" the blacksmith called, as the inquisitor strode away.

Words laced with sarcasm and humor, Caol called over his shoulder, "It doesn't look like I'll be riding today, but thank you for your haste."

The blacksmith bowed awkwardly and returned to his work.

❧Chapter 41❧

"**S**hip at sea!" someone shouted. It was an unnecessary warning, as everyone on watch saw it. This was not their auxiliary forces, which were not due for another few hours, nor was it any other Káliel vessel on patrol or a fishing excursion. It was too large for anything the islanders used. Though she had probably been a merchant vessel originally, this ship was stripped of weight for speed and looked to be manned by mercenaries. The impression of threat was further confirmed as she sped within range of Pháne and the archers on her prow released a volley of arrows. Most passed harmlessly overhead in the dark, but one man screamed curses at the attackers as an arrow sunk into his arm.

Prince Muir caught that much of the action as he scrambled out of the bunkroom. He was not on watch this night and had been trying to sleep. There was little to see in the rolling early spring fog, yet her lights proved that the ship was close enough for the men on the island to define its outline. Muir's fatigue quickly left as adrenaline filled his veins, but without a bow on hand, he could only supervise.

The ship's archers had little luck with their aim as nature conspired against them; the evening's breeze carried most arrows harmlessly away, and its captain knew they were closing rapidly on the reefs that ringed the island. She turned and arched back towards open waters.

Success this night was achieved too easily. If someone wanted to overrun Pháne, they would need to lower anchor and send men ashore. Or perhaps this had been a ruse meant to weaken, test, or distract those in the outpost. In an effort to be ready for whatever their attacker would do next, as Muir was sure they would try again, he roused the remainder of the regiment, equipped everyone with bows, and extinguished or shuttered as many torches and lanterns as was practical. They could not see it, but that ship was still there; it was best they made themselves less of a target as well. If they could hold until morning, relief would come. Another ship would help drive the intruder away…or perhaps capture them to make someone talk.

❧*❧

Staring across the room, Prince Owain set the carafe down with a curious expression. It was near midnight, but neither he nor his guest felt weary; instead of sleep, they had come here to talk. "A visitor? At this hour?" He cast a baffled look at Prince Espen who shrugged. The Hatu prince had even less reason to expect a visitor than Owain had. "Did he say what he wanted?"

"No, sir," the servant replied. "He requests audience and hopes you will welcome him despite the late hour." Clearing his throat with an awkward expression, he added, "He is dressed most peculiarly."

Owain felt a surge of anticipation. "That sounds like something Lord Cliáth would say." Kavan's manner of dress, more like a man of Faith than a lord, was often called peculiar. And it would be much like the bard to arrive at such an hour if he needed help or sought reprieve from Rhidam. He had not heard of Kavan's return; perhaps the bard chose to come here first…or had recently arrived and come to tell him, rather than wait for a message to be sent. Perhaps he had chosen to come here first. "Please, bring him in. You do not mind company, do you, Espen?"

The prince of Hatu shook his head. "I am your guest; this is your home. I do not mind, but whether I do or not is irrelevant." He chuckled as he toyed with his wine glass. "I should like someone to explain this curious habit your family has for asking permission…"

He stopped as the servant ushered a man covered in a bearskin cloak into the sitting room. Owain turned to see why Espen stopped speaking as the hood of the visitor's cloak fell away to reveal the still boyishly handsome face that faded from happy to wary in a fraction of a second. Thick blonde hair hung wild and loose about his face.

There was silence in the room, tense with suspicion. Owain had not expected this, although he had hoped for it. He knew that neither man knew the other but the new arrival glowered as if betrayed.

He growled. "You did not tell me our meeting would be…"

Owain stepped away from the mantle towards his new guest. "You did not notify me you were accepting my invitation. After so many years of one-sided communication…"

"It is the first time you have invited me; there must be a reason. I took the liberty of accepting your invitation, as I think the time has come for me to make my own decisions. But I have no desire for treachery to pass between us."

Owain smiled. "I assure you there is no betrayal. I may have guests as I choose, without any effect on you or our business. There is no threat. Prince Harcourt is here on behalf of Princess Diona."

"Prince Harcourt!" Owain could not tell if his guest was offended or honored to make the Hatu prince's acquaintance. The high edge to his voice gave away a trace of emotion but which one was not obvious. The younger man looked from his host to the seated prince and then crossed the room, his face blank, one hand resting guardedly on the dagger Owain knew was kept upon his left hip in typical Nethite fashion. Please, he thought, prepared to intervene. No violence.

Prince Espen held his ground, standing to meet him but expressing no hostility or offense, as the stranger approached.

"This is a historic occasion; three dynasties meeting under one roof. Whether you arranged it or not, this alone may be worth the risk I take in coming. Prince Harcourt," he said, removing his hand from his knife and offering it instead, "It is my honor to meet you."

"Prince Espen," Owain said, quashing the quaver in his voice, "I would like to introduce you to my cousin…Prince Kjell de Corrmick."

✽

Sir Gabersdon saw movement in the courtyard near the plot designated for burial, but it was too dark, the figures too far away, for him to distinguish what the gdhededhá were doing. Their backs were to the knight and if they were speaking, it was in low enough tones that he could not hear them. The first arrived almost an hour before; the faint sound of their movements roused Balint from a restless sleep and he had watched them ever since. Eventually, several of them carried something bulky into the building while the others remained, their work continuing. Preparing the ground for a burial, he wondered? It was the logical assumption to make. But who had died?

His thoughts flew to Dhybhé in panic and he started to dress. He stopped, however, when common sense reminded him that he would not be allowed to see her tonight since men and women resided in different sections of the chellé. She had been healthy when they huddled together in the library, discussing the artwork in a book she had chosen. If she had fallen ill or died, Balint believed someone would tell him. All he could do was wait.

With another glance at the door, he returned to the window to watch those below, knowing there would be no sleep for him.

✽

Looking quickly beyond the door of Hes á Redh Náós, Caol could see nothing threatening and Tusánt's abilities detected no one near enough to notice their movements. The náós bell rang the second hour of the new day. They, together with gdhededhá Garrett and one strong young man from Saint Kóráhm's, carried their burden and placed it into the wagon Caol had procured for tonight's purpose. Neither the inquisitor, the young man, nor gdhededhá Garrett were dressed in a recognizable manner; when the cart lurched into motion, leaving Tusánt in the náós doorway, the three appeared to be nothing more than traveling merchants or vagabonds.

The inquisitor stopped the wagon a few streets from their destination. It would fall to the gdhededhá to carry their bundle while Caol kept watch for trouble, but taking the cart any closer, where they might be heard, was an invitation for misfortune they did not need.

As arranged, Justice Corbin had patrolled these back alleys recently enough that they were vacant, allowing the trio to pass unhindered, though Caol kept a close eye on the windows and doorways to avoid surprises. From the nearby river came voices rising and falling in argument; Caol stopped the group long enough to determine that the direction of the voices was no cause for concern, then he peered into the street to make sure the way was clear.

No one was there; the guards appointed to watch the warehouse had heeded his orders and left the area unattended. Good. He had no doubt that suspicion of his actions would be the result, that King Hagan would implicate him in the k'gdhededhá's death somehow. But Ártur agreed to cooperate should it be necessary to read the inquisitor, as had Bhríd. Both would lie, if necessary, to protect what they were doing on behalf of Enesfel. It might not be enough for Caol to keep his position, but he would at least have his life and would continue to be involved in the investigation, at the princess' request, as much as he could be from outside the castle walls.

Leaving the gdhededhá in the dark alley, the inquisitor crossed the street, tried the storage building door, and when he found it locked, picked it. It was inched open so he could peek inside, but he did not motion to gdhededhá Garrett until he was sure the building, and the way was safe. The three hurried inside and closed the door behind them. Caol barred it for added protection.

"Just in case."

Due to Bhríd breaking the latch on the cellar door, it no longer locked, making it easy to open, but going down those steep stairs in the dark with their burden was dangerous. Each man knew it was safer without a light and none wanted to see what they were doing, wanted to see the state of the burden they carried.

After many tense minutes of struggling with the canvas bag on the steps, they reached the underground room, also with a broken lock on the door. The sack was opened, and it took biting back revulsion for them to remove the gruesomely tortured body. As Ártur claimed, the corpse showed no trace of decay and since it had been buried in a wooden casket, there was no soil on it that would suggest previous burial. Any dirt, leaves or grass that had been present when the body was originally found had been removed, and pigs' blood had been spread over the table and the floor to lend support of Jermyn's death having occurred here. In the pitch black of the underground room, they were each grateful they could not see it.

"Forgive me, Your Grace," the inquisitor muttered, "for exhuming your remains and leaving you like this…"

"He knows it is for the peace of Enesfel," gdhededhá Garrett breathed uneasily, somewhere to Caol's left. "This is no longer the k'gdhededhá. This is merely a shell."

"Must we stay any longer?" asked the weak voice of the third man.

"No…there is only one more thing." Feeling around in the dark, he found the k'gdhededhá's hand and replaced the ecclesiastical ring upon it, making sure it was the proper hand and finger. Until tomorrow, he thought with a shudder of disgust and nervousness. We will be back for you. Right now, I have to get your brothers home.

❧*❧

The smell of smoke and the sting of it in his throat and eyes brought Kavan abruptly awake to discover he was in a bed in the room they had rented in Pa'aliaka's best inn, with Wortham snoring beside him. The chest was on the bedside table, safe and unopened. There was no fire, not even one in their fireplace as the night was too warm to need one. It was not until Prince Muir's face emerged from the haze in his mind that the Elyri realized the fire he tasted was connected to the prince. A fire on Káliel? Gabrielle!

He closed his eyes to focus on the next image that pushed to the surface of his mind. Myreth was hurt. Kavan could not determine the extent of his injuries, if it was physical or emotional, or anything else of Myreth's condition, and he strained to push the Sight further along that path to learn more.

Instead of showing him Myreth, the Sight shifted back to the fire, refusing to be manipulated. Muir shouted orders, water and smoke surrounded him. A scream. The bard tried to determine who cried out, thinking the voice was Muir's, but instead, Orynn loomed before him, angry, insulted, and bitter. Was Orynn on Káliel? There was Myreth again, his mouth in a tempestuous pout, his dark eyes seething with pain and betrayal.

Then, just as quickly, Kavan's vision cleared. Reeling from the speed of images and from the nausea that came with such an episode, Kavan sat, arms upon his knees, head upon his arms, sheet clenched in his hands, staring out the window across the sea, trying to dispel the pounding in his skull. Sorting out what he was shown would take several hours. If it could be done at all.

He unhitched the donkey from the wagon and kicked the rickety cart over the embankment into the Tegid several yards below the road. Listening for the splash in the darkness, he waited until he could be reasonably sure it had stuck in the viscous river mud. After another fifteen minutes of following the road out of Rhidam, Caol and the donkey stopped and listened again. The land here was open; he would know if he was being watched or followed but it was wiser to be certain than to make assumptions. With one sharp slap on the animal's hairy back, he sent the donkey trotting north. When he could no longer hear its unshod hooves clattering on the packed dirt road, Caol sprinted south back towards the city.

"Damn it! Someone put those fires out!"

They were not large fires, at least not yet. The ship had re-emerged from the fog as anticipated, and renewed its assault on the outpost, launching fiery arrows into the night, the majority of which fell harmlessly into the sea. *Thank k'Ádhá we are not surrounded by forest,* Muir mused, firing his arrow of flame at the attacking ship.

The vessel showed evidence of being ablaze; flames leaped from her port side as she swung out to sea. One last volley was exchanged before she was out of range, but one of the arrows shot from her stern struck a lantern on the outpost's outer rim. It dropped from its peg, shattering as it hit, oil and flame erupting from it. Someone poured a pail of water over the flames, spreading the fire like a carpet across the stone floor. The flames were everywhere, little tongues licking the walls or whole sheets racing up the planks and across the roof. "Take the weapons," the prince cried. "Evacuate!"

A rapping on his door disturbed the healer's sleep, but he rarely slept deeply. His need to be ready to heal on a moment's notice; within a complex that housed over one hundred individuals, attached to a barracks of soldiers, often denied him the luxury of easy rest. Rubbing his eyes, he beckoned his visitor in.

"Pardon the intrusion, milord," said the young soldier sheepishly. "I know it is the middle of the night, but someone brought this to the gate for you." He held out the scroll. "They said it was urgent you get this. With Lord Cliáth missing I thought…"

The healer did not allow him to finish before he was out of bed to snatch the scroll. He opened it hastily, tearing it as he broke the seal, and read it quickly. Any word from his cousin was welcome, no matter what the hour. Ártur did not care if such news woke him or not.

The message was short. Come to the Boar's Garden. Kavan is in desperate need of help. Hurry or he may die.

Kavan! In Rhidam! And in need of Ártur's aid!

Allowing the letter to drop to the bed, Ártur pulled on his trousers and boots, not bothering to change out of his nightshirt, and grabbed his bag in one hand before hurrying through the door with the young soldier on his heels. Not one of the guards he passed in the hall saw fit to question him. He had the required escort and with his healer's bag in hand, each assumed he had business somewhere on the grounds.

His heart pounded as he stepped outside. Kavan! Home! Had he fallen victim to the anti-Elyri violence or was it something else? What about the torture he repeatedly endured that Gaelán experienced with him? What had become of his hands? Where was Wortham? It was not the captain's handwriting on that letter. Whose then?

"Lord MacLyr," called the young soldier. "You may not…"

"I have urgent business outside; a man's life depends on me…"

"You may not leave the grounds without…"

"Fine," he grunted, pushing past the gate attendants and eluding their hands. "You escort me. I'm going now."

❧*☙

There it was again. bhydáni Tíbhyan rubbed the back of his neck to alleviate the tingle that crept up his spine and settled in the muscles above his shoulders. He had thought it was a dream. Now that he was fully awake, he realized it was not, nor was it a purely physical sensation. It was largely a psychic one, a feeling he had not experienced in a long time. He did not have the Sight and he had no way of knowing what had summoned that long-forgotten sensation. But he knew it was a bad omen. A very bad one.

❧*☙

"Lord MacLyr! Wait!" The young messenger and one of the guards at the castle gate hurried into the nighttime streets after the healer, without knowing what direction he had taken or where he was going, while a third ran to wake General Agis or General Zarkosta, whichever he happened to find first. The healer was not supposed to leave the keep without an escort of at least five men. Those were the princess's orders. He had left with two. As he banged on Agis' door, the soldier prayed that, whatever the emergency was, it was worth the healer risking his life. He also prayed that nothing went wrong or it might cost him his head.

❧*☙

On the rocky hilltop, Muir and his men watched the outpost burn, the wooden structure consumed in flames. There was no way to save it; they could only watch as it disappeared into smoke and ash. It seemed the invading ship had won her victory. Or the fire was winning

❧762☙

it for her. Out at sea, loud shouts and screams of panic arose as the orange glow of flame in the fog grew brighter. The vessel was limping away, but Muir suspected she would not get far. At least they had the satisfaction of knowing they had dealt her a crippling blow. For him, the destruction of the outpost was minor; it could be rebuilt, and after being attacked, it was likely the Council would be more determined to keep a presence here. The sole regret Muir had was that his men were going to be hungry and thirsty until the relief ship arrived.

❧*❧

There were no Elyri at the Boar's Garden, the surly innkeeper brusquely snapped, definitely not one matching the description of the White Bard of Bhryell. Nor had anyone brought in a wounded man, Elyri or otherwise. Ártur used each of his senses to search for some indication of his cousin's presence, but there was nothing. Even if Kavan were wounded, if he was here, his proximity should make itself known to the healer. The heads of three late-night patrons turned and eyed Ártur with curiosity and loathing before returning to their drinks and their business.

When Ártur stepped into the street, with the náós bell tolling half past three, the impact of what he had done hit. He had left the keep without escort. He was alone. With the threat of death hanging over him. There was a cold sinking in his belly as he realized the gravity of his situation. The letter had been a ruse, Kavan the one sure temptation that would draw him out without a thought to his own safety.

If he was like his cousin, he could shapechange into a bird and fly to the keep, out of harm's way before he was missed. But he was not like Kavan. The change was not easy for him and when he was anxious, as he was now, it was nearly impossible. He threw back his shoulders, clutched his bag, and started towards the castle with as much bravado as he could muster, hoping the guards who had followed would catch up with him soon.

❧*☙

Stepping out of the k'dhín bhólibh, Tusánt was relieved that tonight's efforts had gone smoothly, that gdhededhá Garrett and his subordinate were back at Saint Kóráhm's and the hardest part of their efforts was over. He could, he hoped, sleep at last. But before he made it across the nave to the thóres door, shouts of confusion in the street stopped him in a cold panic. Dear k'Ádhá, he thought. No one could know about their deeds already!

He ran to the náós door to see two Lachlan guards stopping in the street to catch their breath, both of them looking about in panic.

"What is it?" the gdhededhá called, praying it was nothing that required his attention. He was tired. Not too many more hours and it would be dawn.

One of them shouted back, "Lord MacLyr is missing. Is he here?"

Tusánt grasped the doorpost to remain standing. Not Ártur. Fatigue forgotten, the gdhededhá hastened towards the gate.

"I have not seen him…may I assist in…?"

"No offense, gdhededhá," said the second man, "but one Elyri alone out here is enough. You're safer in the náós. Keep him here if you see him."

Tusánt knew they were right but he hated not being able to help. "Then at least allow me to…" He closed his eyes and sought the healer's life force. Not in the náós; not anywhere nearby. He was a great distance from them, but still within Rhidam's limits. "That way," he pointed south. "Close to the edge of town, though I cannot be precise without going with you."

"We'll find him, gdhededhá. Go inside; try to sleep…or pray."

Pray he could do. Sleep was the farthest thing from Tusánt's mind.

❧*❧

Both General Zarkosta and General Agis assumed posts at the gate towers, though it was more to oversee the search teams than it was to serve watch. Four separate units of eight men each were sent to locate the healer and return him safely to the castle. The fifth unit was forming. They had yet to wake their royal employers with this disturbing news. Agis hoped they could bring Ártur home unharmed and allow the matter to settle before the first light of dawn. Despite his training and his bravery, the High General did not want to face the wrath of the princess should she find her order had gone unheeded. Nor did he want to disappoint his King.

❧*❧

It was impossible not to hear the commotion in the courtyard since his window faced over it and he had slept with the window open tonight. Hearing Ártur's name amidst the chaos, Gaelán dressed quickly and ran to the healer's room. No one was there, just a letter upon the man's bed. Gaelán picked it up and read it. Kavan had come back and needed help?

But the impressions the young healer received from that parchment were not those of a need for aid. They were deception. A threat! He stuffed the letter into his pocket and buttoned it closed. Knowing where Ártur was going, he fled down the stairs into the courtyard where he found Asta watching the proceedings with wide eyes that searched anxiously for her father.

"Come on!" he cried, grabbing her hand and pulling her across the drawbridge. With so many people racing about, so much activity, no one took notice of the two bolting into the darkness.

"My father…" Her voice was mostly lost into the air as she ran. She could tell Gaelán was anxious, that he knew something, and thus did not try to stop him. He had come with her into the city before. She would go with him now. "Where are we going?"

"You are taking me to the Boar's Garden."

❧*❧

It was the second group of Lachlan guards he had seen. Not standard patrol formation, but men in the streets with urgent purpose. Had his work been discovered already? That had not been part of the plan, unless, of course, something had gone unexpectedly wrong. With a growl, Caol realized that getting home without notice would be trickier than he had planned.

❧*❧

He did not like the agitated feeling crashing over him. Pursuing its source led him to conclude that Ártur was vexed and fearful. Having risen from the bed, Kavan leaned on the sill, watching the light of the half-moon play upon the waves as he tried to understand what he felt.

"Milord?" Wortham sat. "What troubles you?" Your hands?

The Elyri did not reply. The anxiety increased with each passing second. It was unlike Ártur to be terrified; there should be no reason for it. Ártur was supposed to be safe. Though he had chosen months ago not to contact his cousin until he saw the healer face to face, Kavan had to know the cause of Ártur's fear. He had to know the truth. He had to help him.

Closing his eyes, he reached across the hundreds of miles separating him from the man who called him sínréc, and opened his mind to the contact…

❧*❧

He was being followed. He had no doubt about that. He could not see them, nor would his unsettled nerves allow him to accurately determine how many there were. But he knew they were there, in the shadows. It made no difference which turn he took or what pace he set, they remained but a few strides behind. Perhaps he should have stayed at the Boar's Garden and awaited the coming dawn. Though he knew where he was going, Ártur realized he was not making progress, merely traveling in circles as he tried to shake his pursuers. Where were the guards who had followed him from the keep?

Cold sweat formed on his brow, on his palms, on the back of his neck. It made him shiver, as normally Elyri did not sweat. He tried in desperation to think of something, anything that might get him out of this predicament. He had to continue running, stay ahead of whoever followed and hope that help caught up with him before they did, or attempt a shapechange and pray that it worked on the first try.

With a determined effort, he stopped beneath the light of a street lamp and tried to focus his thoughts on the hawk shape he used whenever Kavan persuaded him to fly. Yet he was aware of the eyes of those following him and those of a woman looking out from a window further down the street. Few Teren were aware of that ability; to accomplish it in full view of others was inviting disaster. Fearing what might happen if anyone saw him, and too afraid for his life, he was too anxious to complete the change.

There was a dark passage ahead. If he could make it there, he might be able to make the change before the others, whoever they were, caught up. He sprinted, trying to preserve enough energy for the change, but found when he made it there that each little sound kept him too high-strung to focus.

They were right behind him, more of them than before. He could not go back, only forward, further into the alley, further into darkness.

He stopped.

He was surrounded. He knew it with such certainty that he could not find room in his thoughts for panic. There was no escape as they closed in, shadows in the shadows. Kavan. sínréc. It has come to this. A powerful blow from something blunt and heavy struck him in the small of his back, dropping him to his knees.

I am going to die here.

The End

Character Index Book 3

Agis, General--The only Cíbhóló nomad to serve in the Enesfel military. King Hagan promotes him to Lord High General after Ternce Wyndham retires his post.

Aleski MacLyr--Ártur The oldest son of Sámel MacLyr, Ártur MacLyr's nephew and Kavan Cliáth's cousin.

Anri "Hugh" Heward--A Nethite suspected of involvement with the upsurge of anti-Elyri violence during the reigns of King Arlan and his son Hagan.

Arlan Trebor Lachlan--The youngest son of King Innis of Enesfel. He was the 25th king of Enesfel, responsible for peaceful relations with Hatu, increasing Enesfel's size via the war with Neth, and opening a dialogue with the islands of Káliel.

Ártur MacLyr--Elyri healer, employed by Kings Innis, Donal, Arlan, and Hagan Lachlan. He is married to Syl Cáner and is cousin to Kavan Cliáth.

Asta Deidre Dugan--The daughter of Princess Deidre Lachlan and Lord High Inquisitor Caol Dugan, she is being groomed to assume the position of High Inquisitor.

Avner--One of the five Káliel guards sent by Gabrielle Dilyn to serve Arlan in his quest for the Enesfel throne.

Balint Gabersdon, Sir--Once the youngest knight in Enesfel, he is the Duke of Nelori.

Belda--Diona Lachlan's personal maidservant.

Bhenádíctus, málneag--He was a Teren herbalist. Though never ordained, he wandered the known territories preaching repentance, poverty, and forgiveness. He owned nothing in his life other than his clothing and his walking stick; those in his order take vows of poverty and become wandering missionaries. He died on Káliel in the shrine he built there, though since his body was never found some people believe that k'Ádhá took him directly to heaven. He became the patron of travelers, the poor, and those in need of spiritual forgiveness and enlightenment.

Bertram Earl Lachlan--The eldest son of Arlan Lachlan and twin of Diona Lachlan, he was killed at the age of nine by a Coryllien dagger in a skirmish between Caol Dugan and Halstatt Tarmajien.

Bhendhámyn MacLyr--The youngest son of Sámel MacLyr, nephew of Ártur MacLyr. He is a harp maker in the Cliáth tradition who agrees to apprentice Ártur's son Llucás.

Bhílári, gdhededhá--gdhededhá in Hes Índári Náós, Bhryell who witnessed many of Kavan's boyhood "miracles" and is one of the few who has not shunned contact with him.

Bhílycá, málneag--A female Elyri healer who was canonized for her extreme piety and her generous care of the sick. She is particularly known for her work with those suffering from the Great Plague, which she contracted. It ultimately caused her death though she continued to care for the sick and dying up until she could no longer able. She became the patron of healers (particularly Elyri healers) and the terminally ill. After a number of childless women reported having conceived children after visiting her shrine, Bhílycá has also become the patron of women wanting children.

Bhóité--An extremely ancient Elyri, living near the Hatu city of Enda, who was the keeper of the keys that sent Kavan on his quest into the barbarian lands. Also the name of the gentleman to whom Kóráhm entrusted this information many centuries ago, though it is uncertain if these two individuals are the same or different.

Bhríd Cáner, Lord High Chamberlain--A distant cousin of the MacLyr's, employed by King Arlan Lachlan as his chancellor, he resumed the post of Chamberlain upon the death of Guthrie McHador. He is known as the best swordsman in the Five Sovereignties, and is the King's Champion.

Bianca MacLyr Dugan--An orphaned Teren, adopted by Ártur and Syl MacLyr, she is married to Wilred Dugan.

Bowen Lachlan--The 3rd son of King Innis of Enesfel; 22nd king of Enesfel who initiated anti-Elyri violence during his brief reign and was later killed by his own subjects in an uprising backed by Owain Lachlan.

Brenna Weylin Lachlan--Arlan Lachlan's deceased wife, mother of Muir, Diona, and Hagan.

Caol Dugan, Lord High Inquisitor--Originally the son of a member of the Association, now part of the Lachlan court and family, since he married Princess Deidre Lachlan, King Arlan's sister. He has maintained the post of Lord High Inquisitor for his entire time in Rhidam.

Chátá MacLyr--She is the wife of Aleski MacLyr.

Catald Menir--The Duke of Seres, he is one of Enesfel's Generals.

Chethá Llyárá MacLyr--The infant daughter of Ártur and Syl MacLyr.

Charles Gottfrid, Duke--The elderly, bedridden Duke of Erleta.

Charles Nedcalf--A man challenged by Balint Gabersdon for the right to pass to Alberni.

Claide, gdhededhá—The oldest Teren gdhededhá in Hes á Redh Náós Enesfel who serves with k'gdhededhá Jermyn Tythilius

Clianthe Dilyn Lachlan--The daughter of Gabrielle Dilyn, she marries Prince Muir Lachlan.

Cora--A Levonne prostitute.

Coriana Deidre Dugan--Wilred Dugan's firstborn child, granddaughter of Caol Dugan.

Darius Corbin, Lord High Justice--A soldier of the Lachlan army, who rose to the rank of Justice when Minos Cornell assumed the post of Chancellor after the death of Guthrie McHador.

Dawid Coryllien--A figure once thought of as mythical, whose name is connected with the death of many Elyri and Teren during the historical period known as the Persecution. His name was given to the daggers connected with those murders. Very little is known about him in the Five Sovereignties.

Dayly Niall--The eldest son of Duke Symon Niall of Dorshur, he is a close friend and companion of Prince Hagan and Tayte Cáner who spends much time at the castle.

Deidre Dugan-Lachlan--Arlan Lachlan's twin sister, she was the wife of Caol Dugan, mother of Wilred and Asta Dugan. She died of pneumonia when her daughter, Asta, was two years old.

Delins--a peasant family in a small village outside of Rhidam who house an Elyri bard who is later found dead.

Denyan--One of the five Káliel guards sent by Gabrielle Dilyn to serve Prince Arlan in his quest for the throne.

Dhábhiyhá Coryllien--The true birth name of the man who came to be known as Dawid Coryllien to the people in the Five Sovereignties.

Dháná MacLyr--The wife of Tám MacLyr, mother of Sámel and Ártur MacLyr, Kavan Cliáth's aunt.

Dhybhé--An Elyri jeweler who settled in Nelori with her brother, only to have her brother disappear and then be kidnapped herself while under Sir Balint's care.

Dhyóti--An unidentified individual mentioned in Kóráhm's journal

Diona Cordelia Lachlan--The only daughter of King Arlan Lachlan; heir apparent after the death of her father makes Hagan king.

Dórímyr, k'gdhededhá--The highest religious leader in the Faith of Elyriá.

Drebhoti --A mythical/historical figure connected to the staff that Kavan needs to cleanse the thol below the Rhidam keep.

Elys--The former fiancée of Ártur MacLyr.

Eridel--A young harper whom Kavan meets while in Hatu during his quest for healing.

Espen Harcourt, Prince--The second son of King Geir of Hatu, he is the brother of King Noreis.

Everard, Sherriff--Sherriff in Levonne

Felicity Colson-Menir--The daughter of former General, Duke Hewett Colson, wife of Catald Menir, who rules as Duke and Duchess of Seres.

Flannery McGrannis--The former squire of Bhríd Cáner who is elevated to the post of Chancellor upon the death of Minos Cornell.

Friid, Captain--Owain Lachlan's Captain of the Guard at his home in Fiara, Enesfel.

Gabrielle Dilyn Lachlan--Prime Magistrate of Káliel, mother of Clianthe and Piran, she is the wife of Owain Lachlan.

Gaelán Ágdhrán Cáner--The youngest son of Bhríd Cáner and Madalyn Dubuais who has shown to possess the Elyri healing talent despite being half-Teren.

Galvin Ethelwyn--The Duke of Wexel.

Garrett, gdhededhá--The acting head of Saint Kóráhm's while its Khwílen Kesábhá is in Elyriá attempting to gain ammunition to confront k'gdhededhá Dórímyr.

Geir Harcourt--The single heir of King Perren Harcourt of Hatu, he becomes king during Girvin Lachlan's reign and dies during Arlan's.

Gernadus Farley--One of three men accused of murdering an Elyri man and leaving his head upon the signpost of Dhágdhuán Náós in Rhidam; the only one of the three to be caught. He is currently being held prisoner in Rhidam.

Guthrie McHador--Once the general of Enesfel's army under Kings Innis and Donal, he reared Prince Arlan and assisted him in his bid for Enesfel's throne. He remained at court as Arlan's Chamberlain and died during the fight with Neth that resulted in Enesfel obtaining the territory surrounding south of Lake Curo.

Hagan Guthrie Brennan Lachlan--The youngest child of Arlan Lachlan, he is the 26 king of Enesfel.

Hazen--A female dedhá serving in Hes á Redh Náós, Rhidam during the reigns of Kings Arlan and Hagan Lachlan.

Horace--The bartender of the Merry Sow tavern in Levonne.

Hwensen--k'gdhededhá Dórímyr's personal aide

Idal Gottfrid--The second oldest son of Charles Gottfrid of Erleta. He and his brother Kent have purchased a modest home in Rhidam, which is currently under suspicion by the inquisitor and Princess Diona.

Innis Trebor Lachlan--The 19th King of Enesfel, Prince Arlan's father.

Izbin--Balint Gabersdon's squire, he is left in charge of the Nelori estate when Balint goes to Rhidam to place himself at King Hagan's disposal.

Jermyn Tythilius, k'gdhededhá--A former brother in the Order of Saint Kóráhm in Clarys, Elyriá, he was ordained as the k'gdhededhá of Hes á Redh Náós Rhidam and is later murdered in the outbreak of violence.

Jilletta McPhelan--The daughter of General Liron McPhelan, she is greatly interested in Prince Hagan and the prospect of being his queen.

Jorges, Sir--Sir Balint Gabersdon's Captain of the Guard, who is apparently responsible for the kidnapping of the Elyri woman Dhybhé from the Duke's Nelori estate.

Kavan Kóráhm Cliáth--Last of the Cliáth's, only child of Rístyrd and Llyárá, cousin of Ártur MacLyr. He is an admired harper, possessor of the Sight, holder of great psionic capabilities. Known as the White Bard of Bhryell for his tremendous musical talent and unique physical appearance, he was employed by Arlan as his court bard until his flight from Rhidam to the lands south of Hatu. He is also the Duke of Alberni and the founder of Saint Kóráhm's Abbey.

Kent Gottfrid--The third oldest son of Charles Gottfrid of Erleta. He and his brother Idal have purchased a modest home in Rhidam which is currently under suspicion by the inquisitor and Princess Diona.

Khweltz Coryllien--The stepfather of Kóráhm, he was the father of Dawid Coryllien.

Khwílen Kesábhá, gdhededhá--Once an aide to k'gdhededhá Dórímyr, he was selected abbot of Saint Kóráhm's Abbey in Alberni due to his gifts of oratory, learning, and painting.

Kjell de Corrmick--The youngest son of Loris of Neth, he is the brother of King Merkar de Corrmick and is the current heir to the Neth throne.

Kóráhm di Curnydhá, málneag--Elyri málneag for whom Kavan was named, also known as Kóráhm the Rón by many in Elyriá because of some controversial writings he made before the time of his martyrdom. Few of his books are available and he is not commonly discussed. Originally born in the town of Ergoth, he is the half-brother of Dawid Coryllien.

Leord Stold--One of Caol's connections in the Association, second in command to the leader of the Rhidam chapter.

Liron McPhelan--One of the generals in the Enesfel military, he is the father of Jilletta McPhelan.

Llyárá Cliáth--The wife of Rístyrd Cliáth, mother of Kavan. She died during the plague.

Llucás Phaedr MacLyr--The oldest child of Ártur and Syl MacLyr.

Llyr--A mythical/historical figure learned to be a gdhededhá and a fighter, responsible for the creation of the chalice Kavan seeks in connection to the thol below the Rhidam keep.

Logros--One of the five Káliel guards sent by Gabrielle Dilyn to serve Arlan Lachlan in his bid for the throne of Enesfel.

Madalyn Dubuais Cáner, Duchess--The Duchess of Levonne, she is the only woman in Enesfel to have control of her own lands; she is married to Bhríd Cáner.

Maicel, málneag—One of the Elyri saints, sometimes seen as the patron of merchants and tradesmen.

Merkar Rousset de Corrmick--One of the sons of the late King Loris of Neth, he is currently the ruling Neth king.

Mílne MacLyr--The only daughter of Sámel MacLyr, Ártur's niece, who was murdered by a Nethite hunter during her attempts to bring aid to the oppressed Nethites under King Loris' reign.

Minos Cornell, Lord High Chancellor--Once in the service of Innis Lachlan, he is one of the few men to remain in the Lachlan employ up to the time of Arlan's ascension. He first took the post of Lord High Justice, and then later took the title of Chancellor when Guthrie McHador's death left a vacancy in Arlan's staff. Before his death, it is learned that he is part Elyri.

Muir Innis Lachlan--The bastard son of Owain Lachlan and Brenna Weylin Lachlan, he was raised as Arlan Lachlan's son. Upon reaching adulthood he gave his land and title as Duke of Alberni to Kavan Cliáth and relocated to Fiara with his father. He is married to Clianthe Dilyn and lives on Káliel.

Myreth--A singer of extraordinary talent he is a man of unknown mixed heritage who was raised in the cloister of Gorbesh.

Narn--The name of someone suspected of being connected to the anti-Elyri violence in Enesfel, possibly a Cíbhóló nomad.

Noreis Harcourt--The current king of Hatu, he is the elder brother of Prince Espen Harcourt.

Onea Pantel--The woman who heads the Fiara branch of the Association.

Ordelia Cornell--The oldest of seven children, five of whom are girls, of Duke Rostryn Cornell, the son of Minos Cornell of Theron.

Orynn--A member of all three known races (k'kairá, Elyri, and Teren) she was chosen by Kóráhm and her own people to make contact with Kavan and assist in his quest for healing, redemption, and the items needed to cleanse the thol below the Rhidam keep. She is known among the people in the barbarian territories as k'ílshwythnec, "she who sees," because of her tremendous knowledge of the past, present, and future.

Owain Ustes Lachlan--He was believed to be the 5th child of Innis, son of Ula de Corrmick of Neth; he was the 24th king of Enesfel. He is actually the only child of Guthrie McHador. He relinquished the throne to Arlan Lachlan and has lived in the Neth city of Fiara since then. He assumed the title of Duke of Fiara when the area of Neth south of Lake Curo seceded and became part of Enesfel. He is the father of Muir Innis and Piran Guthrie Lachlan.

Phaedr Cáner--The brother of Bhríd and Syl, he joined Prince Arlan's forces and lost his sight, then his life, for that cause.

Phyóná Térari--A distant relative of the MacLyr's and Cliáth's who died during childbirth. Kavan served in her funeral Gathering when he was an altar boy.

Picus, k'gdhededhá--The senior gdhededhá in St. Paul's Náós in Levonne.

Piran Guthrie Lachlan--The son of Owain Lachlan and Gabrielle Dilyn-Lachlan.

Puncilla--A madam in Rhidam, murdered for her alleged engagement to an Elyri man.

Qol--A member of the race known as the phae k'kairá who has been serving as k'gdhededhá in the cloister of Gorbesh, and acting as the keeper of the relics Kavan seeks.

Rankin, gdhededhá--A Teren gdhededhá in Hes á Redh Náós, Rhidam.

Renfrid Valdis--The current king of Cordash.

Reynold--The sheriff in Nelori.

Rostryn Cornell--The son of Minos Cornell, he becomes Duke of Theron upon his father's death.

Sámel MacLyr--Ártur's older brother and Kavan's cousin. He is a harp maker in the Cliáth tradition, like his father.

Sigrid Niall--The daughter of Duke Symon Niall of Dorshur and the younger sister of Dayly Niall.

Sósáná--Kóráhm's mother; little is otherwise known about her.

Syl Cáner MacLyr--The wife of Ártur MacLyr, she is also a healer, and sister of Bhríd Cáner. She is the mother of Llucás and Chethá.

Tám MacLyr--The father of Ártur MacLyr, he is a harp maker in the Cliáth tradition, and uncle of Kavan Cliáth.

Tayte McHador Cáner--The eldest son of Bhríd Cáner and Madalyn Dubuais, he is the heir to the Levonne estate.

Ternce Wyndham, Lord High General--He served as both Owain's second general, then as first general. He was asked to keep his position by King Arlan and has served as such since Arlan's ascension, retiring from the post upon the monarch's death.

Tíbhyan --Elyri bhydáni, who was Kavan's private tutor. He is the oldest man in Bhryell and one of the top 10 sages in Elyriá.

Tusánt, gdhededhá--The only Elyri gdhededhá serving in Hes á Redh Náós, Rhidam.

Tymothy Borlad, k'gdhededhá--The appointed Teren head of the Faith in Cordash.

Urian Jayr--A wandering gdhededhá of the Order of Saint Bhenádíctus who joins Kavan on his journey.

Valesce--A resident of the Gorbesh cloister and personal aide to k'gdhededhá Qol.

Valgis, gdhededhá--A newly ordained Teren gdhededhá from Levonne, currently serving in Hes á Redh Náós, Rhidam.

Wace Elotti--A Cíbhóló nomad turned bounty hunter, heralded as the best in the Five Sovereignties.

Walga--An elderly woman, possibly phae, who acts as caretaker of the shrine where Kóráhm once lived in Ergoth.

Waljan--One of the five Káliel guards sent by Gabrielle Dilyn to serve Prince Arlan in his quest for Enesfel's throne.

Wilred Douglas Dugan--The son of Caol Dugan and Deidre Lachlan, he is the acting Duke of Durham, husband of Bianca MacLyr, and father of Coriana Dugan.

Wortham Delamo, Captain--Captain of the five elite Káliel guards sent by Gabrielle Dilyn to serve Arlan. He is the closest of Kavan's friend and considers himself the bard's protector and servant.

Yhsábhel--A woman with whom Kóráhm was involved at the time of the Persecution who was murdered in the violence by Dawid Coryllien.

Yorick Zarkosta, General--He had joined Arlan's quest for the throne, and has risen to the rank of General in his years of service since then. He acts as the Captain of the Lachlan house guard when not in a state of war.

Zelenka--A young woman from Gorbesh with whom Wortham Delamo falls in love and who travels with them when her mother dies.

Elyri Phonetics

á--ä (as in m**o**p)
a--ă (as in c**a**t)
ae--ā (as in **a**ce)
ag--ä (as in m**o**p) (HE**)
ai--ī (as in **i**ce)
au--aủ (as in **ou**t)
é--ŭ (as in b**u**t)
e--ĕ (as in b**e**t

i--ē (as in b**e**)
í--ĭ (as in s**i**t)
ó--ō (as in g**o**)
o--ŏ (as in m**o**p)
u--ū (as in bl**ue**)
y--ē (as in b**e**)
yh--y (as in **y**es)

b--b
bh--v
c--k
ch--ch
d--d
dh--j
gae--gwā
gdh--zh (as in vi**s**ion)
gh--g (as in go)
gk--<u>k</u> as in loch (HE)
h--h
hw--w (breathy, as in whale)
k'--k
k--k

l--l
Ll--l
m--m
mh--m (slightly breathy)
n--n
ne--nyä
p--p
ph--f
r--r
s--sh
t--t
th--th (as in thistle)
z--z

· **C** is always pronounced **K** but the letter **K** is most often used to designate this sound. **C** mainly appears at the beginning of some proper surnames and place names and occasionally in the center or at the end of a word. This is believed to be a carryover from the earliest days of the Elyri language, or to have been influenced by the Teren languages, but Elyri linguists and scholars have not yet determined its significance. However, in keeping with this unspoken, unexplained rule, no Elyri have first names, or middle names, starting with **C**.

· The combination **gk** (pronounced as in the German ich) occurs only at the end of words unless there is a verb suffix or plural suffix behind it, and only in those words of High Elyri origin.

· The letter combination **ag** occurs at the end of words of High Elyri origin. If the combination appears elsewhere in a word, it will either be as a product of two words having been combined or will be the result of a suffix having been added. Though some Standard Elyri words have retained their **ag** ending, most words carried into the standard will have the **ag** combination replaced with **á** when written, though they sound alike when spoken.

· The **H** sound only appears in High Elyri words and in some names carried over from ancient sources; Standard Elyri derivatives will normally drop the **h** from the original word but there are exceptions to the rule

· Double **L**'s are found at the beginnings of words, single **l**'s in the body or at the end. When words do have the double **L** in a location other than the beginning, it is always the result of two words being combined into one.

· In High Elyri, there were no naturally occurring **B, P,** or **ow** (as in cow) sounds. These did not get introduced until Elyri acquired their current religious faith. Even then, the sounds were not commonly used until the standard Trade tongue influenced everyday life. These sounds mainly appear in proper names or religious settings.

· The combination of the letter **ne** occurs almost exclusively at the end of a word and is always pronounced **nya**, regardless of where it occurs.

· The **ee** sound at the beginning or end of a word is always represented with an **I**. In the center of words, it is represented by a **Y**. When the **ee** sound is represented in the center of a word by the letter **I,** it is a result of two words being combined into one. In some cases, as with the name Cliáth, the original words may no longer be known. The few exceptions where Standard or High Elyri words begin with a Y for the ee sound are believed to have originated as intentional misspellings.

· There is no **S** sound in the Elyri language. S's are always pronounced **sh**.

· The letter **Z** appears only in the High Elyri or in words derived from the High Elyri or originated as misspellings in one of the Teren languages and were absorbed back into Elyri in the aberrant form.

<u>Elyri Grammar</u>

In most Elyri words, the stress falls on the second to last. Words where the stress falls on the final syllable (or on the first syllable in words with more than two syllables) are either names, the result of an Elyri translation of a Teren word, caused by the addition of a prefix or suffix, or the result of a word being truncated, having dropped the last syllable over time.

The **k'** at the beginning of a word signifies importance or singularity. It is applied to a word that can have a common meaning and a special meaning: k'tyne would be a favorite niece or female cousin, whereas tyne is simply a niece or female cousin. In the case of the phae k'kairá, when the Teren translated the term into "the Others" it is the **k'** that indicates the O to be capitalized; not just any others but the Others.

The Elyri written language does not have additional characters for capitalization. The first letters words may carry a dot beneath them to signify that the word is a proper name, a place, or a title, but first letters of sentences are not capitalized.

Sentence breaks are characterized by either a new line of text or by a symbol that looks similar to an s. This has resulted in many mistranslations from Elyri into other languages.

Nouns

Noun forms of verbs do not have gender. When these nouns are made plural they take the plural inclusive suffix sur.

The prefix **íl** added to a verb makes it into a noun; the word then means "one who" as in "ílDaeni"-one who instructs, i.e.: teacher.

Some nouns are formed by adding the prefix **ai** to a verb; the verb dhesá means touch, aidhesá also means touch but is a noun. Not all verbs can accept the **ai** prefix.

-thé: the standard plural suffix

Nouns ending in **I** are both singular and plural and do not take the -**thé** ending

Elyri monetary denominations are both singular and plural.

There are other exceptions to the singular/plural rule, most being words carried over from the High Elyri. High Elyri contains very few words that are NOT both plural and singular. Any exceptions to the rule are noted.

Some words have gender. A word ending in **ne** is feminine and a word ending in **dhá** is masculine. Both are made plural in the same way (with the **thé** ending). Some gender-neutral words that have been altered from their original form may have either ending.

Some words in Standard, those referring to a group that includes both male and female individuals, require the **-sur** ending, creating the plural inclusive form of the word. The same ending exists in High Elyri.

Adjectives

There are few adjectives in the Elyri language. Instead of saying someone is beautiful, or wise, and Elyri would say they possess beauty or they possess wisdom.

To modify such qualities, an Elyri speaker would say:

bhykólé aelá shwyth: She possesses wisdom. Teren: She is wise.

ochbhykóle aelá shwyth: She possesses more wisdom. Teren: She is wiser.

utbhykólé aelá shwyth: She possesses the most wisdom. Teren: She is wisest.

naimbhykólé aelá shwyth: She possesses no wisdom. Teren: She is not wise; or She is a fool.

The few adjectives that do exist come through the High Elyri and are believed by most linguists to have their origins in some language other than the Elyri.

Verbs

When **ibh** modifies a verb (ie: is singing, is looking) it is attached as a suffix to the verb. In all other instances, it is a separate word (bhydáni ibh gaeth: He is bhydáni.)

When **im** modifies a verb (ie: was singing, was looking) it is attached as a suffix to the verb. In all other instances, it is a separate word (ílDaeni im gaeth: He was a teacher)

There is no "be" in the Elyri language. Whereas a Teren would say, "He will be singing" the Elyri would say "He will sing." Instead of "I will be there" it would be "I will come" or I will go"; instead of "I will be here" it would be "I will stay", "I will attend," or "I am here."

Rather than using verbs such as "strengthened" or "beautified", in Elyri they would say "given strength" or "given beauty"

Verb Tenses

(present) do, does	(past) (ár) did, have done	(present) (ibh) am, are, is doing	(past) (im) was, is, were doing	(future) (ád) will do, to do, be done
aelá	aelár	aelibh	aelim	aelád
ándás	ándásár	ándásibh	ándásim	ándásád
árá	árár	áráibh	áráim	árád
bhaeá	bhaeár	bhaeibh	bhaeim	bhaeád
bheken	bhekár	bhekibh	bhenim	bhekád
bhair	bhairár	bhairibh	bhairim	bhairád
bhólon	bhólár	bhólibh	bhólim	bhólád
chóne	chóneár	chóníbh	chónim	chónád
daeni	daenár	daenibh	daenim	daenád
dhesá	dhesár	dhesibh	dhesim	dhesád
dhys	dhysár	dhysibh	dhysim	dhysád
donai	donár	donaiibh	donim	donád
ghlaiph	ghlaiphár	ghlaiphibh	ghlaiphim	ghlaiphád
ghytae	ghytár	ghytibh	ghytim	ghytád
kelém	kelémár	kelémibh	kelémim	kelémád
mairós	mairár	mairibh	mairim	mairád
naeth	naethár	naethibh	naethim	naethád
yháth	yháthár	yháthibh	yháthim	yháthád
zene	zenár	zenibh	zenim	zenád
zólágk	zólágkár	zólágkibh	zólágkim	zólágkád

Verb/Noun Tenses

	noun form 1(íl)	**noun 2(ai)**
aelá	ílAelá (one who owns)	
ándás	ílAndás (one who honors)	aiándás
bhaeá	ílBhaeá (one who asks)	
bheken	ílBheken	
bhair	ílBhair (one who accepts)	aibhair (acceptance)
bhólon	ílBhólon (one who purifies)	
chóne	ílChóne (one who brings)	
daeni	ílDaeni (one who instructs)	
dhesá	ílDhesá (one who touches)	aidhesá
donai	ílDonai (one who endures)	aidonai
ghlaiph	ílGhlaiph (one who sleeps)	aiglaiph
ghytae	ílGhytae (one who threatens)	aighytae (threat)
kelém	ílKelém (one who passes)	
mairós	ílMairós (one who heals)	aimairós
naeth	ílNaeth (one who finds)	
zene	ílZene (one who gives)	
zólágk	ílZólágk (one who reveals)	

Verb Tenses (High Elyri)

(present)	(past)(-ár)	(future)(-es)
aelás	aelásár	aeles
bhánys	bhánár	bhánes
dytae	dytár	dytes
ghai	ghaiár	ghaies
síndóbhaene	síndóbhaenár	síndóbhaenes
zugdhu	zugdhuár	zugdhues
tyreth	tyrethár	tyrethes
pháló	phálóár	phálóes
scenyhur	scenyhár	scenhyures
elzen	elzenár	elzenes

Verb/Noun Tenses (High Elyri)

(noun 1) (bhe-)	(noun 2) (ae-)
bheaelás (one who owns)	aeaelás (possession)
bhehánys (one who makes music)	
bhedytae (one who obeys)	aedytae (obedience)
bheghai (one who does)	
bhesíndóbhaene (one who forgives)	aesíndóbhaene (forgiveness)
bhezugdhu (one who protects)	aezugdhu (protection)
bhetyreth (one who knows/scholar)	aetyreth (knowledge)
bhepháló (one who buries/gravedigger)	aepháló (grave)
bhescenyhur (one who names)	aescenyur (name)
bhelzen (one who gives)	aeelzen (gift)

Foreign Phrase Index

ELYRI WORDS

HE: High Elyri   SE: Standard Elyri

n--noun   v--verb   adj—adjective
adv--adverb   prn--pronoun   prp--preposition
pl--plural   sng--singular   psv—possessive
pl in--plural inclusive

á (ä) (prp)--HE/SE; and, also, together with, together

Ádhá (Ä-jä) (n)--HE/SE; god; k'Ádhá-supreme deity in the Elyri monotheistic religion

Adhár (ă-JÄR) (n)--HE; first Equal day, referring to the Holy Feast day on the spring equinox or any festival, party, or religious observation in honor of that day.

aelás (Ā-läsh) (v)--HE; Have (has), possess, own

aemárdhesi (ā-mär-JĔSH-ē) (n) (sng and pl)--HE; blessing

aendhá (ĀN-jä) (n) (pl: aendáthé)--SE; A father's male relatives, including his father, grandfathers, uncles, brothers, and cousins.

aene (Ā-nyä) (n) (pl: aenethé)--SE; A father's female relatives, including his mother, grandmothers, aunts, sisters, and cousins.

aepháló (fä-LŌV) (n) (sng and pl)--HE; resting place, burial site, cemetery, grave

aesíthaen (ā-shĭ-THĀN) (n) (sng and pl)--HE; wish

aeslag (ĀSH-lä) (n)--HE; Loved one, beloved, lover; occasionally interchanged with kyá and sínréc. This word carries almost sacred connotations and is rarely used outside of some intensely passionate, spiritual, emotional relationship. It is believed that in a person's life, while one could have several lovers, they can have only one aeslag, thus many hesitate to use the term at all and may only apply it to someone in their past when they are old and nearing death.

ágdháni (ä-ZHÄ-nē) (n) (sng and pl)--HE; the title for any Elyri trained in the use of nature's energy. Humans have no word that can be used, though they often translate it as sorcerer, wizard, or some other similar term. In common science fiction parlance, it can be translated as psionist. In sources predating the earliest known High Elyri documents, this word would be translated the same as dhesádhá.

át (ät) (prn)--SE; I, me, myself

átaelás (ä-TĀ-läsh) (prn psv)--HE; mine, my

áti (Ä-tē) (prn)--HE; I, me, myself

bhánys (vä-NĒSH) (v)--HE; 'make music'.

bhánys (vä-NĒSH) (v)--SE; sing, sings

bhólon (vō-LÄN) (v)--SE; purify, purifies

bhydáni (vē-DÄN-ē) (n) (sng and pl)--HE; This is both a title and a social standing. It can be translated teacher, master, sage, or wise one, though it actually encompasses all of these meanings. The title is given to those who, through their exceptional psionic capabilities, wisdom, and intelligence, have demonstrated their worth. Psionic ability is the key to the title, though great ability without wisdom and intelligence will not gain the title. With the title comes the privilege of teaching their knowledge to the children, particularly their psionic knowledge. Each city, town, or village will have at least one bhydáni. Either the bhydáni will ask another into their ranks, or, in the event that a location has no functioning bhydáni, the inhabitants will select someone to fill the position. In extremely rare cases, someone can become bhydáni by accident; they accept mentorship of someone and others begin to ask for the privilege of learning from them as well. By becoming an unofficial teacher, the individual has become bhydáni. A little less than 2/3 of all bhydáni are female.

chellé (CHĔL-ŭ) (n) (sng and pl)--HE; home, house, dwelling, residence; also frequently used to as the shortened form of chellé hábhai, or Seeking House, the residences of various religious orders.

dedhá (DĔ-jä) (n) (sng and pl)--SE; priest or monk; the term makes no distinction between the two. The shortened form came into use after the Teren came into the lands and adopted the Faith as their own.

dhábhyne (jä-VĒ-nyä) (n)--HE; Honored Mother, nurturer. While this term can apply to one's biological mother, it is mainly used to address any woman who is clearly one's elder or superior, or as a term of respect to any woman (not a young girl) with whom a person is not familiar.

Dhágdhuán (JÄ-zhū-än) (n)--HE; the Intercessor, considered to be the founder of the Faith because his death is said to make it possible for mortals to reach the divine,

dhe (jĕ) (pn) (pl: dhethé)--HE; You; occasionally interchanged with the Standard form dhi

dhi (jē) (pn) (pl: dhithé)--SE; You.

dhín (jĭn) (n) (pl: dhínthé)--SE; a chamber or small room

dó (dō) (prp)--HE; also

dytae (dē-TĀ) (v)--HE; obey, obeys

gaethaelás (gwāth-Ā-läsh)(prn psv)--HE; his

gdhededhá (zhĕ-DĔ-jä) (n) (sng and pl)--HE/SE; priest or faith teacher or disciple; the term makes no distinction between them.

ghai (gī) (v)--HE; do

ghaies (gī-ĔSH) (v)--HE; will do, will be done

hábhai (HÄ-vī) (v)--HE; look, search

haeles (HĀ-lĕsh) (n) (sng and pl)--HE; friend, companion

hes (hĕsh) (n) (sng and pl)--HE; heart

ibh (ēv) (v)--HE/SE; Is, are, am; its translation is dependent upon the rest of the sentence.

íd (ĭd) (prp)--HE; if

ílMairós (ĭl-MĪ-rōsh) (n) (sng and pl)--SE; healer, physician.

it (ēt) (pn)--HE/SE; this/that. The rest of the sentence implies its translation.

íth (ĭth) (prp)--HE/SE; the

k'aendhá (k-ĀN-jä) (n) (pl: k'aendáthé)--SE; A favorite paternal male relative, including father, grandfathers, uncles, brothers, and cousins.

k'dhín bhólibh (jĭn vō-LĒV) (n) (pl: dhín bhólibhthé)--SE; Purification Chamber; a place within the naós where the Faithful confess their hearts to k'Ádhá and receive forgiveness and blessings from the gdhededhá

k'elyryhánag (k ĕl-ēr-ē-ÄN-ä) (n); when Kavan first encounters the word, it has no translation as it is a word outside of any forms of the languages spoken, but it appears to be the word from which Elyri was originally derived.

k'gdhededhá (k zhĕ-DĔ-jä) (n) (sng and pl)--HE/SE; The Elyri designation for the male individual who is elected as the head of the Faith.

k'ílshwythnec (k ĭl-SHWĒTH-nyĕk) (n)--HE; She (who) sees; Prophetess. The K indicates a particular individual. Any prophetess would be ílshwythnec.

k'rylag (k RĒ-lä) (n) (pl: k'rylagthé)--HE; Once Kóráhm chose the word rylag for his method of travel, k'rylag was carried over into standard Elyri and came to refer strictly to the Gates, not a standard gate.

kyá (KĒ-ä) (n) (pl: kyáthé)-- SE; Beloved, dearest one

kyag (KĒ-ä) (n) (pl: kyágthé)--HE; Beloved, dearest one.

Kyne (KĒ-nyä) (n) (sng and pl)--HE/SE; The High Mother, the Matriarchal ruler of Elyriá. It includes the translation "Mother ruler", "Mother protector", and "exalted mother". Since nearly all Elyri families can trace some familial link to the Bhíncári, the Kyne is both a figurative, and near-literal, mother of all Elyri. This position is both hereditary and elected, chosen from among all of the women in the Bhíncári family.

lásánai (LÄ-shän-ī) (n) (sng and pl)--HE; my master/lord or mistress/lady; one to whom an individual has chosen to be subservient. This is a strictly voluntary status which may or may not be acknowledged or honored by the one being given superior status, but it gives the title bearer no more power over the speaker than the speaker wishes to allow. Not to be confused with a title of nobility or landholders since there is no such status in Elyriá. It can be used for either women or men.

Llaethlágárá (LĀTH-lä-gār-ä) (n)--HE; The mountains separating Elyriá from Neth and Enesfel.

málneag (mäl-NYÄ-ä) (n) (pl: málneagthé)--HE; it can mean one who possesses a quality of blessedness, sacredness, or holiness; its most common translation into the Trade languages is saint.

náós (nä-ŌSH) (n) (sng and pl)--HE/SE; a place of worship, temple; also occasionally used to refer to the altar.

nuáth (nū-ÄTH) (n) (sng and pl)--HE; son

onyhéc (ÄN-yŭk) (n)--HE; True humility.

phae k'kairá (fã k KĪ-rä) (n) (sng and pl)--HE; The name given to the race of beings who inhabited the territory of the Five Sovereignties before the Elyri arrived. By the time the Elyri came, all that remained of the k'kairá (as they are sometimes called) were crumbling stone circles, mounds, huts, some of which bore written symbols upon them. Unlike most High Elyri words which end with the ah sound, this one does not end with the letter combination ag.

phain (fīn) (prp)--HE/SE; of

Pháne (FÄ-nyä) (n)--HE; An island in possession of Káliel. Its name is translated as tiny or small.

rásai (rä-SHĪ) (n) (sng and pl)--HE; greatness, renown, fame

redh (rĕj) (n) (sng and pl)--HE grace, sometimes used as forgiveness in a religious sense

rón (rōn) (n) (sng) (pl: rónthé)--SE; one whose beliefs run contrary to the teachings of the Faith; a heretic

rósádhá (rō-SHÄ-jä) (n)--HE; Literally translated as the Wounds of the God, it refers to the manifestation of the death wounds of Dhágdhuán which inflicted many saints and holy individuals. These include punctures in both wrists from where the founder was hung by his wrists, sometimes accompanied by the burn of a rope on the left wrist, punctures in both ankles where his feet were secured to the pyre post, possibly the scars of ropes on the ankles as well, and, very rarely, the marks of burning flesh on the lower body.

rylag (RĒ-lä) (n) (pl: rylagthé)--HE; gate, doorway

serbháló (shĕr-VÄ-lō) (n)--SE; A form of Elyri wine with almost no alcohol content, used only for the purposes of religious ceremony.

síndóbhaene (shĭn-dō-VĀ-nyä) (v)--HE; forgive.

sínréc (shĭn-RŬK) (n) (sng and pl)--HE; This word has no direct translation. Blood kin with a special bond is about the closest it can be described. Any blood kin can be sínréc, but saying "he is my cousin," is different from saying "he is my sínréc" (or "he is sínréc."). It is sometimes used for non-relatives who are extremely close.

só (shō) (adj)--HE; Small, little, tiny, not much, a small amount.

sóáne (shō-Ä-nyä)--HE; a word that serves both as an exclamation of praise and a plea to be redeemed; most often found in a religious setting or context.

thóres (THŌ-rĕsh) (n) (pl: thóresĕth)--SE; the room or rooms in a náós that serves as clergy offices and residences.

tydhá (TĒ-jä) (n) (pl: tydháthé)--SE: Male cousin or nephew.

Udhár (ū-JÄR) (n)--HE; Old year, used to refer to the end of year Holy Feast day on the winter's solstice or any festival, party, or religious observation in honor of the passing from the old year to the new.

záryph (zä-RĒF) (n) (sng and pl)--HE/SE; winged beings connected to the realm of the holy; angels

Translations

aesíthaen át aemárdhesi dhi　　　I wish you blessings

aelás Khweltz Córíllyén ibh it aepháló, dó chellé phain gaethaelás nuáth íth k'málneag aelás rásai
> "This is the final resting place of Khweltz Coryllien and the home of his son, the great málneag"

"dhábhyne? dhe ibh k'elyryhánag?"
> "Honored Mother? You are k'elyryhánag?"

dhábhyne, dytae áti. síndóbhaene áti, átaelás haeles íd ghaies áti.
> "Honored Mother, I will obey. My friend will not forgive me if I do otherwise."

Pronunciation of Elyri Names

Ágdhrán (Ä-zhrän)
Aleski (ăl-ĔSH-kē)
Ánásair (ĂN-ä-shīr)
Ártur (är-TŪR)
Bhendhámyn (VĔN-jä-mēn)
Bhílári (vĭ-LÄR-ē)
Bhílycá (vĭ-LĒ-kä)
Bhíncári (vĭn-CÄ-rē)
Bhóité (vō-Ē-tŭ)
Bhríd (vrĭd)
Bhryell (bhrē-ĔL)
Cáner (KÄ-nyär)
Chátá (CHÄ-tä)
Chethá (CHĔ-thä)
Cíbhóló (kĭ-VŌ-lō)
Clarys (klär-ĒSH)
Cliáth (klē-ÄTH)
Dhábhiyhá (jä-VĒ-yä)
Dháná (JÄ-nä)
Dhybhé (jē-VÄ)
Dhyóti-(jē-Ō-tē)
Dórímyr (DŌR-ĭ-mēr)
Drebhoti (drĕ VÄ tē)
Elyri (ĕ-LĒR-ē)
Elyriá (ĕ-LĒR-ē-ä)
Elys (ĕ-LĒSH)
Gaelán (GWÄ-län)
Hwensen (HWĔN-shĕn)
Kármár (KÄR-mahr)
Kavan (KĂ-văn) (in Elyri his
    name is spelt Kabhan)
Khwílen Kesábhá (KHWĬL-ĕn
    kĕsh-ä-vä)
Kílyn (kĭ-LĒN)
Kóráhm di Curnydhá (KŌR-
    äm DĒ kūr-NĒ-jä)
Llucás (LŪ-cäsh)
Llyárá (lē-ÄR-ä)

Llyr (lēr)
MacLyr (mäk-LĒR)
Maicel (mä KĕL)
Mílne (MĬL-nyä)
Mórne (MOR-nyä)
Phaedr (FĀ-dŭr)
Phyóná (fē-Ō-nä)
Rístyrd-(rĭsh-TĒRD)
Sámel (SHÄ-mĕl)
Sósáná (shō-SHÄ-nä)
Syl (shēl)
Tám (täm)
Tíbhyan (TĬ-vē-ăn)
Tusánt (tū-SHÄNT)
Yhsábhel (ĒSH-ä-vĕl)

<u>The Five Sovereignties - City Legend</u>

Enesfel

1-*Rhidam
2-Alberni
3-Bryn
4-Chantel
5-Dorshur
6-Durham
7-Erleta
8-Jardin
9-Kamin
10-Kilmacud
11-Levonne
12-Nelori
13-Seres
14-Talladegah
15-Tarsee
16-Theron
17-Wexel

Cordash

1-*Aralt
2-Anzet
3-Ediug
4-Eleva
5-Jassett
6-Kakkoris
7-Korr
8-Liatti
9-Lindumn
10-Matina
11-Pesek
12-Sebring
13-Trallan
14-Verbier
15-Vioe
16-Vron
17-Wynett

Elyriá

1-Clarys
2-Ánásair
3-Bhastyán
4-Bhórdh
5-Bhryell
6-Cármycá
7-Cylleá
8-Dhánthes
9-Ibhórys
10-Káská
11-Khwíncanon
12-Rísóri
13-Sábhóne
14-Sídhári
15-Turyn

Hatu

1-*Natrona
2-Avarrou
3-Cran Ufa
4-Drisoge
5-Enda
6-Fa Ruqi
7-Furr Katio
8-Kílyn
9-Palil
10-Wasilla
11-Yd Haszafni

Neth

1-*Glevum
2-Fiara
3-Gorea
4-Mawr
5-Nogero
6-Pravek
7-Ruidoso
8-Venago

Káliel

1-*Káliel
2-Jaffe
3-Mara Qin
4-Pháne
5-Shola

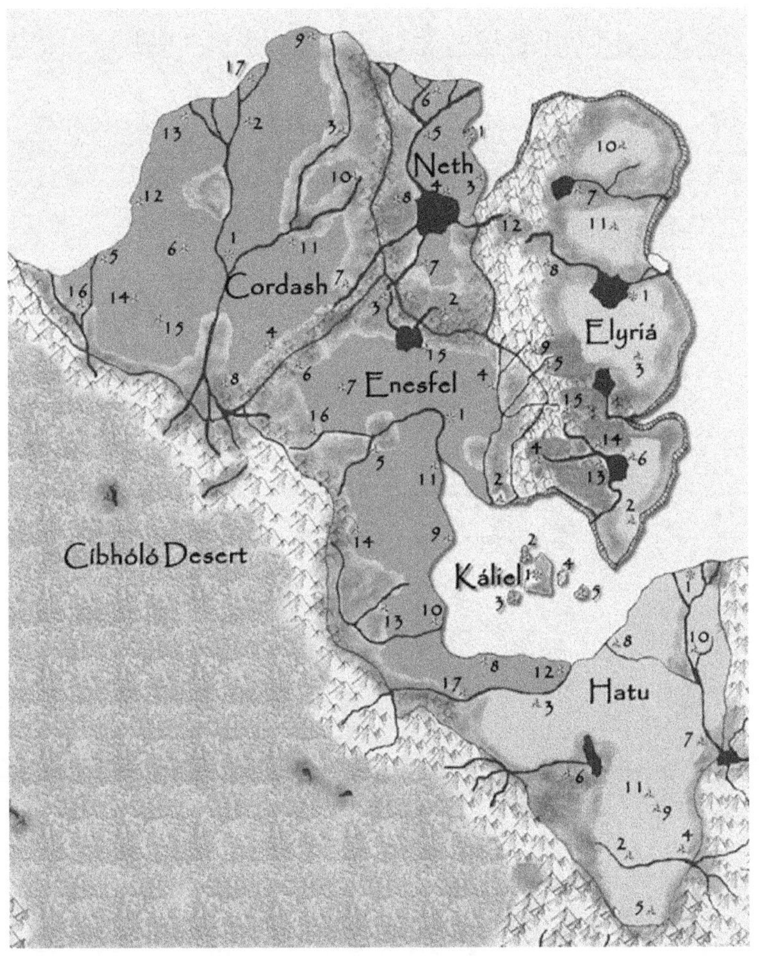

The Five Sovereignties

The Southern Lands - City Legend

1 - Hatu city of Enda

2 - Fikahr

3 - Ergoth

4 - Yashir

5 - Zabin

6 - Gorbesh

7 - Pa'aliaka

⊕ - Monastery of Gorbesh

Southern Lands

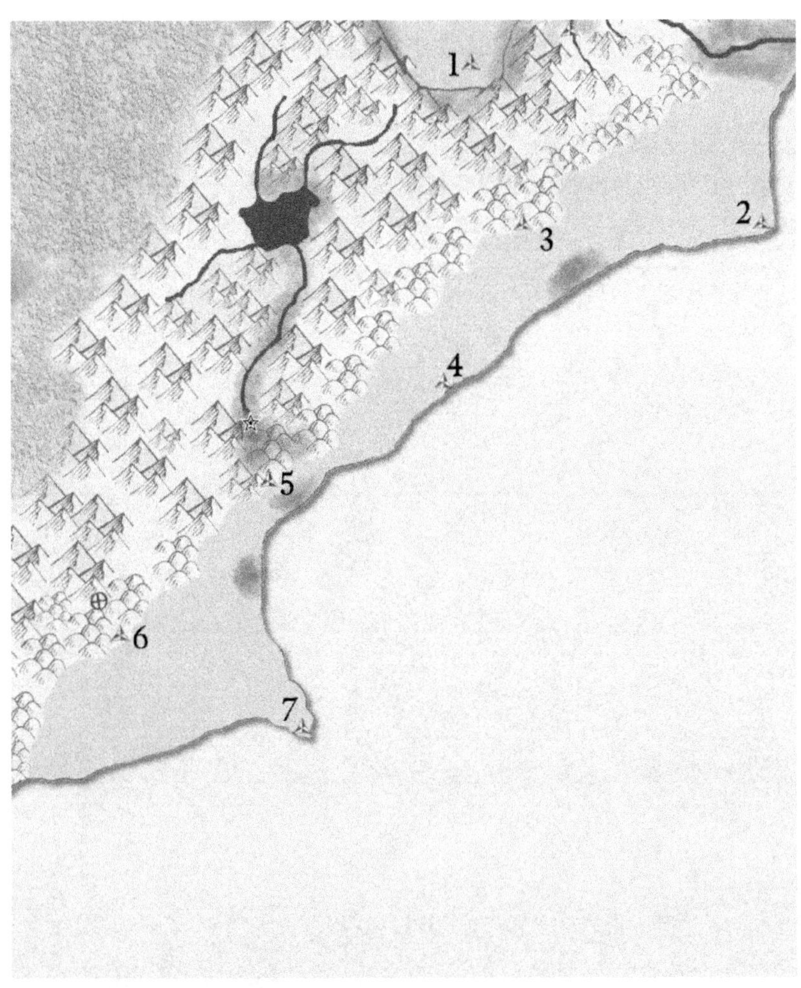

<u>White Prodigal</u>
<u>Kestrel Harper Saga Book 4</u>
(excerpt)

In the courtyard, the King waited with eight men at arms and two servants, none of whom were Captain Delamo or the men from Káliel. Their absence made Kavan scowl for reasons he could not explain, but he was far enough away that King Hagan could not see his face. Deciding that the discomfort was little more than the after effect of the night's dreams, Kavan reached the horse being held for him and swung up on it as the King smiled in greeting.

"My apologies for the delay." He could have placed blame upon Gaelán and Sóbhán but saw no reason to. If the King wanted an explanation, he would ask for one.

"You are here, that is what matters. It cannot be a long ride, I am afraid; my sister has asked for an audience and I received word that Sigrid, her brother, and her father will be arriving later. I must be here to welcome them."

The young woman arriving unannounced, and apparently unexpected, brought the scowl back to Kavan's face, but he hid it easily as his horse skittishly sidestepped away from the nearest soldier. Dayly Niall was Hagan's best friend; their visiting should not surprise Kavan. The Nialls had been a frequent fixture in the Lachlan court throughout King Arlan's reign. Today, for the first time, the unanticipated nature of the visit suggested to Kavan that Duke Niall was vying for deeper political favor from the King. There was great advantage to be found in having both of his children in the King's sphere of influence. Like many others, Duke Niall was a politician, a man who constantly sought power from the monarchy, but this was the first time Kavan felt uncomfortable with the man's actions. The children could not be faulted, as it was their place to obey their father's wishes, and the bard knew he could not warn Hagan away from either his best friend or his intended bride. He could, however, advise caution when dealing with their father, and he intended to do that as soon as their trip got underway. The soldiers with them would be intent on watching the city streets for danger, which would allow Kavan and the King opportunity to speak freely.

The cobbled streets of Rhidam were beginning to come alive as the King's entourage passed through the castle gates. Merchants' shops were opening, tradesmen and craftsmen were lifting their shutters and setting out samples of their wares to tempt passersby, and some residents were already roaming the streets in search of daily needs, a visit to the náós for spiritual feeding, or to call upon friends, relatives, or business associates. Word spread quickly that the King was in their midst and a crowd began to form around them as Rhidam's citizens sought access to their King.

Words of thanks and praise greeted the young monarch and people pushed between Kavan's horse and King Hagan's as they attempted to touch the King in their gratitude. The mass executions, and the peace the people had known since the arrival of the gdhededhá for the vote, were working in the King's favor. It was the first time in Kavan's recollection that the majority of people in a crowd sought not to touch him for blessing, but focused on someone else. It was vaguely unsettling but it was also, he believed, as it should be. The less of a focus Kavan was for these people, the less likely he would be seen as a threat to the kingdom. It was time to put that notion to rest.

There were some, of course, who took the opportunity to make contact with the White Bard, men and women who hoped for miracles for reasons none but them knew. Little by little his horse was pushed further away from the King's as the crowd thickened, and a prickle up his spine that settled at the base of his skull, began to suggest that this situation was wrong. Giving the people access to their King, allowing Hagan to solidify his rule by raising his popularity with the masses he governed, had its benefits, but there was danger to such a situation as well. There was certainly danger to Kavan, who was separated from both the King and the guards and was thus a target for those who sought the expulsion and destruction of Elyri in Enesfel.

An exchange of glances among the guards suggested that they were thinking the same thing, at least when it came to the safety of the king, and they began to shoo the crowd back, with words, with firm but gentle gestures, and with some degree of force when needed. Little by little, Kavan edged his horse closer to the King, eager to be back in the circle of the soldiers' protection. The prickle at the back of his skull flared with heat and pain, making him wince. The movement of his head made him notice someone between him and the King, someone in a dark, wide-brimmed hat that hid his features from view. The person, the menace, was facing Kavan, a death threat he was certain, but when the figure reached him, the jostling of the crowd as the soldiers pushed and pulled people away from King Hagan, made the figure spin away and lose his hat as Kavan was almost pushed off of his horse. By the time the bard steadied himself in his seat, the figure was gone, the hat trampled beneath the horses' feet as the guards urged the animals forward and away from the disappointed throng.

The threat had passed. Kavan had been spared.

His pounding heart settled as they left the thickest of the crowded streets and neared the bridge over the river that would take them beyond the city limits. That threat had been close, and none of those with him had noticed. It was right that they should protect the King at any cost, but not having Wortham with him, his own protection, made Kavan reconsider the wisdom of this ride. Being a target did not surprise him, but how close the killer had gotten did. He would have to rethink his actions when he chose to go out into the midst of people who had once loved him. That realization made him sad.

Senses turned outward around them, his thoughts swarming around what had nearly happened, he did not notice the King's horse drawing nearer to his until they bumped together and the King, apparently startled by the unexpected contact, swayed in his seat and nearly toppled into Kavan's lap. "Easy, My Liege," Kavan murmured, using both hands to steady the King. The touch on the King's shoulders brought dizziness over Kavan and he realized then how pale and discolored the young man's face was.

"I'm fine, Lord Cliáth…a little dizzy. I think we should…"

The King did not finish. His blue-gray eyes rolled back in his head and he slumped sideways into Kavan's arms and off of his horse. Catching him, the bard twisted to dismount and saw a trail of red spreading down the monarch's pale beige leggings and onto the sides of his gray horse. There was too much of it, spreading from a point where a small silver edged orange jewel was embedded into his thigh. With one hand behind the King's head, Kavan pulled the coin-sized item free, revealing the slender pronged teeth that had held it in place. Removing it, however, allowed the blood to flow more freely, but touching it also told Kavan something which made his soul cold.

"What have you done?"